To:
Friends of the West
Bridgewater Library
Read & Enjoy!

FALLEN
BRANCHES

E. B. NADDAFF

PAGE PUBLISHING, INC.
New York, NY

First originally published by Page Publishing, Inc. 2015

ISBN 978-1-68213-066-7 (pbk)
ISBN 978-1-68213-067-4 (digital)

Printed in the United States of America

DEDICATION

The story of the 'rogue and the mouse' was set aside, half finished, when I returned to the workforce when my children entered college. My dear daughters, Nadine, Madeline, Nannette and Martine; my lovely daughter-in-law Linda, my sister Jeannette, and an old and treasured friend Colette, prodded and encouraged me to reread, edit and finalize the manuscript. Their book club's positive reviews were the catalyst that pushed me to just get it done and pursue publication. But especial thanks and appreciation must go to my much loved granddaughter Shannon, who worked diligently with me through three edits! (I put in too many semi-colons, she deleted them!) We shared many laughs during that time, and she kept me focused, since writing can sometimes be a lonely process as words and characters knit themselves into a story. My love and heart-felt thanks go to all of you, dear Ladies! You made it happen! Thanks go as well to Kelly, from Page Publishing who guided this novice from start to finish.

CHAPTER ONE

In the blue-gray brightness of dawn's first light, a striped cat, returning from nocturnal roving, skittered over the wall that surrounded Lord Roderick Merrington's London townhouse. Nearby, a saddled stallion waited patiently by the wall. Though untethered and free to roam, the animal merely shifted his weight at the sight of the cat, the sound of his hooves echoing eerily in the predawn stillness. The mighty beast was obedient, and his restlessness came from fatigue and hunger. Raising his head, he snorted once and then emitted a soft whicker.

In an elegant bedroom upstairs, scented with sandalwood and jasmine, Emory Guersten heard the stallion's signal and was roused from slumber. He withdrew an arm from under his sleeping companion and threw back the covers. The room was chilled, for the hearth held only the ashes of last night's warm fire. The beauteous blonde beside him stretched her ripe body, lying with her eyes closed, but now, she too was awake.

"Stay awhile," she whispered as she caressed his strong body with one hand without opening her eyes. The handsome man removed her cool fingers one by one, though he found her supple ministrations not at all unpleasant.

"I must go," he said, drinking in her soft-skinned loveliness with passionate eyes. "Did you not hear my friend's call?"

"This friend's call is the only one I hear," she replied seductively, reaching for him again.

Naked, Emory stepped quickly from the bed and out of her clutches, clambering for his clothes before he changed his mind.

Her violet eyes still heavy with sleep, Lady Edwina Merrington watched her lover dress just as she had so many times before. This night of passion was over, but there would be others. "When will you come again?" she asked.

He shrugged. "Your husband is in residence too, my sweet, and we must be discreet. Besides, I must return to the midlands this week for certain; it's been a month at least since I've been to Guersten Hall to see my father. He's probably livid by now!"

Naked herself, Edwina slipped from beneath the satin sheets and crossed the room to Emory's side just before he buttoned his breeches. "Won't you give me what I want before you go?"

Emory chuckled and pushed her hand away, no easy task. "I know what you want, Edwina, and why, but I'll not leave my calling card this morn! I've sired no bastards thus far . . . Nor will I."

"But the babe wouldn't be a bastard," the blonde hastened to say. "My Lord Merrington is prepared to claim any child I bear as his own . . . his heir. Think of it as insurance, my sweet, for me. Someday I'll be a wealthy widow. When that time comes, you can claim us both again."

Emory kissed his beautiful paramour one last time and drew a silky robe about her shoulders. "Always planning ahead, aren't you, Edwina? You and your insurance! Take care your collateral doesn't turn blue in this cold room," he added, slapping her backside soundly. "Go back to bed. I'll let myself out," he added, pulling on his boots.

The handsome man departed quickly, and Lady Merrington went to her window and watched until he reappeared in the court-yard below. He turned, mounted, waved once, and then clattered away. "You're a fool, Emory Guersten," she thought idly, before returning to the warmth of her bed. "A fool!"

At the other end of the big house, unseen by either of them, Lord Merrington sat sleepless in a chair by his window, one bandaged foot propped upon a footstool before him. He looked down at his limp member, lying useless against his thigh. Only Merrington and his physician knew what ailed it, and as he watched his wife's lover ride away, his own thoughts paralleled hers. "You're a fool, Guersten, m'lad! We both are!"

In the town of Portsmouth, near the sea, many miles away from Merrington's towering townhouse, a foggy gray mist, heavy and damp, greeted early risers. Fog was a natural occurrence here, and few took notice of it. Snug inside Miss Phillipps's Academy, one of the brown-clad matrons climbed the stairs and tapped on a door on the second floor. "Are you awake, Miss Brenham?" The matron listened for a moment, and then tapped again. "Rachel?"

Inside, Rachel Brenham stirred from her slumber and went to the door. "Yes," she answered. "I'm awake. Is it time for first bell already?"

"No, my dear, but I wonder if you'd pop upstairs to see that new girl, Martinson. She's been whimpering half the night."

"Oh, the poor child," said Rachel, concerned. "Of course I'll go, Matron. Just give me a moment to dress. And don't fret about her any longer. I'll take her to the kitchen. Perhaps Cook will make us some cocoa."

In the midlands, far away to the north, the early morning sun was finally rising, spreading slowly across the countryside, taking the last elusive shadows of dawn with it. Its rays found Brenham Manor, touching first the dove-gray pantiles of the roof, then the long mullioned windows and lastly the soft-pink bricks.

The manor was newer than most of its neighbors in this part of England, and thirty years of warm summers and harsh winters had taken no toll. It was a pretty house, fronted by a tiny courtyard that suggested two separate wings while in reality there was only the main house, two stories high. Two long verandas ran along its sides, their roofs supported by decorative columns. In the summer, wisteria and purple clematis climbed those columns, spreading fingers of color across the tiles, but the vines were withered now, for it was late October, and the nights had become cold and crisp, hinting of an early winter.

Benjamin Brenham, Rachel's father, had stirred long before the first sunbeams had danced along the floor of his bedroom. He slept alone, had these many years, for his early habits greatly disturbed his wife. At the rear of the house, she now occupied a room of her own, although it was joined to his by a little sitting room that they had shared jointly through the early years of their marriage. Slowly though, Benjamin's accounts and papers had spread to its very corners, and it was now his study. Rarely did Louisa trespass there.

A faint odor of cheroot lingered throughout Benjamin's paneled and masculine bedroom. By his edict, the maids did little here, only dusting and changing the bed linens. It was an arrangement that suited Benjamin just fine, for it was a comfortable room, and a pleasant one, and he was damned if he would have it fussed over. He finished dressing, pulling on calf-length riding boots, and hurriedly went through the study and out into the hall. Although Louisa's door was ajar, her room was still dark and quiet.

At the top of the stairs, Benjamin passed by Rachel's empty room and the smaller one occupied by Rebecca, his youngest daughter. Next to it, Lydia Blackburn slumbered on, long released from early risings by lack of duties. Lydia had been in Benjamin's employ for nineteen years, first as nursemaid to both his daughters and then as governess. She filled neither role now but was such welcome company to Louisa that Benjamin kept her on, for his business required that he remain away from Brenham Manor for weeks at a time.

Downstairs, bright sunlight splashed across the entrance hall, reaching nearly to the bottom of the staircase. The wainscoting took on a honey-colored hue in its golden light, and Benjamin noted it and was pleased. It was mahogany, imported from Honduras, and it had cost him a fortune when he built the manor. Oh, he remembered, how he had fumed over the cost! But the farsighted architect had insisted upon using it and no other, and Benjamin long ago recognized that the man had been right; the tones of the wood were exquisite in any light, but breathtaking at sunrise.

In the tiny family dining room, Mrs. Crocker, his cook, had tea and a basket of warm buns waiting for Benjamin, and anxious to be out of the house, he consumed the light meal standing. When the gray-haired cook returned to her kitchen, Benjamin followed her there.

"I'm sure I need not remind you that there will be only Lydia for supper tonight, Agatha. The rest of us are going to Guersten Hall to dine."

"Lordy, sir," said Agatha with a motion of her hand. "I knew that about ten minutes after the invite came. Why, Rebecca tripped in here, petticoats a-flying, swooning with delight at the thought of spending an entire evening in the company of that handsome Edward Guersten."

Edward! Benjamin was somewhat surprised, having thought that matter long since put to rest. But he made no further comment and, turning, crossed the blue-tiled floor in long strides to leave the kitchen by its rear door. Drying her hands on a muslin cloth, Agatha watched as he made his way through the storeroom, pungent with the mixed fragrance of rich spices and aged cheeses. "Really," she said aloud to herself, noting Benjamin's quick step. "Unless I miss my guess the master is a bit excited about the evening's invitation himself."

Agatha was right. Benjamin *was* excited, and once outside, he moved quickly across the open courtyard, still cool and shaded at this early hour. Clearing the end of the wall that enclosed Rachel's garden, he grumbled, finding his mount not waiting.

But the groom had already left the stables, and when the lad saw the master, he nodded politely, dropping the rein he held. Benjamin tapped his riding crop against his boot top, and the old horse raised her head. Spying Benjamin, the mare trotted to his side and stood quietly, waiting to be nuzzled.

Patch was a skewbald and none too pretty at that, with random white patches splashing her gray coat. In fact, one fell haphazardly over an eye, giving the mare a somewhat cockeyed appearance. The animal was ten years old and had come to Brenham Manor as a filly when Rachel was just a child. At that time, for some still-unexplained reason, Rachel was quite jittery about riding, and when Emory Guersten had taken a bloody spill practically at her feet one day, the girl's apprehensions turned to outright fear.

Rachel was eight then, and Benjamin had purchased the gentle skewbald for her ninth birthday, hoping to erase her fears. They were too deeply ingrained, however. While Rachel had given the animal its name, such as it was, that was about the extent of her relationship with the mare. When coerced, she rode Patch the length of the circular drive and back and often even insisted on a lead, and so Benjamin had taken to riding Patch himself. Eventually, man and beast became attached to each other, and between them now existed a camaraderie of sorts that Benjamin found pleasant, though admittedly he was not much of a horseman.

Once mounted, the horse turned away without prodding and headed for the open fields. They went up an incline, edging toward a well-trodden path that led past a copse of almost leafless birches. The sun felt good against Benjamin's back, and clearing a thicket of evergreens, they crested a last ridge, emerging from a stand of mature pines to come upon a rock-strewn promontory, one familiar to both of them.

Whenever Benjamin Brenham was in residence at his midland manor house, he came here, sometimes even when the weather was disagreeable, in fact. The little bluff sat high above the terrain of the surrounding countryside, and from it Benjamin could see across to the neighboring estate of Guersten Hall, looking down on its tall windows and symmetrical roof tiles. Below the house, broad lawns swept down a rambling incline dominated by large clumps of now dormant rhododendrons. At the foot of the slope, the land bottomed out, and here a gurgling brook had been dammed with boulders just enough to slow the rushing of the waters. The resulting pool was not large, but it completed the pastoral composition of the landscape nicely. An octagonal summerhouse squatted nearby, nearly hidden from view in summer by bowers of lilacs and rhodendrons, its domed roof covered by vines of trumpet flower, now all bare and snaky.

On the far side of the oval pool, the path rambled on once again, curving away into a dense stand of evergreens. The children had long ago christened those trees Small Wood. That wood and the wide fields beyond were not part of Benjamin's holdings, for the spring-fed brook marked a natural boundary between Brenham Manor and the great estate owned by George Guersten.

Patch stirred beneath him. With an easy movement, Benjamin dismounted, stretching his long legs as the horse moved away to graze lazily on the last of the summer grass. In a distant field, a small flock of birds suddenly took to the air, and Benjamin watched them soar together through the cloudless blue sky.

Though not particularly handsome, Brenham was a tall man with clear gray eyes and finely chiseled features that made him attractive nonetheless. His jaw, firm and square, was clean shaven, his hair still thick although well streaked with gray. Only his long sideburns belied his years; they were almost completely white.

Benjamin was nearing sixty, a strong man with a robust constitution. His figure was still as lithe and lean as it had been at thirty, and many a portly gentleman at his club envied that straight back and light step. His figure gave great style to the latest in gentlemen's fashion, and often his London colleagues hastened to Crofts, his tailor, asking to be turned out exactly like Benjamin Brenham.

One of London's most successful businessmen, Benjamin was also one of its wealthiest. While his demeanor was not unpleasant, it masked a strong will and a tongue that could be harsh. He was a hard taskmaster; at his warehouses each man had few doubts about what was expected of him. Service at Brenham Manor was no different. Hard work meant success, reasoned Benjamin, and his own appetite for hard work was insatiable. It, along with his application to duty and a considerable measure of good fortune, had enabled him to become wealthy while still a young man.

The morning sun rose higher, and dragging her rein, Patch moved farther away as Benjamin settled himself in the sun, knowing that the mare would not wander. He propped his back against a craggy boulder and sat quietly, gazing across the open space toward Guersten Hall.

What he wouldn't give to own that estate! He loved it, more than his own, if the truth was known! But Guersten Hall was not for sale, Benjamin knew, and never would be. The Hall had been in the Guersten family for more than four hundred years now and would continue to be passed from father to son in unending succession. The present George Guersten had two unmarried sons, and the eldest would inherit when the old man died. And yet, fully aware that the estate was unattainable,

Benjamin continued to come here, sitting for hours on end whenever he could, hypnotized by the view. The big house beckoned to him, it seemed, and he was at a loss to explain the strange feeling that oftentimes overtook him. He already had most of the things that men worship—money, position, a family, and a grand estate of his own. Despite it all, still, there were times when he felt rootless.

Sitting there, Benjamin's mind wandered; he mused about his life, every event sharply in focus. Years before, he never dared hope that he would be considered gentry, almost, with a manor and a London townhouse of his own, for his beginnings had been rather common. He had never known his father; not that he was a bastard, mind you, for Benjamin had a cracked and yellowed parchment that proved otherwise. But his father had been a seaman, and as many seamen do, he had simply never returned to the young woman from the docks who had borne his child. In all likelihood, he was dead, lost at sea, perhaps.

Benjamin's boyhood had been spent near the docks, where he started his first full employment at fourteen as a roustabout for Jonathan Wittenham. Wittenham was a wealthy London bachelor whose corporate enterprise was a hodgepodge of import-export warehouses, ratty tenements, stinking breweries, and a motley collection of dockside brothels and taverns. The young boy had especially liked the warehouses, fascinated with shipments bound for and coming from most of the far corners of the world. There were teas, spices, and gossamer silks from the Orient, fantastic marbles from Italy, wines from Spain, and great merchant ships were loaded with steel from Sheffield, wool from Bradford, and fabrics from the looms of Manchester, all bound for the new nation across the ocean.

Yet a considerable portion of Jonathan Wittenham's wealth came from ill-gotten means, squeezed from the misery of London's teeming slums. About the time Benjamin turned seventeen, Wittenham recognized his intelligence, and also the fact that the lad was trustworthy. Promoted, Benjamin became a clerk in Jonathan's dingy Thames-side office, an ill-lit place with unwashed windows, reeking of sour stout from a nearby brewery. Benjamin worked hard, and though lacking in formal education, he could read and write a legible hand, and most importantly, he was quick; very soon he was entrusted with Wittenham's brewery collections.

Naturally, the docks were familiar ground to Benjamin, but as always, he was benumbed by the hopelessness of the place. Often as he made his assigned rounds, he was set upon and spit at, for in the slums, Jonathan Wittenham was much disliked. Benjamin was especially moved by the children, ragged urchins with distended bellies whose mothers spread-eagled for the price of an ale or rotgut gin. The young man hated them all—Wittenham, the unkempt and disheartened trollops, and the bedraggled poor, who made little or no effort to improve their own lot, or that of their children.

Wisely, Benjamin kept good accounts, and when he was twenty-two, he was able to give Wittenham proof that Shipsley, his chief clerk, was pocketing money from the rental accounts. Shipsley was sacked that very day, and Benjamin was quickly ensconced into the senior position. Peculiarly, and despite the great difference in their ages, Wittenham believed that he and Benjamin were friends, and since the circumstances much favored Benjamin, he let the old man think what he would.

In the months that followed, Benjamin was welcomed at Jonathan's townhouse, often taking supper with the old man and his young niece. Quiet, shy, cloistered by her uncle, Louisa Wycliffe openly adored Benjamin. She was Jonathan's only living relative, the daughter of a deceased sister. She was also Jonathan's chink in the wall of respectability, for none of his more genteel clients knew of his squalid enterprises. Few would have approved; while they might not make any effort to aid the poor and homeless themselves, neither would they think to turn a profit off such misery.

In no time at all, Benjamin began escorting Louisa to the theater or to an occasional Assembly and enjoying carriage outings in St. James Park. Even so, during this period of his life, Benjamin lived an almost temperate existence, saving his sovereigns and spending only what was necessary for clothing and lodging, for he was patently determined to be wealthy one day, although at that particular time he envied no one, not even Wittenham and his wealth. Driven by determination, he was willing to bide his time, taking his opportunities as they appeared and making them when they did not.

The course of Benjamin Brenham's young life was quite suddenly altered, however, when one rainy spring day a consignment of goods was readied for haulage to Guersten Hall, in the southern midlands. The roads were muddy, the shipment valuable, and to ensure the safe delivery of the cargo, Wittenham instructed Benjamin to accompany the heavy dray to its destination. Benjamin naturally obeyed, and he was never to be the same again, for no other singular event in his life ever affected him as profoundly as his first glimpse of Guersten Hall that late afternoon in May. *The young man who had heretofore envied no one, coveted nothing, suddenly wanted everything!*

Now, up on the bluff, Benjamin's reverie was broken when the skewbald nuzzled her master's shoulder. "Yes, I know," he murmured. "'Tis time we went down."

The mare waited patiently, for she knew her master never left this spot willingly, or quickly. Scrambling lightly to his feet, Benjamin gazed again across the open space toward Guersten Hall and, shielding his eyes with his hands, searched out the huge chestnut tree that marked the pillared entrance to the mansion's drive. From his position up on the bluff, he looked down on the great house, its detailing clear despite the distance. Rose-colored pantiles were seen, and the chimneys were plainly visible, silhouetted blackly against the sky. Still unwilling to leave, Benjamin draped an elbow around the boulder and, standing motionless, remembered that strange sense of predestination he had felt that long-ago spring day. He had known then just what it was that had troubled him so often, had clearly identified that indistinct sense of not belonging, which had haunted him wherever he went. Benjamin had returned to London with every facet of that journey to the midlands etched forever in his mind. All could be recalled at will—the crunch of the gravel in the drive, the scent of the early lilacs, the glint of the sun on the windowpanes. He *belonged* there; that much he knew! And he knew, too, that he must somehow find a way to go there, live there, become part of those lovely midlands. There, he felt certain; he could establish some sense of permanency in his life. He became determined; he would find an opportunity, or make one!

It had come about both ways. Taking stock of his position in life, Benjamin realized that a simple clerk could work half a lifetime and barely save enough to keep a humble cottage somewhere, let alone a great midland manor, even if such a property were to become available. Only a few days later, he escorted Louisa to yet another of those boring afternoon tea dances, and during the intermission, while she waited demurely under a potted palm, Benjamin dutifully fetched refreshments. A small group of nattily dressed dandies pressed around the punch bowl, and he had to wait his turn. Nearby, two elderly gentlemen scrutinized the young fops disdainfully, caring not that they might be overhead.

"Look at them! Prancing around like barnyard cocks, hoping to be noticed by some fair lass about to become an heiress."

Benjamin remembered freezing in his tracks. *Of course! Louisa!* Why hadn't he thought of it before? Louisa was Jonathan Wittenham's ward and niece. She was also his only living relative. *Louisa Wycliffe would be an heiress one day!*

Determined, that summer Benjamin became even more attentive, pressing his suit with great subtlety, a not-unpleasant task, for Louisa was not without her virtues, and she delighted in Benjamin's attentions. And while he wished Wittenham no ill, the following February the old man developed a racking cough, which worsened rapidly, and by midsummer, he was confined to his bed. Benjamin found himself making frequent trips to the small but elegant house near Waterloo Place, bringing the old man's ledgers to his bedside, and through the late summer, he discovered firsthand the enormity of the Wittenham bailiwick. He made himself invaluable to Wittenham, and when the old man died before winter came round again, Benjamin knew he had assessed the situation correctly. Louisa Wycliffe did indeed become an heiress, and the heiress turned to him for comfort and advice, for she had been devoted to her uncle.

Benjamin and Louisa were married not too long afterward, and as she had bent to her uncle's will completely, so she gave in to her new husband, whom she adored. To the extent that he could, Benjamin returned that adoration, and while Louisa found no fault with him whatever, neither did she find him to be passionate. Though he remained attentive, Benjamin was simply far too serious for outward demonstrations of love. Louisa did not object, and she retired to the background as Benjamin took her uncle's place as head of the business.

He turned his immediate attention to the many brothels and taverns in Wittenham's holdings, disposing of them quickly and profitably. Even so, Benjamin's first year as head of the huge conglomerate was a difficult one, for all his familiarity with the extent of it. He spent long hours poring over the thick ledgers in an attempt to plot a future course for the business and, finally, deciding he needed a trustworthy agent, retained the services of a solicitor, one Joshua Durklin, a partner in an established Chancery Lane firm. Early on, Durklin and Sharpe, Esq., had assessed the changes that industry and the railroads would bring to England in the thirties and forties. Their firm welcomed the new wave of businessmen openly, and Benjamin and his newfound fortune were no exception. Durklin urged Benjamin to join the Pembroke, a newly chartered men's club at Temple Bar whose membership included many of the wealthiest men in London. The connections could only be helpful, Durklin told Benjamin, and they were just that, as it turned out, for only a month after joining the club, Benjamin's dream of becoming part of the midlands was realized.

At the club, he overheard a conversation, learning that old William Guersten was contemplating the sale of two choice pieces of property. One, a hunting lodge in the north country, with vast forest acreage, held absolutely no interest for Benjamin. The second, however, was a tract of rich pastureland in Buckinghamshire that actually abutted the boundaries of Guersten Hall! Benjamin was beside himself! He instructed Durklin to move quickly, to make the purchase, at any price.

Ready capital made all the difference, and Benjamin's dream was realized! Soon afterward, he contracted with an architect to construct the present brick manor house. When Louisa found herself with child that spring, Benjamin became adamant that his son would be born in the midlands. They moved into the house even before the interior work was finished.

The birth had proven difficult though—Louisa's labor long and agonizing. And the longed-for son did not survive his first hour. In the months that followed, Louisa became withdrawn and even more quiet, overwhelmed by the child's death. As for himself, Benjamin remembered, he had become bitter, hurling himself into his work as never before. In his heart he began to believe they would be childless forever, and for eight long years such was the case. Then, the year Benjamin turned forty, Rachel was born, and less than two years later, Louisa gave birth to another daughter, named Rebecca. Again, Louisa suffered greatly during her confinements, and Benjamin realized that there would be no male heir. Bitterly, he resented the loss of his son and resented too, without being aware of it, that both surviving infants were girls.

Beside him, Patch snorted suddenly, and Benjamin turned in time to spot a small brown rabbit dart into the thicket on the far side of the boulder. He realized with a start that the sun was quite high now; he had remained on the bluff longer than usual. Still, he felt good, excited about the coming dinner party. It had been some years since he and Louisa had last been invited to Guersten Hall, and he wondered what exactly George Guersten had meant when he had referred to "a matter I wish to discuss with you." Perhaps it had to do with the wooden bridge that spanned the brook; it might be in need of some repair, and the work should be done before the onset of winter. *Yes, that must be it,* thought Benjamin, shaking his head. Since Rachel had gone to school, the Brenhams had seen little of any of the Guerstens, save Edward. *Edward!* The idea of that jackanapes sneaking into the summerhouse to meet Rebecca! Still, Benjamin admitted to himself, that vixen would entice any man—and Edward *was* a man now. Shaking his head again, he mounted Patch and hurried down the ridge.

Intending at first to return directly to the house, Benjamin decided at the last moment to ride to the bridge and examine it. It wouldn't do for George Guersten to think that he was not attending to his end of their bargain. Years before, they had agreed that Benjamin would make all necessary repairs but that he was welcome to cut the needed timbers in Great Guersten Wood. That deep forest lay in the northernmost corner of George's estate, its encroaching tree line held back by wide fields bordered with hawthorn hedges.

At the bridge, Benjamin completed his inspection, then turned and cantered back up the road toward the rear of the manor house.

Behind it stood the stables and a large barn, and byres and pens for hens and pigs. The dairy cows were already in the pasture, grazing contentedly, even though the grass was sparse.

Benjamin whistled loudly. The groom heard the master's call and came around the corner of the barn, waving. He gave a loud whistle of his own, and obediently Patch trotted off.

Striding across the lawn, Benjamin went into the house to find the morning room and library empty. He went up the stairs two at a time and strode into the sewing room, where Lydia was trying to pin Rebecca into a gown of blue velveteen.

"Father! Tell me! Do you like it? How do I look?" she cried.

"You look lovely, my dear, as usual," Benjamin said to her. Pointing with his riding crop, he turned to Louisa. "Isn't that neckline a trifle low for one so young?"

Before Louisa could respond, Lydia let out a loud sigh. "Child! If you don't stop squirming, you're going to get stuck again!" she admonished through a mouthful of pins.

"I am not a child!" Rebecca replied, stamping her foot for emphasis. "I'm seventeen!"

As always, Benjamin smiled at his youngest daughter. She was a little minx, spoiled beyond redemption, but she was lovely, and she could always cull a smile from him. Rebecca was slender and fragile, so much so that she appeared elfin almost, with dark shining curls piled atop her head. The blue velvet enhanced the hue of her eyes, dark blue, like her mother's, fringed with long thick lashes. That Rebecca was excited was obvious, fidgeting and turning, with two bright spots of color flushing her cheeks. Lydia threw up her hands in despair, muttering to herself. She had been on her knees for more than half an hour now, and if the dress were to be finished by early evening, Rebecca would simply have to cooperate. With a wave of his hand, and another smile, Benjamin left the sewing room and went down the hall to his study.

Louisa followed him there, entering just as Benjamin settled himself at the polished mahogany desk, its top already well strewn with papers.

"Can Agatha bring you anything from Coltenham? She's going in to visit her daughter who hasn't been well since the birth of that last child. She will be back before dark, and Lydia will be content with cold ham, and a little peace and quiet to go with it."

"Just the mail . . . But isn't she away rather late?"

A short time later Benjamin saw the cook leave the yard in a little trap, with Rodney Stanton at the reins.

Rodney was Agatha's son-in-law. She had approached the master about finding employment for him at the manor some years before. Once, Rodney had steady work as a liveried coachman, but many a good teamster had lost the source of his income when the railroads started carrying passengers, and the winding tracks had finally overtaken Rodney's route between Peterborough and Norwich, on the coast. With seven children to feed, only Agatha's presence at Brenham Manor had enabled the Stantons to make ends meet.

Rodney's position was officially that of stable master, but he doubled as gardener and handyman, too, and his wife occasionally assisted Agatha in the kitchen whenever the Brenhams entertained, fattening their income even more. Benjamin expected full measure from them all, but he paid fairly for it. No one had ever called him niggardly.

Only recently, Agatha's granddaughter Ferne had come to Brenham Manor to live and work, sharing one of the little rooms under the attic eaves with Mellie, the other housemaid. The oldest of the Stantons' daughters, Ferne was fifteen and had been engaged by Louisa partly because she knew the Stantons needed the extra money, but mostly because she, always considerate of others, knew that Agatha was now nearing sixty.

Hired as cook-housekeeper when Brenham Manor was still under construction, Agatha Crocker had moved her family from Aylesbury to Coltenham thirty years ago. There was only Bessie now; Agatha's husband was long dead, and her only son had been killed in the mines while still a lad. Quick and efficient, Agatha was loved by them all, but she knew her place and kept to her rooms when her work was done. Behind the serving pantry, she had a tiny sitting room with an adjoining bedroom, the two rooms warmed by a potbellied coal stove. Even Benjamin, upon occasion, had warmed his hands at that little stove.

The chattering in the sewing room went on the better part of the morning, but eventually the house quieted, and as the sun climbed even higher in the October sky, the study became flooded with light. The Aubusson carpet, with its bright florals, lent soft color to the room while Benjamin busied himself with his accounts, unaware of the passage of time. About two o'clock, Louisa returned to the study carrying a small tray of bread and cheese, with a steaming mug of mulled wine and an assortment of fresh fruit.

"I'm sorry to be so long," she said, offering him the tray. "I insisted Rebecca lie down and rest awhile, and it took longer than I expected to get her settled."

Rebecca had been a seven-month infant, small and puny. No one had been more surprised that the scrawny babe survived her first winter than the doctor himself, but his subsequent predictions unfortunately proved all too correct. Rebecca was never strong, and always her health had to be guarded zealously. Each rigorous winter left its mark on the frail child, sick frequently with long bouts marked by racking coughs and high fevers that left her weak and lifeless. Late spring and summer usually found her recuperating slowly, soaking up the bright sunshine, strengthening lethargic limbs. Her last serious brush with death had been at fifteen, and her recovery then had been slow and agonizing . . . and incomplete.

Through it all, though, Rebecca's personality remained vivacious, ebullient, yet she was spoiled and demanding at the same time. When bedridden, she was terrified to be left alone, and Louisa and Lydia, with Agatha spelling them, spent long hours by her bedside. Bleary eyed and fatigued, they sat even while Rebecca slept, lest she awaken alone to have that horrible cough triggered by fear. Yet once her strength was renewed, Rebecca pleaded to be allowed to come downstairs or go out of doors, and her cajoling usually convinced some member of the household to set aside better judgment and grant her wishes. Benjamin was especially susceptible to the girl's wiles, his sternness vanishing at the first sight of that radiant smile.

"She will not sleep," said Louisa now, handing her husband a linen square. "Of that I am certain. She is so excited about this evening she can hardly contain herself. All I have heard all morning is *Edward* . . . *Edward* . . . *Edward!*"

"Hmm . . . So I understand. Perhaps I should have another talk with her about that young man. I thought my wishes were made clear in that matter, but apparently I was mistaken."

"I know," Louisa said softly. "Every time a horseman passes by the house, she goes flying through the halls in a most unladylike manner, thinking it might be Edward. Just the same, Benjamin, she is young and fancies herself in love, and I find it difficult to be harsh with her."

Benjamin studied his wife, more attractive now than at any time during their long married life. As a young woman, Louisa had always been thin and small bosomed, had worn her dark hair in a severe chignon. Now, at fifty-one, it was more gray than his, and she dressed it in soft curls that framed her face, and extra pounds had added flattering fullness to her figure.

"Come. Sit by my desk while I lunch," he said on impulse, his voice suddenly gentle. That gentleness was noticed by Louisa immediately; raising her head, she glanced at her husband and took the chair he indicated.

"You know," she said, settling herself, "I always suspected it was Rachel who was smitten with Edward. After all, they spent a great deal of time together as children when Rebecca was ill, and they shared many the same interests. I often wonder if you had not sent her away to school—"

"Edward stands to inherit nothing," Benjamin said rather tersely, interrupting her. "He is second son, and the entire estate will go to Emory. It is the reason I discouraged Rebecca. It can come to nothing."

Rather abruptly Louisa stood up, crossing the room to stare blankly out the window. After a long moment, she turned to face her husband. "Just why *did* you send Rachel away?"

Her question momentarily stunned Benjamin. Louisa had never asked it before, not once in the five years Rachel had been away from home. Louisa had accepted his decision to pack the child off to school just as she accepted all his decisions, without question. She had voiced no objection even to the choice of the school itself, so far from Brenham Manor. Yet now, after all this time, she wanted to know.

"Come, sit down, Louisa. Perhaps we should discuss this further."

Arranging her skirts about her, Louisa took her seat again. She watched as Benjamin paused to cover his bread with the sharp Leicestershire he enjoyed so. "Do you recall the morning Rachel left for Portsmouth?" he asked tenderly, sipping the still-warm wine. "Do you remember the tears . . . and the hysterics? It seemed then that all the child ever did was weep!"

Louisa's eyes brimmed and the room fell silent for a moment, as both of them recalled the pale bedraggled child who was literally thrust into the carriage that morning—her body too thin, her arms and legs too long, her brown hair lifeless and poker straight. *And the tears!* Weeping herself, Louisa had run from the drive even before the coach departed. Later, she had avoided Benjamin for days, causing the first real misunderstanding in their marriage, though she never questioned his judgment.

It was Lydia Blackburn who had accompanied Rachel to the new school in Portsmouth, near the sea. She had returned days later and taken to her bed. "That child wept all the way to London," she reported. "And just when I began to think she might stop, we would pass another milestone, and the tears would start anew."

But when the coach neared Portsmouth, Rachel had finally stopped sobbing, and at Miss Phillipps's Academy, she had followed the matron up the stone steps, never looking back. Lydia had wept at that, struck by the child's misery.

Now, in the sunny study, Louisa looked at her husband and nodded, without speaking, as Benjamin continued, his voice controlled and careful.

"When Rachel was fourteen, I began to think about her future . . . marriage, to be exact. I know she was young then," he added, noting Louisa's look of surprise, "but the girl is not exactly a beauty. A suitable marriage may have to be . . . well, arranged."

Since both Rachel and Rebecca would inherit Benjamin's fortune one day, he explained, it was imperative that the choice of husbands for them be considered carefully. He knew that nobility and aristocracy had no quarrel with arranged marriages, but not, if you please, with the daughters of merchants and tradesmen, bankers and businessmen, however wealthy they might be. No, they kept their titles, passing them between themselves like prizes. Oh, here and there some impoverished nobleman married off a daughter to a banker's son, but no title went with the lass, and usually no dowry either.

Louisa interrupted. "But just what does this have to do with your decision to send Rachel to Miss Phillipps's? Even at fourteen, Rachel was intelligent and well read. Lydia has done a fine job as governess, and it is unfair to fault her because the two girls are so different. Perhaps because of her health we have spoiled Rebecca; she is headstrong and somewhat undisciplined, I'll admit, but Rachel has always been withdrawn, preferring her books and music to company."

Benjamin quartered a fresh pear before answering, cutting it neatly with a small pearl-handled knife. "I know I have everything most men ever want, Louisa, but I do not have sons. Unless the girls marry well and provide me with grandsons, all I have worked for ends with me."

Above all a practical man, it had suddenly come to Benjamin one day that Rachel and Rebecca should be capital assets, and yet he had been forced to admit that perhaps neither of them was marriageable, despite his fortune. Both were a bit ungraceful, and Rachel was terribly plain to boot. While Rebecca was lovely enough, she was sickly. In any marriage, both girls would be expected to produce sons and heirs, and there was considerable doubt as to whether Rebecca could fulfill that role. A few years of schooling though, Benjamin said, would provide them both with poise and grace. They would learn to manage a large estate and be prepared to assume their proper niche in society.

"And that was why I sent Rachel away to school," he ended. "Not just for the sake of her education alone, but more because I wanted to give her every advantage. I realize that little can be done about her appearance, but perhaps her position as our daughter will . . ."

Benjamin left the sentence unfinished. "Do you understand now, my dear?" he asked his wife.

She did understand, and he was probably right, Louisa thought. But to be so businesslike about it all . . . What was it he had said? *Capital assets?* She shook her head, and Benjamin, noting it, covered her hand with his.

"I know that her departure upset you greatly, dear, but it had to be done. I intended for Rebecca to join Rachel at Miss Phillipps's also, but then she had that bad winter two years ago, and I see now it cannot be."

No, in Rebecca's case, they would have to hope that beauty alone would suffice. Rachel would be home in the spring, and perhaps then, she could convince her sister to modulate her voice and descend a staircase in a ladylike manner, without raising her skirt to show most of her leg.

A racket from the hallway interrupted their conversation; the maids were bringing steaming buckets of water up the backstairs for Rebecca's bath. It would soon be time to dress for the evening dinner party. Benjamin kissed Louisa's forehead as she left the room. While she was not upset, just now, all the same, it would be nice when Rachel returned home again. Louisa had missed her firstborn sorely.

She went out into the hall and then stopped, standing quietly for a long moment, then turning, went back into the study.

"One last question, Benjamin. Why did you instruct Miss Phillipps's to keep Rachel at the school through her holidays and over the summers? Surely a homecoming would not have upset your plans."

Her husband turned to stare out the window, just as Louisa had done a short time before. "I would never have had the courage to send her back, my dear, if she had ever repeated that dreadful scene."

Pensive, Benjamin spent the rest of the afternoon in the study, trying to complete his paperwork before retiring to his room to dress for dinner at Guersten Hall. As he shaved, he wondered just why that great house drew him so. It was puzzling, in view of the beauty of his own estate. Except for sons, and a continuing heritage here in the midlands, Benjamin's roots were about as deep as they would ever become, he supposed, for one not born gentry. He could not fathom his feelings; he did not really try.

He left his bedroom later, dressed in buff-colored trousers and a rich brown frock coat. In the end though, he had to wait for both his wife and his daughter. He fumed, for Benjamin disliked tardiness, and checking the time frequently on his heavy pocket watch, he paced the large entrance hall with his greatcoat slung over his shoulder. Finally, the ladies descended the stairs together, but not before Benjamin's ill humor surfaced.

"Dammit, Rebecca! You've spent all day getting ready, and *still* you can't be on time!"

Rebecca laughed merrily and, picking up her skirts, dashed down the remaining stairs and planted a loud kiss on her father's cheek. "But, Father! Wasn't it worth it? I feel so beautiful tonight!"

She was beautiful, and Benjamin's anger faded quickly. The blue dress fit her perfectly, its bodice molding her young breasts tightly. She seemed to have filled out a little, he thought, watching her, as Louisa came down the last of the stairs, lovely herself in a gown of lavender brocade. Full puff sleeves and bared shoulders were flattering, and she smiled up at Benjamin, unable to decide whether it was father or daughter who was more excited about the evening.

The shiny phaeton was already waiting in the drive, and Benjamin hurried them into it. He preferred to handle the matched bays himself, for the journey to Guersten Hall was not a long one. The black-maned team would cover the distance in short order.

The Hall lay about two miles past the wooden bridge, and the phaeton wheeled swiftly through a long stretch of road wooded on either side by full-grown silver beeches with half-bare branches. The dirt road was firmly packed, and the clip-clop of the horses' hooves filled the night air as the carriage emerged from under the trees. Moonlight played across the fields to their left, and just ahead, the road turned to meet them in a sharp curve. Benjamin reined in the bays there, for many a light carriage had overturned rounding that curve, he knew. As they neared their destination, he sat up straight in his seat, gripping the reins tightly in his hands. His heart quickened, as it always did when he neared that great house. Suddenly, the phaeton crested a low hill. *There was Guersten Hall!*

CHAPTER TWO

The mansion was magnificent. The original Guersten Hall had been erected more than four hundred years before, consisting then of a castle-like structure and a cavernous Great Hall. The Great Hall still stood, though long unused, but all that remained of the fortress were two round castellated turrets that had been incorporated into the architecture of the present mansion after a disastrous fire necessitated rebuilding. That was more than two hundred years ago, and *that* George Guersten had spared no expense in the creation of an edifice many likened to a cathedral without spires. In fact, the huge second-floor salon was complete with a rose window.

In bright sunlight the bricks of the Hall would be mellowed and cream colored, but in the moonlight they appeared almost white, with long purple shadows flickering among the overhangs and window casements. Seven tall windows flanked each side of an arched double doorway, illuminated now by lighted torches, and on the second floor, three huge oriels projected from the front of the house, the masonry ornately carved below their window lights. Each bay had four tall windows, the outer two angled and paned with stained glass, whose colors reflected across the moonlit lawns.

High above the ground, the tiled roof sloped inward, its length broken by small dormers with latticed windows. This was the attic floor. There, thirty small rooms sat under the eaves, and in decades long past, all had been occupied by house servants.

Benjamin turned into the drive, passing by tall iron fences and heavy gates. He wheeled past the enormous chestnut tree his eyes had sought earlier that day from his perch atop the bluff, its girth tremendous, its branches spreading easily twenty feet around.

Stones snapping sharply under the weight of the carriage, they ambled up the long drive to a high porte cochere that loomed ahead of them on the dark side of the house. It was attached to the end of the building like an afterthought, and in truth it was, for George Guersten's mother had insisted on its construction when she first came to Guersten Hall as a young bride. She had refused to use the double-doored front entrance, no matter how ornate, because it opened directly onto the manicured lawns. She much disliked the wind and inclement weather and was fearful the sun would blemish her alabaster complexion.

Tonight, every window on the lower floor blazed with light, and many on the upper floors as well. Lighted torches had been hung on the round stone pillars, and Benjamin halted the carriage in their meager light. A groom appeared silently from out of the darkness to steady the bays, and Edward Guersten himself suddenly stepped onto the threshold of the stone archway, the heavy oaken door thrown open behind him. Clambering down from the phaeton without waiting for assistance, Rebecca sped to his side and impulsively threw her arms about his neck. In deference to her father, Edward merely brushed her forehead with his lips while artfully disengaging himself from her arms. Indignantly, Rebecca threw back her curls and swept haughtily past him, but she was smiling, and Edward knew she was not angry, for they loved each other dearly.

Entering the house as a group, they proceeded through a long gallery that extended the length of its front, balanced at the far end by a matching doorway that opened onto the formal gardens. At either end, a wide circular staircase with marble steps rose to the second floor.

Tall suits of armor and chain mail lined the walls, interspersed with framed portraits of Guersten ancestors, long since dead, all illuminated brightly by hanging lamps and crystal chandeliers.

Halfway down the gallery, the little group turned and entered an immense reception hall whose frescoed ceiling soared majestically two stories above them. A grand staircase of sculptured marble dominated the space beneath. Along the sidewalls, life-size statues on high pedestals were spaced, and high above them hung four large tapestries representing the family ancestry.

Their cloaks were taken just as Edward's father appeared at the top of the high stairs. The old man descended slowly, as his daughter hovered close behind, although he refused any offer of assistance and tottered stiff-kneed down the stairs by himself. It had been nearly eighteen months since either Benjamin or Louisa had seen George last, and both were unprepared for the change in his appearance.

George Guersten was seventy-five years old. His hair was snow white, short and thick around his neck and ears, thin and unkempt across the crown of his head. Always portly, he still had an ample rounded paunch, but somehow he seemed shrunken, thought Benjamin, watching him, and now he walked with a pronounced shuffle.

George's pleasant countenance remained unchanged though; the pink face was still round and cheerful, the twinkling blue eyes still clear. He was given to much animation, his conversation well punctuated by quick movements of his head and broad hands, and despite his advancing years, he was still sharp and alert. His mental faculties were as keen as ever.

Louisa had always been fond of George, for he was truly a kind and gentle man. In her eyes, his only fault was his sons; they were given to arrogance, and both were familiar faces at London's gaming tables. Save a matter of months, Ermaline, George's only daughter, was the same age as Rachel. And Rebecca and Ermaline were soon seated on a small settee in a corner of the room, their heads together, gossiping about the latest London fashions. Ermaline was more than a little plump, with reddish-blond hair worn severely parted and restrained by a narrow ribbon. Her dress of gray silk had long sleeves and a high neck, and without adornment of any kind, it flattered neither her coloring nor her figure. She too could be rude and unpleasant at times, Louisa knew, but tonight Ermaline had chosen to be friendly, and the two girls were chattering amicably.

"I've not been into London for several months," said George when they were settled with goblets of fine Madeira. "I understand many changes are taking place."

"Not just in London, George, but up and down the entire country," replied Benjamin.

He knew. He had just returned from a fortnight spent in Liverpool, where his firm had contracted for more warehouse space. There was no doubt about it, he stated flatly; the railroads would continue to bring great change to England. They had already done so in many of the shires, where the workforce was changing from agricultural to industrial. As the factories increased production, they required more and more workers, and men and women were leaving the farms and dairies in droves. Around the new factories and mills, the villages and towns were changing rapidly, too. With some mills already operating two and three shifts, hordes of workers were crowded into unhealthy tenements. Sniffing out profits, the mill owners themselves had purchased large tracts of land and constructed row upon row of cheap wooden tenements, back-to-back, all sharing reeking communal privies. Undoubtedly, Benjamin added, there would soon be many new social problems to contend with—housing, sanitation, education, and public health.

Edward concurred with Benjamin's assessment in passing, remarking that sooner or later the workforce itself would reject the standards imposed upon it. Had not some of the mills already suffered labor disputes, strikes, and lockouts? There had been violence; there would be more.

In the city itself, Benjamin went on to say, there was much new construction as rat-infested buildings, decrepit and ancient, were torn down and replaced with vast warehouses and other handsome new structures, many three and four stories high. New hotels and fashionable shops rose from the rubble of outdated buildings, and more were planned.

"Yes, London's face is changing," Benjamin said in closing. "The emphasis now is on money . . . and those that have it." It was clear that he referred to the merchants and tradesmen.

The reminder was unnecessary though. George Guersten didn't need to be told that a way of life was changing for England's aristocrats and landed gentry. For many of them, up to their ears in debt, their estates encumbered, their workers fleeing to the mills, the future looked bleak, indeed.

When dinner was announced, Edward and Rebecca lingered in the drawing room for several minutes after the others adjourned to the dining room. They reappeared quickly, however, happy and smiling, Rebecca starry eyed, her cheeks flushed. She had never looked more beautiful, and Louisa had to admit they made a striking couple, for Edward Guersten was extraordinarily handsome, standing nearly six feet, straight and slender, with wavy hair, thick and dark, and eyes that were bright blue and smiling. He had the high Guersten forehead, but not the broad chin typical of his forebears, and he wore a small, neatly trimmed mustache. Tonight he was elegantly attired in blue trousers and a black waistcoat.

Soft candlelight reflected sparkling crystal and silver cutlery in the splendid dining room. A polished compote with tall tapers and fresh chrysanthemums centered the table, their distinct fragrance wafting throughout the room. The walls were covered with carved panels, ornately embellished with gold leaf, the floors thick with oriental carpets that muffled their footsteps underfoot. Even the high ceiling was fancy, sculptured in bas-relief.

Chatting pleasantly, they dined sumptuously on succulent ham, thick slices of roast beef, and pheasant stuffed with chestnut dressing. There were fresh vegetables and crystal carafes of cooled wine. Dessert was tiny fruited turnovers, freshly baked and still warm, served with coffee.

Ermaline ate everything, and it passed through Louisa's mind, watching her, that the girl was unhappy, eating more than she needed as solace. No wonder she was so plump!

They returned to the lovely drawing room after dinner, to a fire that had burned low in the grate, although the room remained pleasantly warm. Louisa became engrossed in polite conversation with Ermaline, but her attention was drawn again and again to Edward and Rebecca, settled on the little settee in the corner. They sat holding hands, obviously enthralled with each other. *No good can come of this,* Louisa thought to herself, remembering Benjamin's words earlier that day. He would never sanction their betrothal, and she must discuss the matter with Rebecca tomorrow for certain. The girl was heading for heartbreak.

Together, George and Benjamin went into the oak-paneled library for brandy and cigars. Shortly, they were seated before the fireplace in big wing chairs of brown leather, and pouring brandy, George offered Benjamin a panatela from an ebony calamander on his desk.

"What is it that you wish to discuss?" asked Benjamin, neatly cutting the cigar's tip. "I examined the bridge today, and only minor repairs are needed to the planking. The understructure looks sound."

The old man smiled and drew deeply on his cigar, exhaling the smoke slowly. "It has nothing to do with the bridge, Brenham. I have a proposition to put to you. All I ask is that you hear me out before making any response."

"As you can plainly see," he said, continuing, "I am an old man. Oh, I have a few good years left in me perhaps, but it troubles me that Emory has not seen fit to marry and provide me with an heir. I won't beat about the bush. I wonder if perhaps we cannot agree to an . . . arrangement, you and me . . . a betrothal . . . between Emory and your daughter Rachel."

Stunned, Benjamin straightened in his chair. *He was thunderstruck!* He could not, in fact, believe he was hearing correctly. *This was what he had always wanted!* How many times had he been tempted to suggest just such a match himself, but had not, fearing rebuff. *His mind raced!* Ever since he had first seen it, he had coveted Guersten Hall! Emory was a wastrel; Rachel was weak. *Benjamin would have control in all but name, through her!* His face registered his utter surprise, and mistakenly the old man took it for disapproval.

"Hear me out," he muttered, "as we agreed."

Personally, George did not approve of arranged marriages. His own second marriage had been arranged, simply because his own father had found himself in a like position thirty years before. George's first wife, Isabelle Englefield, had come to Guersten Hall when they were both twenty. Sadly, the young woman died in childbirth not a year later, taking her infant to the grave with her. Inconsolable, George vowed never to marry again, for he had loved Isabelle very much. But, determined to ensure the continuity of his great estate, George's father, old William Guersten, from whom Benjamin had purchased his land, had arranged marriage with Abigail Prendergast. Dead set against the match at first, George had come to understand his father's position. He was sole surviving son, and the lands would be returned to the Crown unless he married and sired some sons of his own. When they were wed, George was already well into his forties, and Abigail was twenty-three, a beautiful but peculiar young woman with raven hair and strange green eyes. Married to an older man, she was miserable, but dutifully she bore his children. George was near to fifty when Emory was born. Edward followed four years later. But forced upon each other in a loveless marriage, George and Abigail became estranged, avoiding each other after Ermaline's birth. Years later, when Ermaline was nine, Abigail had been found dead on the landing of the marble staircase, her neck broken.

What George did not tell Benjamin now was that he had suspected that the woman was simply mad. Abigail was given to long periods of deep depression and had taken to roaming about the great house and its grounds in the dead of night. For her own protection, George had finally ordered that she be locked in her room; how she had managed to open her door the night she fell had never been explained. Yes, said George, arranged marriages were admittedly distasteful, yet now, well past the age of seventy, he found it necessary to prod his son into just such a union.

"I am aware," he continued, "that both Emory and Edward are undisciplined, but I am sure that once Emory is wed, he will settle down and assume his responsibilities as master of Guersten Hall."

Again, Benjamin brightened. *The proposal was even better than he imagined!* Emory would not have to wait until the old man's death to assume the position of master; evidently George planned to relinquish the title at the time of Emory's marriage.

Benjamin considered that young man. Emory was six years older than Rachel, and although they had known each other since childhood, they had ever been cool and distant to each other. Rachel disliked Emory intensely, that much Benjamin knew, but just what Emory thought of her, he could only imagine. Benjamin envisaged Rachel as he had seen her last, weeping and wringing her hands that morning she departed for Portsmouth. Could Emory accept such a plain and weepy woman as his wife? Would he? Benjamin put the question to George.

"Emory is a dashing young man about town, as I understand, with quite an eye for beautiful women. Will he consent to this arrangement? Once married, will he continue his lifestyle, leaving Rachel here to wonder when he'll return to the Hall again?"

Rachel had been gone five years. By now, she had no doubt matured into a genteel young lady, and she would be properly enlightened about her role as wife and mother. But just the same, she would still be plain and unassuming. Might not Emory have some strong objections about that?

"Wouldn't Rebecca be more suitable?" Benjamin added. "At least she's attractive."

George was pouring more brandy for them. He set the decanter down with a bang. "I'll see to Emory," he said gruffly. "And as for Rebecca . . . absolutely not! For two reasons, Brenham, and since we need to speak frankly, I'll tell you both. First, I want heirs. Rebecca's not strong enough to bear children. One pregnancy—nay, one winter here and Emory would be a widower, of that I'm certain!"

"Perhaps," replied Benjamin in a flat voice. "And the second reason?"

"The second you should be aware of already. Rebecca's in love with Edward . . . and he with her. I want no triangles under my roof. That would be outright folly," the old man stated.

As it was, no man could ever be certain he wouldn't be cuckolded, but he'd have to be a damned fool to invite it! In his own house yet, and from his brother at that! No, Rebecca was out of the question.

Once more, Benjamin was taken by surprise. *Edward again!* How was it that he had not realized all this himself? He turned his full attention to George, still speaking in his gentlemanly voice.

"There is no need to make a decision tonight, Brenham. Think it over. We can meet again when you have done so. If you believe that Rachel would be unhappy here, say so. I assure you, good fellow, there will be no hard feelings on my part. I'll simply make other arrangements."

Other arrangements? Benjamin's rising spirits now sagged. If Guersten believed he was cool to his idea, then perhaps the offer would be withdrawn. Benjamin couldn't let this chance to gain control of Guersten Hall escape. He made his decision without hesitation.

"There is no need to put off a decision. I accept your proposal, George."

The two fathers shook hands, and it was done! Rachel and Emory were pledged. Since the hour was late and the two men had been closeted in the library for some time, they agreed to meet again soon to discuss the dowry and the wedding contract. The actual wedding arrangements could be made later, when a date was set. Perhaps in the spring, Benjamin said, when Rachel returned from school.

Rejoining the others, neither man mentioned their agreement, and soon afterward Benjamin prepared to depart for Brenham Manor with his family. Edward fetched Rebecca's thick mantle, and the two of them proceeded before the others out into the long gallery. There they stood in the shadow formed by the curve of the circular staircase, locked in embrace.

"I must see you again, my darling," whispered Rebecca. "Meet me tomorrow. Say you will," she pleaded.

"Your father grows suspicious as it is, Rebecca. Besides, it's much too cold to meet in the summerhouse."

"I'll not be cold if I can be with you," she murmured into his chest. "I can't bear to be parted from you."

"Nor I you, but we must be sensible. Give me a few days . . . I'll talk with Father. Perhaps he will speak to your father on our behalf. Trust me, my love. I'll work something out."

Rebecca threw her arms about Edward's neck and pressed her body close to his. They kissed, long and deep, until they heard the others approaching, then they separated quickly and went outside. There,

Edward covered Rebecca's hair with the fur-lined hood of her cloak, in a fond gesture.

"I love you," he said huskily, and handed her into the carriage, just as her parents emerged from the mansion.

It was colder now, the moon half hidden by clouds. During the homeward journey there was little conversation in the phaeton, for each member of the Brenham family was lost in private thought—Benjamin excited about his pact with George, Rebecca mooning about Edward, and Louisa wondering what words she might speak to her daughter on the morrow about her relationship with Edward.

The climax of Rebecca's grand night of excitement was extreme fatigue, and she went directly to her bedchamber upon their return to the manor. At her dressing table she sat for a long time in the semidarkness, lighting only one small lamp. She unpinned her hair and brushed it loose, and she slowly undressed, laying the lovely blue gown over a chair. Before donning a warm nightdress, she studied her naked body in the framed mirror, twisting and turning from side to side. "I don't *look* any different," she said to her image, "but I *feel* so different!" The slim hips and small, firm breasts that reflected in the glass were those of a girl, yet Rebecca knew the love that filled her heart had surely changed her. She was a woman now, a woman who loved and was loved in return. Smiling, she crept under the covers and was asleep almost instantly.

Louisa, too, was tired, but once in bed, she found she was unable to sleep. She relighted the bedside lamp and tried to read, but concentration escaped her, and propped among the lace-trimmed pillows, she pondered again what it was that she was going to say to Rebecca tomorrow.

A soft tap sounded at her door, and Benjamin entered, now changed into a maroon silk dressing gown.

"Well, what problems of the world did you and George Guersten settle tonight?" Louisa asked, surprised to see him at this late hour.

Benjamin sat down on the edge of his wife's bed and took her hand in his own. In an excited voice, he told Louisa of George's proposal and his own acceptance. The news stunned Louisa. She withdrew her hand.

"Rachel . . . and Emory? Oh, Benjamin! I'm amazed you would ever agree to such a thing! Rachel is so sensitive, and Emory is . . . well, he's a scoundrel! Rachel and Emory . . . married?" she repeated. Voice trailing away, Louisa steepled her fingers before her lips, all the while shaking her head. "Not Rachel," she went on a moment later. "Rebecca, perhaps. Though young and spoiled, she could adjust . . . Marriage would be a lark to her."

"Good heavens, Louisa! I *offered* Rebecca to Guersten. And I, too, recognize that Emory is a spirited young man and that Rachel is withdrawn. I'm well aware that they are opposites, but George won't accept Rebecca. He wants heirs. He doubts Rebecca could survive one winter in the draughty hall over there, let alone bear children. He could be right. And there's another drawback."

"Edward," said Louisa without hesitation.

"Yes, Edward. Guersten believes they love each other."

"I believe it myself after watching them together this evening."

"Nonsense! Edward's a handsome young man, and his attentions have turned Rebecca's head. A month in London and it will be some other dandy she fancies herself in love with, you'll see." Benjamin paused, for Louisa continued to shake her head, rather vigorously. "Louisa," he went on, "I know that Emory has a reputation for being a libertine, that he gambles and drinks too much, but half the fancy gentlemen in London fit that description! You need have no fears. Emory will not mistreat or abuse the girl, George will see to that. Just why he settled on Rachel I cannot say, but I do know this—wastrel or not, Emory is still a good catch on the marriage-go-round. He stands to inherit a fortune, and someone as plain as Rachel couldn't hope to make a better match."

His wife was still not convinced. "In all the years we have been wed," she said to Benjamin, "I have never disputed a single one of your decisions. I question this one. I think you are about to make a serious mistake in judgment, and my concern is not only for Rachel . . . and Emory even, but Rebecca and Edward as well."

This time it was Benjamin who shook his head. "My dear, Rachel will be mistress of Guersten Hall! There will be nothing there for

Edward . . . or Rebecca. Once London society discovers an old family like the Guerstens has accepted Rachel, other doors will open for Rebecca."

Louisa pursed her lips, tapping her fingers on the counterpane. "What will you do now?"

"Well," said Benjamin, standing, "I shall write to Rachel, or course, but for now I shall tell her nothing of these plans. She will come home for the Christmas holidays this year, and we can announce the betrothal then. The wedding can be planned for springtime. And as for Rebecca," he added, "after the holidays, we'll take her down to London for the February cotillion. Some new gowns, a few parties, and I guarantee, inside of a month she'll forget all about Edward Guersten."

"Then you won't reconsider?" Louisa asked in a quiet voice.

"No," he said firmly. "I gave my word to Guersten . . . and I much favor this match. The matter is closed."

Benjamin removed his dressing gown, and Louisa knew he intended to remain the night with her. He had never had a great physical need of her, and he came to her room infrequently now. As she moved over to accommodate him, Louisa wondered just what it was about the evening that had stirred him to seek release. Benjamin blew out the lamp.

In the morning, he left Louisa's bed before the sun came up, turning up in the stables soon after. He saddled Patch himself and headed for his haven on the bluff. As he left the barnyard, he heard the cock crow, heralding the sunrise.

"Ha, my friend! I beat you this morning!"

As usual, Benjamin spent several hours atop his bluff, quietly gazing into the distance, reconsidering the events of the previous evening. He was positive he had made the right decision, and equally positive that Louisa would come to the same conclusion sooner or later. He never considered what Rachel would think and, likewise, gave no thought to Rebecca's feelings.

After a light lunch, Benjamin rode again to Guersten Hall and sought out George Guersten. The old man was clearly surprised to see Benjamin again so soon, but when he explained that he must return to London in a day or two, the two men huddled again in the library to complete their business. When George presented the finished document to Benjamin for signature, it was inked with a grand flourish. Secretly, each man was sure he had outwitted the other.

CHAPTER THREE

In the summerhouse the next day, Rebecca waited for Edward to come to her. She waited in vain; he did not appear. On the third day after the dinner party, Benjamin left the manor at daybreak and returned to London. That very afternoon, Rebecca donned a riding habit and went to the stables, waiting impatiently while Pollux was saddled.

Pollux was hers, a beautiful roan gelding, given to her when she was twelve, and time and time again Benjamin had thanked himself that he had spent so little on the animal's acquisition because he was not ridden very often. Between Rebecca's lengthy illnesses and her fluctuating interest, Pollux had grown fat and lazy. Though exercised regularly and well cared for, Pollux had lost his wind, and he tired easily. Still, the gelding suited Rebecca just fine, for he was very gentle and patient, and even Louisa rode him upon occasion.

Despite her infrequency in the saddle, Rebecca rode well enough, and now she trotted down the lane to the road, turning in the direction of Guersten Hall. She was hatless, her dark curls restrained only by tortoise shell combs and a blue ribbon. Her riding skirt of dark blue wool was topped by a smart double-collared cape over a matching jacket.

Keeping Pollux to a comfortable trot, Rebecca traveled along the wooded road and clattered over the bridge. When she reached the entrance to Guersten Hall, she turned up the drive brazenly, to be spotted by a groom who scurried forward, meeting her under the portico.

"Is Master Edward here?" she inquired of the lad.

Assured that Edward was at home, Rebecca sent the young man to fetch him. He did so, glancing back over his shoulder several times. *Let them cluck,* Rebecca thought, uncaring, knowing full well that all the Hall's servants would soon hear of her visit. True, ladies, especially unmarried ladies, were not supposed to call upon gentlemen, but Rebecca had kicked over the traces long ago. Besides, by now she would have walked barefoot all the way to Guersten Hall just to spend an hour with Edward.

He appeared barely a moment later, a wide grin warming his handsome face. Pulling himself into a jacket, he ran to her side.

"Surprised?" Rebecca asked.

"Indeed . . . and pleasantly so!"

"I just had to see you, Edward. I waited for you for two whole days. Why did you not come?" She frowned, pretending to be miffed.

"Ahh, Aunt Adele arrived the morning after you were here with your parents. She's still here now, with Charlotte and Olivia. Will you come in for a while?"

"No, Edward. I came to see you. If you're occupied, then I shall ride alone."

Edward, standing close beside Pollux, smiled up at Rebecca. He ran his hand up under her riding skirt, grasping her bare leg. She shivered at his touch, and it was all she could do not to leap from the saddle into his arms.

"I was hoping you would say that," Edward said with another grin. "My horse is being saddled now. Another hour with Cousin Charlotte and I'd go mad!"

Adele Chandler was George Guersten's youngest sister, a half sister in truth. When George's mother died of typhoid, his father married a second time. Martha Sheridan had borne several children, most of them sickly, and only Adele and an older sister now survived. Married to a wealthy Italian count, that sister had taken permanent residence in Italy. But even had Caroline resided locally, the two sisters would have had distance between them. Adele preferred the company of her half brother to that of her true sister. In short, Adele was a Guersten, Caroline was a Sheridan.

Adele's marriage to Sir Hugh Chandler had been arranged, and it was mutual in only one respect; they could barely tolerate each other. Adele was a very attractive woman, but cold as ice, and while Sir Hugh was quite unattractive, short and chunky, he was a virile and sensuous man. That virility chafed Adele.

The Chandlers owned three elegant mansions. Besides Greystone, at the other end of Great Guersten Wood, there was a large London townhouse and a fine summer estate at Norwich, by the sea. But regardless of where they were in residence, Sir Hugh soon became involved with the newest of the housemaids, and Adele had come to Guersten Hall now after another of their endless scenes. After a short stay with her brother, she would continue on to Greystone, where she would remain through the Christmas holidays with her daughters.

"If only he would take a proper mistress," Adele complained to George. "At least the girls would be spared these embarrassing escapades."

But unknown to Adele, however, neither Charlotte nor Olivia found their father's escapades embarrassing. In fact, it appeared that both of them had inherited the licentious side of his nature. As a result, Edward had spent the past two days trying to avoid their searching hands.

As they rode away from the house, side by side, Rebecca laughed merrily at Edward's narration of his cousin's clumsy clutches.

"I hardly dare undress," he said, exaggerating, "for fear they'll pop out from under my bed!"

"You'll fare no better with me," Rebecca teased. "Do you wish to escape my clutches also?" She moved her horse closer to his and grabbed at his thigh with a gloved hand. Laughing, Edward pretended to beat her off with his riding crop.

Rebecca nudged Pollux with her heel, and the gelding broke into a gentle gallop. With Edward following after, they rode in silence for several miles down a road that tunneled into the deep forest. It was a dark and quiet place, and when the road turned and meandered down into a small green valley, they came to a stop. Below them, Greystone and some other large country estates sat half hidden by stately elms and oaks.

Above them, high on a sunny slope, stood a small abandoned woodsman's hut that Rebecca and Edward had discovered earlier in the summer. Rebecca turned Pollux off the road and climbed a narrow path for some distance, dismounting as the way became overgrown and blocked by low tree limbs. As she led the gelding, she could hear Edward crashing noisily through the underbrush nearby, embarked on a path of his own, and she smiled, knowing he was trying to reach the old hut before she did.

It was centered in the middle of a sun-splashed clearing, and when Rebecca reached it, Edward's horse was already tethered outside. It was warm in the sun, and the exertion of the climb had left her quite breathless; she rested for a moment before entering.

Hidden behind the door, Edward waited for Rebecca inside. The little stone hut was quite dilapidated, with a door that hung half off its hinges and a thatched roof that sagged rather threateningly. Sunlight streamed through its opening onto the earthen floor. A fieldstone fireplace formed one wall; on either side of it, two gaping window openings yawned at the forest. Except for a straw-covered pallet shoved against the far wall, a broken cupboard and a small table were all that were left of the rustic furnishings. The place served its purpose though, as a rendezvous site for the young lovers.

As Rebecca stepped over the sill, Edward seized her from behind, pinning her arms to her side. Feigning escape, she squealed and squirmed until she had turned herself around, to stand happily captured in the circle of his arms. She lifted her own arms to hold him tightly, closing her eyes in delirium.

"Oh, Edward, Edward! How I do love you!" she murmured, before he parted her lips with his. Engulfed in his embrace, she sagged against him lightly. In time, he loosened his hold, but did not release her, and they embraced again and again. Rebecca became conscious of his mounting desire, and it was she who moved away first.

Without a sound, she removed her short cape and spread it across the straw pallet, which lay bathed in sunlight. As the sun's rays highlighted Rebecca's bountiful dark hair, Edward was struck again by her extraordinary beauty. *How he wanted her! Not just here ... and now, but always!*

He crossed to her side, and locked in embrace again, they fell to the pallet together. Rebecca's jacket was closed by a line of small buttons, and Edward opened them slowly, one by one. Underneath, Rebecca had worn nothing, not even a camisole, and when Edward's warm fingers touched her bare breast, she shivered with excitement. Tightening her arms around his neck, she thrust her tongue deep into his mouth.

"You little hoyden!" Edward cried out happily. "Next you'll be coming to me naked! I'll wager you've nothing underneath here either!" He ran his hands up under her riding skirt, higher and higher, only to learn that he was right. He laughed raucously, slapping her bare bottom lovingly.

"Turnabout is fair play," she whispered in his ear, fumbling with his breeches until she found what she was seeking.

The lovers remained in the little hut for nearly two hours, barely leaving each other's arms in all that time. Their lovemaking was wild and fierce, almost primitive, and when it came time to leave, Rebecca was still so ecstatic she could not button her jacket properly. Edward kissed her nose and nibbled at her ear.

"Look at you," he said. "You look like a dairy maid fresh from a romp in the hay. You're covered with straw, your hair has come undone, and one side of your jacket sits higher than the other. What have you to say for yourself?"

Rebecca giggled unabashedly. "I often wondered why dairy maids always look so rosy!"

"We must go," he said at last, giving Rebecca one final kiss. She straightened her hair and brushed the straw from her skirt, and they proceeded down the path arm in arm, leading their horses. At the edge of the Small Wood, they parted. "I do hope your father can help us, Edward," Rebecca said there. "Surely he won't object to our marriage when he sees how much we love each other."

"I'm afraid it is *your* father who is the obstacle, my darling, not mine. But don't fret ... Tonight Father wants to see both Emory and me in the library. I'll speak to him about us afterward."

"Goodness, sounds serious. What's it all about?"

"Your guess is as good as mine, but it must be important. He gave Emory explicit instruction to turn up sober."

Promising to meet in the summerhouse the next day, Edward departed and returned to Guersten Hall, while Rebecca quietly entered her father's house through the front door and tiptoed up the stairs to her room. Smiling to herself, she put the crumpled riding habit away, lest anyone spy its condition.

This evening at Guersten Hall was to be Adele's last as her brother's houseguest; on the morrow she would continue on her way to Greystone. There, she would line up all her maids, scrutinizing each with an eagle eye, trying to determine which among them would be likely to capture Sir Hugh's roving eye when he arrived. That one, poor girl, would be banished to the scullery long before Hugh returned, to spend her days scrubbing blackened pots and wondering just how she had offended her mistress. The lass would remain there only until Sir Hugh sniffed her out, for he was wise to his wife's ruse.

Tonight George had insisted that all dress for the evening, a habit not enforced of late, and now, before dinner, the family was gathered in the downstairs drawing room, all handsomely garbed and on their best behavior. Adele sat in queenly majesty, wearing apricot-colored silk, her hair piled into an elaborate coiffeur, complete with an apricot-colored feather. Charlotte—vain, pale, and blonde—was fetchingly gowned in light green, while Olivia, darker than her sister, wore a saffron-yellow taffeta. Only Ermaline was drably dressed, in a green watered silk so dark it first appeared to be black.

Edward was exceedingly handsome tonight, having topped his yellow strap-down trousers with a blue embroidered waistcoat. Charlotte nearly swooned at the sight of him, but under Adele's sharp eye, both she and her sister were forced to be demure and ladylike, and both kept their hands to themselves. Much relieved, Edward relaxed visibly and began to enjoy himself. George had come down wearing a favorite brown coat and sat chatting affably with his sister, though one eye went continually to the clock on the mantel. Emory was tardy, and after half an hour, Edward was sent to fetch him. He returned, announcing that Emory would not be hurried.

In his own good time, Emory finally swaggered into the drawing room. Judging from the brightness of his eyes, it was obvious that he had already been drinking, and though his father frowned, he helped himself to the sherry then being offered to the ladies, deftly lifting a stemmed goblet from a passing tray.

Except for a gold brocade vest, Emory was dressed entirely in black. His expensive cravat stood stiffly starched, its lacy ruffles standing tall, and at his wrists, delicate lace peeped from beneath his cuffs. On his finger was a large gold ring, a boar's head with sparkling green eyes. Smiling broadly, and with no apologies for his tardiness, he moved with casual grace around the room, greeting first his aunt and then his cousins. The evening marked the first time Emory had been home for dinner in many weeks; if he noticed his father's scowl at all, he simply ignored it, and with glass in hand, he went to stand beside Edward. Slouching carelessly against the wide mantel of the fireplace, Emory stood with one elegantly booted foot resting on the fender, sipping his wine.

There was little doubt they were brothers, for their coloring was nearly identical, but Emory towered over Edward by a good four inches, and he alone had inherited his mother's strange green eyes. Emory was muscular, with wide shoulders and a broad chest, and the tight-fitting trousers he wore outlined his long, lean thighs nicely. Charlotte and Olivia were well taken with him too, but Emory pretended not to notice. After all, it was his policy never to waste time on women he couldn't tumble.

Although his features were not as remarkable as Edward's perhaps, Emory was still ruggedly handsome. His hair was very dark, almost black, thick and full. His forehead was high and straight, and from beneath dark brows, the green eyes glinted icily. Clean shaven, he had a wide nose and lips that were full and well shaped. But there was a flaw—for over his left eye a jagged three-inch scar traced raggedly to his temple. Most of the time that scar was almost indiscernible, but it was a weathervane of sorts, for whenever Emory was angry, or excited, it stood out on his forehead like a streak of red lightning.

Dinner was enjoyable, however late, and surprisingly Emory made an effort to be polite and congenial, exchanging pleasantries with his cousins and enamoring Adele with his lazy charm. Afterward, she shepherded the younger women up the wide staircase to the second-floor salon, where a fresh-laid fire warmed the room, and the four of them were soon settled around a card table for an hour of play before retiring.

In the meantime, the two brothers proceeded into the library, and by the time George joined them some minutes later, Emory had already poured a second brandy. He sat slumped in a great wing chair, his feet planted upon his father's desk.

The old man thumped the soles of Emory's boots roundly with his walking stick as he approached the desk. At that, Emory jumped to his feet, spilling the amber liquid across the front of his lacy cravat. Ignoring him, a scowling George glanced across to Edward and pointed in silence to a nearby chair. Obediently, Edward moved away from the fireplace and sat facing his brother.

"Damn!" said Emory crossly, loosening his cravat. He removed it, examining the spreading stain with a frown.

"Stoddard will never get that white again," offered Edward, as George sat down heavily at his desk. Opening a drawer, he removed a thick ledger. He was grumbly.

"I remind you, Stoddard's position is that of cook, not housekeeper . . . nor laundress."

"Well," growled Emory, "this place sorely needs a housekeeper. My bed linens haven't been changed in a fortnight, and there's dust everywhere."

"What this place really needs is a mistress," remarked Edward thoughtfully, thinking of Rebecca.

Intently, George looked from one to the other, and then paused to light another lamp on the desk. "That is precisely why you have been summoned tonight."

Edward sat straight in his chair. "Father!" he exclaimed. "*You're* not contemplating matrimony, pray tell!"

"No," replied George in a quiet voice. "Emory is to be the bridegroom."

Emory scrambled to his feet again upon hearing that, sucking in his breath noisily. "The hell you say!" he shouted in a loud voice, flinging the goblet he held onto the hearth, while Edward, with sinking heart, slumped into his chair, sensing that his vision of marrying Rebecca was about to disappear like smoke in the wind. Patiently George bid Emory take his seat again and told them both to give him their undivided attention. Pointedly, he picked up the pearl-studded stickpin Emory had just removed from his soiled cravat.

"And what did this little bauble cost me?" he asked Emory with deliberate sarcasm.

"About thirty pounds, I'd guess," replied his son with equal sarcasm.

"Nay," said George. "Closer to sixty, and that's no guess." He fished among a pile of papers on his desk and pulled out an engraved billhead, passing it to Emory. And then he withdrew another, and yet another. Regent Street, Bond Street, Piccadilly! Half the tailors and bootiers in London were represented in that stack. There were others too, private clubs and jewelers, even hotels and livery stables. "A good share of this debt is in your name also," he said, turning in his seat to face Edward. He then proceeded to admonish them both, waving the fistful of papers in their direction for emphasis. The harangue went on for some time. "And I daresay neither of you could begin to accurately assess the total of your outstanding gambling debts," he ended, finally.

For once, Emory offered nothing in his own defense, and when Edward squirmed uneasily, George went on. "The bald facts are, gentlemen," he said laconically to his sons, "we are nearly broke."

"Bankrupt?" asked Edward, incredulous.

"That's impossible!" snarled Emory. "Why, there's . . . there's . . ."

"There's no cash," finished his father bluntly.

Emory poured himself another brandy, while George pretended not to notice. "I suppose part of this is my own fault," the old man said with a sigh. "I have been woefully lax in your discipline, but listen well to what I have to say."

Essentially, they weren't bankrupt, he told them in response to Edward's query. After all, the estates were worth a fortune. There was the Hall itself and its surrounding acres; why, the timber alone and the lush meadows would bring thousands of pounds if he were to sell them. There was also the London mansion at Eaton Place. It, too, was an elegant property, although it was in some disrepair and had been largely unoccupied for years, except for a staff that had been cut to the bone already. And lastly, George said, there was a summer retreat with considerable acreage in Lancashire that had come to him as part of Abigail's dowry.

"For years I have met your debts, lads, and I assure you, they have been substantial. As for myself, I care not. I am an old man and will soon take to my bed. The truth is, if it were not for your sister, I would leave you both to stew," he told them.

The handsome brothers looked at each other uncomfortably as George's somber voice droned on. He had been well past his prime when his children were born, and their mother had spoiled them disgracefully. He admitted that he and Abigail had held little love for each other, and George had abdicated his parental responsibilities in lieu of harmony. After Abigail's death, he had suddenly discovered that he and his children were strangers. But now, he said again, he was an old man, and his only concern was Ermaline's marriage prospects. Until recently, they had been few, and George had truly feared Ermaline was doomed to a spinster's life, for while the girl was attractive enough, she was colorless and devoid of personality. That, coupled with her brothers' reputations as gamblers and wenchers, had closed any number of avenues to matrimony.

Accordingly, George had encouraged Ermaline to spend more time in London and Norwich with her aunt Adele and her cousins in an attempt to expose her to young men of her own age and circumstances. Now, at last, the old man reported, that exposure seemed to have borne fruit. The eldest son of an old and once titled family wanted to take the girl to the altar.

"Well, then, that would seem to solve your dilemma neatly," said Emory, crossing his long legs.

The old man raised a finger. "Ahhh," he said, "but what of her dowry? For the young man's father certainly expects a dowry. And a sizeable one at that."

"Can't you dispose of some property, Father? Or borrow the needed cash?" offered Edward.

"I agree," remarked Emory. "You have more than enough collateral for any loan."

George became exasperated, drawing in his eyebrows. *God!* Did they understand nothing? Both suggestions would have disastrous results for all of them, particularly Ermaline. Property was a yardstick of a man's wealth, and if George were to dispose of any of his estates, or seek out a loan, it would signal to all interested parties that he was strapped for cash, perhaps encumbered. The young man Ermaline had hooked would wriggle himself free, no doubt, and the driveway outside would be ten deep in creditors, all demanding their money.

"No," he said, "we must appear to be financially sound, at least until Ermaline is safely married."

His sons said nothing. Neither of them had ever given much thought to money. They spent their quarterly allowances freely, never questioning the source. Edward gambled away that much and more each month, and Emory wasted his on the pursuit of women, both highborn and low, wherever he found them. Their father had always met their debts, until now.

Without appearing to do so, Emory studied his father over the rim of another glass of brandy. His father's face seemed much as it always had, for George was already old when the boys were born. But now, Emory noted that while the round face was unchanged, his father's hands were veined and wrinkled, and his body seemed to have lost some of its volume. He *is* an old man, Emory thought, surprised that he had never noticed it before.

Behind his desk, George folded his hands across his rounded paunch, and his eyes narrowed once again. He looked directly at Emory when he spoke. "Let me repeat! I am not concerned for myself. Let your creditors beat at the door, I care not. By the time the courts adjudicate, any claims will be against your inheritance. However, that will be too late for Ermaline, and I remind you . . . if she remains unmarried, she will be your responsibility . . . forever."

Emory silenced his father neatly with a wave of his hand. He understood his position as firstborn son, and he was fully aware of the obligations that were inherent in his future role as master of Guersten Hall. He needed no reminders of them now, wanted no further harangue. Still, he was more than a little rankled.

"I see . . . So I am the bait for Ermaline's fish," he said sarcastically, pouring yet another brandy. This one he passed to his brother, and then he poured another for himself. "And who's to be the blushing bride?"

His father frowned. George was acutely aware of Emory's attitude toward women, and matrimony itself, for that matter, and he tried to soften the blow by explaining that the list of available females was rather short. Most of George's own friends were dead already, and those that weren't were marrying off granddaughters by now. Those few that were independently wealthy would find Emory unacceptable because of his reputation, since his appetite for beautiful women was hardly a secret. Proud mamas were known to whisk their virgin daughters safely behind locked doors whenever Emory Guersten appeared.

Emory chuckled to himself, hearing that, remembering how many of those same locked doors had been opened by the fair damsels themselves, all unknown to their mamas of course, and their husbands, in some cases.

As for the rest of George's friends, he went on, many now found themselves in circumstances similar to his own. They had few assets outside their estates, and so the dowry was sure to be small. Thus, George explained, he had looked to those people who dealt on a daily basis in the money market—merchants, tradesmen. They had ready capital, and lots of it, and furthermore, most were seeking the chance to move up in the closed circle of aristocratic society. They would consider the dowry money to be an investment, and a good one, for the Guersten name still commanded some respect, despite all the brothers did to destroy it.

"No . . . merchants and tradesmen . . . they'll not be so particular about reputations," George concluded.

"And whose daughter is to be the lucky pigeon?"

George hedged.

"Her name, Father!"

"Now listen, Emory," said George crossly. "I had to weigh many factors, and I—"

"Just tell me the name, Father!"

"I struck my proposal with Benjamin Brenham."

Edward was as surprised as Emory. *Not Rebecca!* he thought. *It can't be! She is in love with me! No, no! Not Rebecca!*

Emory was thinking exactly the same thing, but for an entirely different reason. He thought Rebecca childlike, and she was far too small bosomed for his taste.

"*Not Rebecca!*" they both chorused in unison.

"Of course not, you fools," said George, almost shouting.

Edward was greatly relieved to hear that, and his handsome face relaxed, but Emory sprang to his feet again, spluttering on his brandy as he did so. For then he understood! *Rachel!*

He was furious! He went into a terrible rage. Instantly, the red streak flashed across his left temple, and he stormed about the library uttering profanities and pounding the mantelpiece. Granted, he had an obligation to Ermaline and his father, but this? *This was too much!*

"Me? Married to Rachel Brenham? *Never!* She's . . . she's . . . *My God, Father! She's a mouse!*"

Emory pictured Rachel as he had known her, thin and flat, her eyes always red from weeping. "Never!" he shouted again and again, continuing to pace the length of the room. George said nothing as Emory vent his rage, and in time, when he ceased his rantings, he returned to stand before his father's desk with his hands on his hips. "What in God's name persuaded you to settle on her?" he snarled.

Wordlessly, his father opened another drawer and removed a copy of the betrothal agreement. "This," he said, pointing to the inked figure that represented Rachel's dowry.

Raising his eyebrows, Emory whistled softly and passed the sheet to Edward, who examined it grimly but said nothing as he handed it back. For all Emory's jaded lifestyle, he was no fool. Money talked, and he could name half a dozen families who would swallow their pride and accept Rachel sight unseen if they but saw the figure scratched on that document. Still, his tone remained derisive.

"And what did you promise away, besides my body, at that price?"

"Nothing. Brenham was in an extremely generous mood. I merely . . . suggested . . . a figure and he chose to nearly double it. He seemed satisfied that Rachel would be mistress here at the Hall."

"I'll wager he was! But what did you tell him initially? Or did you simply confess that you needed his cash to marry off your own daughter?"

"Mind your tongue! Brenham thinks I want heirs."

Heirs! Good God! Emory was momentarily stunned again. There was an angle even he hadn't considered yet. He was a sensuous man, he appreciated beautiful women, and the thought of sharing his bed with a hysterical drab made his blood run cold. His anger returned, heightened by the knowledge that, in truth, he had little choice in the matter. He was trapped! If he rejected Rachel, he was saddled with Ermaline, forever perhaps—and a great stack of unpaid bills to boot. On the other hand, if he accepted the mouse, and her sizeable dowry, they would all live happily ever after. *Except for me,* he thought with a sneer.

Once again Emory reached for the brandy, and this time he filled his glass almost to the top. "Very well, Father. It seems I'm licked! But understand this! Don't hold me to my . . . husbandly duties. Rachel will have my name only, for I'll not share her bed, and I'll not change my ways. You may take it or leave it!"

Downing the brandy quickly, Emory set the goblet down so hard its stem snapped, and without another word, he stormed from the library, slamming the door roundly behind him.

For a long moment Edward, grim and stony faced, sat stock still. He was heartsick, his hands trembled. Marrying Rebecca was now out of the question. If Brenham was prepared to offer such an exorbitant dowry for Rachel, then he certainly must have plans for Rebecca also. Secretly, aware of his brother's desire to remain a bachelor, Edward had hoped that Rebecca might one day be mistress of Guersten Hall. Instead, it would be her sister. Sadly Edward recognized that he had nothing left to offer Rebecca, for he had no income other than his allowance, and it was simply not enough.

That Edward was deeply troubled was obvious to his father, and he sensed intuitively that it concerned Rebecca, for the old man had long ago recognized that they truly loved each other. "Speak, lad. What is it you want to discuss?" he said sympathetically to his son.

"It was nothing, Father. It can wait," he said in a quiet voice.

With that, Edward left the library dejectedly and went to his room, moving in the darkness to his childhood haven in the turret.

During the night, a great storm broke over the midlands, and for hours the wind howled through the trees, whistling down the chimneys. Well before dawn, the rains came, in great slanting sheets that slashed against the mansion, rattling the windowpanes. In angry gusts, the shrieking wind tore the last of the October foliage from the trees, and the wet leaves stuck wherever they fell. The gurgling brook soon became a torrent, and great rivulets of water formed deep gullies as the rainfall followed the contours of the land on its journey to the sea.

In his bedroom, Edward brooded in his windowed turret, staring dully out into the night. The ancient turrets stood three stories tall, and as children, both Emory and Edward had their own rounded retreat, spending long hours searching the horizon in vain for a dragon to slay. Emory no longer used his, but as he had grown, Edward's turret had become a haven of sorts, and hours ago he had climbed the three steps that led to it, to sit watching the occasional lightning flashes and listening to the wind.

Sleep was impossible. His mind was far too troubled. He knew only that somehow he must formulate some plan that would enable him to marry Rebecca. Before dawn, he decided upon one, and carrying a lighted lamp, he went quickly and quietly down the hall to the large square room that had been his mother's. Closing the door, he set the lamp on a low table.

The furniture was shrouded in dingy dust cloths, and the unheated room was terribly chilled. In the center of one wall stood an enormous wardrobe, one end of which was a myriad of small cubbies and drawers. These were originally intended for toilette articles and gloves, but Abigail Guersten had used them for jewelry. As a bride, she had been presented with a heavy case containing the Guersten family jewels, a fortune in priceless gems. But Abigail had chosen never to wear a single piece, preferring instead her own heirlooms, given by her father. She had stuffed all the Guersten pieces into little drawers, keeping her own in a little casket in the largest cubby. It was this enameled casket that Edward searched for now. It was gone. The cubby was empty.

There seemed to be no explanation for the mystery, for Edward found upon inspection that as certain as he could tell, none of the Guersten heirlooms were missing. But though he searched the room again carefully, he did not find the casket.

The sound of Edward's rummaging about disturbed Emory, sleeping on the other side of the wall, and he came to his mother's bedroom to investigate, barefoot and wearing only a loose-fitting nightshirt, unbuttoned clear to the waist. The garment had been thrown on hurriedly, for Emory slept naked. When he spied his brother, he closed the door and crossed to Edward's side.

"Christ, man . . . you woke me. I thought a window had blown open. What on earth are you seeking at this hour?"

Briefly, Edward explained both his dilemma and his solution to it. Without any money, he could not possibly hope to marry Rebecca, and so he had decided to pinch one good piece of the Prendergast jewelry. It would be his stake, he said; with funds garnered from its sale, he would go to the gaming tables, where hopefully he could win enough to come back and claim Rebecca. Then they would run away together, assuming that once they were married neither of their fathers could do much about it.

"I wouldn't count on it, Edward," said Emory. "Brenham's a powerful man. Don't underestimate him. And where will you live? In some dusty garret somewhere? A lass as delicate as Rebecca? Be sensible, man!"

But Edward would not be deterred. In desperation, he began to circle the room again, searching everywhere for the enameled box. Sitting on the shrouded bed, Emory watched him for several moments and then shook his tousled head.

"I'm certain you won't find it . . . If it were in this room, Father would have found it already."

"Father? Are you saying that he doesn't know where it is either?"

"Apparently not," replied Emory. "We had quite a row about it some months back. Seems he believes I pawned the pieces to pay for my . . . shall we say, sport?"

Crestfallen, Edward returned to the wardrobe and opened several of the drawers, examining the Guersten pieces that lay within.

"I'm half tempted to take one of these," he said somberly, withdrawing a black leather box from one of the cubbies. He opened its hinged cover. It was lined with black velvet and contained some of the best pieces in the entire collection. All matched, there was a small coronet set with diamonds and pearls, a bracelet with similar stones, and a pair of pearl earrings. In the center of the rich velvet lay an elaborate pendant on a heavy chain. It was made of platinum, V shaped, and set with large diamonds. The single teardrop pearl that hung from it was enormous. Lustrous, it glowed almost phosphorescently in the dim light of Edward's lamp.

"What should I take?" he asked his brother hesitantly.

Emory could see that Edward was determined to follow through with his foolhardy scheme. The jewelry he held in his hand was a bridal set, worn traditionally by Guersten brides for generations. Somehow, Emory could not picture that delicate coronet atop Rachel's straight brown hair. He pointed to it.

"Take that . . . Only the pearl is worth more, but I fear Father would have a stroke if he ever found it missing."

Edward agreed and, pocketing the sparkling coronet, returned the leather case to its place in the wardrobe, and the brothers left the room.

"It's strange," Edward said wistfully as they stood in the long hallway. "I love Guersten Hall and all its ancient heritage. I have never wanted to live anywhere else, and I'd hoped to continue that heritage with sons of my own someday, working to make the estate self-sufficient as it was in the old days." He sighed wistfully. "I want to stay but find I must leave, and you want to leave and find you must remain. Is that fate?"

"Bah!" said Emory scornfully. "It has nothing whatever to do with fate. It's merely an accident of birth!"

It was no secret to any who knew him that Emory was miserable in his role as inheritor. From childhood he had longed to go to sea; the happiest summers of his entire life had been those spent as a boy at Aunt Adele's oceanfront estate, tramping the beaches and exploring hidden coves. Even in London, where he was a familiar figure on the docks and quays of the great Thames, it was the majestic schooners and clipper ships that drew him there, and not, as many believed, the harlots.

"When will you leave?" he asked Edward now, both of them shivering in the cold hall.

"As soon as I talk with Rebecca . . . tomorrow, or the day after." He extended his hand to his brother, and Emory took it. "Perhaps I'll see you now and again at your London club," added Edward.

"Perhaps," replied Emory. "I still think you're a fool, Edward, but I wish you luck! As for myself, I'm going back to bed. My arse is frozen!"

The midland storm lingered, with heavy rains that did not cease for three long days. Edward knew that Rebecca could not meet him in the summerhouse. Her health fragile and guarded, she would be forbidden even to leave the house in such dampness, and so, when a weak sun poked through the clouds on the fourth day, he hurried to the Small Wood and waited under a canopy of dripping trees for his Rebecca. His wait was in vain, though, for Rebecca did not come to the summerhouse. The very next morning, the sun finally rose in earnest, round and bright in a cloudless sky, but the day was unseasonably cold nonetheless. In frantic desperation, Edward galloped madly back to the Small Wood. Not half an hour later, he spied Rebecca running down the slope to the summerhouse, her blue cape billowing like a sail behind her.

Edward dismounted and tethered his horse, then raced across the narrow footbridge to meet her. With outstretched arms, the lovers flew to each other.

"Love!" cried Rebecca breathlessly. "I tried but I just couldn't slip away. I saw you here each day, but I was unable to leave the house. Forgive me," she whispered, kissing his warm lips.

"Hush, hush. Come, I must talk to you." Edward led Rebecca to a nearby bench and seated her there. Tenderly he pulled her cloak about her body and lifted its hood to cover her hair.

"Can your father help us?" Rebecca inquired. "What did he say?"

"We met in the library," Edward said in a serious voice, avoiding the directness of her question. "There is a setback, dearest. We cannot be married just now."

A low moan passed from Rebecca's lips, and she began to cry wet tears that streamed down her cheeks. Distraught himself, Edward sought to comfort her, gathering her into the circle of his arms as she sobbed out her disappointment against his rough jacket.

"But we must, Edward . . . We must! Dear God, I cannot wait!" There was an urgency in Rebecca's voice that Edward sensed but did not pursue.

Instead, patiently, he explained to her that Emory was soon to be married, and when wed, it would be *his* wife who would be mistress of Guersten Hall. At the moment, Edward had a home there, but that was all. Rebecca's anguish was intense, and Edward realized she knew nothing of the plans by her father and his, and not wishing to add to her sadness, he did not reveal that Emory's chosen bride-to-be was her own sister.

"I have only my allowance now, and it is not enough. I am going to London. I have a plan, Rebecca, and when I get enough capital, I shall return for you. Will you go away with me then?"

"You know I will," she sobbed. "But what will I do in the meantime?"

"You must be brave," Edward whispered huskily into her hair. "I love you more than anything in this world, and I will return for you. You must believe that, trust me."

They kissed, again and again, but by now Rebecca was shivering almost uncontrollably, and he feared she would take a chill, for it was still damp and raw despite the sun. Rising, he insisted that Rebecca return to the house.

"No! Don't leave me!" she cried hysterically, clutching at his collar. "Please, Edward. Don't go!"

"I must, my love. And when I return, I must not find you ill. You must guard your health as never before . . . for me, because I love you."

Knowing that her mother would see them together, but suddenly not caring, they walked across the damp grass to the front door of the manor house. There, before the open door, the lovers parted.

"Don't cry, Rebecca. Be strong and let me remember you smiling. I won't be long, I promise."

Tenderly, Edward kissed his beloved one last time, and then he turned and ran down the lawn past the summerhouse and across the footbridge. Rebecca never saw the unshed tears brimming his eyes.

Once in the saddle, Edward galloped back to Guersten Hall. There, he left his horse under the shadowy portico while he went to his room to pack a small bag. An hour later, he was well on his way to London.

CHAPTER FOUR

At Miss Phillipps's Academy in Portsmouth, Rachel Brenham sat alone in the small room that had been hers for five years, her father's letter spread once more across her lap. The letter had arrived several days ago, and Rachel had read it at least twenty times since then. *At last! I am going home,* she thought, smoothing the paper flat. In all the years she had been at the academy, not once had Rachel ever pleaded to return home, ever whined for holidays and vacations. Like her mother, Rachel had come to understand that her father's will was stronger than hers, and it was his will that had made Miss Phillipps's her home. In the beginning, it had been difficult, especially when most of her classmates journeyed homeward twice a year while she remained in place at the academy. In that, though, Rachel was not alone, for there were others who remained also, boarded over until the semester began again. Several of them were orphans whose thoughtless guardians considered their Christian duty well done if they provided the hapless girls with proper schooling. Some others were daughters of widowers; one had parents who were missionaries in some far-off place, and two jolly sisters were always at the academy while their father tramped the seas conducting the admiralty's business.

Rachel returned the letter to its envelope, smoothing the wool of her spice-brown dress and closing her eyes, picturing Brenham Manor in her mind. *How she longed to be there now! She had been away so long!* Her eyes filled as she thought of her mother and Rebecca, and she fought back unshed tears, just as she had done so often all these years. But she did not weep, would not weep. *Never again!*

She remembered how bitterly she had wept the morning she left her father's house for this place. Halfway to Portsmouth, she had recognized that the carriage would not be turned back, that her tears had been for naught. She ought to have known that straightaway after seeing her father's stern face and grim-set mouth.

Rather resolutely for one so young, Rachel had been forced to come to grips with her own weaknesses, determining then and there to develop an inner strength and some self-reliance. Never again would she resort to weeping! Instead, she would learn to accept whatever it was that life held for her and try to put a sunny face on those things that were distasteful.

Miss Blackburn had misunderstood her silence; that much Rachel knew. But she had been forced to turn her back on her old governess that day, not out of spite, but simply because she knew that another tearful farewell would have destroyed her newfound resolve. That very first night at the academy had been the most difficult. Alone and frightened, Rachel had lain in the darkness of a strange room with tightly clenched fists, gulping deep breaths to hold back rising hysteria. For the first time in her life, she made a genuine effort at self-control and was surprised to learn that she was able to conquer her fears. The rest had been much easier.

Rachel was exceptionally bright. Alert and curious, she had excelled at her lessons and soon became one of the better students at the academy. As her outlook on life changed, her physical appearance altered also, though admittedly that alteration was gradual. Her nervousness disappeared, and at night she slept soundly, and as Portsmouth's sea air whetted her appetite, ever so slowly she began to gain weight.

During this past year, most of her scholastic studies had been completed, and Rachel had grown from girl to woman. Even so, she had still not sought permission to return to Brenham Manor and the midlands she loved so. She had waited, obediently, to be summoned. Because she was naturally friendly, Rachel had filled her days assisting others, and she was most helpful with those new students who arrived weeping and on the verge of hysteria. She felt some kinship to them, remembering her own first night, and the matrons never understood how the calm young woman was able to assuage their fears. Thanks to Rachel though, many a terrified girl had settled quickly into the no-nonsense routine of the school.

Only an hour ago Rachel had returned from a friendly chat with the headmistress in her cramped little office. Her father's letter specified that her departure for the midlands be sometime after the tenth of December, but Rachel was now desperate to leave sooner, anxious to test the maturity and confidence she felt in herself. Besides, she was eager to spend some time in London shopping before returning to the midlands. She would stay at her father's townhouse, she assured Miss Phillipps, and if he were not in London, then she could continue on to Brenham Manor herself by public coach.

Listening to Rachel's plans for departure, the matron was highly skeptical, but she was won over by the young woman's calm confidence in herself and finally gave her consent. After all, she reasoned, the girl had been kept at arm's length from her family all these many years . . . and Miss Phillipps had received a separate letter from Benjamin Brenham, sensing that there was something cryptic in it. Whatever it was, she felt now, it surely boded not well for Rachel, or her future, of that she was certain. *Let the girl go,* the matron suddenly decided. *Let her try her wings, have a little excitement on her own before her father consigned her away to be the wife of some stuffy shipping clerk somewhere,* for Miss Phillipps had received such cryptic letters before. She understood what was written—and what had been omitted. Normally she would never have risked the reputation of her school for any student, but Rachel was different, and Miss Phillipps liked her. *Yes,* she thought, *let her go, and if Benjamin Brenham fumes, so be it!*

The headmistress did insist, however, that one of the matrons accompany Rachel as far as London and, further, thought it best that Rachel stay at a certain small house near the very edge of the fashionable shopping district. "Your father may not even be at his London offices, my dear," she said to Rachel. "The house may be closed, and the servants will not be expecting you. Besides, I'll worry less."

She explained to Rachel that Margaret Morton's discreet establishment was merely a London brownstone, like dozens of others, but Mrs. Morton boarded only select young ladies, and secretly Miss Phillipps knew that no one was allowed out of that house after dark without permission or escort. Eager to be on her way, Rachel quickly agreed to the arrangements, promising to send word to her father's warehouse the moment she arrived in the city.

Excited, she hurried away into Portsmouth, where she ordered a new traveling dress and a sleek new bonnet from the milliner's. The night before her departure, she dined privately with Miss Phillipps and the other matrons. The monastic women were a small but pleasant group, and they chattered together gaily. All were terribly fond of Rachel and would miss her. Among them, they decided that Clarissa Wheeler could be spared to accompany Rachel to London. Clarissa would visit with her sister and then return again to the academy a day later.

On the day of her departure, Rachel awoke to find the sky heavy with gray clouds, the wind whipping fallen leaves around her window. Terribly excited, she dressed in her new finery, deterred not by the grayness. With a critical eye, she studied her image in the wood-framed mirror. The frightened child who had been delivered to these doors five years before was gone. In her place now stood a beautiful young woman, poised and confident; all vestige of the old Rachel disappeared forever.

This new Rachel was tall and slender, the brown velvet dress fitting snugly to the contours of her body, accenting its lush curves. Rich brown hair was neatly coiffed in dark shining curls that lay against a long and shapely neck. Rachel's complexion was flawless, her cheeks flushed ever so lightly with color, and her luminous eyes, large and dark brown, were deeply fringed with thick sable-colored lashes. Her mouth was full and perfect, the lips pink and sensuous, showing straight white teeth when she smiled.

Anxious to be away, Rachel quickly added the last of her toilette articles to the two small trunks containing her possessions. She was almost ready, and stopped to tie on her bonnet and buttoned a short cape around her shoulders. It too was velvet, trimmed with braided grosgrain. Finally, carrying a matching muff and a small beaded reticule, Rachel descended the worn wooden stairs for the last time.

At the last minute, Miss Phillipps suffered some reservations about letting Rachel leave before the time stipulated by her father, but there was no changing Rachel's plans now, and her smiles dispelled the older woman's apprehensions. The headmistress sighed. "It has been a long time since you saw your father last, my dear," she said. "You are not the child you were, though he may not recognize that fact at once. Be patient with him and those around you, and bless you always in all your endeavors."

"I would have thought," the woman added, in her nasally voice, "that you would have tired of the color brown by now," referring to the uniforms worn at the academy, even by the matrons. "But you look lovely, Rachel . . . You will turn heads, I am sure." Turning to Clarissa, she added, "Miss Wheeler, you must frown all the way to London, if necessary!" Everyone laughed then, for Clarissa's frown was legend at the academy, having curbed many an evil thought and deed.

Amid confusion and much chattering, Rachel's luggage was loaded on a little wagonette that would take her and Miss Wheeler to the depot to catch the London-bound coach. Though there was much hand waving and calling out as the wagonette left the small quadrangle and headed for Portsmouth, Rachel, her eyes on the future, did not look back.

The sun peeped out from behind the clouds momentarily at intervals, but it remained cold and windy, and they found the dingy depot to be noisy and crowded. Miss Phillipps's observation was quite correct, too; every head did turn, the gentlemen taking note of Rachel's fine figure and the women enviously scrutinizing her expensive costume. But Clarissa's stout figure followed Rachel's slender one like a shadow through the depot to the waiting coach, and no one accosted her.

Until the very last moment before departure, there were only five passengers for London. Then, a foppishly dressed young man hurried into the carriage, spurred on noisily by his friends. Rachel suspected a conspiracy of some sort and smiled, knowing Clarissa 's reputation as chaperone. When the coachman mounted the driver's box, she settled back in her seat, and shortly the heavy carriage clattered across the cobblestoned yard and passed through the high gates. *She was on her way!*

Through the city limits and its lesser outskirts, progress was slow, but once the huge coach turned onto the London road, the horses lengthened their stride, and soon Portsmouth was far behind them. Stopping twice at inns along the coach road, the horses were watered and rested, and the passengers were given time to leave the carriage briefly to stretch their legs. At the halfway station, all four horses were unhitched and replaced with a fresh team while the passengers ate their dinner, seated before a warm fire in the inn's dining room.

The young dandy who boarded at Portsmouth found Rachel quite cool and unresponsive whenever he attempted to make conversation, and at the rest stop, he retreated sullenly to the tavern on the far side of the inn yard. When it came time to board the coach again, he reeked of claret, and Clarissa peered at him suspiciously from under the brim of her bonnet.

During the stop, the wind had mounted, coming in healthy gusts that shook the coach from side to side. Ahead of them, Rachel could see dark storm clouds gathering and thought surely it must rain very soon. Eventually, the sun disappeared for good, and when the rain came, it fell in great heavy drops that splattered noisily against the window beside her. The lurching of the coach and the drumming of the rain soon lulled Clarissa to sleep; sitting directly across from Rachel, she nodded off, her head tilting sharply against the padded cushions.

Other passengers became engrossed in full-stomached solitude, and some of them dozed, too. The air in the coach became stuffy and warm; Rachel unclasped her short cloak and untied the ribbons of her bonnet. At the last stop, the dandy had somehow managed to seat himself next to Rachel, and he saw his opportunity now. Soon Rachel was surprised to find she was being crowded in her seat. Discreetly she moved away, closer to the window, deliberately turning her face away from him, but the young man was not put off. He pressed closer, taking advantage of Clarissa's nap. His greatcoat lay folded across his lap, and under its cover he suddenly covered Rachel's hand with his, moist and clammy, and at the same time she felt his thigh pressing intimately against hers. She tried to withdraw her hand, but he only tightened his grip and leaned closer, his breath foul from the sour wine.

Rachel was tempted to call out or to nudge Clarissa's foot, next to her own. But then, if she were to be independent, she thought, she must be prepared to handle such situations herself. At her breast, she wore a topaz brooch; with her free hand, she unclasped its pin, long and sharp. Without a qualm, she stuck the young man in the thigh. He shrieked loudly and released her hand just as Clarissa's head shot up. The matron glared at the man, who had now moved as far from Rachel as possible. Even the other passengers, roused from their naps, frowned at him.

Looking across at Clarissa, Rachel shrugged her shoulders with a look of complete innocence on her face. On guard now, Clarissa folded her arms across her ample bosom and sat frowning clear to the next way station. There, the misguided fellow left the coach, and Rachel overheard him making arrangements for return passage to Portsmouth.

Except for the weather, the rest of the journey passed uneventfully. It continued to rain steadily, and the unpaved tracks in the dirt road became puddled and muddy. Progress was slowed considerably, but the horses plodded on, while the coachman sat atop the box covered with a tarp that did little to keep him dry. At the very last stop before London, the ladies refused to even step from the coach, for the inn yard was a quagmire.

Despite her excitement, even Rachel was now weary, her back stiff and her bottom sore from the jolting ride, and as they rumbled on, she too finally dozed, only to be awakened by the sound of hoofbeats thundering at last on cobbled pavement. *They had entered the city!*

She could see little from the window of the coach, for it was completely dark as they rolled into the sprawling yard of a huge coach house, where torches and lamplight reflected against the wet stones. Despite the weather, the yard bustled with activity; great heavy coaches arrived and departed with regularity, and both the dining room and the alehouse were crowded. Mail sacks and packages, as well as passengers and their luggage, were transferred from one coach to another, while ragged stable boys unhitched and led away lathered and sweating beasts, and hostlers brought fresh teams from the livery. The noise was incredible, and for a moment Rachel became confused by it all. Where would they ever find transportation to Mrs. Morton's amid this disorder?

Struggling with weariness, Rachel fretted that her lovely new dress was well rumpled, its hem damp and muddied. She led Clarissa to a dry spot under the long overhang where they waited for their luggage to be off-loaded. There were people everywhere, coming and going, pushing and jostling. Rachel had never realized before just how crowded London was.

Clarissa watched Rachel like a hawk, as though expecting her to falter, and sensing this, Rachel's resolve returned. *This will never do,* she thought, and mustering her energies, she left Clarissa sitting atop one of her trunks and went into the inn. There, amid the clamor, she managed to catch the eye of a young potboy struggling with an armful of heavy tankards. She explained her quandary and was in luck; the lad knew of a trustworthy driver with a small curricle for hire that would take Rachel to Mrs. Morton's and then deliver Clarissa to her sister's for half a crown. The boy himself transferred their luggage, and Rachel tossed him a coin, thankful for his assistance.

The hired curricle clip-clopped along, threading its way familiarly through London's cobblestoned streets, headed for Mrs. Morton's. They were really closer to Clarissa's destination, but her loyalty to Miss Phillipps demanded that Rachel be delivered safely to Mrs. Morton's first. Once there, the two women parted hurriedly as soon as Rachel's trunks were taken inside. It was cold and windy, though the rain had lessened.

It was Mrs. Morton herself who showed Rachel to a snug room on the second floor. While it was quite small, it was exceptionally neat and comfortable, and it contained a wide bed. There was no fireplace, however, and the room was extremely chilly until a stooped old man appeared with a small brazier and a pan of burning coals.

"'Tis small, me dear," he said, smiling, pointing to the brass brazier, "but t'will warm this little room in no time, and I'll be back with a warm brick for ye bed. 'Tis cozy ye'll be."

Again struggling with her fatigue, Rachel decided not to go downstairs for her supper, but Mrs. Morton would not hear of a guest going to bed without something to eat. In no time, a tray was prepared and brought to Rachel's room, and the smell of warm biscuits alerted her growling stomach, for she had not eaten in several long hours. Sitting at a little table, she uncovered the tray eagerly to find the fare upon it simple but adequate—shepherd's pie, biscuits, and fresh butter, washed down with a steaming mug of strong tea—and she was pleased to finish her meal with a piece of delicious Sally Lunn leftover from Mrs. Morton's afternoon tea. Rachel ate every crumb on the tray.

Contented, she turned the covers on the big bed and changed into a long nightgown. She was comfortable now, and without waiting for the promised warming brick, she climbed into bed and blew out the lamp. The little brazier gave the room a pink glow, and feeling warm and secure, Rachel snuggled deeper under the covers. It was then that she remembered vaguely that she had not sent word to her father about her arrival in the city. *Well,* she thought drowsily, *it can wait until tomorrow,* and promptly fell asleep.

How long she slept, she never knew. When she finally opened her eyes and sat up in the soft bed, the curtains were still drawn, and the little brazier had been filled again with glowing coals. The supper tray was gone, and her traveling dress and cape had been carefully sponged and brushed and now hung from a sturdy wall hook. From the hallway, Rachel heard gay chattering and knew that it must be late. Jumping from the bed, she hurried to the window to open the draperies.

Heavens! It must be coming up nine o'clock, she guessed, judging from the position of the brilliant sunshine. Only a puddle here and there remained from the previous day's downpour; the streets were washed clean again. Her window overlooked a tiny front yard, and Rachel saw two fashionably dressed women leave the house, passing down a short walk to the street. The brownstone was closer to the shoppes than Rachel had imagined. *I can go about on foot,* she realized.

She unpacked her trunk, hanging only what she would need in the next day or two. She was pleased to note that her day gowns were barely wrinkled and was glad she had packed them with care before leaving the academy. Hurrying, she made her toilette and dressed, choosing a rich taffeta of lustrous blue, adding a crinoline for fullness. Over it she wore a long fur-trimmed pelisse; it was brown, and not new, but it was warm and lightweight, just right for the weather. As she finished dressing, she was drawn again and again to the window, anxious to be out of doors in such golden sunshine.

Before leaving the room, she pinned a ridiculous little hat atop her curls; its tiny ribbons bouncing merrily as she went down the stairs, humming to herself. Margaret Morton met her in the hallway by the front door.

An older woman, usually stern-faced, Mrs. Morton melted into smiles when she spied the breathtaking creature in brown, and Rachel was obliged to outline her plans for the day over tea and scones in the sunny dining room. "Of course you can walk to the shoppes, Miss Brenham, but certainly you can't be planning to walk all the way to your father's warehouse! And alone at that! His offices are right on the docks . . . And you so beautiful every scoundrel in London will be following! No, my dear, you return here at one o'clock, and Mr. Tremblay, whom you met last night, will take you in my little cabriolet. I admit it isn't fancy, but it will get you safely through the narrow streets, and once you catch up with your father, he can decide what to do with you."

"Very well," agreed Rachel. "This morning I shall proceed to Scofield's to make some selections, and I'll return at one."

On the main thoroughfare, Rachel found the sidewalks and shoppes crowded. Fancy-dressed ladies and gentlemen strolled about slowly, window-shopping and stopping to gossip with one another. Along this street, with its expensive and stylish shoppes, the contrast in society was not apparent. The London poor were not in evidence; no beggars or ragged urchins were to be seen, no streetwalkers plied their trade, no drunken derelicts slept in doorways. Here, sleek landaus and phaetons waited by the curb, their passengers adding to the mosaic of colors, the gentlemen in tight-fitting trousers and tall hats, the ladies gay in rustling silks and velvet, their sweeping skirts held wide with layers of petticoats and small hoops.

As she wandered from window to window, Rachel was enthralled by it all. It had been so very long since she had last been on a real shopping excursion, and here she was, alone and independent, on her own and ready to make selections to her wardrobe that were far more stylish than the brown uniforms that were de rigueur at Miss Phillipps's Academy.

The windows were filled with an array of brightly colored fabric and clothing, as well as sparkling jewelry, furs, leather goods, and bric-a-brac. Rachel stood fascinated by the displays, and several gentlemen nudged one another when they spied her—beautiful face aglow, figure obvious even under the shapeless cloak.

The entrance to Eleanora Scofield's elegant little shoppe was on a side street, and Rachel forced herself to turn away from the busy boulevard. There was far less foot traffic in the narrow lane, and she found the entrance easily. She was surprised to find its windows filled merely with fresh flowers and green ribbons, for Eleanora Scofield made it policy never to advertise her wares in her shoppe window, since all of her creations were originals and no two were ever exactly alike. Stepping through the door, Rachel found herself in a delightful little reception area, all done up in green and white. A young maid appeared, took her name, disappeared, and in only a flash Eleanora herself scuttled from the salon at the rear of the shoppe, a look of utter surprise registered on her face.

"My dear Miss Brenham, your father told me to expect you, but I am certain he said December! You are a month early!"

Clearly dumbfounded, Rachel stared at the woman openly. Father? Expect her? December. None of it made any sense to her!

Nor to Mrs. Scofield, at that moment, but unknown to Rachel, her father had visited Eleanora upon his return to London, just days after agreeing to George Guersten's plan to betroth Rachel to Emory. With her future position as mistress of the Hall in mind, Benjamin had instructed Eleanora Scofield to gather the very best in fabrics and to prepare some designs for his daughter, who was finishing school. He knew that Rachel would require a complete new winter wardrobe and another in the spring. And while he had said nothing to Eleanora of betrothal or marriage, she was astute, suspecting the wardrobe to be a bridal trousseau, but now, since no engagement ring adorned the girl's slender finger, Eleanora wisely made no mention of a trousseau.

"Your father left some rather specific instructions, my dear, but I am hardly prepared. However, let me take your cloak, and I shall show you what I have. We'll begin there."

She took Rachel's pelisse, having already assessed that it was not one of her creations. Noting its obvious wear, she passed it silently to a maid with a wave of her hand and led Rachel to a private sitting room which contained two green velvet chairs and a long work table. In one corner stood a tall triple mirror and a round dais, used for fittings. Across the room, a silk screen hid a dressing alcove. Sunlight poured through two long windows, draped and swagged in the palest of pink, its rays splashing across the carpeted floor.

Eleanora excused herself and left the room for several minutes, while Rachel tried to fathom how this woman could have possibly been expecting her. All her mother's clothing came from Scofield's, had for years, but a seamstress from Aylesbury had usually visited Brenham Manor whenever Rachel or Rebecca required gowns or dresses, saving Louisa the long trip to London for the children's fittings. And of course, Lydia was quite nimble with needle and thread.

In her workroom on the second floor, Eleanora stood silently, her mind working furiously. She was as confused as Rachel! At Benjamin's request, she had already sketched some designs, but they just wouldn't do! She was positive that Benjamin had mumbled something about a girl a little plain, thin, and small bosomed, and her designs would have craftily enhanced that girl. But the auburn-haired young woman waiting downstairs was a beauty! *That face!* thought Eleanora. *And that figure!* No, her designs were all wrong for Rachel, and she tossed them into the little fireplace between the windows. She could hardly wait to drape that figure with satins, watered silks, and *peau de soie*, even though it meant starting all over again.

Eleanora was a small and energetic woman, well into her fifties. Her shoppe was almost unknown until Benjamin Brenham brought Louisa to it many years before, recommended by Crofts, his tailor, and just as Crofts had benefited from Benjamin's patronage, so had Eleanora. The wives of Benjamin's associates hurried to her shoppe simply because Louisa did.

She was both designer and seamstress then, but through the years she had expanded her business and made a small fortune in the process. Twenty seamstresses now toiled in a large room upstairs, and four young men in smart green livery were kept busy delivering large parcels and hat boxes, all marked with the distinctive green-and-white Scofield stripe. Her clientele now was fairly exclusive—the wealthy, women of title, and one or two of her better creations had even been designed for members of the royal household.

Briskly she clapped her hands, and several assistants appeared at her office door as if by magic. She gave them all hurried instructions, and they scurried off to rummage through storerooms and locked closets. Eleanora was excited, looking forward to the task of dressing the beauty downstairs, and she returned to the little room where Rachel waited gazing out of the window into a small courtyard. The assistants streamed in carrying bolts of laces and satins, rich brocades, and an assortment of trim. Some were left on the tables, but many were rejected by Eleanora at a glance—too gaudy, too stiff, too heavy. Boxes of beading and semiprecious stones were rejected, as were trailing boas and flashy feathers. Eleanora stamped her small foot soundly.

"No, no, no!" she cried. "Can't you see the young lady doesn't need them? This one requires no camouflage."

Studying Rachel's figure again, Eleanora surveyed the long neck, the sloping shoulders, and the high, firm breasts. She measured the tiny waist, taking note of long slender arms and legs that ended with slim ankles. *Perfect,* she thought. Rachel's lovely face and that graceful figure would be adornment enough for her creations!

But the pile on the table grew anyway, and Rachel was astounded by the variety of colors and textures. Eleanora set to work, measuring, draping, and discussing ideas freely with Rachel as she did so. She made several quick sketches and gave confusing instructions to her patient helpers. The activity was frenzied, and the room soon became littered with fabric and yards of ribbons and braid.

The two women found they liked each other despite the difference in their ages. That was not surprising, for Eleanora was an artist, charming and congenial, and Rachel was outgoing, with an acute sense of style and color that Eleanora admired in one so young. The morning sped away, and soon it was time for Rachel to leave. Eleanora set appointments for the next two days and walked with Rachel to the front door. Rachel was quite breathless, having been draped and undraped, measured and pinned all morning long. Eleanora smiled.

"I know it all seems confusing right this moment," she said reassuringly. "But you will see, my dear. When you come tomorrow, I will have made order here. There will be final sketches and designs for your approval, and my girls are ready. You will see," she said, patting Rachel's arm. "You will see."

Returning to Mrs. Morton's, Rachel took a moment to freshen herself before Mr. Tremblay assisted her into the small cabriolet. Turning away from the fashionable shopping district, they wove their way through the streets, headed toward the docks. The further they went from Mrs. Morton's brownstone, the more it became apparent to Rachel that most of London's masses were terribly crowded and, for the most part, terribly poor. The housing was decrepit and squalid, the streets so filthy that yesterday's rain had made no inroad at washing it away. Rachel was glad that the drop-hood of the little carriage was in place, for the inhabitants of the area scrutinized the passersby intently. They missed nothing, noting the cut of a coat and the turn of a boot; even the sun glinting off a metal button caught their eye. A few gentlemen passed by them on horseback, moving smartly, their riding sticks held prominently for all to see, and even old Tremblay kept his fingers curled loosely around the butt of his whip. Rachel shuddered. It must be a frightful place after dark, she thought, glad she had heeded Mrs. Morton's advice not to walk.

Years before, her father's offices had been moved to a vast loft over one of his warehouses. Today, as every day, the enclosed yard was a beehive of activity, for Benjamin Brenham exacted full measure from all his employees. Heavy drays and wagons were briskly loaded and off-loaded, the goods they held piled in tall stacks to be counted and labeled for reshipment and delivery. There were horses everywhere: cart horses, great Cleveland bays, and teams of hefty Clydesdales. It was noisy, and the stench assailed Rachel's nose. A stack of crates had toppled, a mistake someone would pay dearly for, and the pungent aroma of blended whiskey mingled with that of dung, molasses, and spices and dozens of others Rachel could not identify.

The burly warehousemen stopped their labors at the sight of Rachel, staring brazenly as she alighted from the carriage and passed by them. Their lecherous glances unnerved her, and she was again thankful she hadn't come alone. She went up the stairs to the offices, to be met near the stairs by a young accountant, already stooped and squinting from years at his trade.

"'E's not 'ere, Miss Brenham," the man said almost apologetically when Rachel explained her mission. "'E left London yestiday . . . 'ad to go to Manchester 'e did, to see about some waggins. Mr. Potter's clerk 'ere, an' 'e can tell ye when ye father's likely t' return."

The man escorted Rachel to Mr. Potter's outer office, a small and dingy place with a worn carpet. Mr. Potter and Benjamin had once worked together in Wittenham's office many years before, and when Benjamin took over the business after his marriage to Louisa, Potter had moved into the position of chief clerk. Now, the younger accountant left Rachel there to wait, nervously offering her the only chair, for Potter was occupied in his office with another caller. Rachel refused the seat, preferring to remain standing, for the chair was rickety and badly soiled. She paced the floor while waiting, stopping in surprise when she heard a woman's voice filtering from Potter's office, knowing that no women were employed on these premises.

"Mrs. Bailey sent me, sir. I came for her money."

"Mr. Brenham isn't here," stated Mr. Potter flatly. "But he left this bank draft for Mrs. Bailey."

Rachel heard the woman mumbling, and then Mr. Potter spoke again, rather gruffly. "Yes, yes, go on . . . speak up, girl. I've other business."

"Well, sir, Mrs. Bailey wants Mr. Brenham to know she'll need more money . . . what with another child coming an' all, sir. The last one was sickly, and the doctor still hasn't been paid yet."

"I see," said Potter. "Tell her not to be concerned, it's an oversight, I'm sure. Mr. Brenham is a generous man, as you well know. But he won't return from Manchester for at least ten days . . . perhaps longer, for he'll stop at his manor house before returning to the city. Tell Mrs. Bailey that."

"Yes, Mr. Potter. Will he come to see her? She's sure to ask."

"Doesn't he always? And no doubt, if he cannot, the extra money will be included with her December stipend. Be off, now!" he growled.

Rachel had not meant to eavesdrop, but the door *was* half open, and their voices carried clearly to the outer office. She was shocked! Her father and another woman? It couldn't be possible!

She was still standing in the same spot by the window when the door opened wide and a young maidservant in a gray cloak and bonnet emerged from Mr. Potter's office, closing the door behind her. The young women stared at each other for a brief moment, and then the servant girl hurried past and went down the stairs.

Rachel leaned against the wall. She closed her eyes and pressed her gloved hand against her lips. She felt ill; her stomach churned. The air was suddenly fetid, and she actually felt faint. *I must get out of here,* she thought, and without waiting to speak to Potter, she left the building swiftly, passing the startled accountants once more. Skirts dragging on the splintered steps, Rachel dashed down the stairs. Outside on the loading dock, the din and the noxious odors almost made her retch.

Mr. Tremblay spotted Rachel's white face and knew at once that something was amiss, and with his help, she scrambled into the cabriolet, her cheeks burning. Fortunately, under its folding hood, she was hidden from the prying eyes of the draymen, and waving Tremblay on, she took a perfumed handkerchief from her reticule and touched it lightly to her damp brow.

It simply cannot be true, she mused. But it must be! Had she not heard it with her own ears? Rachel knew little of the ways of men and their mistresses, but she was not totally ignorant; she knew these things happened, and frequently, she guessed. Many wealthy men maintained mistresses privately, quite apart from their respectable public images. But her father?

The dock area fell behind them, and when they turned up a wide street in a middle-class neighborhood, Rachel sighted a slight figure in a gray cloak and bonnet rounding the corner ahead of them. All at once she was curious. Who *was* this Mrs. Bailey? Rachel bent forward and spoke to Tremblay.

"Slow down, please. I must know where that young woman goes."

"But, miss . . ."

"Please, Mr. Tremblay. I'm all right now, and it cannot be far since she's afoot."

Two streets and two turns later, the girl in gray entered a large brick house set close to the street. Nothing about its exterior gave any clues to its inhabitants. It was solid, well built, and well maintained, as were those around it, and while Trowbridge Road was not the most fashionable of addresses, it was obvious that the upkeep of a house this size required a considerable outlay of capital. And her father paid that cash, monthly it seemed! For a mistress!

Rachel had seen enough and bid Tremblay drive on. Her head was pounding miserably, and she could not think clearly. When they returned to Mrs. Morton's brownstone, she hurried straightaway to her room, where she sat perched on the bed for nearly an hour, bewildered by her discovery. She thought of her mother. How hurt she would be if she even suspected the existence of someone like Mrs. Bailey. Well, Rachel would never be the one to tell her; that was certain. But what on earth would she say to her father when he returned to Brenham Manor? How could she face him? *It will all be so awkward,* she thought. *Brenham Manor! Home! And how am I going to get home?* She suddenly wailed.

She stood, crossing the room to hang her pelisse on the wall hook. Standing before the wardrobe, she caught her image in the mirror and suddenly burst into laughter. Her clothes were untidy, the ridiculous little hat sat askew, and one of her curls hung lopsidedly over one ear.

You little fool! she told herself. *You wanted to be on your own, yet the very first day, you end up hiding in your room like a frightened child. Why, in another instant you'll be weeping!*

It was true, and Rachel chastised herself roundly. Her first crisis and she had resorted to typical womanly tactics. *My God!* She had become nauseous, nearly fainted! It must never happen again, she vowed. She would have to learn to keep her head, no matter what the circumstances. So her father had a mistress! It had nothing to do with her. Who knows, she thought, it might even happen to her one day! She was a woman now, and she must be prepared to see and hear things that might shock her. Why, any girl in the streets knew more about life than she did!

Stiffening her spine, Rachel regained her composure, biting her lips to add some color, just as Mrs. Morton knocked on her door. "I just came back from the green grocer, and Tremblay said you were not feeling well. Is anything wrong, Miss Brenham?"

"No, no," said Rachel quickly, opening the door. "Everything is fine. It appears my father left the city already, and Mr. Tremblay mistook my disappointment for something else."

"Dear, dear! What will you do now?" asked the older woman.

"Why, I shall finish my shopping as planned, and Friday morning I will take the Peterborough coach to Coltenham. I will wait at the inn there until someone fetches me to my father's house."

A public coach? If Mrs. Morton had her doubts, Rachel gave her no time to express them. "I do hope supper won't be delayed," she said, changing the subject, "for I am famished. Will we have your Sally Lunn again? It was especially delicious, and it is such a favorite of mine."

The compliment did it; the older woman relaxed, convinced that this pretty young thing would give her no cause to worry, and on Friday, Mr. Tremblay could see her to the coach. "Just listen for the bell, my dear," said Mrs. Morton when she left Rachel's room. "It will signal supper."

The rest of Rachel's week passed in a bustling flurry. Each morning she arrived at Mrs. Scofield's very early, and the two women sat together over coffee, poring over Eleanora's sketches and notes. Rachel made her selections, making some changes, but finding the collection on the whole to be very satisfactory, and Eleanora's girls were set to work at once.

Rachel found the fittings to be tiresome, and she was unable to stand still for the pinnings. "I think I will make a horsehair mannequin of your figure," said Eleanora, finally. "It will make the fittings easier on both of us, and you won't have to return for more of them. Most of your choices will be completed before you leave the city, for I have six of my best girls working just on your selections. The remainder will be delivered to Brenham Manor before Christmas."

Rachel slipped away from Eleanora's shoppe one afternoon long enough to purchase several pairs of shoes and a pair of shiny black riding boots. At a new Parisian shoppe on the boulevard, she selected sleek leather breeches to go with them. Eleanora was shocked at the very sight of them.

"Why, you'll look like one of the stable boys!" she sniffed. "Sidesaddle is the only acceptable riding position for young ladies, and furthermore, you're going to look so fetching in your new riding dress that you'll never wear those . . . those . . . trousers!" she finally spluttered.

Rachel laughed merrily at Eleanora's disdainful expression, and when the older woman saw herself reflected in the triple mirror, she too laughed, as her assistants stared in disbelief, for Madame rarely ever smiled, and yet here she was, on her knees, giggling like a schoolgirl.

At last, Rachel completed her shopping, with time to spare, and set about purchasing small gifts for her family. A handmade lace shawl shot with silver thread was chosen for her mother, and she selected an engraved leather fob for her father's watch. For Rebecca, she found a small leather diary with a lock, sure to please, Rachel thought. Lydia and Agatha Crocker were not forgotten, and for them Rachel found hardbound books filled with pictures of faraway lands.

By the end of the week, the weather changed again, turning cold and raw as Rachel made ready to leave the city. She had added another trunk by now, a rather large one, filled almost exclusively with her new clothes, wrapped in Scofield green tissue paper. Rachel was impatient now, eager to be on her way, for all at once pangs of homesickness had overtaken her.

Her first meeting with her father was still days away, for he was in Manchester yet. *But tomorrow this time,* Rachel mused, *I will see Mother . . . and Rebecca, again.* She knew that her arrival would be such a surprise to them all, and she was glad, for it marked a new beginning. It was not *poor little Rachel* who was returning to them but a grown woman, a woman whom they would have to learn to accept as an entirely new person.

Rachel's spirits were buoyed by her week in London. Alone, she had accomplished what she had set out to do, and she made several new friends at the same time. It had all been like a final exam, a test, which she had passed comfortably. Her days of weeping were truly behind her now, and she knew she could face whatever it was that the future might hold for her.

CHAPTER FIVE

Before the Peterborough coach reached its first way station it began to snow. Apprehension became evident on the faces of all the passengers not long afterward, including Rachel's. The howling wind set the coach to rocking, the temperature began to fall, and in no time the visibility was so bad that the horses were slowed to no more than a fast walk.

"We'll not make Peterborough tonight, I fear." The dignified old man who spoke accented his remarks by shaking his gold-topped walking stick in the air.

"Hmphh! We'll be lucky if we even make it to Aylesbury," stated another of the passengers. "How that fellow up there in the box can even see the road in this blow is beyond me."

"The poor chap must be half frozen out there," added the first gentleman's wife sympathetically, all the while bundled warmly herself in a heavy cloak of good wool.

The coachman *was* cold, even though he wore a heavy greatcoat that was waterproof and would keep him dry at least. He had tied a long muffler across his top hat, wrapping it over his ears, and sat hunched against the biting wind, one foot braced against the brake lever, at the ready lest the wheels of the coach leave the road. He let the horses assume their own lead, set their own pace. The team would be replaced with a fresh one at the inn at Aylesbury, and the animals knew the way to their own stabling as well as he did.

Fortunately that morning, Rachel had chosen her traveling outfit with care. Its long skirt and jacket were wool, and her cloak was lined with fur, with a roomy hood which offered warmth and protection from the cold and the elements.

Some of the other passengers were not so lucky. As the journey progressed, Rachel became friendly with a young woman near her own age who traveled with two small children. In the cold coach, both children now shivered, for their outer clothing was of poor quality, and one, only a babe, had no mittens on his tiny hands. More than once Rachel offered to hold one of the children, but neither would leave their mother's arms.

Time passed interminably for all the passengers as the coach rocked along, for there was nothing to be seen from the window except whirling whiteness. Steadily losing time, they soon found that they were two hours behind their scheduled arrival at Aylesbury Inn.

"Worst blizzard I can ever recall, this early in November," commented an older man plaintively, just as the coach, lurching sideways without warning, came to a sudden stop. The team had lost the road, now little more than a track anyway under the fallen snow, and up in the box the coachman tried to remain calm. He wasn't lost, but he knew it would take some doing to get the heavy coach back onto the road. Climbing down from the box, he came round to the door and rapped on the window. One of the passengers rolled it down slowly.

A gusty blast of cold air whistled inside the coach as the round red face of the driver loomed up out of the silent whiteness. "Doona fear," he shouted against the wind. "We'll soon be under way again. We're near t' Aylesbury, an' they're lookin' out fer us, nae doot."

Three heavy lanterns were passed inside, to be lighted out of the gusting wind. The coachman then hung one on either side of the coach and, climbing up to his box, hung the third one high. Perhaps the lights would be spotted by someone watching for the overdue coach, although the experienced driver admitted to himself that the chance of that was slim; once on the open road each coach was more or less on its own. Besides, the wind would likely blow the lanterns out anyway.

The blinding snow continued to fall, mounting against the underside of the coach, and after a time, even the coachman's carefree concern turned to outright worrying. He knew that if he did not find the road at once and lead the horses onto it, then the coach was doomed. It would become stuck fast, for this storm was sure to last the night.

Inside the coach the passengers began to feel the penetrating cold, for even the meager warmth provided by their body heat had escaped from the interior when the window was wound down. Even Rachel felt the bite of cold toes despite the fact that her boots were better made than some of the others. She observed that the infant's little fingers were now nearly blue, and he slept fitfully in his mother's arms. With a sign to the child's mother, Rachel took the baby from her, drawing him close to her own breast, wrapping him in her voluminous cloak. The tiny tot struggled for a few minutes, but then, as the warmth of Rachel's mantle surrounded his chilled body, he fell into a sound sleep. With only one child to comfort, the young mother bundled her older child just as Rachel had done, and he, too, soon slept.

During the next moments, the horses strained repeatedly to return the coach to solid ground, while inside, all the passengers sat in silence, putting no voice to the fear that gnawed at them, all aware that the wind, and the drifts created by it, was their enemy. Before they could despair, however, the voice of the coachman sounded, and in the distance another voice answered, both of them barely heard over the howling of the wind.

"We're found!" cried one of the passengers, peering futilely out his window. Unexpectedly, the door beside Rachel was suddenly yanked open, and whistling wind and blowing snow came flying into their faces once more. In one move Rachel swept forward, bending low, sheltering the sleeping child's face with her wide hood, as a man's voice boomed directly over her head.

"Is everyone all right in here? The coachman says you have infants . . . Are they warm enough?"

The voice was deep and resonant, but crouched over the child as she was, Rachel could not see its owner's face. What she did see was that he was astride a huge horse, one which whinnied and snorted, pawing the ground with a great hoof. Only the man's ungloved hand was visible to Rachel as he leaned from his saddle above her, bracing himself on the doorjamb. It was the hand of a gentleman, with long well-shaped fingers and square manicured nails. On the ring finger was an impressive gold ring, formed in the shape of a boar's head, with glinting emeralds for eyes.

"Shut the door, man . . . and be quick about it!" cried one of Rachel's seatmates after assuring the man that the babies were safe.

Laughing pleasantly, the stranger shut the door with a bang. When Rachel peered out the window, he had disappeared from view; she saw nothing but snow. Curious, the old man sent a younger one to see what was happening outside; his return brought more snow and cold into the coach, but his words were encouraging.

"Some crazy galoot half in his cups has come to rescue us, riding the biggest beast I ever saw! He's a sight, he is! Cape's blowing wild in the wind, wide open, and him with only a shirt on underneath! Bare chest showing, it is!"

"My word! A sot? How can someone like that possibly be of any assistance to us?" worried the black-cloaked lady.

"He told the toff to ride postilion . . . and follow him," the other said, explaining that the coachman would ride astride the lead horse in the team as the stranger led the way to the shelter of the inn.

"But will the team follow that black beast?" inquired the older man. "An' will they even find the road in this damn storm?"

"Y' can't see the road at all out there! But the coachman 'pears to know the chap, claims that he knows these parts well, even if he is half gone with ale! If we can just get out of this drift, we should be . . ."

Even as he spoke, the coach rocked back and forth for several long minutes; it scraped, and swayed, and then was free of the drifted snow that imprisoned it. Progressing slowly, the coach moved forward, and about an hour later, they came abreast of the inn at Aylesbury. In the wildness of the night, Rachel thought surely that they would have missed it completely had it not been for the stranger's guidance, for the inn sat well off the road, and only between gusts of wind were the lighted windows visible at all.

The great two-storied main house that formed Aylesbury Inn was made of Portland stone and sat surrounded by long low-slung outbuildings. The stranger now led the snow-shrouded coach through the gates of the yard and right up to the door of the barn, where the passengers dismounted to find themselves under a brightly lighted overhang, which joined the barn to the kitchen of the inn. Still holding the sleeping infant wrapped protectively in her cloak, Rachel stepped down from the coach.

The tall stranger who had rescued them had ridden on into the barn, and she saw him there now, unsaddling his horse in the dark shadows at the far end. The animal was huge, a jet-black stallion, wild and fierce looking. Never before had Rachel seen a riding horse that big, and she stared in awe as the beast pranced around and around, snorting and pawing the wooden floorboards. As the passengers moved toward the inn, Rachel overheard one of the burly hostlers talking to their coachman.

"'E's a darin' one, he is! Brought in three coaches so fer t'night. Drunk or sober, nobody knows these roads like 'e do. An' that stallion! Did ever ye see the likes o' him before?"

Admitting to herself that surely she never had, Rachel followed the others to the back door of the inn. Aylesbury was near to a well-traveled crossroad; because of the severity of the storm, great coaches such as theirs were still arriving, but none were departing, and the place was crowded to the rafters. All the male passengers tossed their coats and cloaks atop a heap that was already mountainous, and migrated naturally into the tavern on the far side of the dining room. The innkeeper's buxom wife, her face flushed bright pink from the heat of a great open hearth, hustled the newly arrived women and infants into the warm kitchen until she could make room for them upstairs. She seated them next to the blazing fireplace and, shouting noisy commands to all, settled them with their backs to the warm bricks. All five of them would have to share one room, she said jovially, but they would be warm at least, for the room she had in mind was right over the kitchen. The wee ones would be safe, she added, setting wooden bowls before them.

After a hearty supper of steaming Brunswick stew and hot dumplings, the ladies were ushered directly up the back stairs to their assigned room, for there was simply no place to sit downstairs. In the tiny room, none of them bothered to undress; their trunks were still in the coach anyway. Rachel and the young mother took the double bed, sharing it with the two infants, now well fed and wearing clean napkins. The older woman, fatigued by the day's overlong excitement, curled up on a small pallet with her back to the chimney wall and was asleep almost immediately. Part of the garret, the tiny whitewashed room had a low ceiling; it was spotless and comforting, and now that they were all both warm and dry and their stomachs were full again, they all grew drowsy.

Settling down to wait out the storm, all were soon asleep, except Rachel. Wide awake, she was suddenly overcome by homesickness, brought close to tears when she realized she was almost near enough to Brenham Manor to go by horseback, if need be. *Tomorrow,* she said to herself over and over. *Tomorrow, I will be home!*

Twice during that night, Rachel slipped from beneath the quilts to peer through the little window that overlooked the yard of the inn. The snow still fell, swirling around the inn, forming great drifts near the fences and outbuildings. Once, she saw the great black stallion and his mysterious rider leading yet another snow-covered coach up to the door of the barn, and hours later, she was certain that she heard his booming voice downstairs in the kitchen calling for more ale, followed by the shrieks of the serving girls when they brought it.

By dawn, the snow had stopped, but the sky remained gray and threatening, and it was bitterly cold outside. Every able-bodied man and boy about the place turned into the yard to clear away the snow. The coaches had already been delayed far too long, and their drivers moved about the barn, carping and bawling, trying to sort out both their passengers and their teams. Many of the coachmen added two extra horses to the regular six hitches, knowing that the extra horse-power might be needed to combat drifting. Besides, they reckoned, even if conditions on the open road were not too bad, their extra pull would help make up for lost time. As it was, there would be no bonuses this trip. The innkeeper and his wife busied themselves heating large flat stones in the fireplaces of the kitchen and the dining room; wrapped in old carpeting, they would keep the passengers' feet warm, for the journeys would take longer than was usual, and the bitter cold was penetrating. Rachel commiserated with the coachmen, who would need to sit outside on the box without protection from the wind.

The confusion in the yard mounted and many local residents showed up at the crack of dawn, surrounding the inn with sleighs and pungs, in the hope that those passengers already near their destinations might opt to be taken directly to their homes for a few coins of the right size. Rachel's coach stood near the entrance of the barn, and as the driver checked his teams, she joined the others there. Everyone was wearing wrinkled clothing, and the men were in bad need of shaves, but still, all were in good spirits as they stood about joking of their communal misery.

As Rachel prepared to step into the coach, she heard a loud commotion in the barn, behind her. There, the great stallion, rearing and kicking, with nostrils flared wide, had the stable boys running for cover. Near the door, the brawny hostler boxed the ears of a young stable lad, who trembled in fear as the beast screamed again and showed his teeth.

"Damn you, brat! Told you t' stay away from 'im, I did! Won't let anyone near 'im but 'is master . . . y' knows that! If'n 'e spooks t' others I'll lay y' backside bare, I will!"

"I was only going to feed him," stammered the frightened lad.

"'Is master will feed 'im when 'e sleeps orf 'is ale! Till then, keep away from 'im. Take care of the gray an' the cob, like I tol' yer!"

The man and the boy backed away from the animal, and he quieted, but his eyes remained wild, and he shook his maned head and stamped the floor fiercely. He was fearful and yet magnificent, with a long arched neck, sleek flanks, and tapered legs. The gentlemen were still discussing the attributes of the beast as the coach hauled out of the yard, heading at last for Coltenham.

"Rare piece of horseflesh, that! Never saw any finer."

"Nor I! Dare say he and his owner actually saved our lives last night!" remarked the older man with respect.

"Aye! Liked to have thanked him proper, but he never showed his face."

Rachel considered the animal's owner for a moment. From what little she had seen of him and what she had pieced together from others at the inn, the man must be gentry. But what sort of gentleman went tearing around the countryside during a blinding blizzard, half gone with ale, and half dressed at that! *No matter,* she mused, *if not for him, I might now be sitting frozen somewhere along the London road.*

Even without the hindrance of new snow, it took them more than four hours to reach the outskirts to Coltenham, so deep was that which had already fallen. Not many miles after that, they turned into the yard of the Old Priory Inn. The Old Priory was not the handsomest of structures; it sat, squat and low, almost by itself in the middle of a yard, its stables and barns placed well to the rear. Several other coaches sat scattered at random angles to each other in the yard, but not a great deal of activity was noticeable.

Old Priory, and the large barn behind it, dated back to the days of good Queen Anne. The building had stood empty and abandoned for years, its cloistered wall broken through, until some shrewd and enterprising entrepreneur threw open its doors, in supplication almost, bidding weary travelers enter and rest. They did, and business flourished. The inn was only a way station, but it was the only one of any account on the much traveled road between Aylesbury and Peterborough.

Just the same, few passengers ever stayed the night, except in circumstances like last night's ferocious blizzard, for in truth, the Old Priory was not noted for its accommodations or its dining room either, for that matter, and only one small corner of the huge building was set aside for it. Here, under ancient but still sturdy timers, it was the refectory turned tavern, which was the hub of activity.

The village of Coltenham itself lay surrounded by gently rolling hills, lush meadows, and great forests, all ripe with valuable timber and game. Every square foot was owned by wealthy aristocrats, titled noblemen, and an occasional misplaced merchant like Benjamin Brenham, accepted to their outer circle as a peer because of his coinage.

Most of Coltenham's villagers were employed by the landowners in one capacity or another, even the women and children, except those that answered the call of the sea or them that hired out to the mill owners up north. Since the countryside was well dotted with great estates, it was only natural that the tavern at Old Priory would be the gathering place for all, rich and poor, employer and hireling alike, for the inn served as post office, and the only doctor for miles around kept a small room behind the kitchen wall. In the tavern itself, news and gossip, and many an outright lie, were passed freely over dripping tankards of ale. The place had seen many a celebration, its share of brawls, and had even been used as a courtroom once or twice.

Leaving her traveling companions, Rachel stepped from the coach for the last time, grateful to escape its lurching and swaying. She saw her trunks stowed outside the inn's door and hurried inside. Home was only an hour or so away now, and she hoped to hire a sleigh and make immediate departure for Brenham Manor.

But champing at the bit to be under way, Rachel was forced to wait yet again, for the innkeeper was busy outside with a departing carriage, while his wife filled in at the bar in the tavern. Rachel heard loud laughing coming from that room and the noisy clank of tankards rapping on wood. She paced up and down in the dining room, a starkly simple room, its high ceiling marked by wide oaken beams, rough hewn and blackened by soot. Eventually, Rachel was sighted by the innkeeper's wife.

"Dear lady . . . I knew not you were here. 'Tis my fault for not checking," she said. The woman was raw boned but slender as a girl, with a thin face and tired eyes. Wisps of scraggly hair escaped from beneath her mobcap and lay limp against her neck. She was friendly enough though and, still apologizing, produced a pot of tea and some sweet cakes, as if by magic. She listened as Rachel explained her need for transportation to her father's house, on Great Guersten Wood Road.

The woman nodded thoughtfully, but frowned. "My dear," she mewed, "there ain't be a soul 'ere jist now wot can take 'e, except me lad . . . an' 'e's on an errand jist now. But 'e'll be back afore the hour is up, an' if it don't start t' snow agin, then ye'll be orf to the manor in no time flat. Me lad has a sled, and a fine mare, an' 'e know t' way."

When the lad finally returned, Rachel was quite disturbed to discover he was really little more than a boy, in his very early teens at the most. His father, who had since returned to the inn, assured Rachel that the boy was familiar with the road. "And make haste, lad," he added, draping an arm around his son's shoulder. "It is sure to start snowing again, and I want you back before it does."

Rachel spoke to the innkeeper. "It will be nearing four when we arrive at the manor, and it will be dark, or almost so. If it is snowing then, why perhaps the boy should stay the night. There are comfortable quarters for the stable boys in the barn; he can sleep there."

All agreed that was most sensible; the mare had been out the better part of the day already, and if any drifting were encountered on the open road, she would be well spent by the time they reached Brenham Manor. Given the conditions, and the oncoming darkness, the return trip might be risky, especially for one so young.

And so, with Rachel's largest trunk lashed securely to the front seat next to the lad and her other two stowed in the rear of the sled beside her, they departed at once from the inn. The waxed runners of the sleigh moved swiftly over the snow along the open road, but once they turned onto Great Guersten Wood Road, the way at once became more difficult and torturously slow, thought Rachel, half out of her seat with the excitement of nearing home. They had just passed the halfway point in their journey when it began snowing again, thick fluffy flakes that made it hard to see any distance. There was no wind, no blowing, as in yesterday's blizzard, but once it began to get dark, Rachel knew they would find it difficult to see the landmarks at the edge of the road. Looking around, she noted there was no lamp or lantern of any kind in the sleigh.

Between stands of pine and evergreen, they made fairly good time, for there was little drifting under the close-packed trees, but each time they emerged from them, they were faced with high drifts, some impassable, which forced them to leave the road completely to skirt them. After one such skirting, the boy *whoa'd* the mare to a stop, admitting reluctantly to Rachel that he was confused about his bearings. Climbing down from the sleigh, she studied their surroundings in the fast-fading light, solemnly hoping that none of the familiar landmarks had changed during the time she was away at school. She threw off her mantle and squinted through the falling flakes, up to her knees in the deep snow. Ahead of them stood a long line of leafless trees, and she recognized them. "I see our mistake," she said, offering reassurance to the boy. "We must backtrack a short distance. We are on the wrong side of that high stone wall."

Somehow the lad was able to turn the sleigh without tipping it over, and then, retracing their route, returned at last to the barely discernible road. The winded mare was wheezing heavily now, and Rachel was grateful for *her* sake, as well as their own, that their journey was to be one way this night.

She peered ahead, remembering. Once past those barren trees, they would enter a long grove of full-grown evergreens where the going would be easier. On the other side of that grove should be a low hill and three great oaks, which had stood for centuries and now marked the entrance to Brenham Manor's service lane. *She would be home!*

Suddenly though, once they entered the grove, everything went wrong. Some of the younger trees were bent nearly to the ground under the weight of the accumulated snow, and near the edge of the road a great mass of white dropped without warning from one of them, landing just in front of the mare with a loud swishing sound, as the young tree sprang erect again. Startled, the animal snorted, and stood on her hind legs in the harness. The lad, also startled, leaped from the sled and ran to her side, just as the nervous mare reared again. This time, one of her forefeet struck the boy sharply on the side of his head; he fell to the ground, unconscious, landing directly under the mare's flailing hooves.

Rachel watched in horrified silence. It had all evolved in a matter of seconds! The animal was spooked, apt to bolt at any moment, and the injured boy lay deathly still just under her feet. Rachel's childhood fear of horses returned with a rush that overwhelmed her, and she sucked in draughts of the cold, clean air of the forest, trying to stifle it. Her heart was pounding so loudly she could hear it. *Don't panic! Keep your head!*

Climbing down from the seat, her breath coming in heaving gulps, Rachel pulled the lap robe from the seat behind her, and moving very slowly so the animal would not be frightened further, she used it to cover the mare's eyes. Although still trembling, the horse quieted almost at once as timidly Rachel bent over the boy.

His scalp was torn, bleeding profusely, staining the white snow beneath his head in a dark circle that widened even as she watched it. *What to do? Try to move him? Cover him and go for help?* Rachel ruled that out quickly; it was nearly dark now and getting colder, and she realized that if she left him here alone, perhaps she would be unable to return to this exact location again. *The boy would freeze to death!*

Gingerly, she touched a clean handkerchief to the lad's wound, startled to see how quickly it became sodden with blood. The sight of it decided her. *She couldn't leave him! She wouldn't!*

Reaching out her hand, she touched the animal's flanks. The trembling stopped, and when the mare was quite still, Rachel grasped the boy under his arms and dragged him to the side of the sled. There, she struggled with her two smallest trunks, moving them into the front seat, and returned her attention to the boy. Eventually the bleeding was staunched, and bending over his unconscious form, she rubbed his face with cold snow until at last he opened his eyes. He looked at her groggily, but he was conscious, at least, and somehow, with his feeble help, Rachel managed to get him into the sleigh, protecting him from the elements as best she could, using the thick lap robe, which she removed ever so carefully from the mare's eyes.

Rachel regained her courage. *Well,* she thought, *I shall have to walk.* The front seat was taken up by her trunks; she couldn't manage the reins anyway, so the animal, still quivering occasionally, would have to be led. She gathered the reins in her hand, spoke reassuringly to the mare and, hesitantly, led the way out of the grove.

Impeded by her long skirt and the weight of the heavy fur-lined mantle, which dragged in the snow, Rachel was surprised to find how slowly they progressed, and how quickly she became fatigued. She slogged onward without pausing to rest or catch her breath. She knew that she was only about two miles from her father's manor house, though it could not be seen through the falling snow; but soon she did spy a light in the stables. Deciding to take the sled directly there, Rachel hurried toward the service road, only to find her way blocked by a large tree branch, fallen from one of the oak trees.

An omen, she thought, prophetically. Since childhood, fallen branches had always seemed to her to have some unusual significance, to be an indication of some change soon to come into her life. Normally, its presence would have caused her great anguish, but just now she was too tired to concern herself about it very much. "We'll just have to go around," she said to the mare, "and wonder about it later."

Getting around it was not a simple matter, however, for the branch took up most of the road and the ground to the right of it dropped away sharply into a steep ravine. Holding her breath, Rachel maneuvered her way around the branch, inching the runners of the sleigh through some of the broken branches and along the very edge of the drop-off. She turned, pulling the mare in the general direction of the lane, now heading directly into the driving snow.

She was physically exhausted, her feet were frozen, and she was still concerned about the boy crumpled in the sleigh. She had come nearly two miles on foot in deep snow, the heavy cape dragging interminably at her shoulders. She unclasped it now, lifting it onto the sleigh with great effort, and leaned wearily against one of her trunks for a moment before continuing on, at a far slower pace. Her legs seemed leaden, her breathing nearly as labored as that of the mare. Ahead, the light in the barn glowed like a beacon, ever brighter, ever nearer, as Rachel headed toward it, her mind completely blank now. Only the light mattered any more.

Inside the warm cocoon of the barn, Rodney Stanton was spreading hay for the saddle horses when his dog began to bark steadily, running back and forth before the wide stable doors. At first Rodney suspected that Mutton had heard the wail of the wind, but then he heard it too, a faint calling, repeated again and again. Thinking that perhaps someone might be signaling from the big house, Rodney opened one of the barn doors wide.

There stood Rachel, although Rodney would not learn until later just who she was. Half frozen, she staggered into the barn, still holding the mare's lead tightly in one gloved fist, her bare head covered with snow, her skirt stiff and wet to the knees.

Opening the other door wide, Rodney led the exhausted horse inside, sled and all. The ice-caked runners skewed across the planks as Rodney, closing the doors against the wind, shouted for one of the grooms who were tending the cows in the adjoining dairy.

"Come quick, Jeremy, and bring some blankets. Hurry!"

Rachel faltered, her weight sagging against the mare, her lips blue and her jaw so stiff she could barely speak. She pointed to the pathetic figure huddled under the snow-covered lap robe.

"H-h-he's injured," she managed to stammer in a weak voice. "His head . . . it's bleeding. Help him."

Young Jeremy dashed into the stable barn then, carrying an armful of blankets, as instructed. He stopped dead in his tracks and stood looking at Rodney, dumbfounded, as the beautiful girl in wet clothing slithered to the floor at his feet in an exhausted faint.

Quickly, Rodney assessed the situation. He had recognized the boy, for the innkeeper was a friend of his, but neither Rodney nor Jeremy knew the identity of the young woman lying on the straw-strewn floor. The boy's injury was obvious, but the young woman suffered from exposure and exhaustion.

Deftly, he examined the boy's wound. As a veteran coachman, he saw at once that it had been wrought by a blow from a horse's hoof. Rodney had seen many like it before. The wound was deep, but its own swelling had checked the bleeding, and together he and Jeremy moved the weakened lad to a warm bed in the quarters they now shared at the rear of the stables, both of them glad to see the boy was fully conscious now.

"He'll be all right," Rodney said to Jeremy. "Head wounds are sometimes wont to bleed badly, but he'll have a wicked headache come morning. Keep him quiet, and I'll dress that cut as soon as I take the lass up to Agatha."

Rodney didn't know what else to do with her. She must be removed from those wet clothes at once, or she would surely catch pneumonia, and it would be unseemly to strip her bare here, before Jeremy and the boy. Besides, Rodney had nothing dry to put on the girl. No, Agatha would know what to do. Wrapping Rachel in her own cloak, he and the dog left the barn by the side door, stepping out into the wind and snow.

"Go, Mutton! Go! Scratch at the door and let 'em know I'm coming!"

The dog raced ahead, barking frantically, taken with Rodney's excitement. The distance to the big house was not far, but Rodney found that the girl's wet wool weighed almost as much as she did, and twice he had to stop to shift her weight in his arms. When he turned the corner by the little walled garden, he was relieved to find that Ferne was standing in the doorway with a lamp held high.

"Father! Is that you? What have you got? Who is that you're carrying?"

"Stop your shouting, girl! No need to stir the whole house! Fetch your grandmother, and be quick about it!"

But Agatha had already heard the commotion and came across the blue-tiled floor toward them, spreading a dark shawl over her shoulders. She stepped aside as Rodney passed through the door with his burden, and as Rachel's cloak fell away from her face, long strands of wet hair spilled across her features.

"It's a girl, Granma . . . a girl! Who is she, Father? Where did you find her? How did she get here?" Excitedly, Ferne fired off one question after another, without waiting for answers.

"For heaven's sake, Ferne, be quiet!" said her grandmother sternly. "Fire up the stove and put some water on to boil. Make yourself useful!" In the same breath, she turned to Rodney, pointing. "Put her on my bed . . . The poor thing looks frozen half to death."

Gently, Rodney laid Rachel on the bed and bent to remove her stiffened boots, relating to Agatha how the girl had led the horse and the sled with the injured boy right up to the door of the stable.

"Just blew in with the snow," he said, widening his eyes, as Agatha lifted the wet tresses away from the lass's face. Rodney heard a gasp, turning to see Agatha staring hard at the young woman on the bed, a look of utter bewilderment clouding her eyes.

"Good Lord! It's Rachel! The master's daughter! I know it is, Rodney. I'd know that lass anywhere . . . for all she's changed!"

Agatha turned back to the bed, rubbing Rachel's face and hands briskly, repeating her name, over and over. "Rachel! Rachel! Can you hear me? Speak to me!"

Ferne was all set to rush upstairs and call Louisa down to the kitchen, but Agatha quickly quelled that idea. "No need to upset the mistress just yet. Get the smelling salts, and some towels! She'll be all right!"

As she began to unbutton Rachel's jacket, Rodney turned away, heading for the door. He would return with the girl's trunks later in the evening, he said, but just now he was needed in the barn to care for the boy and his wound.

"Keep the trunks till morning," advised Agatha. "I'll keep Rachel here in my room for the night. Why, the mistress would faint dead away if she caught sight of her now!"

The housekeeper knew that the mistress rarely came into the kitchen after dinner, and in the morning, Rachel could offer her own explanations as to how she happened to arrive at the manor under the most bizarre circumstances imaginable! "Last I knew she was in Portsmouth," Agatha muttered to herself, passing the smelling salts under the girl's nose again.

In due time the salts roused Rachel; her eyelids fluttered, and she opened her eyes, gazing hard at the unfamiliar ceiling. The sight of Agatha's tearful face brought everything into focus, and she cried out, "Agatha! Am I home? Am I really home?"

"Yes, dear child," crooned Agatha, sobbing softly. "You are home, safe again at Brenham Manor."

Agatha took charge again, stripping the wet clothes from Rachel's chilled body and rubbing her briskly with thick towels. She dressed Rachel in one of her own roomy nightgowns and a pair of hand-knitted bed socks. Afterward, she brought hot tea, well laced with rum and lemon and, as a last gesture, brushed those tangled tresses into some semblance of order.

"You stay right there in that warm bed, dear. Sleep . . . Do as I say, child. You were always strong, but you could take a bad cough. Rest there till morning."

"But . . . Mother . . . I should go to her!"

"Hush! Your mother's been waiting five years, Rachel. One more night won't matter. Now sleep . . . Sleep."

Rachel was much too tired to argue or resist, and she snuggled under the blissful warm blankets. She inquired about the innkeeper's boy before she slept, relieved when Agatha assured her he was all right and well taken care of.

"Rodney has seven young 'uns of his own . . . He'll watch over the lad. Now rest. In the morning you can greet your mother and your sister, and I'll fix a fine reunion breakfast for all of us."

Rachel slept the sleep of the exhausted, soundless, and dreamless, while Agatha hovered over her during the night, watching for the first telltale signs of fever or congestion. Fortunately, none appeared.

CHAPTER SIX

Sunlight came soon after first light. It was brilliant, blinding to the naked eye as it reflected off the white snow, bathing the ice-covered trees in silver. All across Buckinghamshire, the snow lay deep and drifted, long blue shadows darkening the ground under the trees and in the hollows formed by the glistening drifts.

When Rodney brought Rachel's trunks up to the big house just after sunup, his report on the injured boy was heartening. "He ate a pretty good breakfast, but his head is hurtin' fearful. I'll have Jeremy take him back to his father in the sled he came in. That mare is rested and frisky now, rarin' to go."

Rodney planned to go into Coltenham village himself this morning, wanting to make certain that his own family had come through the blizzard safely. He would bring Jeremy back then, along with two of his own boys. "Goin' to need plenty of help shoveling out," he told Agatha.

She gave him a list of supplies to be gathered from the village, admonishing, "And don't forget the mail, like last time. And I'll be needing lots of fresh eggs and milk this morning, before you leave."

In her blue-tiled kitchen, Agatha set about getting breakfast, special this morning in honor of Rachel's return. Buried under the covers,

Rachel still slept, and about half after seven, Agatha woke her. "Here you go . . . hot cocoa. Make yourself presentable, and I'll tell your mother you're here."

"Wait, Agatha. Let me go up myself. I want to surprise her."

You'll surprise her, all right, thought the housekeeper. *Just wait until she sees you!* Poor plain Rachel had turned into a breathtaking beauty, from the top of her head right down to her toes. Agatha had toweled that lovely body dry last night, and she knew. Chuckling, she popped a pan of muffins into the oven. *And wait until your father returns! He's in for a bit of a surprise, too!*

Without fussing, Rachel prepared herself quickly, brushing her long hair into uncontrived curls and tying them with a ribbon. She removed a blue-and-white striped morning dress from one of her trunks, and Ferne shook out the wrinkles, oohing and aahing over the rest of the trunk's contents.

A few moments later, Rachel emerged from the little back bedroom, placing her empty cocoa mug on Agatha's worktable. The housekeeper was cutting thin slices off a pink ham and, without looking up, advised Rachel that no one stirred yet upstairs.

"Well . . . I shall stir them, eh?" said Rachel, passing through the serving pantry to the hallway between the dining rooms. She stopped under the main staircase at the back end of the foyer. From just that spot, she could see into all the rooms except the library. Without warning, her throat constricted, and she became choked. *How good it was to be home! How she had missed this lovely manor!*

Rachel wandered from room to room, finding that some had been refurbished in her absence. The salon was now decorated in gold and green; the morning room in yellow and white, hung with colorful print draperies that let in the bright morning sunshine; and in the music room, only the carpeting had changed. The walls were still covered in ivory, with creamy draperies embroidered with gold fleur-de-lis for accent, and the Wedgwood blue carpeting was attractive and made the room seem larger, thought Rachel.

In the library, the paneling was polished to its familiar golden luster, and the rows and rows of red and green leather-bound books still marched around the walls in soldierly alignment. Before Rachel went away those shelves had always been disordered, with books lying open all over the house. She smiled now and ran her fingers over the stamped bindings, searching for her favorites. Finding one, she placed it with great care on a little table and, removing a second volume, opened it to a random page and placed it facedown on one of the window seats that faced the courtyard. "There! I'm home again!" she said aloud to no one in particular.

She climbed the stairs, holding her skirts above her ankles and, at the landing, turned and went directly to her father's study. The door to his bedroom was closed, as it always was when he was away, but her mother's door was slightly ajar, and she tapped on it lightly. Instantly there came a response from within.

"Is that you, Rebecca?" asked Louisa softly, as Rachel pushed the door open wider and peeked in. The curtains were still drawn, and the room was in semidarkness, but already Louisa was sitting on the edge of her bed, pulling on a lace-trimmed dressing gown. She slept lightly, always attuned to Rebecca's needs, and had already slipped her feet into waiting slippers. She stood up, tying the ribbons of her gown as Rachel spoke.

"May I come in, Mother?"

"Of course you can come in, Rebecca, but what are you doing up so early? Are you ill?"

At that, Louisa raised her head, seeing at once that the figure stepping across the threshold was not Rebecca, and her question died on her lips. She went to the window, throwing open the draperies. Turning, she recognized Rachel instantly, but surprise arrested her voice, and she was silent. No matter, all at once they were embracing, laughing and crying at the same time.

"Rachel . . . Rachel! How? When? I don't understand! When did you arrive?"

Rachel kissed her mother once again. "I'll explain everything over breakfast, Mother. For now . . . I wanted only to surprise you. Sit down and let me look at you."

Louisa sat on the edge of her bed, gladly, for her knees trembled, and she was quite breathless. "No," she whispered to Rachel, "let *me* look at you! I can't believe it! You're all grown up!"

Rachel knelt at her mother's side, the striped skirt billowing about her in a graceful circle, as Louisa took her daughter's face in her hands and studied it. It was such a lovely face, long and oval, with a high forehead and finely arched brows. And those eyes!

"How did you know it was me, Mother? I thought perhaps you wouldn't recognize me," said Rachel.

Her mother smiled. "Every mother knows her own child, and I'd know those brown eyes anywhere. Only the last time I saw them they belonged to a scrawny little girl, and they were filled with tears. Whatever became of that little girl? Where did she go?"

"She's gone, Mother. I have come in her place, and now that I have, I am never going away again."

The moment was precious, and they sat together on the bed without speaking, their arms around each other, until Louisa lifted her head, prodded by her thoughts. "But where is your father? Did he not return with you? Agatha always wakens me when he arrives during the night. How did you get here, Rachel? And during this frightful storm! I just don't understand!"

"To the best of my knowledge, Mother," said Rachel, getting to her feet, "Father is in Manchester. I came alone. It's a long story, and I'll tell you all of it later, but for now, Agatha is preparing a big breakfast for us all. Do get dressed while I wake Rebecca and Lydia. We can go down together, as we used to."

Louisa watched in silence as her firstborn moved gracefully to the door. It was all so confusing! At the door, Rachel turned.

"Hurry, Mother. I shall be right back for you."

Ferne had already slipped up the back stairs to open Rachel's empty room, and since it was so cold in there, she bent to light a small fire in the hearth, rattling the grate noisily as she did so. On the other side of the same wall, Rebecca wondered about the noise. It had been years since she had heard anyone in that room, and wearing only her nightdress, she opened her door and stepped into the hall, just as Rachel left her father's study.

The two young women stood still, studying each other, for each had changed considerably, and then Rachel smiled and moved nearer. It took Rebecca only a minute or so to connect the sounds coming from the empty bedroom and this lovely girl, and she ran to her sister's side.

"Are you . . . you're not . . . you are! You are!" she squeaked.

"Yes, I am," said Rachel, laughing as they hugged each other tightly.

Her hair tousled, her feet bare, Rebecca was still half asleep. She stifled a yawn. "I must be dreaming . . . It can't be December already!"

Besieging Rachel with questions and refusing to leave her sister's side even long enough to dress, Rebecca pulled on a warm dressing gown and, carrying her slippers, followed as Louisa and Rachel went down the stairs arm in arm. At the bottom, standing straight and stiff, Lydia Blackburn waited for them, familiar in black bombazine, with white lace cuffs and collar starched and spotless. Rachel greeted her warmly, running down the last few steps, and it was Lydia who suddenly burst into tears and ran weeping into the library. Without hesitation, Rachel followed her there.

"I thought perhaps you might still blame me for that day," sniffed Lydia.

"On the contrary! I'm glad now that it was you who accompanied me that day. Had it been Mother, I would have been taken kicking and screaming into Miss Phillipps's and most likely would have emerged the same way. Your sternness helped me to be strong, and I shall be forever grateful."

Rachel hugged her old governess and left the library, allowing Lydia an opportunity to regain her composure. Only a few moments later she rejoined them in the dining room, holding in her hand the leather-bound book Rachel had placed on the window seat not an hour before. "Will you look at this," she remarked, shaking her head vigorously. "Already! You must learn to be neat, Rachel!"

It was almost as if Rachel had never been away, and they all laughed merrily, for Lydia Blackburn had made that exact statement, and others like it, hundreds of times while the Brenham girls were growing up. "You must learn to stand straight; you must learn to speak softly; you must learn to sit like a lady," she would say. Her list was endless!

Around the dining room table, they chattered and laughed like schoolgirls, even Louisa and Lydia, while Agatha kept Mellie and Ferne scurrying from the kitchen with platters of griddle cakes, fluffy omelets, thick slabs of ham, and feathery popovers. There was fresh butter and cream, as well as cheeses and Agatha's own strawberry preserves, taken from the larder. *Oh,* relished Rachel. How she had missed Agatha's grand cooking!

In a voice that was clear and cultured and reflected her happiness, Rachel brought the others up to date, telling them of her decision to depart from Miss Phillipps's ahead of schedule and her grand week of shopping in London. Once, she hurried from the room, returning with the gifts she had chosen for them and was especially pleased at Rebecca's excitement over the locked diary. As they lingered over their breakfast, Rachel regaled them with the story of the stranger on the wild stallion who had rescued her coach from the snowdrift.

"In his cups, you say?" inquired Lydia, quite unbelieving. "Why, it's a wonder he didn't carry you off!"

"Under my great cloak, he didn't even see me, and besides, I was not alone, and had a child in my arms. He must have thought it mine."

"All the same, you'd better not let your father hear about that little episode. He'll not find it amusing, I'm sure of that!"

It was Agatha who spoke, and rather sternly, catching Rachel's eye. Quick to glean the meaning of the housekeeper's statement, Rachel nodded and changed the subject. It probably *was* best to keep the rest of her adventure to herself, for Benjamin Brenham wouldn't think much of an unmarried woman traveling alone at any time, let alone during a raging blizzard!

"We must have a party to celebrate Rachel's homecoming," said Rebecca then excitedly. "As soon as Father returns, we can invite all our neighbors, the Chandlers, if they are still at Greystone . . . and the Guerstens," she added, thinking of Edward.

The Guerstens! Louisa dropped her fork, and it fell against her plate with a noisy clatter that startled them all. *Emory!* In her excitement at seeing Rachel once again, Louisa had completely forgotten the commitment the two fathers had made. *Rachel was promised to Emory!*

"Is something wrong?" inquired Rachel from across the table, looking quizzically at her mother.

Louisa shook her head, completely at a loss for words, and sat staring blankly in Rachel's direction. The strange moment was evaporated by Rebecca only seconds later and was put out of mind.

"You must learn not to be so careless," Rebecca said in a stern voice that mimicked Miss Blackburn, and even Lydia joined in the laughter. Agatha, returning to the kitchen, wiped her eyes with her apron, thinking how happy they were.

In time, Rachel crept away up the stairs to her own room, a room now warmed by the afternoon sun streaming through the tall windows and a small fire that Ferne had laid in the grate. Rachel studied the room, pleased to see that nothing had changed. Across a chair lay an old familiar quilt, faded and worn, and she paused to finger it pensively. It was hers, and how she had cried when her mother had refused to pack it. "Miss Phillipps will think we're paupers," Louisa had said, hiding it.

Rachel's room was fairly large, with rich polished furniture and a great canopied bed. As a child, she had needed steps to climb into it. She looked now, smiling to find them still tucked underneath the bed. She had exacted a tearful promise from her mother that nothing would be changed while she was away, and Louisa had kept that promise. The old blue counterpane and draperies were still in place, and the patterned carpet still brightened the room. She paused before a wide bookcase that stood between the windows. *Hardly neat rows these!* The books were stacked on their sides in some mysterious order known only to Rachel in those days before she had gone away to school. She stirred the coals in the grate and spent another hour rummaging through a box of childhood mementos, wondering just why she had deemed them worthy of saving. She swung on the bedpost, as she had so many times before. *How she loved this room*, and suddenly she was choked once again by the realization that she was really home . . . to stay.

Ferne had hung most of Rachel's gowns and frocks in the tall wardrobe, but the big bed was littered with green tissue paper and piles of lacy underclothes and beribboned nightgowns. Ferne would be back to right the disorder, and until she did, Rachel went to her favorite window seat, one that overlooked her little walled garden below. For another hour she sat, her knees pulled up under her skirts, musing about her homecoming. Nothing had gone as planned. Her father had been away from London, and Rachel had learned quite by accident about Mrs. Bailey. What a shock that had been! And then she had been trapped in a blizzard, only to be rescued by an unknown stranger on a wild stallion. And to top it off, the journey from the Old Priory had been nearly disastrous; she had arrived home with an injured boy, wet and half frozen herself. Still, she had kept her head when it mattered most, and both she and the innkeeper's son were safe. With quiet pride, Rachel felt satisfied with her own conduct.

"How Rachel got that sleigh around that branch without toppling it into the ravine, I'll never know," Rodney said admiringly to Agatha sometime later in the kitchen. As they waited for servings of stew to cool, Rodney elaborated about the huge tree limb that he and Jeremy had been forced to move from the roadway that morning before they left for the village.

Forgetting all about the branch, Rachel remembered it that night for some reason as she climbed the stairs just before bedtime. She was certain that it was portentous, another omen of something to come in the future. Something was soon to happen that would change the course of her life in some great way, and she crept into bed wondering just what it might be. But then, so much had happened during the past week, perhaps finding the fallen branch was anticlimactic, she thought.

Her first encounter with a fallen branch had occurred when she was eight. Then, at her father's insistence, she had been riding, and on the far side of the Small Wood she had spied Emory Guersten galloping toward her. Emory taunted Rachel relentlessly whenever they met, and to avoid him, she had turned her mount into the trees, only to find her way blocked by a branch fallen across the narrow path. Having spotted her though, Emory galloped into the woods after her without slowing the stride of his horse. The animal shied at the sight of the fallen branch, and Emory was thrown from the saddle into its outstretched branches. He received no broken bones that day, but his face and arms were badly torn and bloodied, and his forehead was scarred permanently. Rachel remembered now with some consternation how she had become hysterical at the sight of him.

Ever since then, it seemed to Rachel that whenever she saw a broken branch, something happened soon after. Some of the events were insignificant, she knew now, and most were not evil, but to a frightened child, they had been near disasters—the loss of a treasured trinket, another of Rebecca's illnesses, her own departure for the academy.

Now, safe in her own bed at the end of her first day home, Rachel put all thought of the branch out of her head. She wasn't a silly schoolgirl any longer, and she was certain that she could handle whatever change that branch foreshadowed, if indeed such things were possible!

The days that followed Rachel's return were happy ones for all of them; because of the storm, they had no visitors, and Rachel spent many hours alone with her mother. They became closer than ever before, although neither suspected that the other was withholding a secret.

For her part, Louisa could not bring herself to tell Rachel that she was promised to Emory Guersten. She hoped, in fact, never to have to tell her. Benjamin would arrive in the midlands in another day or two, and she would broach the subject again then. Now, more than ever, Louisa was positive that it was a bad match. Rachel was beautiful, graceful, and charming; she would have dozens of suitors if the betrothal was dissolved. Louisa felt certain that Benjamin would agree once he saw his daughter again.

As for Rachel, she now saw her mother in a new light, soft and feminine, and felt a rising bitterness toward her father whenever she thought about the conversation she had overheard. It was too much to accept—a mistress, a child! And another on the way, apparently! How would she ever be able to conceal what she knew from him? It was all too disconcerting, and Rachel tried not to dwell upon it.

The reunited sisters also became closer; only now they were friends as well as siblings. They sat together in the music room on sunny afternoons, which pleased Louisa no end, for the pianoforte had been used rarely during Rachel's absence.

On one of those lazy afternoons, the two young women sat bent over a tapestry of garden flowers, and punching the needle through the fabric, Rebecca told Rachel of her love for Edward Guersten.

"I love him so," she said, her delicate face serious. "And he loves me. But I know that Father will never sanction our marriage. What am I to do, Rachel? Perhaps you could speak to him when—"

"I could try, I suppose," Rachel said, interrupting, "but I daresay nothing will come of it, and you must recognize that. Where is Edward now? Why does he not approach Father himself?"

As close as the sisters had become, Rebecca could not bring herself to confess that Edward was even now making arrangements for them to elope. "He has gone to London," was all she said in a low and whispered voice. "He . . . had some business there."

"Have you spoken to Father yourself?" asked Rachel. "I am sure he thinks you too young, but perhaps if he understood . . ."

"I tried," sighed Rebecca, pacing the floor. "He refused to hear a word of it. He told me outright to forget Edward . . . and marriage, or he would send me away."

At that, Rebecca burst into tears, deep wracking sobs that shook her slight body. Rachel gathered her sister into her arms and tried to comfort her, but the tears continued. "I must marry him," said Rebecca at last, wiping her tearstained face. "It is all I live for now."

Promising to do whatever she could to help the lovers, Rachel finally succeeded in getting Rebecca to lie down. Descending the stairs again, she shook her head. While it was clear to Rachel that Edward and Rebecca truly loved each other, it was Benjamin who must be convinced, for nothing would be done without his consent.

Two days later, Benjamin returned to Brenham Manor, arriving just before midnight. Expecting him, Louisa joined him in the dining room where he took a late supper. Benjamin was buoyant and greeted her with a warm embrace, for his trip to Manchester had been a complete success.

"I should have been here hours ago, but traveling is difficult. We are in for more snow, I fear."

Agatha brought another pot of tea and then left the room. While Benjamin finished his supper, he told Louisa of his trip and of his accomplishments. He had struck an agreement with several distillers in the north, contracting to handle the exporting of their blended whiskies. They had met in Manchester, where Benjamin had ordered several large wagons from a wainwright there. All would be constructed with heavy-duty springs, and all would be able to handle considerable tonnage. Benjamin intended to transfer the crates of whiskey between his own warehouses and the London distributors using his own wagons and teams.

"I have designed a special reusable crate that will hold forty-eight bottles. While I cannot deliver any cheaper than the railroads, I can do the job faster, and with the special crates, I can reduce the losses caused by breakage."

As it now stood, the distillers were standing losses that were both heavy and expensive. The crates were loaded and off-loaded half a dozen times or more between the distilleries and the London market. Even those crates which were not dropped or toppled were badly jostled, and the bottles, packed only in straw, cracked readily. The distillers were familiar with Benjamin's business expertise, and they promised to ship exclusively with him if his plan turned out to be profitable. At the same time, Benjamin had guaranteed to handle their overseas shipments directly from his London and Liverpool warehouses, eliminating some of their agents' fees. His firm was familiar with outbound shipping, and he could ascertain that the goods arrived dockside in time to catch the earliest sailings. There were sometimes several weeks between sailings to American ports and other remote destinations, and many an unscrupulous agent had deliberately allowed a shipment to miss a sailing in order to collect warehouse fees during the interim. Benjamin planned to hire drivers and teams from the great coach lines that had suffered during the expansion of the railroads. He would buy Clydesdales for the most difficult routes, and his men were already contracting with inns and liveries along the old coach roads to stable the alternate teams.

"What about the time between shipments?" asked Louisa. "Those animals will have to be fed and stabled. How can that be profitable?"

"I thought of that, my dear," Benjamin replied, reaching for another of Agatha's light biscuits. "On the return trip north, they can deliver the casks of wine that I import from Spain and southern France. I usually pay for their haulage to Scotland ... That saving will more than make up for the stabling costs. Perhaps in time I can make a similar arrangement with the pottery manufacturers. Their breakage is astounding, too."

He had no plans to go into the freight business, but the damaged goods had simply become an expensive problem to the importers and warehousemen. When the manufacturers lost money through breakage, so did he, because the unmarketable goods took up valuable space in his warehouses for months sometimes, waiting for insurance companies to settle claims.

Benjamin was tired yet highly pleased with the results of his trip. Louisa knew it wasn't the best time to approach him about Rachel's betrothal, but he had to be told that she was home, and sooner or later Rachel herself must be told about the coming wedding.

"I wanted to speak to you before you slept," Louisa began tentatively. "It's about Rachel . . . and Emory. You simply must reconsider their engagement, or at least postpone it."

Hoping to discuss the subject rationally, Louisa had meant to raise it carefully; instead, the words just tumbled out, and she gave Benjamin all her objections once again, toying nervously with a teacup all the while. As she knew he would, Benjamin became vexed.

"Dammit, Louisa . . . This is folly! We have discussed this already any number of times. The matter is closed! I shall not reconsider, and in truth, I don't want to, for the arrangement benefits Rachel greatly. When she comes home next month, we will announce the engagement as planned."

Vexed herself, Louisa's voice became strident. "But you haven't seen her, Benjamin! When you do, you will see . . ."

Something in the tone of her voice alerted Benjamin. His mouth became grim, and he frowned. He interrupted her. "You speak as though you have seen her lately. Explain!"

"She's here now," said Louisa, nodding with her head down. "She came home five days ago," she added meekly.

Incredulous, Benjamin wiped his mouth with his napkin and demanded the details of the girl's arrival—how, when, and who had accompanied her. Louisa knew the truth would infuriate him more, but she had never lied to her husband, and did not do so now.

"Rachel came alone," she replied, lifting her head to face him directly. "By public coach from London, because you weren't there. She made her own arrangements, and was none the worse for it."

He did indeed become angrier, sure that the girl had somehow compromised her reputation . . . and his. He had arranged a very satisfactory marriage for Rachel, and on her own, she gadded about the countryside by herself! He pounded on the table with a clenched fist, and the teacups danced in their saucers. What if Guersten heard about it? What if there was a scandal! George might feel free to renege on their agreement . . . and rightly so!

Benjamin was talking nonsense, and Louisa told him so rather indignantly! Just the same, her arguments fell on deaf ears. Benjamin remained adamant; the plans would not be changed, and refusing to discuss it further, he stomped out of the dining room and went into the library, where he stood brooding before the fire. He said not a word to Louisa when she came to bid him good night. Sorry that she had upset him so soon after his arrival in the house, she kissed his cheek tenderly and started up the stairs. Benjamin called her back in a sharp tone.

"I want to see the girl . . . tonight!"

"Now?" asked Louisa, turning on the stairs. "My dear, it's quite late . . . and you're tired and upset. Can't it wait until tomorrow?"

"Now!" he thundered.

"If that is your wish, Benjamin, I'll wake her."

"It is! Send her to me here!"

Slowly Louisa went upstairs to Rachel's room to wake her, advising that her father had returned and that he demanded to see her. "And he's angry," she warned the girl.

"But why?"

"Because you came early. Because you came alone. I couldn't lie to him, Rachel. I'm afraid Miss Phillipps will have to answer for her folly. She should have followed your father's instructions to the letter."

"Folly, indeed! That's ridiculous, Mother. Besides, the decision to leave was my own, and I shall make Father see that."

Rachel brushed her hair into a semblance of neatness and then returned the silver-backed brush to the dressing table. She drew on a loose-fitting satin robe, one trimmed with wide lace at the throat and sleeves. Even in the middle of the night, she looked lovely, her dark eyes velvety and her smooth cheeks still pink from sleep. In the hallway, Louisa kissed her daughter.

"I shan't go down with you, dear. Be patient with him. He remembers only the child that you were. You're a woman now, but his anger may prevent him from seeing that just now."

How odd, thought Rachel, going down the carpeted stairs silently. Miss Phillipps's parting words had been in much the same vein. Proof, it seemed, of the changes these past five years had wrought. And so! Her father was angry! Well, she too was vexed.

Rachel's relationship with her father was not especially close, had never been. As a child, she had thought him cold and businesslike, and in his turn, he had found her withdrawn an overly emotional. Nevertheless, Rachel had never feared him, for all her timidity, nor did she now. She squared her shoulders, determined to maintain her newly found independence no matter what. She raised her hand to tap on the library door, and then thought better of it. That was timid, childlike. Instead, she rapped loudly, opening the door wide without waiting for Benjamin's response.

When she swept in, Benjamin was just about to seat himself in a wide armchair, and looking up, he froze in an awkward half-standing, half-sitting position. Rachel pretended not to notice his obvious astonishment, and crossing quickly to his side, she embraced him and kissed his cheek.

"How wonderful to see you again, Father," she said in a delightful tone. "How I've missed you! You're looking well!" He was too, although his hair had more gray than Rachel remembered.

Clearly, Benjamin was baffled. He continued to stare, blankly, unbelieving, as Rachel stepped away from him to pause beside a tall writing desk. *How was this possible!* It was Rachel, but he barely recognized his own daughter! *She was stunning!* There was no semblance to the girl he had seen last. The silence then became awkward, and to cover it, Rachel kept on talking, as Benjamin, rather heavily, sat down at last.

"I'm sorry I missed you in London," she said to him. "I arrived just after you left for Manchester." She went on, mentioning briefly her shopping excursion in London, and she spoke openly of her pleasant lodgings at Mrs. Morton's. But when it came to the matter of her homeward trip, especially the last leg of it, there were some deliberate omissions in her story.

"Sit down, Rachel!" Benjamin seemed not to have heard her narration.

Obeying, Rachel sat on a small chair near her father's side. His eyes fell on her shining hair. It had always been so lifeless, now it lay thick across her shoulders, the ends curling upward, gleaming lustrously in the firelight. The satin robe that Rachel wore was full and voluminous, yet still it revealed the contours of her youthful figure. Her hands, half hidden under rich Honiton lace, were slender and shapely, he noted, studying his daughter in silence broken only when the fire snapped loudly and one end of a burning log fell from the grate.

Benjamin's surprise was genuine, and having been forewarned, Rachel knew of his anger, but at the sight of him, her own had cooled. Perhaps his too had passed. Tenderly, she reached out a hand and touched his arm.

"Mother said you wished to see me, and I'm glad we did not wait until tomorrow to meet again." Seeing him now, it seemed even more incongruous to Rachel that he could have taken a mistress. She longed to ask him pointedly about Mrs. Bailey but dared not, afraid that it might spur his anger again.

Benjamin cleared his throat. "Yes . . . I was . . . I wanted . . . You've changed, child," he ended lamely.

Rachel threw up her hands and rose to her feet. She crossed to the fireplace and stood looking into the flames. *Child!* He had seen her, yet still he called her child! She spun around and faced him.

"Of course I have changed, Father. I'm no longer a child! Do you not see that?"

Swiftly, Benjamin recovered himself. "I see only that you have grown," he said sternly. "It was imprudent of you to leave school on a holiday without a proper traveling companion. I would have sent Miss Blackburn, or perhaps come for you myself."

"*Holiday!*"

Rachel was aghast! Here was a turn she had not foreseen. *Holiday, indeed!* She had missed all of her holidays for five long years, and when Benjamin's letter arrived, naturally Rachel assumed that she was to return home for good. Even Miss Phillipps herself had not indicated otherwise.

"Surely there can be no question of your returning to the academy," Benjamin said. "There is still the spring semester to complete."

"*There can and is, Father!*" stated Rachel, raising her voice. "I am home, and I have no intention of leaving again. My schooling has long since been completed. Surely you must have read those lengthy reports Miss Phillipps sent you every half year."

Her father sat quietly, tapping his fingers silently on the padded chair arm. A look of indecision crossed his countenance; he opened his mouth as if to speak and then closed it again. Yet, in that very split second, understanding came to Rachel like a bolt of lightning! *Of course!* How could she have been so blind! There was some purpose behind her father's letter, some reason why she had been summoned home at last. It explained everything—his anger and the long glances her mother had given from time to time these past days. She turned and faced the fireplace once again, trying to hide the fact that she was trembling.

But Benjamin, ever alert, had seen that look of recognition as it flitted across Rachel's face, and he knew that she understood that something had been left unsaid in his letter. He was unsure now just what to say to her. Perhaps, after all, it would have been wiser to discuss it all tomorrow, or even the day after, just as Louisa had advised. He noted her trembling; he suspected that she was weeping.

Rachel disarmed him completely by turning again to face him. She spoke in a clear voice, and there were no tears.

"Tell me now, Father."

Benjamin rose to his feet and came to stand next to his daughter. He was surprised to find there was no pretense. Rachel was quiet and composed.

"Very well, my child; had I realized you were so . . . so changed, I would have handled this matter differently, but you are right. It is now in the open, let us have it out. Let me start from the beginning."

Still standing side by side before the hearth, Benjamin related to Rachel, just as he had related to her mother earlier, exactly why he had decided to send her away to school in the first place. Uninterrupted, Benjamin spoke for several long moments. He spoke plainly of his meeting with George Guersten and his hopes for Rachel's future. Rachel said not a word as her father explained the terms of her betrothal, spoke of the engagement to be announced, and mentioned the wedding to follow in the spring.

Rachel's silence came from shock. *Her brain was reeling!* As a result, she heard only smattering of the details . . . Guersten . . . betrothal . . . wedding! She was wide-eyed; for the second time in two weeks, she was hearing the unbelievable! Knowing her voice would betray her emotions, Rachel choked back bitter tears and said nothing. Her face was drained of color, and she knew that her father believed she would become hysterical at any moment.

Initially, Benjamin was alarmed by her silence. At his very first sight of her, it had flashed through his mind that Louisa might be right. Rachel's speech and mannerisms were charming, and for one split second he considered that a better arrangement just might be secured for her. But then, as he pictured her at Guersten Hall, as its mistress, he was again quite sure his plan was perfect after all. Her beauty, coupled with Guersten's station, would be all that was needed to crack the nut that was London society. Granted, Benjamin was now unsure just how much control he would be able to exert over this new Rachel, if any, but nonetheless, he still felt that through her he would have access to some of the most exclusive drawing rooms in London. Rachel would take society by storm, and hopefully that society would accept Rebecca as well.

Yes, Benjamin was certain, Rachel's future was secure. She should be grateful; instead, she stood there, unspeaking, her beautiful face devoid of all expression. Suddenly, Benjamin's anger flared anew.

"Have you nothing to say?" he demanded.

Rachel thought for a long moment before she spoke. "And what of Rebecca? Does she know about this . . . betrothal?"

"Rebecca? What has she to do with it?"

"She has much to do with it, Father. She loves Edward deeply. She told me so, and I believe it to be true. And while Edward and I have always been good friends, what of him? Will he accept me when it is Rebecca he wants?"

Benjamin was confused. He had not used Emory's name, but then, neither had he used Edward's. He frowned and shook his head.

"Edward? Accept you? You misunderstand, Rachel. The betrothal has nothing to do with either Rebecca or Edward."

Rachel looked at her father blankly, and then, stunned, sank to her knees and buried her face in her hands as understanding finally settled upon her. Benjamin thought she would faint, so white was her face when she raised it, and her whispered voice was barely heard.

"Not Emory, Father! Please . . . not Emory!"

Now she fought to control her tears, and she stifled a scream. *No . . . not Emory!* It would be too much to bear. Rachel could see him now, torn and bloodied, mocking, taunting, and riding her down! *No! No . . . not Emory!*

Tenderly, Benjamin lifted his daughter to her feet. She must understand, he said. Emory would inherit; he was firstborn son. She would be an heiress someday, and it was proper that her husband have some station. She would have wealth, position, jewels, a country estate, a London mansion. What more could she want?

"Dear God, Father, have pity on me! I don't love him! I doubt I ever could. I haven't seen him in years, but it doesn't matter. We simply can't stand one another!"

His anger rising again, Benjamin paced the floor. *Such foolishness!* "Love! You sound like Rebecca. Don't be so romantic, girl. There are more important things in marriage than love. Emory may have his faults, I daresay, but he is a gentleman. He won't mistreat you. You have nothing to fear from him. He will be your husband."

"Yes," Rachel retorted, feeling angry and trapped. "He'll be my husband, though he detests me! And when I have done my duty and presented him with an heir or two, what then? Will I be abandoned in the country, like Mother, while he spends his nights in London with a mistress? I understand it's quite the fashionable thing to do these days!"

It was a cruel thing to say. It was meant to sting, as blindly Rachel wanted to hurt him as he had just now hurt her. She watched for some sign that he understood her meaning. There was none; Benjamin merely looked at her blankly again.

"That was a foolish remark, Rachel. What has your mother to do with this?"

Mrs. Crocker tapped on the library door just then. Sadly, she noted the hang of Rachel's head, but she could only guess at its cause, for Agatha knew nothing of the betrothal.

"Can I bring anything before I retire, sir?"

"Some brandy, please. And two glasses," replied Benjamin. When it came, Rachel still sat, her face pinched and white, valiantly holding back her tears. Benjamin poured two small brandies and handed one to his daughter.

"Drink it, my dear. You look ghastly, and it will calm you."

"I am quite calm," Rachel said very softly.

She was, but she was also deeply hurt that her father could plan away her future without consulting her. That deed, coupled with her knowledge of his mistress, now created a chasm between them, one that perhaps would never be bridged.

"I would have chosen another time and another way to tell you of this," Benjamin said with a grim face, "but perhaps it is just as well that it is out in the open at once. When you become reacquainted with Emory, I am sure you will find him pleasant enough. He is not an unattractive man."

"And if I refuse?" Rachel glared at her father with brittle eyes.

Benjamin bridled. *Damn!* Things were getting out of hand! All of a sudden his decisions were being challenged, first by Louisa, now Rachel!

"Refuse? On what grounds? Listen well, Rachel. The truth of the matter is this . . . You're not getting a pig-in-a-poke, but Emory thinks he is. He has no idea you have changed; he believes he's getting the Rachel of old. And yet he gave his consent in this matter, simply because his father wished it. It's about time you showed some respect and did likewise."

Rachel stormed to the door at that, the brandy still in her hand. *A pig-in-a-poke was she!* At the threshold she turned, her brown eyes blazing with fury. She upended the glass, swallowing the fiery liquid in one gulp. It burned and made her eyes water, but she would be damned if she would let her father see that. She left the room, slamming the door deliberately as she went out.

On the stairway, gasping and fanning her face with both hands, she leaned on the balustrade as the brandy burned its way to her stomach. She heard her father's footsteps behind her and hurried up the stairs to her room. It was senseless to talk further tonight; they would only argue.

In the darkness of her room, she threw herself across the bed. She felt beaten. *Oh, God . . . not Emory!* She clenched her fists and took deep breaths to keep from weeping. The unaccustomed brandy went at last to her head; it made her dizzy, her temples pounded until she couldn't think. Despite her battle, some tears welled from her eyes, trickling across her cheek. She lay there a long, long time before she fell asleep.

When Benjamin finally mounted the stairs himself, the hall clock was booming. Two strikes sounded. He listened at Rachel's door but heard nothing. The door was ajar, and he pushed it open slowly. The lamp from the hallway fell across Rachel's sleeping face. Benjamin saw the tears staining her cheeks. So, she had wept, after all! Just the same, her self-control had been formidable, and he admired her for it. He picked up the old quilt that lay on her chair and, covering her, left the room and went to his own.

There he sat, fully clothed, for another long time, troubled by the way his meeting with Rachel had gone. He was tired, and he had been angry when he should have been gentle. He had not been prepared for such a transformation in her, and she, in her turn, had been shocked by his revelations. Benjamin recognized that he had handled the matter badly, and he was aware that a gap had been formed between him and his daughter. However, though it troubled him, he never considered changing his mind, and his last conscious thought before sleep overtook him was of Guersten Hall!

CHAPTER SEVEN

In the morning Agatha tried vainly to recreate Rachel's homecoming breakfast. She might have saved her energies, for Rachel herself remained in her room with a pounding head. Louisa brought a headache powder and urged the girl to take it. Her own nerves were equally frazzled, and she was furious with Benjamin for his handling of the matter. But Benjamin had already reproached himself in that regard and wished to hear no more about it. "Enough is enough," he fumed, retiring to his study.

Since there was no further need for secrecy, Louisa informed the other members of the household of Rachel's betrothal to Emory Guersten. Noting their mistress's obvious consternation, Lydia and Agatha wisely passed no comment, but they lamented and shook their heads in private.

Rebecca was another matter. She was horrified at the news and dashed straightaway to her room in hysterical tears. That dear Rachel should turn out to the very person who had caused her separation from her beloved was especially difficult to bear. While Rebecca loved her sister dearly and understood well that Rachel was an unwilling party to the coming marriage, still, the news was crushing all the same.

The entire day was one of misery. Bravely, Rachel made an attempt to be cheerful, only to discover that she was unable to carry it off, even though she had decided to let the matter of the betrothal lie a few days. Then she would approach her father again, rationally this time. She must learn just how deeply he was committed, and why; if she kept her head and made a viable case for herself, perhaps she could change his mind. At any rate, she thought, the fallen branch had surely turned out to be a harbinger of change, after all—for marriage was certainly a change!

In the cheery library that evening, Rachel sat with her mother before the fire, but Rebecca, morose and fatigued, went silently to her room. If only Edward would return! She needed him, now more than ever.

From the bottom drawer of a tall highboy that stood between her windows, Rebecca removed the diary Rachel had given to her. It was locked; the key lay safe between Rebecca's delicate breasts on a long chain that she wore constantly about her neck. She had been thrilled with the gift and had written her first entry the very day it had been presented. Heartsick, she knew there would be no correspondence between herself and Edward during his absence, and she had seized upon the leather diary as a substitute. Now, each night, she entered her letter to Edward, pouring out her heart in a fine script.

My darling, she began and, writing on, told him that she had just learned at last the name of the person who was Emory's intended bride. *If only you had told me, I would have flown away with you that day, riding pillion, if need be.* Rebecca filled the rest of the page with the outpourings of her heart and ended by adding, *This date . . . I am sure. I am with child.*

She had suspected it for weeks. At first, the realization had alarmed and frightened her, but then, a satisfying sense of fulfillment enveloped her, and she had almost willed it to be true, though not daring to think what her father was going to say! Edward's departure had been so sudden that they had not exchanged remembrances, and she had nothing of his except the tiny secret tucked under her heart.

Without removing the chain from her neck, Rebecca locked the little book again and returned it to the drawer, forcing it into its hiding place inside a brown fur muff. She went back downstairs and joined the others, unable to bear her loneliness another moment. Playing cards at a little table pulled close to the fire, Rebecca's melancholy faded for the moment.

"It will snow again, unless I miss my guess," announced Agatha, carrying a tray of hot chocolate and cookies to them later.

Her guess was on the mark. They awoke next day to find themselves snowbound in a world of white. Winter had arrived in earnest this time, and the new cover, added to the earlier accumulation, blanketed the countryside to great depths. The roads were nigh impassable, and only a brave horseman or two passed by the manor in several long days. Always, the sky remained gray and bleak; windblown drifts and continually falling snow frustrated Rodney's efforts to clear the drive and the walks, and he finally settled for a narrow path between the big house and the barns until the weather cleared for good.

Unknown to any of them, that was to be months away, for the snows that year were some of the worst England had seen in recent times. All across the continent, in fact, winter was exceptionally severe, all the way to Russia, and for many long weeks the temperatures in the midlands remained well below freezing. At Brenham Manor, great cords of firewood had been stacked in the long shed that lay on the lee side of the kitchen wall; they would all be warm anyway, but others weren't so lucky. In search of food and fuel, poachers encroached upon Benjamin's woodlands, as well as those of old George Guersten, and it wasn't until spring that the immensity of the woodcutting was realized by the land owners. Hardly a rabbit or deer was to be found by then, and the locals, unable to drag away full-grown trees in the deep snow, had hacked away viciously at young saplings.

"I hope they choked on the smoke," Benjamin was to say later in a bitter voice.

Trapped as he was in the house, Benjamin was miserable. Inactivity nettled him, and his ill humor surfaced frequently. Instinct told him that the weather, curtailing his shipments, would cut sharply into his profits. In winters past, he found such to be true, and the snows had not been so heavy then, nor the gales so fierce.

Daily he stood fuming before a huge map hung in his study, on which the locations of his warehouses were marked in black. All of them were on or near the wharves, and he could readily guess the effects of the storms on shipping, delaying departures and causing late arrivals. He was only partly right; few ships departed at all, and daily, great vessels limped to the piers with toppled masts and icy shrouds, their cargoes saturated with seawater.

Despite his black mood, Rachel knew that if she were going to speak with her father again concerning the betrothal, its announcement date now a mere month away, it would have to be soon. At the first sustained break in the clouds, Benjamin would bolt from the house and head for London, even if it meant going all the way on horseback.

She found him one dreary afternoon before his map, his arms clasped behind him. He was glum, but Rachel hid her trepidation and tried to be cheerful.

"What is this large area here, Father?" she asked, pointing to a great inked square near the waterfront.

"That is the main warehouse, near the East India docks. That's where my offices are."

Rachel nodded, almost sorry she had asked. That was where Mr. Tremblay had taken her that frightful day she learned of her father's mistress. She pointed again to the map.

"And the red . . . and the blue?" There were many of those.

"The red are freight transfer stations," said Benjamin. "The blue are distributors of the goods I import. They are the most important since they represent the points at which I receive payment." The other colored squares on the map were all yellow, and there were only a few of them, mostly placed above the border into Scotland.

"They are earmarks for future expansion," he said and explained to her the recent contracts he had framed with the northern distilleries.

"I had no idea the business extended this far," Rachel commented, passing her hand across the top of the map.

"It burgeons itself, it seems."

"Will you expand further?"

Benjamin eyed his daughter with a cocked head, and Rachel thought he seemed pleased she had asked. Pointing to a large globe mounted in an elaborate wood stand, he said, "I think not. If I do, it will be here . . . in the states across the sea."

Turning the orb, he indicated several cities along the eastern coast of the United States: Boston, Philadelphia, Baltimore, Charleston.

"There's a fortune to be made there in shipping," he added. "All I would need is warehousing. I might even manage the distribution myself."

He gave Rachel a quick smile. Her beauty and the changes wrought during the time she was at school still amazed him, and each time he saw her, it seemed he was amazed anew. Today she was especially lovely in a long sleeved dress of light blue wool.

"But I'm sure, daughter, that you didn't come up here to discuss my business, now did you?" he asked astutely.

Rachel moved about the room slowly, fingering some of the art treasures he had acquired from faraway ports. There was a small Oriental figurine made of white jade, a Meissen vase, and a jeweled scimitar from India laying on a shelf in a glass case. When she turned to face her father again, he saw that she was totally a woman; there was no trace of girlishness in either her movements or her answer to his question.

"I confess I didn't, Father. I want to know where I stand."

Still standing before the globe, Benjamin set it to spinning wildly.

"For the sake of brevity, Rachel, let me say this. Nothing has changed, nor will it."

Rachel found his words bitter, dashing her hopes of reasoning with him. How well she recognized the set of that firm jaw.

"Rachel," he said suddenly, before she had time to frame a response. "Let us suppose I were to dissolve the agreement I made with Guersten, if I chose. Will you sit here and pine for a knight in polished armor? Visit London, perhaps? Will you attend balls and fetes, fluttering behind a fan, hoping that someone of equal station or better notices you? And if you are chosen, will it be for yourself alone . . . or your inheritance? You may never know until it is too late."

"There is some truth in what you say, Father, but there are other avenues open to me, surely."

"Ah . . . other avenues," said he irritably, sitting down at his desk. "You could be a matron . . . or a governess, perhaps! Lydia has been here nearly twenty years. She considers this to be her home, as do I, but if I choose, I could let her go, and she would have no recourse but to make do with whatever annuity I choose to grant. How about a seamstress?" he suggested brightly. "You have seen them at Scofield's, and Eleanora treats them better than most, believe me! Working in poor light until their eyes go bad, and then they're out on the streets! So much for your other avenues!"

Rachel considered his words. He was right, of course. What could she do? Even though her father was wealthy, England's unmarried women had few rights, and even fewer chances to exercise them.

"A woman of your beauty, someday to be wealthy, must secure herself in a sound marriage," said Benjamin, interrupting her thoughts, "lest every blackguard and fortune hunter in England come calling."

"Emory is himself a blackguard!" Rachel cried out.

"But not a fortune hunter! The Guerstens have wealth of their own. Emory's . . . wildness can be tamed, and the alignment of your two fortunes and properties will bring great power to your heirs, politically as well as economically. No doors will be closed to your sons and daughters."

"You've considered everything, haven't you?"

"I've given great thought to your future. A proper marriage is part of that future."

"Marriage should be more than an arrangement of property," said Rachel simply.

"Nonsense! Marriage is what you make of it!"

"And love? What of love? Am I not to love . . . and be loved? Or am I only to be . . . aligned!"

"Bah!" scoffed Benjamin. "Love is the stuff of women's novels. In the real world it doesn't exist!"

Rachel's trepidation gave way to heartache. She seated herself in a chair beside her father's desk. In the little study, they conversed for a long time, but Benjamin was convinced he was right, and in the end Rachel was forced to yield simply because she had no other choice.

Privately she had spent considerable time weighing her options; now, in the study, she came to realize that really she had none. She must obey, but in the end she decided to make some demands of her own. She cleared her throat and began.

"Very well, Father," she said in a subdued tone. "I will abide by your wishes, and I will try to do so without malice. But I have a petition to make, and I beseech you to grant it."

"Go on," said Benjamin warily.

"I am aware that my dowry is most generous, but control of it will pass to Em . . . my husband. I would ask that you set aside some small amount of money that I might draw upon, as I alone see fit . . . without accountability, for I will not ask him for anything!" she concluded through clenched teeth. "He will not make me grovel!"

Her vehemence surprised Benjamin greatly, but he was so relieved that she would now consent to the wedding without further argument that gladly would he settle an allowance on her.

"That can be arranged easily, Rachel. I will instruct Durklin to set aside . . . say, two thousand pounds per annum, the terms written to be untouchable by any but you. Will that suffice?"

Rachel gasped. Was he assuaging his guilt, perhaps? The amount was ridiculously high, but Rachel smiled graciously, prepared to accept it. "It is far more than I expected, Father, and I thank you for your generosity."

She smoothed her hands across the front of her dress, swallowing hard, and Benjamin saw she had yet another request to make of him, one not so easily spelled out.

"There is something else, Rachel?"

Rachel blurted it out. "I wish to dispense with the announcement, Father, and have the wedding over at once. If it must be done, then let it be done quickly, or I shall lose heart!"

"But there's no time!" spluttered Benjamin. "Surely you want a grand wedding, and—"

"I want nothing of the kind!" retorted Rachel. "If Emory Guersten agreed to accept me as his bride, then there has to be a reason, and after we are married, I suppose I shall learn what it is. Until then, I shall not see him, nor have him advised that I'm any different than he remembers me. Let him continue to believe he's getting a *pig-in-a-poke*! I beg of you, Father, do not tell him or his father that I have changed."

"But your mother, and Christmas!"

"Mother will do as I ask, of that I am sure, and as for Christmas . . . After the wedding, I shall go to Guersten Hall. I will spend my Christmas there, as is fitting, for it will be my home then."

Bravely, Rachel fought back rising tears. She had been away for so many Christmases, and the one coming was to have been so special. She had looked forward to it with such longing! But she would become a Guersten on her wedding day, and her place was at the Hall. Benjamin agreed with her there, feeling a little dismayed, watching her anguish. Though he had forced a new role upon her, Rachel was keenly aware that the execution of that role rested solely with her. Emory had always intimidated her, had always managed to reduce her to tears. They had been children then, but she must not allow him ever to do so again. She was a woman now, and she must command her own destiny, that of it which was left to her, at any rate.

Benjamin listened in amazement, realizing again the enormity of the change that had taken place in his daughter. It was more than just physical, and he fully understood that for the first time since their reunion. He also understood, and clearly so, that he would have no control over Rachel once she became mistress of Guersten Hall. That realization was unsettling to him. He had won . . . but had he? The young woman who stood before him now was strong, sure, and determined. She would make her own way, would not require his counseling, and for a fleeting moment Benjamin Brenham felt a pang of sadness. Was it for Rachel or for himself? He couldn't say.

At Rachel's insistence then, the date of the wedding was moved forward to the fifteenth of December. Stunned, Benjamin listened to the rest of her demands. It would be a small wedding, she said, with few guests, only those neighbors who chose to trudge through the deep snow for the ceremony and a small supper afterward.

"Whatever will I tell Guersten?" asked Benjamin lamely as Rachel prepared to leave the room.

"Tell them anything you like," she said. "Emory always claimed I was peculiar. For certain he'll be convinced he's getting the poor, plain Rachel of old!"

Benjamin went at once in search of his wife, telling her of Rachel's demands and the change in plans.

"Oh, the poor dear," Louisa muttered, wringing her hands. "The poor, poor dear."

"I think not," interjected Benjamin. "In fact, my dear, I suggest that you save some of your sympathies for your future son-in-law. Something tells me that young man is going to need them."

Benjamin prepared to go to Guersten Hall. He knew that George and Emory must be told at once about the new date, and he wondered just what Emory was going to think when he learned that Rachel desired the wedding date moved forward by four full months.

The snow had stopped momentarily when he left the house, but the wind still blew in powerful gusts that took his breath away as he made his way to the Hall astride Patch, following a rough path broken through the snow by an earlier rider. At the Hall, high drifts still lay against the double doors, and snow was piled clear to the glass of the windows on the first floor, although the long drive had been shoveled as well as could be from the gates to the portico.

Benjamin found George alone in the upstairs salon. Bored, Ermaline had gone by sleigh to Greystone to visit with her cousins days before, and Emory and Edward were both in London. A maid ushered Benjamin up the marble staircase, where George waited at the top, his hand extended.

"Sorry to drag you all the way up those damn stairs, Benjamin, but they ruin these stiff knees of mine."

Small wonder, thought Benjamin, looking back down the steps he had just climbed, for they were actually two full flights broken by a large landing in the middle. He had never been on the second floor of the Hall before, and he saw now that on either side of the stairs a broad corridor stretched the width of the house. There seemed to be dozens of doors, almost all of them leading to bedrooms, as George pointed out.

The spacious salon was located adjacent to the top of the stairs, and they entered through tall white doors, ornately carved and gilded. The walls were covered with expensive white moiré, and all the woodwork matched the double doors. On each sidewall stood a massive fireplace, each made of dark green coriander. The tall Grecian figures that supported the heavy mantelpieces were made of the same mottled marble. Benjamin thought this room a trifle warm, and well he should, for a roaring fire blazed in each twin hearth.

The room was used only by the family and private guests, and the furniture was comfortable and inviting, four settees and assorted easy chairs grouped before the fires, with small tables scattered among them. The prisms of crystal chandeliers caught the firelight, the colors reflected again in gilded mirrors hanging over the mantels. Rich rugs and expensive objets d'art pointed the room, and glorious landscapes and pastoral scenes lined the walls. It was a charming room, yet Benjamin's eye was drawn again and again to a round rose window that faced the door. It was enormous, with pink tinted glass and delicate tracery.

"It's beautiful," he said admiringly. "It must be something to see with the sun streaming through it."

George chuckled heartily at that. "I imagine it might be, but you see, one of my damn fool ancestors couldn't remember which way the sun rose and set! As a result, the window is never fully illuminated, but it serves some usefulness as a conversation piece just the same."

The rose window was flanked on either side by tall French doors that led to a narrow balcony overlooking the roofs of the original Great Hall and the kitchen below. Behind it was a conservatory and a small courtyard, and in the distance Benjamin saw the enormous carriage house, the stables, and other outbuildings. He was swamped again by the pull of the great estate.

Following George's scuffling figure across the room to a fireside, Benjamin sat where he indicated, but the old man himself remained standing, with the tails of his frock coat parted, warming the seat of his pants at the hearth.

"You'll set yourself afire, my friend," Benjamin said, smiling.

"Already have, to tell the truth," grinning himself and cocking his head. He showed Benjamin several small holes and scorch marks on his trousers. "Can't stand the cold! What brought you out in it?"

As briefly as he could, Benjamin told him of Rachel's desire to push the ceremony forward.

"Bride a little eager, is she?" George cracked in good humor.

Despite the light tone to his voice, the news troubled George. Emory had drawn barely a sober breath since that night in the library as it was, and his father knew well this new revelation would provoke yet another nasty scene.

"On the contrary," said Benjamin, ignoring the tease, "Rachel is merely tremulous and wishes the formalities behind her. She especially desires a small wedding, and I would oblige her."

In compliance with Rachel's request, Benjamin did not now tell George that his daughter's physical appearance was radically altered, merely stated that she was well raised, modest, and benefited from an exceptional education. Rachel understood her duty and would perform it graciously.

"She will give you no cause for concern," he added proudly. "You will find her an asset to your house."

George's concern, however, lay not with Rachel at the moment, but Emory. He would misread this development, no doubt about it, thinking Rachel so eager to be his bride that she could not wait until spring to be married. But still, there was a bright side—a small wedding would save a fortune in hard cash. All those many guests who would not have to be quartered or fed, for Guersten weddings had always been expensive and elaborate affairs, lasting two or three days at least. Further, this change meant that Ermaline's betrothal could also be moved forward by a matter of months. "Not a bad turn of events at that perhaps," said George, rubbing his chin thoughtfully.

Still, he disguised his satisfaction and attempted to appear justifiably doubtful, though he agreed in the end to be at Brenham Manor with Emory at the appointed time.

"Your house must be in a dither," he said, changing the subject. "Women like time to plan these things."

Benjamin threw up his hands and laughed. "Little you know! They were in a stew over the decorations when I left. Come hell or high water, tomorrow I leave for London!"

"Decorations, eh? Perhaps I can help there. The conservatory is choked with plants, though I doubt there's anything in bloom. Suppose I send over some greens and whatever else might be appropriate?"

"That's most kind of you," Benjamin said, taking his leave. "Louisa will be most appreciative."

Nearly a week passed before Emory finally returned to Guersten Hall, and when he did, he arrived well in his cups. The house was nearly in darkness, and the hour was late when George heard him staggering slowly up the staircase. He met his son on the high landing.

"Come into the salon. I want to talk to you. It's important."

"Can't it wait, Father? Stoddard is fixing me some supper, and then I'm going to bed."

"Have it sent on a tray . . . It has to do with the wedding."

Emory snarled but stumbled into the salon and dropped into the nearest chair, a dark scowl spreading over his handsome face. His clothes were rumpled, and he badly needed a shave.

"Ah . . . the bride has reconsidered, perhaps? Is there to be no wedding?" He gave a loud sigh and made a long face, pretending sadness.

"No, Emory. In fact, it seems that Rachel wants to have the ceremony over and done with as soon as possible . . . the fifteenth, to be exact."

A cruel smile curled Emory's lips, and then he started to laugh, the sound of it filling the room to its corners. The maid who brought the supper tray was much amused, for Emory had been unusually unpleasant of late.

"So!" he said in his deep voice. "Instead of being reluctant, it seems my little mouse is anxious to turn down the covers on the bridal bed! Remember what I told you, Father. I—"

"Emory!" interrupted George in a sharp tone. The maid was still in the room, and George was certain that whatever Emory was about to say would be unkind. When the door closed behind her, George faced his son. "I know what you told me, but hear this and hear it well! Rachel is to be your wife, and she will be mistress here. She is entitled to your respect, especially before the servants, and I demand that you give it. What goes on in your bedroom is your own affair."

Despite not having eaten in more than a day, Emory suddenly lost his appetite. He picked at the food on the tray, glancing all around the room, and George knew he searched for something stronger to drink than the coffee Stoddard had sent up.

"There's nothing here. Drink your coffee. It will clear your head."

Chewing halfheartedly on a biscuit and sipping the hot brew, Emory slumped further into his chair. Stoddard had seen his condition; the coffee was extremely strong. Emory wrinkled his nose at its bitterness.

George took a chair beside his son. He would be glad himself when the wedding was over. All this tension was wearing on the nerves.

"I know you are discontent, Emory, but don't make a fool of yourself because of it. Keep to your ways in London, if you must, but here at the Hall there must be decorum. I gave my word to Brenham that you wouldn't abuse the girl."

Emory frowned. The jagged scar turned bright pink. "I have no intentions of laying a hand on her, Father, and well you know it! But what's their hurry?"

George didn't know and said so, adding that he suspected the girl was probably unhappy with the match also. She had returned from school earlier than expected and didn't want to return. There was no real reason not to be married at once.

"You should call on her, Emory," he suggested. "Perhaps the idea of marriage will not be so distasteful once the two of you become acquainted again."

"Court her? Never! She'll have my name . . . no more! She's damned lucky to get that!"

With that, Emory stormed angrily from the salon, stomping noisily down the stairs. In the dining room he lifted a decanter of claret from the sideboard and went into the library, slamming the door behind him. He fumed. Was there no escape from that mouse? Call on her? Court her? Ha! She'd be lucky if he even showed up for the ceremony!

Brooding, he sat before the dying embers in the hearth and refilled his glass frequently. The wine stuck in his throat every time he envisioned Rachel Brenham. Emory's prowess as a lover was widespread. He was a rogue, yet women were drawn to him, and those women were always beautiful . . . and always willing. He was certain he would be the laughingstock of London when he turned up with Rachel on his arm. *It was too much!*

Emory had always fancied himself a confirmed bachelor. He could not picture himself tied to one woman, even now, with circumstances about to force him into marriage. To actually stand beside Rachel and exchange vows! The more he thought about it, the more impossible the idea became.

Staring gloomily into the fire, a sudden thought came to him. Some months before, one of his companions had found himself party to an arranged marriage, only the lady was French and would not cross the channel until she had become his legal wife. The marriage was performed by proxy, since the gentleman in question would not leave his mistress, about to bear his child. *A stand-in!* thought Emory. He wouldn't have to take the bloody vows himself! It was a rotten thing to do, he knew, and his father would raise an awful stink, but the more wine he consumed, the more firmly the idea became fixed in his mind.

He sat there most of the night, drinking all the while. Just before dawn, he lurched across the room to his father's desk and, taking quill in hand, scratched out a document in a barely legible hand. It gave his father authority to act as his deputy. George could appoint someone to represent him at the wedding. Emory scribbled his signature at the bottom and set the paper inside his father's ledger book, where he would be certain to find it. Then he buttoned his green reefer and left the room.

Outside, the first gray light of dawn was just appearing. The yard was still shrouded in murky shadow as Emory wobbled his way to the barn and stumbled to a stall near the door. He brought oats and water to the horse stabled there and went to fetch his saddle while the animal was feeding. A few moments later, he had saddled the great black stallion and led him into the yard.

"Come on, Sultan. It's back to London for you and me!"

With one hand on the pommel, Emory swung himself into the saddle and galloped wildly down the path, racing under the portico and down the long drive. Out in the road the deep snow failed to impede them; they fairly flew along the trodden track, for Sultan's strides were long and powerful, and his silky mane and long tail undulated in the wind.

That icy wind sobered Emory quickly. He tore across the bridge and passed by the gates of Brenham Manor, but when he reached the entrance to the service road, guilt-ridden, he pulled the big stallion to an abrupt halt. Sultan pawed the snow nervously, snorting noisily in misty breaths, while Emory sat rigid in the saddle, gazing through the early morning grayness at the house spread before him.

His bride-to-be was asleep somewhere on the second floor of that house. For a moment Emory wondered what Rachel must look like now. How long had it been since he had seen her last? Five years? Six? Perhaps his father was right; he should call on her. He could at least be kind. She was a victim too, and there was no need for animosity. He could return to the Hall now, retrieve the insulting document, and burn it before his father even knew it had been written. Theirs would be a loveless marriage, but they could be friends, at least.

Sultan pranced fitfully under his rider, and a great fallen tree limb suddenly caught Emory's eye. It was snow covered, lying just where Rodney and Jeremy had placed it. Instantly, Emory recalled another day, another branch. He touched his temple, fingering the long scar. And then he remembered Rachel, weeping, hysterical.

"Hah!" he cried, and raising his hand to the bricks of Brenham Manor, he shouted into the morning silence. "Farewell, little mouse! Farewell!"

Turning the stallion, Emory headed for London. Galloping away like a madman, he was out of sight in a matter of seconds.

CHAPTER EIGHT

Brenham Manor was in an uproar, the turmoil spreading to every room. Lydia hurried from floor to floor looking frightfully busy, but in truth accomplishing very little, while Louisa and Agatha sat with their heads together in the dining room, bent on planning an elaborate wedding dinner. Finally, Rachel felt compelled to intervene.

"There will be no more than forty guests, Mother, if that, given the snow. A simple buffet would be much more appropriate."

Yet even that caused Agatha to lament; she needed more time, she wailed. There were errands to run, but the blocked roads rendered any trip to Coltenham out of the question. Once, while drawing water in the pump room, Agatha opened the outside door and shook a clenched fist at the still falling snow.

Only Rachel remained calm, and it was just that calmness that unnerved Louisa, who suffered the guilt Benjamin had escaped by returning to London. One afternoon, she climbed the stairs to Rachel's room, raising the subject of suitable bridal attire.

"If only you would give us more time, my dear," she said to Rachel. "We could obtain a proper wedding dress."

Rachel, however, was not concerned about a proper wedding dress and, to Louisa's great dismay, flatly refused to wear a bridal veil.

Pulling several of her new frocks and gowns from the wardrobe, she spread them across the bed for inspection.

"Any one of these is suitable, Mother. It is just a matter of deciding."

The one chosen was a simple but elegant oyster white moiré with a bell-shaped skirt and fitted waist, its bodice and long sleeves made of finest lawn, delicately embroidered here and there with tiny rosebuds. A wide bertha edged with seed pearls formed the collar, and while Mrs. Scofield had added a wide sash of bottle green velvet for color, Rachel now removed it, substituting a length of off-white satin that was almost a perfect match to the moiré.

In the salon the largesse from George Guersten's conservatory provided ample greenery for decoration, but romantically, Rebecca still fretted over the lack of fresh-cut flowers for her sister's bridal bouquet and decided to cover Rachel's prayer book with white lace and tiny ribbons. Happily, Lydia pounced on the task, thankful for any chore that gave her weary legs a rest. When she returned the book to Rachel later, a small gold cross hung from its bookmarker, and Rachel was touched by her old governess's thoughtfulness.

The snow finally stopped falling in the days just before the wedding, but other than that, little improvement was marked in the weather. The sun never appeared, and each day the threat of more snow remained imminent. Heavy gray clouds hugged the very treetops, as if deciding just where the next foot of precipitation was to be dumped.

Benjamin returned from London the day before the wedding in a sleigh rented in Aylesbury. With him was the Anglican bishop, a fusty old man who tottered into the house, reeking of dust and tobacco. He was patently as dull as the weather; the only thing that seemed at all alive about him was a heavy gold cross which reflected bright points of light whenever he moved. He creaked up the stairs to his assigned room, to remain there until just before the ceremony.

Surprisingly, in view of the weather, by late afternoon that same day the manor was half filled with guests. A scant few were business associates of Benjamin's, but most were neighbors from nearby estates. Adele Chandler and her daughters arrived at the same time as old Squire Paxton and his dour wife. Sir Hugh remained at Guersten Hall, to come with George tomorrow. Two elderly spinsters, the Warrington sisters, arrived late in the day; they sat in the library like two fat brown spiders, side by side before the fire, continually sipping tea.

"I swear I don't know where they put it," whispered Ferne to Mellie. "They never leave the room!"

When at last she spied one of the brown sisters creeping up the stairs after supper, Ferne chortled with glee. Nudging Mellie, she pretended to be emptying a chamber pot.

It was well after midnight that night before the house finally became quiet, but even so, sleep did not come to Rachel. She lay wide-eyed in her bed, pondering her future. This was her very last night in her own bed! Tomorrow she would sleep at Guersten Hall . . . beside Emory! The very thought of it sent shivers up and down her spine; she knew of the physical relationships shared by men and women, and she understood her duty to Emory in that quarter, but just the same, it was all a bit frightening. Why, she thought, she had never even been kissed, really. True, she had shared some stolen kisses as a schoolgirl at parties and dances, but no man had ever held her in his arms, or approached with lovemaking in mind. Would Emory be gentle? Rough? What if he should hurt her? Would she become hysterical? One thought led to another, and soon vivid pictures were dancing about in Rachel's head until she sat upright in her bed. Such thoughts were unladylike.

If only she had a confidante, someone who might answer her questions and lay her fears to rest. But Rachel couldn't ask her mother. Louisa was certain to be evasive if Rachel put such thoughts into questions. She was tempted to seek out Rebecca; no doubt she and Edward had shared many passionate kisses, but what could Rebecca really know about the physical intimacy of love, that secret world that took a man and woman beyond kisses?

She knows no more than I, assumed Rachel, nestling under the covers again. The remaining hours of the night dragged by interminably, and she heard the tall clock in the foyer sounding them ominously as dawn approached. Soon it would be her wedding day, and she would belong to Emory Guersten. Would he someday learn to love her? If not, would he be kind to her at least? Or would he be unchanged, plaguing her with taunts and intimidations?

Rachel knew not the answer to these questions and was still pondering them when at last her weary eyes closed and she slept, to stir not an hour later. Then, she opened her dark eyes slowly, not wanting the dreaded day to begin. At the window she drew back the blue draperies to find that the weather matched her mood. It was bleak and gray, and snowing again, harder than ever.

Agatha brought up a breakfast tray, covered with a fine white cloth, and bustled around Rachel's room in false cheeriness, trying to lighten her spirits, for the girl's pinched face left the older woman heartsore.

"The guests are breakfasting, and everything's topsy-turvy downstairs. I thought you might relish a little quiet before the ceremony."

Bless her! Going downstairs was the last thing Rachel wanted to do just now. The ceremony was set for ten o'clock. That would be soon enough!

Knowing it was Rachel's favorite, Agatha had made a fresh batch of Sally Lunn especially for her that morning. Rachel's appetite had completely deserted her, but to please Agatha, she nibbled at the warm sweet cake while Rebecca dashed in and out, sharing her sister's tea.

In deference to Rachel's sad mood of dejection, Rebecca tried to be appropriately solemn, but she was excited and hopeful all the same since there was some chance that Edward might appear for the ceremony. Many weeks had passed since Rebecca had seen Edward last, and now she had a special secret to share with him.

"After all, they are brothers," she exclaimed, looking out the window for the tenth time. "Oh, Rachel, you don't think the snow will keep him away, do you?"

"If I'm lucky, maybe it will keep Emory away as well," remarked Rachel dismally.

"That I doubt," murmured Rebecca, shaking her pretty head in her sister's direction. "Besides, I'm sure he will be very glad he came once he sees you."

Rachel scoffed aloud at that. "If only he'd made some effort to see me!"

Rebecca lifted her eyebrows quizzically. "But you distinctly said you didn't want to see him!"

"I know that . . . and I wouldn't have seen him even if he had come. But if he had tried, a note even . . . I would know that he had given some little thought to me. No, Rebecca, I know Emory is in this against his will also, just as I am."

"But why? Why would a man agree to take a bride he obviously detests?"

"Who knows? But go now and dress, for they will be here shortly, and I must make myself ready. Here's to love and marriage," she said scornfully, raising a teacup to Rebecca.

By the time her mother came into her room later, Rachel was calm once more. She had brushed her hair into a smooth knot and enclosed it in a snood woven of fine velvet ribbons. Across her brow, soft ringlets were held in place by several pearl-encrusted combs set in a precise half circle. The effect was lovely; to pronounce it, Rachel wore no other jewelry.

"I still think you should wear a veil," fretted Louisa, "if only a short one."

Still adamant on that score, Rachel would hear no more about it. She refused to cover her own face, wanting to see Emory Guersten's clearly when she took her place by his side. It was the only part of the ceremony she looked forward to.

The last straggling guests were reporting that traveling was dreadful and getting worse by the moment. Nine thirty came and went, yet still the Guerstens had not arrived, as upstairs, having been dressed for some time, Rachel sat miserably on the window seat, staring out at the whirling flakes.

"I'm concerned," Louisa said to her husband when she returned to the lower floor. "If only she would show some emotion! Anything . . . even tears at this point! But she's so calm! No tears, no anger, no smiles . . . nothing! She just . . . sits there!"

Benjamin shrugged guiltily, relieved when Louisa hurried off to greet the old bishop just descending the stairs in slow and deliberate steps. By this time, most of the guests were already seated in the salon, but Benjamin continued to pace the foyer floor nervously, peering repeatedly out the door in search of the Guerstens. *Whatever was keeping them?* he wondered. Yet despite his vigil, it was Rodney, working to keep the drive clear, who first spotted George Guersten trundling up the road in a lumbering coach pulled by six matching bays. Arduously, they hauled into the drive, stopping at the entrance to the little courtyard. At the sight of them, Benjamin's jaw dropped measurably.

Upstairs, Rebecca came running to fetch Rachel, and together they hurried to the front of the house to watch the bridegroom's arrival from a window. The driver dismounted from the box and then moved around to open the door of the coach, carefully assisting George Guersten to the ground. In the doorway, Benjamin remembered his manners just in time and hurried forward to meet him, while Ermaline was next helped down from the coach. Quickly, they all turned and hurried into the house, for the swirling wind clutched wildly at their cloaks, threatening to blow them down. Now, thought Rachel, with her nose pressed to the glass, she would glimpse Emory, and before he had a chance to see her. But the falling snow made it difficult to see anything, and though she squinted hard, Rachel had to strain to see the man who stepped from the coach and hurried inside after the others. Wearing a dark greatcoat and a tall top hat, he was noticeably short and noticeably stout. He was not Emory Guersten!

The sisters waited, but no one else dismounted. The coach was empty; the coachman closed the door, and then he and Rodney led the team of grays around the back to the stables.

Rebecca was greatly disappointed, as discerned by her face, for it was evident that Edward would not come that day.

"And neither, it seems, will Emory," said Rachel, perplexed. "But who is that man?"

Not having seen his face, Rebecca didn't know, and the two young women went together to the top of the landing and leaned over the railing. Just below them, the late arrivals were removing their wraps in the foyer. Perplexed by Emory's absence, Louisa, escorting Ermaline into the salon, signaled to Benjamin over her shoulder, imploring him to get to the bottom of the mystery.

"I recognize him now, without his top hat," whispered Rebecca to her sister. "It's Sir Hugh, Adele's husband."

But Rachel's attention was elsewhere, listening to her father's voice, stern and gruff, rising up the stairwell as he spoke to George.

"Good God, man! A coach and six? When a sleigh is clearly the order of the day? No wonder you're late!"

"My sincerest apologies," said George humbly. "I saw my error as soon as we left the Hall. We became stuck almost at once and had to wait while they added more horses. You know how much I dislike the cold. The thought of riding in an open sleigh in this weather set my bones to aching. I stand chastised."

"But where is Emory? Why is he not here?"

An expression of discomfort settled over George. He glanced toward Sir Hugh, and then took hold of Benjamin's arm. "There is something I must tell you. Where can we talk?"

Benjamin pointed to the library door and followed the old man across the foyer. It was then he spied his daughters peering over the balustrade. Rachel's face was pale, drawn.

"Go to your room," he said to her in a curt tone. "I will come to you in a moment."

The two men then passed into the library, and Benjamin closed the door behind them, leaving Sir Hugh standing alone at the bottom of the staircase. He looked up, eyeing the two young women standing at the top of the landing. In his fifties, Hugh Chandler's round face was heavily jowled, adorned with a long drooping mustache. With pudgy hands, he withdrew his spectacles from the pocket of his coat and slipped them over his nose. Something was notably amiss! Sir Hugh had agreed to stand in for Emory, at George's request. Just why, he wasn't sure, but he had been led to understand the young man's aversion to the bride was ... well, to be charitable, she was supposed to be quite unattractive. Sir Hugh knew Rebecca by sight, and Benjamin himself had just called the other by name. Rachel! Why, she was beautiful! What did it all mean?

Rachel's own thoughts followed much the same track. Something *was* quite wrong, and she was determined to learn what it was, and quickly! Without hesitation, she rushed down the staircase, sweeping past the astounded Sir Hugh, and went into the library without knocking. She found her father and George Guersten huddled together near a front window. Closing the door with authority, Rachel crossed resolutely to where they stood.

"What is going on, Father?" she demanded of him. And to George, she said, "Where is Emory?"

Benjamin whirled about at the sound of her voice. His face was stricken, his jaw clamped tight. "I sent you to your room," he said sternly.

"I am not a child, Father, and today of all days, do not treat me like one!" she answered angrily. "This wedding has turned into a charade! What is the delay?"

"Leave us!" bellowed Benjamin, his face contorted with such rage that Rachel knew at once that it was not only her presence that had raised it. What in the world had George Guersten been telling him?

Reaching for Rachel's arm, Benjamin tried to propel her toward the door, but she pulled away from him defiantly to stand facing them both, her hands clenched into tight fists at her sides.

"Tell me! And be quick about it, or I shall make such an almighty stink that even the bishop will come running!"

Despite Rachel's outburst, her father moved again to oust her from the room, and would have, until George interrupted.

"Let her stay!" he said sharply. "She has a right to know."

Releasing Rachel's arm, Benjamin sat down heavily on the window seat, just behind her. Lowering his head dejectedly, he stared in silence at his boots. George Guersten, though, remained standing. Leaning upon his ebony walking stick, he stared in disbelief at the young woman before him.

So this was Rachel! Poor, plain Rachel . . . all grown up! George now wondered just why Benjamin had neglected to mention that she had grown to such a beauty, as he observed her carefully, swiftly appraising her lovely face, the tiny waist and perfect bosom. Everything about her was superb, he noted, and it struck him that he had never seen a woman so beautiful, except perhaps his own dear Isabelle. So this was to be Emory's bride, he thought. *But, oh, good Lord, was she angry just now!* Standing before him, Rachel's cheeks were flushed to a brightness, and her blazing eyes now darted from one man to the other.

Without a word, George withdrew the proxy document Emory had scribbled from an inner pocket and handed it over to her. It was nearly illegible, and it took Rachel several minutes to decipher the scrawl.

She looked up, dumbfounded, to her father and then to George.

"But why? This insult is madness!"

"Indeed it is!" said George with some conviction. Long had he thought his son a fool; now he was convinced of it. If only Emory had heeded his advice, called upon the girl! It pained him to think of it, but George had little choice now but to release Rachel from the commitment made by her father, and he said as much, while Benjamin struggled to his feet.

"Why did you wait until today to tell me . . . us? How long have you known about this?"

"I found it only yesterday," said the old man, pointing to the document Rachel still held in her hand. "And that is the truth, Brenham, whether you care to believe it or not." He leaned heavily against his walking stick. "I hoped against hope that Emory would come to his senses and return to the Hall before today, for I favored this match greatly even before I saw Rachel again."

Then, turning slightly, George spoke directly to her. "And now that I have seen you again, my dear, I am doubly sorry. My son is a fool! You have spirit, and I like that. I see blessed little of it these days. You would be good for him."

Unexpectedly, in a sudden, angry movement, Benjamin tore the offending proxy paper from Rachel's fingers and, crossing to the fireplace, tossed it onto the smoldering ashes, where it fluttered against the grate without igniting. Then, he turned again to George, berating him soundly. George was supposed to have seen to Emory! If the young man found the marriage so distasteful that he preferred to run away, why, then George should have warned them!

The old man sighed, agreeing with everything that Benjamin said, adding that Sir Hugh had been prepared to stand in for Emory. Naturally, under the circumstances, the wedding would be cancelled. He would return Rachel's dowry money promptly.

"Just a moment," interrupted Rachel. "And what of me? After all, it is I who has been humiliated!"

She was indignant! By tomorrow this time everyone in the shire would know that she had been left at the altar by Emory Guersten. She would be the object of pity and whispered gossip, and no doubt some ribald jokes as well! Then too, many might even believe something to be seriously wrong with her; perhaps no one would ever propose marriage again, assuming incorrectly that the Guerstens must be justified in withdrawing. After all, were they not one of the oldest families in the shire? *No!* Rachel was adamant; she would not go back to being poor Rachel again for the rest of her life! Anything was preferable to that—even marriage to Emory Guersten!

In a lightning move, she snatched the scorched document from the grate. "The reputations of both our families are at stake, Mr. Guersten, and I have my pride. If you are agreeable, I suggest we get on with the ceremony as planned. Mr. Chandler is acceptable to me as proxy. I will deal with Emory in my own good time."

For quite some while, even though he favored the match himself, Benjamin remained unconvinced, so offended was he by Emory's conduct. Calmly though, Rachel made him understand that her position was untenable. As for George, he was thrilled! How he liked this girl's spunk! Why couldn't Emory have found her himself?

Finally, it was agreed. They would proceed with the wedding, Sir Hugh standing for Emory. By then it was nearly eleven o'clock, and when Benjamin opened the door of the library, he found Louisa and Rebecca waiting in the morning room with Sir Hugh, the strained faces of all three registering their confusion and anxiety, while the guests crowded at the door of the salon, already whispering among themselves.

Benjamin spoke quietly to his wife. "Come, my dear, tell your guests to be seated. The ceremony will begin immediately. Emory will not be present, but Sir Hugh will stand for him."

"I don't understand any of this," whispered Louisa under her breath. "Where is he? Whatever will I tell them?"

"It's a long story, Louisa, and I'll explain it all later. Emory is in London. For now, just say that he is ill and has been taken to bed."

Hmmph! Not far from the truth, thought Sir Hugh dryly, standing off to one side, for it was almost a certainty that Emory was probably sharing someone's bed this very moment, and clearly the young man was ill if he considered the likes of Rachel Brenham to be unattractive!

Dutifully, though still confused, Louisa went to wake the old bishop, who had dozed off under a potted palm while waiting for the bridal party. Rachel returned to her room for her prayer book. George's blue eyes sparkled brightly as he watched her come rustling down the stairs again. *Things couldn't have worked out better!* Ermaline would have her husband, and for the first time since his own dear mother died, Guersten Hall would have a mistress to reckon with. Rachel would keep the servants in line, for certain, and George knew that if and when Emory returned, this willowy young woman would cut him down to size in short order. Secretly, George hoped it would be soon. *Oh, how he hoped it would be soon!*

When the old bishop took his place, Sir Hugh stepped before him and composed, but somber faced, Rachel took her father's arm, and they stepped to the door of the salon. The room had been decorated simply, using the many greens from Guersten Hall and some evergreen boughs collected by Ferne and Jeremy. Tied with white ribbons, they were festooned over the mantel and around the doors, their fragrance filling the room with balmy scent. Rachel squared her shoulders, and father and daughter moved across the floor of the salon to stand before the stooped bishop. Sir Hugh took Rachel's icy fingers in his, and the ceremony began.

It was over in minutes, and afterward Rachel remembered little of it, except that her knees trembled. Instead, her thoughts had gone continually to Emory and his humiliating effrontery, and she had had to struggle valiantly to retain her composure. It was not self-pity or hysteria that she felt, but anger—anger that welled in her breast and stuck in her throat. Emory Guersten would pay for this humiliation, she vowed. She would see to that!

As Rachel mingled with the guests later, none was aware that anything untoward was amiss. She was charming, even making proper apologies for her indisposed bridegroom. Most of them departed shortly after the buffet was spread, for outside a light snow still fell. Agreeably, Sir Hugh offered to deliver the old bishop back to his parsonage, and he left early with the old man tucked safely into a sleigh beside him. It was then Sir Hugh's avowed intention to go straight to London, search out his nephew's haunts, and tell him personally what a damned fool he was!

Alone in her room, Rachel changed into her brown velvet traveling costume, packing a small wicker trunk with those things she would need in the next few days at Guersten Hall. The rest were already packed and would be sent over when the snow stopped. Now, methodically, Rachel collected her silver-backed brushes and combs and a nightdress, adding them to the trunk, all the while staring in disbelief at the wide gold band that now adorned her left hand. It had belonged to Emory's mother, and now it was hers. She was a Guersten.

Solemnly, she bid farewell to her sister, to Lydia and Agatha, and when her father offered to escort her to Guersten Hall himself, Rachel declined. She knew that her father had been as openly shocked at the day's event as she, but now, faced with departure, Rachel was suddenly resentful that it was he who had been responsible for pairing her with Emory in the first place.

"I'm not a child, Father. I will go with George and Ermaline in the sleigh. I am a Guersten now, as you wished."

Standing in the little courtyard, Rachel said a sad good-bye to her mother. Louisa wept openly, and Benjamin, himself distraught, made no move to comfort her. And so, at three o'clock on a snowy afternoon, calm and dry eyed, Rachel left Brenham Manor for her new home at Guersten Hall.

CHAPTER NINE

Well-waxed runners whispered quietly as the sleigh slipped along the wooded road toward Guersten Hall. Darkness would come early this night. Already, long purple shadows writhed and danced under the windswept trees, and stealthy fingers of blackness stretched across the road before them. It was quiet, the sound of the horses' hooves muffled in the snow. All that could be heard was the tinkling of the little bells on their harnesses, a merry sound, but a bit out of place under the circumstances, and the eerie humming of the rising wind.

Miserable at the start of the short journey, Rachel listened to it moaning through the tops of the tall evergreens. The cold air had cooled her resentment toward her father, yet for some reason now she recalled her last farewell from Brenham Manor, equally sad, when she had cast off for Miss Phillipps's Academy in Portsmouth. She had been but a child then; she was a woman now, a married woman! *My word,* she thought distractedly, *and to think I spent most of last night fretting about sharing a bed with Emory! Ha!* She covered her rosy lips with a gloved hand and laughed aloud, thinking that if and when Emory Guersten *did* return to the Hall, he had already forfeited the right to share her bed. His insulting behavior today had seen to that!

Beside her, huddled deep into his greatcoat and a lap robe, with a long muffler wrapped clear to his nose, the sharp tones of that laughter startled George Guersten. The girl was remarkable, he thought. Most brides would have been reduced to tears hours ago by the day's events, but this one sat with straight back, actually finding something amusing about her plight! George already admired his brand-new daughter-in-law; she was strong and sensible, everything his own children were not. Just the same, he knew she had been used shabbily by all concerned, each for their own purpose, and the old man vowed to make it up to her somehow.

The horses were halted under the Hall's portico, yet not a single soul came out to greet them. It was quite dark now, but none of the outside lanterns had been lighted, and George fumed, as in the darkness Rodney assisted his passengers from the sleigh, speaking to Rachel as he did so.

"If ever you need assistance, Miss Rachel," he said in a low voice, "I am at your service. You have only to send word."

"That is most kind of you, Rodney, but this will be my home now, and I am certain to be well cared for."

Though George was pleased overhearing Rachel's reply, Rodney himself was not so sure. While he knew neither Guersten son well enough to speak to personally, he had heard many a rumor about Emory's drinking and carousing at local inns and taverns. Rodney held Rachel in high regard and ruefully returned to his sleigh, promising to return George's coach and matched grays when the weather permitted.

The total darkness that enveloped Guersten Hall extended inside as well as out; the long gallery was pitch-black, and in the drawing room, while one lone lamp burned feebly, the hearth was empty and the room was unbelievably cold. By this time, George was openly furious. He thumped on the marble floor with his walking stick.

"Bah! Servants! Damn the lot of them!" he added vociferously. "Well, you're the mistress now, my dear," he added, "and I pass them to you gladly. I hope you can bring them into line. But I must warn you, you'll have your hands full, for they're a shiftless lot. Sack 'em all and start anew if you see fit."

In response to the echoed pounding, a young serving girl hurried from the dining room, and George exploded his wrath upon the hapless girl.

"Where the hell is everyone? Where is Stoddard? Damnation! Is this any way to greet your new mistress?" he thundered. "Hurry now, light the lamps. Get a fire going in that grate at once!"

"Yes, sir," stammered the girl fearfully, watching George's ebony stick as it whizzed above her head, for the man gesticulated wildly with it as he bellowed. "I'm sorry, sir," she said. "There's a fire in the upstairs salon. It's right warm there, sir. Is there anything else, sir?"

"Send Stoddard to me at once! I want to know what she's planned for supper. And have Mrs. Guersten's things taken to her room. And for your sake, it better be ready!" he finished, glowering at her.

"It is, sir," the girl said, curtsying. "The girls are just finishing up, sir."

The red-faced maid took their things, and the three of them started up the marble steps to the salon. They moved slowly in deference to George's stiff knees. He, refusing assistance from either of the young women, maneuvered the stairs deftly with the aid of the balustrade on one side and his walking stick on the other, even if it was one step at a time.

"You must forgive this confusion," he mumbled to Rachel as they neared the top, "but Emory's letter threw me into a tizzy, I confess. When we departed for your father's house this morning, I was not at all sure there would even be a wedding."

George had spoken softly. Ermaline, ahead of them, knew nothing of the scribbled document, assumed only that her brother was off yet again on another one of his drunken sojourns. Ermaline liked her new sister-in-law, admiring Rachel's beauty and calm poise. Not once throughout the awkward day had Rachel given way to the anger and humiliation Ermaline knew she was enduring. The two women had hardly known each other growing up, though their two family estates bordered each other. Ermaline now hoped that they would become friends; perhaps Rachel would become the sister she had always yearned for.

Many, many years had passed since Rachel had last been inside the Hall, and she was struck again by the vastness of the place as they passed into the salon. Ermaline would give Rachel a guided tour of all the rooms on the morrow, but for now George himself offered to show her to her room. The lamps in the long corridors had been lighted at last, and their flickering light danced against the gilded oak, outlining the soft relief of carvings and tracings. Long runners woven in burnished reds and blues extended beneath their feet, and while the decor was admittedly luxurious, still, everywhere Rachel was able to spot telltale signs of shoddy housekeeping—dust and unswept corners, even cobwebs here and there. She made mental notes of all the shortcomings.

The master and mistress of Guersten Hall had always occupied separate bedrooms, one located on either side of the salon. Rachel was ushered into the room that Abigail Guersten had last occupied, and before her, generations of other women who had played out their roles as mistress of the Hall.

It was a large square room with two massive windows, covered now by heavy draperies of patterned velvet. Everything was dusted and polished, and a pleasant fire crackled in the grate, yet the room was still cold and barren. Its walls were not white and cheery, like those in the salon, but dark and heavily paneled in aged oak. There was a great beamed ceiling and a monstrous medieval bed that stood on a raised platform against one wall; a half canopy with velvet curtains extended above it. A tall secretary was placed precisely between the windows, and there was a dressing table in one corner, its bulk neatly balanced by a chaise and small table in another.

Before he left her to change for supper, George opened several drawers and cubbies of the wardrobe that lined the wall across from the bed and, without fanfare, beckoned to Rachel. All the spaces were filled with trays and lined boxes containing what Rachel assessed to be a king's ransom in priceless jewels!

"The family gems . . . passed from bride to bride for generations. They are yours now, Rachel. As Emory's wife, you are entitled to them. I hope you will see fit to wear some of them."

Rachel took little solace in the bridal bequeathment, however, and none at all in the fact that she had right to them simply because she was Emory's wife. She put the jewels away and, changing quickly into a dress of dark green wool, hurried back to the warmth of the salon's fires, eager to be away from the dark and cavernous room that would be hers. There, she found Ermaline, and together they whiled away a rather pleasant hour, all things considered, until George joined them for supper.

The repast prepared by Stoddard was simple, delectable pork pies and breast of young chicken, washed down with well-chilled cider and topped by bowls of preserved fruit slices, well smothered in thick new cream.

For more than a month, Stoddard had listened with a sympathetic ear to Emory's sour grumblings about his future bride, especially her supposed lack of beauty. Darting in and out of the dining room, she was quickly captivated by Rachel's friendliness and charming manner, as well as her beauty, and Rachel further endeared herself to the older woman by passing praiseful comment on the light crust that encased the juicy pork. Until this very moment, the cook had secretly sided with Emory, knowing his yen for a pretty face. Tidying up after the meal, she assessed Rachel's satiny complexion and auburn tresses for the tenth time and found the new bride not wanting.

"*Eeeee!*" she said to no one in particular. "The lad must have a bolt loose! Or else t' drink is gettin' to 'im." Like Emory, Stoddard herself was expecting a new mistress remarkably plain of face and figure. "If that be plain," she said, chuckling heartily, "then I be Cleopatra!"

Though George did all he could to make Rachel feel comfortable and welcome, the rest of Rachel's first evening at Guersten Hall was awkward. George sat with her in the library, making small talk, and just before bedtime, he offered her a tiny brandy. Rachel accepted it graciously since her head had begun to pound again. Perhaps the brandy would enable her to sleep, help her to forget the awful events of the day. As they went up the high stairs once more, George reached across and took his new daughter-in-law's slender hand into his own.

"My dear Rachel," he said. "I sincerely hope you will be happy here. Though your marriage has gotten off to an unfortunate start, do not be disheartened. You are young, and you have great strength. All will work out for the best, in time. Somehow I just know it."

Once alone in her room, however, Rachel dropped dejectedly onto the long bench that stretched before the foot of the bed. Even though the room was large, the walls closed in around her ominously, while outside the snow storm still raged, though it could be neither seen nor heard through the heavy draperies. It was her wedding night, yet she was alone, abandoned by her husband, who was probably miles away in London, sharing someone else's bed, or at best, besotted by drink somewhere. For just a moment Rachel's composure threatened to crumble, and she came close to tears.

But she stood resolute, just as she had that very first night at Miss Phillipps so long ago. To others, at first glance, it might appear that she had everything any woman could ever yearn for; the wardrobe contained a fortune in fabulous gems, and all around her was magnificent, if dusty, opulence. Sitting alone on her bench though, Rachel was starkly aware of the absence of the one thing that guaranteed happiness, that one thing that, in its absence, was suddenly more important to her than great wealth or glittering jewels. *That was love!* Her relationship with George and Ermaline would develop compatibly and congenially, of that she was certain, but as far as Emory was concerned, the marriage was a sham!

And so it remained, for Emory did not return to the Hall in the days following the wedding, much to his father's great consternation. With Ermaline's help, Rachel quickly became settled in the mansion, becoming familiar with its many rooms and long corridors. Soon she was exploring the house by herself, wandering through the halls, studying the many portraits and tapestries to be found there. On the second floor, opposite the great staircase, a tiny wrought iron balcony projected out over the reception hall. In days long ago, trumpeters and musicians occupied this perch, announcing titled guests and providing entertainment for them. In the tapestry nearest the balcony, a helmeted figure sat in dignity astride a great black stallion. Ermaline explained its significance.

"The first Edward Guersten," she said, "who fought beside Athelstan, grandson of Alfred the Great, and helped expel the Danes from England in the tenth century. He was granted this land for his bravery, but he and his heirs continued to follow their sovereigns into battle, and it wasn't until the end of the fourteenth century that the Great Hall was built and the Geurstens finally became gentlemen."

In her tours about the house, Rachel continued to find signs of neglect and disorder. The morning room was bright and sunny, but the white marble fireplace was black with soot, the furniture covered by shabby purple velvet. In the cold ballroom, there were icy puddles on the dirty floor where melting snow had trickled under the French doors, and Rachel had to wipe smudges from the glass in order to view the terrace and formal gardens outside, now drifted over by wind-whipped snow.

The music room, too, was unused, its windows draped and shuttered. Delicate chairs with torn upholstery were piled haphazardly in one corner, and Rachel found the draperies to be rotted and water stained. It struck her that such neglect was more than just shoddy housekeeping. It was almost as if someone had snapped a pocketbook shut, unwilling or unable, perhaps, to expend the money necessary for upkeep.

It was natural then that the library would come to be her favorite place. It was a sizeable room, pleasant and inviting, with high oaken ceilings and bookcases containing at least twice as many books as did the library at Brenham Manor. A movable spiral staircase with a small platform enabled Rachel to examine those that were hidden away on the topmost shelves. Many of them were very old, she discovered one day with interest, their parchment pages brittle, their print faded. She guessed some of them were probably valuable as well, for the type in some appeared to have been set by hand, and a few were actually hand-lettered.

On a dusty bottom shelf, Rachel unearthed a long row of old journals pertaining to the estate's history and its management. The earliest entries had been made two hundred years or more before, and the very last inscription recorded simply, in a spidery scrawl, the expenses for Margaret Guersten's funeral. That was Emory's grandmother, thought Rachel, but after that entry, the remaining pages were blank. Either

George maintained his own journals, or in all his years as master of the Hall, he had not seen fit to keep them.

Three steps and a low railed platform enclosed a windowed turret in one corner of the room, and it was here that Rachel confiscated a gateleg table for a desk and established a study of sorts. Here she would keep her household accounts and see to the supervision of the staff. She retrieved the housekeeper's key ring from Stoddard and toured the house from attic to wine cellar once again, learning which key opened each door. On her fourth morning at the Hall, she finished her inspection by going to the kitchens.

She came downstairs before breakfast that day dressed in a simple house gown of brown merino, the soft wool falling in gentle folds from her waist, her hair tucked neatly inside a lace-trimmed morning cap. Unannounced, she descended the steps that led to the kitchen. Her entrance went unnoticed for a long moment while she stood on the bottom step, surveying the kitchen.

It was a huge place, bathed in morning sunlight despite the fact that the windows were placed very high, for the room was actually below ground level. One wall was dominated by an enormous fireplace, tall enough for a man to step into without stooping, its inner wall lined with an assortment of niches used for baking and a number of warming ovens. The great spit stood empty now, but it could easily roast a whole deer or even an ox. Through the years, the redbrick floor had been polished and worn smooth until it glowed with a dull patina wherever the sunlight touched it.

A great black range stood near the fireplace, with neat rows of cabinets and shelving running along the walls beside it. In the middle of the room, Stoddard was busy preparing breakfast at a square worktable. Her kitchen was immaculate! Why, it must be the cleanest room in the whole house!

Just then a small child suddenly appeared from a nearby doorway, struggling mightily with a cook pot filled with water. The thin girl was bedraggled, wearing a torn dress and a soiled apron. Her legs were bare, only a pair of wooden clogs protecting her feet from the bare bricks. Rachel guessed the child was eight. She was nine.

The weight of the pot became at last too much for her, and she set it on the floor with a thud, spilling some of the water. Staring at Rachel, she offered an awkward little curtsey, just as Stoddard began to scold without turning from her work.

"Wipe it up, Annie, and be quick about it!"

At the silence, Stoddard spun around, coming forward quickly when she spied her new mistress standing on the bottom step, embarrassed to be caught carping.

Effie Stoddard was a short woman, her thinness accented by a long nose and pointed chin. Her pinched features gave her a shrewish appearance, but in reality she was friendly enough. Well taken with the beautiful woman who stood before her, Stoddard offered a smile. She had been in service at Guersten Hall nearly forty years now. She had watched Emory grow from boy to man. He was her avowed favorite and, because of it, had always excused his rude behavior and sharp tongue. Stoddard had known from the start of Emory's objection to his arranged marriage, but after meeting his new bride, she had joined the ranks of those who thought him a fool. Her new mistress was not snobbish and demanding, as Miss Abigail had been, but gentle and considerate, as well as lovely. Why didn't the dolt come home?

"Good morning, ma'am. Why didn't you ring?"

"I came to view the kitchen, Stoddard. Beginning today I will assume my proper duties as mistress. Henceforth, in matters pertaining to the household, you will deal directly with me and not Master George."

"And relieved to hear that, I am," said the older woman, smiling. "My place is here in the kitchen. I don't manage well above stairs. Those maids try me patience!"

"I shall reckon with their shortcomings soon enough," Rachel said firmly. "The discipline may come hard after this laxity. You may hear some grumbling at the table, but see that they keep their places."

"Aye, ma'am, but I doubt they'll yawp, at least in my presence. As you can see, here I rule with an iron first. 'Tis on the other side of yon door me trouble starts," she said, pointing up the stairs.

Rachel laughed. "I shall submit a menu each day. You are to adhere strictly to it, making no changes without consulting me."

She toured the rooms off the kitchen then, passing from the buttery to the larder, and then from the storeroom to the laundry. In the scullery she was surprised to discover yet another little girl, this one busily scrubbing potatoes. The child was as ill-dressed as Annie, now hard at work mopping the buttery floor.

"Whose children are these?" asked Rachel of Stoddard.

"They be the daughters of Stevens, the dairyman," replied Stoddard. "Pug found them hiding in the barn the night of the first snowfall, half dead with cold, both of 'em hungry. Stevens was on a binge, and I hadn't the heart to put them out again, what with the weather 'n' all, only to have them abused again. Master George said he didn't mind me keeping them, so here they be."

"I see," said Rachel soberly. Good heavens, child abuse on the estate!

The potato scrubber, named Becky, was a pretty child, with dull and lifeless dark brown hair. Her ribs could be seen under the thin fabric of her dress, and scrawny legs protruded like matchsticks from beneath its ragged hem. Something about the child reminded Rachel of herself at that age, and she had been abroad in that terrible blizzard, too. For some unexplained reason, Rachel felt a kinship to the child.

"Stoddard," she said, turning at the foot of the stairs a few minutes later, "this work is much too hard for them. They are far too young, and both of them are undernourished. Set them to work polishing the silver for now until I decide what to do with them. And feed them, for heaven's sake! I will send Flossie and Amanda to you as kitchen help; put them to work as you see fit. Betsey has agreed to take charge of the laundry and mending for an extra pound a month. That leaves six for above stairs, more than enough I think."

Ensconced in her position as mistress, Rachel ran the staff ragged for days, while George beamed his satisfaction openly. Politely but firmly Rachel let them know exactly what she expected of them all, and woe to them that shirked! Every occupied room was torn apart, cleaned and set to rights again, and the smell of strong soap and beeswax permeated throughout the house. The music room was cleaned and reopened, and despite the weather, windows were thrown open. The stable boys were set to clearing away the snow from the terrace out-

FALLEN BRANCHES

side the ballroom, after which they were quickly put to work beating carpets. The maids took the draperies there, to shake accumulated dust from the thick folds. The house began to shine.

The two little waifs were removed from their cold garret over the storeroom and given warmer quarters on the third floor. Betsey was assigned the task of remaking gray uniforms to fit them both, complete with aprons and mobcaps, and they were given warm stockings and new shoes. By now, both of them openly adored Rachel, and one of them was always near, willing to fetch or carry for her. She was grateful for the steps they saved her, but still, she felt badly for them, having learned that they had no mother.

Rachel's days were full. Her trunks arrived from her father's house, there was the supervision of the staff, and she busied herself with her ledgers, making inventories of the linens and silver, planning menus. Her nights were another matter.

Stoically, Rachel refused to dwell on Emory's absence, and already the bedside table in her room was piled high with books. Just the same, she came to hate those moments spent alone in that dark square room.

Christmas came and went without fanfare, a marked cry from what she had envisioned it would be. Neither Edward nor Emory returned to the Hall, although the Chandlers did come to dinner on Christmas Eve. Then, George's round face glowed with pride as he led his sister from room to room, showing off the fruits of Rachel's labor. On Boxing Day, accompanied by Ermaline, Rachel sleighed across to Brenham Manor to visit her mother and Rebecca. Her father had been held captive in London by the continuing bad weather, and in that regard Louisa was thankful, for Rachel and Benjamin had not spoken since the day of the wedding, and she hoped that time would set things to right again. She noted with amazement how Rachel had adjusted to her new position.

By January, George was even more impressed with his daughter-in-law and harbored strong resentment against Emory for his contin-ued humiliation of her. If Rachel had any misgivings about her new role, she kept them well hidden. Her disposition was sunny at all times, and for the first time in years, the household ran smoothly; meals were pleasant and on time, and the staff performed efficiently. But it was the

153

change in Ermaline that most endeared George. Following Rachel's lead, the girl at last began to show some interest in the Hall, in her appearance, and to George's utmost surprise, in books! Usually sullen and somewhat dispirited, Ermaline now became animated, chattered incessantly, and made intelligent observations for a change. George's relief knew no bounds, for secretly he had long feared that Ermaline had inherited a touch of her mother's tendency toward depression.

One afternoon late in the month, Sir Hugh stopped at the Hall to visit George. His face was puffy, and one eye was swollen shut. George, shocked, led him into the library.

"My word, Hugh! How did you come by that eye?"

"Outside White's, three days ago. Compliments of your firstborn."

"Emory? I don't believe it!"

"Well, it's true enough. He was waiting for a hansom, and while I meant only to reproach him for his neglect of Rachel, I got no further than stating simply that I had stood for him, adding that she was certainly a beauty. With that, he struck me!"

"But why? Didn't he say anything?"

"Only that he would not stand for any ridicule about his wife. Afterward, he stormed away. Even now I'm not sure what it was all about."

"Nor do I," said George. "Was he sober?"

"Oddly enough, he was! Perhaps he felt I was having a joke at his expense."

George nodded in agreement. "Maybe," he said. "Not that it excuses his behavior, though! Did you see him again?"

"No, and I certainly shan't seek him out," said Sir Hugh with a grimace. "But I did see that stallion of his at Aylesbury Crossing as I passed through earlier today."

"Are you certain?"

"Aye, quite! There's no mistaking that beast, even with one eye shut!"

When Sir Hugh departed, George went up the stairs to his room, to come back down only moments later, wearing well-worn riding breeches, having decided to go to the inn at Aylesbury Crossing himself find his son and drag him home! Emory had played the fool long enough!

Pug, one of the grooms, watched him trot away from the stables half an hour later, but neither Rachel nor Ermaline even knew he had left the estate.

The sun went down; dinnertime passed, and still George did not return. Alarmed, Rachel settled in the library to wait for him, an unopened book in her lap. Something was wrong, she sensed it. She waited, roused by a commotion on the kitchen stairs sometime later.

It was Stoddard, who came to fetch her, and jumping to her feet, Rachel met her at the door of the library. Standing behind the cook, in a high state of agitation, was Peter Hubbardston, stable master at the Hall.

"What is it, Peter?" asked Rachel before the handsome man could speak. "What is wrong?"

"I don't know," he said in a worried voice. "The master's horse returned alone just now. We're saddling now to start a search for him. I don't know what else to do."

"Could he have been thrown?"

"I doubt it, ma'am. Master George rides well, and Hunter is one of the best mounts on the estate. If the master fell from his saddle, Hunter would have remained with him. I fear the master sent him on, Miss Rachel. Wherever he is, he is unable to remount."

"Wait for me. I'm going with you."

Rachel changed quickly, slipping into her leather riding breeches and a warm jacket, while Peter and the others waited for her under the portico. There, Peter brought forth George's brown stallion, and without a thought for her childhood fears, Rachel climbed onto Hunter's saddle.

The riders split into two groups and proceeded single file along each side of the road, searching in complete silence, lest they miss the master's call. The little group passed by Brenham Manor and the other estates at the foot of Great Guersten Wood Road and then gathered in a loose circle when they came to the Coltenham road.

"Not a trace," said Peter dejectedly. He looked at his pocket watch in the light from a lantern. "It's nearly midnight now. If we don't find him soon, he may freeze to death." Turning in his saddle, he spoke to Rachel. "Which way was he coming, ma'am? Where had he been?"

"I don't know," said Rachel in a worried tone. "He left without a word to anyone."

"Who saddled for him?" called Peter to the circle of grooms.

Pug pressed forward. "I did . . . but he said naught about his destination."

Not quite sure what their next move should be, the little group rested in silence for a moment. It was a clear night, but there was no moon, and except for the meager light reflected by the snow, it was awfully dark. In the quiet of the night, only the creaking of their saddles and the puffing of their mounts was heard.

"Coltenham is closer," said Rachel, deciding. "We will go that way first. If we do not find him, we can double back and head for Aylesbury."

Peter nodded. "Very well, Miss Rachel. But stay alert; watch Hunter."

"I don't understand."

"He can't talk, ma'am, but he knows where he left his master. If Hunter starts to handle badly, he just might be trying to tell us we're going the wrong way."

Peter was right. Not a mile up the road, Hunter started to balk and lagged back, moving so slowly that soon Rachel was bringing up the rear.

"Peter!" she called.

"I see him," replied the young man. "He's usually steady, ma'am. Do you trust him enough to turn around?"

But Hunter had already planted his feet firmly and laid back his ears; Rachel doubted she could have coaxed him another foot toward Coltenham. She turned him easily.

"Yes," she said, "and let us hurry. Hold your lanterns high and look sharp."

They found George nearly an hour later, lying exactly where he had fallen. He was barely conscious, and his lips were a dismal shade of blue. He tried to speak when he saw Rachel, but a low throaty moan was all he had the strength for.

Peter pointed to the ground where the snow had been trampled in a wide circle around George's prone figure.

"Just like I said, Miss Rachel. My guess is he fell from the saddle, and Hunter stayed until the master sent him on when he realized he could not remount. God knows how long he has lain here!"

"He'll need a doctor. Pug, will you go?"

"Ahhh!" said Peter scornfully, "and you'll have to wait while he sobers up! There's a new man, ma'am, in Peterborough. A Dr. Ferguson, a Scotsman from Edinburgh. If Pug rides hard, he and the doctor should arrive at Guersten Hall just before daybreak."

"Go ahead then, Pug. But hurry!"

All the way back to the Hall, it was Peter who cradled the old man in his strong arms, and once there, he carried him up the stairs and put him to bed. The old man was stripped and toweled and settled under the covers at last in a warm nightshirt. Rachel stayed by his bedside for the remainder of the night, refusing to rest, and when Dr. Ferguson arrived near dawn, it was she who met him on the stairs.

In his thirties, the doctor, a darkly handsome man with thinning hair and piercing gray eyes, climbed the stairs with his mouth open, quite flabbergasted at the sight of Rachel, still wearing her tight breeches and high riding boots, her hair disheveled and her cheeks still rosy from the night air.

"Thank you for coming so promptly," she said to him, unaware of her appearance. She explained what happened. "I fear he has been taken with a stroke."

Pacing nervously, Rachel and Ermaline waited in the hallway just outside George's door while Dr. Ferguson examined his new patient. When he exited an hour later, Rachel hurried to his side.

"You were right about the stroke, but it's far too early to say just how bad it is or what damage may have been done. My more immediate concern is pneumonia. There is already congestion and some fever."

"Will he die?" whispered Rachel, suddenly frightened for the old man, whom she had come to love.

"I cannot say," replied the doctor, stroking his chin, "but his chances are not good. Y'd best face that. He is an old man, and who knows how strong he may be."

Typically, Ermaline, high-strung and nervous, became nearly hysterical when she learned of the severity of her father's illness, retreating to her room, to remain there, tearful and brooding. It was Rachel who assisted the doctor in making the patient comfortable, and then she readied a guest room for him. When she finally went to her own room again to change her clothes, it was already late morning.

As she bathed and dressed again, this time in a green morning frock, Rachel thought about Emory. *Emory! Damn the fool!* Would he never come home? Now, when George needed them most, neither of his sons had presented themselves.

George was no better the next day; his breathing became labored, and the fever began to climb. Resolutely, Rachel went into the library and penned a short note. It was addressed to Emory. After it was sealed, she sent for Peter.

"You are the only other person on the premises who has his wits about him," she said. "You must take Hunter and ride hard for London. Seek out Mr. Percy Tisbury, the solicitor, on Fleet Street. He will know best where you would be most likely to find my . . . my husband," she finished, nearly choking on the dratted word.

"Give Emory my letter and tell him he must make all haste. Be certain that he understands his father may die!"

By the time Peter returned, four days later, George's condition was critical; he was nearly comatose. To make matters worse, Peter's report was not good. He had scoured the entire city and found no trace of Emory.

"Tisbury was most helpful; in the end he suggested I leave your note with him. Emory is sure to show up the first of the month for his allowance draft, Tisbury says. He'll deliver your letter then."

"That may be too late," moaned Rachel woefully. "By the first of the month your master may be dead!"

CHAPTER TEN

But George Guersten did not die. Instead he clung tenaciously to life, lying still and white in his great canopied bed, breathing with marked difficulty in deep bubbly rasps that anguished those that heard them. For more than a week, his condition remained unchanged, neither worsening nor improving. Then, very slowly the fever began to subside, his breathing eased, and his sleep was peaceful again for long hours at a time. Occasionally he would open his eyes; each time he did so, it was Rachel he saw. She was always there.

Toward the end of February, Dr. Ferguson and Rachel left George's sickroom together one day, passing down the marble staircase side by side.

"And how is our patient today, Duncan?"

"Out of the woods, I'd say, but he is far from recovered, Rachel. He'll not walk again, and that left arm will forever be useless. All in all though, he's lucky to be alive, given his age. His faculties are good, but you may notice some slurring of speech now and again."

"He hasn't said much of anything so far. Have you told him . . . about his legs?"

"Aye, but I needn't have bothered. He's nobody's fool, Rachel. He knew."

At the bottom of the stairs, Stoddard came toward them from the back of the house, just tying on a clean apron.

"Ah, there you be, ma'am. And you, Doctor, will ye be staying for tea?"

"Please do, Duncan," said Rachel, taking his arm. "Join me and Ermaline."

"I wish I could, but I have a croupy child to see yet, and my clinic will be full when I return to Peterborough. I shall call again on Sunday; might I join you then?"

"Come early, take Sunday dinner with us," Rachel said on sudden impulse. "My sister Rebecca will be here. I would like you to meet her, and there will be Ermaline, of course, and George's sister Adele . . . and the cousins. Oh my," she said, placing her fingers across her lips. "Unless all that female company would make you uncomfortable."

"On the contrary," laughed Duncan, "I shall fancy myself most fortunate."

Rachel gave him a warm smile. "Sunday then, at three."

The doctor prepared to take his leave, Rachel escorting him to the door. More than a month had passed since that fateful night George had fallen in the snow, and during that time Rachel and Duncan Ferguson had become friends. Rachel admired the man greatly, as much for his intelligence as his friendship, and Duncan had never known any woman quite like Rachel, so beautiful and charming. Stoddard watched them turn the corner into the long gallery, chatting easily together. She saw something no one else had yet discovered; Rachel had found a new friend, but the doctor, *puir laddie*, had fallen head over heels in love.

Duncan Ferguson came to dinner that Sunday, and most of the Sundays afterward, enjoying himself immensely each time. In the drawing room his pleasant wit entertained them all, and in the now refurbished music room, he raised his voice in song, his mellow baritone blending nicely with those of the young women as Rachel accompanied them at the piano. Duncan was enthralled by Rachel's vivaciousness, amused no end by Charlotte's empty-headed chatter, and he succeeded in impressing even Adele with his quick intelligence and old-world charm. She, always perceptive, soon spotted what Stoddard had shrewdly seen, noting the quick turn of Duncan's head whenever

Rachel spoke his name or entered a room, and she saw how hungrily his eyes followed wherever Rachel went.

George's improvement continued as winter waned, and one bright day Adele stopped at Guersten Hall with Charlotte and Olivia, all on their way to London for the February cotillion. The girls chattered excitedly, begging their cousin to join them. Rachel agreed, encouraging Ermaline to go.

"Your father is out of danger now; there is no reason you cannot go."

Still, Ermaline was hesitant. Her engagement was to be announced in April, the wedding planned for September. Thinking of her own empty marriage, Rachel wondered if perhaps Ermaline's reticence had something to do with Henry Rowland. She raised the subject when she and Ermaline were alone.

"Do you have any reservations about your coming marriage? About Henry, perhaps?"

"None," answered Ermaline quickly. "Henry loves me well enough . . . and I him, and I am excited about living in London, truly. The Rowlands have a grand house in Knightsbridge; we will live there, I suppose."

"Then I fail to understand your reluctance to join your cousins. It will be your very last ball before you become a married woman."

"But I do want to go!" cried the girl. "It's just . . . Oh, Rachel," she moaned. "You always manage to look beautiful, no matter what you wear, while I always seem to choose the wrong gown, the wrong color . . . And I'm so plump! It never bothered me before, but now it does. Just once I'd like to be beautiful, for Henry's sake! Why, I don't even have a decent ball gown to wear to the cotillion!"

She burst into tears then, collapsing in a billow of dark taffeta upon the bed.

"So, that's it! Dry your eyes, Ermaline! There is a solution!"

Rachel went to her desk in the library and wrote a letter of introduction to Eleanora Scofield, requesting that she take Ermaline under her wing. Eleanora would know dozens of ways to camouflage Ermaline's extra pounds, choosing fabrics and colors that would heighten the girl's plain coloring yet enhance her red-gold tresses.

Finishing her note, Rachel scratched her signature across the bottom of the ivory sheet and, after folding it, sealed it with wax and handed it to Ermaline.

"Give it to Madame . . . and leave everything to her. Trust her judgment; there is none better in London at any price. You'll see, a little boning, a longer bodice . . . you'll be the talk of the cotillion, and Henry's eyes will pop, I guarantee!"

"Do you really think so?"

"I know so! Eleanora is a genius. You will adore her, and if you are satisfied, then give her leave to create your bridal dress and your wedding things . . ."

"But . . . the cost!" interrupted Ermaline, a look of doubt shadowing her face. "Scofield's must be frightfully expensive! Father has asked that I . . . well, *frugal* was the word he used."

The reference to money brought Rachel up short, a sudden thought flashing through her mind. Money! Was that the reason she had been chosen as Emory's bride? The niggling suspicion had come to her once or twice before, but each time, she had dismissed it. It was true; there was neglect here at the Hall when she first arrived, but perhaps it was just that, neglect, having nothing at all to do with money, or the lack of it. After all, she reasoned, the house had gone a long time without a mistress or even a proper housekeeper, for that matter. Once again, Rachel cast the idea away and, turning, hugged Ermaline tightly.

"Then I may go to Scofield's?"

"Of course, you may! I will assume responsibility. You shall have your trousseau!"

Pink with excitement, Ermaline kissed her sister-in-law happily. Self-expression was difficult for her, and though she tried hard to express her gratitude, she stumbled badly over the words. Without sisters, Ermaline's childhood had been lonely, for she had hardly known her strange green-eyed mother, and her relationship with her cousins, though certainly companionable, was somewhat reserved. Until Rachel came to Guersten Hall, Ermaline had neither a close friend nor a confidante. Now she had both.

"Say no more," said Rachel. "We are sisters now, are we not? Now hurry! I will send someone to help you pack, for Adele is anxious to be away, and she will surely fume if you keep her waiting."

Only minutes later, Rachel encountered Adele herself in the grand salon. She had just left her brother's room, and a deep frown etched her brow.

"He's sleeping again," she said.

"And how did you find him today?"

"It's sad," sighed Adele, "terribly sad. He's just a shell of his former self. He looks like an old man."

"Stuff and nonsense!" cried Rachel indignantly. "He is an old man, Adele, yet his mind is as sharp as it ever was. Only his legs are useless now."

"Nonsense yourself!" snapped Adele, bridling under the criticism. She pointed at Rachel with a jeweled finger. "He'll never leave that bed, and it won't be long before he becomes senile."

Shaking her head vigorously, Rachel sat down beside the older woman. "That's where you're wrong," she said gently. "He *will* leave that bed, and soon! Duncan . . . Dr. Ferguson is going to bring him a comfortable wicker chair . . . on wheels. George will have the run of the house again, even the grounds once the weather improves."

Idly, Adele tapped her fingers on a nearby tabletop, noticing the half smile that passed Rachel's lips at the mention of Duncan's name. If Emory did not come to his senses, and soon, she thought, his beautiful bride was going to fall in love with another man. *Serves the fool right, too!*

"Well, who knows," she said, getting to her feet. "Perhaps you and the good doctor have something there at that. But what of the stairs? And who will dress him? Sooner or later, Rachel, my brother is going to require a manservant."

Rachel agreed. She had thought about it herself lately, had hoped instead that at least one of George's fool sons would return before this time came. Rachel's position was difficult. A young man would be required to carry George up and down those high stairs, and a strong one at that. Until such time as her wayward husband chose to return,

Rachel felt that to have such a man in residence at the Hall would only invite criticism.

"There's been enough talk, Adele. I dare not jeopardize Ermaline's betrothal with more. For now, perhaps the stable master can continue to be of assistance; at least he sleeps in the carriage house."

Adele nodded agreement. The girl was wise beyond her years. The hurried wedding and Emory's continued absence had kept tongues wagging the better part of the winter. Years before, there had been all that unsavory talk about poor Abigail's death on the stairs. It would take only a rumor or two to dredge it all up again.

"You've grown quite fond of my brother, haven't you?" asked Adele.

"Indeed, I have," responded Rachel, as the two women moved to the door of the salon.

"I am devoted to him and wish only that I could do more for his comfort. If only Edward and Emory would return! George has called for them, again and again, and I know their continued absence hurts him deeply."

"Hmmph! They are nincompoops! Both of them . . . especially Emory! Perhaps I shall seek him out myself when I reach London. Daresay he won't blacken my eye!"

Remembering poor Hugh's bruised and swollen face, Rachel smiled sympathetically.

"Do that, Adele, but pray, speak only for your brother . . . say nothing in my behalf. I will speak for myself when the time comes."

"You're a remarkable young woman, Rachel, remarkable. You have every right to despise Emory, yet I see no anger, and you have yet to shed a tear, from what Ermaline tells me."

"I am done with tears," Rachel said, proceeding down the stairs. "And I do not hate Emory; on the contrary, I feel rather a sadness for him. After all, he was born here at Guersten Hall, yet it is I who am home."

Adele departed straightaway, chattering charges in tow, and for a few days afterward, the house seemed empty and quiet. Rachel welcomed the solitude. When George was awake, she sat by his bedside, reading aloud to him, or else they chatted, if that was the old man's preference, while Rachel busied herself with needlework. Some days she brought his mail to him and wrote the necessary replies at his direction.

Thus, that particular Sunday, only Rebecca and Duncan joined Rachel for dinner. As the three of them left the dining room afterward, Rebecca suddenly paled and would have fallen to the floor had Duncan not caught her. Scooping her slight body into his long arms, he carried Rebecca to the library while Rachel went to find the smelling salts.

Duncan laid Rebecca on the sofa, noting her swollen ankles with some dismay when he rearranged her skirts. He met Rachel at the door and took and smelling salts from her trembling hand.

"She'll be all right," he said kindly in light of Rachel's apprehensions. "Will you send for my case and a light blanket?"

Nodding, Rachel sped away up the stairs herself, where Duncan's case still lay on the bench at the foot of George's bed, while Duncan turned his attention again to Rebecca. He found her alert, her dark blue eyes swimming with tears. With one foot, he pulled a nearby footstool to a spot beside the sofa and sat down awkwardly, elbows draped across his bony knees.

"Well?" he said to Rebecca, breaking the silence.

Rebecca stared into Duncan's gray eyes. They were gentle eyes but, still, uncomfortably piercing.

"You know, don't you?" she said with a catch in her voice.

"About the child? Of course! I've known for some time! What amazes me is that no one else has spotted it. You must know you cannot keep it hidden much longer."

Rachel tapped on the door just then, and Duncan went to retrieve his bag. "Meet me in the morning room," he whispered. "I'll be there in just a few minutes."

Weeks ago, Rachel had explained to Duncan, in much detail, about Rebecca's lengthy illnesses, and he examined the girl carefully now, keeping in mind her fragile health and delicate body. Through it all, Rebecca said not a word, merely watched him intently, noting each scowl and frown that flickered across his brow. At last, when Duncan crossed the room to open the draperies again, Rebecca spoke.

"What shall I do?" she asked simply.

"To begin with," the doctor replied, "you must remove those tight stays, at once . . . and if you are concerned for the well-being of that babe, you must keep them off. And then, of course, you must inform Rachel . . . and your parents."

Rebecca covered her face with her hands.

"They must be told, Rebecca, and soon. If you find it disturbing, perhaps . . . or embarrassing, might not Rachel tell them for you? That way there would be no recriminations, no scenes that would add to your distress."

Pale and wan though she be, Rebecca sat bolt upright on the sofa, drawing the thin blanket about her.

"Understand me well, Duncan! I am not . . . embarrassed! My grief comes only from the knowledge that I have broken my parents' trust, for I love them dearly. But I love Edward more, and to bear his child will bring my heart full measure, though I may lose my life in the bargain. My days are numbered! I know full well that I cannot survive many more of those awful attacks; I accept it as His will. The child is my legacy, therefore, the only mark I shall ever make in this world."

"In that you are mistaken, Rebecca, for you have left your mark in the hearts of all who know you, including myself. You have borne your cross well."

They discussed the matter further, and Duncan insisted that she rest. In the end, she agreed to let him advise Rachel of her condition, and then, he said, together the sisters could decide just how and when they would reveal this disastrous development to their parents.

The door to the morning room stood open, and Duncan saw Rachel standing before the window, gazing across the greening gardens. In her hand she toyed with a porcelain figurine taken idly from a small table. She turned sharply as Duncan crossed the threshold, closing the door behind him.

"She's all right, she is resting," he commented.

"What happened to her? What brought on that fainting spell?"

Duncan made a gesture of silence. "Rachel . . . how much do you know of Rebecca's relationship with Edward?"

"In truth, very little. Only what she has chosen to tell me. That they love each other dearly, wanted to marry, had not my own . . . had circumstances favored them more. Why?"

"She is going to have a child, Rachel. Edward's child."

Rachel gasped. The color drained from her face, and the figurine slipped from her fingers, to fall to the parquet flooring at the edge of the thick carpeting, where it smashed into a dozen broken pieces. Rachel looked at them dumbly for a moment, and then took a chair near the window.

"If I heard that from anyone's lips but yours, Duncan, I would not believe it! She admits to it?"

Duncan laughed dryly, and his hand covered Rachel's. "There's no denying it, my dear. I have suspected it for some weeks now, and when you go in to see her in a few minutes, you will wonder yourself just how you missed it."

Rachel's eyes widened. "You suspected? Yet you said nothing? But why?"

Lord! Duncan thought to himself. That would have been unthinkable! Doctor or no, he was a guest in Rachel's house, and one does not repay a kind hostess by suggesting her unmarried sister is pregnant! Pointedly, he ignored her question.

"I judge her to be ending her fourth month or starting her fifth. Your father must be told at once," he said, "lest he discover it himself his next trip to the midlands."

"Will she . . . Is everything all right?"

Duncan pursed his lips as he groped for an answer.

"For the moment, but even without her long medical history, Rachel, Rebecca could have some problems. She's not strong, and she's small . . . in all the wrong places. Before long she may find it necessary to take to her bed, conserve her strength for the ordeal ahead. It's not called labor without good cause."

"Will you see her through her time, Duncan?"

"Gladly, as though she were my own sister; but let me remind you, that decision is not ours to make. Rebecca is an unmarried woman; your father may prefer the services of someone else."

Rachel considered that for a moment. It was obvious that she would be the one elected to break this shocking news to Benjamin. Emotionally, the scene would simply be too much for Rebecca. Rachel's relationship with her father was at an impasse; he had been infuriated, as well as humiliated, the day of her wedding when George Guersten appeared without the bridegroom, arriving with Sir Hugh and an insulting letter of proxy instead! And then Benjamin had been even more shocked when Rachel defiantly demanded the ceremony be conducted anyway, choosing to be mortified as an unwanted bride rather than face the disgrace and probable spinsterhood that went with being left at the altar. Benjamin's secret dreams of storming London society with two beautiful daughters had crashed around his feet, for could society be expected to accept Rachel, lovely though she was, when her own husband continued to reject her? She sighed. Since that stormy December day, she had not spoken to her father; now, when she saw him next, she would bring him news that could only cause further abjection and debasement. The chasm between them would widen.

"Perhaps he might prefer the services of someone else," Rachel told Duncan, yet she suspected that when Benjamin learned of Rebecca's pregnancy, the revelation would either enrage him so that he would disavow her or crush him so badly that he would be unable to function in her behalf. In effect, Rebecca would be abandoned. "Either way," added Rachel, "the decision may be mine, by default, and I choose you."

She squared her shoulders, offering Duncan a weak smile. If Rebecca were to lean on her for support, then Rachel would have to be strong. The tall doctor had no doubts about her strength, had already seen it displayed during the worst days of George's illness, and promising to return in a fortnight, he departed, off to Edinburgh to collect George's new wheelchair.

Rachel went immediately to the library, where, after a few awkward moments, the sisters flew into each other's arms. There were no tears, no recriminations, and as Duncan had said, Rachel wondered how on earth she had ever missed her sister's condition, for there was no mistaking the puffiness of her face, the fullness at her breast, or the dullness of her usually shining tresses.

"I was certain that you, of all people, would be the first to discover my secret . . . especially when I began to spend so much time here at the Hall."

"To avoid Mother?"

"Oh, no," replied Rebecca, "not Mother! It is Agatha's sharp eyes I seek to avoid. I am positive she knows or, at the least, suspects, but poor Mother has been much preoccupied since your wedding, and she and Father have had several terrible scenes. She was dead set against your marriage to Emory from the start, and she blames Father for the way things have turned out for you."

That news troubled Rachel, because the relationship between her parents had always been one of pleasant compatibility, but returning to their more immediate problem, the two women agreed that Rebecca herself would break the news to her mother that very evening, and Rachel was elected to tell Benjamin as soon as he returned again to the midlands. At the moment, none of them knew when that might be, for he was still assessing winter-storm damage to his business and untangling back-ordered shipments. His last letter to Louisa had been posted in Liverpool.

"Well, when he comes . . . he comes," said Rachel matter-of-factly, not relishing the task before her. Rebecca prepared to return to Brenham Manor; as they parted under the porte cochere, Rebecca kissed her sister tenderly.

"For any trouble I have caused or may cause you in the future, forgive me," she whispered. "It's just that I love him so, Rachel. I love him so very much."

Climbing into the carriage, Rebecca sat in the very center of the upholstered seat, her back straight, her chin held high. She was a tiny and pathetic figure, waving forlornly as the carriage rolled down the drive.

Pondering her sister's parting words, Rachel lay awake in her lonely bed that night for hours. Would her own heart ever know a love to compare with Rebecca's adoration for Edward—a love so deep, so complete, that she would willingly jeopardize everything for it, perhaps even her life? With some measure of despair, Rachel realized that she stood alone. Those around her looked to *her* for strength and support:

George, Ermaline, and now Rebecca. Rachel had no one—her husband, who refused to take his place at his side; her mother, who had little strength to give; and her father, whose estrangement with her soon to be complete at their next meeting. No, she had no one . . . except perhaps Duncan, she thought, drifting off to sleep. Yes, she could lean on Duncan.

In a twinkling, it seemed, the weather changed, surprising them all by its suddenness. A quick thaw set in, bringing unusually warm days that were bright and sunny; the heavy snows began to melt steadily, and soon patches of bare ground were to be seen on the southern slopes of the estate. At night the temperatures remained mild, and the land became shrouded in a thin fog-like mist that disappeared rapidly once the sun came up again.

On one such misty night, an elegant carriage drew up under the portico, and from it stepped Percy Tisbury, George's London solicitor, very distinguished looking in a gray frock coat and silk cravat, carrying a thick portfolio of papers tucked under one arm. Tisbury was an older man, his face hidden by a full beard and heavy side-whiskers. Frankly, Rachel thought him to be stuffy and uncommunicative, with an air of perpetual preoccupation about him.

The man went directly to George's sickroom, even took supper on a tray there with the old man. Though Rachel readied a room for him, the two men were still huddled together when she retired for the night.

George and the solicitor conferred yet again the next morning, and then Tisbury departed hurriedly, without taking lunch. Rachel had no time to wonder about the purpose of his visit though, for no sooner was he gone than Dr. Ferguson arrived with George's new rolling chair strapped to the rear of his carriage. It was an uncomplicated contraption, a simple chair of unfinished wicker with a rolled back and side arms, and a padded seat, the whole mounted on a low wheeled platform.

Jubilant, Rachel promptly sent one of the maids to fetch Peter from his chores, watching excitedly as he and Duncan maneuvered the chair up the marble staircase. There, Rachel was overtaken by doubts.

"What if he doesn't like it?" she asked of Duncan. "He may refuse to use it!"

Duncan shrugged. "There's that chance, I suppose, but he seemed warm to the idea of mobility when I first suggested it. We'll soon see," he added. "Wait in the salon while Peter and I lift him in; with any luck, we'll join you there shortly."

They did just that, with George nestled comfortably in the wide seat with a blanket spread across his knees. An impish grin wreathed his round face when he saw Rachel, who ran to his side.

"I would have been heartbroken if you had been stubborn about the whole thing."

"So I hear," he said, patting her cheek tenderly with his good hand. "Ferguson told me. I feel like a damn fool in this oversized perambulator, but I couldn't let you down now, could I?"

And so, each day George was able to leave his room for longer periods of time, and slowly, but steadily, his strength returned, although his legs would remain forever useless, as Duncan predicted. Daily, Peter came up from the stable to help the invalid bathe and dress, giving assistance wherever it was needed. The stable master was a strong young man, and soon he was lifting George in and out of the wicker chair with ease.

In the salon, Rachel set a small round table into place before the French windows, and each day she joined George there for a light lunch. One day she found him sitting in his chair before the open windows.

"Come look," he called when he saw her, pointing toward the stables.

Most of the estate's riding horses had been taken from the stables to a nearby paddock, and even from this distance Rachel recognized Hunter, sleek and dark, cavorting friskily around the enclosure.

"Spring will be early this year," the old man said with some conviction. "Mark my words. Somehow they know it, too."

"He's truly a magnificent animal," commented Rachel as they watched Hunter's playful prancing for some moments.

"Only one better on the estate, and that's Emory's black."

"That may be, my friend, but this one saved your life. Did you know that?"

"Yes, Peter told me. He also told me that you had ridden Hunter that night, said you handled him well, too. I'm glad, for now that I cannot ride any longer, I wish you to have him. A gift, shall we say, token of my regard."

Rachel was touched and immensely pleased as well, for she had ridden Hunter several times since that dreadful night in January, and each time, she felt unaccountably sure and confident on his broad back. A slender-legged stallion, Hunter was all brown, even to his eyes, except for an identical patch of white splashed on each fetlock. Besides being handsome, he was intelligent and obedient, and as Rachel's confidence grew, she discovered she actually enjoyed her outings in the saddle for the first time in her life. It was often that she chided herself these days for those unnecessary childhood fears.

"Hunter will be yours, regardless of whatever should happen now, my dear," George said. "Remember that."

His mood changed. The round face, pale but cheerful just moments ago, was at once sober and drawn, and Rachel saw his wrinkled hands were clenched tightly in his lap. Plainly, something troubled him. She had caught him watching her recently, as if he was assessing her thoughts. At first, she assumed it was the excitement of the new rolling chair and the freedom it brought him, but now Rachel saw it had nothing to do with the chair. Then she remembered; Duncan had brought the wheelchair not an hour after Tisbury left Guersten Hall for London. That morning, before he departed, the unsmiling solicitor had given Rachel a long and studied look, a peculiar gaze, a mix of open admiration and guarded scrutiny at the same time. Yes, she thought, Tisbury's visit was surely behind George's melancholy mood.

"Tell me what troubles you, George. Perhaps I can help . . ."

"Ah, you have done so much already, and there's the rub," he said, interrupting. "You have become very dear to me, Rachel, and I bask in our mutual friendship. Still, I have done you a great disservice, and coming so close to death has made me realize that it must be put to rights, even should I diminish in your esteem."

He motioned Rachel to silence when she made to speak, and choosing his words carefully, he related to her the entire sordid story about her marriage to Emory, why it had been arranged, why she had been chosen. He told about the debts his sons had incurred and the cash needed for Ermaline's dowry. He revealed everything, even the naked truth that it was her supposed drabness that Emory had fled from on their wedding day and that it was the cause of his continued absence, even now.

Amazingly, Rachel heard it all without flinching. Nothing George said really shocked or surprised her; it was as if she already knew somehow. *So!* The lingering suspicions she had harbored about money were well founded after all, for all she had ignored them, and she had long ago recognized that Emory's objections to her were physical. In fact, she had seen to it that he remembered yet the poor, plain Rachel of old; what was it her father had called her that awful night . . . *pig-in-a-poke?* Still, the spoken truth did cause Rachel's anger to rise.

"So!" she said, her voice tinged with scorn. "Sight unseen, he determines I am unworthy to share his bed, so unredeeming in character or appearance that he chooses to neglect his father and absent himself from his home rather than face me!"

She sprang to her feet in a quick movement, pacing the floor, back and forth, back and forth. "And what of Edward?" she asked, halting before the open window. "Is my presence here so offensive that he, too, avoids home and family?"

"No, no," George hastened to assure her. "Edward's absence has nothing to do with you. He is in love with Rebecca, you know that already, and when he learned that Emory was to be wed to you, Edward simply recognized that your father would never consent to their marriage, especially not without some source of income more than his allowance alone."

Long speeches pronounced the old man's slur, and he paused to catch his breath before continuing. "Edward thinks me a fool, but I am aware of the valuable coronet he took with him when he left for London . . . one of his mother's pieces . . . yours, as it turned out. No doubt he's gambled it away by now in a vain attempt to win enough to come back and claim Rebecca."

Rachel returned to her seat, feeling more sadness at Rebecca's predicament than her own. The delicate clock on the mantel ticked ever so loudly, filling the room with its sound. She looked across the room at George's sad face.

"What are we to do now?" she wondered aloud.

"I leave that up to you, Rachel. Tisbury has been instructed to do your bidding in this matter. 'Twas why he came. That part of your dowry which I earmarked for Ermaline's betrothal is still intact, but the rest has been spent to meet my son's debts and the cost of operating the estate. You may seek release from this farcical marriage anytime you choose, and I will make any settlement you care to name, short of the Hall itself. By right, that must go to Emory, even though in truth you deserve it more, but you may strip it, Rachel . . . Take whatever you please, jewelry, artwork, anything. It will be small compensation for the humiliation you have suffered at the hands of my son . . . and me," he added in a voice she strained to hear.

Rachel was confused. "Do I understand correctly? You advocate annulment?"

George nodded. "It should be a simple matter. You certainly have enough grounds, from what Tisbury tells me . . . an unconsummated marriage, a drunken husband, fraud, and he assures me it can be done quietly, without scandal."

"Assuming I were to do that," Rachel said, turning to face her father-in-law directly, "just where would that leave Ermaline?"

The old man shook his head dejectedly. That was the most painful part of all. There might be some slim chance that Henry Rowland loved Ermaline enough to accept her without a dowry, but more than likely, his family would exert pressure upon the young man to disavow the engagement and seek another bride, especially if there were *any* scandal concerning an annulment. That being the case, Ermaline would have no choice but to remain at Guersten Hall with her brothers. In recent months, she had blossomed, partly because of her coming marriage, but also because of Rachel's presence at the Hall. George feared the loss of both would turn the girl into a bitter spinster.

"But that will be my cross to bear," he said brokenly, "for I engineered this disastrous situation. I should have released you the moment it became apparent Emory's objections were so deeply rooted, but after the wedding I was certain that everything would work out once he saw you, and who knows, perhaps it would have. Only a man of stone could not love you, my dear."

The old man's torment was too painful to watch, and Rachel turned away, stepping out onto the balcony, where she paced back and forth within its narrow confines. George's statement was true enough; her marriage to Emory was a farce. She had been his wedded wife for more than three months now, but she had yet to lay eyes upon her bridegroom. Clearly, this situation could not continue much longer, nor did Rachel wish it to. In the space of time since George became ill, she had found herself drawn to Duncan Ferguson and suspected the quiet doctor needed only some small sign from her before he declared his love. Duncan would never be wealthy, but he was a fine man, and someday he would head a great hospital. While it was true he stirred no passion in Rachel's heart, still, many marriages survived with much less amicable relationships. *And who knows,* she opined, *in time I might come to love him dearly.*

Yet, on the balcony, watching the horses frolicking in the paddock, Rachel knew full well that she was hopelessly fooling herself. There were others to be considered now, and they could not be discounted. There was Ermaline, for one, and now there was Rebecca. Rachel concurred fully with George's assessment of Ermaline's predicament. If her future plans were to crumble now, so close to fruition, Ermaline would indeed be bitter and no doubt sink into a melancholia from which she would never be roused. But Rebecca's circumstances went beyond a broken heart, and it seemed to Rachel there were some fundamental rights involved as well, for the child Rebecca carried was a Guersten. Surely, when Edward returned, he would marry her at once, and unless Rachel's own marriage bore fruit, high unlikely given the present circumstances, Rebecca's child would be rightful heir to Guersten Hall, if only through succession.

As far as Rebecca was concerned, there was still another angle to be considered, too, for who knew what turn Benjamin's wrath would take when he learned of her condition. If he should turn his back on Rebecca, then she would need a safe haven for her lying-in; as long as Rachel was mistress at the Hall, that haven was assured.

And so, Rachel determined she was yet again the victim of circumstances. Admittedly, she knew that George would never turn Rebecca out. Still, for now, Rachel decided, it was best that she retain her position as Emory's wife, and with a sigh, she turned and went inside. There, she pulled her chair close to where George sat, unmoving and gloomy in his wheelchair.

"Lift your spirits, dear George, before you become ill. I have decided that, for now at least, there will be no annulment. I cannot be a party to Ermaline's grief, and there is another reason, equally important, perhaps more so. It concerns Edward and Rebecca."

The old man's head shot up. He looked at Rachel quizzically.

"Oh, Lord!" he said hoarsely. "I can almost guess."

Despite the seriousness of the matter, Rachel grinned.

"That's more than I did. I had to be told."

"It was bound to happen," he said, running his good hand across the top of his forehead. "Love like that always bears fruit."

Briefly, Rachel imparted to him the information Duncan had given her, stressing Rebecca's poor health.

"So you see," she said softly, "I must stay. Rebecca may have need of a place to go, for Father has not yet been told. Besides, the child is a Guersten; it is fitting it is born here at the Hall."

"As all Geurstens have, Rachel, in the very bed you now occupy. You are right . . . Rebecca should come here. Still, are you positive that you wish remain?"

"As of this moment, I see no other alternative. Mind you, I am not a martyr. The arrangement you struck with my father was abominable, for it touched the lives of far too many people . . . myself, Emory, Edward, Rebecca. It has wrought discord between my parents, where none existed before, and it has created a canyon between my father and me that may never be breeched. Consider Ermaline, too! She would be miserable if she but suspected that her happiness came at the expense of all these others. Nay, George, your plan was disastrous, but it is done, and cannot be undone. We can only go on and try to make the best of it. To my thinking, that necessitates my remaining just now."

The old man placed his good hand over his eyes and hung his head as Rachel rose to leave the room. When she reached the door, he called her back.

"Rachel!" he cried in a croaking voice.

Turning, Rachel saw the tears and the despair in his eyes and hurried back to his side, falling on one knee before him.

"It's not a sacrifice, George, believe me! I did not mean to imply that it was. I have been happy here, under the circumstances, truly. For now, let us see the child born and Ermaline safely wed, and then, when Emory returns, we two alone will decide what course our marriage is to take."

"And what of your dowry money?"

"Use it as planned. We'll square accounts later, you and I, after your son returns."

"That may be sooner than you think, Rachel. I expect that both he and Edward will be returning to Guersten Hall any time now."

"How can you be sure?" she asked.

"When Tisbury was here, I instructed him to cut off both their allowances. I should have done it before, but as of the first of the month, they'll both be penniless unless Dame Fortune smiles on them at the gaming tables. They'll not even be able to afford decent lodgings!"

"Now, George," Rachel said, teasing in an attempt to lift him from his doldrums, "you know perfectly well that Emory will always find a bed for himself . . . somewhere!"

"True enough, but when he cannot afford proper stabling for that stallion of his, he'll bring the beast back to the Hall. Nothing but the best for him! I've never known a man to care for an animal as much as Emory cares for that black!"

"Well, then," said Rachel, rising. "There's nothing further to discuss. Everyone will soon be here at the Hall, perhaps even Rebecca. And isn't Edward in for a shock when he arrives? Perhaps I can give Emory a jolt as well . . . I'd say he's got it coming, wouldn't you?"

George's round face split into a grin. "Aye! Aye! That he does!" he said. "And if I'm allowed to take sides, I'll stake my money on you, Rachel. Go to it! Rattle 'im around a bit!"

Rachel winked at her father-in-law as she left the room, rewarded with another smile.

"Emory, m'boy," George murmured as the door closed behind her. "You've met your match! *Damned if you haven't.*"

CHAPTER ELEVEN

Leaving her canopied bed early the next morning, Rachel crept to the windows, throwing open the heavy drapes and securing them with their braided and tasseled cords. Outside the sun was shining brightly, glinting starkly on the few patches of melting snow that remained in the yard below. The sun's bright rays never reached her bedroom, however, and even now, with the draperies spread wide, the massive room was still dark and shadowy. How she disliked it! Even during the daytime a lamp was needed to read or write.

She was out of sorts this morning, having slept poorly, tossing and turning fitfully until the bed linens were twisted and wrinkled. She had wasted little time ruminating about her decision to remain at Guersten Hall; it was the right one, she knew. Simply put, Rachel's presence at the Hall guaranteed the birthright of her sister's unborn child. But Emory was another matter! It was when Rachel dwelt upon his imminent return that the inner turmoil began. He was being forced to return, and more than likely, he would arrive annoyed and resentful, and probably half tipsy as well. Undoubtedly, he would immediately set about remounting his old campaign to intimidate and humiliate her. The mousy girl of Emory's childhood had always disintegrated under his barbed taunts and threatening stances, but now Rachel felt ready for him. Poised, collected, she was certain she could remain unruffled by his derisive actions, might even counter them somehow. Once, Rachel had been willing to take her place beside him, bear his name, his advances, his children. Now, she felt freed from that commitment, but still, she knew well that theirs would be a stormy relationship.

While Rachel finished dressing, Hunter was saddled and brought around to the portico. She had chosen a full skirted riding dress of ruby velveteen, then, at the last minute, changed her mind, stripping off the heavy costume, slipping instead into her comfortable leather breeches and shiny topped boots. Today she was in no mood for a quiet canter, one leg slung over a lady's saddle; she wanted to race with the wind on Hunter's strong back, catch the morning breeze on her face, and fill her lungs with the clean, cold air. Clutching gloves and saucer-brimmed hat in one hand, she clattered down the stairs and went outside. There, by the mounting block, waited Hunter, who now required resaddling, for the stable master had assumed Rachel would ride sidesaddle. She followed the groom to the barn, where the swap was accomplished good-naturedly.

Rachel discovered that it was indeed a glorious day, unusually warm and glittering with newness under a cloudless sapphire sky, one of those rare days that slip unannounced between the passing of winter and the real coming of spring. There was a good deal of activity around the stables this morning, and she watched as half dozen grooms led an assortment of saddled horses from the barn. Once mounted, the group thundered off down a well-rutted road that led to the back of the estate.

Seconds later, squinting in the dazzling sunshine, Peter himself emerged from the barn, leading two horses, one a sluggish bay mare, and the other Hunter, who nudged Rachel's shoulder affectionately.

"Where are they off to so early?" she inquired of him as he handed her up to the saddle.

"We're just running them, trying to work off some of the winter fat. Take a look at Makira here!" he chuckled, slapping the mare's rump.

"I've a mind to run myself this morning. Would you mind some company? Perhaps you could show me the working side of the estate at the same time."

"My pleasure," Peter said amicably, "but you won't find much working, I'm afraid."

They moved off down the road at a hard gallop, exhilarating in the ride. Hunter reveled in the exercise, stretching his long legs until he had pulled away some lengths ahead of his stable mate. At the next turn in the road, Rachel halted, waiting by a tall spruce until Peter caught up to her. The overweight Makira was breathing heavily but seemed to be enjoying the outing regardless, and Hunter settled down to an easy lope that kept him and Makira shoulder to shoulder as Peter pointed out the landscape to Rachel.

The rutted road meandered for miles along the outer acres of Guersten Hall, and topping a low rise, Rachel saw before them great expanses of gently rolling hills, open fields of rich farmland and soon to be green meadows, all neatly squared and bordered by overgrown hedges of hawthorn, forsythia, and barberry. Tumps of last year's yellowed grasses stood like sentinels within the squares, guarding the empty fields. All along the way broken stiles and missing gateposts were plentiful, Rachel noted, their state of disrepair standing in mute testimony that the fields had lain fallow for many years.

Even so, the beauty of the estate was still breathtaking, and Peter, it turned out, was familiar with every inch of it. There were trees and shrubs of every kind and description, and he named them all, directing her attention to the very first of the spring flowers, bright purple crocuses, peeping their saucy heads through the blanket of snow. Nearby, golden carpets of lemony winter aconites had popped up as if my magic; beside them, blue scilla and fat clumps of violets were already well leafed and budded. Peter veered off the road, leading Rachel to a long row of pyramidal spruce trees, planted many years before as a windbreak. There, under their crowded branches bloomed waxy snowdrops and more winter aconites.

"Are you superstitious?" he asked her, pointing to a giant fir standing alone in a little dell, its sweeping lower boughs dipping nearly to the ground. Although the tree itself seemed healthy, a few of the boughs were gnarled, with grotesquely misshapen cones and ragged branches.

"Some call it witches broom," Peter explained, "and most folk hereabouts make a point of avoiding it. In the old days it would have been pruned away long before it became this unsightly."

"What causes the malformation?" Rachel asked, curious. She didn't believe in witches and, except for the mystery surrounding fallen branches, didn't think of herself as superstitious.

"Who knows? Insects perhaps, or some sort of infection. It's not common, but it appears now and again . . . just enough to keep the superstition alive anyway."

Turning their horses from the edge of the dell, a large flock of caterwauling sparrows swooped down from above and disappeared before them into a magnificent hemlock. The birds settled for only a scant moment, chirping harshly, and then they flittered right out again to continue their quest for the last of the winter berries. The fields abounded with birds during summer, Peter told Rachel: finches, thrushes, starlings, and small meadow pipits, as well as crows and rooks. There were goshawks, and even a falcon or two swept down from the forest above them, he added.

The lands of Guersten Hall were expansive, but even while enjoying the ride, Rachel became disturbed as they proceeded further along the winding road, chagrined at the needless neglect that was evident about the place. Many of the barren fields were choked with clumps of gorse, and everywhere unsheared hedgerows had grown into massive hillocks of tangled twigs and scraggly branches.

The road wound past the untended orchards, situated on a cool north slope where the trees would not be tempted to burst forth their blossoms too early on days such as this. Row upon row of apple, pear, plum, and cherry trees stretched endlessly, standing in soldierly alignment, their branches broken and twisted by years of lashing winter winds. Without pruning, many of the limbs had become crossed and stunted, while underneath runty offshoots struggled to grow. In another section of the orchard, black walnut and hazelnut trees had fared little better.

"Do they bear any fruit?" asked Rachel from her perch in the saddle.

"That they do, Miss Rachel, surprisingly good yield considering, but much of it just drops to the ground, and since it is not thinned much of the fruit is small, and some of it wormy as well." He laughed. "And the birds manage to get most of the cherries as soon as they begin to pink."

Dismayed at the unproductivity of the land, Rachel shook her head forlornly. Her appallment at the sight of the orchards turned to open indignation when she spied the dairy farm, though. A barn and low-stone farmhouse, both solidly built years before, still stood straight and sound, but both were now in urgent need of paint and repair. Neither had been whitewashed in a long time; both were gray and grimy, and the roof of the farmhouse sorely needed new thatching.

The barn doors hung wide, and Rachel dismounted and went inside, only to be disgusted at what she found: piles of foul-smelling manure, dirty straw in the stalls, and water troughs that were splintered and nearly empty. The condition of the milking room was equally disgraceful, littered with debris and scattered with a number of buckets reeking sour milk. Glad that she had not eaten anything that morning, Rachel held a lacy handkerchief to her nose and hurried out into the fresh air, an angry look marking her lovely countenance.

The ultimate responsibility for these intolerable conditions lay with the dairyman, Stevens himself, no doubt about that, fumed Rachel, but how and why had they gone unnoticed for so long?

The master was very old, reminded Peter, and seldom made rounds of the estate as he had in the old days, and Emory, who long ago should have assumed responsibility for the estate's operation, simply took no interest. Wisely, Peter said no more, already uncomfortable for having said as much as he had. It was certainly not his place to criticize.

At the farmhouse, the dairyman's two sons, both in their early teen years, sat at a scarred wooden table, eating cold gruel. Rachel didn't need to be reminded that no woman attended these premises, and observing the dirty kitchen, she was thankful now that Becky and Annie had remained at the mansion. But she was further distressed to note that one of the lads bore the marks of what appeared to be a recent beating.

Their father had taken the cows to the low pasture, they told Peter courteously, in answer to his question, all the while gawking guardedly at Rachel's boyish breeches.

The dairyman's wife was dead six years, Peter explained when they went outside again. Until she died, Stevens had been a good dairyman, and even now, when he was sober, he worked hard and was kindly, but apparently the woman, patently overbearing, was the driving force behind her husband. Now, without her nagging influence, Stevens seemed incapable of functioning as he had before. When he was drinking, frequently it seemed of late, he became belligerent and abused his children.

Remounted, Rachel and Peter turned their horses toward the low pasture, for Rachel was determined to seek out the dairyman and chastise him. They came upon him wending his way back to the farmhouse on foot, stopping often to pull at a flask he carried in the pocket of his kersey coat. When he spotted the two riders, he stepped off the path respectfully and tugged at his cap.

Stevens had never before laid eyes on Rachel, but he recognized her at once, for both Annie and Becky had given their father a glowing description of the new lady of the manor, singing praises to her kindness, and Stevens himself had fingered the stuff of the little gray cloaks his daughters now wore and saw their once cold feet warmed by stockings and sturdy shoes.

The dairyman was a broad-shouldered man, stocky and florid faced. Now, having spent the night in his clothes, as usual, he stood before them unshaven and disheveled, fixing Rachel with a placatory smile. Mistakenly, he assumed her kindness and generosity to be feminine softness and, thus, was totally unprepared for the rebuke she administered.

"Stevens, you have two weeks to remedy the slovenly condition of Home Farm," Rachel said sternly. "If, at the end of that time, I am not satisfied, you will be dismissed summarily, and without references."

The tone of Rachel's voice and the severity of her words sobered the man, almost at once. "But, ma'am," he whined, twisting his cap between his hands, "tha's a gran' task ye've set me to. I'll need help."

"You've got more than enough help for the size of the herd, Stevens; you'll get no more!" Her reply was flung scornfully. "Use your boys! They are young and healthy. Perhaps if you fed them better and ceased your abuse, you would find them more cooperative."

Stevens grasped the reality of the situation then. It dawned on him that the mistress meant what she said. His job was on the line.

"Aye, ma'am, aye. I'll do that, ma'am. I don' want to lose my place here. I'll work hard, ma'am, b'lieve me, I will."

"See that you do, you won't get another warning. Now empty that flask," Rachel said crossly, pointing with her stick, "and get started." She glared down at the hapless dairyman from her seat in the saddle. "Remember, you have two weeks. For your own sake, make sure that I hear nothing of drunkenness or child beating in the interim."

Yanking firmly on Hunter's rein, Rachel turned and started for the high road. As Peter moved to follow, Stevens clutched at Makira's halter with an outstretched hand.

"Put in a word for me, will ye, 'Ubbardston? Tell the lady how 'tis been since m'wife died," he pleaded.

Peter spun Makira in a tight half circle, nearly knocking the man down. "Stop your whining, you sot! How many times did I warn you that this moment could come? If you need a woman's knee in your back before you can be a man, then go get another! Times are hard; the shire is bursting with sturdy wenches only too glad to wed a widower with steady work. Just see you don't lose that work, man, you are on very shaky ground. Hear me, your mistress only looks delicate; she exacts full measure! Remember it!"

The dairyman, worried and crestfallen, jammed his cap onto his tousled head, muttering a muffled curse. Basically he was a good man, and though his sniveling was annoying, Peter felt some compassion for him.

"She'll check on you well before the two weeks are up, count on it," he told Stevens, motioning toward Rachel's retreating back. "She saw the inside of that barn, knows the herd must be filthy. Run the cows through the stream while the sun is still high. I won't let on that it wasn't your idea."

Peter found Rachel resting on a fallen log, her face flushed to a rosy pink. As she removed her hat, the rounded chignon coiled at the nape of her neck came loose, and long glossy tendrils of auburn silk trailed lazily across her shoulders. The young man was frankly amazed at her natural beauty, evident even in the ridiculous outfit she wore.

She flashed him a bright smile.

"The sun is warmer now, or could it be my anger overheats me?"

"Now that you have spoken to him, I think you may be surprised by Steven's efficiency," Peter said. "It's just too bad the rest of this neglect cannot be as easily corrected." His gaze wandered across the open fields and down into a valley that spread before them. At the foot of the hill lay a tiny hamlet, the gray stone cottages nestled together in a half circle. It was a rustic scene, and the little hamlet, surrounded on three sides by sloping hills, seemed cut off from the rest of the world.

"I've never come this far before. Is that still Guersten land?"

"Aye, it's Guersten land all right. Those hills mark the boundary on this side of the estate. Everything on the far side of them belongs to Squire Paxton."

Peter pointed to the little hamlet. "Years ago that village was home for the estate's workers, but most of the cottages are empty now. Beyond that vill, there's a stream and an old stone bridge, and then a duck pond and some sheep pens. It's very scenic."

"It sounds idyllic! Can we return to the house that way?"

"The road winds through the park, practically to the front door."

"Then let's go that way, unless I am keeping you from your duties."

Removing a heavy timepiece from an inner pocket, Peter glanced at its worn face. "We've time," he said, "if we do not tarry. The master expects me at half after eight to be shaved, and I'd not like to keep him waiting."

"How is it that you know so much about Guersten Hall, Peter?" asked Rachel as they trotted down the lane toward the cottage.

"Why, I was born here," he answered. "Right down there in one of those cottages. My grandfather was garden superintendent here at the Hall until he became too old to work. I grew up at his side."

"Did your parents work on the estate, too?"

"No, I'm an orphan. My grandparents raised me. My father was a mate in the King's navy. He died at sea, and my mother died of consumption not long after I was born."

"Oh," said Rachel somberly. "I'm sorry to hear that."

"Don't be," he said, putting her at ease with a smile. "I never knew either of them. Gaffy and Granmam were all the family I ever needed."

Time was forgotten as the sole remaining inhabitants of the tiny hamlet came out to meet the new mistress of the estate. All were quickly captivated by Rachel's charm, just as the house staff had been, and if the ladies were at all shocked by her attire, Rachel never knew it. After all, as the old gamekeeper's horsey wife pointed out later, the rich can afford to be peculiar. A pleasant lot, most of the cottagers were middle-aged or better; when the economy of the estate faltered, they had opted to remain at Guersten Hall on half wages rather than chance the fates in Manchester.

It went without saying though that Rachel's favorite would at once be Peter's grandfather. He was a scrawny little man, slightly built, with a wizened old face, leathery and suntanned from his years outdoors. As a toddler, Peter's fractured English had contorted the word *grandfather* into Gaffy, and the name had stuck. Gaffy he was to everyone, including his wife. In fact, no one had called him Martin in years.

Now in their eighties, Gaffy and Granmam shared a tiny three-room cottage on the very end of the row, nearest the edge of the sandy stream. There, Gaffy sat whittling in the sun, his back pressed against the cottage wall. His old face beamed with pleasure when he spied his only grandchild.

"Petey, m'lad," he chortled merrily, hopping to his feet. "It does me tired eyes good to see ye this bright morn. Granmam," he cried, "come see what the wind blowed down from the big house!"

Granmam appeared in the doorway of the cottage. She too was tiny, pink, and plump, with bunned white hair. Surprisingly agile for their years, neither she nor Gaffy made any attempt to hide the fact that they doted on Peter.

"I say!" said Gaffy, winking at Rachel as the young man embraced his grandmother. "Who's this bit o' fluff ye brought with ye? She be the comeliest groom I ever saw!"

Rachel giggled as Gaffy slapped his knee roundly, but Peter was embarrassed.

"Gaffy!" he said in a dignified tone. "This is the new mistress of Guersten Hall. She is Master Emory's new wife."

Gaffy squinted hard at Rachel for a moment and then chuckled. "Well, my lady, the damage already be done. No offense meant, ye understand?" And he winked again. "Master Emory's wife, ye say? So the lad do have some smarts, after all!"

"Gaffy!" Peter spluttered, but Granmam wisely stepped forward before the outspoken old gent could make matters any worse.

"Mistress, would you care for a cuppa tea and some hot scones? 'Twould certainly be my pleasure, despite what this old fool may be saying next," she said with a grin, giving her husband an elbow.

What a happy household, thought Rachel. No wonder Peter was so easy to get along with. Not a soul on the estate seemed to dislike him.

"I would love to join you, but I must return to the manor now," said Rachel, laughing as Gaffy feinted a poke at Granmam's ribs in return. "Perhaps I might come another time."

"My word! Do stop in anytime you are out riding. Tomorrow, perhaps?" asked Granmam, her voice betraying her eagerness to have Rachel at her table.

"Agreed!" said Rachel quickly, just as eager to spend some time with the rare couple.

As Peter unhitched Hunter and Makira from a nearby fence, Gaffy thumped his grandson roundly on the back.

"Now, Petey," he mumbled under his breath, "when're ye goin' to find y'self one fetchin' like that? Me and Granmam want to see some wee ones before we go to that garden up there." And he jerked his thumb skyward.

"Awww, Gaffy, give over. Relax, you'll get your wee ones just as soon as I find me a girl who prefers the smell of the good earth to perfume and toilet water. Then you watch me strut my stuff!" he added with a grin, jostling his grandfather.

"Well, Granmam! That's some gel now, ain't it?" Gaffy waved gaily as Rachel and Peter rode off across the stone bridge.

"Aye," said his wife, turning to go back into the cottage. "Too bad she don't wear a skirt though. Them breeches don't do her justice."

Gaffy settled onto his stool again, resuming his whittling. "Thet be your opinion," he said to himself. "I thought 'twas t' other way round. She the one done the breeches justice!"

Rachel turned and waved one last time, hearing the sound of his cackling as it carried across the stream.

"Is he always that chipper, Peter?"

"Lord, yes . . . and it's getting worse! He thinks that because of his age he can get away with saying whatever he chooses!"

Increasing their pace, the two riders headed back to the manor, but Rachel still had time to view the duck pond and the sheep byres, noting that there were few ducks and fewer sheep. The land that lay before them was flattened, all of it bordered by woods. Centered amid vast squares of empty fields were ten huge copper beeches, all growing in a near perfect circle. In summer their intertwined branches and foliage formed a cool and leafy glen, informed Peter, adding that those fields were the most fertile in all the valley. Like all the others, these, too, lay fallow.

Inside the boundaries of the manor's park, with its ornate plantings and winding paths, they put their horses once more to a hard gallop, racing along a pathway that ran adjacent to a shallow stream, bordered to its very edges with graceful weeping willows that swept the ground. Once again, Hunter easily outdistanced the tired Makira, and Rachel pounded over a little bridge and on up to the house, waving to Peter as she went.

Rounding the corner of the mansion, Rachel found a strange coach parked under the porte cochere. Rich and expensively upholstered, two liveried footmen were just removing a number of trunks from the boot, while the coachman steadied four black horses. Noting the large and gilded *R* emblazoned on the door in fancy script, Rachel rode past the startled footmen, hardly prepared to greet guests in her breeches. She entered the house through Stoddard's kitchen, a beehive of hectic activity.

"Thank heavens yer back," she said breathlessly to Rachel. "Ermaline returned from London just now . . . with the Rowlands in tow."

Rachel dashed away to the second floor by the back stairs, nearly colliding with Ermaline, in a cloud of moss-green silk, just emerging from her father's bedroom. The two women embraced fondly.

"My word, Ermaline!" cried Rachel excitedly. "You look stunning!"

She did, too, in a dress with a nipped-in waist and a pleated bodice that flattered and slimmed her. Her hair was piled atop her head in a style that added stature and lengthened her neck. Her smile attesting to her happiness, Ermaline beamed radiantly.

"Well? Tell me for heaven's sake! What did Henry think?"

"Just as you said," replied the happy girl, linking arms with Rachel as they went down the corridor. "His eyes popped! From the moment I arrived at the ball, he hardly left my side, and he insisted on personally escorting me back to Guersten Hall. His father came to finalize the betrothal documents and to visit with Father . . . or so he claims, but I really suspect he thinks that suddenly we two need a chaperone!"

Sitting on the bench at the foot of her bed, Rachel removed her riding boots. Oh my, she thought to herself, ever so grateful that she had decided against George's offer to leave the Hall. Ermaline would surely have cracked like a bone china cup if the betrothal had fallen through under these circumstances, what with Henry and his father present downstairs.

"And your father? What did he say when he saw you?"

"Very little," said Ermaline in a soft voice, "but he hugged me tighter than I can ever remember in my whole life, and with only one arm, too. It must be my new clothes!"

"Hogwash, you ninny! It's you! It is the change in you that pleases your father so, not your clothes."

Ermaline was suddenly embarrassed by Rachel's attentions and turned toward the door. "I must get downstairs," she said. "Stoddard is laying breakfast for our guests, and Father is waiting to be shaved. Such confusion!"

"I know! I certainly picked the right morning to detain Peter, didn't I? But . . . how on earth did you get here so early? And where are Adele . . . and the cousins?"

"Aunt Adele has long thought she should start looking for husbands for those two, and duly impressed by my miraculous transformation at Scofield's, she has decided the time is now! Both Charlotte and Olivia have fittings with Eleanora this week. As for your other question," she said mischievously, peeping around the door, "we stopped the night at Aylesbury Inn, for Henry insisted I was far too fragile to travel the rest of the way without resting. Can you imagine! Me . . . fragile?"

Rachel laughed, pleased at her sister-in-law's happiness. "Oh, be off! I'll join you in the dining room when I'm presentable."

After a quick bath, Rachel went downstairs again, breathtaking in a full-skirted morning dress of the softest yellow. The pale color creamed her flawless skin, enhancing her dark eyes magically. Hearing voices in the drawing room, she crossed to the door, fully expecting to find Ermaline and the Rowlands.

Instead, it was Peter, and with him was George, now freshly shaved, ensconced in his wheelchair. He was dressed in a crisp morning coat and even held his gold-topped walking stick. Caught off guard, Rachel was speechless.

"The others are in the dining room," said Peter. "The master insisted on coming down."

"High time I did, too!" said George firmly, grinning at Rachel. "Come, come, Rachel!" he said, gesturing wildly with the walking stick. "Push me into the dining room. We've kept our guests waiting long enough."

Choking back tears of happiness just to see his presence on the ground floor once more and in the dining room, when she saw him, it was Ermaline's turn to become choked. The moment needed no words; George patted his daughter's cheek lovingly, and then he took his place at the head of the table. At the sideboard, loaded with an assortment of food and sweet rolls, everyone filled their own plates and gathered informally around the table. Ermaline catered dotingly to her father, while Henry watched her every move, as if he couldn't quite believe his own good fortune.

The Rowlands were two peas in a pod, it seemed, only their years belying the fact that they were father and son and not brothers. Both were thin and dark complexioned for Englishmen, with jet-black hair and matching face whiskers adorning their aquiline features. Both were soft-spoken and obviously turned out by the same tailor in impeccably cut frock coats.

"I'm sorry to have kept you waiting," said Rachel politely to the elder Rowland, making apologies for not being present to greet them. "I went for an early morning ride, and I fear I resembled one of the stable hands by the time I returned."

"Not quite, my dear . . . not quite," said Henry's father. "We saw you as you rode by the window of the drawing room."

Rachel blushed prettily. "Ah! My secret is out."

Noticing her blush, Rowland tactfully changed the subject and turned to George. "Congratulations are in order, Guersten. Henry has received appointment to the Queen's Counsel. It bodes well for his future as a barrister."

The younger Henry accepted their congratulations graciously, if uncomfortably, for he was rather a bashful young man, and this time it was Rachel who changed the subject, putting the red-faced fellow at ease.

After breakfast was done, Ermaline and Henry, anxious to be alone for a while, wandered into the music room. Henry blushed again, hotly, as Ermaline herself, grinning almost lecherously at Rachel, closed the door behind them. Clearing a spot on the end of the dining room table, George and the elder Rowland remained there to finish their business, choosing not to bother with shifting the wicker wheelchair to another room.

Rachel, left to her own devices momentarily, went into the library. At her little gateleg desk, she planned the next day's meals and rechecked her household accounts. Sometime later, after the Rowlands had departed, she spied a horse-drawn wagon hauling up the service drive with a load of vegetables. She sent for Stoddard.

"Was that the greengrocer I saw a few minutes ago?" she asked when the cook entered the library.

"Aye, ma'am. He's on his way to Lady Paxton's, and he stopped by out o' politeness, we bein' old friends an' all. He's having a cuppa tea in the kitchen. Is something amiss?"

"No, no, Stoddard. I merely wondered why he stopped. Did you purchase anything?"

"Just a few carrots for my stew tomorrow. We've gone through the last of what was left in winter storage. You got something on your mind, ma'am?" asked the cook, cocking her head.

"I was simply curious," replied Rachel, stepping down from the turreted corner of the room. "You may go. Enjoy your tea with your . . . gentleman friend."

"Hmmph!" mumbled the cook as she headed back to her kitchen. "Gentleman friend, indeed! Just some bloke I've known for thirty years who likes my cookin' better 'n me!"

After the door had closed, Rachel dropped onto the long sofa, tucking one leg under her yellow skirt. "My word!" she said to the picture above the mantel. "This place is madness! Here we are, sitting on the most fertile land in the valley, yet we buy carrots from a traveling greengrocer! And Cook pours tea for him, to boot!"

The ridiculousness of the situation made Rachel laugh aloud. She was the daughter of a businessman; whatever would Benjamin think if he knew—him who could rub two coins together and come up with a third! As she laughed again, she shook her head, her eyes falling upon the old Hall journals, long since moved to a place of prominence in a glass-fronted bookcase near the fireplace. Withdrawing two of them, Rachel carried them to the window seat in the turret. There she made some remarkable discoveries.

Guersten Hall had been highly productive in years past, totally self-sufficient, even marketing some crops for cash. Rachel studied the entries closely. Four hundred tuns of cider one year, three hundred another. Hops sold to a London brewer; lambs, geese, and ducks sold at Covent Garden; and on one page, an entry listing a number of surpluses distributed to the poor that particular year. *Surpluses,* thought Rachel, *and here we are purchasing carrots for a pot of stew!*

After lunch, George retired to his bedroom for his customary nap, but not before he informed Rachel that he would be down again for dinner. From this very day, he said, he would take his evening meal in the dining room again, with whatever members of the family were present. The announcement buoyed both Rachel and Ermaline, but she was little company for the rest of the day, mooning over Henry and her approaching engagement party, and so, alone again, Rachel returned to the library. This time she carried the stack of journals to George's immense desk and, clearing a work area there, set about perusing the ledgers carefully, item by item, making copious notes in a journal of her own.

"Do you have a kitchen garden, Stoddard?" inquired Rachel of the cook when she came into the room with tea and a light snack some hours later.

"Aye," said the surprised older woman, lighting the desk lamps, for Rachel had been too absorbed to notice the fading light. "But there's naught in it but herbs and such. I never had time nor knack for anything more. Remember, 'twasn't always like this," she added, indicating the now spotless library with its polished furniture and gleaming glass fronts. "Till you came, I spent most of my day on the stairs, I swear, trying to get them layabouts to finish their work." The cook was stern, seemingly unmindful that the corps of maids she referred to was anything but layabouts these days.

But Rachel was only half listening. "Ummm," she said, continuing with her writing.

"Have you got something in mind, ma'am?"

"It's only an idea. Now leave me . . . Let me get back to work."

The very next morning, Rachel rose early and galloped through the park, straight to Gaffy's little cottage. There, bursting with pride that Rachel had sought them out, Granmam spread a crisp cloth and a tasty breakfast before her mistress. From the back of the hearth, she pulled a small crock of beans, baked with crumpled bacon on top, and there were eggs and hot scones heaped high with sweet jams and thick buttery cream. While Rachel enjoyed every morsel with gusto, she enjoyed the company of Granmam and the sharp old gentleman with the weather-beaten face even more.

Returning to the manor, Rachel went again to the library and closed the door, and once again the next morning, she rode out to the cottage by the stream. This time, seated around the tiny table with Gaffy and Granmam, Rachel learned even more about Guersten Hall's productive past. Deciding to reveal to Gaffy the plan that had been buffeting about in her head these past days, Rachel explained in detail just what she had in mind. To her great surprise, and greater pleasure, Gaffy thought it a good one.

"Aye!" he said, slapping his palm on the tabletop. "'Tis a sound plan, my lady, and Petey's your man, yer right about that. An' ye can count on me t' help, too. Though me back's no good, me brains are still good for pickin'."

And so, Rachel presented her plan to George that same day. Seeking his opinion, she spread her journals across his desk and shared her notes with him. The old man kept shaking his head, looking first at Rachel and then back to the extensive jottings she had made.

"But, Rachel," he said at last, more than a little flabbergasted at the extent of her research. "Farming? For profit? It's never been done before at Guersten Hall."

"I see," said Rachel, somewhat amused by his surprise. "But, does that mean we shouldn't try even?"

"It's not that, I don't doubt your wisdom, my dear. You've got a good head on your shoulders. It's just that the Guerstens were always . . . well, gentlemen, not farmers!"

"Yes, and you'll still be gentlemen when you are forced to sell off valuable land to maintain your lifestyle. Your estate will shrink, acre by acre, and what do you think the men who buy that land will do with those acres? Cut the timber and till the fields . . . for profit! We badly need income, George. Ermaline's wedding will deplete almost all of our ready cash, and although all our creditors have been paid, it won't be long before we are in debt again."

The room was silent. Slumping against the back of the wheelchair, George considered Rachel's words. She was right, of course.

"Still," he said slowly, "I don't know. Really, Rachel, I just don't know. Perhaps we ought to wait. Tisbury tells me he may have a buyer for the Lancashire estate. Those profits should carry us for a while."

"A buyer, eh? A gentleman, no doubt, seeking a country house where he can spend his weekends communing with nature," said Rachel in a voice just tinged with cynicism.

"No," remarked George. "As a matter of fact, he is a businessman, and I understand he has already bought up much of the surrounding countryside."

"And?" inquired Rachel expectantly.

"And he promptly put it to the saw and the plow," admitted George a little sheepishly, realizing he had proven her point.

"You see? Your way of life is fast going by the boards, George. In one or two short generations, no one will be able to afford these great estates. If we are to salvage any of this," she said, waving her hand about the room, "then we must make the most of our assets. Since our best asset is the land, we should work it."

"You've given considerable thought to this, haven't you?"

"I have. I feel certain it can work, and so does Gaffy. At least it's worth a try."

"But, Rachel, you will require cash to begin. You yourself just admitted there is precious little of that about."

"I have cash, George, money of my own, accessible only to me. I am willing to contribute what is needed to the plan, that much faith do I have in the land. As I told you once before, we'll settle accounts later, you and I."

"All right, put the cost aside for the moment. What about manpower? Farming is backbreaking work, and most of the able-bodied men in the shire have gone to work in the mills. Even our cottages have nary a man that's not past his prime."

"True, but they'll work for me, I'm sure of it. We can begin on a small scale, with just a few acres, and perhaps we can lure back some of the others with an offer of half rent."

"Why not?" she continued, noticing George's raised eyebrows. "The cottages stand empty anyway, and if we dispense with the rent, or half of it, in lieu of part of their wages, well . . . at least the vill will be productive, too."

"Furthermore," she said, still on the subject of manpower, "there are far too many grooms. Half of them at least are going to work in the fields, a fact they'll soon learn."

"That won't set well, Rachel, I can tell you that. Grooms are a special breed, not happy unless they are around horses. No, they won't like it at all!"

"But they will be around horses, my friend," said Rachel, chuckling. "Plow horses! The next cut in expenses will be made in the stables anyhow, so it's a draw. This way, they keep their jobs, and somehow, I think they'll prefer plow horses to the ironworks of Peterborough or the looms of Manchester."

The old man now laughed heartily. She had an answer for everything!

"Very well," he said, fingering Rachel's journal. "It appears you've thought it all out. Then go to it! Give it a try; you have my blessing."

"I hoped you would say that! I've invited Peter to take dinner with us this evening. We can iron out the rest of the details then."

"And then . . . when will you begin?"

"At once, I hope, but that depends on Peter, for he will be my right hand. What little he doesn't already know, Gaffy does. We will succeed, you'll see."

And so, over the dinner table that night, Rachel's plan, as it came to be known, was set into motion. Ermaline, bored by conversation concerning crops and equipment, left the table as soon as the meal was finished. Peter, neat and presentable in a well-cut frock coat, was in complete accord with the plan, and too, knowing the soil as he did, he was as confident as Rachel that it would succeed.

Only a few real decisions needed to be made that night, all of them accomplished without difficulty. Rachel would establish a line of credit in Aylesbury and another in Peterborough, providing funds which Peter could draw upon to purchase stock and replenish unusable equipment. Pug was chosen to move into Peter's position as stable master, one that Pug had long since earned through years of loyal service to George. At the same time, Peter agreed to remain in the carriage house to assist in George's care until either Emory or Edward returned.

"Give me a week, Miss Rachel," said Peter, preparing to take his leave. "I'll make an inventory of what we have and what we need, and I'll divide the men into crews. By this time next week, we should be able to get rolling. We still have time to set in some cool-weather crops like turnips and cabbages and such."

"I can hardly wait," said Rachel, openly excited about the challenge of the whole thing. "And please, Peter," she added, "after tonight, let's forego the formalities. Just plain Rachel suits me fine."

Just plain Rachel, my foot! thought George, toying with his walking stick. Peter, returning to the carriage house later, was thinking exactly the same thing. Plain indeed!

CHAPTER TWELVE

Not unexpectedly, the weather turned seasonably cool once more, raw and damp; it rained steadily. Out of sorts after her freedom out of doors, Rachel wandered aimlessly from room to room, finding little interest in anything. Then too, she had learned in a recent note from her mother that the overcast skies and swirling night mists had affected Rebecca's mood also.

"Your sister seems listless and depressed," wrote Louisa, "and has been fretting since we learned that your father will return on Thursday next. Do come cheer her when the weather lifts."

Poor Rebecca! Waiting nervously for the other shoe to drop. Perhaps Rachel herself ought to be more uneasy about Benjamin's imminent return, but she had resigned herself to the fact that he would have to be told about the child. Her only concern was to intercede on Rebecca's behalf, to break the news without making matters worse.

Disturbed by the note, Rachel prepared to go to Brenham Manor that day, inviting Ermaline to join her. That one, though, declined. Still daydreaming over the stolen kisses she had shared with Henry in the music room, she preferred to spend her time examining her wedding trousseau for the hundredth time. And so, bundled in the brown cloak that had seen her so serviceably through the blizzard months before,

Rachel climbed into an enclosed curricle and headed for her mother's house. Going much too fast, the carriage lurched from beneath the portico, rocketed down the drive, tossing Rachel about helplessly in the back.

"Slow down, lad!" she shouted to the driver, one of the youngest boys in the stables. "We'll overturn on the curve!"

But even at a slower pace, the young driver soon ran into a problem of another sort when one wheel of the carriage became lodged between two planks on the wooden bridge that spanned the brook. With a jolt, the curricle shuddered to a halt, as Rachel, shaken, climbed down to survey the situation.

"My God, lad," she said breathlessly, straightening her cloak. "Don't you know how to maneuver this thing?"

Apologizing in a contrite little voice, the lad admitted he had little experience.

"I'll attest to that! Why didn't you say so back in the barn, for heaven's sake! Pug could have chosen someone else for the job."

The young boy was openly distraught and hung his head. "You see," he mumbled, "old Pug, he ain't like Peter. He didn't give me a chance t' speak, and 'sides, I dassn't talk back. Pug frowns mightily on back talk."

"Back talk! We could have been killed!"

Thoroughly chastened, the lad clambered down from his seat, holding a light whip in his hand. Deftly, Rachel removed it from his grasp, tossing it away.

"That was your mistake! You don't need it! This old nag has been pulling this buggy far longer than she cares to remember. Just speak to her gently, and she will take you wherever you want to go without any problem."

Rachel then examined the front wheel, stuck fast between the planks. "I think you'll be able to back it out yourself," she said, patting the poor horse's flanks, "but I'm going the rest of the way on foot. Take her back to the stables and have Pug check her mouth."

"But you can't walk, ma'am!" blurted the anguished lad. "You'll be soaked!"

"I much prefer that to getting killed," said Rachel, drawing the hood of her cloak over her hair. "No one need know of this mishap, laddie," she added, suddenly feeling a little sorry for the wretched groom. "But next time, do speak up!"

The boy smiled weakly as Rachel started off, much relieved that he would not have to face Pug's wrath when he returned to the barn. Rachel too was thinking of Pug as she made her way along the muddied road. It was easy to understand that Pug would not have the same rapport with the younger grooms that Peter did. Peter, young, efficient, and likeable, would spot the best in each man and exploit it wisely, while the other, older and probably taken with his new authority, would see only the faults and weaknesses of those under him. Rachel hoped there would not be problems in the stables, especially now, in view of the soon-to-be shortened staff there. Perhaps Peter could put a buzz in Pug's ear, without letting on that anyone else had noticed the developing disharmony.

The rain was falling in earnest again; it was a cold rain, accompanied by strong gusts of wind that fluttered Rachel's cloak and tugged at her hood. Quickening her steps, she arrived at the front door of the pink brick mansion but not before she was thoroughly drenched. It was Rebecca herself who opened the door just as Rachel reached for the heavy knocker.

"I *knew* you'd come today!" she said with a smug grin. "Whenever the weather is at its worst, we can count on you to be out in it, and usually on foot at that!" she added, pointing to Rachel's sodden slippers.

Laughing, the sisters went inside, and after Rachel was warmed and dried, they shared a leisurely lunch with their mother. The rest of the day sped away quickly. Frankly, Rachel did not believe Rebecca to be all that listless and depressed. Although she tired easily, Rebecca admitted she felt well enough, but by now, however, her maternity was very obvious. Even the soft fluid gown she wore, cut in the new empire style, failed to hide the burgeoning roundness of her slender body. Benjamin Brenham was no fool! He would spot Rebecca's condition the moment he laid eyes upon her. It was knowledge that alarmed and unsettled Rachel.

When Rebecca had gone to rest, Rachel cautioned her mother not to mistake weariness for depression. As Duncan had explained, it must be expected that the child growing within would sap Rebecca's meager strength.

"Our more immediate concern is what Father is going to say . . . and do when he sees her," Rachel said.

Not known for his diplomacy, Benjamin's words could be sharp and cutting, as well Rachel knew. If he became angry and inconsiderate, Rebecca's delicate health might be affected. Rachel and her mother conspired over their teacups and, accordingly, decided that Rebecca should be kept out of their father's sight until Rachel had approached him first. As insurance, she would be spirited to Guersten Hall, to remain there until Benjamin's reactions had been tested.

"Let him vent his wrath on me," said Rachel. "At the very worst, I shall be reduced to tears."

As she spoke, she looked out the window, surprised to find that darkness was already falling. Although a thin mist still hovered close above the meadows and lawns, the rain had stopped, but ominous clouds scooted low before a rising moon. Setting her teacup on the low table, Rachel got to her feet.

"I must go," she said to her mother. "I've stayed much longer than I intended. Bring Rebecca to Guersten Hall on Sunday. Duncan is joining us for dinner then, and he can examine Rebecca once more. Perhaps it will put your mind at ease."

Choosing to forego another carriage ride, Pollux was saddled and brought around to the front door, while Rachel herself went to fetch her brown cloak, hung to dry by the side of the stove in the familiar kitchen. It was still too damp to put on.

"You shouldn't be riding alone at night, Rachel. It's much too dark," complained Agatha, wagging a plump finger in Rachel's direction.

"Nonsense," replied Rachel, unafraid. "I'll only be out a few minutes at best. Besides, no more buggies for me today, thank you. I've had enough jolting!"

Grumbling, but knowing Rachel was determined, Agatha removed a blue cape from its hook by the door. "Put this on. At least you'll be dry," she said and wrapped the garment around Rachel's shoulders.

The linsey-woolsey cape, plain and unassuming, belonged to Ferne. Anxious to be off, Rachel fastened its simple clasp at her throat and went out to the lighted courtyard, where Jeremy helped her into the saddle, peering all the while down the dark road. Hesitant and doubtful, he looked up at Rachel.

"Perhaps I ought to go with you. I heard a rider passing on the road awhile ago."

In the doorway, Agatha began to cluck again, while Louisa wrung her hands.

"Oh, Lord, Jeremy! Not you, too!" snorted Rachel. "I can be halfway to the Hall before you're even saddled. Rest easy, all of you! I'll avoid the road and go through the Small Wood and then cut across the meadow." And so saying, Rachel tightened the reins and spurred the roan gelding forward. With a wave of her hand, she was gone, disappearing around the corner of the house.

Over in the road, that same rider heard by Jeremy earlier now swayed precipitously in the saddle. He was drunk, or nearly so, crooning aimlessly as he sauntered along, chuckling merrily at his own ribald lyrics. Coat and shirt open, he seemed impervious to the chill night air and creeping dampness. In spite of his insobriety, the tall rider was in no danger of being unseated, for horse and rider were as one, the animal much accustomed to carrying his master in an inebriated state. The high-stepping stallion, usually given to much prancing and pawing, was subdued, as though fully understanding that unexpected movements could pitch his master to the ground.

Presently, the handsome stallion raised his great maned head, sniffing at the night air with flared nostrils. With pricked ear he listened intently to detect once again the faint and muted sound that had not escaped his acute hearing. Then, sure of its source, he whickered softly, alerting his master. But the man leaning forward in the saddle was already alert.

"Ah, you heard it too, my friend?" he said to the animal. "In a bit of a hurry, I'd say. He's coming fast."

The moon, just topping the tall trees, broke from behind a low-lying mass of dark cloud, bathing the open fields in a strange pale light, its peculiar eeriness accentuated by the wafting mist that hugged the wet ground. Into that weird light, Pollux, carrying Rachel, burst forth from the Small Wood and moved swiftly across the open meadow.

To the besotted rider in the road, the woman on the galloping horse appeared as an apparition, for Rachel's long hair and her mantle streamed away behind her, and the gelding's feet and lower legs were invisible, shrouded in the drifting ground mist.

"Well, well! What have we here!" said the man with a wild laugh, yanking on his reins. "Can it be the wine, or do I see a ghost? No matter, Sultan, 'tis a fine figure of a woman, and I think we should take a closer look!"

Ever ready for a conquest, the man had the black over a low stone wall in a flash, and then they thundered across the meadow at a hard gallop in hot pursuit of Rachel and the roan gelding.

Hearing the thudding of Sultan's hooves behind her, Rachel turned nervously in the saddle, glancing over her shoulder. She spotted the racing stallion and his rider coming toward her at top speed, seeming to have materialized right out of the mist. With a terrifying shock, she realized that she was about to be ridden down.

She spurred her mount onward, but Pollux had been galloped hard already; he was nearly winded, had no reserve of strength to give, and his pace did not quicken. The tireless stallion, on the other hand, with superb strength and a longer stride, gained on them steadily.

Her heart pounding, Rachel knew that the rider would shortly come abreast of her, and she decided upon a course of action just as she neared the edge of the meadow. Though the stables of Guersten Hall were some distance away, the lights of the mansion itself could be seen through the darkness, and she turned Pollux sharply, heading for the high stone gateposts of the mansion's drive, more than a little relieved when she heard the gelding's hooves crunch upon its gravel. Surely this madman, whoever he was, dared not follow to the very door of Guersten Hall itself!

But dare he did, uttering a maniacal yell that chilled Rachel's blood as she pounded up the long drive. The rider, following right behind, was so close now that she could actually feel the huge stallion's hot breath at her shoulder.

In a matter of confused and terrifying seconds, the moon became obliterated by clouds once more, and Rachel, stifling a rising scream, was blanketed by the darkness of the night just as Pollux, well spent and panicked by the scent of the fearful stallion, reared without warning. Struggling frantically to keep her seat as the two animals jostled side by side, Rachel was suddenly seized from her saddle by a long arm that reached out and encircled her waist. Alone, the riderless gelding sped off down the gravelly drive, while Rachel, aware only of the empty space that had yawned beneath her, clutched wildly at the arm and shoulder of her abductor to keep from falling to the ground. Then, as the huge beast came to a halt, Rachel was drawn to safety across the black's saddle.

Trembling, frightened half to death, she lay sprawled precariously against her abductor's chest, gasping for her very breath in the pitch-black night. She was aware of a great roaring in her ears, not realizing that in anticipation of falling she had been holding her breath. Now, her body sagging heavily against the muscled arm that held her captive, she could feel his warmth through his open shirt and sensed his fingers, touching lightly to her hair. She became aware of an odor of tobacco and the smell of strong wine.

"Well now, Sultan," declared he in a deep voice that rumbled in Rachel's ear, pressed roughly against his chest. "Not a ghost at all, but a woman ... warm ... and fragrant," he said, breathing in Rachel's perfume while continuing to stroke her silken tresses.

Then, quite boldly, his hand moved away from her hair to roam freely along the length and contours of her body, touching first her soft breast and then moving down to her shapely hip. In the darkness, his head bent low, and Rachel knew his lips were awfully close to hers. The only sound heard was her own breathing, pulling in and out in short frightened gasps.

The driveway, so very, very dark, was briefly illuminated in that mysterious light again, and just as suddenly fell dark again, as the moon darted fleetingly behind another fast-moving cloud. In that split second, Rachel saw nothing, for her abductor's face, shadowed and indiscernible, remained hidden. Yet in that same instant, her captor had gazed upon the most beautiful face he had ever seen! It was pale, ashen, appearing marble-like in the eerie light, with carved and sculpted features that stirred him. He drew his breath in slowly.

"And a beauty she is, too, Sultan," he exclaimed, while the stallion stamped the ground. "Aye! A beauty!"

Brazenly, the man touched his hand again to Rachel's breast, this time slipping his fingers under the edge of her bodice, while his lips pressed ever nearer.

Rachel came alive at that indignity, regaining her senses with a cry. She tensed her body, unconsciously doubling her hands into fists, only to find that the fingers of one were still coiled around her riding stick. Again and again, she lashed out with it blindly and was rewarded when she felt it strike flesh.

Bellowing loudly, her captor clapped a hand to his ear, his hold upon her body loosening ever so lightly. Needing no urging, Rachel wriggled free, dropping quickly to the ground.

The man cursed, and loudly. Mistakenly, he had believed her to be frozen by fear, unable to move even, let alone capable of mounting some defense against him. Her wild swings and competent movements had taken him by surprise. Dismounting, he started after his elusive captive, but Rachel was much too quick for him. Scrambling to her feet, she began to run. Lighter, more agile, and unhindered by wine, there was little doubt she would outrun him, and he knew it. In drunken desperation, he made one last lunge at her, just catching the hem of Ferne's mantle between his fingers. He gave a sharp pull, and Rachel was brought cruelly to her knees as the bone clasp pressed savagely against the base of her throat. She heard his triumphant laughter, and sensing he was about to fling himself atop her in the darkness, Rachel opened the simple clasp and rolled away, all in one quick-witted movement. Then, springing lightly to her feet, she raced up the stony drive without looking back. Fairly flying, she passed under the portico and, springing up the steps, burst into the long gallery. There, safe inside, she closed the door and, with quaking heart, slammed the bolt home.

Out in the drive, having indeed thrown himself on the ground, the madman, now on his knees, gathered in the voluminous linsey-woolsey cape, cursing again when he discovered it to be empty. After groping futilely in the dark, he became amused by the absurdity of the entire escapade, and raising his voice in uproarious laughter, he pulled himself into the saddle.

"Ah, Sultan . . . our beautiful ghost has gotten away! A servant, I'd guess, by the feel of this cape. But come, I tire of the chase, and I have developed a thirst that cannot be ignored."

Had Rachel but glanced out of the window just then, she would have seen a great black stallion and his amused rider trotting away from the Hall. Moonlight danced across the lawns as they proceeded through the park, their movement parting the swirling mists that bordered the stream and lingered under the weeping willow trees. At the edge of the woods, horse and rider turned onto a path known only to them, to emerge half an hour later in a spot close by the Old Priory Inn. In a hidden corner of the crowded taproom, Emory Guersten would muse over his wine, trying to recall again and again that lovely face seen so fleetingly in the moonlight.

Meanwhile, totally overcome by her awesome experience, Rachel, now safe, shivered uncontrollably. She might have been kidnapped, or raped! Murdered, even! She was flushed and overheated just moments before, and now an icy river of perspiration trickled down her back. She hurried to her room, unseen by anyone, and huddling before the fireplace, she lifted her hands beseechingly to the warmth offered there. She was reminded again of her ordeal when she examined her clothing; her skirt was muddied, the bodice of her blouse gaped open, and the ribbons of her camisole were untied. Even looking at them recalled her terror, and she stripped them off, discarding them quickly in a heap on the floor.

She tugged at the bellpull, wanting a bath, hot and steamy. While waiting for the hot water, she wondered if she ought to alert Peter of the episode. But then, she reckoned, surely that man, whoever he was, wasn't about to wait around to be caught; he had probably disappeared as soon as she made good her escape. The search would surely be fruitless, and for just that reason, Rachel felt it made little sense to alarm either George or Peter. Besides, she surmised correctly, from then on George would fret incessantly whenever she left the house alone to ride out on Hunter or even to visit her mother again. She wanted complete freedom now to oversee the plans so recently instituted, and so, she decided not to mention the attack to anyone.

Pleading a headache, Rachel did not dress for dinner that night but remained in her room, taking supper on a tray. Sore, bruised, and still shaking, she went to bed early, fervently wishing she hadn't gone to Brenham Manor. But before sleep came, she considered again the man who had ridden her down. He had appeared so suddenly behind her, rising out of the very mist, it seemed. Who was he? What had he wanted? She could only guess at that, and with a shiver, she remembered the touch of his fingers on her breast, the scent of his masculine body, so close to hers. Just the same, Rachel remained indignant at the liberties he had taken! And that sweating stallion! Lord, what a ferocious beast!

Long after everyone in the mansion had gone to their beds, Emory Guersten returned to the Hall. By the time he left the inn, he was very drunk, but even so, he had climbed into his saddle without help, for to assist him meant approaching that snorting stallion, and none dared.

Reaching the barn, Emory slithered from the saddle. Lurching dangerously, he unsaddled and stabled Sultan. Then and only then did two sleepy-eyed grooms bring oats and water for the animal, placing the buckets a safe distance from the black's stall. His mount fed, Emory draped a long arm around the neck of the nearest groom.

"Hey, lad," he slurred, his knees buckling. "Can y' gi' me a hand to m' bed?"

With that, he passed out, and the grooms carried him from the barn. As they passed by the end stall, Sultan looked up from his oats and gave a loud, shrieking whinny, as if warning the lads to handle his master with care. But the lads were young, and they were strong, and in short order Emory's wine-riddled body was secure in his own bed. There, it was Stoddard who undressed and covered him, and then left him to sleep.

CHAPTER THIRTEEN

Awakened by the sound of Stoddard's tapping, Rachel rubbed her eyes sleepily as the cook, once admitted, crossed the room to place a tray of steaming coffee and warm sweet rolls on the bedside table, and then proceeded to the windows, opening and fastening the draperies. The early morning light did little to brighten the vast room, for the sun wasn't even up yet.

"Is something wrong, Stoddard?" asked Rachel, concerned.

"No, ma'am, but I know ye didn't eat proper last night, and thought perhaps you might like your coffee a little early this morning."

"Early, yes," mumbled Rachel, groaning, "but this is ridiculous!"

"Ah, yes, ma'am, but . . . well, you slept through the commotion last night, and I just wanted to warn you . . . Yer husband has finally come home."

Rachel sat bolt upright in the bed, wide awake at that.

"My hus . . . Emory? Here? At Guersten Hall?"

"Aye," said Stoddard, nodding her head briskly, pleased to be the first to carry the news to her mistress. Hovering over the bed, she fluffed Rachel's pillows and propped them against the bedstead. Wincing from her bruises, Rachel lay back against them.

So! At last! How often had she wondered what her own reactions might be when Emory finally returned to the Hall! Anger? Trepidation? Or simple relief for George's sake? In truth, just now, Rachel felt nothing. It was simply too early in the morning, and besides, she was stiff, and her throat hurt where the clasp of Ferne's cape had bitten deeply against her windpipe last night. An ugly purple bruise still formed in just that spot, one that Stoddard did not fail to notice, her forehead skewered into a deep scowl.

"It's nothing," said Rachel, closing the ribbons of her nightdress. "A slight mishap. Now tell me more about Emory's arrival. You spoke of a commotion. Am I to assume then that he arrived drunk in the dead of the night?"

"He . . . was a little under the weather, ye might say," replied the cook, not wanting to make matters worse for her favorite. She placed the footed tray across Rachel's lap and handed her mistress a crisp napkin, while Rachel grinned up at her suspiciously.

"Come now, Stoddard! It was late! He was drunk, and more than likely he was carried in! Now, isn't that closer to the whole truth?"

"Well, now that ye mention it, he did require a little assistance. Those stairs, ye know . . ."

Putting down the creamer, Rachel broke into amused laughter, while Stoddard squirmed uneasily, caught watering the truth.

"Your partiality shows, Effie. But, out with it! Just why have you waked me at this ungodly hour?"

"Awww, Mistress . . . I'm no good at this, but might I be pleading with ye to be a little easy on the lad? Nobody ever took the time to set any standards for him, and so he set his own. Not meanin' no disrespect, but Miss Abigail, she was never overly fond of her children, and none of them knew much love as they grew up. Oh, 'tis true she spoilt them, especially Emory, since he was firstborn, but that was just her way to strike back at Master George, don't you see? She was terrible unhappy, him bein' so much older than her an' set in his ways. There wasn't ever any love between them. They was forced together."

Rachel returned her cup to the tray.

"Really, Effie! You overstep! You're as familiar with the situation here at the Hall as anyone. I too was forced into marriage, and Emory's behavior has only made a bad situation that much worse. He has much to answer for."

Humbled, Stoddard studied the floor and then busied herself, straightening the bedcovers.

"I know that, and I'm sorry I spoke out of turn. It's just that the Guerstens, they're family to me after all these years, an' by now, I've come to be real fond of you, too. I'd not like to see either you or Master Emory unhappy."

Effie Stoddard had never married. Having come to Guersten Hall as a young woman, she had first served old William Guersten and the invalid Miss Martha, then George and Miss Abigail. Now, nearing sixty, Stoddard wanted only to end her years in service to Emory and Rachel, especially those two, for now she adored them both.

Aware of this, Rachel was inclined to be tolerant, and she spoke gently to the older woman.

"I harbor no resentments, if that is your concern, for it is not my nature, but by the same token," she said, stretching her long legs beneath the covers, "I have endured enough. Whether we will be friends or enemies is up to Emory."

Knowing she could ask no more of her mistress than that, Stoddard prepared to remove the tray. The next move was up to Emory, just as it had been all along. She started for the door.

"Where is he now, Effie?"

"Why, in his room, ma'am. T' other side of yon wall." With a jerk of her head, Stoddard motioned to the wall behind Rachel's bed. "He'll sleep for some time yet, I think."

"I dare say he'd like to, but wake him, Effie. Ply him with strong coffee, and let George know the moment he is on his feet. Emory can begin his explanations there, and . . . in case his mood be sour, I shall defer my own meeting with him until this evening."

By now the sun was up, and hoping that an early morning ride would work out some of the stiffness that had settled in her shoulder, Rachel searched in the wardrobe for her riding boots, turning back to the cook with an impish grin.

"One more thing, Stoddard," she said conspiratorially. "Emory has kept me waiting a long time, and I've a mind to let him stew some.

Inform the others, not a word to him all day about me. Let him continue to think what he will. Understand?"

Nodding, Stoddard was grinning herself as she left the room.

"Tell Pug to saddle Hunter," Rachel called after her. "It looks like it's going to be a grand day."

"Don't it, ma'am? Now, don't it?"

The brew that Stoddard sent up to Emory's room awhile later was hot, strong, and bitter, but even so, it was midmorning before he was on his feet and even later before he was fully dressed and freshly shaven. He felt awful; his head ached ferociously, and he was plagued by a sour stomach. Had he been left to his own devices, he would have crawled back into bed.

But the time for reckoning was at hand. Summoned to the library by his father, Emory proceeded slowly down the polished marble stairs, sullen and ill-tempered. Ever since that night he had first learned Rachel Brenham was to be his wife, he had been miserable. Nothing had changed; he was still miserable. But miserable or not, Emory knew that a meeting with his new bride was inevitable now; it could not be prolonged any longer. She was his wife, and she was here at the Hall.

He had conducted himself rottenly, even cowardly; that much he admitted. At first, having sped to London after weaseling out of the ceremony, Emory had truly intended to return; many times, in fact, but on each occasion he was forestalled by his memories of Rachel as a child, memories that danced around in his head mockingly until he stilled them with wine.

And thus, the days had turned to weeks, the weeks to months, until only days ago, in Tisbury's office; Emory had been momentarily sobered by two startling facts. It was April already, and his funds were gone.

He paused at the bottom of the staircase, passing a hand across his aching brow. Around him the vast reception hall fairly sparkled. Daylight streamed through the tall windows of the gallery, highlighting the glossy marble and the subtle colors of the wall hangings. Gone was the dust, and gone was the faint musty odor of mildew that had long emanated from the nearby ballroom. But all that sparkle escaped Emory's usually observant eye, and he saw none of it. *God, he felt ter-*

rible! And how he dreaded the meetings today. His father would be angry, as had right to be, but there would be a scene, and probably another when he met Rachel. *Probably? Ha! Positively!* he thought. *Complete with tears and hysteria!* He groaned audibly, his resentment renewed, and went into the library.

Seated behind his mahogany desk, George looked very much to Emory as he always had. Smaller, a little pale perhaps, and seated in a wicker chair instead of his usual leather; other than that, Emory saw nothing amiss. The platform and wheels of the chair were hidden by the desk, and enveloped in his own misery, he never noticed his father's useless arm.

"*So!* You're home!"

"Yes, as you can plainly see, Father. You seem well."

The old man raised his gold-topped walking stick and would have struck his son's outstretched palm with it had not Emory pulled away his hand just in time. Indeed, his father *was* angry!

"A remarkable observation, Emory, considering you arrived dead drunk in the middle of the night after a prolonged absence. Let's see," said George sarcastically, counting on his fingers. "Well, over three months."

Emory's head throbbed with pain. He decided to say nothing; his silence only enraging his father more.

"Well! Speak! What have you to say for yourself?" he thundered. "I take it you ran out of funds?"

"Look, Father," said Emory irritably, "dispense with the small talk. You know damn well I'm out of funds. You saw to that when you cut off my allowance!"

"Aye! I did, and I'm sorry I didn't do it sooner!"

"Was it your idea . . . or Rachel's?"

Furious at Emory's effrontery, George raised his walking stick again. Emory backed away to a safe distance, dropping into one of the wing chairs near the fireplace. He sat with one knee slung over the chair's arm, glowering sullenly across at his father.

"You're as insolent as ever, Emory. We shall discuss Rachel soon enough. For now, forget her."

"I've tried, Father," replied Emory impertinently, thinking of his aching head. "Oh, how I've tried! But I find there isn't enough wine in all of England to accomplish that feat!"

George exploded. "Now see here, Emory," he shouted at the top of his voice. "That's enough! Hold your tongue!"

They eyed each other warily, and finally Emory shrugged. It had gone far enough. George, his face flushed, was now lathered into a high state of agitation. He was old, thought Emory guiltily, and his anger was justified. In tacit agreement, the needling ceased, and George's temper subsided.

"I want an accounting, Emory. Where have you been?"

Closing his eyes for a brief moment, Emory rested his pounding head against one of the leather wings.

"Exact your pound of flesh, if you must, Father, but there's nothing to tell really. I've been running . . . Now I've stopped. I was going to return at Christmas but chose to remain in London instead. And then, in February, I went to Kent as Lord Merrington's houseguest. I've only recently returned from there."

"You mean Lady Merrington, don't you?"

"All right . . . Lady Merrington, if you prefer. She's a young woman, Father, married to a man much older than she is. Can she be blamed for wanting a little diversion now and again?"

"Diversion, my foot! Hmmph! *Laid* is a better word! She's older than you, and vain and boring as well. Reminds me of Charlotte! How many times must I tell you, Emory . . . Never play the fool with another man's wife. Not that Merrington gives a damn . . . He needs an heir to retain those estates, and since he can't do it himself, he looks the other way while some jackass accommodates his wife. Don't let it be you! You've estates of your own to see to."

Emory ignored his father's last remark, but still he laughed, despite the criticism.

"Don't worry, Father, if Lady Merrington finds herself with child this spring, even she won't know who's responsible. They were six deep about the place when I left."

"It's not a matter for jokes, Emory. Your behavior has been inexcusable, and I am quite disappointed in you."

"Please, Father! No more! Not today!"

"Be quiet!" George said snappishly, his voice rising again. "I shall make no long harangue. It would fall on deaf ears, anyway. But all the same, there are some simple truths to be laid bare here. You drink too much . . . gamble too much . . . and your morals are disgraceful!" Each of Emory's faults was emphasized by a *whomp* on the desk with the gold-topped walking stick.

"By whose standards, Father? Am I worse than any of my peers?"

George grimaced disgustedly. "Peers! Hmmph! Snotty louts who think themselves gentlemen because they were born on the right side of the blanket and because they belong to all the right clubs. Bah! It's men like Benjamin Brenham and Tisbury, even Peter and Gaffy, who make the wheels turn in this world, while you and others like you waste your youth chasing skirts and drinking yourselves to death night after night. In all the best clubs, of course!" he sneered.

Getting to his feet, Emory paced about the room, perching at last on the back of a long sofa.

"All right, all right!" he said crossly. "I get your drift. Get on with it!"

George cleared his throat. "Clearly, your way of life cannot be tolerated any longer, nor will it. You have had far too much time on your hands, perhaps that is why you turned to wine and cards . . . and whoring. But now that you are home again, all that will cease. Immediately!"

"My God, Father! My friends will think I've turned into a damned prig!"

"Frankly, I care not what your friends think! Wastrels, the lot of them," answered the unsmiling George. "They are as worthless as you are." He paused, and then resumed his tirade. "You've been given every advantage, and to what end? Despite your education, you cannot even manage your own estates!"

This time it was Emory who sneered, and his needling resumed. "Maybe I should have made the grand tour, Father," he said. "Perhaps there was something I missed."

"And what, pray tell, might that have been?" snarled George scornfully. "Laying women and learning new vices? You were well schooled without traveling to Paris and Vienna to learn more. But silence! I've heard enough!"

Bristling, Emory moved again, this time to the unlighted fire-place. Rakishly he hooked his thumbs over his belt and leaned his back against the mantel, while his father pointed a finger in his direction.

"Hear me," he said, "and hear me well. From now on you will be expected to participate in the management of this estate. You will present yourself at mealtimes, sober and properly dressed. You will be civil at all times—to me, your wife, your sister, and the servants—and since it is patently clear that you cannot approach the gaming tables without losing half a year's allowance, you will not gamble, for I will no longer stand your losses. Any further drunkenness on your part will certainly incur my wrath, and as far as women are concerned, I remind you, Emory . . . You are a married man. Granted, you did not stand beside Rachel and exchange vows, but you are no less married because of it. You have a wife; you will behave accordingly. Under the circum-stances, Rachel is to be excused if she spurns your advances and refuses you admittance to her bedroom, but I warn you, take care to conduct yourself as the gentleman you claim to be."

Emory listened to his father's critical intonement without moving a muscle, but he was furious all the same. His scar, inching redly across his forehead, offered mute testimony to that. His entire lifestyle was turned upside down—all because of that damnable mouse!

"Dammit! You go too far, Father! I am not a monk!"

"Silence!" shouted George, cracking the walking stick on the desktop again. "I mean what I say. I will not see that young woman humiliated again! She has been tested sorely by this family and found not wanting."

"There are a number of things of which you are not aware of yet," he continued, his voice growing softer as he thought of Rachel's goodness. "They will become obvious to you very soon. Until then, remember this, I owe her much, perhaps my very life, for it was she who found me and saw me through my illness, and it was she who encouraged my recovery."

"Illness? What illness?"

Emory wracked his brain. Returning from Kent, he had gone directly to Tisbury's office, in need of funds. That was a week ago. He was certain Tisbury had made no mention of his father being ill.

"Why didn't Tisbury make mention of this?" he demanded.

"He was instructed not to. I did not want my illness to serve as your excuse for returning to Guersten Hall. Face it, Emory . . . You did not come home because of me, or because of Rachel. You came because you were out of funds, and only for that reason. In the end, it was your own hide you were concerned about . . . yours and the black's."

"This illness . . . it was serious, I take it?"

"Serious enough," replied George, "considering it nearly took my life and left me crippled."

So saying, George gave a push with his good arm, and the wheelchair rolled away from the desk. Emory stared blankly, shocked and incredulous, suddenly seeing the wicker chair for what it really was. He saw the blanket and his father's left arm lying helpless against his side. With a low cry, he fell into the wing chair again and buried his head in his hands.

"If you want the details," continued George in a stony voice, "get 'em from Peter. I owe him much, too. I needed you, Emory, both you and Edward . . . Yet neither of you came. Peter scoured the entire city for you, and Rachel even left a note with Tisbury for you."

Emory hung his head. *My God, the note! Now he remembered!* Before he even went to Kent, he'd called at Tisbury's office one morning, seeking an advance against his quarterly allowance. He'd been half tipsy that day, he recalled, and he had laughed heartily at the contents of Rachel's note. *I still have it somewhere,* he thought now detachedly.

Grimly, with a drawn face, Emory looked across the room at his father. When he spoke, his voice came in a choked sob.

"It was delivered, Father, only I ignored it, I'm ashamed to admit. I thought . . . I thought it was a ruse . . . that Rachel was trying to trap me into returning to the Hall. I'm sorry; can you forgive me?"

George expelled a long, whistled sigh. As if Rachel need resort to ruses! Suddenly the old man realized he was tired, very tired; he wanted to go to his room to lie down. Half turning in his chair, he tugged at the nearby bellpull, and when it was answered, he sent for Peter. While waiting, he silently studied Emory, who still sat with bowed head before him. Inexplicably, the old man was filled with gentle compassion for his firstborn son, who had known little love as a boy, and even less as a man.

"Yes, I forgive you, son. After all, much of this is my own doing. We've got to live with our faults, you and I, but I must tell you straightaway, Emory, that as far as Rachel is concerned, I have taken sides. Whatever happens now remains to be seen, but do not hurt her, Emory, I warn you. It would be the last straw."

Peter arrived, tapping lightly at the door, and a moment later, as George rolled past Emory, he laid his hand on the top of his son's still-bowed head. It rested there for only a moment, in a profound and wordless gesture, and then George was wheeled from the library.

Emory remained sitting for several anguished minutes, and then, rising slowly, he went to his father's desk. His head still hurt something awful, but now there was an ache in his chest, too. He poured himself a large brandy, downing it neatly, and still clutching the decanter, yet only half aware of doing so, he left the library and headed for his room. His father's empty wheelchair sat at the foot of the staircase, the still-warm blanket folded neatly in the seat. Heavyhearted, Emory went to his room and closed the door.

With the decanter always close by, he remained there in the rounded turret most of the day, leaving the room just once, and then only long enough to tend to Sultan's needs. In the barn, Ferne's cape, which had been draped across the black's saddle the night before, now hung limply on a hook just inside the door. Emory never saw it, if he remembered the incident at all.

As usual, when drinking, he misread everything. Brooding guiltily, at first he blamed himself for the turn of events, and then, typically, as the contents of the decanter lowered, he shifted the burden of guilt to others. First, it was Tisbury—if only the man had told him his father was ill. And then it was Edwina Merrington—if only she hadn't lured him away from London with her lush body. On and on it went, full round to Benjamin Brenham; from there, it was only natural that the ultimate blame would shift again to lie with Rachel. The memories flooded back, mocking . . . mocking.

Realizing the decanter was half empty, Emory heeded his father's stern admonition and, replacing the stopper, threw himself across his bed. By now he was peevish, a little angry, and without knowing it, more than a little jealous that Rachel had been able to ingratiate herself into the household so easily. Why, even his father was openly taking sides!

Moodily, Emory schemed about the meeting yet to come with Rachel. *How shall I behave? Perhaps I should be charming and play the gallant! No, then she will assume I want to spend the night with her, and there will be tears and hand wringing. Hmmm . . . Perhaps I should be forceful and demand my rights! No, that wouldn't do either . . . There would surely be hysterics!*

In the end, before he dozed off, Emory conceitedly decided that he would just be himself. *I shall dress very carefully,* he thought vainly, drawing a hand across his handsome face. *Perhaps I shall swagger a bit, too.* Ah, yes! That was the route to go! He would intimidate Rachel, just as he always had. It was so easy to do, and it always worked. A look, a posture, it had even happened that without speaking a single word he had been able to reduce her to tears. Best of all, his father could accuse him of nothing!

It was Rachel who came downstairs first that evening. In the dining room she set about arranging the pretty centerpiece herself, made colorful with early irises and daffodils from Gaffy's sunny garden. Stoddard waylaid her at her task.

"There's a problem, ma'am. I should've told you before this, but it slipped my mind . . . It's the stuffed oysters. Master Emory . . . he don't like stuffed oysters. Never did."

The menu had been planned days ago, before anyone could know of Emory's arrival, and while Rachel admitted to herself that perhaps she might have checked with George as to Emory's likes and dislikes, still, it was too late to alter anything now.

"Just tell the girls to keep the duck and the vegetables at his end of the table," she said to the cook.

"That's just as bad. Brussels sprouts . . . he don't like them either."

Annoyed, Rachel waved her hand. "He isn't a guest, for heaven's sake! Off with you! Just remember, the wine stays at my end of the table."

Joining George and Ermaline in the drawing room for sherry, Rachel suddenly tensed as they awaited Emory's arrival. She paced the room expectantly. This first meeting would be so awkward, and she much preferred to be alone with him. She finished her sherry, returning the crystal goblet to its place on the tray.

"I prefer that he not have an audience to play to," she said, winking, adding that she would wait for him in the music room.

Shaking with mirth, George nodded, and even Ermaline smiled. How well they all knew Emory! At the door, Rachel turned.

"If we are delayed, go in to dinner. We will join you when the formalities are done."

Purposely closing the double doors to the music room, Rachel seated herself at the piano. Not ten minutes later, Emory descended the stairs, splendid looking, dressed fully in black, his ensemble set off by an emerald-green waistcoat that showed beneath his tailored frock coat. He had taken great pains dressing; his hair was perfect, and he had even shaved again for the second time that day. Tonight he was exceptionally handsome, and he knew it. Straightening his cravat, he tugged at his ruffled cuffs one last time, then, swaggering shamelessly, entered the drawing room.

Ermaline looked away. It was either that or laugh openly at the sight of his cock-o'-the-walk stance. The posturing quickly faded, as Emory, surprised to find Rachel not present, became convinced she was even now cowering somewhere in the big house, afraid to show herself. Relaxing, he turned his attention to his sister, greeting Ermaline warmly, noting the lowered neckline that enhanced her figure so marvelously and the sleek curls piled so intricately atop her head. She was expensively dressed in a long-waisted gown of pale peach taffeta. Was this fair creature really Ermaline? Plain, ordinary Ermaline? His astonishment was hard to hide.

"There is ever so much to tell you," said Ermaline, planting a sisterly kiss on Emory's cheek. "But not tonight. Your wife awaits you."

With his walking stick, George motioned across the hall to the music room, with its closed doors. Very carefully he poured some sherry into a glass, handing it to his son.

"Well you know how I frown on your drinking, but this once I think you may have need of this. Drink it, for the next few moments may prove a little difficult for you."

So! I was right! The little mouse is still a little mouse!

"And how shall I greet the fair Rachel? With a kiss, a bow, or a handshake?" he asked with a trace of sarcasm.

"A gentleman always does what's right, Emory, remember that," George replied, referring to their earlier conversation. He looked at his timepiece. "We shall meet you in the dining room on the quarter hour."

Emory's petulance gave way to resentment again. It doesn't take that long to crush a mouse, he thought, and downing his sherry, he ushered himself out of the room with a flamboyantly executed bow.

"Well," said his father, turning to Ermaline, "he's as arrogant as ever, but he seemed sober, and he was dressed properly. It's a start."

Crossing the reception hall in long angry strides, Emory paused outside the music room. *By God!* he mused. *She'll probably be wearing gray . . . No, worse! Brown! And her hair will be done in a bun!* Glowering resentfully at the closed doors, doors that Rachel herself had obviously shut, Emory felt his anger rising even more, burning the back of his throat. *Damn! I'm beginning to feel like the outsider, and it's my house!*

Reaching out with both hands, he pushed open the double doors with as much force as he could muster. They flew apart wildly, and one struck against the wall with a loud clatter. Stepping inside, he slammed them shut behind him, deliberately creating another racket.

Rachel, unflinching, sat at the piano, her back to him. Only a single missed note of a melodious air gave evidence that she had even taken notice of Emory's abrupt and noisy entrance. He glowered even more, convinced that she should have jumped from the bench at that racket.

Instead, Rachel continued with her music, ignoring him completely. Fuming, Emory advanced fully into the room with thumping heels, only to come to a dead stop midstride. Something was wrong, and his confused brain sought vainly to assess what it was. The shadowed room was lighted only by two wall lamps, and soft candlelight flickered off a back that was much too curved, hair that was much too lustrous, and a gown of rich sea-green silk that could not be mistaken for gray or brown in any light.

Unmoving, Emory remained in the center of the room, totally confused, mentally thanking his father for the sherry. Though the music had stopped, Rachel still sat with her arms extended along the ivory keys, and Emory stared at them, long and shapely with well-turned wrists and slender hands. At last, Rachel dropped them to her sides and, turning slowly, rose to her feet, proudly lifting her face for her husband's scrutiny.

His jaw sagging visibly, Emory withdrew, reacting much the same as if he'd seen a ghost. He had, in fact! His head spinning, the events of the previous night filtered back. *Her!* The same fragile being that had lain across his saddle so fleetingly! His senses stirred as he remembered the supple curves of that soft body. *But how can it be?* How can that ghostly spirit be standing here in the music room at Guersten Hall? Be his wife?

Yet Emory knew, as he continued to stare unabashedly, there was no mistake. Impossible though it was, that flawless face was the very one he had seen in the moonlight. She was beautiful beyond words, her forehead high and smooth, her cheekbones rounded, a complexion that was perfect, and those dark eyes he had first seen fraught with fear now returned his gaze steady and sure. They were deep and luminous eyes, surrounded by curving lashes.

Swiftly, Emory's experienced eye drank in the rest of Rachel's appearance; he noted her hair, drawn into a simple and exquisite coil, with several long curls resting lightly against her neck, and her gown, equally exquisite, baring smooth shoulders and exposing rounded breasts with its low décolletage. Here and there, tiny pearls nestled in draped folds, and the barest wisp of green silk formed a sleeve on each upper arm, while sweeping folds of the rich fabric swirled about her feet. At the hem, a delicately pleated petticoat of filmy mousseline de soie peeped from beneath the overskirt, drawn up and draped at one ankle. For jewelry, Rachel had chosen only the pearl earbobs from the Guersten jewels and a slender ribbon tied about her throat, leaving the adornment of the gown, as Eleanora had planned, to its wearer.

The narrow ribbon about Rachel's throat swamped Emory with guilt, for it did little to hide the dark bruise beneath it, a bruise he knew at once had been inflicted by his own hand. He was unable to speak. Only moments before he had barged into the music room, swaggering, conceited and angry, having hoped to intimidate Rachel by his very presence. Now it was he who was discomfited and bewildered. His distracted mind raced; try as he might, he could not associate this lovely woman with the picture of the old Rachel so firmly etched into his memory, one enlarged upon with great liberty so frequently during these last months.

The silence, and Emory's staring, became embarrassing, and Rachel moved across the room to stand before him. Her perfume enveloped him hauntingly, reminding him again of the previous night. Somehow, he was certain, standing there, that Rachel was unaware that it was he who had chased her across the Small Wood meadow, and he was greatly relieved, for he was just now beginning to realize what an utter ass he'd been. Perhaps she would never know, he considered hopefully.

Raising her eyes to meet his, Rachel was amazed, as she had ever been, at the greenness of his. She waited for him to speak, and when he did not, she moved again, this time to the double doors of the room.

"This is all very clumsy, Emory, you must agree. We have been thrown together, and we have much to discuss, but since you choose not to speak, or cannot, come . . . Let us join the others at dinner. We can talk later," she said in calm, clear voice.

Emory groped for words, but none came, and though he nodded his head in mute agreement, still, he didn't move.

"Your arm," said Rachel softly.

Woodenly, Emory pulled the doors open and then offered Rachel his arm. It was the wrong one, but she took it graciously anyway, and they proceeded to the dining room that way, with Rachel on the wrong side.

Joining the others, Emory carefully drew out Rachel's chair, while George gave his daughter-in-law a conspiratorial wink, and Ermaline covered her lips with her napkin to hide a smile.

To Rachel's mind, the highlight of the relaxed meal came when Stoddard entered from the serving panty carrying a silver salver. She went directly to Emory's side.

"In honor of yer homecoming, Master Emory, we cooked up two of yer detestables." And she uncovered the divided salver to display generous portions of stuffed oysters and Brussels sprouts.

Emory helped himself to both, staring all the while at Rachel.

"That was thoughtful of you, Stoddard . . . very thoughtful, indeed."

The sight of Stoddard's "detestables" on his plate, though, seemed to rouse Emory from his daze, and pushing them unobtrusively to one side, he pleased his father no end by being charming and amusing through the rest of the pleasant dinner, though his eyes never left Rachel's face.

CHAPTER FOURTEEN

Put at ease by Rachel's unpretentiousness, it wasn't very long before Emory regained his composure and found his tongue. He relaxed, and throughout the dinner the conversation remained light and pleasant. Once, caught pushing both the oysters and the Brussels sprouts discreetly to the side of his plate, Emory smiled engagingly at Rachel, and by the time the dessert was served, even she began to fall victim to his easy charm and pleasant chatter, understanding why women were so readily attracted to him. Alternately witty and amusing, Emory was both polite and attentive, and also thoroughly bewitched, completely captivated by Rachel's astonishing beauty. As for old George, he was beside himself, hoping that somehow a lasting relationship would develop between the handsome young couple sitting across the table from each other.

George signaled to Ermaline, and they left the room, leaving Emory and Rachel privacy to begin to settle their differences. Emory ushered Rachel into the library, made comfortable with a banked fire and drawn drapes, where he began by uttering sincere and humble apologies for his past behavior. He was ashamed, he told her, and regretted his actions lamentably. Pouring Benedictine into small glasses, he handed one to Rachel.

"Father feels he owes you much, but I am the one who is in your debt, and decidedly so. I've been a heel, Rachel, and I'm sorry, very sorry. My humiliation of you personally is unpardonable. I beg your forgiveness, but fully understand if you choose not to give it."

Throughout their long conversation, he continued to offer apologies, as they discussed that snowy wedding day when he did not appear, and his father's critical illness, when again he did not appear, and the duties Peter had assumed in caring for George, when he was needed and yet again did not appear.

At this point, again, Emory begged her forgiveness, furious with himself all the while. Hadn't his father advised him months before to call on her ... court her? "Aaah! If only I had listened to him," he muttered inaudibly under his breath, castigating himself for being such a fool! He knew now that one sight of this new Rachel would have pleasantly changed the course of both their lives. "I've been a fool!" he said to himself again and again.

Glass in hand, Emory assumed his favorite position, his back pressed against the mantelpiece, while Rachel sat before him on the long sofa. Her long legs were curled daintily beneath her, the rich green silk ballooning about her like frothy sea foam. While pretending not to, Emory watched her intently, finding it quite impossible that this lovely creature could be the very same Rachel he had known and despised so as a boy. Her beauty was stirring, and more than once he felt the flush of desire wash over him.

Rachel was studying him just as intently. She had not even begun to assess her own feelings about his return to the Hall or what changes it might bring to her own life. It was all too new. That he was due a serious dressing-down was clear; he had it coming, but Rachel had observed George carefully during dinner, and it was equally clear that the old man sorely wanted some peace and harmony under his roof. For the hundredth time in a month, Rachel considered again the matter of Ermaline's future and Rebecca's pregnancy, and then, setting aside the bitter words of denunciation that were on the tip of her tongue, she bowed to George's sentiments, opting, too, for peace. Still, her words were intoned harshly.

"For your father's sake, if no other, I prefer to see harmony here at Guersten Hall," she said to Emory. "And I will not belabor your remorse just to see you squirm. But I warn you, do not mistake my charity for weakness," she added. "I was not your choice, nor were you mine, but we are married, nonetheless. My bedroom is off limits to you under the circumstances, but perhaps we can be friends, at least."

Coloring hotly, Emory offered a salute with the tiny liquor glass. "That's a lot more than I deserve, as you say, under the circumstances, and in time," he replied hopefully, "who knows."

To that, Rachel offered no response, even while admitting to herself that he was certainly most attractive, as he had always been. His muscled frame filled the well-cut coat to perfection, and the green vest lent extraordinary depth to those emerald eyes. Even the scar that traced its way across his forehead somehow seemed only to add to his striking virility. Just the same, Rachel was not willing to concede anything beyond friendship. In name, they were man and wife; it was enough. It simply made more sense to live under the same roof as friends rather than adversaries.

They conversed at some length, moving on to touch upon a great many subjects—Rachel's years at Portsmouth, the changes evident in Ermaline—but when the subject of his father's illness was raised again, however, Rachel said nothing. That was a matter Emory alone would have to cope with, and judging from his guilt, it might not be easy for him. As for Rebecca, Emory was not at all surprised to learn of her approaching motherhood, for he, better than any, knew just how much Edward loved her.

"By now," he remarked lightly, "Edward has probably called at Tisbury's office, and like me, with pockets empty, will be along any day now. Once they are married, it will soon be forgotten."

Rachel wasn't so sure, but she let the matter drop, as somewhere in the house a noisy clock chimed eleven times, the sound caroming softly throughout the lower halls.

"I had no idea it was so late," she stated. "I like to rise early. I enjoy riding out at dawn when all is fresh and clean."

"You ride?" exclaimed Emory, plainly surprised. "I distinctly recall that you were never very fond of riding."

"True, but thanks to Hunter, I have gotten over my fears."

"May I join you? Would I be imposing?"

Rachel shook her shining curls. "No, as a matter of fact, I am anxious to see that black of yours. Is he all your father claims?"

"That and more! Did he tell you that I won him? One of the few times I did win at cards, now that I think of it!"

Emory remembered that long-ago night precisely. The black's previous owner, a notoriously cruel chap, thought to trick Emory, certain that he would be unable to claim his win, for the beast was half wild, unruly, and even dangerous. But Emory had an uncanny way with horses that few knew of, and his blood had raged when he spied the whip marks and dried blood that spotted the animal's hide. The cruel bloke was thunderstruck when, eventually, the excitable black allowed Emory to remove a bloodied bit from its mouth and then followed him docilely to a nearby stable. There, Emory had tended the animal's wounds himself; since that very night, he had never ridden another horse, and to this day, no one but he could approach the stallion without it raising a ruckus.

At the foot of the marble staircase, Emory said good night to Rachel, taking her cool hand into his own on impulse, kissing her fingertips lightly. His mother's gold wedding band gleamed dully in the somber light thrown by the trimmed wall lamps, and again, he was troubled by ignominious guilt. She was his wife, yet he had treated her sorely. He cursed himself, knowing he had forfeited his husbandly rights. If only he had acted more the man and less the bounder, he might this very night be welcome in her bed. He felt a powerful urge to sweep Rachel into his arms, as the dim light outlined her beautiful face, but with difficulty he let the moment pass, knowing such an action would only estrange her. It was too soon, he said to himself. *Much too soon.*

Confused by the look of open desire that had flooded Emory's strange green eyes, Rachel withdrew her hand and, in a rustle of silk, turned and disappeared up the stairs. Emory remained where he was until he heard the sound of her door closing.

"Sleep well, little mouse . . . Sleep well."

Stepping outside, he stood for a while under the portico, with one foot on the mounting block, exhaling the rich smoke of a thin cheroot in clouds that lay heavy on the night air.

"*Damn!*" he said finally, kicking the stone block.

When morning broke, cool and bright, Rachel dressed in a sable-brown riding skirt, adding a short Hessian jacket trimmed with jaunty gold braid. She coiled her hair into a light snood and, without knowing why, topped it with a small brimmed hat, its long feather dipping rakishly over one shoulder. She looked devastating. And Emory, waiting by the stairs, whistled appreciatively.

"*Very* smart, Rachel. Would that we were headed for Rotten Row this morning! I would be the envy of every man there!"

Freshly shaven, wearing snug gray breeches and high black boots, Emory looked very masculine this morning. A full-sleeved shirt lay open at his neck, showing a wide expanse of chest. In contrast to yesterday morning, he felt remarkably fit, with a clear head and a settled stomach. Furthermore, he was buoyed by the knowledge that it had been months since he had risen so early.

While he proceeded to the stables to see about their horses, Rachel went to give Stoddard the day's menus before hurrying after him, anxious to meet his notorious black. At the barn, she found Hunter saddled and ready to go, and paused to nuzzle the brown stallion's nose before stepping inside the open door.

There, pleased to see his master and anxious for a fast-paced morning run, the rambunctious black was prancing about excitedly in the middle of the floor. He flicked his inky tail ominously, uttering muffled neighs, while two grooms cowered inside a nearby stall. Emerging from the tack room just then, carrying his saddle, Emory spotted her and nodded, laying a hand on the black's flank.

"Steady, Sultan! Steady! She's a friend."

But even before Emory had uttered the animal's name, Rachel knew! She had seen that beast before! The blizzard! The barn at Aylesbury Inn! And even more recently, the night before last! The night she was ridden down!

She leaned against the wall, steadying herself, and in doing so, one hand brushed against Ferne's linsey-woolsey cloak, hung on a peg by the door, probably by one of the grooms that infamous night. Horrified, Rachel gasped aloud, yet even without that further bit of evidence, she had been sure. There was no doubt! There simply wasn't another horse like that in all of England!

"You!" she shrieked, throwing the cloak at Emory's feet. "My God! It was you!"

Dismayed, Emory dropped his saddle and ran to her side. "Rachel! Hear me!" he cried in a wretched voice. "Everything can be explained!"

He reached for her arm, crushed by the disgust that he read in her eyes. She pulled away from him, while the two grooms watched in amazement.

"Don't touch me!" she screamed over her shoulder as she ran outside. "Pug!" she cried. "Help me mount!"

In another second she was gone, disappearing down the road to the back of the estate. Swearing profusely, Emory returned to the barn. Quickly, he set about saddling Sultan, but by the time he finished, Rachel was already out of sight. Not knowing what else to do, Emory set out after her.

He was heartsick, realizing now that he had been foolish to suppose even for a moment that Rachel would never know, never guess that it was he who had chased her that night. She was too discerning, too alert. *But not now!* he fumed. *Not now!*

For months he had avoided the Hall because he could not bear the thought of being married to a woman who was less than beautiful, only to learn that just the opposite was true! Rachel was more than beautiful; she was perfection, and suddenly he had been so hopeful. True, he had humiliated her, even hurt her physically; the bruise on her throat attested to that, yet Rachel had not been bitter or malevolent. On the contrary, she had seemed willing to accept his apologies, had even extended friendship. For his father's sake, she had said, but to Emory, bedazzled by her beauty and overcome by the realization that she was actually his wife, it was more than enough . . . for now! All he needed was time; he would do the rest. He would make amends, court her. He would have her in the end. He must! Forlornly, he galloped on, knowing he had fallen into an abyss he never dreamed possible, drawn irresistibly to a woman who scorned him.

Ahead, Rachel followed the rutted road, trotting now. Cannily, Emory cut across the greening fields, putting Sultan over the scraggly hedgerows again and again. Just before Rachel reached the park, Emory intercepted her, bursting from the trees and forcing her to rein Hunter to a quick halt. She glared at him with a contemptuous look that would have withered a lesser man.

"Get out of my way!"

"No! Not until you let me explain."

"There's nothing to explain! As usual, your actions have spoken for you."

Emory had already admitted, freely, if only to himself, that he was in the wrong, but somehow her attitude angered him. His temper flared. He became belligerent.

"I've already said I'm sorry, dammit! I'll say it again if you wish to make me crawl!"

"Sorry?" spluttered Rachel. "You snatch me from my saddle, put me in fear of my very life, and now think it enough to be sorry?"

"I didn't know it was you," Emory said contritely. "And besides, I wouldn't have hurt you."

"That's enlightening," she snapped. "And just what were your intentions that night . . . kidnapping, murder . . . or rape, perhaps?"

Emory said no, but it was an untruth. He had never forced himself upon any woman; he'd simply never had to. But had Rachel not escaped that night, surely he would have taken her, or tried to; that much had her beauty stirred and excited him. No woman, in the many he had bedded before, had ever touched his inner emotions so intensely, though that encounter in the drive had been so very fleeting.

Still, stung to the core by her contempt, Emory tried to make light of the situation. "Look here, Rachel . . . you're my wife. A man doesn't rape his own wife!"

"But you didn't know that then!" she said harshly. "You admitted as much!"

Emory laughed softly. "So I did, so I did. Well, I confess . . . when I saw the cape I thought . . . Well, no matter."

Again, Rachel was horrified. "A servant! That's what you thought, isn't it?" she demanded. She shuddered, thinking of Ferne, so young and tender. *Damn the man!* He was despicable! He reached out, and Rachel lashed at him in a swift motion, but he was just as quick, catching her slender wrist. He held it in a steely grip.

Rachel saw the boar's head ring then, the brilliant emeralds sparkling greenly in the morning sun. Suddenly, she was wild with fury. She remembered the night of the blizzard! Well, before that stormy night she had already been betrothed to him, yet it was clear that from the very start he had cared not a whit about her. She heard again the shrieks and peals of the serving girls as Emory romped with them in the kitchen below her crowded little room. She recalled his absence on their wedding day, and her wedding night . . . spent alone! Her cheeks burned with anger and humiliation.

In turn, Emory saw the flames of fury in her eyes, and without warning, he pulled her fiercely against his chest and kissed her. His lips closed roughly over hers as she clutched at his shirtfront to keep her seat. Her lips flamed, and she felt his tongue probing relentlessly. It was a searing embrace, over almost before it began; still, it left Rachel giddy and breathless, and her color mounted even further.

Watching her, Emory became petulant, and he laughed, amused at Rachel's embarrassed confusion. It was bitter laughter, raucous, grating harshly in her ears as she righted herself. She straightened the cocky little hat with her free hand, for Emory still held the other in a tight grip.

"I'll apologize one last time for my past behavior," he snarled at her, "especially for that bruise on your pretty little neck." He flicked lightly at her throat with his riding crop. "But that, my dear," he added, "is the end of it. I was a damned fool to believe you would think better of me if I spoke in soft terms and played the gallant. I am what I am! You'd better get used to it!"

"How dare you!" hissed Rachel, her eyes flashing.

"I do dare! I am your husband, have you forgotten? And you are my wife." He let go of her wrist. "Now, if you wish to run to Father, you may. It makes little difference to me if you choose to tattle." He leaned forward in his saddle, looking down at her, and touched his riding crop to her chin.

"That kiss, by the way, was delightful, for all you didn't help."

"You're an animal! As wild and unpredictable as that stallion you're riding."

He flashed her a wide grin, revealing marvelous white teeth, and patted Sultan's long neck. "Why, thank you, my dear . . . I guess we are alike at that."

He turned the big black, tipped a nonexistent hat in Rachel's direction, and then disappeared into the woods, leaving her sitting in the middle of the road, frustrated and angry.

"You beast!" she shouted after him. "You're an arrogant rakehell!" But he was gone; her parting words were unheard. She dismounted and, leading Hunter, walked through the park and back to the manor. He had bested her, just as he had always done. The truce was ended; the intimidation had begun.

Proceeding to Coltenham, Emory went to the Old Priory's tavern to pick up the mail, he told himself, yet he spent an hour in the taproom nonetheless despite the early hour. When he returned to the Hall, George was in the dining room having his breakfast. Hungry now, Emory joined him.

"Where's Rachel?" he asked his father matter-of-factly, wondering if he knew that they had already quarreled. Apparently not, he decided, else his father would surely make mention of it. Kissing Rachel had been a serious mistake, Emory knew that, but at the time, he had been unable to help himself. She had been so close, and she was so damned beautiful, even with fury coloring her face. Then too her scorn and contempt had crushed him, coming as it did now, just when he wanted so badly to gain her favor. He was sure that he had bungled everything, that she would avoid him now.

"She rode off with Peter about an hour ago," said George in answer to Emory's question. "They're going to start plowing today. Peter thinks they can begin planting in a few days."

"Plowing? Planting? Whatever are you talking about, Father?"

"Why, just what I said! It's a plan Rachel came up with . . . raising produce and livestock . . . enough to maintain the estate sufficiently and a good deal extra to market."

"Market?" Emory broke into laughter. "Marketing produce? My word, Father! Whatever for?"

"Why, for profit! What else?"

"Profit?" Emory roared again at that, as he filled a plate from Stoddard's well-stocked sideboard. He sat down next to his father and shook his head.

George nibbled at his toast. "Go ahead, laugh," he remarked. "I had my doubts, too, but now I think Rachel is on to something. Squire Paxton was here the other day, and he agrees. We are one of the last great estates in this area to come round to this way of thinking. Others have been turning a profit on their land for some time," he finished.

"So, the good squire is a gentleman farmer now, eh?"

"Not exactly. He leases his land to someone else who works it. But does it matter? Either way, the land produces income, and even you cannot deny that we badly need income."

Emory poured coffee for himself from a china pot. "And what about Rachel's dowry money?" he asked guardedly.

"What about it? A portion of it was set aside in turn for Ermaline's dowry, remember? The rest went to pay our debts . . . or yours, I should say. One hundred and twenty pounds, Emory, just for the care of that black alone!"

"It's gone, then?"

"Just about," explained the old man.

As it was, he told Emory, he felt he had lucked out concerning Ermaline's betrothal party. The elder Rowland was making a bid to regain his family's lost title. Using young Henry's recent appointment to the Queen's Counsel as ploy, Rowland hoped to impress some people with connections to the court, choosing to hold a gala engagement party at his elegant London townhouse. Naturally, George had consented, for it represented a tremendous saving for them all, enhancing Ermaline's future.

"Even so," George added, "by the time her wedding expenses are met, I shall have less than three hundred pounds cash money to see us into winter."

"I see," commented Emory, waving a napkin. "Essentially it is gone, and Rachel's . . . plan, I think you called it, is going to save us all from ruin, is that it? I'm afraid I shall need convincing," he scoffed.

His breakfast finished, George laid down his napkin and rolled away from the table.

"Rachel's journal is on my desk in the library. Study it, Emory. It's quite detailed, you'll find. We can discuss it again later if you like, but just now, Ermaline is going to push me onto the ballroom terrace while the sun is still warm . . . First time I've been out of doors in ten weeks," he added, smiling broadly.

Sprawled on the sofa in the library, Emory studied Rachel's journal at length, lured by his curiosity. *Well, she's thorough, I'll give her that,* he thought, scanning the journal's many entries. With Gaffy's help, Rachel had plotted the course of the agricultural enterprise carefully, right down to the number of fields to be plowed and the yield she expected from each. On one page she had even estimated her hoped-for profit . . . a respectable several hundred pounds. Emory was impressed.

With the journal propped against his solid chest, he was still stretched out there when Rachel returned to the manor later on. He heard her coming, and when she entered the library, still wearing the brown riding habit she had worn that morning, her beauty took his breath away.

When Emory's head popped up from the sofa, Rachel stopped abruptly, still smarting from his rough treatment of her earlier in the day. She turned and was almost ready to leave the room when she thought better of it. Sooner or later she must make a move to stand her ground, fend off his intimidations. Why not now?

As if reading her mind, Emory watched in amusement as Rachel pointedly opened the paneled door as far as it would go, then secured it with a heavy doorstop.

"Really now, Rachel, none of that is necessary. I promise to behave myself."

Having had enough of his promises, Rachel ignored him, deftly plucking her journal from his fingers as she swept across the room and up the steps to the little gateleg desk. He followed her there, stopping just long enough to pour himself a brandy along the way. Climbing the steps, he settled his long frame on the padded window seat.

"You've done your groundwork well," he told her with grudging respect. "But still, how can you be sure of the success of your . . . er, plan, I believe Father calls it?"

"I suppose we can't, really," she said, scratching some new entries into her journal. She answered without looking up, determined not to let him know that his presence bothered her. "Just the same," she continued, "it seems to me that the production end cannot fail. The land is sitting there, fertile and well rested, as you surely know. All that was required was an outlay of capital and the acquisition of manpower and equipment. Neither presented an insurmountable problem."

Holding the brandy glass up to the light, Emory studied its contents with interest. "Do tell! I was led to believe our coffers were just about empty. May I ask where this . . . capital comes from?"

"You may, although it is none of your concern," said Rachel rather curtly. "I have capital of my own, and I will save you the trouble of asking . . . Not a penny of it can be touched by anyone save myself."

"Tsk, tsk, Rachel. You sound as if you don't trust me."

"As if your past behavior gives reason to!" she retorted.

Emory bristled. Springing to his feet, he drained his glass and came to stand just behind her. Leaning closer, he rested one hand ever so lightly on her shoulder.

"It's not your money I want, my dear," he whispered into her ear before moving away to refill his glass.

He was needling. Blushing hotly, Rachel tried to ignore him. She closed the journal and placed it in the glass-fronted bookcase, as Emory dropped into a nearby chair.

"Tell me more about this plan. It will require laborers. Where do you propose to find them?"

Rachel replied that she had already found her field crews, enough to start the planting, at any rate. Further, she added, there were plenty of idle men scattered throughout the shire, men who had been displaced by machines, forced to accept poor wages or lose their cottages. Many had, in fact. These were the men Peter sought out; for half rent and half wages, they now worked at Guersten Hall and would share in the fruits of their labors.

"The air is clean here in the midlands, and there are no dreary tenements. We can guarantee their children will be well fed, at least," said Rachel.

Emory scoffed noisily. "There's little profit in feeding children!"

She was aware of that, and for just that reason, all the families newly situated in Hall village had older children who could also work somewhere on the estate, their wages determined by their usefulness. One young lad who had some experience as a carpenter's apprentice was now busy repairing broken stiles and rebuilding pens and byres. Another had been assigned to Stevens, as an increase in the herd had been planned. Still others were hard at work under Gaffy's supervision, weeding and beautifying Guersten Hall's once famous formal gardens. Then too, all these nimble youngsters would be needed later, in the orchards, she added, thinning fruit and picking the ripened harvest.

"No . . . if we have any problems at all," Rachel added, stepping down from the turret, "they will come at harvest time, for none of us knows the first thing about marketing, you see."

"And if you fail? What then?"

"Why, then I shall distribute the surplus to the needy, just as your grandmother did in her time. At best, I will be out a few hundred pounds!"

As she spoke, Rachel threw up her hands in a carefree gesture, and her face was wreathed in an infectious smile. Emory watched, fascinated. Lord, she was lovely! He got to his feet as she prepared to leave the room, unable to stop himself from moving close to her. When she stepped past him, his arms flew out and drew her into an embrace. She extricated herself neatly, pushing against his chest with both hands.

"There will be none of that!"

"And why not?" said Emory cockily. "We are man and wife, are we not? And furthermore, I thought we were going to be friends."

Intimidating again, he caught Rachel's eyes and held them, while a mischievous half smile played about his lips. Calmly and unswervingly, Rachel answered his gaze and was exulted when it was he who looked away first.

"We are man and wife in name only, Emory . . . by your own dictum, if you recall. It was *you* who refused to share my bed, and it was *you* who absented yourself, sending another in your place."

"Dammit, I've already apologized for that, time and again!"

"I know that, but apologies won't wipe the slate clean. Understand this . . . I've had my fill! Being attacked by you the other night was the last straw. We are man and wife because of a set of circumstances over which I had no control. I came to Guersten Hall because I had no choice. I remain here because of my pride, your father's illness, and my duty to Rebecca. I am wise, at last, to your game of intimidation, Emory, and shall not fall victim to it ever again. I warn you, mind your manners!"

Rudely, Emory laughed at her, slapping his thigh at the same time.

"You? Warn me? Really, Rachel, don't be absurd! You haven't changed *that* much! I can still snap you like a twig anytime I choose. Besides, I have rights."

In a bullying gesture, he stepped forward, but Rachel held her ground, did not step backward as he had expected, nor did she move a muscle.

"Nonsense!" she fired off at him as he pressed even closer. "It was bad enough that you left me at the altar with your proxy, but you made a serious miscalculation when you chose not to claim those rights on your wedding night. Then, I would have submitted dutifully to you, drunk or sober, and honored those vows still ringing in my ears. But now that I have learned the truth, Emory Guersten, I owe you nothing! I am your wife, and I will be civil to you. Nothing more!"

"Now see here, Rachel! You go too far! I am master here . . . Have you forgotten that?"

"Master, indeed! You can't administer this estate and you know it, so step aside and I will do it in your stead!"

Spluttering with rage by now, Emory was tempted to strike her, went so far as curling his fingers into a fist.

"And what makes you so certain that you are in control?" he demanded.

"Money! My money!" shouted Rachel right back, her hands on her hips. "For it's my money that will maintain this estate, at least until the crops are harvested."

"Christ, Rachel, this is England! What belongs to the wife belongs to the husband. It's the law!"

"Not this, Emory. It's out of your reach, I saw to that! The moment you try to lay claim to it, the allowance will be cut off, and with it your father's comfort and peace of mind in his remaining years. You avoided the Hall when he needed you most . . . Will you now begrudge him the care he needs or the comforts he deserves in his old age, as well? Without my money, Emory, everything grinds to a halt. You won't even be able to afford clean straw for that black of yours!"

With that, Rachel whirled and hurried from the room, while Emory, stunned by her outburst, stood rooted to the floor. It wasn't just the sting of her words, but more the fact that she had dared to speak them, and it came as a shock to him to realize that she no longer feared him. Typically, for him, his emotions went from towering rage to grudging respect, intermingled with the knowledge, in his heart, at least, that her fury was justified. He had it coming.

So! he thought, when his temper had cooled. Rachel had bared her claws, turned into a hellcat, claiming that she was wise to his intimidations, his *game*, as she put it. He poured himself another drink and raised his glass to the open door.

"Well, we shall see about that," he said aloud, tossing down his brandy. "Yes, my little mouse, we shall see about that!"

CHAPTER FIFTEEN

Rachel waylaid George in the upstairs salon later that very evening. The day had given way to a wild night. A cold rain and draughty winds buffeted against the French doors, threatening to burst them open. In an attempt to escape from the damp chill, George had maneuvered his wheelchair frightfully close to the flickering fire. He was miles away, lost in thought.

"Here, here," said Rachel, moving the chair away from the hearth. "You'll set yourself afire."

"Hmmm . . . how odd you should say that, Rachel. Your father made that very statement only a few months ago, in this very room, matter of fact." He patted Rachel's hand. "A lot of water has gone over the dam since then, hasn't it, my dear?"

"Yes, and there's more to spill yet, I'm afraid. I want to talk to you about Rebecca."

Emory, slouching in a chair behind them, and unseen by Rachel, stood up in a movement so sudden that Rachel jumped. George frowned, having noticed Emory's black mood and Rachel's forced pleasantries during dinner. His eyes narrowed, watching them, as Emory crossed to the fireplace. With a sooty poker, he stirred the logs and added another.

"Perhaps we ought to convert to coal, Father. It's cleaner and more efficient, and you can get quite close to a coal stove without going up in flames."

"Bah!" said George, waving his ever-present walking stick in the air. "Wood was good enough for my ancestors, and wood is good enough for me!"

"Besides," contributed Rachel, "the wood is free. We cut the logs ourselves in the Great Wood. The coal would have to be purchased and transported."

Emory turned to face his wife. "You're right, of course!" he snarled, and sneering, he stalked from the room, muttering all the while, "As if I don't know where the damned logs are cut!" When he was gone, Rachel took a seat near George's wicker chair.

"Oh, dear," she groaned. "I think I spoke out of turn."

"Don't fret," sighed the old man. "He came in here an hour ago, clearly spoiling for battle. I let him down; I'm just not up to it tonight. Besides, one quarrel a day should be enough, even for him."

"I was hoping you wouldn't hear about that," Rachel replied softly, remembering the dreadful scene in the library earlier.

"Ah, well . . . I was in the dining room taking my tea early, and the door was open . . ."

"I'm sorry, George. I know you dislike unpleasantries, but really, I had to put him in his place."

"Think nothing of it! You handled the situation just right, I think, only I know Emory, and I feel it my duty to warn you. He will accept that putdown as a challenge, mark my word. He'll try to regain the upper hand. Be on guard for it!"

Rachel smiled. So, again the gauntlet was thrown. Before she could make any further reply, Emory burst into the room, without knocking. In one hand he carried a crystal decanter.

"I seem to have mislaid my glass," he said in a polished tone. "Have you seen it? Ah, *there* it is!" He crossed the room and retrieved the glass from a little table next to the chair he so recently vacated. "Well, ta ra! I'm away to my room."

He went out, shutting the door behind him.

"You see, my dear?" said the old man. "There are plenty of glasses right downstairs, just where he found the decanter. Emory knows full well that we both disapprove of his drinking. He was hoping that one of us, at least, would make an issue out of it. But come, come," he added, changing the subject. "What's this about Rebecca?"

"She'll be here on Sunday, bag and baggage, for my father is due any time now."

"Well, it is only right that she come here, as I said before. She is welcome, whatever happens. Tell her that. We'll have a full house on Sunday, then?"

"A full table," replied Rachel, kissing him good night. "Eleven, to be exact."

The great house became still. Abed, Rachel had just pulled up the covers, preparing to blow out the lamp when there was a loud thundering at her door. She jumped, quite startled by the noise. It wasn't knocking; it went beyond that. Someone was pounding, first with a fist and then with the flat of the hand. Throwing off the covers, Rachel was just about to step out of her bed when Emory shouted.

"Rachel! *Rachelll!* Open this damn door! I want to talk to you!"

Rachel sat poised and tense on the edge of the bed. What nonsense was this? He sounded almost drunk; she could tell by the slurring of his speech. Emory pounded again . . . and again.

"I know you're not asleep, Rachel," he cried. "Open this door! I'm y' husband! I have a right to come in."

He rattled the knob, and Rachel got off the bed, drawing on a filmy negligee over her nightdress. The door was not locked; from her very first night at Guersten Hall it had never been locked. All Emory had to do was turn the knob. He could walk right in!

Rachel recalled her father-in-law's words, spoken just hours before. Emory would challenge her, he had warned. Squaring her shoulders, she went to the door, stood a moment, and then pulled it open.

Propped on one elbow, Emory was leaning nonchalantly against the doorjamb, his fist raised to pound yet again on the thick oak door. He was wearing only a nightshirt, and the contours of his muscular body were outlined beneath it in the dim light of the hall. Brazenly, he grinned down at her.

"Did I frighten you, my dear?"

He wasn't really as drunk as she had thought him to be, and intuitively Rachel recognized what he was up to. He was merely playing his *game* again. Clearly, he had no intention of bursting into her room, content to satisfy himself with the knowledge that he had undoubtedly terrified her.

"Go back to bed, you drunken fool!" she hissed at him. She looked up and down the hall, expecting to see Ermaline or one of the servants coming at a run, and she was much relieved to see that he had not yet disturbed the entire household. "Go to bed!" she repeated angrily.

"Whatever you say, Mistress Guersten," Emory mumbled with an unsteady bow. He turned and sauntered off toward his own room. Surprised that he had given up so easily, Rachel watched him go, not amused when he pretended to stagger and stumble. But Emory's next move came as a complete shock; approaching his own door and the circle of light that flooded from it, Emory reached down and grabbed the end of his nightshirt. Chuckling, knowing full well that Rachel was still watching, he peeled it off in a quick movement that barely ruffled his hair. Stepping into the lighted doorway, he started to turn around.

Rachel was too quick for him. When his bare bottom came into view, she drew in her breath and shrieked; she whirled, leaping back into her room and slamming the door shut, all so quickly that her negligee was caught fast in the jamb. Turning the knob a bit, she snatched the fabric free and then bolted the door.

Returning to her bed, Rachel sat stock still for a few moments, and then began to giggle, softly at first, but soon laughing uncontrollably. She threw herself across the bed and buried her face in the pillows, as tears of laughter filled her eyes.

On the far side of the wall, Emory gloated. He poured himself another drink. When he heard Rachel's bolt shoot home, his befuddled mind assumed he had won the match. Parading around the room stark naked, he stopped now and then to press one ear to the wall that separated them. He listened intently, chortling aloud when he heard muffled sounds coming from the other side.

"Ha! She's weeping! Good . . . my backside must've upset her!"

He pounded on the wall and raised his glass high. "Here's to you, little mouse!" he shouted gleefully. "Forget not who is the master around this place!"

Rachel laughed all the harder at that, while Emory, quite pleased with himself, jumped into bed and pulled up the covers. He was asleep almost instantly.

In the morning, Rachel was awakened by a repeated tapping at her door. The room was still dark. *What time can it be?* she wondered. Was it him who came back again?

"Come in," she said defiantly.

"I can't," returned Stoddard. "The door's bolted. I brought yer coffee."

"Since when did you take to locking y' door?" she asked once Rachel admitted her.

Shrugging, Rachel went to the windows, searching for a plausible answer. She opened the draperies just in time to see Emory and Sultan leaving the stable yard. Emory was watching her window; he waved gallantly. Rachel snapped the draperies closed again.

Damn him! she thought. He knew now that she rose early and went riding every day. Did he intend to spoil that too, waylaying her when she least expected it?

"Leave the coffee!" she fumed. "And don't worry, Stoddard, you won't find my door bolted again. I'm not afraid of him!"

"Him? Who?"

"Never mind! Go away!"

Bewildered, the cook left the room, muttering to herself. Rachel did not touch her tray; instead, she got dressed hurriedly, choosing her comfortable leather breeches and a lightweight jacket. Downstairs, she went into the dining room, where Stoddard was laying the sideboard.

"Tell Master George I will join him here for breakfast at nine," she said, drawing on her gloves.

"Emory said the same thing. Are ye riding out together?"

"Decidedly not!" Rachel snapped.

Stoddard went back down the stairs to her kitchen, talking to herself. "Ah, Emory," she mumbled, "me thinks yer the burr under m'lady's saddle this morning. Step lightly, laddie, step lightly."

Once outside, Rachel marched across the wide yard to the stables. She was earlier than usual, but Pug had seen her coming. Tightening Hunter's girth, he handed Rachel the reins. Her leather breeches were old hat now to the stable boys, and without a word, Pug tipped his cap and cupped his hands. With his help, Rachel boosted herself into the saddle, and pointedly, she turned Hunter in the opposite direction of the one taken by Emory.

Eventually, Emory trotted down the hill that led into Hall village. He did a double take when he spied Hunter tethered outside Gaffy's neat little cottage. Sultan was lathered, for Emory had spent most of the last hour crisscrossing the estate at a hard gallop trying to find her.

"She fooled us, Sultan. She knew I'd look for her, so she's been hiding here like a mouse in a hole."

Not wanting a scene at the cottage, Rachel went outside at once when Emory arrived. This time it was his turn to gasp. He did, sucking in his breath when he spied Rachel's leather breeches. Patently, Rachel ignored him, preferring to use the mounting block rather than accept his help into the saddle. With a smile and a wave for Gaffy and Granmam, she trotted away before Emory was even mounted. When he caught up again, they rode side by side for a while in silence. Finally, Emory pointed to her breeches.

"I hope you're not trying to prove who wears the pants around here, Rachel."

"Why no, Emory," Rachel said sweetly. "Besides, there's no need, is there, since we both know already."

Wishing it were her neck, Emory's fingers tightened around the reins, and he gritted his teeth as their eyes met. Glinty green gave way to sable brown, eyes so strikingly clear that Emory saw his own reflection in them. He had thought to find them red rimmed and swollen.

"You're looking remarkably beautiful this morning, Rachel, for someone who spent the night weeping."

With a derisive laugh, Rachel turned on him. "You fool," she said. "I wasn't weeping; I was laughing!"

She jammed her heel into Hunter's side and rode away, while Emory sat in the middle of the road, doing a slow burn as Rachel's laughter trickled back to him over her shoulder.

And so it went. Daily, the friction between them mounted; the very air became charged whenever they were alone together. While Rachel continued to keep her busy schedule, Emory followed her around idle, usually with a glass in hand. One moment he was pleasant and charming, the next he needled and teased, and though Rachel gave as good as she took, she soon tired of fending off his advances. Emory never missed an opportunity to touch her, coiling an arm about her waist or trailing his fingers lightly across her breast. He never passed her door without tapping, and nightly he pounded on the wall that separated them, hoping to raise some response. There was none, and to the best of her ability, Rachel ignored him. It wasn't easy, for whether he was being charming or obnoxious, Emory Guersten was very persistent.

That Sunday dawned bright and sunny, but within two hours, dark clouds blotted out the sun, and it began to drizzle. By noon it was pouring steadily.

Sir Hugh Chandler arrived first, in a small closed carriage; neither Adele nor the girls were with him. Instead, he brought with him a powerfully built man of about thirty, recently engaged by Sir Hugh to be George's new manservant. Standing half a head taller than Emory even, Angus Maxwell-MacKinder was every inch a Scotsman, with any number of years in service as a valet behind him.

"His last employer passed away recently," explained Sir Hugh to George, seated by a window in the drawing room. "He comes well endorsed, and he was highly recommended by Dr. Ferguson, who knows your requirements. He's a likeable chap, though I must admit a bit stiff and formal."

"He seems a bit down in the mouth to me," replied George, peering through the doorway at Maxwell-MacKinder standing in the reception hall.

"Not really. He's a family man, and his wife and children are still up in York. I suspect he's just lonely. If he works out, perhaps they can join him later."

Sir Hugh left the drawing room, and George summoned his new man to his side.

"Stand easy, lad," he said to the younger man. "Have you ever been employed in the midlands before?"

"No, sir, Mr. Guersten. I've never been this far south even, in fact." MacKinder's voice was soft, and he spoke with a curious Anglicized burr.

"Well, you'll like it here, I'm sure. After you've been here awhile, you'll wonder how you ever stood those damned moors. Sir Hugh tells me you have a family."

"Yes, Mr. Guersten. A bonnie wife and two bairns, sir, both boys."

"Good," said George. "A man needs sons. Sir Hugh assures me your credentials are in order, and I'm certain we shall get on well enough. However, there are a few things I would like to impress upon you. Because of my impairment and the intimate duties you will be called upon to perform, ours will, of necessity, be a personal relationship. I find Mr. Guersten much to stiff for my taste. When we are alone together, I wish to be called George. Is that clear?"

"Yes, sir," replied MacKinder in a respectful voice.

"Furthermore," continued George, "there is no way on God's earth I can get my tongue around Maxwell-MacKinder every time I need you. I shall call you Angus."

MacKinder nodded.

"Lastly," added George, cocking his white head, "you will soon discover a number of relationships under this roof that may trouble you at first. Foremost among these is that of my son and his wife. Emory puts up a noisy front, but Rachel is a stalwart young woman. She can handle him. Just ignore their bickering. Do you understand?"

MacKinder didn't, but he shook his head anyway.

George covered his mouth. "They're newlyweds," he whispered.

"Oh," said the valet, not at all sure how that explained anything.

"And Angus," added George, "there must be an empty cottage in Hall village that would suit your family; we'll have you all back together again in a month's time. Now, wheel me out there."

With his stick, George motioned to the reception hall, where Emory and Rachel stood arguing at the foot of the stairs. The dispute was over MacKinder's quarters. Emory had summoned one of Pug's boys, instructing the lad to take MacKinder's bags up to the third floor.

"No," interrupted Rachel. "The second floor is better. He should be at hand in case your father needs him during the night."

"The third floor," insisted Emory, "with the rest of the servants. We'll string a bell."

Rachel won. Angus was settled in a small but adequate room at the top of the back stairs.

"You'll be quite comfortable there," she said, turning to MacKinder. "It has good light and a small fireplace. Peter will explain your duties, and Stoddard will help you get settled. I'll meet with you tomorrow to answer any questions you may have."

As George predicted, Guersten Hall was full that day. Adele's coach rumbled up the drive not too long after Sir Hugh's, and Ermaline, a vision in bottle-green silk, rushed down the stairs to greet her cousins. The change in her was quite remarkable, and at any other time Emory would have been duly impressed by it, but today, like every other since his return to the Hall, his eyes were for Rachel alone.

Lounging against the marble balustrade, ever-present glass in hand, Emory watched and fumed inwardly, feeling a bit like the outsider. The whole family, it seemed, had succumbed to her charms. He was fairly seething when Duncan Ferguson arrived and he saw Rachel greet him so warmly. During the introductions, Emory was quick to note how Duncan's hand rested ever so lightly on her arm, and how she allowed it to remain there. *Christ,* he thought, *I'm her husband, but I can't touch her!* Despite those feelings, Emory was forced to be polite to the tall doctor; after all, hadn't the man saved his father's very life? Jealousy again overwhelmed Emory. For him it was a new emotion, one he couldn't cope with.

His heart softened, however, when he saw Rebecca, her gentle beauty heightened by her advancing pregnancy. Still, she looked so fragile and delicate that Emory feared for the child she carried, and he sent out a silent message for his brother's quick return.

Dinner was announced, and in the dining room Rachel's instructions had been carried out letter perfect. The appointments on the lace-covered table were just right; silver gleamed, crystal sparkled, the table laid with a dainty set of old Limoges that Emory could not recall seeing in years. Its pattern was a simple one, and Rachel had chosen a low centerpiece of shiny leafed greens from the conservatory to complement it. Mixed among the dark green foliage were clumps of star-of-Bethlehem blossoms, waxy white and tinged with bright green edges, a perfect foil for the tall white candles set randomly among the leaves.

"My word," George said, echoing Emory's thoughts, "I haven't seen this china in a long time."

"And the centerpiece is exquisite, as well as unusual," remarked Adele, as they all took their places.

Rachel flushed with pride; she touched her fingertips lightly to the little star-of-Bethlehem flowers.

"The green and white took my eye," she laughed. "They remind me of Scofield ribbons."

All the ladies present were by now familiar with Eleanora's distinctive packaging; they murmured their consent, though Rachel's comments flew by the gentlemen without recognition.

The meal that Stoddard produced was superb. It began with a robust soup, included a tenderloin of beef so large it was trundled from the serving pantry on a cart, and ended with a rich cake smothered with clotted cream and brandied peaches, served up in a silver dish.

Ermaline and her cousins went to the music room afterward, while Rachel and Rebecca settled in the green-and-rose drawing room with Louisa and Adele. The gentlemen stood as the ladies left the room, all except George, and then settled themselves around the table again to enjoy their cigars and brandy.

"I understand you've just returned from London, Doctor," remarked Sir Hugh.

"Aye, and a more squalid place I've never seen," answered Duncan.

Emory interrupted. "Oh? I rather fancy the place myself," he said, blowing smoke. "The clubs, the salons . . ."

George laughed roundly and turned in his seat toward the doctor. "Did you know, good Doctor, that there are near a thousand clubs in London? I venture Emory could tell you the decor in at least half of them."

Twirling his brandy, Emory scowled darkly under the criticism.

"Ah, well," said Duncan, easing Emory's discomfort, "I'm outside that circle, anyway. Mine was a business trip; a colleague is working with the Bow Street coppers, and there is an opening on his staff. He wondered if perhaps I might be interested."

"And are you, Doctor?" asked Sir Hugh.

"No, not at all, as it turned out," Duncan replied. "While I'm not averse to working with the poor, I prefer to help the children and not the scurrilous types my policeman friend sees daily."

"They are a sorry lot, all right," George agreed, "but I wonder if we can blame them. For hundreds of years their lives have been almost unaffected by the changes engineered by those at the top. Somehow, I have a feeling that this industrial revolution will change the order of things in this world. Nothing will remain as it was . . ."

"Come, come, Father," interjected Emory. "It will be years before any of these things radically change England, let alone the world."

"You're wrong," sighed George, shaking his finger in Emory's direction. "In your lifetime alone, more changes will be wrought than you can begin to imagine. You young ones must alter your thinking . . . be ready for them."

"I agree," commented Sir Hugh. "Very soon we shall discover our world drastically enlarged as communications and transportation improve; there will be a greater demand for British goods, and in turn, we will ourselves be flooded with all manner of foreign goods, from China silks to Spanish oranges."

"To say nothing of good rum and fine brandy," joked Emory, raising his glass.

Duncan finished his brandy and stood up. "If you please, gentlemen, I have patients to examine. I'll start with you, George, if you've no objections, and then I'll take a look at Rebecca. Rachel tells me her mother is concerned about her well-being."

Emory called for MacKinder, and effortlessly, Angus carried George up to his room. After his examination, the old man was returned to the lower floor, and Rebecca wearily climbed the long stairs, followed by her mother and Duncan.

It was quite late in the afternoon, already dark and still raining heavily, when Louisa and Duncan came back down the stairs and rejoined the others in the drawing room. Rebecca remained upstairs, resting on Rachel's big bed.

"All's well," Duncan assured Rachel when he saw her anxious face, "but see if you can't get her to rest more often."

Emory, leaning on a chair off to one side of the room, watched them jealously with icy eyes, until Rachel moved away from Duncan's side and went to join her mother on the little loveseat in the corner. Only then did Emory take a seat, just near the door, and thus, he was the first to hear the heavy portico door slam with a muffled thud. Cocking his head, he heard soft footsteps as they moved along the long gallery at the front of the house. They stopped near the door of the reception hall.

"*REBECCA!*"

The shout, croaked but loud, filled the vast space beneath the vaulted ceiling with reverberating echoes. Everyone in the room started; all save George scrambled to their feet and went to the door of the drawing room.

"It's Edward!" cried Emory, just as Edward shouted again.

"*REBECCAAA!*"

Edward stood at the entrance of the marble entrance hall, soaked through to the skin. Rivers of water runneled from his cape and puddled at his feet. His hair was plastered wetly to his scalp. He was thin, haggard, and unshaven, and there were deep circles under eyes that stared unseeing at them all, though he fixed his attention on Louisa.

"Where is she?" he demanded of her. "I know she's here!"

Drawn by the shouting, Ermaline opened the door to the music room, Charlotte and Olivia crowding close behind her. Adele, slipping from her position next to Rachel, crossed the reception hall in front of Edward and shooed the younger women back into the room, closing the door again.

A soft whimper then attracted their attention, and all eyes turned to the staircase. Rebecca stood at the top, leaning heavily on the balustrade with one hand, clutching at one of Rachel's dressing gowns with the other. The loose coat did little to conceal her rounded abdomen. Her hair, loosed from its ribbons, fell free about her shoulders in a dark mass. Another pathetic moan escaped her lips.

Edward stood frozen, looking up. On shaking limbs, Rebecca started down the stairs toward him, the dressing gown fluttering lightly over the steps behind her. Her eyes never left Edward's face. At the landing she wavered, unable to proceed further, and still clutching the balustrade, sank slowly to her knees.

Concerned, Rachel made a move to go to her sister's aid, but Emory, behind her, slipped an arm about her waist.

"Leave them," he said in her ear, in a voice shaky and low.

Over and over Rebecca whispered Edward's name soundlessly, seen but unheard as it formed on her lips. At last Edward moved; in the space of a second he was on his knees at Rebecca's side. For a long moment they did not embrace, nor even touch each other. Then, while water dripped about them, Edward collected his beloved Rebecca into his arms, enveloping them both in the sodden cape. Rebecca was still holding the banister in a tight grip; one by one Edward unwound her cold fingers from the icy marble, and picking her up, he carried her up the stairs to his room.

George coughed discreetly. "Come," he said, "love is a private matter."

Emory's arm was still coiled loosely about Rachel's waist; he turned her slowly until she faced him. She raised her face and, looking up at him, saw the passion that smoldered behind his green eyes. Her own heart pounded rapidly, too, though she couldn't say why.

"Someday," Emory whispered hoarsely to her, "I hope you will look at me like that."

Releasing her abruptly, he stepped around the corner and went out the portico door. Ignoring the downpour, he walked Edward's bedraggled horse to the stables.

CHAPTER SIXTEEN

An eerie quiet settled over the mansion, and all of them were locked into their own thoughts by the scene of raw emotion that had unfolded on the stairs. For Rachel, the adoration Rebecca held for Edward served as a profound reminder that the love of no man graced her own heart. Even worse, she admitted to herself, she knew so very little about love. Why, even Emory, rogue that he was, fully understood what had passed between the reunited lovers that rainy afternoon.

Having been prepared by Rebecca, Edward's reunion with his father took much the same vein as Emory's. There was surprise and shock, followed by guilt, but where Emory had retained his arrogance still, Edward was almost pathetic in his despair. On his knees, he begged his father's forgiveness.

"I was wrong, Father," he said, sobbing freely, "and I'll do all in my power to right that wrong, but just now my only concern must be Rebecca. I never should have gone away, should have confronted her father and confessed our relationship instead."

"I doubt it would have done much good at the time," said George in somber tones. "Her father had other plans for Rebecca then. Now, in her condition, he'll be forced to relent, but be warned, Edward . . . He won't like it! Men like Brenham don't like to be backed into corners. Then too, you stayed away so damned long, even I began to wonder if you hadn't seduced and abandoned the girl."

"I didn't, Father, I swear! It simply never dawned on either of us that Rebecca might have a child. When I saw her on the stairs, I thought my heart would stop."

Edward's absence was explained away in a minimum of words. He had turned away from the gaming tables empty-handed, having lost all he had gained from the sale of the pilfered coronet. He had called upon every source he knew, but none could, or would, make him a loan, and fraught with despair that he had failed Rebecca miserably, he'd borrowed a page from Emory's book and spent the last of his change getting drunk. When he awoke, he found himself aboard a Jamaica-bound spice ship, well at sea.

"Shanghaied?" asked his father in disbelief.

"So I believed, but the mate showed me my signature, entered into his log. It was just a drunken scribble, but it was mine, all right. I'd thought to run away, I guess, but my troubles were just beginning, for the *Wood Lark* was a sluggish merchant ship, and I was just a lowly seaman, and not a very good one at that. I puked all the way over, and all the way back. I was too ashamed to write, and you know the rest . . . As soon as we docked, I hired a horse and came straight home."

"Well," said George with a measure of sympathy, "you've passed from boy to man, son. 'Tis unfortunate you chose to do it the hard way, but your love for Rebecca seems to have survived intact. Hopefully, we can arrange to get you married at once; time will do the rest."

Still, Edward fretted. "When I think how Rebecca has suffered," he wailed, "all alone . . ."

"Not alone, Edward, not alone," interrupted his father, making a silencing gesture with his good hand. "Here at the Hall everyone has been understanding, knowing just how much you two really do love each other. Besides that, Dr. Ferguson has been looking after Rebecca's health. She has had love and consideration, Edward, thus far, and there have been no recriminations. But," he warned, "Brenham knows naught of this yet, for he's been away some months himself."

Briefly, George explained to his son how last winter's storms had taken their toll on Benjamin's enterprises. "Aye, it was a hard winter for those who make their fortunes in shipping," he concluded. "And it will be months yet before the insurance companies straighten out the mess. No doubt, when Brenham returns to the midlands, he'll be in a vile mood anyway, so you'd best prepare yourself to stand and face his wrath!"

"What do you think he will do?" Edward asked querulously.

"Well, my boy, if he doesn't kill you first, he may just force you to marry the girl!" said George, poking Edward with the tip of his walking stick. Then, in a more serious tone, he offered some advice.

"Go and discuss it all with Rachel, Edward. Follow her lead; she's got more good sense than the rest of us put together. She'll know best how to handle this matter."

Edward cornered Rachel that same afternoon on the far side of the garden while Rebecca napped in a darkened bedroom. Troubled and grim, he led his sister-in-law to a stone summerhouse set atop a little rise that overlooked acres of hedgerowed fields. Below them, the spread of patterned greensward was broken here and there by the color of freshly turned earth, and a surge of pride coursed through Rachel's breast at the sight of it all. She turned her back, however, on the pleasant scene, for Edward's problems demanded all her attention. She found his evident despair distressing, as he paced back and forth before her on the stone floor.

"For heaven's sake, Edward, do sit!" she blurted.

"What shall I do first?" he asked her bluntly, settling opposite her, his elbow on his knees.

"Are you still anxious to marry Rebecca?"

"Of course!" he shouted, jumping to his feet again. "Now more than ever!"

"Please sit down, Edward! I was more than certain you would say that, and it being so . . . why, then, you and Rebecca have only to choose the day. The rest of us will abide by whatever you two decide. But it should be soon, Edward, very soon. Rebecca is anxious to become a bride before she becomes a mother, and time is running out."

"There is still the matter of your father." Edward's simple statement was accompanied by a look that reflected the shame he felt.

"True," replied Rachel, tapping a finger against her white teeth, "but just the same. Don't worry yourself to death about it. It's simply a matter of who will bell the cat." She smiled ruefully. "Who will it be? You . . . or me?"

"Why, *I'll* tell him, of course!" said Edward, leaping to his feet yet again. "I've never considered otherwise, despite my behavior."

"Yet I know his moods so much better than you," Rachel said frankly. "And then too, Mother can back me . . ."

"No!" cried Edward, resuming his pacing. "I won't hear of it. To do so would be cowardly, and I've been cowardly long enough. I shall face his wrath alone. After all, I *did* seduce his daughter!"

A contemplative smile crossed Rachel's lips hearing that, one that she could not hide. As if Rebecca hadn't been a willing party to that seduction! Even Edward managed a weak smile, which erased the tragedy from his handsome features momentarily. The doomsday air faded away then, as both of them turned at a shout from the garden, where Emory appeared in view, carrying Rebecca, doll-like and fragile, in his arms.

"Look what I found on the path," he said jovially, depositing Rebecca on the bench next to her sister, and then, while Edward hovered over her protectively, Emory offered an arm to Rachel.

"Come," he said. "I'm sure Rebecca didn't wander this far from the house just to be with us."

While Rebecca blushed happily, her hand safely enclosed in Edward's, Rachel stepped down from the summerhouse, prepared to leave the lovers alone. Edward caught her eye.

"It's only a matter of when, then," he whispered.

Rachel nodded. "He returned last night, I hear. I suggest you go at once, while your courage still rides high."

"Whatever was all that whispering about?" queried Emory, as they headed back up the path to the manor house together. Enamored by her nearness, he was aware only of her arm, draped lazily through his, and of her woodsy perfume, its haunting fragrance wafting up to him with each step she took. It was a distinctive blend, an unnamed scent given to her by Eleanora Scofield, who had known intuitively that it was right for her. On any other, that particular fragrance would seem unnatural, its outdoorsy scent out of place, especially in a crowded drawing room.

Rachel waved to George and Ermaline settled on the ballroom terrace and, withdrawing her arm, started up the terrace steps.

"I think," she said in answer to his question, "that your brother has finally grown up." Behind her, Emory frowned, wondering if her remark was somehow a putdown of him.

Upon rising the next morning, Rachel learned from Effie that Edward had already ridden to Brenham Manor and returned; he was at that very moment in the morning room with Rebecca. Slipping on her riding clothes, she joined them there. Ruffled and shaken, but still in one piece, Edward offered her a weak smile.

"How did it go?" Rachel asked hesitantly.

Edward shrugged. "Well enough, I guess. Your father railed quite a bit, as was his due, but all in all he managed to control his rage. Most of what you see," he said, referring to his own dishevelment, "was caused by quaking knees and a churning stomach."

"But what did he say, specifically, when you told him about Rebecca?"

"Well, actually I didn't have to tell him. He already knew!" Always shrewd, Benjamin had surmised from Rebecca's absence and her mother's demeanor that something was amiss. He had weaseled the story from Louisa. "I'm ashamed to say the worst of his wrath had already fallen to your mother," Edward now added, while Rebecca wept softly, thinking of her poor mother, so gentle, so weak, pitted against Benjamin's terrible shouting and violent table-thumping.

"He's forbidden us to wed! I know it!" she sniffed, as Rachel tried to comfort her. "You just don't want to tell me!"

Over Rebecca's head, Rachel looked askance at Edward, whose pale face was wreathed suddenly in smiles.

"On the contrary, love," he said, falling on one knee before Rebecca. "He is *forcing* me to marry you, 'pon pain of imprisonment, he swore!" Passionately, Edward kissed his beloved's fingertips. "I can't think of any punishment I'd relish more!"

But Rebecca, distraught, found nothing amusing in Edward's words.

"What do you say? That he intends not to pursue the matter further? I don't ..."

"Hush, sweet." Edward drew her to her feet. "Go wash your face and join me for breakfast. My stomach is settled now, and suddenly I'm ravenous!"

On swollen feet, Rebecca headed for the door obediently. "I'll go," she said, "but I still don't believe Father gave in so easily."

"Nor do I," said Rachel when the door closed. "Just what *are* you saying, Edward? Surely there's more to this than what you told Rebecca."

"There is," he said, drawing a hand through his tousled hair. "Your father was expecting me ... last night, from what I gather. Only his pride stopped him from coming here and having at me."

"But what happened ... exactly? Where was Mother all this time?"

"I never saw her. Ferne admitted me to the library, and your father wasted no time giving me a proper tongue-lashing. I'm not complaining, I had it coming, but I fear his wrath now turns devious. While I'm delighted that he demands I marry Rebecca, you know that, still, I'm not sure what his reasons for doing so may be. Frankly, I suspect he seeks vengeful pleasure ... throwing us to the wolves, so to speak. He stated he intends to write Rebecca and the child out of his will, apparently to thwart me, for he believes I only want his money, through Rebecca."

"I don't believe it!" said Rachel, openly shocked. "It's small and petty, not at all like Father. Did he actually tell you that?" she asked, turning to Edward with narrowed eyes.

"Not in so many words, but he inferred as much, all the same."

"But that's preposterous, Edward. My father believes the Guersten fortunes to be secure; it was one of his sounder reasons for pushing me into marriage with Emory. He cannot know how low our finances are here at the Hall."

"I'll wager he suspects something by now. He seemed not to believe that I really want Rebecca to be my wife, that I've always wanted her. He scoffed openly when I spoke of love, perhaps because he knows that's all we have now."

Rachel dropped into a chair, shaking her head from side to side. "Poor Rebecca! The money matters not, but his scorn will crush her, for she adores Father."

Benjamin had abandoned Rebecca, just as Rachel had suspected he might. Without funds, how could Edward possibly care for Rebecca's needs at this point in her maternity? Rachel recalled again that night she had made her decision to remain at Guersten Hall, now more thankful than ever that she had done so. As long as she had breath, she vowed, she would see to it that her sister had proper care.

It was time to confront her father, Rachel thought, getting to her feet. She would go to Brenham Manor and have it out. After Hunter was brought around, she mounted quickly and galloped straightaway across the fields, thundering through the Small Wood and across the wooden footbridge. At the manor, she found the front door half open, the kitchen cat perched on the sill, sunning herself.

Angry at her father's renunciation of Rebecca, Rachel stamped her booted foot, sending the poor cat scooting for cover across the courtyard. At once, she was ashamed, for the damned cat had done nothing, but such was the temper of her mood.

She found her mother in the morning room, sitting idle and pensive, with puffy cheeks and reddened eyes. Under Louisa's sleeve, even now, an ugly bruise was forming on one forearm, in just the spot where Benjamin's fingers had curled so cruelly. Though Rachel was never to know that, she was dismayed by her mother's general air of sadness, for there was little that could be offered to cheer her.

"Why didn't you wait, Mother?" was all she said. "We had already agreed that I would tell him. Barring that, you should have left it to Edward."

"I know," sighed Louisa, "but your father demanded the truth, and I couldn't put him off or lie to him. I've never lied to him. No, dear, it was best that I do it." She sighed again, and tears watered her eyes. "He was so angry! At Rebecca! At Edward, and most of all, at me," she added in a hurt little voice that cut Rachel to the quick. "But at least he's not angry with you this morning," Louisa ended, trying to smile up at her daughter.

"He will be soon enough," said Rachel, "for I mean to have it out. It is why I rode over."

"Oh, Rachel, do be careful! Don't stir him up again. He's threatened to cut Rebecca out of his will ... cut her off without a penny, and he'll do it, too. Your father isn't one to make empty threats. If he suspects that you shielded her, he'll cut you out, too. He blames *me* for not keeping closer watch on your sister, and perhaps it is my fault, but let it lie so! Remember, dear, he is hurt, and just now he is bitter and unhappy."

Slapping her riding crop across an open palm, Rachel spun around to face her mother at that. "Is he?" she cried. "And what of us? Rebecca, you ... me? That day in October when he met with George Guersten, he gave little thought to anyone's happiness except his own. Ah, Mother ... there is more to all this than just a desire to see a daughter well married, and I won't rest until I learn what it is."

"I think I know what it is, at last," said Louisa, laying her troubled head against the upholstered chair back. "I pieced it together, and I despise myself for being so blind; I should have guessed years ago. For some thirty-odd years now your father has spent his every free moment up on that bluff, staring across toward Guersten Hall. In the rain, the cold ... whatever the weather, still he went there."

"Guersten Hall? Do you suggest, Mother, that all this came about because Father covets Guersten Hall?"

By now Rachel's head was spinning. For months, she had been pummeled by one new and startling fact after another, each seeming more preposterous than the one before it. But this one was patently ridiculous, or so she believed at that moment.

"You may think so, Rachel, but it is the truth all the same. His beginnings were humble, you see, and despite all this," Louisa said, waving her hand in a sweep that took in the elegant room, "despite his wealth, the position he's earned, apparently he's ever been discontent. Even with me, perhaps!" She moaned, "Oh, how could I have loved him all these years, yet never suspect that he was so dissatisfied? Not that it matters, I guess; I couldn't give him what he wanted anyway."

"And what does he want, Mother? An estate? He has one! And he has great wealth, thanks to your inheritance! How could Guersten Hall add any measure of happiness to his life?"

"Lineage, perhaps," said her mother. "He hinted at it once or twice. Heritage, a past . . . a future. And George had those sons . . ."

Rachel picked up her gloves, preparing to leave. "Rubbish!" she said indignantly. "You make him sound like a neurotic old woman!" although secretly she was convinced her mother might be right. At the door, she turned to face her mother, who remained in her chair.

"Just think," she muttered, thrusting one hand angrily into a glove, "if he had only minded his own business, had allowed Rebecca to marry Edward in the first place, then he would have *exactly* what he covets, for the child Rebecca carries is presently the only heir to Guersten Hall. Father would have administered the estate in all but name, for George Guersten is an old man. He's also cash poor, by the way, and for a comfortable allowance, Emory would gladly have remained forever in London, childish and irresponsible, content only to savor life's vices to the fullest. Do you not see it, Mother? Father would be happy, Edward and Rebecca, too. Once Ermaline is safely wed, George will be content in his dotage, and all Emory ever wanted is to be rid of me!"

"And you, Rachel? What of you?"

"Me? I would be free, too, Mother, free to search for a love that can fill my heart completely, as Rebecca's does, for if there is one thing I have learned since leaving the academy, it is that! Without love, all else matters naught!"

Slamming the door behind her, Rachel mounted again and, soon afterward, crested the ridge at the top of Benjamin's bluff. There, her father sat stone-faced, his back pressed against his favorite boulder, while Patch nibbled at new shoots of grass just off the path. Dismounting, Rachel tethered Hunter near the same spot and approached her father, who did not speak, nor move, nor offer any sign whatever that even acknowledged his daughter's presence.

"Don't ignore me, Father! I came to talk to you."

"If you've come to tell me about Rebecca and her bastard, save your breath," he said without turning. "I've already heard the sordid story twice."

"What about Rebecca? She'll not be the first bride to stand before the vicar already pregnant, and she'll not be the last. Once wed, it will all be forgotten."

"Not by me!" snarled Benjamin.

Rachel's anger surfaced anew, as her father, having caused them all such needless grief, now sat, stiff and unyielding, pretending to be the injured party.

"Dammit, Father, don't take that pained tone with me!" cried Rachel, shocking Benjamin and surprising even herself at how easily the words rolled from her tongue. "Though you may find it easier to place the blame elsewhere, it's *yours* all the same, for Rebecca was already pregnant that night you and George blithely penned away my future! And it happened right down there . . . under your own nose!" she added, pointing to the vine-covered summerhouse which stood below them at the foot of the bluff. "They should have been allowed to wed months ago, for any fool could see they were hopelessly in love. Instead, it was me you married off, and that more to feed your own ego and secure yourself a place in society!"

"Oh, I know all about that!" she said, noting his furtive and startled expression. "But know this, even if my marriage to Emory had been sound, it might not have mattered, Father, for that society you covet doesn't always bend that far. To some, class distinction still exists. Despite his sons' behavior, George Guersten will still be a gentleman with his pockets turned out, while *you*, in spite of your money and your careful manners, will always be a merchant. You have great wealth and prominence in your own right; why is it not enough?"

Prodded by Rachel's denunciation, Benjamin's temper loosed in an explosion of bitter wrath, all of it aimed directly at her. He leapt from his place by the boulder and whirled, facing his daughter, his face purple with rage, for she had dared to finger the truth, something even Louisa had feared to do. A frightful quarrel then ensued, during which Rachel thought surely, again and again, that he would strike her in his rage. She stood her ground against him, pressing her point defiantly on

Rebecca's behalf. She made no progress on that score, though, for as the shouting continued, Rachel learned that Edward's suspicions were quite correct; Benjamin had indeed learned that the Guersten coffers were depleted, and therein lay the rub!

In January, it seemed, when Rachel and Emory were not seen anywhere socially, as Benjamin had hoped and planned, he sought to learn why. His discreet ferreting turned up the fact that Emory had still not assumed his new role of bridegroom, had not yet returned to Guersten Hall, ignoring Rachel completely, in fact. Further digging had uncovered news of Emory's diversionary side trip to Woodleigh Grange, in Kent, and there was no doubt, given his reputation and Lady Merrington's, that Emory went there at her invitation, and not the Lord's. Benjamin was appalled at the affront to his daughter and to his own pride as well. Then and only then did he do what he should have done in October . . . would have done, had his daughter's intended husband borne any name but Guersten. Using the same discretion, he sent Durklin about the city, seeking . . . and finding, the truth about George Guersten's net worth. In the end, while the old man's assets still outweighed his liabilities, Benjamin knew that it was Rachel's dowry, his own money, that had allowed Guersten to meet his debts, keeping his assets intact.

Those cold facts had drawn Benjamin up short, and he knew then that he had been bested by the old man. Worse, George Guersten had clearly gotten the better of the bargain, for besides the dowry, admittedly generous beyond belief, there was Rachel herself! Not the plain and weepy one remembered by them all, but a new one—accomplished, capable, and so beautiful! Too late had Benjamin realized she was worth her weight in gold in the marriage market. Furthermore, the giving away of his daughter, and a small fortune to boot, had brought him no closer to the possession of Guersten Hall, either in name or fact. And now, to complete his humiliation, there was Rebecca, well swollen with child by yet another Guersten, who, Benjamin believed, sought only to align himself to Brenham wealth.

It was all too much! Bellowing with rage, Benjamin's voice roared over the treetops, so loudly that Patch laid back her ears and trembled.

"Don't blame us because your pride has been bruised," hissed Rachel, standing her ground before him. "Just tell me what you mean to do so that I might plan for Rebecca and her child. Is it true that you intend to remove them from your will?"

"I do!" thundered Benjamin. "And perhaps you should suffer the same fate for harboring her! What do you say to that, missy?"

"Do it if you will," said Rachel in a calm and quiet voice, looking her father straight in the eye as she said it. "The die is cast! You forced me into marriage with a man who detests me, a marriage in which I have already suffered one repeated humiliation after another. If it pleases you now that I suffer the indignity of poverty as well, so be it. But know this, Father . . . you will not beat me, for I shall work the land at Guersten Hall with my own two hands, if necessary, to provide for myself and those of us at the Hall."

Benjamin caught his breath, choked by surprise. "You would provide for the Guerstens after the way that old man duped me? Hmmph! He's a fool, and you're a bigger one!"

"Let us say that George was foolish, Father, and he freely admits it. The rest of them are victims, no different than I."

Benjamin put an end to the argument by brushing past his daughter, and seizing Patch's rein, he mounted and turned to leave.

"As you wish," he said curtly. "I take responsibility for your presence at Guersten Hall, and accordingly I will see that you are comfortable. Your allowance will be continued, and your inheritance will be assured. But as for Rebecca, keep her! I wash my hands of her!"

"Father! How can you? Have you forgotten she's sickly and . . ."

"She seems to have forgotten it herself, in her romping with young Guersten. Despite your silly prating about love, Rachel, I believe Edward to be a fortune hunter, and neither he nor his bastard child will *ever* see a penny of mine. Now get out of my way! I've seen enough Guerstens for one day . . . you included."

With that, he rode away, and Rachel was left alone on the bluff, now curiously silent as the last echoes of her father's ranting and raving faded away. She was empty, felt sad, knowing the breach between them was now impassable. Oddly, now that she wanted to weep, no tears would come. With heavy steps, she started down the bluff, leading

Hunter all the way to the Small Wood before she mounted. Once in the saddle, she stared for a long time at the beautiful brick house where she had spent her childhood. Then, turning slowly, she rode back to Guersten Hall.

It is truly my home now, she thought, turning up the Hall's stone drive. *Mine and Rebecca's. For better or worse, our lot is cast with the Guerstens.*

CHAPTER SEVENTEEN

Rebecca and Edward were married the following Friday evening in a simple ceremony held in the library at Guersten Hall. Besides the family, only Louisa and Dr. Ferguson attended, Benjamin having already flatly refusing to see another daughter become a Guersten.

When the old vicar wheeled up to the porte cochere in a battered landau some minutes late, he was helped into the library by his assistant. After the young couple signed his register, the old man scrutinized their signatures closely for a long moment, and then, still bending over the book, tapped the page with a gnarled finger, peering through his wire spectacles at them.

"Did I not wed thee two already?" he asked in an ancient voice. "I confess being poor with faces, but I remember well thy names. I am sure I joined a Guersten and a Brenham in wedlock, not yon back."

"That was my brother, sir," replied Edward.

"And my sister," chorused Rebecca.

Redeemed, happy that his memory was not failing, the bishop cackled into his whiskers, looking pointedly all the while at his younger aide, who was not above whispering that the old man had outlived his usefulness.

For the ceremony, Betsey, the Hall's seamstress, had hurriedly fashioned a make-do wedding dress from a bolt of silk-faced satin found in an upstairs armoire. The powder-blue fabric was worked into a dress of draped folds, and over it, gathered and flowing, a swath of blue lace fell from shoulder to floor, completing the camouflage of Rebecca's advancing pregnancy as well as ever could be. Admittedly fragile and pale of cheek, Rebecca was truly beautiful as she stood beside Edward, her blue eyes brightened visibly by the blue of her gown.

There were no flowers and no music, just the brief rites that saw Rebecca and her unborn child, by the placement of Edward's hastily acquired ring, become Guerstens. Once done, the vicar and his aide departed, and Stoddard laid a small supper in the dining room for those that were hungry.

It was there that Rachel learned that her mother had quarreled bitterly yet again with Benjamin, and he, angry with them all, had stormed back to London, telling Louisa, from the steps of his carriage, that he did not know when he would return. Seeking reconciliation, Louisa was prepared to follow him. Rachel intervened.

"No, Mother," she advised. "Let Father's anger cool before you see him again. I will be in London ten days from now for Ermaline's engagement ball, and I'll call on him then. Perhaps by that time he will recognize that both his behavior and his words were predicated by anger and hasty judgment."

"I hope you are right," agreed her mother. "So much has happened, and his dreams have been shattered."

"Besides," added Rachel, "though Stoddard has promised to watch her carefully, Rebecca may need you while I'm away, for I shall be gone a fortnight, at least."

As night drew nigh, Edward escorted his pregnant bride up the long staircase. Rebecca was weary from the day's excitement, but the lovers were happy at last, and their wedding day, downplayed under the circumstances, would have passed quietly into oblivion had it not been for Emory. He got roaring drunk!

He began drinking shortly after breakfast. By midafternoon, when George admonished him for the second time, Emory became belligerent. Astride Sultan, he rode from the estate, heading for the taproom at Aylesbury. George fretted most of the day, fearing his son would disappear again, but Emory returned in time for the ceremony, well in his cups. His belligerence was now patently obnoxious; he squabbled with the servants and followed Rachel wherever she went, ogling openly. To forestall another battle, she avoided him when she could, ignored him when she could not, and spoke to him only when necessary. In his turn, Emory fumed and burned, watching jealously with those green, green eyes when Rachel accepted a cup of tea from Duncan.

When the doctor departed, Rachel, too, retired. Sitting at the secretary in her square bedroom, she penned a note to Eleanora Scofield, advising that she and Ermaline would be in London soon and offering some suggestions for Ermaline's ball gown. They were only suggestions, however, for Eleanora knew best; her eye for simple design and understated detail was better than any. For some reason, Ermaline had set her heart on something pink, and considering the highlights of her coppery tresses, Rachel had doubts about the suitability of such a color. But Eleanora would know what to do, and Ermaline had promised to abide by her better judgment.

Settling into bed with a book, Rachel heard Emory stumbling about in his own room, just next door. She heard him chuckle, then mutter to himself. She wished he'd simply go to bed, sleep it off. Near ten, Stoddard brought a nightcap of warm milk and spicy ginger cookies to Rachel's room.

"Y' best lock the door, ma'am," she advised when she heard the sound of a chair falling next door. It was followed by loud and vociferous swearing.

"Edward is just down the hall," said Rachel, without looking up from her book.

"Him? He's asleep already."

"Exactly where you should be, Stoddard."

Tarrying, Stoddard tidied up a bit and then left the room. No sooner had she closed the door than she opened it again, popping her head inside.

"If needs, call Angus! He's bigger!"

The disturbance from the next room quieted, and Rachel, propped against her pillows, read on. Engrossed in her book, she heard nothing, until near eleven, when Emory suddenly burst unannounced into her room. Throwing open the door, he lurched inside, carrying a decanter, and approached her bed. Wearing only a nightshirt, rakishly unbuttoned to the waist, and nothing more, his maleness was quite obvious under the white lawn.

While not immediately concerned or frightened, Rachel was flustered and tried to look away, but her eyes were drawn again and again to the sight of him. She blushed hotly, a fact that did not go unnoticed by him, as he stepped up to the corner of the bed and wrapped his free elbow loosely around one of the carved bedposts. His green eyes caught hers and held them, until Rachel was forced to look away.

The look in Emory's eyes began to dismay her then, for it was not desire she saw there, but lust, and even in her inexperience, she recognized it for what it was. As she watched, his lips curled into a presumptuous smirk, and she wondered if perhaps his insobriety was again feigned. She decided it might be real enough this time, though; he reeked of wine, and there were ruby spots across the front of his nightshirt where the wine had splashed and dribbled.

Emory's eyes caught hers, only it was he who looked away, to ogle the bodice of her nightdress, where frothy lace and satin ribbons tumbled from her throat and spread across her bosom. She was well covered, but his lecherous leer left her feeling naked. Her cheeks crimsoned, and her blood rose.

Under the covers, she clenched her fists. Before her, once again, stood the Emory of their childhood, brash, arrogant, and playing his damnable game again. Unless she put him down, and quickly, he would succeed again at that game. The thought disturbed her no end, for there was little doubt that tonight he meant to share her bed, by force, if necessary. She took a deep breath and slipped from the covers on the far side of the bed, the book still clutched in her hand.

"*Mister* Guersten! You have made a mistake. Your room is farther down the hall."

"Missus Guersten," he slurred, mimicking, "I have made no m'stake. I am master here . . . This is m' wife's room. I have a right to share it."

Looking ready to pounce on her at any moment, Emory carefully transferred the half-empty decanter from one hand to the other. His cockiness struck a responsive chord, and Rachel lashed out at him.

"Damn you!" she sneered. "You dare call me wife after all those months you ignored me and your behavior . . . and your drunkenness! You come here now expecting to share my bed! Never! Get out!" she screamed. "Get out!"

Emory straightened. He laughed, and the sound of it maddened Rachel all the more. Raising her arm, she threw her book at him. It sailed across the bed, striking him in the chest, and was followed in quick succession by a small clock and an empty inkwell, both of which missed their mark, striking the wall behind him with a loud noise. Storming to the door, Rachel pulled it open, even before the inkwell's splinters had settled.

"Leave!" she commanded. "At once!"

Even in his stupor, Emory covered well his surprise at being struck, and her tirade of angry words seemed not to disturb him. Just the same, she noted he was no longer laughing when he made one more attempt to grasp control of the situation.

"Or . . . ?" he threw at her.

"Or I'll have Angus throw you out! Now go!"

Passion vanished. Fury took its place, a fury triggered by Emory's realization that his *game* no longer worked. That knowledge, coupled with the contempt she held for him, made his blood boil. Oh, how he wanted to crush her, throw her upon the bed and prove who was master . . . once and for all!

But he made no attempt to move toward her, for one more realization pierced his numbed mind. Slowed by the wine he'd consumed, he was no match for her, as he had previously learned that night in the drive when she'd escaped his clumsy clutches. Glowering darkly, he strutted from Rachel's room and returned to his own, just as Angus appeared out of the gloom of the darkened hallway. He peered suspiciously after Emory.

"I heard a crash, ma'am. May I be of service?"

"Thank you, no, Angus. I dropped my book. Good night to you."

Closing her door, Rachel was tempted, for one long moment, to lock it, but returned to her bed bravely leaving the bolt still unlatched. She had sent Emory away without revealing exactly just how frightened she was. If he were to return again and find his entry barred, he would guess, and any newfound ground in their battle of wits would be lost. Apprehensively, she lay listening for a long time in the darkness, until finally, through the wall, she heard him snoring evenly. Then she too fell asleep.

Days passed, days in which Rachel's patience was tried relentlessly by Emory's discordant behavior. Outside the mansion, the estate ran smoothly, due for the most part to Peter's capable supervision. Acre after acre went under the plow, and where verdant greenness once sat idle, now fields of cabbage seedlings sprouted in straight orderly rows. Crops of turnips, beets, and carrots were sowed, and cultivation began in the strawberry fields, cleared of their winter hay cover, while more beds were readied nearby. Each day a great pile of brush and dead branches, pruned and carted from the orchards, was burned in an empty field. Each day, too, Gaffy made the rounds of the estate, riding about in a little wooden pony cart. He never interfered, merely sought Peter's ear whenever his expert eye spotted something gone awry or some instruction not followed to the letter.

The newly rebuilt byres were soon filled with ducks and geese, while in the meadows, the sheep grazed on acres of new grass. Swelled by the addition of white-faced Herefords and gentle Guernseys, the herd at the dairy had grown. Whitewashed and tidied, the barn was now spotless, and if Stevens still took nightly comfort from his flask, he was at least discreet about it.

Not so for Emory. Things were markedly different inside the mansion. The place was in a constant dither, and he was the cause of it all. His spree of intoxication lasted for days and nights, during which time he continued to quaff wine and ale. He quarreled with everyone, including Stoddard, his favorite, and when his father's plea for sobriety went unanswered, the old man recruited Edward, hoping he might inculcate some sense into his brother's befuddled mind. He too received an argument for his trouble, while Ermaline was reduced to prolonged tears, certain that Emory would never sober up, and just as certain that he would make fools of them all next week at the Rowlands'.

As for Rachel, she refrained from speaking to Emory. She kept out of his way, even missing her morning rides to avoid confrontation. She did, however, make some determined effort to stop his drinking. One by one the crystal decanters disappeared from their ready places in the library, the dining room, and even Emory's own room. In the butler's pantry, Rachel locked the liquor cabinet, pocketing the key, and when Emory forced the lock one day, she transferred the liquor supply elsewhere. In a fit of pique at that, Emory went off to the inn to drink in earnest, and by week's end, even Rachel worried that he would be unfit to travel.

"Damn him!" said George, thoroughly disgusted with Emory's behavior. He drew Edward aside again, advising him to be prepared to take his brother's place as Ermaline's escort. When Edward complained, mostly because he objected to being separated from Rebecca so soon after their reunion, George turned on him.

"You owe me, Edward! Now be the man your brother isn't!"

"Whatever are we to do?" Rachel asked one evening, as she and George sat playing cards in the salon. "We can't let this continue much longer. He will become ill, and besides, it's all so childish."

"It's the grown-up version of a ten-year-old's tantrum, all right," agreed the old man, "and done for much the same reason. But don't fret, he hasn't much money. It will wind down once it's gone, and he'll be back like a maddened bull."

The matter resolved itself a couple of days later, when Emory returned from the inn during the waning hours of darkness. At the time, there was little danger of his behaving like a maddened bull. He was simply too drunk to do or be anything. In fact, no one knew he was even on the estate until Sultan showed up alone at the door of the barn. Once admitted, the stallion, still saddled, found his own way to the stall at the end of the row, while the stable lads sped away in search of Emory.

He was found in the long gallery, sprawled precariously against a suit of armor, cradling a pikeman's staff in his arms. Carried to bed, he was plied with a brew so strong he swore later it had been on the back of Stoddard's stove for at least a week, yet by midafternoon the next day, he was no closer to becoming sober. Intermittently he slept, but when awake, and alone, he undermined the worth of Stoddard's bitter coffee with thirsty dregs from a flask hidden under his mattress.

Stoddard finally found it, and while Emory bellowed and scrambled to recover it, she poured what remained of its contents into the chamber pot. She made another sweep of the room to be sure no other intoxicants had escaped an earlier search and, satisfied, opened the casements wide. Freshened breezes brought the cool night air inside, where they quickly cleared the stagnant room of its boozy odors.

"It's the best way," she said to Rachel, as she threw another blanket over Emory's form. "He must sleep it off, and the night air will clear his head."

Concerned, Rachel listened at Emory's door for any sign of activity before she retired for the night. Not a sound came from within. Many hours later, well dregged with sleep herself, she lay snuggled beneath the covers in her bed, when something woke her. Suddenly!

Her eyes flew open! Her body tensed. She lay surrounded by almost total darkness, with only the strained light of a pale moon filtering into the room near the window. There was no sound, had been none, yet she sensed that something, or someone, was in the room.

Straining nervously to listen, she lay perfectly still, and it was then that a strong smell assailed her nostrils. *Wine! Sour wine! Emory!*

She rolled over, and there he was. Not only in her room, but in her bed! He lay sleeping right beside her, his head cradled against one of her satin pillows, the night covers pulled right up to his chin.

In the darkness, Rachel removed herself from the bed and struck a flint to light a lamp. As the intruding rays spread about the room, Emory merely squinted, squeezing his eyes shut and withdrawing further under the covers.

My God, thought Rachel. *What colossal nerve! How long has he been here?*

"Emory!" she cried sharply, rapping the mound that was his foot. "Get up! What are you doing here?"

Emory rolled over, grinning foolishly. "S'too damn cold to sleep alone," he mumbled.

"Is it now?" said an indignant Rachel. "Personally, I don't give a damn if you freeze! Just get out of my bed!"

Taking hold of the blankets, Rachel pulled them away from Emory's body; the cocoon-like warmth that had surrounded him disappeared in a rush of chilled air. He let out a whoop, flailing his arms, trying to retain the covers. But if Emory was surprised, so was she . . . for he was naked . . . stark naked. And in all her life, Rachel had never seen a naked male before, not even a baby boy! Gasping, she dropped the covers, backing away from the bed.

"Get out of here," she said rather weakly, trying not to look, but looking all the same.

As for Emory, the glaring lamplight and rush of cold air had brought him more than half awake, and he studied Rachel now, luscious in a nightdress of the softest pink, its low bodice cupping her rounded breasts invitingly, while she stood mutely to one side of the bed, squirming under his nakedness. Confused, unsure of her next move, her embarrassment became evident as her color heightened. He laughed, as Rachel gasped audibly at the sight of him.

"Come," he said, patting the warm space where she had lain sleeping just minutes before. "Now we'll sleep, and in the morning . . . who knows!"

Eyes darting toward the door, Rachel took yet another step backward, reaching for her robe with one arm. This time it was Emory who was the quicker; he left the bed in an athletic leap and seized Rachel roughly and urgently into his arms, pressing his naked body hotly against hers. She shuddered, and only by turning her head was she able to avoid his ardent lips. His embrace was distasteful, for not only was his breath unpleasant, but he needed a shave as well.

Emory tried to draw her back to the bed, as Rachel, crushed against his chest with one arm pinned behind her, gave some thought to screaming for Angus. In the end, though, the Scot wasn't needed. Carelessly, Emory suddenly stumbled, tripping over a little footstool which sat beside Rachel's bed.

He went down ponderously, falling with a loud *ooph* as the wind went out of him. Flat on his stomach, he lay perfectly still, holding his head, which had struck the bedpost with a sickening crack. Rachel leaned against the far bedpost to catch her breath, jumping when Emory groaned again, more loudly than before.

"Are you hurt?" she inquired. "Say something!" Surprisingly she was not disturbed by his nakedness any longer, only by the fact that he appeared to be injured, perhaps seriously. There was no blood to be seen, nor even any swelling, but still, Emory did not move. Gingerly, Rachel stepped closer, one step at a time, wondering if perhaps she ought to scream for Angus after all.

She was about an arm's length away when he lunged at her, but she had seen the telltale muscles in the back of his neck tighten and contort, telegraphing his movement, and she leaped on top of the bed just as he grabbed for her ankle. Scrambling off the other side of the bed, she whirled to face him.

"And I thought you were hurt. You're all right, you bastard!"

Emory snorted, starting across the bed on his knees after her. "I will be, if you but share this bed till dawn."

"Share my bed, if it pleases you," shouted Rachel herself, "but it will be with the pillows, not I!"

One by one she picked them up and flung them at Emory, who collapsed with laughter at the barrage. Then, still half in a stupor and exhausted by his efforts to capture her, he gave up and lay still, his upper torso sprawled across her bed, his bare backside and long legs dangling over its side. Snatching up her robe, Rachel stormed from the room, furious at the sight of him. Emory took no note of her leaving, didn't even move when the door slammed shut, and in minutes he was sound asleep again.

Burning from his offensive embrace, Rachel marched down the darkened hall to the grand salon. By the light of a dim lamp she found one of George's lap robes and, curling up in a chair near the door, wondered if Emory would come after her, parading his naked-ness through the halls. Trying to get comfortable in her chair, Rachel cursed his name roundly and cursed the day she became the wife of a drunken lecher, as well. Exhausted, she dozed eventually, but before dawn could announce the coming of another new day, she was awakened by a very long and very loud shriek, a bloodcurdling cry that raised almost everyone in the house. Only Ermaline and George missed the show.

The cry came from Rachel's room, where one of the younger maids, sent by Stoddard with Rachel's usual morning tray, was greeted by the sight of Emory's bare bottom and dangling legs when she opened the door. The contents of the tray were now strewn across the carpeting, and the poor girl had scurried down the back stairs to the safety of the cook's kitchen.

Now sober, and very red-faced, Emory, wrapped in the counterpane from Rachel's bed, crept sheepishly back to his own room. The look he gave Rachel as he passed by her in the hall was especially foul, and as their eyes met, it was he who turned away, while she covered her mirth behind the fringes of George's plaid lap robe.

Emory's sobering up that day was a painful experience for him, surely the worst he'd ever suffered. Remembering Sultan's disagreeable disposition at last, he dressed and hurried to the stables. As long as no one had neared his stall, the black had remained quiet, but he was still saddled. How long now? thought Emory, and his filthy stall was a sorry sight. All this served to subdue Emory, for never before had he neglected his mount, no matter how drunk. He spent two hours in the barn, first watering and feeding Sultan, and then currying his sleek hide till he shone. Later, loosing the stallion into the paddock, Emory mucked out the stall himself.

But shoveling manure that day was not to be his only penance, for he still had his father to face. Once bathed and clean shaven again, Emory looked reasonably presentable for a man who had been drinking steadily for nearly a week, but he was quiet and cowed, sobered by the knowledge that he had surely made an utter ass of himself this time.

As expected, George did carry on, railing at length. Leaning on Rachel's little gateleg table, Emory stared out of the library window, paying scant attention to his father's words. After all, they'd all been said before. So many times!

"You cannot carry on as you have this past week! Your presence is disruptive, yet your absence, under the circumstances, causes us all grave concern."

"You are right, of course, Father," admitted Emory with what he hoped sounded like genuine humility. "I will offer apologies all around. Will that help?"

"Not much and you know it! The situation demands more. You simply must turn over a new leaf."

"Dammit, Father, I have. I live like a monk! No cards, no cock-fights, no women! What more do you want?"

"But more than enough wine, eh boy? You'd put an abbey full of monks to shame on that score!"

When Emory began to pace the floor, George pointed to a chair with his stick. Fitfully, Emory took it.

"I've had a bellyful," growled George. "And since you've already been warned numerous times about your behavior, now I must act. You will be on probation this coming fortnight . . . Oh yes," he said, noting Emory's raised eyebrows. "You're going! You already know what is expected of you as escort to your wife and your sister, and I warn you, one mistake at the Rowlands', one incident in London . . . anything, and I am prepared to wash my hands of you. As of this moment you will be responsible for your own actions or suffer the consequences."

"Which are . . . ?"

"Fail me again, m'boy, and you will learn them soon enough."

"That's unfair, Father. I was forced to come home, yet I am not needed here. Will you have me continue to play second fiddle to Rachel?"

"You are needed, and don't blame Rachel if you cannot see it."

The discussion came to an end, nothing really settled except that Emory agreed—nay, promised—that he would behave while in London, would not abandon his duties in any way.

"It is a covenant, son," said the old man as Emory left the library. "This time I hold you to it."

Exactly at nine the next morning, the Guersten carriage, four matched grays harnessed into position, waited under the porte cochere for its passengers. Rachel, bonnet in hand, was almost ready to begin the long trek to London. She turned as a soft tap sounded at her door, and Rebecca entered, looking unusually flushed. The news she brought was disturbing.

"Bleeding? From where?"

"Where do you think, goosey? It's not unheard of during pregnancy, you know."

"Oh, my," mumbled Rachel, sitting down on the edge of the bed. "It cannot be a good sign. It's far too early."

"I shouldn't have told you. There wasn't much, and I feel fine. Now you'll worry."

"Of course, I'll worry! Rebecca . . . you and Edward . . . I mean . . . you aren't . . . ?"

"For heaven's sake, Rachel, say it! We're both married women now, but the answer to your question is no . . . we haven't."

Her cheeks turning pink, Rachel tried to look stern.

"Just the same, Rebecca, I would worry far less if I knew you were sleeping here, in this room, while I'm gone. It's where you really belong. You know . . . this is where the babe will be born."

"Oh, Rachel, no," cried Rebecca. "I don't ever want to sleep alone again. Let me stay with Edward! I feel so secure with him tucked under my bum at night."

"*Rebecca! Shame!*"

But Rebecca was anything but shamed, and in fact, she giggled with glee as Rachel turned away, pretending to check the contents of her traveling bag for something.

"Nevertheless," Rachel said, her back still turned, "Stoddard will move your things in here tonight, and you are to stay in bed until Duncan has examined you again. No arguments! Edward will see to it, I'm sure."

He did too, but several hours later, halfway to London, Rebecca's well-being still weighed heavily on Rachel's mind as she settled drowsily into the cushions of the coach. Awhile ago they had stopped for lunch, picnicking beside the road from a hamper prepared by Stoddard. The cook had buttered thin slices of white bread, fresh baked in the morning's first batch, adding pieces of tender chicken wrapped in cress.

There were some meat pies especially for Emory, as well as an assortment of sweets and fruit. Only a decanter of chilled wine was missing, conspicuous in its absence. In its place was a container of cold buttermilk, at which Emory turned up his nose, preferring to drink plain water fetched from a brook that burbled nearby.

The grays were fed and watered, while Emory tended to Sultan's needs himself, as usual. The black required no tether, but he followed the coach obediently, never straying far afield from Emory. Earlier, Rachel had been surprised to see the stallion under the portico, sleek and saddled, until she remembered that no one on the estate could care for him in Emory's absence.

"Besides," admitted Emory once they were under way, "I can't spend eight hours cramped in this damnable space. Where will I put my legs?"

Returning to the coach, sated, Rachel found the rhythmic rocking of its body soon made her drowsy. She shared one of the seats with Emory now, he in one corner, she in the other, their shoulders barely touching. It had not been an unpleasant trip thus far, but due to the distinct coolness there was little conversation between them..

Removing her bonnet, Rachel unbuttoned her jacket, and in no time she was napping, while Ermaline, sitting opposite, tried to become engrossed in a book. As Rachel slumped in sleep against Emory's shoulder, he placed his long legs on the cushions next to his sister, toying absently with the corded fringe that hung from the bottom of Rachel's little purse.

Without raising her head, Ermaline watched him for some minutes, and then, nudging his foot, pointed to Rachel.

"She's so beautiful," she said in a low voice. "Why is it that you treat her so badly?"

There was a long pause as Emory considered an answer. "I can't say, Ermaline. I know what I think, and I know what I feel . . . She fascinates me, yet whenever I find myself alone with her, invariably I say the wrong thing or do something boorish."

He was confused. He had known and bedded a wealth of beautiful women, but in all his experience, he had never known one quite like Rachel. So far she had remained totally unmoved by his flatteries, and she did not succumb to his usually effective charm. Her open rejection of him was annoying, but strangely, it also served to heighten his desire.

"Perhaps your problem lies in your attitude. Rachel's not just another easy conquest, waiting to be bedded by some cavalier, Emory. She is a lady, a cut and a half above the likes of Edwina Merrington. It's something you should have recognized months ago."

"Lady Merrington? And what do you know of Edwina?"

"Father told me all about her. In fact, he told me lots of things, Emory, some time ago, before either you or Edward returned to the Hall. Tisbury came to see Father one day, and later he told me of some new financial arrangements he made. He wanted me to understand the details of them, and in the process I learned all about your past escapades . . . at the bar, the gaming tables, and in bed!"

"These arrangements you speak of, how do they involve me?" Emory asked, remembering his father's stern lecture of yesterday.

"They don't. You needn't worry, Emory, they are meant only as contingencies, in case you don't heed Father's warning not to hurt Rachel. He's adamant on that score, Emory, and he's prepared to back it up with action. He's threatened to dispose of all his holdings if you don't come round, and divide the proceeds between me and Rachel, and the child Rebecca carries. The Hall will be sold, and you, and perhaps even Edward, will be written out."

"I don't believe it!" hissed Emory, quite taken aback by this revelation. "*The Hall sold?*"

"I wouldn't test him! You'll end up with only the clothes on your back and that stallion for company! You see, Emory, it's time you realized that whether you like it or not, both your fortunes and your future rest on the happiness of that woman."

Ermaline pointed again to Rachel, whose head now rested squarely against Emory's shoulder. He turned, gazing down at her, her dark tresses brushing against his cheek and her perfume drifting lazily upward, its scent enveloping him. Rachel's hands were folded demurely in her lap, and his mother's ring glittered in the sunlight that streamed through the window of the coach. Her beauty never failed to stir him, and he felt a tinge of guilt at the way he'd treated her.

"Then I guess my fate is sealed," he said to his sister, "for it's clear that she can barely tolerate me. Once I felt that way, too, but now . . ."

"Oh, stop feeling sorry for yourself! She's your wife, isn't she? That's your ring on her finger, Emory . . . Play your cards differently, and you might win a few points. Think about it!"

"I have, Ermaline. But every time I make an overture or try to woo her . . ."

At that, Ermaline burst into loud laughter. She buried her face in her lap, trying not to wake Rachel, and whooped wildly for several moments. When she raised her head at last, she wiped the tears from her eyes and looked across at Emory.

"Sorry, brother; it's just that I cannot believe what I hear! Woo her, indeed! That business the other night was hardly the action of a man set out to woo a lady. Only a brutish dolt, and a drunken one at that, would force his way into his wife's bed."

As she spoke, Emory slumped down into the cushions. "You know about that, too, eh?"

"Know about it? Everyone on the estate knows about it, thanks to Lizzie's hysterical shrieking." Just thinking about it sent Ermaline into another fit of laughing. "I understand old Gaffy laughed so hard he fell off his stool," she cried gleefully. "Oh, how I wish I had been there!"

"Ermaline!"

At first embarrassed, Emory was now angry, maddened by the thought of being the laughingstock of everyone at Guersten Hall. That old feeling of being trapped by Rachel's presence swamped him again; he gritted his teeth and, kicking open the door of the coach, whistled loudly for Sultan. A scant second later, he galloped away up the road ahead of the coach.

Ermaline caught the swinging door and closed it, turning the silver latch quietly, but Rachel had already stirred from her nap.

"Whatever is all the commotion about?" she asked.

"Oh, dear! I merely tried to talk some sense into Emory's head, but I fear all I did was anger him."

"Don't fret about it," Rachel said matter-of-factly as she straightened her skirt. "He'll cool off; he always does."

"Yes, but these ups and downs are so trying. And now he'll resume his drinking and spoil the party."

"I doubt it," comforted Rachel. "He gave your father a promise, and something tells me he'll keep it this time."

Rachel was right. Emory did not abandon them for the nearest tavern, and though he did not rejoin them again in the carriage for the rest of the journey, he remained within sight and sound of it. By the time the tired grays pulled to a halt before the tall brick house facing Eaton Place, Emory's dark mood had passed.

CHAPTER EIGHTEEN

Old Edgerton, the caretaker, met them at the curb. Bald and wrinkled, older than Emory's father even, Edgerton had been a Guersten employee all his life, starting as a boy in the mews behind this very house. He took their luggage inside and up the stairs with a minimum of conversation. On the other hand, Lettie, his wife, was a grandmotherly woman of huge proportions who doubled as cook-housekeeper. She took to Rachel at first sight and happily led her from room to room on an inspection tour of those rooms that were open on the lower floor, all the while maintaining a steady stream of cheery chatter that more than made up for whatever it was that her husband did not say.

While the London house fell short of the princely grandeur of Guersten Hall, it was still elegant in its own right, or would have been had the need for repairs not been so obvious and extensive. Most of the rooms were closed off, with the furniture shrouded in sheeting, but those that Lettie had opened for their arrival were spotless and freshly aired.

Lettie served them tea and, later on, supper in a tiny alcove off the paneled library. There was fresh linen and candlelight, and everything was delicious and filling to the tired travelers.

"I took the liberty of putting the table in here," Lettie told Rachel, hovering over her, "for the dining room is much too large for just the three of ye. Y'd be lost in there."

"But that was Mrs. Guersten's decision to make," interrupted Ermaline in a tone clearly meant to be a reprimand.

However, Rachel agreed with Lettie. "It was a wise move; we will only be here two weeks, and there's no need to open the entire house for so few of us. We can take all our meals right here; it's rather cozy."

Bedtime presented a problem of another sort. While Ermaline occupied the same room she always had in the London house, Edgerton had naturally placed Emory and Rachel's luggage in the same room. It was a guest suite, really, two unpretentious bedrooms with a common sitting room between.

"There was a leak in the master bedroom," Edgerton explained to Emory, "and no mattress in the other."

Since Emory preferred that no one in London, even the servants, who were known to gossip, learn that he was not welcome in his wife's bedroom, he waved Edgerton out and turned to Rachel before she voiced any objection to the sleeping arrangement.

"Look," he said, "let's make the best of it. As you said, we're here only the two weeks. I'll sleep here," pointing to one room, "and you can sleep there. We can take turns ... there," he continued, gesturing toward a little dressing room containing a washstand and a claw-foot commode that hid a chamber pot. In one screened corner, a stack of fluffy towels waited beside a high-backed tub, already filled to the brim with hot water.

"But ... but ..."

"No buts," Emory said, inspecting the steaming tub. "I've already promised to behave this trip. You can lock the door if you're afraid of me."

Rachel was not afraid of him, not anymore, and she was much too weary at the moment to argue the point further. Besides, what did it matter where she slept? "All right," she said, giving in to the arrangements, "but I claim first rights to that tub."

Rachel did not lock her bedroom door that night, nor any other while in London, and to his credit, Emory behaved admirably. Shortly,

Rachel found she became used to his presence, so near at hand. It was strange to lie in bed in the morning, hearing him at his shaving stand, slapping the strop and humming a jaunty tune. Her father had always done much the same while shaving. Did all men? she wondered.

Filled with expectant hope that her parents would be reconciled, Rachel went to her father's townhouse one morning, only to find he was not there. Accompanied by Emory, she traveled across the city to his warehouse in the dock area, and while Benjamin was in his offices, he flatly refused to see his daughter. Hurt, Rachel smiled bravely through watery eyes when Emory offered to go up and confront Benjamin himself on her behalf. "No," said Rachel, turning away. "Maybe it's best to give it time. So much has happened . . . to all of us."

Shopping kept Rachel and Ermaline exceedingly busy the rest of that first week. Each morning they proceeded to Mrs. Scofield's green-and-white salon for fittings. There, Eleanora put her best girls right to work.

"*Aieee!* Two ball gowns in one week!" she cried distractedly, but there was no question that they would be ready. The gown she created for Ermaline was exquisite, layer upon layer of sheer white mousseline de soie, poufed at the sleeves, its skirt belled into a drape that ended in a mass of ruffles and flounces, all caught with clusters of small silk roses ranging in hue from shell pink to deep cerise.

"It's perfect," said Ermaline ecstatically, "exactly what I wanted . . . except . . ."

"Except you had something with more pink in mind, eh?" replied Eleanora. "Is that it?"

Ermaline hesitated.

"Say it, chickadee, you won't hurt my feelings! But look," Eleanora continued, pulling a stiffened petticoat from a closet. It was decidedly pink. "See," she said, slipping the petticoat over Ermaline's head. "We put this on, and then goes the gown! *Voilà!* Now, is that better? Ah, I see that it is," she added, as Ermaline turned happily this way and that before the triple mirror. The deep pink of the undergarment barely showed through the layers of white, but it gave the ball gown's skirt a muted color all its own. "Aah, bridal blush it is," said Eleanora.

"Anything else would be inappropriate for a bride-to-be. Now stand still and let my Simone pin you, that's a good girl."

"And now, my dear," she added, turning to Rachel, "come with me. I want to show you something." Eleanora led the way from the fitting room to her tiny office, where she unwrapped a bolt of light-colored fabric that lay on a cutting table. She held it up for Rachel's inspection. "What do you think of it?" she asked.

"It's gorgeous," admired Rachel, fingering the fabric, a thin material that floated ethereally at the slightest whisper of movement. "What is it?"

"One of the new crepes, from France. I've only used it once before myself."

"The color is . . . odd. Ecru, is it not?"

"It is called eggshell."

"Ah! Well, it is most unusual, Eleanora, but somehow I cannot picture a ball gown made from it. Do you have something in mind?"

"Come . . . I'll show you," said the couturier, taking a key ring from her pocket. She unlocked an armoire that stood between two windows. It was filled with dolls.

"Dolls?" inquired Rachel quizzically.

"Fashion dolls," explained Eleanora. "Every month or so I receive one from a colleague in Paris. The dresses are exact duplicates in miniature of designer originals. They keep me abreast of the latest trends on the continent." She removed one, still wrapped in tissue paper, from its place on a bottom shelf. "This one just arrived. Tell me what you think."

Eleanora removed the paper and stood the doll on a little stand, locking its feet into place with a thin strap. The bisque doll stood about a foot high and was completely dressed, down to slippers and undergarments; she was even holding a tiny fan, fastened to her gloved fingertips with glue. Her dress was a ball gown of the same material which lay on the cutting table, a gown so elegantly simple that it was breathtaking.

The fitted bodice hugged the body; there were no sleeves, just a mass of crystal pleats, gathered and fluted, which dropped off the very edge of the doll's shoulders, covering its upper arms in a flesh-colored cloud. The skirt front was plain, its bottom draped into a great soft swoop. In the back, the skirt fell in huge folds, gathered up into a low bustle, from which tumbled row upon row of flounced pleats, which then swept under the hemline all around.

"I shall make only a few changes," stated Eleanora. She pointed to several tiny purple bows scattered over the dress. "First, we must remove these gaudy ribbons and the sash. Then I shall add some trim. Here . . . and here," she said, indicating the shoulder and hem flounces. "Something narrow, and brown, to match your eyes . . . velvet cording, perhaps . . . or soutache. Lastly, I think a pair of cabbage roses, made from the bolt, to go here, at the dropped bustle. That is all, for the gown must remain uncluttered. The rest is up to you. Wear only topazes, and put your hair up; something elaborate is called for."

"Aaaah, yes!" she sighed, pleased. "The fabric is unique, and the color is one that no other woman could dare to wear. Only you, my dear, only you."

Satisfied, Rachel gave her consent to the design, ordering a number of other frocks and day gowns at the same time, all to be lighter weight, for her entire summer wardrobe consisted of last year's school uniforms, sitting now in a trunk in the attic at Guersten Hall. To Rachel, it was incredible to think that only six months ago she had been a happy schoolgirl.

"I'll have everything ready when you leave London, my pet," Eleanora said through a mouthful of pins. "Shall I send the bill to your father, as before?"

"No," sighed Rachel, again saddened by the reminder of the break with her father. "This time send them all to Guersten Hall. My . . . husband will pay for them," she remarked, but did not add they would be paid with a draft drawn from her own allowance.

Each day the three Guerstens came together for their evening meal. Politely, Emory sat through dinner, trying valiantly to show some interest in the ladies' talk of fashions and fabrics. He was still unable to reconcile either of the women with the girls they had been, and in the confinement of the smaller house, he was able to study both Rachel and Ermaline at close range as they chattered about their purchases. While Rachel's remarkable transformation had already left its indelible mark upon him, his sister's alteration never ceased to amaze him either. Ermaline had always been such a nuisance before, yet here she was, attractive, pleasant, and even witty at times. Between Henry's love and Rachel's attentions, the girl had blossomed, and gradually Emory began to understand why his father felt so beholden to Rachel.

Still, everything was not as idyllic as it seemed on the surface, for repeatedly, one person turned up odd man out that first week in London, and that person was Emory. He rarely left the house, and when he did, it was to go alone to the docks, where he whiled away the hours watching the comings and goings of the man-o'-wars and the merchantmen on the Thames. Where else could he go? he griped to himself. He was forbidden to drink, cards and dice were taboo, and any dalliance with women was out of the question. Frankly, the only woman he wanted now was Rachel, but nevertheless, while the temptation to visit his usual London haunts was overwhelming, he recognized that a chance meeting with any of his old comrades would surely end in his participation of one or more of the outlawed occupations. And so he remained inside, distracted, watching the clock on the mantel tick away slow hours until Rachel returned to the house each day.

Once, he escorted Rachel and Ermaline to the Rowlands' for tea, sitting through a long and dismal hour of teacups and insipid small talk. On another day, he invited Rachel to go riding, and twice he suggested the theater. Each time, she put him off.

"We are much too busy this week, Emory. Perhaps after the party."

As the week progressed Emory became disgruntled. Plainly he was bored, and wisely Rachel sought to defuse him.

"Next week Ermaline goes to Adele's for a visit with your cousins, and I will be freed from my role as chaperone for a while. We can go wherever you like then . . . the theater, or the opera perhaps. Whatever you choose, Emory, all within reason," she added, lest her intent be misunderstood.

Yet even with that promise, by the night of the ball, Emory's distress was hard to conceal any longer. *Or could it be that it had been replaced by something else?* guessed Rachel shrewdly. Pacing in and out of her sitting room, Emory watched her guardedly, as if wondering what her thoughts were at that moment. Later, when she heard no humming while he shaved, she decided that yes, something surely troubled him. While dressing, it was Rachel's turn to study him. Standing off to one side, she heard him swear under his breath, as he struggled futilely with the sleeve buttons on his shirt.

"Will you help me?" she asked, trying to fasten a splendid topaz necklace around her throat. As Emory stepped behind her, she whirled about to face him.

"You've been drinking!" she said, sniffing the air. Though faint, the smell of alcohol was unmistakable.

"I had a single brandy, that's all. I thought it would calm my nerves."

"I see. And what is it that makes you so jittery?"

He hesitated, groping for an answer. "Nothing . . . it's only that this will be our first public appearance together, and I . . ."

He left his statement unfinished and, in silence, finally buttoned his cuffs.

"Yes, go on," said Rachel, fastening her earclips.

"Forget it! I just hope there won't be any scenes."

She turned around to face him again. "Scenes? I don't understand. Do you think I . . ."

"Of course not! It's just that I've behaved so badly, and now I'm hoping . . . ," he said, fumbling for words, "I mean . . . that you won't . . ."

His sentence trailed away again, as he paused, growing uncomfortable under Rachel's steady gaze. "Well," he said at last defensively, "many of the Rowlands' friends are mine, too!"

"And your father's, and Ermaline's as well! Why should I make a scene?"

Could it be, she wondered, that for once he was genuinely concerned about her well-being, troubled perhaps that she might be uncomfortable tonight at the Rowlands'? In view of all that had passed between them, such thoughtfulness seemed out of place, but for the moment, she gave him the benefit of a doubt.

"I'm not as naive as I appear, Emory. I understand that some of the people I'll meet tonight would not bother with me at all if we were to meet under different circumstances. Many have rank and social standing, while I am just the daughter of a businessman. But, relax. Tonight I'll simply be . . . your wife or Ermaline's sister-in-law. The ladies will probably ignore me, and the men will assume I'm bored, and try to bed me . . . for my amusement, of course, never theirs. Doesn't it go something like that?"

There was more than a little truth to what Rachel said, and Emory admitted it. To be sure, there would be many exceptions, the Rowlands themselves and Lord Merrington, for example, who was warmhearted and pleasant to all, regardless of station. But Rachel's extraordinary beauty would make all the difference tonight, Emory knew. Jealous, some of the women might resent her, and their husbands were sure to swarm around like summer beach fleas. Moreover, Rachel's father was worth more than half the lot of them, and they knew it. No, many would be polite, but precious few would extend genuine friendship to her.

"Even so," continued Rachel, facing her mirror again, "you needn't worry. I won't commit any social faux pas, if that is what troubles you."

"Stop it, Rachel!" snarled Emory. "That's not at all what I meant!"

"Then tell me. Just what did you mean?"

Remaining silent, Emory didn't tell her . . . He couldn't. He recalled all those months he had burned over his wine, convinced he would be the laughingstock of all London when he showed up with Rachel on his arm. His reputation as a lover was on the line then, and the situation was now really little changed. It was still on the line, only this time the woman on his arm would be the loveliest in the room, his own wife, yet he had never taken her, never touched her! If his contemporaries but even suspected that Rachel was still a virgin after four months of marriage, he would surely be the laughingstock! But how could he tell her that?

He didn't have to. Understanding at last, she faced him once again, squarely this time. "I see," she said icily. "So! Your concern was not for me, but yourself, as usual. I might have guessed! You were worried . . . worried I might try to get even for past humiliations by embarrassing you before your friends!"

"Now, see here, Rachel . . ."

"No! You see! We leave for the Rowlands' momentarily, and I won't have unpleasantries now. Let us strike a deal," she said, still concerned that he might begin drinking again. "If you promise to remain sober tonight, I will promise to behave in a manner befitting a new bride and devoted wife. None of your friends will learn about our peculiar . . . arrangement."

Fidgeting with his jabot, Emory grunted his consent, caught in a trap of his own making. Stepping before him, Rachel straightened the frothy lace for him, fluffing its ruffles into high peaks.

"I really botched it, didn't I?" he said to her, disgusted with himself.

"That you did! As I told you before, this is Ermaline's night, and I won't let anything spoil it. To that end, I was fully prepared to play the role of loving wife anyway. Your fears were groundless, but a promise is a promise, and I hold you to it."

The Rowlands' house was so brightly lighted that night it glittered like a diamond in the moonlight. The drive outside was full, cluttered with expensive carriages and hansoms, while inside, liveried footmen and maids busied themselves taking wraps and top hats. Rachel and Ermaline, once admitted, were whisked away to a little powder room on the second floor and given the opportunity to adjust their skirts and smooth their curls before entering the ballroom. No sooner had they closed the door, however, there came a tap, and a maid in gray taffeta entered.

"Mr. Henry is waiting for you, Miss Ermaline. They are taking their place for the receiving line."

Nervously, Ermaline jumped to her feet. "I must go, Rachel. How do I look?"

"You've never looked lovelier," Rachel answered in tender sincerity, "and I only wish your father were here to see you. He would burst with pride. Go now, and ask Emory to meet me at the foot of the stairs."

Rachel sat down at the tiny dressing table. Not a hair was out of place, but she fussed with it anyway, as women are wont to do, while the soft sound of female voices filtered through from the next room. There, Lady Edwina Merrington sat chatting with two of her friends, not realizing that the door was cracked open. Alone in the powder room, Rachel was soon able to piece together the identities of the ladies through their conversation, and though she tried not to eavesdrop, it was difficult not to do so. Her surprise grew as, shocked, she realized that they gossiped about Emory . . . and herself.

"He must have arrived by now," remarked Lady Merrington. "Oh, how eager I am to see him again."

"Careful, Edwina. Emory is a married man now, remember?"

Lady Merrington tittered. "My marital state never troubled him! I daresay I shan't let his trouble me!"

"We understand that you prefer them tall and virile, my friend," said a contralto voice, "but Emory won't be alone tonight. His wife will surely be with him."

"All the more reason he'll seek me out," quipped Lady Merrington smugly. "If what he told me about her was only half truth, he'll be ripe and juicy for me."

"Edwina!" cried her companions in unison.

"Do tell me what she looks like," one of them said.

"I've never seen her!" confessed Lady Merrington, toying with silken curls. "Emory described her to me just the once, and swore me to secrecy. But come, let us go down; we shall all see soon enough."

On the other side of the door, Rachel was stunned, unable to move, having never heard a woman speak so brazenly about a man before. She stood up, drawing on her gloves, hoping to quit the room before her presence was discovered, but it was already too late. The door was pushed open, and Rachel found herself face-to-face with Edwina Merrington.

Lady Merrington was petite and lovely, with a magnificent figure that hinted boldly of the joys it held. She was a satiny-skinned blonde, but tonight she wore an elaborate wig of piled white curls, topped with purple plumes. Deep violet eyes seemed even darker in contrast to the gown she wore, fashioned of purple Genoa velvet. White silk roses were draped idly across its skirt, but the bodice lay unadorned. A tiny mole on one bared shoulder captured attention, drawing it down to half-bared breasts that threatened to burst any moment from the fabric that confined them. Clearly, Lady Merrington knew how to make the most of her attributes, and clearly, she was quite surprised by Rachel's presence in the outer room.

"I didn't know anyone was here," she said, eyeing Rachel uncertainly. It was an awkward moment for them both, for there was no question that Rachel had overheard their tantalizing conversation. Pensively, Edwina studied the beauty that stood before her, and then she waved a hand airily.

"Forget it," she whispered conspiratorially. "We were discussing a . . . friend, a charming man who has the misfortune to be married to the most unattractive woman in all of London."

Rachel's eyes widened in further surprise.

"It's true," said Edwina, mistaking that surprise for interest. "She's an absolute mouse . . . by his own lips, mind you." Edwina stepped closer. "He even ran away on his wedding night, rather than bed her!" she whispered behind her fan. And then she changed the subject abruptly. "What an exquisite gown you are wearing, my dear. Is it a Worth?"

Before Rachel could muddle off a reply, one of Lady Merrington's friends took Edwina's arm and pulled her toward the door. Heavy perfume lingered after their exit.

Alone, Rachel sat down again rather abruptly. So! That was Emory's light-o'-love! Once again she was reminded of how little she knew about the things that drew a man and woman together. She could readily picture Emory coupled with Edwina Merrington; they were so alike, so uninhibited and sensual. She knew now, without a doubt, that it had been Edwina's charms Emory had sought that cold night in December when he had been unwilling to claim his bride at Guersten Hall. The thought stabbed Rachel.

Outside the room, Edwina and her companions were nearing the stairs.

"She's quite a beauty, isn't she?" remarked one.

"Who can she be?" the contralto voice inquired.

But Lady Merrington, peering over the railing to the gathering below, didn't answer. "Aaah! There's Emory, there at the foot. Lord, he looks handsome all in black. Makes me think of that stallion of his."

"Edwina!"

"Disappear, you two. Scoot!"

Laughing, Lady Merrington's friends scooted, leaving her alone with Emory at the bottom of the stairs.

"Lady Merrington!" said he, touching his lips to Edwina's gloved hand. "How lovely you look tonight."

"You scoundrel! Why did you leave me alone at Woodleigh?"

"Dear lady, Woodleigh Grange is your husband's estate, and he was in residence. I did not wish to overstay my welcome. Besides, you were hardly alone."

"I pined for days."

Emory laughed roundly at that. "Come now, Edwina, I doubt that. Others were champing at the bit. Which one did you choose to take my place?" he whispered in her ear.

"Does it matter?" she asked, wetting her lips deliciously. "None can follow you any way." Her hand went under the edge of Emory's embroidered waistcoat. "Shall we find a corner to discuss it further?" Turning, she looked up the stairs as she spoke, and Emory's gaze followed her, as did the gaze of half dozen others who stood nearby.

Rachel stood at the top. Starting down, she descended the long flight gracefully, floating effortlessly it seemed, as the ruffled flounces in the hem of her gown fluted and whispered over each step behind her.

"I saw her upstairs," said Edwina, "and I must learn where she got that dress." She sighed. "I say it grudgingly, but I must admit I've never seen anyone more beautiful."

"Nor I," said Emory, catching Rachel's eye.

"I wonder who she is. Someone's daughter perhaps?"

As Rachel reached the bottom step, Emory extended his hand. Rachel took it.

"Nay, Lady Merrington," Emory said. "Someone's wife . . . mine in fact."

Lady Merrington made a peculiar sound. Wide-eyed and choking, her cheeks paled until they nearly matched the color of the wig she wore. Hiding a satisfied smile, Rachel made a polite curtsey as Emory moved to stand proudly beside her.

"Lady Merrington, may I present my wife, Rachel."

"We've already met, *darling*," Rachel said in a forced tone, enunciating the word *darling* so acidly that Emory turned to stare at her in confusion. His experience with women told him that both women were vexed, that something had passed between them already.

Rachel's vexation, though apparent only to Emory, faded quickly. She resented strongly the fact that he had actually dared to discuss her supposed lack of attributes so intimately with Edwina, yet took some satisfaction in the knowledge that it was now Edwina who stood discomfited. That discomfort was almost embarrassing to watch, as Edwina's eyes traveled from Emory to Rachel, and back to Emory again, wondering whether she had been made the butt of some amusing joke. When Emory did not release Rachel's cool fingers, Edwina fanned herself vigorously, and the little group was presently surrounded by others who pressed Emory, clamoring for an introduction to his beautiful wife. In the crush, Lady Merrington disappeared.

"I shall have to explain this matter to Edwina," Emory said to Rachel later as they made their way to the ballroom. "I cannot allow her to believe we've shared a joke at her expense. I will tell her frankly that her surprise at first sight of you matched my own."

"Do that," Rachel said icily, removing her hand from his.

The evening progressed without further incident, and Rachel's introduction into London's society went far better than even she had expected. Her dance card filled rapidly, and though the matrons peered suspiciously at her through their lorgnettes, their sons and husbands went out of their way to make her welcome. The husbands especially so, for when they saw Rachel's loveliness, they gave a collective sigh of relief. Surely, they believed, with such a beauty in his own bed, Emory Guersten would at last cease to plunder theirs.

Mrs. Rowland, a delightful little lady with a round red face, overweight, overdressed, and overheated, flitted from place to place tugging Rachel's wrist, determined that every Lord and Lady, every guest, in fact, should meet Rachel personally, for Mrs. Rowland, too, recognized that the change wrought in Ermaline's appearance had come about through Rachel's coaching. Her gratitude knew no bounds; Rachel could only escape her by dancing until her feet ached.

The ballroom was of grand dimensions, its high ceiling supported by Corinthian columns, its floor glossed by years of loving care. On it, the dancers circled gracefully under the light and heat of hundreds of tapers, becoming a kaleidoscope of color that constantly moved and changed, a chromatic mix of elaborate ball gowns and nobility's bright sashes, well sprinkled with the brilliant reds and nautical blues that set Her Majesty's cavalry and admiralty officers apart from the crowd.

The dining room, where a stupendous ten-course meal was served in shifts all night long, was always crowded, for there were almost as many footmen as diners it seemed, with one stationed between every two guests up and down the long table. Each, with powdered hair and satin knee breeches, was identically liveried in Rowland gray, a fabric woven especially for the Rowlands alone.

After supper, Rachel was finally introduced to Lord Merrington, tucked away in a not-so-busy corner of the balcony that overlooked the dancers. There Merrington remained seated, with both hands resting on a cane. One foot, propped up on a footstool, was swathed in swansdown bandages, for Merrington suffered acutely from the gout. Seeing him, Rachel hoped her surprise did not show; for while Edwina had long ago seen the end of her girlhood, Merrington still looked old enough to be her father. He was an outspoken man with wiry whiskers and tufts of hair that poked out from his ears. As they talked, Edwina stood in wifely fashion behind her Lord's chair, but her eyes were only for Emory. They devoured him.

"Know your father well, my dear," said the Lord to Rachel, boldly appraising her beauty. "Hold 'm in great esteem, too." He nodded to the two women, the pair of them the most attractive beauties in the place. "You two run along and learn to be friends. I want to talk to Emory."

But becoming friends was out of the question, and Rachel knew it. Emory stood between them and always would, and she was shocked by Edwina's brazen lifestyle. As for Edwina, Rachel's matchless beauty, wholesome and natural, confused and threatened her. Jealousy was unknown to her, for she had always managed to be the most flamboyant woman at any gathering, in dress, in style, and in personality.

But tonight she felt challenged, amazed to find her position under-cut by Rachel's dress and manner, both remarkably exquisite in their simplicity.

"Right nice piece o' baggage you've acquired for yourself, m'lad," commented the Lord. Emory laughed, knowing that Merrington's remark was meant as a compliment. In his younger days the Lord had been a rakehell, an inveterate skirt chaser until the gout had taken him out of the running.

"Yes," Merrington added, "it was a smart move on your part, right smart."

"Thank you, m'Lord, but personally, I take no credit for it. My father engineered the whole thing, and there's no use trying to claim otherwise with you."

"Knew it already, m'boy. Perhaps your father has more brains than even I gave him credit for. Brenham's the shrewdest businessman I know, though what he hopes to gain from your match escapes me."

"A place in our society, perhaps," offered Emory idly.

"Through the back door?" scoffed Lord Merrington. "It won't work, and besides, Brenham doesn't need us. Look at them," he said, pointing with his cane to the whirling dancers below. "Itchy husbands on the prowl for a fresh lay, and bored housewives who pretend it doesn't happen until it's their turn to get laid."

"Are we as bad as all that?"

"Y' know we are! No, this isn't your father-in-law's forte. He already belongs to a number of the right clubs . . ."

"Who?" asked Emory absently, as he watched a fat officer in a bright red coat commandeer Rachel and lead her to the dance floor.

"Brenham, you ass! He is your father-in-law, is he not?"

"So he is," replied Emory, brought around by the Lord's acid tongue. "I'd clean forgotten that. I understand he belongs to the Pembroke."

"Aye, one of the few that matters, too. Even we can't join that one! In years to come our PMs and cabinet officers will be culled from clubs such as that. You're a lucky man, Emory. You married a beauty with a fortune. But you'd better keep an eye on both."

"My Lord, I suspect you lead up to something. Advice, perhaps?"

"Damn right! And you need it! Brenham's worth nearly as much as I am, and I don't mean falling down houses and paintings of ancestors nob'dy remembers, either. His fortune is mostly cash, and his property is all income producing. Aye, but the rule of primogeniture won't help you here, lad, and if you continue your boorish incompetency, you'll never control a penny of that fortune. Brenham'll see to that."

Emory resented the criticism. He drew himself up, stiff and uncomfortable.

"My Lord, I . . ."

"Listen, lad, no offense. Don't get uppity. I like you, always have . . . hate to see Edwina using you. Oh," he said, smirking. "Did y' think I didn't know about that? I do. I just choose to look the other way. And don't flatter yourself," he added bluntly. "You're only one of many. Let me tell you something . . . She was a virgin when I married her. Aaaah, that surprises ye! Aye, a virgin, and a blonde beauty, too. But I was like you . . . handsome, ne'er-do-well . . . worthless. She was loyal and true for years, till I neglected her once too often to spend my time whoring and drinkin'. Hmph! When my convivial habits turned out to be confirmed drunkenness, Edwina turned elsewhere. I cannot blame her. How old d' you think I am?" he asked Emory brusquely. "I'll tell ye. Forty-nine, my last birthday."

Emory was visibly stunned. Haggard and drawn, with an unhealthy yellow tint to his flesh and most of his teeth missing, Lord Merrington looked closer to sixty-nine, at the very least.

"'Tis the drinking done much of it, but the whoring took its toll, too. Got the damned pox . . . That's why I can't sire m' own brat; poor thing'd be a halfwit for sure. I'll be dead soon, and unless Edwina can get one on her own, she'll see hard times when I go. 'Tis my confession, lad, take a lesson from it. Stay at home and tend yer own hearth, afore someone else does. And listen," he added, "bring y' wife up to Woodleigh Grange next weekend. Edwina's planning another of those damned parties. Be there!"

Merrington pointed to Rachel as she went whirling about the room, this time on the arm of a villainous-looking fellow wearing a naval officer's uniform.

"Y' better rescue her, lad; that bastard will waltz her right out to the garden and under a bush afore you know it."

As Emory rose to leave, Lord Merrington gave him a playful poke with his cane. "She looks to be quiet, lad. Them quiet ones sure come alive once't bedroom door closes, now don't they?"

Emory's booming voice joined Merrington's thin one in a peal of merry laughter. "That they do, m'Lord that they do." *If only you knew*, he thought to himself as he went down the ballroom steps. *If only you knew*. And he laughed again, remembering flying books and pillows, to say nothing of clocks and inkwells.

"Thank heavens you rescued me," said a breathless Rachel when she was enclosed in Emory's arms shortly afterward. "I couldn't stand that clutching much longer."

"And I suppose they all wanted to take you out to the garden," he said, holding her closer on the pretext of speaking into her ear.

"How did you know? But I really did want that breath of air they offered; it's so stuffy in here."

"But not with them?"

"Certainly not with them!"

"How about me? Will you go with me?" asked Emory as they glided toward the vaulted doors that led to the garden.

"Yes," said Rachel wearily, "and let us go now, please! I'm so overheated!"

Emory led Rachel through the doors and down the terrace steps, aware that half the men in the room had watched their exit.

"So! Suddenly you're not afraid to go for a walk in a darkened garden with me. I'm glad, but I'm also surprised. I thought you didn't trust me!"

"I don't," laughed Rachel. "But tonight you promised to behave . . . for . . ."

"For Ermaline," he finished. "Yes, I know."

The walled garden behind the Rowlands' house was quite unlike any Rachel had ever seen. It was a moon garden, with crushed white pebbles forming an almost luminous path, all the plantings restricted to those whose flowers and leaves were white or near white, reflecting silvery and ghostlike in the light of the evening's low moon. Plants and walks lay bordered by narrow swaths of cropped grass and manicured shrubberies, and here and there pedestaled statues, whitewashed by the sun and rain, stood watch over the promenaders. It was a garden designed with lovers in mind, and Rachel and Emory passed several other couples as they progressed from path to path. Only one of them did Rachel recognize—Lady Merrington, strolling arm in arm with a handsome young man wearing a nobleman's sash.

"Lord Simmsdale's son . . . young Lord Robert."

"Your successor, I take it," jibed Rachel, remembering again Edwina's salacious description of Emory.

Emory stopped on the path and turned to face Rachel, raising his voice. "Now see here," he said, almost shouting.

"Shhh!" Rachel said. "I was teasing. I'm sorry, I shouldn't have."

"Well, well, well!" smirked Emory, taking her arm again. "You apologizing to me! That calls for a drink!"

"No! You promised."

"And you promised to behave like a loving wife before all my friends. Under the circumstances, with the moon there . . . and this lovely garden here," he said, waving his arm about, "I think a kiss is called for . . . just to prove that we are devoted newlyweds. No scenes!" he ordered when Rachel resisted.

"You take advantage!" she hissed.

"I certainly do!" he said jocularly, drawing Rachel to the privacy of a tall shrub. He closed his arms about her, covering her lips with his. Whether it was the moon or the evening's excitement itself, Rachel knew not, but unexpectedly she found the sensation of his embrace not at all unpleasant. Emory's lips were soft and warm as they brushed over hers, and unlike their earlier embraces, this time he was careful to be gentle. There was no urgency in his kiss, and without even being aware of it, Rachel responded to the pressure of his mouth. One arm went slowly about his shoulder, and Emory drew her closer still.

The kiss was long and ardent, and when it was over, Emory was reluctant to release her. Their lips met a second time, and again Emory was passionate, but gentle. But this time Rachel's responses confused her. She pulled away from him.

"Emory . . . I . . . I," she stammered.

"Don't say anything," he said, circling her waist with his arm. "Let us resume our walk."

I can wait, little mouse, he said to himself as they continued around the path, aware, even if Rachel was not, that her response had been both eager and unfeigned. And oh, so sweet!

CHAPTER NINETEEN

No sooner had Ermaline departed with Aunt Adele and the cousins than Emory began to press Rachel on her offer to spend time alone with him.

"Have you ever seen an elephant?" he asked her at breakfast only a day or two later.

"Only in a picture book," she replied, curious and puzzled by his odd question.

"Good! Then I'll take you to the zoo. The elephant pavilion at Regent's Park is something to see. And I hear there's an Italian opera company in town. Does that interest you?"

Rachel was caught up by the excitement of free time also. "Aah, and while we're at it, how about a trip to the National Gallery?"

Before they knew it, they had planned an itinerary that would keep them busy day and night for most of the week. By mutual consent, both of them set aside their past grievances, and not once during that week was a harsh word spoken by either of them.

From the very first outing, Rachel was surprised at the change in Emory. His behavior was markedly different, gentle and attentive, revealing something of himself she had never seen before. He was always proper in his conduct and never once did she find cause to reprove him about his drinking. He was always sober.

Emory knew London intimately, and he showed Rachel, who had previously seen little of it, all the great and important places. He took her also to several out-of-the way places that delighted her no end. There was a little-known chop house, where great slabs of meat were served to them in wooden trenchers, and a bakery where they ate sticky meat pies like children, licking their fingers afterward. Once, in the East End, they watched an outdoor Punch and Judy show, laughing with their foreheads pressed close together. Always, it seemed, they were laughing, as Emory regaled her with one story or another about the people they met and the places they went.

The days flew past. They attended a musicale in a galleried concert hall, strolled through Kew Gardens, ambled about Sotheby's, and walked along the Thames. They went to the theater and the Italian opera, which Emory found absurd, but which Rachel enjoyed immensely. When the weather was good, there were carriage outings and riding jaunts in Hyde Park.

Wherever they went that week, they were at once the most attractive couple there. Heads turned in envy as Emory handed Rachel in and out of Adele's borrowed landau, and when she took his arm upon leaving the theater, many stepped aside to watch them pass by. Often, as at the ball, Emory's friends and acquaintances crowded around, hoping for an invite to join the inseparable pair in their rounds of the city. The silver bowl on the hall table was soon half filled with requests for their presence at all manner of affairs, but they sat, unopened and unanswered, for Emory had no intention of sharing Rachel with a single soul that week.

Egotist that he was, he took smug pride in Rachel's presence at his side, and she, in her turn, was pleased and flattered by the pleasant attentions he showered upon her. She couldn't help herself, was sure that no woman could, for Emory Guersten was a master at being charming when he chose to be.

Tall, virile, ruggedly handsome, impeccable in dress, and exact in his manners, he remained careful not to offend Rachel in any way and, shortly, was thrilled when he realized that she no longer withdrew or hesitated whenever he touched her arm or crowded close in a cab. In no time, Rachel was familiar with all the nuances of his speech, with every gesture of the hand that wore the boar's head ring, and she was oh, so familiar with those green, green eyes . . . for they were always upon her.

Occasionally, there were repeats of the kisses they had shared in the Rowlands' moon garden. Though not passionate, they were shared kisses that brought to life some unknown entity deep within Rachel's being, raising emotions that confused her. Wisely, Emory was cautious, never pressing Rachel for more, and by the end of the week she was even more confused, rethinking her feelings for him. Was it possible, she wondered, for someone to change so radically in one short week? And who was that someone . . . him or her?

Though mutually enjoying their week about town, by Thursday, both of them were exhausted by the pace they had set for themselves and chose to dine at home on Lettie's grilled salmon steaks. During the meal, the conversation turned to Lord Merrington's invitation, an order, really, to spend the coming weekend at Woodleigh Grange. Rachel balked, not wanting to go for several reasons, although at first only one of them was voiced as an excuse.

"I mean no offense, Emory, but I think that Edwina's company can do Ermaline little good."

"Ermaline?" Emory's face registered his surprise, for the invitation had not included his sister.

"She returns tomorrow from Adele's," stated Rachel, "and surely we cannot leave her here alone with just the servants for the weekend. It would be unseemly."

"Nonsense! Adele would be glad to keep her longer, especially if she knew you were about to enjoy yourself for a change."

Not at all certain that she would enjoy herself at Woodleigh Grange, still, Emory was on solid ground there, for Adele most cer-tainly would encourage Rachel to go, knowing the deprivation her social life had undergone for months on end. Besides, Adele, like her brother, still clung to the hope that these two adversaries would some-how salvage something from their marriage.

"Lord Merrington has practically demanded our presence," urged Emory, who saw the invite as a chance to extend his time alone with Rachel. "His influence is powerful, and who knows, someday I may have need of it. We should not disappoint him."

"Are you certain that it will be he who is disappointed if we do not show?" asked Rachel openly, touching upon another of her reasons not to go. Visions of Lady Merrington, blonde and seductive, danced through Rachel's head, for she had heard a number of rumors about Edwina's infamous parties and notorious guest list. Just now, Emory's face was unlined and calm; he was eating well and sleeping soundly. He looked remarkably fit, and his green eyes sparkled brightly, brightness sponsored by their own clarity, and not from a wine decanter. He was presently clean of his addiction to drink, and given a choice, Rachel preferred not to invite backsliding by thrusting among too familiar company.

Furthermore, having noted the hungry desire in Edwina's violet eyes as they watched Emory constantly the night of the ball, Rachel now considered the matter of Lady Merrington herself. What man could resist those charms, flaunted so openly . . . offered so freely? Would Emory? Could he, especially now, in view of her own lack of intimacy with him? Blushing discreetly behind her napkin, Rachel came to grips with the fact that it had now been some months since Emory had lain with a woman last.

"You have nothing to fear on that score, Rachel," he said in an earnest voice, shrewdly sensing the cause of her concern. "I am done with Lady Merrington. I have a wife . . . one that I want."

"But is Edwina done with you?" inquired Rachel simply, letting the rest of his comment pass. "She will be our hostess, and she wants . . ." Turning her head, Rachel studied the candelabra. "I won't be humiliated again, Emory, not there of all places," she said, after a time, flinging forth the words in a low voice that was almost a hiss.

Leaping from his chair, Emory raced around the table to Rachel's side, where he drew her to her feet and crushed her close, all so swiftly that she had no time to resist.

"Rachel! Rachel! Dear one! I shall never humiliate you again, ever. Don't you know, after this week, that it is you I want . . . you I need?"

Crushed against his wide chest as he whispered passionate words in her ear, Rachel wanted badly to believe him. She found his words rang empty. He spoke plainly of wants, openly of needs, but not at all of love. Its absence brought her around to her last excuse—Emory himself and their relationship.

Having enjoyed his company, she now hated to see the week drawing to a close almost as much as he did. Still, she wondered aloud, where were they destined to go from here? Would it not make more sense simply to return to Guersten Hall together?

There, they could learn where their new relationship would take them, discover what the future held. Day and night this past week they had been together, yet Emory restrained himself admirably. She knew he wanted her, and she admitted now to herself that since her opinion of him had so changed, she was physically attracted to him. The thought of succumbing to his advances no longer frightened her; still, she wasn't quite ready for . . . that!

Pressed against his shirtfront, Rachel groped for words. "It will be . . . too . . . awkward, Emory," she said, without looking up. "Thrown together in the same room, perhaps expected to share . . . the same . . . bed."

Emory lifted Rachel's chin. Staring intently into her brown eyes, he devoured them with his green ones before he crushed her against his chest once more. His heart pounded, and his ears rang until he was giddy.

"Oh, Rachel," he whispered in a voice that resounded with urgency and passion, "do you think I haven't thought of that . . . counted on it? I've dreamt about it! Dear God, look at me! I ache with need for you!"

Rachel stiffened. "Stop!" she cried.

"No!" he said defiantly, holding her even more closely. "Don't deny it! I want you, and you want me!"

"But, I don't! Not like that . . . not yet anyway."

"I don't believe you," he said, remembering the kisses they had shared and the way her lips had parted to meet his. She *had* returned those kisses; he wasn't mistaken in that! He couldn't be! But why did she fight it so?

Wrenching herself free, Rachel backed away from him, retreating behind her chair. "You're a fool, Emory!" she cried stiffly. "If *ever* I were to give myself to you, do you think it could be there, of all places? There, with Edwina just down the hall, and you so far into your cups you wouldn't even remember it the next morning? Never!"

Her shouting stopped, and Rachel sped from the room, as Emory, his head reeling as though he were drunk, fell into Rachel's vacated chair. He groaned aloud. "Oh, little mouse," he said, staring at the ceiling, "perhaps I *am* a fool, so wracked in my desire that I keep forgetting you're not like the rest! When will I learn?"

Before breakfast the next morning, a liveried courier arrived with a message that ended the matter. It was from Lord Merrington, penned in his own matchless script. It was abrupt. *Be there!*

Emory passed it to Rachel. She read it, then handed it back.

"So! Then we go."

"Rachel, nothing will happen! I promise . . ."

"Please! No more promises! You've made far too many already, and if you break one, the rest will fall like dominoes. It is actions that count now. Don't tell me . . . Show me!"

And so, in less than two hours they were on their way to Woodleigh Grange, coaching through the Kentish countryside. Though the trip was one Rachel would certainly have preferred not to make, still, she had never been to Kent before, and the landscape, at least, had some redemption. Her eye for quality farmland found much to admire. The scenery was pastoral and peaceful, pleasant villages marking the passing miles. In the country the houses ran the gamut from thatched cottage to palatial manor, some of brick and timber, others of stone and mortar. Sheep grazed in pastures that resembled green velvet, and under the trees, brown-faced cows, their udders heavy with milk, waited patiently for return to the barn. Once, they spotted ducks and geese squabbling like children for space at the edge of a pond, totally ignored by placid swans that floated in the middle.

With Sultan trailing behind, Emory remained at Rachel's side throughout this journey, and as they neared their destination, the boundaries of Lord Merrington's vast lands were pointed out to Rachel.

So vast were they that once inside those boundaries, they rode for yet another hour before passing through an arched stone wall which enclosed the estate's parkland. Through the trees Rachel spied the house itself, enormous and three storied, made entirely of fieldstone. Grown through years of add-ons, it was now a gem of architectural imperfection.

"Quite a rock pile, eh?" said Emory.

"It's all too pretentious."

"Nonsense, just a matter of taste and income."

But Rachel found the inside of the house to be just as horrid as the outside. Great stuffed birds shared shelving with dainty porcelain vases, and the furniture was an eclectic mishmash of periods and styles, some massive, some fragile, some gilded, some painted, but all thrown together until the place resembled a huge warehouse of sorts. Still, one theme coursed unrestrained throughout the manor; it reeked of money. *Everything* at Woodleigh Grange was expensive, if not in good taste.

The place was already well filled with guests when they arrived, most of whom Rachel had never seen before, and in contrast to the people she had met for the first time at the Rowlands', this group made her decidedly uncomfortable. She tried to remain always in the same room with Emory, but repeatedly he was dragged away, to be plied with cards and drink, both of which he steadfastly refused until it became priggishly embarrassing to do so any longer.

Forced to join the ladies in a soiree of idle small talk in Edwina's upstairs sitting room, Rachel detested every moment. Though cool and polite, Edwina was distinctly distant to her, making it quite clear that Rachel's presence put a damper on things. In manners and politeness, Rachel was equal to any, but she found their scandalous gossip shocking. Having previously sampled the favors of half the male guests there, Edwina and her contemporaries occupied themselves by comparing abilities and attributes openly. Now and then, throughout the waning afternoon, couples disappeared mysteriously, only to reappear later, their absence unquestioned by any.

At dinner that evening, Rachel found herself seated half a table length away from Emory, who had been positioned conspicuously to Edwina's right. Though he smiled down the table at her from time to time, it did little to dispel her feeling of being left out, although she certainly did not lack for attention. On the contrary, the mustachioed gallant to her left, a Spanish nobleman of some sort, continually retrieved his dropped napkin, leaning closer each time to ogle her bosom. Unwittingly, the gentleman opposite her played footsie with the Spaniard all during the meal, both of them certain that it was Rachel's slippered foot that had been corralled. In truth, Rachel's satined toes were tucked so far under her chair that she was uncomfortable, and she was decidedly glad to see an end to dinner.

Lord Merrington pigeon-holed her the next day in the conservatory, where Rachel had gone to seek a moment's respite from unwanted attentions. At the moment, she had no idea of Emory's whereabouts.

"And what do you think of Kent, little lady?"

"It is lovely, your Lordship, though I much prefer the midlands. But that is to be expected, I was born there."

"As was Emory."

"Ah, yes . . . well, sir, Emory and I, we do not always see things with the same eye."

"Know that, I do . . . I have ears in London. I know more than Emory thinks I do."

Rachel had no idea what was meant by Lord Merrington's cryptic remark, and to hide her ignorance, she pretended to be interested in the greenery spread about the glass-roofed room.

"Are you having a good time, my dear?" he went on, limping behind as Rachel wandered from table to table. "Be honest."

"Frankly sir, I am not."

Displaying a toothy grin, Merrington hooted with laughter, leaning on his cane for support. "Well, nob'dy ever said that straight to my face before! And what don't you like about my house?"

"Oh, it's not your house, sir! It's . . . it's lovely," Rachel lied. "It's just that I have nothing in common with your other guests."

"Oh? And what's wrong with 'em?"

"Nothing, your Lordship," said Rachel, wanting to shout *just about everything!* Instead, she said, "It is probably me . . . I am not used to being so . . . idle."

"And idle they are, the lot of 'em! You're on the money, there. No, m'girl, I knew you wouldn't fit in, but I had a reason for askin' ye. I want to give y' husband something . . ." He eyed Rachel up and down and waved his cane at her.

"What would you be doing right now if you were home . . . tendin' yer cabbages?"

Rachel giggled, amused at the bluff Lord's reference to her agricultural enterprise.

"You heard about that also, I take it?"

"I did! Told you, girl, I have ears . . . everywhere."

"Yes, I'd be tending my cabbages, as you put it, and there is Emory's father, who needs constant care, and my sister, who is soon to deliver a child . . . and I have my household duties, and my journals."

"Ah, yes," said the Lord. "Edwina did all those things once. So! You don't p'ticularly like my guests, eh? Well neither do I. Edwina invited most of them. Do you read?"

"All the time, your Lordship," said Rachel, confused by the way the conversation jumped around, and in truth getting more flustered by the moment. But then, abruptly, Lord Merrington turned and limped away.

"Well," he said, over his shoulder, "right across the way is the library. Hide in there when they grate y' nerves. Y'll be safe . . . only unused room in the house. Ain't nob'dy opened a book in this house God knows how long!"

Half an hour later, Emory ran into the Lord outside the gameroom.

"It was a mistake to bring Rachel here, m'Lord," he said. "She must find this way of life shocking."

Even as Emory spoke, more couples were pairing off for the evening, and damned few of them with their own spouses.

"Mebbe, mebbe not," mumbled the Lord. "She's holding up fine . . . jus' see no one takes advantage of her innocence, m'lad."

By midnight, when most of the other guests had already gone to their rooms, or someone else's room, at any rate, Rachel was thoroughly fatigued. Stiff from sitting, and bored no end, she sat in one corner of the stuffy gameroom, where Emory was engaged in a prolonged card game with several older gentlemen. Thick with smoke, the room was stifling. All the players had removed their coats hours ago, and sat now in their shirt sleeves.

"Go to bed, Rachel," encouraged Emory between deals. "This game may last for hours yet."

"I'm afraid, "she whispered to him. "I don't like this place."

"Nonsense. You are quite safe."

"You've been drinking," she sniffed, still whispering.

"Aye, but I'm not drunk, as you can see. There's a difference. Now, do go upstairs. I'll join you as soon as I can."

Reluctantly, Rachel stood, preparing to go upstairs, as Emory returned to his seat at the card table. *I might as well be ignored there, as here,* she fumed, crossing the carpeted floor. However, approaching the door, she was met by Edwina, who swept grandly into the room, followed by her ever faithful hangers-on. Pointedly taking up a position just behind Emory, Edwina placed her hands possessively on his wide shoulders, her expensive rings glittering brightly, despite the smoky light.

"Good night, my dear child," she said sweetly to Rachel, giving her a superior smile. "We'll see you at breakfast."

The two women glared at one another across the length of the room and over Emory's bent head. Plainly, Edwina's words were meant as a dismissal, and plainly, she spoke for Emory as well as herself, or presumed to anyway. His company was desired by both of them that night, but for markedly diverse reasons. One was looking for joyous pleasure . . . the other simple protection.

Staring across at her husband for some sign, some word of reassurance on her behalf, Rachel stood for a moment, undecided whether to go or to stay. Emory did not look up; instead, collecting the cards to deal again, he ignored both Rachel and Edwina, his concentration centered wholly on the baize covered table. Consequently, no one but Edwina even noticed when Rachel left the room.

But once out in the corridor Rachel stood with clenched fists, burning at being sent away like a bothersome child. Half tempted to return to the gameroom, she peeked furtively through the still opened door, to see Emory, open shirted, still dealing the cards, while Edwina set another drink before him. All of the men were laughing jocularly at some off-color joke, and Edwina's silvery tones were heard above them all.

Rachel started up the steep stairs to her room, a miserable little box near the back stairs. Whether assigned by accident or design she knew not, though the simple truth was that Edwina, naturally assuming that Emory would bed with her, cared little where Rachel spent her nights, or how.

After closing the door, Rachel paced the floor in swift strides, furious at Edwina for what she deemed an insult, and angry with Emory for his callous disregard for her feelings. Moreover, she was equally angry with herself, for not rising to put both of them in their places. An hour passed, and then another, and Rachel grew angrier still. She did not pretend to sleep, did not undress even, but sat, tense and rigid, on the edge of her bed, waiting for Emory to come to her, as he had promised. In the hall, footsteps fell, and doors closed, as couples changed partners, frequently, from the sound of things. Her own door was locked, fortunately, as it turned out, for the knob was rattled several times.

While Rachel waited vainly, the card game downstairs finally broke, and Edwina approached Emory as the others quit the room.

"Will you have a nightcap with me?"

"Yes," Emory replied. "I want to talk to you anyway."

"Ah," she said, smiling in anticipation of a splendid night of love-making. She tucked her arm through one of his. "Come, we will go to my bedchamber."

"No!" said Emory with an emphasis that surprised her. "We'll use your sitting room, instead."

His suggestion, and the tone in which it was offered, was unusual, for Emory was more than familiar with Edwina's bedroom at Woodleigh Grange, with its lavender draperies and satin bedsheets. She said nothing, though, merely led the way to her second floor parlor. There, she poured a brandy for them both, and then stood so close to Emory that her powerful perfume rushed to his head.

"We are wasting time, darling," she said, seductively, letting her hand wander freely. "I have need of you tonight, and well you know it. It has been a while," she added, whispering.

"And what of all the others you invited?" he said, his eyes suddenly mischievous. "Do you need them, too?"

Edwina waved a jeweled hand airily. " Does it upset you that I share my bed with others? Then I will dismiss them, and be yours alone."

Emory sipped his drink, and then laughed. "Ah, Edwina . . . you'd be tumbling with the coachman as soon as my back was turned."

"And you with the coachman's wife, eh? We know each other well, don't we?"

"Yes, we do, and we've always been honest with one another. That is the reason I must tell you . . . myself, that our liaison must come to a halt."

"But why?" she asked, openly shocked. "I thought you loved me."

"I never told you that, Edwina, and you know it. Mutual gratification brought us together, and it has kept us together. That and friendship!"

"Then why end it? Because you are married? It matters not to me!"

"But . . . there is the rub! Suddenly it does, to me!"

"Aaaah . . . Rachel! I should have guessed, especially after seeing you in the garden the night of Ermaline's party. You seemed quite smitten. Do you love her?"

"I don't know. It is one of the answers I seek."

"Does she love you?"

"Rachel neither loves me, nor wants me," Emory said, putting down his glass. He wandered about the well appointed room, and then faced Edwina again. "She is, in fact, still a virgin. I am barred from her bedchamber!"

"A virgin? Oh, how priceless!" Edwina, wide-eyed at Emory's confession, tried not to smile. "But, oh, poor darling! That is no marriage!"

"Exactly, only a relationship of sorts. But I have never given that relationship a fair chance, Edwina, not since the very first day that my father arranged it. I think I owe that much to Rachel now."

Despite her strong sexual appetite and her exaggerated lifestyle, Edwina Merrington was not a bitch, though she played the part well. She was not in love with Emory, any more than he with her.

In fact, in her own peculiar way, Edwina's heart belonged entirely to Lord Merrington. It was only her body that craved something else. Swallowing her drink, she deposited the fragile glass on the wine table next to Emory's.

"You know I am not as despicable as some would believe. I have never bedded a man who wasn't willing. For now, then, I shall step aside, and let you pursue this, er . . . relationship of yours. If it fails, or you change your mind, you will always find me . . . available."

"Thank you, Edwina. In time, perhaps Rachel will come to understand about us, but even if she doesn't, it would please me to know that you and I will always remain friends."

"But, of course!" she said, pouring another drink into the tiny glasses. "By the way, darling, your secret is safe with me," she added, in a whispery tone. "None shall know that Rachel is still pure as the driven snow."

Away upstairs, in the nether regions of the house, Rachel stirred from the edge of her bed, daring to venture forth from her room in search of Emory. The hallway now seemed quiet, at last, as she crept down the stairs, only to find the gameroom empty. Lured by the sound of voices, she made her way back up the polished stairs, to find herself outside Edwina's sitting room. Inside, Edwina and Emory stood close together, sipping from small glasses and conversing intimately. Rachel was shocked to find Emory there.

"So then!" Edwina was saying, trying not to let her disappointment at losing a night's partner upset her very much, "you have decided that you want this . . . er . . . relationship, to continue?"

Not realizing that the two of them had already spoken at length, Rachel could only guess what that relationship might be, and naturally assumed that Edwina referred to her own affair with Emory. But still, she was not prepared for Emory's reply.

"Why not? I feel I should play it out, see where it takes us.

"And what will you tell Rachel?"

"I don't intend to tell her anything. This conversation concerns only you and me."

"True enough," said Edwina, who admitted to herself that no wife could be expected to understand her husband's intimate involvement with another woman. Hadn't she traveled that road herself, many times? No, the Rachel's of this world would never understand the pull of the flesh that drew women like Edwina to men like Emory, not at all in love with each other, but friends and lovers all the same.

Touching Emory's cheek fondly, Edwina lifted her glass. "I propose a toast . . . to love," she said.

"And the pain it brings," added Emory.

"I prefer the pleasures myself," murmured Edwina, stepping closer to him. She ran an arm about his waist. "Let us share one last kiss, love, before we part."

Rachel, standing in the dimly lit hall, did not hear Edwina's final whispered comment, or Emory's reply. But she did see Edwina place both arms around Emory's neck, and press herself against his length. Then, she closed her eyes and kissed Emory's mouth hungrily. He, in turn, returned that kiss.

Misunderstanding, Rachel recoiled from the sight of them, stunned and deeply hurt. Turning, she dashed away to her backstairs room and rang for a footman. While waiting, she tossed her clothes into the single valise she had brought with her.

"Send for my carriage," she ordered when the startled footman arrived. "And take that bag downstairs."

"Now? In the middle of the night?"

"Now! In the middle of the night! And be quick about it!"

Scurrying close behind the weary footman, Rachel went back down the shadowy staircase one more time. When her carriage drew up, she grasped the door handle and climbed in without waiting for assistance. Hewlitt, the coachman, stood rubbing sleep from his eyes with one hand, checking the gray's harness with the other.

"I am alone," said Rachel from the window. "Let us be away to Guersten Hall!"

"Now? In the middle of the night?"

"You sound like a parrot, Hewlett! Now! In the middle of the night! Off with you!"

The heavy coach pulled away from the manor, and the worried footman turned, hurrying back up the steps. "I must inform the lady's husband," he muttered to no one in particular. "She cannot go alone!"

A voice rang out of the gloom of the doorway. "Let her go!" Lord Merrington stepped into the light.

"But, sir . . ."

"No buts! Wait one hour exactly, and then tell Guersten his wife has gone. One hour, do y' hear?"

"Aye, Emory," said the Lord to himself, "and when y' find her gone, then you'll have to choose, on the spot, between this way of life and hers. Yer future . . . . 'tis hinged on that choice."

The hour passed. Exactly ten minutes later Emory, astride Sultan, galloped out of the stables at Woodleigh Grange. Lord Merrington waited for him by the paddock gate.

"What the hell's the meaning of this, m'Lord?" demanded Emory angrily, reining his horse. "Why did you let Rachel leave?"

"Let us say that it was a test, lad, and you passed with flying colors."

"I don't understand . . ."

"You will, someday. For now, consider it a favor, for I like ye and y' bride. And remember, boyo, always be faithful to the one you want, if you would demand faithfulness in return."

"Little you know," said Emory in a voice slightly tinged with scorn, "though I thank you anyway for the free advice. If you are so damned well informed, then you must know that the one I want doesn't want me!"

"Small wonder, way you was! Them kind you must earn, m'boy." Merrington pointed with his cane up the darkened road. "Her coach should've just about cleared my outer boundaries by now. I'll tell Edwina you said farewell, now, be off, lad, the girl could meet with danger alone! Lots o' robbers out there."

"Aye, lad, a favor," muttered Merrington after Emory had torn up the turf in his haste to be away, "one that I wish't someone'd done fer me twenty years ago."

Miles down the road the grays, under Hewlett's guidance, were carefully picking their way through the pitch black night. Even so, the coach struck every stone in the roadbed, it seemed, bumping and rocking so wildly that Hewlett feared it would tip over.

Inside, Rachel sat fuming, so angry at Emory that she hardly noticed the erratic movements of the coach. *Nothing would happen,* he had promised. *Ha! Everything had happened!* As if resuming his drinking and gambling were not enough, she herself had heard the final insult; Emory and Edwina plotting to continue their illicit relationship, despite the fact that both of them were already married, and despite Rachel's very presence at Woodleigh Grange. *Damn them both!* It had been a mistake to go there. She should have flatly refused and returned to Guersten Hall . . . alone, if necessary. At least there she was needed!

"Damn the man!" she said, out loud. "Damn him and damn his worthless promises. And damn that hussy, too!"

So intent on cursing Emory roundly was Rachel that it took several minutes for her to notice that the rocking of the coach had stopped. She wound down the window glass, poking her head out, only to have a lantern thrust into her face.

Two men stood beside the coach. There was no doubt that they were thieves; one held Hewlett at gunpoint, the other peered up at Rachel.

"Well, well, what d' we have 'ere?" said the huge highwayman, rubbing his groin with a hammy fist. He snatched open the coach's door, while Rachel backed into the seat, cringing.

"Who are you? Wh . . . what is going on?" she demanded, hoping to sound authoritative and brave, yet knowing that her voice betrayed her fear.

"Why, we bein' a robbin' your coachman, good lady," he said, laughing at her. "Now bring y'self down from there an' we'll see what's to be done wi' ye."

He laughed once more, showing broken teeth, and Rachel shuddered as he rubbed his groin provocatively, but she did as she was told. Still, it dawned on her that something she had been reluctant to give willingly, might now be taken forcibly from her. On the ground, she huddled next to the frightened Hewlett, as the two of them cowered before the robbers. One of them reached out a greasy paw toward Rachel's breast.

"Keep your hands to yourself, matey!" said a voice that boomed out of the darkness.

It was Emory, and suddenly the night air was rent by the sound of Sultan's excited neigh, a wicked scream that terrorized the robber's horses. In panic, both of them bolted and fled. In unison, both highwaymen spun around; the one with the lantern held it high, and spying the huge stallion that reared and snarled before him, he dropped the light and took off up the road after the horses. Behind him his partner fairly ran up his back in his haste to get away.

Dismounting, Emory approached Rachel, ashen faced and trembling.

"Are you all right?"

"Oh, Emory!" she wailed, throwing herself into his arms, so frightened at that moment that she forgot she was angry with him.

"Well, now! I shall have to rescue you more often!"

"Don't make jokes," she said, though she didn't loosen her hold on his neck. "Just take me home! Please, Emory . . . take me home!"

Scooping her up, Emory deposited her in the coach, and then climbed in himself, calling out to the coachman, now recovered from his own fright.

"Home, Hewlett! Home to Guersten Hall!"

Underway, Emory tried to comfort Rachel. He wrapped his coat around her shivering shoulders, and removing a lap robe from its place beneath a seat, covered her with its warmth.

"Don't tremble so, Rachel. You are safe now. Come," he said, gathering her into his arms again, "you're exhausted. Snuggle down and try to sleep. We'll talk tomorrow."

They rode in silence for some minutes, both of them glad to be putting Woodleigh Grange behind them.

"We never should have gone," said Rachel drowsily into Emory's shirtfront.

"Oh . . . I don't know," murmured Emory, ecstatic at the way she still clung to him.

"What did he give you?"

"Give me? Who?"

"Lord Merrington. He told me he invited us because he wanted to give you something. What was it?"

A gift? thought Emory. Well, certainly nothing tangible had passed between the two men, but then again, Lord Merrington had presented Emory with considerable food for thought this night. A favor, Merrington had called it.

"Perhaps he did give me something, at that, Rachel," murmured Emory. His confusion began to lift, as he understood the Lord's ploy at last. But Rachel did not hear; she was already asleep in his arms.

In the morning, Emory rode ahead, purchasing breakfast for them and feed for the animals at a country farmhouse. By the time Hewlett pulled the grays to a halt the farmer's shy young wife had an array of hearty fare ready for them in her spotless cottage kitchen. There were eggs and buttery hotcakes, slabs of ham and steamy biscuits. The lass packed a hamper of food to go with them, and later, ushered Rachel into a back bedroom, and bringing towels and a basin of hot water, afforded Rachel privacy to make her morning toilette. In her haste to depart Woodleigh Grange, Rachel had not stopped to change her clothes, and she did so now, exchanging the rose colored evening dress for a simple day gown of cobalt blue with its own matching coat.

Rachel was completely subdued as they set off once again. Last night's angry mood had been replaced momentarily by panic and fright, but she remembered that anger, and its cause, nonetheless. The experience had taught her a valuable lesson, proving, as it did, that trusting a man like Emory was reckless. She must be on guard now, lest she be swayed and taken in by his engaging charm ever again. In choosing not to offend his hostess, Emory had broken his promises to her, had succumbed to cards and drink. Rachel could forgive him that, perhaps, but never, never, for his weakness in succumbing to Edwina's charms, so soon after he had spoken of wanting only her, needing only her. Oh, and to think she had almost believed him! *Bah!* The man could not, or would not, be reformed.

Aware of Rachel's cold and quiet mood, Emory knew that she, like he, was remembering and contemplating the events of the previous evening.

"It's time we talked," he said, leaning forward in his seat. "Why did you run away? It was foolhardy, as you learned."

"I didn't run away," responded Rachel, annoyed at being put on the defensive, and at the prospect of a lecture. "I simply . . . left, and while I'm sorry I put Hewlett's life in jeopardy, still, under the circumstances, I could not remain in that house another minute."

"And what circumstances might those be?"

Rachel stared wide-eyed at him, amazed that he could pretend such innocence. Of course, he didn't know that she had witnessed his shared embrace with Edwina, but even so, he had ignored her most of last night, had let her sit alone in that miserable room for hours; and hadn't he kept silent when Edwina dismissed her like a wayward child?

Without affording Emory an opportunity to offer excuses or make apologies, one by one, she catalogued the reasons why she had fled in the middle of the night.

"It's foolish to discuss it further," she said to him in a flat voice, ending the conversation. "We will only squabble. Once, quite pointedly, you told me that you are what you are, and I must accept it. Perhaps the same holds true of me. Maybe it explains why we are so . . . incompatible. Our mistake was not recognizing it sooner. I do now."

Not surprisingly, Emory became angry under her withering criticism, as the red scar testified, but wisely, he checked his emotions and held his tongue, not wanting to alienate her further. He did not whistle for Sultan, did not run away, but remained in his seat, as silence engulfed them for the remaining miles. Dejectedly, he understood then that the ground gained during that wonderful week in London was now lost, but having closed one door behind him, somehow he would struggle to open the next, and see what lay before him.

CHAPTER TWENTY

Fatigued and glad to put an end to the long and silent ride with Emory, Rachel pressed forward on her seat, peering out the window when the carriage turned up the Hall's stony drive. It was dark again, and Rachel started when she spied Duncan's small Victoria parked under the dimly lighted porte cochere. *Rebecca!*

"Stay calm, Rachel," cautioned Emory. "It is Sunday; perhaps Ferguson merely came by for a visit."

But when they rushed into the house, Stoddard greeted them in the reception hall, and behind her, two maids scuttled up the stairs, one with a kettle of hot water, the other carrying a mountainous stack of linens.

"It is Rebecca!" said Emory.

"Aye!" responded the gray-haired cook, glad to see them. "She went into labor last night, but Duncan was away, so we sent for Dr. Broadman, who left just an hour ago, thrown out by Duncan, who's upstairs, and right now I'm not at all sure just what's happening up there." The long sentence was rambled off with hardly a pause, as Stoddard, looking worried, hustled Emory and Rachel, still in their coats, up the stairs to the salon where the other members of the household waited around for something to happen. Stoddard's rambling served only to heighten Rachel's concern; concern that Emory now shared, as well.

"Tell ye father I haven't forgotten the tea tray," called Stoddard, as they neared the top. "T'will be right along."

"I don't know anything," said Edward, some few minutes later in answer to the many questions Rachel fired off. "Ferguson came to the salon but once, and then only to tell us not to worry. Go and see what you can learn, Rachel. He won't let me in."

"I'm not surprised," she said, sizing up her brother-in-law's appearance as she greeted her mother and George with warm embraces. "Look at you!"

Edward, obviously harried, was considerably mussed, wearing a rumpled coat and two day old whiskers. Rachel chided him, and reluctantly he left the salon to bathe and shave, but only after she had promised to learn what she could from Duncan about Rebecca's progress.

"Why was Broadman here? Why was he thrown out?" inquired Emory of his father and Louisa jointly, while helping Rachel out of her coat. "I believe those were the exact words Stoddard used. What's it all about?"

"It has something to do with medication that Dr. Broadman gave her," offered Louisa, looking tired and rumpled herself. "Rebecca has been in deep sleep ever since; some hours now."

Rachel tapped lightly on the door of the square bedroom, and then entered, closing the door behind her. Rebecca, her eyes closed and her knees drawn up, lay off to one side of the wide canopied bed, one arm dangling limply over the side. Across her pale forehead glistened beads of perspiration, reflected in the light of the lamps Duncan had drawn close around the bed. The tall doctor crossed quickly to Rachel's side when she emerged from the shadows near the door.

"Thank the Lord you have returned," he said, giving her a weak smile. "I can use a level head about now."

"Is she all right? Can I help in some way?"

"So far," answered Duncan, taking the questions as they came, "and yes . . . I'd welcome some help." Rubbing his chin thoughtfully, he observed Rebecca clinically from a distance.

"*Damn* that Broadman!" he cussed. "Dosing her with laudanum, God knows how much. She's in a deep sleep, Rachel, but we've got to bring her round or her labor's going to last far too long."

In words dripping with scorn, Duncan briefed Rachel about Broadman's administrations. At every whimper, it seemed, Rebecca was given another draught of the opiate, and Broadman dosed himself with whiskey each time, as well, from a flask he always carried on his hip.

"I came by just on a hunch," he added, "to find them both drugged." He motioned to the chair where he had found Broadman sleeping off his last draught.

"Who sent for him," inquired Rachel, concerned. "Everyone here knows he is unreliable."

"Ah, well, I guess it was a mutual thing. They all panicked when her pains started and they couldn't locate me, especially after Stoddard revealed to your mother that there had been some bleeding."

"Oh, dear," wailed Rachel, "that began two weeks ago; on the morning I left for London. Does it present a problem?"

Duncan pursed his lips. "Who can say just yet? She has hours to go."

"Well, I want to help. Where shall I start?"

"Change from your traveling clothes, and then let's get her freshened up," he said, each of them unknowingly reassuring the other with their no nonsense approach to the task at hand. "Sponge her down, and change the bed linens. I'll get Stoddard to assist you; she's familiar with this sort of thing. Rebecca's pains may start coming closer soon, but you still have time."

Leaving the room, Rachel returned a scant ten minutes later, tying an apron over a dark day dress. While Duncan went to bolt down some supper, Rachel followed his instructions, and Rebecca was soon resting against cool and fragrant pillowslips, garbed in a fresh nightgown. Rachel brushed her sister's long hair, fixing it in loose braids.

Below stairs, the girls kept the stove fired, and the hot water cauldron was refilled again, while Becky was set to work cutting squares from a bolt of lockram. In the salon, Edward disintegrated into an emotional wreck, and not knowing what else to do, Emory took him downstairs and tried to ply him with brandy, his own customary remedy in times of trial. Wisely, Edward refused the glass that was offered. "Getting drunk won't help Rebecca," he said.

Rachel returned to the salon from time to time to give them all a progress report of sorts, although there was really little to tell. "We must wait," she said. "These things take time, I'm told. Why don't you all go to bed?"

"I won't greet my first grandson in my nightshirt," George said by way of refusal. He tried to sound lighthearted, but the night's progress reminded him of another, so many years before, only then it was his beloved Isabelle who had suffered, torn and bleeding, through the agonies of childbirth . . . her cries that were heard, as Edward now heard Rebecca's. The results of that disastrous night had changed the course of George's life, and while he often thought of Isabelle, could conjure up her beautiful face at will, it was his habit never to dwell upon the son who had gone to the grave with her. Now, the parallels between that night and this made not remembering difficult, and remembering frightened the old man.

Despite his resolve, though, George eventually dozed off, still sitting in his wheelchair, his head propped on a pillow thoughtfully provided by Angus. Rebecca's loved ones were still in the salon at daybreak, but their waiting was not over. All told, Rachel and Stoddard remained with Rebecca nearly sixteen hours, assisting Duncan in what proved to be a difficult birth. As the effects of Broadman's laudanum wore away, Rebecca suffered pitifully. The room reeked of blood, and Rachel worried if her sister could last much longer.

"She's bound to suffer toward the end," stated Duncan, following the course of Rebecca's pains. "The child is good sized for all its early."

"Can't you give her anything?" cried Rachel, as Rebecca screamed again.

Duncan shook his head. "It will only prolong the inevitable now, Rachel. That child means to be born, and it will go quicker if she helps."

"Push!" he shouted at Rebecca, as she groaned under the onslaught of a new and stronger contraction.

"I can't," sobbed Rebecca, weakly, tossing her head from side to side. "I just can't . . ."

"You must!" said Rachel sternly, leaning over to wipe her sister's pale face with a cool cloth. "Your son wants to be born, and Edward is frantic with worry. Now push, Rebecca! Push!"

Biting her lip and clutching Rachel's hand in hers, Rebecca pushed, and pushed again. And yet again, garnering strength from that hidden reserve known only to women; until suddenly she sucked in her breath, her body gripped by one last great and terrible pain. Then, the squall of a healthy infant filled the room.

Thus, shrieking indignantly at the way he was handled, Rebecca's son came into the world midmorning on that bright May day. Surprisingly strong, considering his mother's health and his arrival a good month early, the boy was hale and hearty, weighing nearly six pounds. Brilliant sunshine and fluffy clouds heralded his arrival, and with him came new green shoots and warming temperatures, on air that was heavy laden with the smell of fresh plowed earth, moist and fertile.

"A good omen," said Stoddard, who believed in such things, as she watched Rachel swaddling the child in swansdown.

"A child of the land," commented George later, when Rachel placed the infant in the circle of his one good arm.

After being duly admired, the baby was put to bed, and Edward was allowed some time alone with Rebecca. Half asleep, she sensed his presence somehow, and opened her eyes to find him on his knees beside the bed. Once again she was fresh and clean, her hair coiled loosely about her face. She reached for Edward's hand.

"A son. Edward! A son!" she whispered before he had a chance to speak. "I did it, though how I shall never know. Have you been here long?"

He shook his head, awed by the sight of her. He kissed her fingertips, noting with dismay her colorless skin and the dark circles still forming under her eyes.

"You look awful," he said, bluntly.

"I won't lie to you," she said, in a tired voice. "I feel awful. But don't smother yourself with guilt, Edward . . . I'm happy. Besides," she added, "you don't look much better yourself!"

Clutching her stomach, Rebecca changed her position in the wide bed, moaning as she rolled onto her side to be closer to him. "Don't look so scared. I'm all right, just a little sore."

Tender concern was mirrored in Edward's face, as he positioned a pillow against the small of Rebecca's back, and then, kneeling again, he choked, burying his face in her hair. When he lifted his eyes again, they were brimming with happiness and unspoken love.

"Did you see him?" she asked, drowsily.

"I held him," answered Edward, nodding. "So did his grandfather."

"Umm," mumbled Rebecca, half asleep. "My eyes are heavy. Kiss me and let me sleep."

"I love you," Edward said, leaning to brush his lips against hers. But Rebecca never heard his words, nor felt the touch of his lips; she was already sound asleep.

The child and his mother were the only ones in the house who did sleep for a while. Rachel, now staggering with fatigue, helped Stoddard set the room to rights, and then she and Duncan joined the others in the dining room for a breakfast of sorts, although every one of them was too excited and tired to eat. Their joy at Rebecca's safe deliverance was boundless, and Edward, rejoicing that his wife's long ordeal was over, now took the whiskey that Emory offered, raising it high when George called for a toast to his new grandson. One by one, throughout the morning, the estate's workers made their way up to the big house to congratulate Edward. Each was offered a whiskey, and each in turn raised his glass in traditional salute to the newest Guersten.

The chaos calmed, the house quieted. Stoddard went to her bed and so did Louisa, only she would post a letter to Benjamin before she slept, writing of their daughter's safe deliverance.

"And now, my dear," said George, turning to Rachel, "I think it's high time you and I nodded off, too."

"Oh . . . Rebecca's in your bed," remarked Edward. "Where will you sleep?"

"Right here at the table, I fear," murmured Rachel, who sat with her head propped in her hands. "In a house with twenty bedrooms, can it matter?"

George shifted in his chair. "It can, and does! In your absence, I had Adele's old room done over especially for you. In the whirlwind surrounding the babe, I clean forgot about it. Your mother and Rebecca took care of the colors and the details. It was to be a surprise, and they'll both be disappointed not to be with you when you see it for the first time." He rang for Angus. "But now, if you don't mind, I'm away. I've been in this chair far too long already. My arse is numb and my back hurts. I'll see you all at dinner."

Duncan departed, promising to return on the morrow. The tired doctor had yet to look in on one more last patient before enjoying some well deserved rest of his own.

"Aren't you going upstairs?" Rachel inquired of Emory, at the foot of the stairs.

"I'll nap, I guess, but first I must tend to Sultan, and I need to stretch my legs. I think I'll ride for a while. I don't suppose you'd care to join me?"

"Ride? I should say not! I spent the weekend jolting through the countryside, remember? It's been three days since I've seen a decent bed."

Emory laughed. "You're right of course, but it's so beautiful outside I hate to waste it."

It *was* a glorious day, and Rachel's eye was drawn to the foyer, where the tall front doors had been thrown open and propped wide. Long slashes of sunlight were mirrored on the polished floor, and the fragrance of new grass aired the house pleasantly.

"Angus must have done that."

"A proper butler, he! No side doors for him."

"We ought to leave them open more often. The colors in the marble never looked lovelier." said Rachel, yawning.

"Come; it's up the stairs with you. You're done in."

Rachel turned, looking up the stairs, which loomed up before her like the side of a shiny mountain. She was so tired! How would she ever get to the top?

As if reading her mind, Emory bent and scooped her into his arms, lifting her effortlessly, and started up the stairs. She offered some weak resistance, but one arm went around his neck and she rested her head against his shoulder. Emory, happy and buoyed as always by her nearness, pretended to be lost. "Let's see . . . Ermaline's room is on the left, so Adele's must be over here."

"Ermaline!" cried Rachel, one hand flying to her lips. "Ermaline! Good grief, Emory! We forgot her! We left her in London!"

"Well, I'll be damned!" he said, setting her down. "So we did!"

In their haste to remove themselves from Woodleigh Grange they had driven straight back to Guersten Hall without returning to London. Ermaline was still at Adele's, and now it struck both of them as amusing. They went down the corridor laughing together. George, just drifting off to sleep, heard it and was heartened.

Opening the door to Rachel's new room, Emory ushered her inside with a sweeping motion. He gave the decorating a cursory inspection and then backed out the door, as Rachel turned this way and that, examining this new space with a critical eye.

The room was lovely, all done in mellow greens and sunny yellow, with lots of white for contrast. It was considerably smaller than the dark one near the grand salon, but Rachel didn't mind, for one wall was lined with a trio of wide windows, all of them overlooking the terrace and the gardens. But even more important, the room was flooded with morning sunlight. It was heavenly!

All the furniture was matching; a remarkable oddity in an old manor-house, where pieces had been collected singly over centuries. A green velvet chaise was placed before one window, and Rachel sat there now to remove her shoes. Before her stood an enormous four poster bed, high and wide, its print coverlet strewn with a jumble of pillows, and she flung herself among them, luxuriating in their softness. Oh, it was such bliss just to lie down. She stretched out, for just a moment, she thought, but was too tired to get up again.

Her brain whirled, as drowsily the events of the past days and hours spun through it; disjointed and unconnected by fatigue . . . Emory . . . the baby . . . the ball . . . kisses . . . robbers. In seconds, she was asleep.

Rebecca's recovery from the ordeals of childbirth was torturously slow and equally arduous, and it was never complete, for she was left permanently weakened and more fragile than ever. There were days when she barely left her bed, but now she never fretted at being alone. She had her son for company, and she was enthralled by his tiny presence. Her one desire was to nurse him herself, but that desperate yearning went unfulfilled, for those small and boyish breasts that had so enticed Edward, now swelled and plumped, but the milk that came from them was thin and scant. The baby howled his protests, and Anna Maxwell-MacKinder, small but very buxom was brought to Guersten Hall and promptly installed as wet nurse, oozing enough milk for two babies.

Disappointed, Rebecca resented Anna at first, jealously handing over her son for his feedings. When the child fattened before her very eyes almost, Rebecca set aside her resentment, and the two women soon became friends. During the child's feedings, Anna would settle herself on the edge of Rebecca's bed, and the pale girl would watch in tender amusement as her son searched out and snatched up Anna's rosy nipples, gorging himself on the thick, yellowy fluid. Once, Rebecca reached out a finger and dipped it into Anna's milk, where it dribbled from the infant's mouth; she tasted it and gave a bland shrug.

"It doesn't look, taste or smell like much of anything," she said, "and yet it does so much."

"Like the very stuff that made him, eh?" quipped Anna, sagely.

The baby, who slept soundly in the same spindled cradle his father had used, was adorable. From birth he was the spitting image of his maternal grandfather, dark haired, gray eyed, in all respects a Brenham, so like Benjamin that it was uncanny. He was christened Edward, after his father and an assortment of earlier Guerstens, but from the first he was Little Benjy to all, and no one in the house felt their day complete without passing his cradle to have a finger pressed by that pudgy fist. Even Emory succumbed to the charm of the child, though he flatly refused to hold him or pick him up, for the baby's constant wriggling unnerved him.

Rachel returned her attentions to her agricultural venture after the christening. By now, much of the arable land at the Hall had fallen to the plow, and the scattered fields abounded with a wide assortment of produce in graduated stages of development, from seedlings on up.

Peter was an able overseer, on top of almost every problem even before it developed, but still, they were not without their share of difficulties and failures. There were some personality conflicts to be dealt with, and a field of month old plants that wilted and died without apparent cause. Once several acres of seedlings were washed away in a heavy rainstorm . . . and the rabbits! They were everywhere! Peter had never seen so many, and Rachel wondered if some inner biological voice told them their numbers were nearly decimated in the winter just past?

"Turn the dogs loose at night," said Gaffy, surveying the damage they did one night, "and when ye slaughter any o' the fowls, save the blood. Spot it round the edge of the fields. Rabbits don't like the smell o' blood."

Though often at Rachel's side when she rode about the estate, Emory continued to take no active part in its operation, leaving the direction of Rachel's enterprise wholly to her. He offered no opinions except those that Rachel especially requested. Try as she might, she could not seem to interest him in anything pertaining to the future of Guersten Hall. It disturbed her, for with both brothers at last on the premises, Rachel did not want to assume the reins any longer. But neither, it seemed, did Emory.

And so, in time, some of the decision making passed to Edward. He reveled in it, gloried in it, rising at daybreak each morning to spend hours at a time at Peter's side. Having grown up together on the estate, they were already lifelong friends, and they were alike in many ways. Both of them loved the land, held profound respect for it, and so it was natural, then, that the role of overseer passed almost unseen from Peter to Edward, who took it simply because Emory wouldn't.

Rachel understood that Emory was unhappy, knew that he had never wanted to be master in a landlocked harbor, but Guersten Hall was his inheritance, his birthright, and he had a duty to it and his father. As far as their own relationship was concerned, she knew what it was that he wanted, nothing had changed on that score, but the trip to Woodleigh Grange had spoiled everything, and now Rachel's heart was steeled against his advances.

There the situation remained, until unexpectedly, much to her chagrin, Emory resumed his drinking. He drank at night, through the day, and during dinner, but his conduct was acceptable at all times, his clothes and manners impeccable. He drank, but he did not get drunk, and, as he so often reminded Rachel, there was a difference.

"I feel partly responsible," she told George one day, as they sat playing chess in the library.

"You? How so?" he inquired with raised eyebrows.

"Once we were enemies, and then we became friends. He is ready for more, I am not. It is as simple as that."

"I see," said the old man, capturing Rachel's queen. "And you worry that you will become enemies once more?"

"Yes. I would not like to see that happen, but I am not ready to give my . . . heart. And then too, I am concerned that he continues to let others assume his role as Master here. Me, Edward . . . even Peter."

"It is puzzling, isn't it?" agreed George. He cleared his throat. "Tell me, my dear, just how do you feel about Emory? If I speak out of turn, please say so."

"You have a right to ask," said Rachel, conceding the game, "and if I knew I would tell you. The truth is, I simply don't know."

The Buckinghamshire midlands were shortly graced with summer in full dress. Idyllic days passed by in fleet succession, and nights so warm that Rachel slept with most of the windows open. The crops, and baby Benjy, too, grew and grew.

While in the barn one day, Rachel discovered a small brake cart sitting idle in an unused stall. Borrowing a pointer from Gaffy and his little pony cart, Rachel had it refitted for George, knowing that since he could no longer sit a horse, he would welcome the mobility it offered. She conferred with Pug about the choice of an animal to pull it, and together they agreed upon a stocky bay mare, who was slow, dull, but gentle.

"You must remember," cautioned Rachel, "George can use only one arm, and his legs are useless. She must be obedient."

"Have no fear," reassured Pug. "This one's too slow to be anything else, and she's not too bright, either. If George should drop the rein, she'll stop. She couldn't bolt to save her life." To prove his point, Pug smacked the bay on her rump with a strap. She flicked her tail, then her ears, and finally, turned around to see what it was that had struck her.

Rachel laughed. "She'll do fine. What does she answer to?"

"Told you, she's a might slow." Pug spoke in a low whisper and tapped his skull. "Her stall reads Baybelle, but she thinks her first name is *Giddap* and her last *Whoa.*"

George was beside himself at his newfound freedom. Each day the weather was fair, Angus set him on the leather seat, placed a blanket across his knees, and the old man rode about the estate joyfully. There was room for two in the little buggy, and some days Rachel kept George company, keeping him abreast of every facet of the expanding enterprise.

He had other company, as well, for a little trundle-tailed mutt from the stables took to following him wherever he went. Finally, the old man took pity on the mongrel, and invited him into the seat beside him. From that day on, the pup shared that seat daily with George, surveying the world from behind Baybelle's rump.

Often George and Gaffy would meet, positioning their carts side by side under a spreading elm, and jawing about the changes wrought by Rachel across the breadth of Guersten land. The two old men were pleased with what they viewed from their vantage point under the elms. The estate was flourishing from the attention it had received, and for the most part, the people who dwelled there were happy. Emory was the lone exception.

CHAPTER TWENTY-ONE

When the first strawberries ripened, Gaffy picked the very best himself, presenting them to Rachel one morning at breakfast. One was a berry so fat it had to be cut before it could be eaten. Smothering it with new cream, Rachel devoured it with relish, pronouncing it delicious. Not long after, other crops began to mature. There were rows of beets and carrots, and soon several fields of early cabbages were marked for harvest. The time had come to develop a workable plan to market the expected bounty.

"It better be a good one," said Emory, chuckling. "You're going to be knee-deep in vegetables any day now."

Rachel bristled, wondering if perhaps he was expecting her to fail. Hadn't she already admitted that marketing was the weakest part of the plan? Yet when she pressed him for assistance and ideas, he remained aloof and noncommittal.

She was convinced, just then, that the best plan would be to bypass the local markets, sending the first wagonloads of produce straightaway to London's busy marketplace at Covent Garden. A sturdy wagon and team were already waiting; Peter had seen to that, and two able boys had been chosen to handle that wagon. Both could manage the team, and both were bright, could count and make proper change. There was disagreement to Rachel's idea, however, and when the time came, Edward voiced it. "London is just too far away. The vegetables will be limp before they get there. Furthermore, it necessitates the use of another team, for one pair can't be expected to make that journey without relief. We'd have to buy or rent another, and pay for stabling somewhere near the halfway mark. It defeats your own purpose, Rachel, cutting into your profits before you even see them."

"True enough," admitted Rachel. She turned to Peter. "What do you think? Be honest, speak freely."

Peter, who admired Rachel, and rarely found reason to disagree with her, now looked uncomfortable, but in the end he spoke out honestly. He agreed with Edward.

"I'm afraid he's right. I think we should try to develop a local market, if possible. To that end, I have already spoken to a greengrocer in Coltenham and another in Aylesbury. They'll buy from us if the price is right and the quality high."

"But they can't get rid of a third of what we've got growing out there," said Rachel in a troubled voice, pointing toward a window. "If we flood our own market our price will fall. Perhaps London *is* too far, but there must be something else."

Emory, who had been lounging against the mantelpiece, quiet and seemingly disinterested, now made a move to join them where they crowded around his father's desk.

"May I offer a suggestion?"

"Of course!" said Rachel, welcoming him with a smile, thrilled at his interest.

"The more heads the better. We're all so new at this."

"Edward's right," Emory began. "London is too far, and you really shouldn't send two boys there alone. They'll have full purses coming back, remember, and the world is full of thieves. No, you'd have to free up a man to go with them for protection. There is another market quite close by that you have all overlooked though, a market that is still growing, in fact. Have you considered Peterborough?"

"Of course! cried Peter, slapping his thigh. "Peterborough! I should have thought of it myself. The railways!"

"Exactly," agreed Emory. "The railways!"

"You've lost me," George said. "Will someone please explain the correlation between rutabagas and railroads?"

"The correlation is this, Father," offered Emory, who then proceeded to outline to all of them how the unprecedented phenomena of railway expansion could turn them a profit. The advent of the steam engine had birthed a boom that was still in its infancy, he said. Anyone with a thousand pounds or so, could acquire some miles of track to start a railroad of his own. Consequently, a passenger on just a fifty mile ride might travel three different lines. "Those tracks will soon resemble a pile of jackstraws," he continued, "and someday, somebody will have to untangle them . . . link them to one through way. But right now that expansion means a continuing demand for iron and steel needed in quantity for rails, coaches and locomotives."

"The iron works!" shouted Rachel, understanding at last. Emory nodded. Those iron works were already operating full time, expanding and taking on more workers every day . . . workers who had to be fed.

"A whole new village filled with tenements has sprung up there. Surely those housewives would welcome fresh produce. You're not two hours away," commented Emory.

"We could rent a small stall and set up a tommy shop," Rachel said, excited now by the prospects that lay before them.

"You would do well not to identify at all with that sort of enterprise," cautioned Emory. "They usually sell only cheaper grades of meat and produce, and overcharge at that. Keep your quality high and beat their prices. The ladies will flock to you."

"But how can we distribute without a shop?" asked Edward, caught by the idea but uncertain about its implementation.

"Sell right from your wagon. If you do, there will be no need to rent space or set up a stall. Start with one wagon load a day, undercut the next fellow's prices and you're in. Don't forget, your vegetables will be picked fresh every morning; I doubt any of your competition can boast that claim."

"A tommy shop on wheels!" said Rachel, her faced wreathed in a smile.

"He's right, of course," said George, pleased as punch at Emory's interest. That interest pleased Rachel too, and behind Emory's back she smiled widely at the old man.

The second plan, as it came to be known, worked well, but was not without some difficulties of its own, during startup. These might have scotched the plan, had it not been for Rachel's determination to see it through. The problem arose through no fault of anyone at Guersten Hall, and should have been expected. It was competition.

Everyone on the estate turned out to watch the loading of the first wagon. A team of rugged Percherons, strong and sturdy legged, waited patiently as the vill's workers brought forth the bounty to be offered to Peterborough's housewives. There were crates of carrots and beans, beets and berries, as well as straw packed eggs and greens galore. And of course, there were early cabbages . . . small but plentiful, bushels of them, all round and firm with crisp outer leaves.

Watching, in his usual idleness, Emory picked up a hefty head and tossed it from hand to hand.

"Ah, the English, they certainly do like their cabbages, don't they?"

"The hungry ones do," said his father, from his seat behind Baybelle. "Nothing like cabbage when your belly's empty; it rattles around and lets you know it's there."

"It's plain you have never been the victim of a meager harvest, or struggled through a winter that followed," said Rachel in a sober voice. She retrieved the cabbage from Emory and restacked it in a long crate. Peter then threw a tarp over the whole load to keep it cool on its journey to Peterborough.

"And you have?" inquired Emory with sarcasm, certain her words were some sort of put-down.

"I've read about it," replied Rachel.

"Aaah! Your friend Dickens again!"

"He only chronicles what he sees, Emory, remember that. Fiction is often truth in disguise."

"Good God, Rachel!" said Emory, amazed that a simple statement about cabbages could have gone so far. "You're much too serious. Are you aware of that?"

Rachel ignored him, and turning back to the business at hand, briefed the boys once again on their prices. Peter checked the team's harness for the third time. At last, amid cheers and whistling, the two boys climbed onto the wagon seat and pulled away from under the makeshift loading shed recently erected in the circle of beeches that ringed the fields.

Standing atop a stone wall, Rachel watched them go until they passed out of sight. A short cut would certainly come in handy, she thought, considering the distance the team must travel from the loading shed to the Peterborough road. That distance alone would take near a full hour to travel, and she made a mental note to ask Emory about the possibility of a short cut when his mood improved.

Hours before they were expected, Rachel's boys came back to the Hall. They returned unannounced and without the springed wagon. Tired and bedraggled, one of them sat astride a stout Percheron as the other led the team, the horses still harnessed together.

"What on earth happened?" demanded Edward, who had ridden out to meet them after they were spotted making their way up Guersten Wood Road.

"The lout wot owns the tommy shop set some galoots on us," cried one of the lads. "Not half an hour after we reached the ironworks gate," added the other. "They roughed us up and overturned the wagon for good measure."

Edward grimaced. "Are either of you hurt?" he inquired.

"Naw, jus' a couple bruises is all, but Miss Rachel's produce was spilled all over and we couldn't right the wagon again. We didn't know what else to do so we unhitched the horses and came back."

"You did right, boys. Did they take your money?"

"No. They didn't rob us, only wanted to scare us off. Said we was fringin' on their territory, whatever that means. Made some threats and told us not to come back, they did."

"Intimidation! Pure and simple!" declared Rachel when the story was related to her moments later. She counted the coins the boys had brought back. "Not even sixpence, for a load that should have brought ten times that."

"Were you perhaps on the property of the ironworks when this happened?" she asked, turning to the boys, for she had already explained to them that the tommy shop had permission to operate where it did. Duggan, its owner, had a lease, and they must not trespass upon his rights.

"No, ma'am," they chorused. "We were careful 'bout that. Like you told us, we stayed at the boundary marker. We were on the public road when they jumped us."

"Good, lads," Rachel said. "Then what happened was not your fault, and should have been foreseen by one of us. Go get some supper and some rest. Tomorrow we're going back with another load . . . only this time I'm going with you!"

"Is that wise, Rachel?" asked Emory, though not at all surprised by her announcement; it was typical of her take-charge attitude. "Still, those ruffians might turn ugly."

"Nonsense! Intimidation is just a game, one that I've come to understand quite well! We'll go back, all right, for by now those women have had a free sample of good quality produce, and by now they've talked among themselves. They know our prices are fair. They'll buy from us if we go back, I'm sure of it. It's just a matter of showing our mettle."

"Then I'll go instead," offered Peter.

"Or I," added Edward. "There might be a confrontation."

"That is exactly why it is I who should go," said Rachel. "Any show of strength on our part will only force an equal show by them. Instead, I propose to stare them down and let the ladies make their own choice about where they choose to shop."

Emory laughed aloud. "You have a way of making everything seem so damned simple."

"Perhaps that is just why my approach works best," she replied, grinning up at him.

At dawn's first light the next morning, an old farm wagon was loaded high with more crates of fresh picked produce, and Peter hitched a spare team to its rear. One extra lad was chosen to make the run with them, for the springed wagon would have to be reclaimed and brought back to Guersten Hall.

When Rachel appeared at the loading site wearing her leather breeches and a light reefer, all the boys cheered, her outfit familiar to them all.

"Aren't you afraid you'll be mistaken for one of the lads in that get-up?" twitted Gaffy with a wry grin.

"That is my intent," chuckled Rachel. "There may not be trouble today, and I don't want my presence to provoke it. With my hair tucked under my cap no one will be the wiser."

"Only if they don't study your shirtfront too closely," whispered Emory in her ear.

Pointedly, she ignored him, and mounting Hunter, followed the wagon as it lurched away. "This gallivanting in pants is getting ridiculous," muttered Emory to his brother, when Rachel's strange procession was gone. "She's my wife! Her place is in the house!"

With a broad grin, Edward shook his head. "I wish you luck brother, if you think to put her there!"

Out on the Peterborough road Rachel was overtaken by a few misgivings about her mission. What if Duggan's thugs did indeed anticipate their return, were prepared for it? They could be laying in wait for them even now! *I could be leading these innocent lads into a very messy situation* she worried, characteristically unconcerned for her own safety. On that score, Rachel was quite sure that if there were any trouble, it would die aborning when Duggan's men learned her identity. Her sex and the Guersten name would serve as her shield, but still, if they should slug away and ask questions later . . . what then?

Thinking about it made Rachel nervous, and she turned in the saddle once or twice to look behind her, scanning the roadway over which they had just traveled. It was empty; she saw nothing, but as they progressed further she became certain that they were being followed.

Without alarming the boys, she set a faster pace for the wagon, and soon they moved out of a long wooded stretch, passing into an area bordered on either side by wide grassy fields, with only an occasional stand of trees. Here, anyone following would be obliged to expose himself as his cover shifted diagonally from one side of the road to the other.

She remained alert, watching carefully, and sure enough, spotted a horseman . . . a tall rider on a great black stallion, darting and disappearing into a stand of oaks on the opposite side. With a sigh of relief, she smiled and relaxed, knowing Emory was behind her.

"Step lively, lads," she said to the boys buoyantly. "We're almost there!"

Approaching the toppled wagon, Rachel found it flanked by two small groups of people. Her boys quickly recognized one of them.

"That's the same bunch wot jumped us yestiday! And look! They've got clubs today!"

"So they have, lads, but take a look at what the other group is armed with!" That second group was made up entirely of women, and each and every one carried a small wicker basket or a trug resting in the crook of an elbow. "Our customers, boys! And there are more where they came from."

"But what about the toughies?"

Even as they watched, the roughnecks with the sticks had moved closer to the overturned wagon, and some of the villagers stepped back timidly.

"Keep your pace," said Rachel. "I'll ride ahead and talk to them." Her calm confidence was reassuring to the boys, though Rachel admitted honestly that much of it was acquired by Emory's presence behind her. Her boys didn't know that, however, and they cheered as Rachel went forward to greet Duggan's men, trotting briskly the last quarter mile.

At closer range, Rachel found there were four of them, little more than lads themselves. She rode Hunter almost into their midst before reining, and they were forced to split apart and separate. Divide and conquer, she thought, as from her saddle she peered over their heads and addressed the women from the village.

"Good morning, ladies! I'm sorry to keep you waiting, but the load was heavy. My boys will have the wagon in place shortly and you can make your selections. Tell your neighbors about us!"

One of the galoots raised his club menacingly and shouted up at Rachel. "Now just a minute, boyo . . . ol' Duggan claims this 'ere as his territory. He sez you ain't to sell 'ere and we be 'ere to see you don't."

"By whose authority?" bellowed Rachel in a demanding voice, and if they hadn't already suspected she was a woman, they did so now, turning and looking askance at one another.

"Hey . . . wot gives 'ere?" asked the spokesman, laying one hand on Rachel's booted ankle.

She rapped his fingers with her crop, and the surprised youth loosed his hold at once. "By whose authority?" Rachel repeated. "Mr. Duggan has license to operate a tommy shop on the ironworks property. That license does not extend to the Queen's highway or a public road."

Uncertainty spread across the faces of the little group and they all looked to their spokesman for leadership. "Who sez so?" he demanded of Rachel, though his cockiness was fading fast.

"I say so!" Rachel said, dismounting. She moved into their midst, and since her disguise was worthless anyway, she removed her cap. "I . . . Rachel Guersten, say so!" she stated authoritatively. "You are accomplices in a crime, lads. Mr. Duggan owes me for one basket of broken eggs and most of yesterday's load of vegetables, and there is also the matter of roughing up my boys. That, too, is a crime! If I choose, I can have all of you . . . and Duggan, jailed!"

The ruffians let their sticks drop to the ground. Only their spokesman did so because of Rachel's words; the others were staring openly at the woman before them, awed by her appearance and her breeches.

"From Guersten Hall, lads," said Rachel, pointing to her own boys as they drew their wagon into position beside the toppled one, which lay on its side like a beached whale. "Tell Mr. Duggan that," she added, "and tell him too, that I expect no further trouble, or the bailiff will be upon you all."

Duggan's boys dispersed and Rachel spent the next two hours meeting and greeting the housewives of Peterborough's iron works, who *oohed* and *aahed* openly over the price, the variety, and the quality of Rachel's offerings. Picked fresh this morning she reminded them, and then told her boys to give them all good measure. "Baker's dozen all around."

As the sun rose higher Rachel began to wish she'd brought a proper bonnet, for she could feel her forehead burning, but she kept at her task. There was no further sign of Emory; he never appeared and she wondered if he'd returned to Guersten Hall or perhaps found his way to the nearest tavern. Preoccupied, she did not at first notice the round and whiskery fellow who sat astride his horse some distance away, just watching them.

That fat fellow never approached, never left the ironworks property, in fact, but just sat by the edge of the road, watching, watching. Rachel noted that he spoke to all of the women on the road, both those trudging toward her "tommy shop on wheels," and those returning to the village after making purchases. Before long the steady stream of women that flowed to her wagon thinned and then almost petered out, for after speaking to the fat man, several of the women hesitated and then turned back without making purchases. Perplexed, Rachel watched, and sure enough another . . . and another, turned away and plodded back to the village. It was then that Rachel put two and two together.

"Who is that fellow?" she said to an old woman busy selecting ingredients for her husband's stew. The old lady's reply confirmed Rachel's suspicions.

"Why, thet be ol' Duggan, ma'am. Business at the tommy shop mus' be bad," she tittered, "to get 'im off'n 'is arse. 'E's usually too drunk to set a horse!"

"Hmmm," said Rachel. "But why do these women turn away? What does he say to them?"

"Well . . . 'e cuffs us. Only too glad to cuff us 'e is, for a stiff fee. 'E jus' tells them if they're goin' t' buy from you they have t' pay wot they owe 'im first. 'E knows they can't."

"But that's blackmail!" spluttered Rachel. "Coercion at best! I am going to have a talk with Mr. Duggan," she added angrily.

"Y'd best be careful, dearie . . . 'e's a mean one, 'e is."

Rachel started away on foot toward Duggan, and then thought better of it. She returned, unhitched Hunter and mounted. Intimidation always worked better eye to eye, a lesson she'd learned the hard way herself. Turning away, another thought came to her.

"Tell me," she said to the old woman, "did Duggan pick up any of my spilled goods yesterday?"

The old lady hesitated, not wanting to incriminate either herself or her neighbors. "Look," Rachel hastened to add, "I made no effort to recover that load because I hoped it would be collected by those in the village who needed it. They may consider it a gift. Mr. Duggan, however, is another matter! Now did he or did he not help himself to any of my cabbages?"

Hearing Rachel's words, the woman's face brightened. "Aye, lass! Thet 'e did . . . crates an' all if ye care t' know! Seen 'em in 'is shop m'self."

"That's all I wanted to know, and I thank you kindly for the information."

Rachel rode away, and as she approached the fat man he straightened in his saddle, expecting a confrontation. He watched Rachel through beady eyes, and was surprised when she rode right past him without stopping or speaking.

Cantering at an easy pace toward the village, Rachel sat tall on Hunter's back. Warily, Duggan watched her go, and then spurred his horse into a gallop and rode after her.

"Hey, missus! Where y' think y' be going?"

"Into the village, if it's any business of yours."

"You cain't sell in the village! Y' don't hev a license."

"Sell? You err, good man. I don't have cabbage or a carrot on me!"

"Then wot fer y' going t' the village?"

"Unless you are in authority here, and have the right to ask questions, then I shall answer no more of them. I will only tell you that I go to the tommy shop."

"*My* tommy shop? Wot fer," he snarled, more wary now than ever. "Say . . . wot you up to anyway?"

Rachel did not answer the fat man. Instead, holding her head high, she rode ahead of him through the tiny village square directly to his tommy shop. There she dismounted, and with a great show, hitched Hunter to a rail. A small crowd quickly gathered; women from the tenements and men who poured out of the local pub, all of them sensing that ol' Duggan and the slender lass in breeches were about to have a confrontation of some sort.

Huffing noisily from unaccustomed exertion, Duggan followed Rachel up the dirty steps that led into his shop, nearly bowling her over when she stopped dead in her tracks at the sight that greeted her.

The place was a shambles. Piled high with crates and boxes, the floor and two long tables were littered with rotting fruits and vegetables, and there were flies everywhere. A massive overstuffed chair sat in one corner, the shape of Duggan's round body imprinted permanently into its cushions.

"Jus' wot are you after, missy?" asked Duggan, so close behind Rachel that she could smell his foul breath.

"The name is Guersten, Duggan, and don't you forget it! Now back away!"

"Ol' George's wife be dead ten years . . . and I know the daughter. You ain't her!"

"The name is Guersten, nonetheless," declared Rachel, greatly disturbed by what she saw. She wandered about the tiny store, little more than a stall really, noting with mounting dismay the filth and the smell. A malodorous air of tainted meat pervaded the place, its stench noticeable even over that of rotting potatoes. She went to the door, beckoning to a boy who stood at the edge of the growing crowd.

"Fetch the bailiff for me, will you, lad?"

His color blanching, Duggan moved to a battered wooden table that served as a counter, behind which his four hooligans were already cowering. When the bailiff arrived, Rachel introduced herself.

"I am mistress of Guersten Hall," she said. "Yesterday, one of my farm wagons was deliberately toppled on the Peterborough road, and some of its contents have inexplicably found their way to Mr. Duggan's shop." She pointed to a crate of cabbages that sat on the end of one of the long tables.

"A cabbage is a cabbage," snarled Duggan. "Who can say where it was grown?"

"The presence of fresh produce amid such rot as this is proof enough, Duggan, but if more is needed, there is the matter of those crates. This one," she said, "and this . . . and this, are mine." While speaking, Rachel moved down the length of the table, rapping each of her crates with her riding crop. She turned to the bailiff.

"If you will turn these crates over, you will find burned into their bottoms an identifying mark . . . a ring of ten irregular circles depicting the beeches that grow in a field at Guersten Hall, under which we built our loading shed. The iron for that mark was forged by my farrier, and hangs now on a peg in his workshop."

The bailiff turned over the end crate, exposing the telltale mark burned into the wood, while Duggan perspired uncomfortably. His boys would have bolted then, but the way was blocked by the presence of the villagers, who watched the proceedings in silence.

"Do you wish to press charges?" inquired the bailiff.

"That depends on Mr. Duggan," said Rachel, turning to confront the hapless man.

"Much of this swill is not fit for human consumption and should have been fed to the pigs days ago. I would hazard a guess, Duggan, judging from your prices, that your profits fall somewhere in the vicinity of sixty percent, to say nothing of the additional fees you charge for carrying these people. Further, since many of them can neither read nor write, they have no way of knowing whether your bookkeeping is reliable or not. They must rely on your . . . er, honesty. Your entire operation, Duggan, borders on larceny. Your profits are nothing short of thievery."

"I got me a license! Don't forget it!"

"Ah, yes, the license!" Rachel contemplated that for a moment, and then continued. "The owners of the ironworks are friends of my father-in-law. One is even now a houseguest of Squire Paxton, my neighbor. Why they choose not to hear the grumblings of their people and visit this place, I cannot say. But this I will say! If I were to invite them to Guersten Hall for dinner tonight, by tomorrow your license would be removed, and you would likely be called to face the magistrate in Peterborough."

Duggan gulped, his discomfit mounting, but Rachel gave him no change to speak.

"I'll offer you an out," she said, "if from now on you purchase all your produce from me!"

"Wot?" he cried, with popping eyes. "I cain't afford your prices!"

"Of course you can! Just deduct it from your sixty percent! There is market in this village for four loads of fresh produce a day, at the least. Now, we can each sell two, or I can sell them all, putting you out of business."

"And wot about the money they already owes me?" said the fat man, pointing to the people crowding in the doorway.

"It is debatable whether that money is even due you, Duggan, but if your prices were to drop to where they belong, then these people could pay their debts."

"And wot if I refuse?"

"Come, come, Mr. Duggan! There is still the matter of those charges."

Duggan stared across the tables to the bailiff, who stood silently watching the proceedings with interest. "This is blackmail!" Duggan shouted, having little choice but to agree to Rachel's demands, and knew it.

"You know more about blackmail than I," said she, but in case he would waver, she demanded pen and paper, and inked out a contract of sorts right then and there, the bailiff witnessing their signatures. The paper contracted for two wagonloads of fresh produce to be delivered to Duggan's shop daily, each accompanied by a bill of lading. Duggan was to pay Rachel's driver in cash, and was free to set his own prices. Competition would keep him honest, for if he hiked his prices too high again his trade would fall away to Rachel's tommy shop on wheels, which would be parked at the outskirts of the village.

"Let me give you a bit of advice," Rachel said to Duggan, as she pocketed her copy of the folded contract. "It may not occur to you just now that you have any advantage in this situation, but you do. These women must walk two miles to trade with me, while you are practically in their midst. Clean this place up, paint it, and deal fairly with them, and I daresay before summer's end I will be delivering all four wagonloads to your doorstep each day. It might even be advantageous for you to create your own tommy shop on wheels, and let your boys go about the tenements, selling from the wagon. And if you've a mind to enlarge your scope, I can supply you with fresh killed poultry and all the eggs you can sell. Your income will nearly be the same as it was before, only it will have been gleaned honestly. These people will be your friends, rather than your enemies."

"She's right, uncle," said one of Duggan's nephews after Rachel departed. "Tol' you thet before."

"Mayhap she is," Duggan admitted grudgingly, sinking into his cocoon-like chair, "only time will tell. But it jus' goes t'show . . . watch out fer wimmin wearing pants!"

CHAPTER TWENTY-TWO

Pleased at the way her day in Peterborough turned out, Rachel related her coup to the others at dinner that evening; and even Emory was genuinely happy for her success. The contract with old Duggan meant that a total of eight wagonloads of produce a day were now being distributed in the communities immediately surrounding Guersten Hall, and of the eight, six were on a wholesale basis. As the weeks passed, the pile of coins in the strongbox on Rachel's desk grew and grew, and she flushed with pride of accomplishment. Her *plan*, as George still called it, had proven to be highly successful; feeding them all and providing employment for many, as well as turning a neat profit. And now, more importantly, from manor house to byre, the estate itself was now a prudent example of efficient management.

Still, Rachel did not relax her endeavors; riding out daily she checked on her boys, though much responsibility was turned over to those who showed that they could handle it.

Under the summer sun Rachel's velvety skin slowly acquired a golden color; she was more beautiful than ever, a fact not missed by Emory, or anyone else for that matter. Buoyed by her success, she was reasonably happy, but Emory's idle resentment began to grow again; he became restless, smoldering much of the time, and their battle of wits continued. They took turns besting each other, one entanglement coming hard on the heels of the one preceding. There the situation remained, much to the distress of George and Stoddard.

In July the haying began; according to the old Anglo-Saxon calendar July was traditionally the month of haying, Gaffy explained. Still, he added, much would depend on the weather, calendar be damned. If it should rain on a field of just cut hay, little damage would be done so long as the weather cleared again at once. But once the hay was cured, a sudden shower could be disastrous; the dried hay would likely rot. "Ye must remember," he warned Peter, with a wag of his finger, "niver cut more than ye can load in a day once 'tis dry."

There was little danger of that though, for the hay was cut by hand. Working several fields at once with long handled scythes, the men began shortly after dawn each day, when the fields were still glistening with the morning dew. Rachel watched in rapt fascination as the sharpened scythes, in rhythms of their own, repeatedly bit into the juicy grasses and sweet timothy. A small army of boys with pitchforks followed in the swathes made by the scythers, scattering the new mown hay for drying. The next day all returned to the fields, this time with rakes, sweeping the cuttings into windrows, and soon after the hay was forked onto the wagons, the loads divided between the stable barns and Steven's loft at the dairy.

It was hard work, hot and prickly under the blazing July sun, often in a race against the elements. On one blistering afternoon the men were loading the hayracks to mountainous heights, working at breakneck speed ahead of a bank of ominous thunderclouds that soon blotted out the sun. To Rachel's surprise this day, even Emory pitched in, and stripped to the waist, the muscles of his strong back rippled as he flung fork after fork to the top of the rack. The rain held off, the storm eventually moving harmlessly away into the distance, with only a lively display of heat lightning marking its passage. Rachel couldn't help thinking how much smoother the work went when he helped.

Summer peaked. One sultry afternoon in August, while George and Rebecca napped, Rachel sneaked into the nursery where little Benjy lay cooing in his cradle. He flailed his arms excitedly when he spied his aunt, kicking the covers off to expose fatted thighs, pink and dimpled. Rachel changed his napkin and then tiptoed from the room, hugging the child to her bosom.

"Come, little one," she whispered, kissing his nose, "I will take you for a walk in the garden."

Emory found them there some time later, playing with a basket of kittens; Rachel sitting upon the grass with the contented baby in her lap, he chewing on his fist, playing gleefully with chubby toes.

"Ah, there you are! Anna has been looking for you both. It seems it is past the little fellow's dinnertime."

Rachel smiled as Anna removed the child. "I think he can afford to miss a meal or two; just look at those fingers."

One by one Rachel picked up the furry kittens and deposited them into their basket. Watching, Emory was swamped with emotion at the sight of her. In the humid afternoon air Rachel's dewy skin was flushed pink, her daintily sprigged day gown plastered to her body with damp perspiration; so tightly that the outline of her breasts was seen through the thin fabric.

A surge of desire coursed through him, and Emory dropped to the ground beside her. "Rachel, I must talk to you."

"Please, Emory . . . I know what you are going to say."

"Do you now? Then you must know why I am forced to say it. Why won't you understand? Since my return to Guersten Hall I've not touched any woman . . . a man has needs, and it's perfectly natural to look to one's wife to fulfill those needs. How many lonely nights must I endure?"

"My nights were lonely, and my days too, for that matter. You cared little then, and even now you speak only of yourself . . . and your needs."

As she spoke, Rachel saw Emory's eyes change; the greenness turned icy, his forehead reddened. He gripped both of her arms and pulled her close, startling Rachel with his strength.

"I can take you by force, you know," he muttered, "any time I choose, and no one, not even Father, could say that was not my right."

"You can do that; perhaps one day you will," Rachel answered calmly. "But once done what then? For each and every time you take me after that it will have to be by force. It amounts to assault."

Emory let go of her arms, then sprawled himself across the grass. "I won't assault you, Rachel. I want only to introduce you to the kingdom of love. Barring that, a plain old fuck will do!"

Rachel drew in her breath, shocked and taken aback by his insult, spewed out so unexpectedly. "You are rude . . . lewd, and . . . crude!" she said, spitting out the words in a curious singsong rhyme."

"And you, my dear, are virtuous, pious and ridiculous!" he retorted, mocking her.

Gathering her skirts, Rachel leaped to her feet. "Well then, we are even. I shall not try to reform you, don't try to corrupt me."

A week went by. Two. Silence fell between them again, and for a while solitude reigned, until Emory's wild nature surfaced again. It was inevitable, as he smoldered anew, for one with his temperament and inclinations could hardly be expected to sit night after night across the dinner table from a woman as beautiful as Rachel, and not seek fulfillment.

One evening Emory made an attempt to attain that fulfillment. The encounter was unplanned, quite unexpected, but he seized it eagerly when it came. Only this time, he tried a different strategy.

The evening was hot; no breeze rippled the curtains in Rachel's room. They hung limp and lifeless against the sill. Sleepless, Rachel drew a peignoir over her nightdress and went down the stairs to the first floor. The cool marble felt refreshing under her bare feet, and she was momentarily tempted to go outside and walk through the garden. Instead, in search of something new to read, she went into the library, where Emory sat in a half-darkened corner, holding a glass in his hand. Unprepared for his presence, Rachel drew the filmy robe closer to her body.

"I didn't know anyone was here."

"Stow your fear," Emory said. "I won't attack you, it's much too hot. And I'm not getting drunk either," he added when Rachel's knitted her brows in a frown of disapproval at the sight of his glass. He held it out to her.

"Chilled sangaree . . . just the thing for a hot night. Will you have some?"

Unexpectedly, Rachel said yes, and Emory served her from a frosty pitcher standing on a little wine table. Then, in the semi-darkness, he watched as she sipped the cooling sweetness. God, she was exquisite! Her hair, pulled away from her forehead, exposed perfect bone structure; as a child those cheeks had been so damned thin, he remembered, but now they were rounded and smooth. He refilled her glass, and in time, when Rachel found a book that looked promising, she took the glass and returned to her room, then stretched out on the green velvet chaise to read, and when she looked up again, Emory was leaning against the doorjamb, holding the cold pitcher in one hand.

"I had Stoddard refill it. When I told her it was for you she filled it without a blink. I'll have to remember that; it might come in handy some night."

Rachel laughed at him. It had been some weeks since he had last thrown over the traces, but still, Rachel supposed it did seem to him that everyone in the house monitored everything he drank, and the missing decanters had yet to be returned to their usual places. "It is cooling," she said at last. "Will you join me this time?"

From that moment on the evening took one strange turn after another, though Rachel was never to understand how any of them came about. Emory closed the door and took a distant seat near the open windows. Rachel laid aside her book and they chatted easily and pleasantly, discussing the crops in the fields, her choice of literature, and his.

"I like Thackeray myself," Emory stated.

"I find him too formal. He seems to write only about the rich. Dickens is my choice."

"How well I know," he said, recalling the incident over the cabbages, which now amused them both.

Refilling both their glasses, Emory somehow was soon seated on the end of Rachel's chaise. He kept his desire well hidden, and between the heat and the wine Rachel was soon relaxing languorously against the green velvet. Emory regaled her with stories of his years away at school, and when she wasn't looking, he refilled glass again.

"Do you know," he said at length, edging over closer, "we've been in the same room now for over an hour without squabbling? That hasn't happened since we were in London together."

"Ah, London! We did have some good times that week, didn't we? The walks by the Thames, the rides in the park . . ."

"We were friends that week Rachel and I think about it often. Do you?"

She did, but she was reluctant to admit it. In truth, she didn't have to, for her eyes told Emory all that he wanted to know. Over the rim of her glass brown caught green and locked in a steady gaze.

Emory leaned forward over Rachel's half reclining form, and slowly one arm went around her waist. With his free hand he caressed her throat, as Rachel's heart pounded loudly in her breast. Surely he must hear it! Was it that look? Those mysterious eyes? The wine? She never knew, and without realizing it raised her face, offering her lips to him.

He took them, covering them with his own, in a kiss that grew in ardent intensity, from gentle pressure to sensuous fervor. The heat of Emory's passion fired them both; Rachel's lips parted willingly and rose to meet his again and again, while his trembling fingers sought to untie the last inadequate ribbon that kept him from those magnificent breasts. He bent to kiss her neck, her throat . . . and both of Rachel's arms went instinctively about his shoulders.

She held him tight, and in her embrace, Emory was overtaken by a most delightful sensation as he felt that voluptuous body melt under his own. It marveled him, he who had taken so many women before. Why should this one, even in her innocence, be any different, thrill him so?

Above his own passion Emory sensed that deep within Rachel there burned a fire that once kindled would make her his slave forever. He set about kindling it, pressing her body into the cushions beneath her, and spreading his length against her. When she struggled, he silenced her objections with another kiss. She returned it, and moaned softly as the peignoir fell away at last, revealing full and rounded breasts, barely constrained by the thin batiste of her fragile nightgown. Emory cupped one perfect breast in his warm hand. Rachel froze, experiencing and understanding for the first time the depths of pleasurable emotion that overtake a man and woman entwined in one another's arms. She had never dreamed such feelings existed, and she was astonished by her own responses, and how naturally they came.

"Oh, Rachel, Rachel! You're so beautiful . . . so damn beautiful," Emory groaned, pressing his lips to hers again. "I want you . . . I need you!", he said, getting bolder.

"Emory . . . this has gone too far," she whispered, though her own lips still reached for his and she made no attempt to push his hand away.

"Don't deny me now! My body burns for you! I must have release! See?" he said, taking her hand and guiding it to his turgid member, eager and demanding in its hardness.

Why not submit? Rachel thought to herself, tempted. After all, they were lawfully man and wife, it was wholly natural. Then that single thought took Rachel back to her wedding night, and suddenly she was furious with herself for her weakness in succumbing to his handsome face and his smooth charm. Had she not spent that night alone and rejected, sitting on a bench in a dark room while he cavorted with Edwina Merrington in London? She had been ignored, humiliated, and even now he professed nothing for her beyond lust. With a hiss she gave Emory a push and rolled out from under him, her movement taking him by surprise.

"Did you think to ply me with wine and seduce me?" she demanded.

"But . . . but . . . I thought . . ."

"You were wrong! Go away!" she cried, retying the ribbons of her peignoir again, although the spreading warmth in her loins gave lie to her words.

"Christ, Rachel," shouted Emory, his face contorted with anger. "You confuse me mightily!"

"You're confused? Think of me! I've been reeling ever since you returned to this house! One moment you abuse me and in the next you seek to caress me!" She threw up her hands. "Oh, go away, and take your wine with you!"

With a snarl Emory left the room, slamming the door as he went, so violently that a picture leapt from the wall. Afterward, Rachel sank into a seat before her dressing table, thoroughly shaken. *What is the matter with me?* She looked at her own reflection in the glass, staring intently at her own body, still rosy and flushed from the nearness of his. Her nipples stood erect, piercing the fabric of her nightgown, and her heart continued to pound wildly. He wanted me, she thought. He would have taken me, I would have let him! Her knees trembled, as she realized with a start that she had wanted Emory almost as much as he had wanted her. And it had all seemed so natural; their bodies had fitted together perfectly.

Bewildered by her own emotions, Rachel made her way to the windows, seeking some cool night air. She stood there for a long time, peering out into the empty night. Once, the sound of a nightingale came to her from somewhere far off. It was a lonely sound, even in its sweetness, and it haunted her. "Oh, Emory, Emory! Why do you torture me so?"

The rest of that night was miserable; she lay sleepless and troubled, and it irked her doubly to see Emory the next morning, heading for the stables, seemingly not the least bit upset at having been rebuffed. He was whistling cheerily as he headed down the stairs.

In confused frustration, Rachel tried to put it all out of her mind. She turned her full attention to Ermaline's approaching wedding.

The invitations were posted, the manor house was cleaned and aired top to bottom; guest rooms were readied and menus planned. Since the influx of expected houseguests necessitated the need for more help, Rachel turned to her neighbors. Aunt Adele, Squire Paxton and others farmed out their servants, and Rachel divided the borrowed maids and footmen into day and evening shifts. Mrs. Crocker came from Brenham Manor to assist Stoddard with the cooking. Agatha's forte was desserts, and Stoddard relinquished a long table under the windows of her kitchen and assigned three of Greystone's best pastry makers to help her, while she herself supervised the rest of the kitchen staff in preparing enough food for the two hundred plus guests.

"There is no way we can outdo the lavishness of Mrs. Rowland's ball," Rachel said wisely at dinner one night, when Ermaline brought forth some rather grandiose ideas as they discussed the arrangements. "We would be foolhardy to even try, but we can dazzle them with simple goodness; good food, well prepared and nicely serviced, much of it grown right here at Guersten Hall. I have a flock of spring lambs set aside for slaughter and we can fill every room in the house with flowers fresh from our own gardens. Even Mrs. Rowland can't top that!"

"Is she ever wrong?" was all that Emory offered, when Ermaline looked to her brother for an opinion.

But Rachel had no time for childish animosity and petty bickering; there was too much to be done, and the days flew by until only three remained before the ceremony. That morning, Eleanora Scofield wheeled up to the portico in a splendid enameled carriage, all gold and garish green, drawn by four white horses whose green leather harnesses sported striped Scofield ribbons a-fluttering wildly in the breeze. Both her drivers and two footmen were also clad in the same famous colors.

"I know, I know!" she laughed, as Rachel and Ermaline examined her carriage in bemused fascination, "it's overdone," she admitted, "but no more so than Lady Merrington's gaudy wheels. I passed it on the road some hours back, going so slow you'd think they were carrying eggs!"

"Eleanora! Don't you know it's bad manners to overtake the carriage of a social better?"

"Hogwash!" cried Eleanora. "I hold my head up in the best of company, and 'sides, the way they're creeping along they're apt to miss the ceremony. I've got a bride to dress!" she announced, turning to Ermaline, "and there's no better time for that final fitting than right now!" All business, Eleanora herself supervised the unloading of the coach's boot, and soon a dozen or more striped boxes were strewn all about Ermaline's bedroom. The country maids gaped openly as Ermaline's bridal trousseau was unpacked and lifted piece by piece from them. The garments were shaken to remove the wrinkles, and then hung about the room in gay disorder. The last box, larger than the rest, held Ermaline's wedding dress, and Eleanora shooed everyone, including Rachel, from the room before opening it.

"We must find a place where I can work undisturbed; some place we can hide the dress until the ceremony." Ermaline thought for a moment and then pointed to a tiny dressing room off her bedchamber, so little used she had almost forgotten it was there. After dusting it herself, Eleanora called for sheets and linens to cover the floor, after which she set right to work putting the final stitches into the magnificent dress.

It was truly a breathtaking creation, and would remain the subject of much fashion-talk for months to come. Eleanora had made it her business to learn that Rowland brides were traditionally presented with diamonds on their wedding day, and she had created a dress that would serve as perfect foil for the splendid necklace already set in platinum by a chosen London jeweler.

Simplicity, ever Eleanora's trademark, was the motif of the dress. Accordingly, its neckline was low, its bodice completely unadorned. "We must not out-dazzle Henry's gift, even by jewels of your own," she said, pinning the fabric taut against Ermaline's jutting breasts. Great pouffy bishop sleeves were sheer, ending in long cuffs of delicate lace, and the long pointed waistline that had served Ermaline so well already, was utilized once again. Rushing from under its full skirt poured yards and yards of pristine white mousseline de soie, the hem awash in beading of tiny glittering stones and blushing pearls that outlined dainty flowers on Italian lace. The hat that perfected the costume was a beauty too, a large crowned affair concocted to encompass Ermaline's upswept hair. Its brim was curved and dipped, fully swathed in silk tulle shot with pearls.

Rachel meanwhile, was kept solidly occupied elsewhere in the house, solving a myriad of last minute problems that sometimes threatened to upset her carefully drawn plans. As she worked, bustling from floor to floor, she fumed, disturbed by Eleanora's news of Lady Merrington's imminent arrival at Guersten Hall. In the garden, in fact, she griped openly about it to Adele, as the two of them strolled along the path selecting blossoms for the dinner table.

"I only sent the blasted invite because I had too!" Rachel said, stamping her foot for emphasis. "Your brother and Lord Merrington are old friends, but I dared hope that Edwina would have the good grace to decline."

"Lord Merrington is even more closely aligned to Henry Rowland, and just now has become his benefactor in Henry's quest to regain the Rowland earldom. The Lord's presence here was to be expected."

"His, yes . . . but hers? I can't bear it, Aunt. Am I to be humiliated again, and under my own roof?"

"Perhaps you worry needlessly," tutted Adele. "Though hardly industrious, Emory has at least remained sober these past few weeks, has he not?"

"Yes, but he is vexed with me just now, as usual, and it has been a long time since he has . . . I mean . . ." Blushing prettily, Rachel pretended to examine a yellow day lily.

"Lain with a woman? Come, child, perhaps it is time we had a little talk, you and I." Adele led the way to the stone summerhouse, now sparkling with new paint and gay cushions.

"Does it bother you that Emory became entangled with Lady Merrington and others like her?" asked the older woman.

"All that was before our marriage, Adele, but by the same token I cannot be friends with her knowing that . . ."

"That he bedded her?"

"It goes beyond that. Edwina is so . . . wanton and Emory likes her for just that quality."

"Exactly, my dear," advised Adele, arranging her skirts around her. "Men have need of women like Edwina, and you would do well to look the other way when Emory feels the need to expend his passion elsewhere."

"Aunt! What are you saying? That you approve of such liaisons?"

"Rachel, Rachel," Adele said, softly patting Rachel's hand. "It is not a matter of approval. Men have their needs. They can be . . . messy, and most inopportune, sometimes. For a price, some trinket, say, others can be enticed to fill those needs."

"Do I hear correctly?" asked Rachel, dumbfounded. "You look the other way when Hugh dallies with others? I don't understand; you are ever complaining about it!"

"Of course, I complain! And loudly, too! It is expected of me, and it serves as a reminder to Hugh that I expect him to be both discreet and select about his choice of companions."

"And what of love, Adele? Do you feel nothing for Hugh?"

"Certainly, I do! He is my husband, is he not? But the type of love you refer to doesn't exist, and it isn't necessary to a good marriage."

"You sound like my father," said Rachel in a rather distraught tone. "He too, denies the existence of love, but can you compare my marriage to that of Rebecca and Edward? They adore each other; their moments alone together are bliss, while mine are hell."

Adele wagged a pointed finger. "Only because you have not performed your wifely duties, my dear."

Rachel leapt to her feet. "Duties be damned! If succumbing to husbandly advances is to be deemed only a duty, then it is one which I shall never perform! You are wrong, Aunt," she added, fitfully pacing the length of the summerhouse in long strides.

"There must be something here!" she cried, pounding her breast, "and there must be trust and understanding, giving and sharing. These are the qualities that mark my marriage a failure . . . and without them I can never go freely into Emory's arms."

"Bah!" snorted Adele in disaccord. "My role in life was chosen for me, just as yours was, and if once I dreamed of romantic interludes with some handsome charmer, I soon put them out of my head." She laughed. "Hugh's appearance alone dispelled them; always so short, so stout, even as a young man. No amount of love could change that."

"Who knows?" sighed Rachel. "Maybe if he believed you loved him for himself he'd feel six feet tall and handsome to boot!"

Adele laughed delightedly at that, but shook her head from side to side in disagreement, just the same. "Believe what you will then; for myself, I have cautioned my daughters to marry well, perform their duties, provide the expected heir, and then leave the capers in the bedroom to those who get paid for it!"

Strangely, there were tears in Rachel's eyes when she left Adele in the summerhouse and went back to the house. Poor Hugh! What a lonely man he must be, always seeking love, never finding it. And Charlotte . . . and Olivia, doomed to an equally loveless life simply because their mother didn't believe it existed.

In the library, George looked up from his letter writing, and spotting the half dried tears on Rachel's cheeks, became disturbed, certain that Emory had put them there. "Is something amiss, my dear. Do you wish to talk?"

Rachel stepped behind the old man, bent and gave him a kiss. "It's nothing," she said, patting his shoulder affectionately. "Adele thought to allay my anxiety over Lady Merrington's arrival, but somehow she has only managed to make matters worse."

George snorted. "Adele is hardly one to be giving advice to the lovelorn, though I suspect she meant well enough." He watched as Rachel went to the window seat and threw herself upon it, her lovely face stripped of its usual composure. George guessed that Edwina's presence at the Hall would cause Rachel more pain than she was letting on. Pushing his chair away from the desk, he rolled to the door and slammed it closed with the butt of his walking stick, then made his way to the far side of the library. He came to a halt at the three little steps, just below where Rachel sat.

"Daughter, would you be offended if I passed comment on the same matter?"

"Certainly not, we've always been able to talk, have we not?"

"Aye, we have, but I've in mind some things a man does not usually say to a lady."

"Let me be the judge of that," Rachel answered, moving to sit on the top step, so that their eyes were on the same level.

"I take it," George began, "that you do not believe that Emory and Edwina are done with one another?"

I know so, Rachel wanted to say, but she merely nodded without divulging the conversation she had overhead that night at Woodleigh Grange. They've plotted to continue, hammered her brain, and she knew, if George did not, just how badly Emory needed a woman.

"Hear me, Rachel. Emory assures me he is through with her, and I believe him, but even so, it is natural that they should remain friends." Here George paused, actually blushing. "Edwina was the first woman with whom Emory was intimate," he said pinkly, choosing his words with care. "He was young then, and I tried to prevent it, but intimacy was inevitable for a man of his inclinations, and in Edwina he found an ally. They are alike in so many ways; both of them free and spirited, with passionate natures, like two wild things in the forest. Emory moved on to other conquests, many of them to his shame, but always, he returned to Edwina. Do you have any idea why that is?"

Shyly almost, Rachel looked at her father-in-law, spreading her hands in an I-don't-know gesture.

"Only in intimacy did Edwina demand anything from Emory," continued George, "and even then, she gave as much as she took. With others, he had to go through the motions and pretenses of those silly little games men and women play before they'll drop their defenses and respond to the call that brought them together in the first place; the courting, the baiting, the fawning . . . and the whispered lies! Bah! Some couples even play that ridiculous game *after* marriage! But Edwina did not . . . Emory needed only to go to her and say: I want you . . . I need you, and she fulfilled his wants, answered his need."

"Why do you tell me this" Rachel asked suddenly, her head bent as she studied her shoes.

"Perhaps in the telling you might come to understand Emory a little better, my dear, that's all. He is only a man, no better, no worse than most of us."

"But does he not love her, even though he is reluctant to admit it?"

"Heaven's no!" scoffed George. "Men don't love women like Edwina! She is his friend! They were lovers, but they do not love. There is a difference."

"Life is full of differences that I don't understand, I fear."

"You will, in time. For now, you need only understand what role a woman like Edwina plays in a man's life. She is his sister, his mother . . . all women, wrapped into one grand package! He can go to her naked and not feel naked; he can go to her drunk or sober, happy or sad, she welcomes him. He can be a man, or a little boy; he can be brave, or cowardly, still she welcomes him. He can rant or swear, pound out his frustrations on her body, yet still she remains his friend."

"And if he marries, or falls in love? What then?"

"Ah, Rachel! There is the wonder of it all! For if that woman I just described is his wife, too, or the woman he loves, happy is he! And envied! It happens now and again." The old man paused and smiled at Rachel before continuing. "Ideally every man should know a woman like Edwina. Lord knows, there would be fewer misfits among us. Know this; whenever you hear of a happily married man or a man who has kept the same mistress ten, fifteen . . . twenty years, you will know that man has found such a woman."

"And have you known such a woman?" Rachel asked timidly.

A faraway look came into George's blue eyes and it was a long time before he answered. "Yes," he said. "Isabelle was that woman in my life, and when she died I never needed another. Perhaps that explains why poor Abigail was so unhappy. She understood it not."

"Does any woman?"

"Hell, no!" he said good-naturedly. "You women measure each other by your own yardsticks, and accordingly, you see each other as threats and rivals. But Edwina is not your rival, Rachel; she never has been. She really has little to do with the present state of your marriage."

"You may be right about that, George," said Rachel, rising from the hard step, "and keeping that in mind, I will try to think kindly of her, but it will be difficult. For some reason I cannot explain, I still resent her coming."

"Ah, me girl," thought the old man as Rachel left the library. "Do y' not know jealousy when you see it?"

Climbing the stairs, Rachel contemplated her father-in-law's words. Emory need only say to Edwina, "I want, I need you," and she would fulfill his want, answer his need. *He said those same things to me*, she thought, *just nights ago, and if he'd only added "I love you," then perhaps I might have fulfilled his want, answered his need.* Now, with Edwina rattling toward Guersten Hall, who would Emory choose to answer that need? His friend, or his wife?

In the end, neither was called upon, for Rachel was swamped by her duties as hostess. Besides, her last encounter with Emory had put even more distance between them. But Edwina was something else! Her inability to service Emory's randy needs were determined by quite another matter altogether.

Lord Merrington's coach, still making its turtle-like pace, finally drew up before Guersten Hall. The Lord, gout and all, stepped down, turned around and handed his wife to the ground. Pink and blonde, Edwina was as beautiful as ever, even if she seemed a bit pale. Rachel determined at closer range that Edwina Merrington was uncharacter-istically scrubbed clean; she wore no rouge, no lip color, and her hair had been twisted into a simple knot, half hidden under a fashionable bonnet. But it was Edwina's costume that caused commotion among those standing on the steps to greet her. Though made of some silky and expensive fabric, it was plain, brown, and it was buttoned to the very neck. It made Edwina appear very chic, very lovely, and very, very pregnant.

"Pregnant?" whispered George, looking suspiciously at Emory, who in turned looked at Rachel, now ushering her latest houseg-uest into the manor. Rachel only scowled at him, and he knew from the quizzical expression on her face that she was doing some mental counting.

"He's so doting!" whispered Edward, watching the limping Lord help his wife up the stairs. "You'd think he planted the seed himself."

Not too much later, Lord Merrington waited in the library with George and his sons for a carriage to be brought around, for Merrington was most anxious to make a grand tour of Rachel's "cabbage patch," as he put it. Waiting, the gentlemen sipped a brandy, while upstairs, in anticipation of the evening's ball, Edwina rested in a darkened bed-room. Neither Rachel nor Emory had spoken more than a dozen words to her; she had even brought her own maids and they hovered over the mother-to-be as though she were a queen in a hive. It was natural then, that the conversation in the library turned to her delicate condition.

"Yes, she's pregnant, m'boy," the Lord said, thumping Emory on the shoulder. "And I owe it all to you!"

Gulping, Emory blanched, nearly dropping his glass. "Me?" he said, dumbly. "How so, Lord . . . how so?" One hand shot behind his back, his fingers counting off the months. He had last lain with Edwina seven months ago; at best she was only five months along.

"The child isn't mine!" Emory blurted, without thinking.

"Course it isn't," replied Lord Merrington. "Didn't mean to imply 'twas. 'Tis mine, in fact!" he added proudly.

"Well, I'll be damned! But, I thought . . ."

"Know what you thought, and you thought rightly. But now my physician says my condition is some improved. Awhile back me 'n'

Edwina talked it over and weighed the risks. She decided she wanted the child badly enough to take them. We're gambling, we know, but the heir will be my own!"

"And happy I am for you," said George, pumping Lord Merrington's hand. "You're wife is brave; the risks are many,"

"We both know that; she could catch my disease or something could be wrong with the bairn, if it survives at all."

"I'm puzzled, Lord," said Emory. "How does your . . . success relate to me?"

"That weekend you came to Woodleigh Grange with Rachel done it," said Merrington, limping to a chair. "Thet wife of yours is just as responsible, maybe more." He wagged a crooked finger at Emory. "That girl came here to Guersten Hall under awkward and difficult circumstances, yet she made the best of it, never complaining. She's gritty, and I admire her."

"I, too," commented George, his white head bobbing up and down.

"And as for you," continued the Lord, pointing to Emory, "you chose on the spot that night to give up an established way of life when you chased after her, left behind your clothes, y' friends . . . everything, even though you knew then there was no guarantee y'd find happiness! You were gambling, and Edwina and I figured we could do as much. After all, we loved each other once; we'd just lost sight of it!"

As they waited under the portico for Angus to position George in the open carriage, Emory turned to the Lord. "Here I thought you had done *me* the favor that night."

Merrington nudged Emory with his cane. "Call it a trade-off, lad. Tell me, did y' find love?"

Grimacing, Emory tried to make light of the matter. "I'm afraid not. Rachel and I, well, our differences are too ingrained, I guess. Neither of us can change."

"Nonsense! You are both too stubborn, is all! Neither of y' wants to be the first to say I love you. Say it, boyo! Look at me! Haven't felt this good in ten years! Now, shall we go? I want a peek at Rachel's cabbages before it gets dark!"

Later, brushing Sultan's satiny hide, Emory contemplated Merrington's pointed remarks. *I love you!* Emory had never thought to say those words to Rachel. He had never said them to any woman, in fact; not as a lie in the pursuit of conquest, not in jest, no matter how drunk . . . never, not even to Edwina in the throes of passion.

Yes, both he and Rachel were stubborn, there was no question about that, and each was equally strong willed, too. Emory faced what he believed to be the facts; Rachel did not love him, probably never could. His more dominant personality had plagued her from childhood, and she was unlikely to forget that. He had tormented her, argued and fought with her, and more recently, chased her down and throttled her. No, he reckoned, though she had forgiven his boorish behavior repeatedly, she was not the type to simply forget it, and therefore, would never be the first to say *I love you,* if ever she said it.

"And neither will I!" he announced to the stallion, who neighed, as if approving Emory's misguided stand. "What happened when we were children is done with," added Emory with finality. "Most of the rest is her fault as much as mine. She's so damned bossy!" he thundered, "and so damned righteous!"

He slapped Sultan's round rump and threw down his brush. "Now if only she wasn't so damned beautiful, eh fellow? And if only I didn't want her so damned bad!"

Sultan fed and watered, Emory returned to the house just in time to meet Rachel, coming down the marble stairs in a rustle of silk. She had dressed early for the evening, for a small ball, followed by a midnight supper had been planned for the entertainment of their houseguests. Now, spying Rachel's beauty, Emory's self-induced animosity melted quickly. She was wearing his favorite gown, the same sea green silk she'd worn that night he returned to the Hall. Standing close to her, he drank in her perfume, and was decidedly fascinated by the way the dress clung magically to her curvaceous figure. Now, as then, she was beautiful, the only change in her costume being the addition of the magnificent Guersten pendant. The heavy opalescent pearl lay nestled between her breasts.

"You haven't even begun to dress! she snapped.

"I've been in the stables," he said, admiring her openly.

"That much my nose told me! And will you stop ogling?"

"I was just admiring your . . . er, pearl," he teased, lifting the valuable gem from its bed against her flesh.

Brushing his hand away, Rachel retrieved it, just as Angus approached them. The Scot, doubling as butler tonight, was very proper in his garb, looking taller than ever all in black.

"A gentleman in the morning room, sir," he said, addressing Emory. "A Mr. Landseer," he added.

"Oh, yes," said Emory over his shoulder, bounding up the stairs two at a time. "Merrington invited him. He's an artist of some sort. See to him, will you, Rachel?"

He vanished up the stairs, and Rachel, who still had half a dozen things to see to, was forced to turn and head for the morning room. There, an attractive man, dressed in dark brown, stood admiring a framed landscape. He turned as she stepped over the threshold.

"You must be Rachel, ma'am!" he said quickly, "though my friend Merrington's description was most inadequate!"

"I'm afraid you have the advantage, sir."

"The name is Landseer," the man said. "Edwin Landseer, madam, painter of dogs, horses, and sundry other animals, come to crash your wedding festivities at Lord Merrington's second hand invite. He tells me there is on this estate one of the finest stallion's in all England. My curiosity piqued, I packed my oils and here I am!"

"We are certainly glad to have you," replied Rachel graciously, "though just where we shall put you I'm sure I do not know!"

"Oh, but I do!" she expostulated only seconds later. *Edward's room!* He would need little prompting for a chance to double with Rebecca. They had already worn a path between their rooms.

"There is a turret there that overlooks the stable yard from a distance," she said to the man. "You'll be quite comfortable. I have heard of you, Mr. Landseer. Do you intend to paint Sultan?"

"Aaaah, even his name is majestic. I do! I do!" added the friendly Landseer, "though if ever I were to turn my talents to portraiture, I would start with you, in that exquisite green gown. You are a most beautiful woman, madam."

Blushing under the artist's praise, Rachel led the way from the morning room. "Angus will show you to your room. I shall send up a tray and some hot water. Join us in the ballroom at your leisure."

"You are most kind," Landseer said to her, as Angus gathered up his valises. "But tell me, is there not time for me to see this fine horse first? I've heard so much, you see."

"All of it true, too," confirmed Rachel. "Yes, go . . . see for yourself, but beware, the beast likes none but Emory, and his temperament makes him awesome."

That brief conversation was the last that Rachel had with Mr. Landseer for several days. The artist all but took up residence in the stables, and the turret in Edward's room, with its good light, was soon turned into a miniature studio.

CHAPTER TWENTY-THREE

The chandeliers in the long ballroom glittered brightly, their lights reflecting a thousand times over in the many mirrors and polished glass of the French doors, thrown wide open by Rachel. Dozens of flower arrangements extended the gardens across the terrace into the ballroom. Taking their places on a little dais placed before the sliding doors leading to the music room, the musicians began to play, and the dancers took to the floor.

From one end of the room, George and Lord Merrington watched the gaily dressed guests whirling and dipping, and Merrington's foot, gout and all, bobbed up and down in rhythm to the pulsating music. Primly, Edwina sat near him, leaving his side not once all evening, although she did allow Emory to escort her to the banquet table around midnight. Still, not once did any man take Edwina in his arms and spin her about the floor or turn her on the garden path. She was the model of decorum, ignoring every man present, her behavior as chaste as her costume, a royal blue affair, its deep décolletage demurely stuffed with flocked tulle. All evening long, the Lord smothered his wife with solicitous attention.

"She certainly draws full measure from her maternity, does she not?" asked Ermaline of Rachel during a lull in the music.

"Ladies, ladies!" whispered Emory, stepping between them. "Have some charity! Edwina is past thirty, and this is her first child."

"One she needs badly if Merrington is to retain his estates," he added in Rachel's ear, after claiming her for a dance. "Can you not be tolerant?"

"I'm sorry I gossiped, but I find it difficult to like her."

"She likes you!"

"Only because I have a handsome husband."

"Oh, you admit I'm handsome?" The emerald eyes curled with laughter.

"Tonight you are, and well you know it! Only the peacock in the garden outshines you!" Emory *was* handsome tonight, wearing a plum colored frock coat over dove gray trousers, sleek and form fitting that hugged his rugged thighs and outlined his masculine body. By now, Rachel was most conscious of that body, having seen it in various stages of dress and undress, and having felt it pressed warmly against hers on more than one occasion. She knew too, that they made a most attractive couple as they went spinning about the ballroom. *Aaah*, if only they brought each other pleasure instead of pain.

As if echoing her thoughts, Emory tightened his hold on Rachel's waist and deftly steered her toward the garden. "I demand my token kiss," he said in mock seriousness. "If you refuse I shall get drunk, or throw a tantrum at the very least."

"Why, that's blackmail!" she cried, but she went with him out onto the terrace anyway, and from there they made their way into the garden. The September night was lovely, the air comfortably warm under a midnight blue sky awash with stars. The moon, nearly full, cast romantic shadows along the path to the summerhouse.

"Are you really jealous of Edwina?" asked Emory, abruptly, as they strolled between the flower beds.

"I'm not jealous!"

"Oh, but you are," he said, "though you need never be again. You are woman enough for me, Rachel. Am I not man enough for you?" He strutted outrageously, throwing out his chest, and smiled down at her.

"You are a shameless braggart!" exclaimed Rachel, laughing at his posturing. "And now I must go back inside, we have guests."

"My kiss . . ."

Emory was in a remarkably affable mood, one achieved naturally for a change, since he had not had anything to drink in several days. Rather than risk souring that good mood, Rachel turned up her face, only to discover that the kiss was a mistake. A sensuous thrill shot through her body and her emotions surged upward. Her heart began to pound, and the memory of that recent episode in her bedroom flooded back, bringing with it desire that had taken her ten days to bury. Its reappearance confused her anew as it coursed unrestrained through her body. Emory's lips were warm, as his arms tightened about her.

"About the other night . . ."

"Let us forget it," she said, her knees weak. "It is already in the past; let it remain there."

"Add to it my dalliances with Lady Merrington. That too, is past. Now she wants only to be a respectful housewife . . . to bear her Lord's child."

He turned Rachel until the moonlight flooded her lovely face. Tracing its outline with his fingertips, he pressed her even closer. "And I want you, Rachel . . . only you, and somehow I mean to have you."

Some peculiar quality in Emory's voice made Rachel's heart skip, as he gathered her closer still, her face buried against his throat. It had occurred to her once that there was not a serious bone in his body. Drunk or sober, when he was not intimidating or threatening, he was usually bragging or jesting. But now, held tightly in the circle of his arms in the romantic moonlight, his soft words conveyed none of these things. Controlled yet passionate, they were the naked words of a man tormented by desire, and his passion, his nearness, the moonlight, all combined to excite Rachel. She looked up at him, to find his green eyes flooded with that desire. Her lips parted to meet his in passion. It was a long kiss, a thrilling kiss.

"Why do you fight me so?" he groaned in agony, as his mouth lifted from hers.

Regaining her composure, Rachel stepped back. "You are wrong," she said, straightening her gown. "It is you who fights."

She slipped away from him then, a little unwillingly, knowing that remaining would surely lead to a commitment. Back up the path she went, and crossing the terrace without looking back, re-entered the ballroom. Emory followed a short distance behind her, and Lord Merrington, who had watched them go out, now turned to Emory when they reappeared singly.

"Trouble, lad?"

Straddling a small velvet chair, Emory watched Rachel make her way to the other side of the ballroom. Turning, their eyes met and held, then Rachel looked away. "No, m'Lord," Emory said to Merrington, "our little game continues yet, is all."

Under a sky as blue as old George's eyes, Ermaline and Henry Rowland were wed in the garden of Guersten Hall the next day. This time the old vicar had no trouble discerning either the bride or the bridegroom, and before a makeshift altar banked with garden lilies, he united the happy couple in matrimony. Brilliant points of light flashed from Ermaline's throat as Henry's gift caught the afternoon sun. Nattily attired all in gray, young Henry barely took his eyes from his bride, and more than once, his responses had to be nudged from him.

"Love is everywhere at Guersten Hall, it seems," said Emory, standing close beside Rachel. With his hand, he indicated Ermaline and her new husband, now surrounded by well-wishers, and then pointed to Edward and Rebecca, wandering off to the summerhouse to be alone. Lastly, Emory gestured to Edwina Merrington, whose doting Lord hovered over her protectively over on the terrace. "It seems to be a disease, my dear," he added, laughing. "Take care you don't catch it!"

Before the newlyweds departed for an extended honeymoon on the continent, Ermaline, with Rachel's assistance, changed into a two-piece traveling dress of green silk faille. The little curtains on her bonnet matched the material of the gown's bodice, tissue thin white silk, flocked with green dots.

"A gift from Eleanora," said Ermaline of her bonnet, as together they finished the last of the new bride's packing. "It seems she will have me carry her colors clear to Switzerland and back!"

"Nonetheless, she has served you well," replied Rachel, handing the last little valise to a waiting maid. "No bride ever looked more beautiful. Now hurry! Henry is eager, and your father waits in the library to say his good-bye."

"I am ready," said Ermaline, "and just as eager as Henry, if the truth be known. But first, how can I ever thank you, Rachel? You made it all possible."

"No, Ermaline. *You* made it possible, by casting off the shroud in which you had cloaked yourself."

"Still, how can I ever repay you?"

"Your happiness is payment enough. I ask no more."

Embracing, the two young women made their way to the stairs, where Ermaline grew serious. "Your marriage to my brother is difficult for you, I know. If ever you grow weary of his antics, remember, we are friends as well as sisters. Perhaps I can smooth your way for a change."

"His quicksilver moods can be a trial at time, but I'm not ready to admit defeat yet."

Arm in arm, they descended the stairs, proceeding to the library, where their pleasant laughter brought joy to the old man.

"Henry's love has made you beautiful," said George to his daughter as they kissed each other good-bye.

"Not just Henry's, Father," whispered Ermaline, on her knees before him, "but yours as well, now that I know I have it. For the first time in my life, I am sorry to be leaving Guersten Hall."

"Don't be, daughter. It is time for you to exchange one home for another, without looking back, as Rachel did. Our love goes with you."

Their farewells said, the couple departed, and by the next day the last of the houseguests had also departed, one by one, until only Edwina and Lord Merrington remained. And, of course, Landseer, the artist.

Since his arrival, Landseer and Emory had become fast friends, drawn together by their mutual admiration of superb horseflesh. Furthermore, if Sultan was to stand still long enough to be sketched, then Emory's presence was required. Yet, even though Sultan was often restless and given to prancing, Landseer was still able to capture all of his wildness faithfully on his canvasses. Working on several of them at once, the images were so lifelike that once Rachel was tempted to put her fingers into the wet paint to touch the remarkable likeness portrayed there.

While the affable Landseer was graced with Rachel's company, Lady Merrington was not. To the best of her ability, Rachel made every attempt to avoid being alone with her, and by Friday, as Edwina's visit to Guersten Hall drew to a close, it was she, therefore, who sought out Rachel. Edwina approached her in the little room off the conservatory, where Rachel had gone to arrange some fresh blossoms into a bouquet for the tea table. Blocking the doorway artfully with her hooped skirts, Edwina presented Rachel no opportunity to continue her evasions.

"I'm sorry you have seen fit to avoid me," she said frankly to Rachel. "I had hoped that somehow we two might be friends. At any rate, I owe both you and Emory my thanks."

Despite Edwina's offer of friendship, Rachel remained decidedly cool to her. "Yes," she said, "Emory explained that you felt our presence at Woodleigh Grange had prompted some . . . soul searching, but the decision you and your husband made, was, after all, your own. I pray only that it brings the happiness you seek." Then Rachel tried to change the subject, steering it to the expected heir. "Do you now return to Kent for your lying-in?"

"No," replied Edwina. "The second leg of our journey will take us to my Lord's ancestral home in Northumberland. It is his birthplace, and he wishes his own child to be born there also."

The conversation lagged, and as Edwina watched, Rachel jammed one blossom after another into a flower holder. The two women had so very little to say to one another.

"You don't like me, do you?" asked Edwina with remarkable candor. Rachel's reply was equally candid.

"Our backgrounds are too diverse, and you already know how much I disapprove of your lifestyle."

"But all that has changed! Surely, you can see that! It is the true reason we travel to Northumberland. Perhaps after a long absence, some of my . . . notoriety will diminish. Don't you believe that I can change, or that it will last?"

"Time will tell," said Rachel, rather curtly, snipping unwanted leaves from some thorny roses. As before, a deafening silence fell between the two of them.

"Come, come, Rachel. We are skirting the issue!"

"Which is?"

"Which is Emory . . . of course!"

Laying down her scissors, Rachel turned to the door. Edwina stepped aside and let her pass, and then followed Rachel into the humid greenness of the conservatory itself. One behind the other, the two women passed among tables of ferns, dotted here and there with splashes of bright color; a tropical blossom, a rare orchid, some flower that ordinarily would have drawn accolades. Today, nature's exquisite achievements went unnoticed and unclaimed. Then, at the end of the row, Rachel suddenly halted, turning abruptly to face Edwina.

"You are right. Emory *is* the issue, and has been for some time. I resent your liaison with him. Surely you must be aware that it caused me much embarrassment."

Edwina tossed her blonde head and sniffed.

"Don't be stuffy, Rachel. You make it sound as though I lured him from your very bed! We both know Emory was never welcomed there, is not now welcome! Besides, he was far from chaste at the time of your marriage, and the truth is, had he not followed me to Kent last winter, then he would have sought someone else's company, for he was determined to put distance between you then."

"I don't dispute those facts, but is it not also a fact that both you and Emory plotted to continue your illicit . . . er, relationship, I believe you called it? That was in the spring, and it is needless for you to deny it. I learned of it firsthand!"

"So that's it! One of my maids reported that you were seen in the corridor outside my apartments just before you fled Woodleigh Grange. Well there you err, Rachel! I met with Emory that night after the card game, true . . . but it was a meeting of friends, not lovers."

"Friends, indeed! I saw you embracing with my own eyes!"

"Did you, now? A farewell kiss, love, nothing more, and I make no apologies for it. Emory is my friend, and he shall remain so! My husband, too, cherishes that friendship, despite the differences in their ages. The Lord does, in fact, intend to name Emory as guardian of his heir, should misfortune fall upon us both before the child reaches his majority."

Wide-eyed, Rachel received that bit of news with astonishment. Emory? Overseer to all of Merrington's wealth? Guardian to the future Lord Merrington? Why, Emory had thus far shown little inclination or ability to administer even his own estate, and Rachel said so!

"Do not confuse his ribald attitudes about life with incompetence, my dear," cautioned Edwina with a tut. "Despite his attitudes, Emory is quite capable, and in time he will assume his responsibilities, performing them well, as have countless others before him, my own husband, for one. To that end, it was Emory who chose to end our . . . liaison, as you have labeled it. His own stated intent was to return here to Guersten Hall, and to concentrate all his energies upon it . . . and you. Especially you! Now he wants only to give your marriage a fair chance, his own words, I might add. Perhaps if you were more receptive to his advances, he might have put his old ways behind him already."

"Do not lay Emory's shortcomings at my feet!" cried Rachel, hurling the words at Edwina in a near shout. "I will hear none of it!" she added. "I have done quite well by Emory; running his house and his estate, caring for his father and his sister. None can fault me there!"

"Perhaps not, love, but sooner or later, however talented you are, you must stop being a manager and a housekeeper, and be a woman. Only a woman can hold a man like Emory."

"And if I choose not to hold him? What then, eh?" snapped Rachel, cutting before Edwina on her way from the conservatory.

At the door, Edwina reached out, grabbing Rachel's sleeve. She held the fabric tightly. "Then you are a fool, Rachel Guersten! A fool, plain and simple!"

The Merrington's finally departed, to Rachel's utter relief, taking the renowned Mr. Landseer with them, although that one promised to return as soon as he replenished his oils and canvases. The borrowed maids and footmen were returned to their own places of service, and Rachel gave her own house staff time off in rotation, for a deserved holiday.

Weeks passed, weeks in which the abundance from the Hall's fields continued to flow unabated to the midland's supper tables. Rachel's strongbox filled to the top and then overflowed. The last of their creditors were paid off with the coins, and Peter purchased whatever materials he felt would be needed for the early plantings, next spring. Already planned, the second summer's venture was to be on a larger scale, with extended acreage going under the plow. This time, no one disputed the merits of Rachel's "plan." Even Emory, openly, deemed it a success.

"We'll need a lot more men next year," Peter said one morning, as they sat astride their horses, watching the loading of the wagons. Crate after crate was handed up and carefully positioned, and today, early apples were added to the assorted bounty, which already included tart peaches and juicy grapes.

"We'll find them," said Rachel in a confident tone. "Once they hear how well those in Hall vill have done, perhaps some will even seek us out."

Eventually, the remaining coins in Rachel's box were sorted and divided equally among the estate's workers. Since no one in the big house took a share, not even Peter, who refused his, all the portions were larger than the original half wages that Rachel had promised. The extra coins, and the knowledge that they would be warm and well fed through the winter to come, further cemented the loyalty of the vill's people.

"Anything collected after the first of October will be clear profit," Rachel announced to George, as the last man was paid off. Only three weeks later, when she proudly showed George the box again, its bottom was already covered. It later turned out that Rachel's original estimate of profit was off a bit . . . the final tally would show almost a hundred pounds more than even she had anticipated.

For a month or more the weather remained pleasant. The days were warm and sunny, the nights seasonable. Then one morning, the midlanders awoke to find themselves awash under a teeming downpour that continued for days. The ground became sodden, and great quantities of black midland mud were transferred from field to cottage, as the workers, despite the cold wetness, went about their business as best they could.

With spirits as gray as the weather, Rachel curled up on the green chaise in her room to read one afternoon. The rain had lessened, but the air turned crisp, and the ominous sky remained heavy and threatening. The house was silent; Rebecca and her son napped, Emory and Edward were out somewhere in the fields, helping to free a mud-mired wagon. Engrossed in her book, Rachel read on, while the china mantel clock ticked away one hour, then another. Finally, she looked up from the pages, realizing with a start that the light was almost gone, and that the room was quite chilly. Her door was ajar, and a strong draft crept over the floor. In the hall, she set about finding the cause, reasoning that somewhere on the second floor a window had blown open.

Tracing the cold draft to Ermaline's now empty bedchamber, she found all the windows to be secure. The room itself, though, was nearly as cold as outside, and plainly she detected the freshened smell of damp earth.

Investigating further, Rachel found the door to the tiny dressing room open, the same little room that Eleanora had confiscated as a work room. The sheeting, now completely saturated with rain water, still lay on the floor, and both windows were blown wide apart, not having been latched properly when the room was last used.

Latching the latticed windows, Rachel called for two maids to remove the wet sheeting and mop the puddles before the water seeped into the library below. Moving about the tiny room, she wondered if perhaps her own room, a duplicate of Ermaline's, might also have a dressing room.

In her own room she looked for a telltale doorway that might reveal the presence of a similar room. If there was one, it was completely hidden by the massive wardrobe that held her clothes. Her interest piqued, Rachel summoned Angus, and if the Scotsman found her request for assistance unusual, he remained mum about it, as together they edged the heavy wardrobe from the wall. Behind it, as she suspected, was a door.

Through it, Rachel found the tiny room that was twin to Ermaline's, but this one was cold, dark and musty, even though its windows were closed and secure. She spread wide the ragged draperies that covered them, eyeing the place. One wall was piled with a cluster of unused furniture that included a broken chair and a carved bed without a mattress. A long table was placed against the inside wall, and under it were two old trunks, their high rounded tops covered with dust. Otherwise, the room was empty, the floor bare.

On her knees, Rachel opened one of the unlocked trunks. It was filled with an odd assortment of bric-a-brac, among which she found a toy cannon, a silver thimble, and old porringer and a child's tea set made of pewter. Secreted between layers of folded clothing were some wrinkled ribbons, a few collar studs, a cloisonné brooch and a snuff box. Digging deeper still, Rachel retrieved a cameo powder box and a man's gold watch with an exquisite hunting scene engraved on its cover.

Rachel was almost certain that these possessions had belonged to Emory's mother. But why were they secreted away in a hidden room? There seemed to be nothing of any value here, at least in the first trunk. Who would squirrel away such a motley collection so carefully?

The contents of the second trunk confirmed the collector's identity. Laying on the very top was a small color portrait of a young woman dressed all in black, with raven hair and emerald eyes. The rest of the trunk was filled with more clothing, mostly baby garments, all packed away with loving care. *So!* Abigail Prendergast *had* loved her babies, after all, just as Stoddard believed, calculating to spoil them only to torment her husband.

Rachel laid most of the baby clothes on the table above her. The bottom of the trunk was lined with a number of books, arranged in a peculiar pattern that saw all their spines upturned. Only someone with an interest in old titles would have disturbed those ancient books, and Rachel was that person. After drawing out one or two of them, she spied something large and bright colored beneath them. Curious, she removed the rest of the books, dumping them unceremoniously on the floor beside her. There, on the very bottom of the trunk were two items; one a portrait of a small child . . . Emory, Rachel guessed . . . the other was an enameled jewelry casket. Opening the cover she found it filled to the top. *The Prendergast jewels!* The very same pieces that George believed Emory had taken and squandered away!

All of the jewelry was old, their settings quite archaic, but all were of excellent quality and well set just the same. The size of the stones took Rachel's breath away; diamonds of all sizes and shapes, and sapphires, big as her thumbnail. And there was an emerald brooch that must be worth a thousand pounds, at least.

Leaving the contents of the trunks strewn about the room, Rachel sped away to find George, eager to reveal this cache to him at once. He was alone in the salon, rolled close to a freshly laid fire, with one blanket across his knees and another over his shoulders.

"This place is like a barn!" he complained when he saw Rachel.

"I know! But be glad it is!"

She explained about the opened windows in Ermaline's room, and told him how she had searched and found her own tiny room, realizing there must be a balance in the architecture.

"I knew that," said George, "though I'd forgotten it. What makes it so important?"

"Come! I'll show you," Rachel replied, wheeling her father-in-law down the cold corridor and into the tiny dressing room.

"What the hell is this mess?" he asked, looking at the circle of books and bric-a-brac scattered about.

"It was all in the trunks," answered Rachel, parking his chair next to the long table.

"Why, those are Abigail's trunks, the same ones she brought with her from River Park. Always wondered what became of them."

A moment later he pounced on the gold watch when Rachel handed it over to him.

"It's mine!" he cried. "Given to me by my father as a memento of my first kill. See the stag on the back? Got him with one shot!"

He opened the watch and wound it, pleased and surprised to find it still kept time. "Abigail was a peculiar woman, for sure . . . and it appears she was a bit of a packrat, too! Anything else in there of value?"

"This might interest you!"

George's jaw dropped when he recognized the little enameled chest that Rachel placed across his lap.

"Abigail's jewel case! My word! I thought Emory'd taken it!"

The old man opened the case, smiling broadly when he found the cache of jewels intact, but it was a smile that died quickly on his lips.

"And to think I accused Emory of stealing them . . . his mother's jewels, when they were right here all those years, just where she hid them!"

"Why would she do that, George? They were hers, she didn't have to secret them away."

"Can't really say. Maybe she thought I was going to take them from her. I'll confess something to you. Abigail suffered from far more than simple melancholia. She was half mad long before she ever reached womanhood; she was terribly unhappy here at Guersten Hall. I think her mind must have snapped, and I've always suspected she threw herself down those stairs that night."

The thought of it made Rachel shudder, as she replaced the baby clothes in the trunk. "Just the same," she said without turning, "only a woman who loved her babies would pack away their things so carefully. And perhaps she loved you, too, in her way. That watch was the only thing of yours in here. Abigail must have known how much it meant to you."

"Did, too! Never was without it, not from the day my father gave it to me. We tore the house apart when it disappeared. I wanted to give it to Emory when he made his first kill, but then it became lost, and anyway, Emory refused to hunt."

"Refused? Why?"

"Couldn't bear to kill the forest creatures, or so he claimed. Frankly, I always thought that streak of gentleness out of character with the rest of his behavior."

After securing the dressing room again, Rachel and George went to the square room near the salon which Rebecca now used, and together, they returned the enameled casket to its rightful place beside the Guersten heirlooms.

"I'll have Tisbury dispose of them, Rachel," advised the old man. "The stones will bring a good price and the proceeds will ensure that we'll never have to worry about money again. This cache, coupled with what you accomplished in the fields means that Guersten Hall is once again worth a fortune, a lot of it in hard cash. It is all your doing, for no one else would have ever thought of that little room, and I would have gone to my grave thinking my son was a thief. As usual, I owe ye!"

Disdaining his thanks, they joined the others in the salon, where they had gathered for tea. As they entered, Stoddard was berating Emory for a trail of muddy tracks. On the spot, she made him remove his dirty boots and carted them away. Drawing up a chair, he pushed his toes toward the fire, not the least affected by the cook's rebuke.

"The storm's coming back," he announced. "The wind is rising again and the barometer is falling fast. We're in for a real blow this time!"

Emory's words turned out to be more than prophetic, for later that evening the rain returned in earnest, falling in a downpour so heavy that Rachel was unable to see anything from her windows. The wind howled and gusted, dispatching fingers that plucked at the shutters and tiles of the big house, rattling the windows in their casings. Chilly drafts whistled down the chimneys, and once, ashes and embers alike came flying into Rachel's bedroom, blown from the hearth, and the curtains billowed and fell as though they had a life of their own.

Around midnight, thunder clapped without any warning, and flashes of brilliant lightning streaked the dark sky. The first white crack brought Rachel from her bed, and while the booming thunder that followed was still resounding, she reached for a robe and fled to the hallway. There, she collided with Emory, nearly bowling him over.

"It's a wild one, eh? Are you frightened?" he asked her with a grin.

"I seem to have spooked myself," she admitted, suddenly feeling foolish.

"Come on," he said, reluctantly letting her go, but still holding her loosely in the circle of his arms. "Storms always make me hungry. Let's go down to Stoddard's kitchen and see what she can round up."

Stoddard, familiar with his habits, was expecting him. There were pastries on the table, and meat pies warming in the oven. She welcomed Rachel, and then poured them cider from a cask, to be heated on the back of her stove. With a half dozen others, also unable to sleep, Rachel remained there in the kitchen with Emory for the rest of the night, while nature spent its wrath upon the midlands. Like all storms, this one, too, finally passed, and when dawn broke, a brilliant sunrise seemed to mock Rachel's childlike apprehensions.

Emory went directly from the kitchen to the stables, as Rachel hurried to dress. She sought out her father-in-law, each of them anxious to learn what damage the storm had wrought across Guersten land.

"Will you take ol' Baybelle's reins or shall I?" asked George, once they were settled in the little buggy.

"You'd better do it," cautioned Rachel. "I've got a very bad case of the jitters this morning."

Evidence of the storm's fury lay scattered all about the estate. The stream that ran through the park and past Hall village was choked with rainy runoff, almost to Gaffy's door. It boiled and bubbled, gurgling madly on its route to join the Thames. Elsewhere, a flock of confused chickens were perched atop a toppled henhouse, squawking noisily as they wondered where to deposit their eggs, and everywhere shrubs and bushes lay plastered flat against the ground.

"They will survive," George said, "give them a few days. But just think, if this storm had struck before the harvest, my girl, why, you would have lost half your crop!"

As it was, the last of the apples had been blown to the ground, and in the orchard near the low pasture, some wandering cows were enjoying the unexpected treat. Just past the scene, the little buggy crested a low hill, and Rachel suddenly clapped both her hands to her face. She swallowed hard, wringing her hands at the same time.

"My dear! Whatever is wrong? Why should a broken tree frighten you so?"

Before them stood a wounded elm, victim of the brutal storm, sheared in half by a bolt of lightning. It had been rent in lopsided portions; one large branch now lay upside down on the ground, still attached to the tree's trunk by tangled strands of torn bark.

"It's a sign! A sign! I know it! Something dreadful is about to happen!"

"Nonsense, Rachel! It's merely an old tree that didn't weather the storm. It was probably ripe with disease and half rotted anyway."

But Rachel wouldn't be consoled. "No! No!" she said in a trembling whisper. "It's an omen! I've only seen one this bad before . . . the very day Emory fell from his horse."

"But that was years ago, Rachel! You were a child then."

"True, but do not think my present distress something left over from childhood. It's real, George, I feel it. Something awful is going to happen!"

Encircling her shoulders with his one good arm, George tried vainly to comfort Rachel, as they sat in the little buggy stopped in the middle of the road. With little prompting, Rachel blurted out her lifetime fear of fallen branches, telling her father-in-law how each sighting had seemed a prelude to some unfortunate event . . . bad news, a sickness, some failure. Before each of Rebecca's worst illnesses she had seen one; before Emory was thrown, again on the night of the blizzard, and even before her marriage.

George listened quietly to her tumbled words, unable to offer anything that might belay her fear. He noted the tears that stained her white face, and saw that her poise was completely gone. She was like a little girl again, frightened of the unknown. He wished Emory were with them.

"I have never put too much stock in omens or signs, myself," the old man said at last, staring at the splintered tree as if it would tell him something. "I don't mean to belittle your fears, lass, they are real enough, I can see that. I just don't know what to say to you."

"Say nothing, dear George," Rachel said, her voice strained and barely audible.

"Just be careful! Someone in this house is vulnerable . . . you, or Rebecca! The child perhaps! Take care! Someone is in danger!"

CHAPTER TWENTY-FOUR

That someone was Rebecca. Only days later, a sudden October squall developed while she took air in the park with the baby and Anna. Dark clouds sped before the sun and the temperatures dropped in a matter of minutes. As the first splatters of windy downpour splashed through the half bare trees, the two young women ran for the house. Anna, carrying Benjy, raced ahead, her skirts hiked to hasten her way. Rebecca followed behind, hurrying across the wet lawns, dodging cold raindrops all the way. The three of them arrived at the garden door sopping wet, and while Anna and the child were fine, and remained so, within days Rebecca had developed an ominous cough. Before week's end she was abed, imperiled by a fever that worsened hourly. Never again would she leave that big canopied bed that had become hers before Benjy's birth, for by the tenth day Duncan declared her to be in mortal danger, and by the end of the second week she was terminal. Her frail body wracked constantly by violent spasms of coughing, Rebecca wavered between periods of lucidity and a coma-like stupor induced by a drug that Duncan administered to lessen the pain in her chest. Daily, Louisa and George sat, sad and helpless in the salon, knowing too well that Rebecca's health was ebbing away, hour by hour.

This time it was Edward and Rachel who vigiled beside her bed, each of them troubled and heartbroken.

Awaking from restless slumber one afternoon, Rebecca found Rachel alone beside the bed, staring emptily into the long shadows playing about the edge of the room. Snapped from her reverie, Rachel lit a lamp, offering a small circle of light around the bed. She straightened Rebecca's bed linens, and touched a hand to her sister's cheek, to find Rebecca's skin taut and dry, parched by the relentless fever that refused to go away.

"Can I get you anything?" asked Rachel softly.

"No, but sit. I would talk with you while there is still time, Rachel. Death is near."

"Do not speak of it! Do not give up," hushed Rachel. "You must rest, conserve . . ." She paused, her words silenced by Rebecca's fluttering hand.

"Hear me, please!" Rebecca's voice was low and hoarse, and Rachel strained to hear it. Despite her illness, there was an urgency in her sister's voice that would not be denied, and kneeling by the bedside, Rachel brought her ear closer to Rebecca's lips.

"Do not be afraid, Rachel, for I am not," whispered Rebecca, struggling to breath. "I am ready." She fell silent, looking wistfully around the vast room and then she smiled. "Why is it that you disliked this room so much? I have always loved it. I've been happy here."

She paused, as if searching for words. "You have been good to me, Rachel, and I love you for it, but while I have strength, I seek one last favor. It concerns Father . . . why has he not come?"

That Rebecca could not see her anguish, Rachel hung her head. "I cannot say, dear. Perhaps he is still away from London and our messages have not reached him. Mother sent two through Potter already, and a third went off this morning. He may come yet."

"And he may not. Perhaps he no longer recognizes me as a daughter . . . not that disinheritance troubles me," she said resignedly. "I wanted only to spend the last of my life with Edward, and I have. I have found fulfillment, but now I want to see them all brought together . . . Father, Edward, and Benjy. Unite them Rachel, make Father accept my child."

"Pride does strange things to a man, Rebecca, and Father believes his to be injured. He may not understand, even now, and in the end it may make little difference as far as his will is concerned. But you needn't worry, dear, for neither Edward nor the child will ever know want, I'll see to that."

"You don't understand, Rachel! I care not about the money! Benjy is a Guersten. He will spend his childhood here at the Hall, and when he is old enough, I would see him strike out on his own. Money is unimportant."

Rebecca fell silent. Only the sound of her labored breathing was heard in the stillness of the hushed room. She closed her eyes, lying so still that Rachel wondered if perhaps she slept again. When at last she spoke again, she did so without opening her eyes again.

"My love for Edward was not meant as betrayal of Father, tell him that. I simply followed my heart. But that love has torn my family asunder, and if I am to go to my grave without remorse you must repair that damage. Act in my stead, Rachel. Make peace with Father for me, however long it takes. I am flesh of his flesh, as Benjy is of mine. Let them know and love one another. Bring them together, Rachel, prom- ise me . . ."

It was Rachel's turn to fall silent. What could she say? Reunion seemed an impossible task, for Benjamin Brenham wanted no reunion with his family . . . not with his wife, nor his daughters, let alone a grandchild he still considered to be a bastard. Rachel had not seen her father since that morning, many months before, when they quarreled so bitterly atop the bluff. He had refused her attempts to see him, and all of her letters had gone unanswered. What more could she do now, when plainly, Benjamin wanted no part of them?

The inevitable became avoidable no longer, and Rachel faced it then. Rebecca was going to die . . . and soon. If a simple promise brought contentment at this late hour, then Rachel would give it, and concern herself with its fulfillment afterward.

"I promise," she said to her sister, fighting back the tears. "Benjy will know his grandfather. Somehow . . . someday, I will bring them together."

"Then I am happy," murmured Rebecca. With some effort she removed a satin ribbon from under her pillow, handing it to Rachel. From it dangled a small key which fit the diary brought from London as a gift. "It is hidden in my brown muff," said Rebecca, "in the bottom of the wardrobe. Later, when the pain is gone, give it to Edward. It is my only gift for Benjy. I want him to know how much I loved him. Now go," she said to Rachel. "I am very weary, and I hear Edward's step."

Rebecca succumbed not long afterward, in that great bed that had already claimed a dozen or more of Guersten Hall's women. To the end, Edward was with her, their hands joined in wordless union, for everything that required words had been said already. Rebecca had kissed her son, and voiced her love for her husband for the last time.

"Do not withdraw from the world, Edward," she had said to him. "A life of loneliness will not prove your love for me. Benjy is that proof. You are a man and you are young; for his sake you must marry again. Do not cripple him with the love that you would give a woman." To Rachel, her words were simpler still. "Follow your heart, wherever it leads."

During that long last night, a quick passing storm buffeted the midland countryside with heavy rain and crackling lightning. It was soon over, and in the morning sunshine bathed the house in warm light, just about the time Duncan appeared in the doorway of the salon. All turned in sad anticipation of his words.

"I found them both asleep," he said. "Exactly when she passed, I do not know. Does it matter, now?"

Rachel rushed from the room, brushing past Duncan, framed in the doorway. Down the long staircase she went, heavily, like an old woman. Louisa handed a shawl to Emory. "Go after her," she said. "It's her first brush with death, and they were unusually close."

Outside, Rachel headed toward the sunny gardens, but the bright-faced flowers and gesturing statues seemed a mockery in view of her sadness. She turned, and proceeded across the broad lawn that fronted the house, moving slowly at first, almost painfully, until at last she was overtaken by an urge to run, to escape from the emptiness that engulfed her. Wooden legs, following a command of their own, carried her across the grass and into the park. When Emory emerged from the house, he saw the last flash of her blue skirt as she disappeared under a weeping willow by the stream. He found her there, under its sweeping branches, sobbing almost hysterically in despair. Tenderly he wrapped her mother's shawl about Rachel's shoulders, and then enclosed her in his arms. She did not resist, but leaned against him for support, and when her legs gave way beneath her, Emory slumped to the ground with her, cradling her in his arms while she sobbed out her grief. How long they remained there he didn't know, but at last Rachel became still.

"I'm all right now," she said softly against his shirtfront, sensing his concern. Surrounded by the sound of the willow's rustling branches, Emory wet his handkerchief in the stream and wrung it out, then dabbed at Rachel's tear stained face. Helping her to her feet, they turned and together, walked slowly back to the manor house.

There, Duncan was just departing. He beckoned to Emory, calling him aside as Rachel went into the house. "Despite my admonitions," he told Emory, "Rebecca was again with child. I see little point in telling Edward, now. He has sorrow enough," Duncan added, climbing into his Victoria.

"She left one and she took one," said Emory, solemnly, as the two men shook hands. "Almost as if it were planned."

Duncan picked up his reins. "Aye, seems that way, doesn't it?" he murmured, before rolling away.

Under an overcast sky, Rebecca was buried on a gentle, sunny slope that overlooked Brenham Manor's summerhouse and the Small Wood. Remarkably, that spot had been suggested by Emory, who knew Edward would be reluctant to place his beloved in the Guersten family plot, so deep among the cold pines in the Great Wood. Only the men on the estate attended the interment, the women remaining behind in the Hall, bringing small comfort to one another. Benjamin Brenham was very conspicuous in his absence, a fact that only added to their grief.

Edward disappeared the very next day. His bed went unused and his horse was gone from the stables before daybreak. None saw him leave, and when darkness fell, he had still not returned. George fretted over his absence.

"The lad's despondent," bewailed the old man. "He's apt to do something foolish."

"Nonsense, Father. Edward's got more good sense than that," said Emory.

For once, Rachel agreed with her husband. "He just needs time to be alone. Besides, Edward would never abandon the child, of that I am certain."

Rachel believed what she said, but by the afternoon of the third day, even she became concerned. Emory scoured the grounds, went to the gravesite half a dozen times, and searched the summerhouse. On the unlikely chance that Edward might have elected to drown his sorrow in drink, Emory went to the tavern at the inn. None had seen Edward.

Rachel remembered something later that same day, and about an hour before sunset, came down the stairs wearing her breeches and a warm jacket, the same outfit she had worn during her search for George.

"Once, Rebecca told me of a spot that was special to them both," she explained to the old man, pulling on her gloves. "Perhaps Edward has gone there."

She planned to go alone, and once in the saddle, Angus handed up a small bundle to her, containing one of Edward's jackets, some food and a flask of brandy. "Just in case he is not ready to come down," she told George, before leaving the drive.

She hadn't gone half a mile, just turning up the road that led through Great Guersten Wood, when Emory galloped out of the forest behind her. In a few long strides Sultan overtook Hunter.

"Must you always come crashing through the trees at me," she demanded.

"I've decided to go with you," he announced, as Sultan pranced sideways in high placed steps. "You might get lost."

"I know where I am going, and I'll be back before it gets dark."

Emory gave her a charming smile. "Since I'm already here, I'll go anyway. Perhaps I can convince Edward to be sensible."

"Does it not occur to you that Edward's actions just now are quite sensible, to him at least?" She nudged Hunter forward. "But suit yourself . . . come if you wish."

"Just where are we headed," inquired Emory as the two stallions moved side by side down the rutted road.

"To an old woodsman's hut in the high forest. They used to meet there, and I have a hunch that is where Edward went."

The trodden path that Rebecca had spoken of was found easily enough, and both horses climbed up the side of the slope, one behind the other, until at last it became necessary to dismount because the path narrowed.

"The rest of the way is by foot," Rachel said. "Wait here for me."

Strangely, Emory offered no argument, and took Hunter's rein. Taking the bundle from her saddle Rachel started up the path. It was narrow and winding, and the climb was steep. Shortly she found herself at the edge of a small clearing, dappled with the fading sunlight. The stone hut, sitting on the other side was streaked with long shadows thrown by the late afternoon sun. Though perched high on the slope, the hut had no surrounding view; in every direction there was nothing to be seen but a forest of mountainous evergreens, all dark and gloomy, nodding and bending in the wind. That wind had set the trees to humming, and they moaned audibly in a low and ceaseless wail.

Given Edward's mood of sorrow just now, Rachel thought the spot must surely be the loneliest place on earth.

She approached the hut, stepping through a half broken doorway, pausing to adjust her eyes to the darkness inside. On a straw pallet, Edward sat huddled against a far wall, his head buried in his arms. Moving to his side, Rachel placed the cloth bundle beside him.

"I knew it must be you," he murmured, without raising his head. "Rebecca once told me she revealed this place to you."

"Are you all right?"

When he didn't answer, she stooped, opening the bundle. "We were worried," she said simply. "I brought some food." She poured some brandy into the flask's cover and nudged Edward's foot, handing the cup to him when he raised his head. Obediently, he tossed it down, making a face as the strong liquid burned his throat and traced its way to his empty stomach. After returning the cup to Rachel, he leaned his head against the wall again, gazing skyward through the caved-in roof. His face was pinched and ashen, his eyes sunken. He looked older.

"I must go away for a while, Rachel. Can you understand that?"

"Yes," she said gently. "I can. But you have only just returned to the Hall, and perhaps your father will not." There was a pause. "You have decided?"

"I cannot stay here just now . . . without her. I need time."

"Where will you go?"

"I gave no thought to that. I only know I must go."

"Will you come back?"

"In time, for my heart is here . . . and my son."

Stiff from stooping, Rachel stood, looking around the weather-beaten old hut. It was a peculiar place for a lover's tryst, to say the least, so bare and empty. And yet . . . her eye caught Edward's saddle, left near the stone fireplace. Centered carefully on it was a tortoise shell comb that Edward had found near the straw pallet. Rebecca's! Even in this desolate spot, so much of her remained.

"Are you ready to come down?"

"Soon, but not just yet."

"Do you want me, or Emory, perhaps, to stay with you."

"No," he said. "I need to be alone."

"Then I will leave you," replied Rachel. At the door she turned, studying Edward's forlorn figure. "There is always some way to make the best of a bad situation," she said. "To that end, I have an idea that might interest you. When you are ready, return to the house and let us talk. And Edward, take heart! Rebecca was doomed from childhood, but you gave her the child. You made her happy!"

Edward came down from his hideaway retreat a few days later. He looked in on his son, and then joined Rachel and his father, who were in the library.

"I'm glad you decided to return, boyo," said George to his son, now presentable again, having shaved and bathed. "I have something to say to you . . ."

"Now, Father, you can't convince me to stay. I must . . ."

George waved his walking stick in the air. "No, no, son. Rachel made me understand that point, but I have . . . we have," he corrected, smiling at Rachel, "an offer to put to you."

"What kind of offer?" inquired Edward. Whatever it was, he could see it excited the white haired old man considerably. His round cheeks were even pinker than usual, so eager was he to have the idea out in the open.

"It concerns River Park, the Lancashire estate where your mother grew up. I won't beat about the bush, son. Would you be willing to go there and try to duplicate what Rachel has done here?"

"I'm not sure I understand what you mean by duplicate. Do you mean . . . farm it? Crops, herds, the whole bit, as was done here at the Hall?"

George nodded. "You won't have it half as easy as Rachel did, in fairness, I warn you of that." He didn't mean to imply that Rachel's task had been a simple one, it was just that at the Hall, at least, they had known exactly what they were up against; the shortfall of cash, the state of disrepair, the shortages in the herds and the lack of equipment. Even so, they knew the worth of every man in the vill, and there was no doubt about the richness of the Hall's black soil. Solemnly, George directed his remarks to Edward.

"At River Park your task will be monumental. I've been there only once in the past ten years and even then the place was in need of major repair. Now, I understand, every outbuilding needs a new roof, and even the manor house leaks badly. Jackdaws have nested in half the chimneys, and you'll be lucky to find a decent mattress anywhere in the whole house. But . . . read it for yourself," he said, passing a thick folded paper to his son. "Tisbury's man in Manchester prepared that report when I contemplated selling River Park last spring. Whether or not the land is suitable for an enterprise such as Rachel's is something you will have to determine for yourself, and I will accept your judgment in the matter. If you decide to go with it, there is still time before the snow comes to make enough repairs to see you comfortably through the winter. Acquiring manpower, materials and new herds will be your immediate order of business, and you'll have to do it alone, or nearly so, for we can spare only one man from here. However," he added, bobbing his head merrily, "we'll make him a good one. You can take Peter with you, if he's a mind to go. I'll not force a man from his home, you see."

"He'll go," injected Rachel. "I've already spoken with him about it."

"Well, there you are," said George, smiling. "I'll wager the two of you can set the place to rights in no time."

Though still a little bewildered about the whole idea, Edward liked the proposal well enough. He glanced first to his father, then to Rachel, and again and again to the report he still held in his hand. "The same thing?" he asked, "sell from the wagons, chickens, eggs . . . whatever?"

George nodded. "Whatever, if it can be done. Pair o' good Percherons, a springed wagon and all you can pull from the earth. You'll be in business!"

It was now past the dinner hour, and the old man half turned in his seat, ringing for Angus.

"Wait, Father! What about a market? What about money?"

"The market is ready-made," Rachel said, getting to her feet. "Even better than here, in fact. The backside of one of those infamous textile mills lies just across the river from the estate. Indeed, only a stand of trees separates River Park from one of that mill's new slums. Carperton, who owns it all, bought up the neighboring estates two years ago and now wants River Park, as is, to construct more slums and another mill on our side of the river."

"And there are more mills and other tenements within an hour's ride over good roads," added his father. "People, Edward . . . people who have to eat, and who are already paying a premium price for rot."

Edward turned to Rachel. "And the money? Is that ready-made also?" he asked, for well he knew how much of Rachel's own money had gone into ridding Guersten Hall of its debts.

"Matter of fact, it is," stated George, before Rachel could reply. He then told Edward of her discovery of the little casket, explaining how the Prendergast jewels had been found that cold wet day. Having been subsequently sold, cash was not a problem. "But come," he added, when Angus appeared at the library door. "Stoddard's waiting dinner."

"Father, wait! I still have a hundred questions!"

"Read that paper again, see what you are up against, and then we'll talk again, and include Peter," replied George over his shoulder as Angus wheeled him out.

"Whose idea was this?" Edward asked of Rachel as they headed for the dining room together.

"I confess I've toyed with it a time or two, but the logistics of the whole thing requires that it be implemented by a man. And now, in light of your need to be away, I thought it tailor made for you." At the dining room Rachel stopped and took Edward's arm. "You see, Edward, if you just leave, idle and without direction, your sorrow will linger interminably, but if you are busy, in time the future will not seem so bleak without her."

He choked back a half smile. "That's so, I guess," he said in a low voice, "but what if I fail? And how will you manage without Peter?"

"Don't concern yourself with failure, but if it should happen, then we'll simply offer the place to Carperton, who has wanted it badly for a time now. Your father will add the cost of your investment to the price, and either way we stand to make a comfortable profit out of River Park. And as for Peter," she said, smiling up at Edward, "yes, I shall miss him, and you! Terribly! But perhaps some good will come of it all. In your absence Emory may be forced to assume some responsibility here."

"And if he doesn't?"

"Until he does," Rachel went on; willfully ignoring the fact that Edward, for one, did not believe Emory would ever exert control of his inheritance. "I have your father's expertise, and Gaffy's, to draw upon."

Around a guttering candle in Granmam's fragrant little kitchen that night, Edward and Peter discussed their chances of emulating Rachel's success. In the end, both agreed it should be attempted, though Edward freely admitted he knew precious little about Lancashire, and even less about River Park. He read aloud from Tisbury's report, which declared the estate to consist of three hundred acres, mostly hilly, bordering a narrow but fast moving river not far from Manchester. There was a hundred year old mansion, which, though rambling, was still handsome, plus a carriage house that had been nearly destroyed by fire, and numerous other outbuildings, all rundown and weather-beaten. Plainly, Tisbury's man had not assessed the estate with an eye for agriculture, but Edward repeated Rachel's optimistic commentary about a ready market. At that point, Gaffy joined the conversation.

"Don't forget, lads, one of the largest iron and steelworks in England, mines and all, is nearby in Furness."

"But the shire's not really noted for agriculture," Peter remarked. "What if the soil's not good enough to support a wide range of crops?"

"All the more reason to make the best of what arable land there is. How much plowed acreage is available?"

"Beats me," said Edward, leafing through the report again for the fiftieth time.

"There are no orchards; there is no park, and only grazing land for a small dairy herd, so sheep are out. There's nothing in here about tilled acres, and my guess is that most of the land is rocky, not good for more than potatoes, if that."

Gaffy laughed and slapped his knee. "Well, y' backs'll tell ye soon enough when ye start t' dig, lads. But here's to success, anyway," he toasted, raising high a glass of buttermilk. "If thet lass in leather breeches can do it, so can you!"

And so, on a cold and blustery day, after a hectic week of whirlwind preparations, Edward made a final visit to Rebecca's grave, kissed his sleeping son, and then went into the library to bid farewell to his father.

"God go with you, son," said the old man with a tear in his eye. "Never forget, this is your home. You will always be welcome here."

"Thank you, Father. I know that, but the time has come for me to make a place for myself. For that reason, I'm more than grateful for the chance you now give me at River Park." Edward embraced his father, and then picked up his coat. "I will be back, Father, and until I do, I entrust you with my most precious possession. Take care of him."

Edward headed for the door, and George, smiling far more broadly than was necessary, tossed a salute to his second son, now a man, with the gold topped walking stick.

"Edward, wait! I have something for you!" It was Rachel, calling to him from the top of the stairs, just as he crossed the foyer below.

While he waited, she hurried into the square bedroom, empty since Rebecca's death. It seemed yet to have her presence everywhere, and Rachel caught her breath, choking as a wave of sadness overwhelmed her.

From the bottom of the wardrobe she withdrew a soft sable muff. In it lay Rebecca's diary. The key was in Rachel's pocket just then, but the diary was unlocked. At random, she rifled through the pages once or twice.

The first part of the book was filled with declarations of Rebecca's love for Edward. Some of those passages, penned well before their marriage, were freely written, almost torrid; but most of the later entries dealt almost exclusively with Benjy. Page after page was covered with Rebecca's rambling script, containing open letters to a son who would never know his mother . . . only that she loved him. Some entries were dated far in advance, years ahead, in fact. *Today is your tenth birthday. You are sixteen today,* and *today you are a man.*

Moved, Rachel closed the leather book. Locking it carefully, she returned it to its hiding place inside the fur muff, and then placed it, with the key, in a small wooden memory chest for safekeeping. In the foyer downstairs, she gave the chest to Edward.

"This is for you," she said. "Rebecca left it, her legacy to you and Benjy. When you are ready, read it. It will help to put things into perspective once again."

With their own horses tethered behind, and a hamper of Stoddard's goodies stowed under the seat, the two young men were away only moments later. Peter, neat in his good brown suit, sat next to Edward, his eyes dark, still pale and gaunt from his recent bereavement. A draft of credit, established at a Manchester bank, preceded them. Beyond that, they were practically on their own. What they would find at River Park was anyone's guess.

CHAPTER TWENTY-FIVE

In due time, life at the Hall regained some semblance of normalcy, only now, for Rachel, at least, the pace was quickened. With neither Edward nor Peter to rely upon, the administration of the estate fell solely upon her shoulders once again. From dawn to dusk she was out of the house, and evenings usually found her in the library, busily posting entries into her well-kept journals by the light of a lamp. It was work and work alone that made Rachel's life bearable now, for busy hands and a busy mind, she reasoned, heeding her own advice to Edward, forestalled brooding about Rebecca's death, the alienation of her parents and her father's continued rebuff. Then too, there was Ermaline's absence, as well. She missed all of them.

The last of the crops were harvested, and yet even with the estate's root cellars and larders well stocked, there was still a great deal of work to be done before winter came around again. The days had already grown shorter, the nights colder. Time threatened to become Rachel's enemy.

The apple crop was dealt with first. That which had not already been pressed for cider was sorted and separated; the unbruised fruit was packed carefully with the same care usually reserved for eggs, to be enjoyed as winter eating and baking. The bounty was plentiful, and bushels of striped beefings and other ruddy reds were sent up to the manor's kitchen. Since it was the largest kitchen on the estate, all of the vill's women, including Rachel, gathered there, working feverishly to preserve what they could of the bruised fruit.

Soon, jars and crocks were filled with sweet jams, jellies, spiced apple rings and tart applesauce. Added to the already crowded shelves holding plum, pear and berry preserves, along with pots of honey, they would brighten the fare of families on the estate during winter.

The pruning in the orchards long completed, the boys were moved on to the task of cutting and splitting the winter's supply of logs. At Rachel's suggestion, they ultimately cut far more than was needed, thinning the woods in the process. The surplus was stored in the old and cavernous Great Hall, ordered unshuttered by Rachel for just that purpose. Though dark and gloomy, it was at least dry, and many rows of cordwood were hauled down from the high forest to be stacked under its ancient timbers. Eventually, eighty tuns of cider joined it, the casks stacked in neat rows in the darkened interior.

"Pass the word," Rachel told their greengrocer vendors and Duggan, "there is ready firewood for sale at Guersten Hall, enough to last through the winter. Tell them also that we will not tolerate indiscriminate cutting of healthy trees on Guersten land. Violators will be prosecuted to the letter of the law. We will work out something for those who cannot pay."

Elsewhere on the estate, fences and byres were strengthened, outbuildings battened down in anticipation of winter's wrath. Hay and grains were stored in dry shacks closer to the hen yard and the pigpens, and the sheep were herded into pastures nearer their byres, where they huddled together under the hedgerows for warmth on cold nights.

The hogs were butchered in late November, when they were at top weight, and the hams were covered with salt to cure over the winter in a pungent mix which Stoddard concocted, revealing only that it included black pepper, sage and molasses. They would be smoked in the spring, aged through the following summer, and while none would ever have that indefinable tang that marked a York ham, the families in the vill would enjoy them no whit less.

It was only in the house itself that Rachel had little to do. The staff performed admirably these days, almost without supervision. Somehow Angus had officially and permanently added butlering to his roster of duties, and his Anna was now solidly entrenched in the care of little Benjy. Her own two sons played happily in a corner of Stoddard's spotless kitchen whenever their mother was above stairs. The youngest, a placid and amiable little fellow would one day be Benjy's boon companion.

Predictably, just as the chores wound down, the weather turned bad, and on an especially foul day, with flashes of lightning zigzagging across a darkened sky, Rachel found herself at sixes and sevens, unable to concentrate on anything. Needlework was boring without someone to share it with, and in the library she gave up her search for something new to read and went to the window seat, pushing aside the draperies. There, lost in thought, she did not hear Emory as he entered the room. When he spoke, his voice startled her and she turned on him.

"Am I to be constantly assailed by your unannounced presence?" she snapped, spinning around.

"I am indeed sorry," he said caustically, pouring a fresh drink from a decanter he'd brought with him, though the afternoon was young. "I was half under the impression that this is my house, too," he said. "Does your law of exclusion pertain to the library as well as your bedroom?"

"Your sarcasm is uncalled for."

"As is yours."

Eyeing one another, Rachel became embarrassed, ashamed of her uncharacteristic outburst. She had allowed the dismal weather to color her mood.

"You are right," she said, by way of apology, and turned back to the window. A clap of thunder boomed close by, rattling the window-panes. "This bleakness bothers me, and I'm at odds with nothing to do."

"If we were more compatible we could find much to do on days like this. I mean, we *are* married and all, and we're practically alone in the house."

Rachel turned away from the window, watching as Emory sipped his drink. He was never without it, it seemed, and the sight of it suddenly angered her.

"Isn't it rather early in the day for you to be drinking?"

"It's never too early to drink," he teased, raising his glass. "Will you join me in another?"

"Certainly not! And you don't need another! You're well on your way to becoming drunk."

This time Emory turned on her. "I haven't been drunk since Edward's wedding day, and you know it!"

"And I suppose you expect to be rewarded for that! Well, you'll get nothing from me!"

"That, my dear, is hardly news!"

Smarting under his repartee, Rachel turned away. It always came back to that, for his intent was clear. Well, today Rachel would hear none of it! She side-stepped around him, planning to leave the room, but Emory moved also, and striding across the room before her, swung his arm in a wide arc. Four inches of solid English oak made a very sharp and resounding thud as the door slammed shut.

Furious, Rachel set her jaw. "Open it," she commanded.

"No!" Emory was shouting. "Whenever it comes time for you to face the fact that we are husband and wife, have been for damned near a year now, you manage somehow to evade the issue by putting me off or quitting the room. Well, it won't work this day!"

Rachel had never seen him so angry; never, in any of the many altercations they'd had before. He was bellowing, pointing at her with a long finger.

"We got off to a bad start, I realize," he continued. "I did my best to amend that! I've tried to respect your feelings. I've given you time, plenty of it, but I'll wait no longer, Rachel! You're my wife, and I mean to have you!"

The lightning appearance of that red scar, and something in Emory's eyes, their brilliance, perhaps, flickering with frozen greenness, cautioned Rachel to hold her tongue. *He was bluffing, of course,* she thought, until wide-eyed she saw him begin to remove his coat. Her brain did a somersault! *Here?* she thought, in shock. *Here, on the floor, like a tavern maid, with the servants running about?*

Emory tossed his coat on the wing chair and approached her. Moving backward, she stepped away from him, not stopping until she found her back pressed against one of the bookshelves. She was trapped before him.

"You're insane!" she hurled at him, only to be laughed at.

"Aye! I am! With desire!"

Suddenly, standing before her, Emory's handsome face was all at once freed of its anger. He smiled down at her; was neither threatening nor intimidating, and she admitted to herself, he was far from being drunk. At that moment Emory Guersten was just a man . . . a man who needed a woman, and badly wanted one in particular.

Slowly, he reached out a hand and removed the little house cap she was wearing. Unrestrained, her hair tumbled down and the tresses, thick and luxurious, coiled about his fingers.

"That is how your hair should be, always," he said, looking at her delicate face with its soft skin and dark eyes. "Free and loose . . . it gives you a wanton look."

Barely breathing it seemed, Rachel stood very still, her back ram-rod stiff, her hands clenched before her. Without touching her, Emory leaned forward, pressing his warm lips lightly against hers. Rachel's too, were soft and warm, but they remained unresponsive.

Secretly, she found it somewhat difficult to remain so, for the touch of Emory's lips was pleasant, and she remembered other kisses, exciting kisses that hinted of pleasures that might follow. To compound her confusion now, Emory bent again, bringing his lips close to hers for the second time, inhaling her fragrance, that exquisite mix of lavender and sandalwood. Then he made his mistake.

"Come," he whispered in her ear, taking her arm, "let us go upstairs. I won't hurt you," he added, when she stiffened at hearing the suggestion. "Surely you must know that, just as you surely know that sooner or later, I would take you . . ."

Rachel exploded. Trapped before him, she raised her face to his in contorted fury. "Take! Take! Is that all you know? Take a drink! Take a ride! Take your meals! And am I now to be taken also, at your fancy, the way you take everything else around here! Well, there you are wrong, Emory, for my love cannot be taken! Only given!"

His fury matched hers. His forehead reddened again, and long months of pent-up frustration and unfilled desire surged upward. Without a thought for his actions, he raised his hand and struck Rachel. The boar's head ring, with its roughened surface, caught her on the cheek. Recoiling from the blow, she cried out in pain and shock. It had drawn blood, and Rachel lifted one hand to her face, and then, stock still, stared stupidly at the blood on her fingertips.

Emory was equally shocked by what he had done, and he and Rachel stared at each other in horrified disbelief, hers from the sight of the blood, his from the knowledge that he had drawn it. And then, in one quicksilver instant, their eyes met and locked, and something unseen and unspoken passed between them.

With a soft groan, his arms opened wide and Rachel fell into them. Their lips met in a kiss that burned, a torturous embrace that left them both dizzy.

"Rachel, Rachel! I'm sorry!" he cried, crushing her tightly to his chest between kisses, kisses that she now returned freely. "Forgive me. I lost my head. What in God's name has happened to us?" he moaned, made more distraught when he spied small drops of blood that had spattered across the snow white fichu she wore.

By way of an answer, Rachel only clung to him all the more, burying her face in his neck. "I don't know," she whispered in a muffled voice, "and I'm sorry, too. You're a man and I've tried you so these months."

"No, no! It was all my fault," he said. "I pressed you! It's just that I need you so! I want you so much!"

"And I want you," Rachel whispered, hardly believing that she said those words. She lifted her head and gazed up at him. "At last I can say it, Emory. I do want you! I want your arms about me, and your lips on mine, only . . . I'm afraid!"

Given the revelation that their desire was mutual, Rachel supposed that her heart might be gayer, lighter. It wasn't. Still confused by her responses, she was unsure of her own feelings, yet knew that something was missing from Emory's declaration. Held in his embrace, the words she longed to hear never came. Even if they were not true, why did he not say them? Especially now, when he wanted her so badly? Why could he not bring himself to say that he loved her?

"What makes you afraid? Tell me."

"What happens afterward, Emory, when you have sated yourself? Will our marriage continue as it has, without fulfillment for either of us? The heat of passion cools quickly, and it's the moments between that mark a marriage good or bad."

"And ours is bad . . ."

"It is very bad, and we both know it. Passionate lovemaking may sustain it for a time, but its basic faults will tear us apart again, until we end up despising each other."

They separated and drew apart. Stepping back, Emory took Rachel's beautiful face in his hands.

"And do you despise me now, in view of this?" His thumb fingered the still swelling bruise and the blood clotting on Rachel's cheek.

She stared up at him, and their lips met again, a tender kiss this time, one without promise or passion.

"I don't despise you," she whispered, "but I am not sure what I feel. Now my role becomes harder still, for you know that I share your passion, could match it, perhaps. Will you not use that knowledge to, to . . . hurt me?"

"I've hurt you for the last time, Rachel," he said in earnest sincerity, letting her go. "I don't know what will become of us," he added, "but as much as I want you, from this day on I will wait . . . until you come to me!"

It could be now! Now! If only you would speak of love! At this point, Rachel was unable to define what it was that she felt, but if he loved her, that would be enough! They could make their beginning there, build on it. Her thoughts went unanswered, for Emory never spoke of love. Instead, he opened the library door abruptly. "Don't be afraid anymore. I shall never hurt you again."

Before Rachel could speak again, he was gone, running down the stairs and out through Stoddard's kitchen. Dazedly, she sped upstairs to the safety of her room, throwing herself across the bed, her emotions torn asunder by Emory's erratic behavior. Part of her wanted to go after him, to rush into his arms, to shout that she loved him, whether it was true or not. She wanted him, and afterward, if he were to slip back into his old ways, then she would be no worse off than thousands of other women across the land. If her tormented heart were to know no great love, what did it matter?

"But it does matter!" she wailed, pounding a little pillow senseless. "It does!" If Emory were to stray again, how could she endure abandonment at the Hall, waiting, waiting . . . while he frittered away the hours with women like Edwina? Would she herself one day become another Edwina, searching for someone to love. "No, no!" she cried aloud. "I can't! I won't! There *must* be something more!"

While bathing her bruised face, she managed to still her heart, and reason took control once more. Even still, she knew well that she would never forget those searing kisses she had just experienced, knew well that something deep within her had been awakened at last, something that demanded fulfillment. Rachel knew too, that it was something that was bound to cause her pain.

When she did not come down to dinner that evening, George was unconcerned. Women were always having headaches, and Rachel had far fewer than most. But when Emory did not appear at the table either, the old man suspected they had quarreled again. He became certain of it when he heard Emory, from the library, loudly and rudely demanding another flagon of wine.

"Here, here," he said, waylaying his son at the entrance to the library. "Sit with me awhile," he ordered, blocking Emory's exit with his wheelchair.

"I'm foul company, tonight," warned Emory blackly, but he retreated back into the library just the same, and George watched as he placed the hard won decanter on the desk, though he poured nothing from it. The library rang with silence as Emory toyed with an empty glass. Putting it down on Rachel's gateleg desk, he moved aimlessly about the room. George pointed to the decanter with his walking stick.

"You cannot resume your old ways, son. I meant what I said about that."

Emory sighed, a loud sigh. "My old way of life was hell enough, Father, I see that now. But this is worse!" He groaned. "I cannot go, yet I cannot stay. She will not have me, yet no other woman will do!"

"Aaaah! So it is Rachel, then, eh?"

"Yes! It is Rachel! It is always Rachel, these days!"

The zigzag scar turned pink, then red, as Emory dropped into a leather chair, only to propel himself right out of it a mere second later. He paced the length of the room relentlessly, tortured by his emotions, and the old man knew that the time had come to speak to his firstborn about Rachel, about his inheritance. If Emory exploded, well, that was a chance that must be taken.

"It's time you buried your resentment, son. Step up and take the helm from Rachel's hands. She's steered a wise and true course, my boy, but it's time her duties were more wifely. Do you understand?"

Emory said nothing. Treading lightly, George cleared his throat and continued.

"Are you afraid?" he asked quietly.

"Of assuming my responsibilities? No, not at all. I've been ready for some time."

The old man's chin dropped. "Yet you continue to let Rachel carry the burden? But why, Emory? Why?" he asked in a voice that reflected his disbelief.

"Because she'll leave me!" snarled Emory, whipping himself into a lather. "There's little doubt that she much prefers running Guersten Hall to being my wife and assuming those wifely duties you speak of."

"I'm not surprised, the way you fight with her! But why should her leaving trouble you? Unless . . ." George fell silent for a moment. "You're in love with her, aren't you?"

Grimacing, Emory paced some more. At last he stopped, and stood before a window looking out, staring up at the night sky, his hands on his hips.

"Yes dammit!" he growled, without turning around. He raised his voice and shouted to the window, to the sky. "Yes! Yes! I love her! Truly love her, as a man should love a woman. I love the sight of her face, the sound of her voice, everything about her." Turning, he faced his startled father. "Yes," he repeated, this time in a calmer voice, "I love her! From the moment I saw her riding out of the mist that night I think I loved her. Perhaps I've always loved her, without knowing it, even when we were children. Can such a thing be possible?" he asked in puzzlement.

"All things are possible when it comes to love, Emory. But how came there to be this rancor between you?"

"I'll never really know," groaned Emory. "Always, I guess, without meaning to, she challenged me, and I always felt the need to defend myself." He hung his head. "And of course, there was little to defend. She was right to scorn me, but I know now that I love her, yet all I have ever done is hurt her, caused her grief."

"Have you told her of your love?"

"No," muttered Emory, his voice a barely audible whisper. He didn't look up, but continued to hang his head. "I just realized it myself, only this afternoon. We quarreled again, in this very room, and I struck her. I think it was then that I really knew, but if I had told her then, would she have believed me, just after I had drawn blood."

To George's recollection, no Guersten had ever struck a woman, no matter how sorely tempted, and he was stunned anew by his son's revelation. *Drawn blood! Good Lord!* No wonder Rachel hadn't come down to dinner.

"Then you honestly believe that managing the estate is all that keeps her here, is that it?"

"Isn't it? Except for that she'd be gone in an hour! I'll lose her!"

"Then let her go, son, let her go! It's far better to be a lonely man than no man at all, and Rachel is entitled to her chance at love, also. There comes to each man in his lifetime one supreme sacrifice. Rachel will be yours."

Yet again, Emory shook his head. "No, no!" he cried, not wanting to hear the words.

"She can never love you as you are, Emory. Only the love of a strong and earnest man can win Rachel's heart, and she may have found those qualities in another."

"You mean Ferguson? Do you think I don't know that? That I don't burn anew each time I see them together? He's so damned sure of himself!"

"And he's also quiet, sober and gentle, to say nothing of competent and industrious." Rolling his chair, George moved closer to his son's side. "No one can help you in this dilemma, Emory, but face it! There's no place left for you to hide. You must begin to assume your inheritance, and soon. The longer you cower behind Rachel's skirts the harder it will be for you. Let her go, son. Let her go."

Unable to bear his father's words for another moment, Emory got to his feet, and running from the room, headed for the stables. There, in great haste, he saddled Sultan and thundered away from the Hall at a hard gallop. From the library window George watched his son ride away.

"For once in your life, Emory, be a man. Be a man!" he muttered aloud.

During breakfast only a few days later, one of Steven's sons rushed almost unannounced into the dining room in search of Rachel. "There's a problem at the dairy barn," he said to her, a bit breathless. "We've two Guernsey's calving, and one's having a bit of a time of it."

Pointedly, George looked across the table at Emory, for Rachel was already half out of her chair.

Emory stood up, rising to his feet in a motion so swift that his chair teetered on its legs, nearly toppling over. "I'll go!" he mumbled.

"But," said Rachel, "you don't . . ."

"Christ, Rachel! I've seen a calf born before!" Emory snarled, tossing his napkin to the table.

Observing them, squared off as if to do battle, George knew it was now or never for Emory. He mustn't be allowed to waver.

"Rachel! Push me into the drawing room!" commanded the old man. Bewildered, Rachel looked first at her father-in-law, and then to her husband, who now followed young Stevens out through the reception hall.

"Give over, Rachel," said George in a low voice, once they reached the drawing room. "It's time. Give over."

Thus, in the weeks that followed, Emory claimed his birthright, fully assuming his position as master of Guersten Hall. To his utter amazement, and everyone else's, he found he liked the job. He rose early every day for a change, and while shaving and dressing, nibbled on a meat pasty brought by Stoddard, washing it down with tea. Most mornings he left the house before Rachel was even awake, and when she rode out later, she always found him busy somewhere; in the fields, at the dairy, or in the barn. He would acknowledge her presence, but would then turn back to his business, and each afternoon he would join her in the library for tea. There, he gave her detailed accounting of the day's activities, and Rachel would enter his figures and information into her thickening journals.

At once Emory became quieter, purposeful. He no longer drank, and when he made mistakes, he admitted them. While there were things he needed to know about the operation of the estate, he was determined not to ask Rachel for information. Gaffy's was the only advice he sought, and eventually his night-table was littered with the same books that Rachel herself had used in her quest for information; books on agriculture, animal husbandry, and manuals that explained diseases and the cross pollination of fruit trees.

Not once during this period of time did Emory offend Rachel. As a woman, in fact, he all but ignored her, and while she was certainly pleased by the change in him, she was confused more than ever by his continued coolness.

By mid-December, so thoroughly was Emory playing out his new role, that Rachel's was reduced to enforced idleness. With the house half empty and her outside activities drawn to a halt, there was simply not enough to do to fill her day or occupy her energies. She turned to needlework, but found the endless punching of threads through fabric boring, and though she read, and continued her chess games with George, time was truly now her enemy, loneliness her companion. For the most part she rode about the estate . . . alone, walked in the park . . . alone, spent time in the conservatory . . . alone.

She visited her mother upon occasion, would have gone more often, but Louisa's own sadness served only to heighten Rachel's solitary mood even more. Her only respites came on Sunday's, when

Duncan came to dinner, and those moments spent with little Benjy. She loved the fat little baby dearly, and wrote long letters to Edward detailing his progress.

As Christmas neared, Rachel grew pale; her appetite waned and she began to sleep poorly. In contrast, Emory was now remarkably fit. His already healthy appetite burgeoned, and he retired early most nights, sleeping peacefully until cock's first crow. He drank not at all these days, usually passing up even the table wines. He never gambled, and if he yearned at all for a woman there was little outward evidence of it. He was prompt, pleasant and polite, and his days were filled with industrious activity, all in marked contrast to his earlier ones of wasteful idleness.

All of these changes pleased George no end, just as they did Rachel, but they only added to her emotional turmoil. Every reform she had ever hoped for was now achieved, and in so short a time! She should have been happy. She wasn't, for as that reform took place her own relationship with Emory deteriorated further, simply because she had no way of knowing that it was his undeclared love that drove him, firing his energies from dawn to dusk. She didn't know that it was love that soothed and comforted him whenever he was out of her sight, and love that stilled his pounding heart when he was in it. Just the same, his transformation was not achieved without considerable inner turmoil of his own.

The knowledge that he had always brought her pain, and the sobering fact that he'd struck her, drawing blood chafed him. He wore his guilt like a hair shirt, never without it, and in a strange way it gave him courage . . . courage to wait, until Rachel would come to him.

Rachel knew none of that, and so she suffered under his continued coolness just as she had always suffered at his hand, through intimidation, humiliation, and lately verbal and physical abuse. To her mind, until only recently, he had been rude and arrogant, the insufferable brat on the next estate! He gambled, drank, and was a womanizer! But now, she wailed to herself, pacing her room, now . . . just when she had at last recognized that he was also a man, an attractive man, now, when she had finally admitted to herself and to him that she desired and wanted him . . . now, Emory chose to ignore her completely, making no overtures of any kind.

His calculated coldness raised havoc with her fitful sleep; she became despondent and glum. Dark circles formed under her eyes. George saw them and fretted.

"I did not mean for this to happen, Rachel, when I forced you to give over. I wouldn't see you unhappy for anything."

"I know that," she replied morosely, "but you were right, it was time and he is managing well. He's very capable, just as Edwina told me he would be."

"Aye! He'll make a good master. If only he were a better husband I might worry less."

"Don't! Emory and I, we must work this out for ourselves. Perhaps it was all predestined." She sighed, hands on her chin. "It was a bad match from the start, and now we're down to the bottom line. All of my excuses are gone now . . . Ermaline, Rebecca, money . . . even Emory himself." She sighed again. "If only I knew what he really thought, really felt, perhaps then I would know better what I felt myself."

"He says nothing to you?" asked George, probing cautiously, for he was determined not to interfere, though he was tempted to speak on his son's behalf.

Rachel shook her head. "Not a word. In fact, his callous treatment earlier was almost easier to bear. Now he ignores me. Our conversations are restricted to those dratted journals. His heart is as cold as those icy eyes."

Though he had sworn himself to silence, the old man broke it some days later.

"Tell her, you damned fool!" he said to Emory then. "Tell her you love her and be done with it!"

"No!" retorted Emory. "We agreed, Rachel and I. She will come to me when she is ready. Until then, I'll wait."

"And she's waiting for you! Speak son, declare yourself, or you'll lose her!"

But Emory didn't speak, and there the matter remained. He and Rachel occupied adjacent rooms, were companions at tea and dinner, and once in a great while rode about the estate on some errand having to do with its management, but they were as estranged as if one of them was absent. The big house seemed bigger than ever, and the absence of all those others became more noticeable than at any time previous. The last of Rachel's sparkle disappeared, as did Emory's wit. His booming voice was never heard these days, neither in anger, nor laughter. It was quiet. Too quiet, and George complained about it to Stoddard one day.

"Aye, 'tis like a grave," agreed the cook, "but wasn't it you thet was looking for peace round here some months back?"

George scoffed. "Peace! I'll take their squabbling any day! At least then I knew they were aware of each other!"

Rachel was painfully aware of Emory, though, and he of her, as he waited, as he said he would, for some sign that would announce that her head no longer ruled her heart. It never came, for she was afraid to give it. Often she would look up from her reading to find his eyes upon her, eyes he quickly diverted. Once, handing her up to her saddle, their eyes met and locked. But the moment flittered away, and Rachel bid her heart be still when nothing came of it.

Announced in earnest by the first snowfall, winter came again. One day, it was Emory himself who sleighed Rachel across to Brenham Manor to visit her mother, abed with a cold. Little was said during the short journey. Rachel, bundled under a fur lap robe, sat quietly beside Emory, handsome in a black caped coat, with a colorful scarf about his neck. Fluffy snowflakes, fat and wet, began to fall as the sleigh moved swiftly through the woods, and the brim of Rachel's bonnet was soon covered with white flakes. Hatless, Emory's dark hair soon became piled with the wet stuff, too.

Crossing the wooden bridge, Emory turned his head to find Rachel staring at him. Her beauty and her nearness combined to drive him wild, and as he watched, her lips parted, as if she would say something. Emory raised one hand, and in another second she would have been in his arms, but the spell was broken when the horse missed her stride and the sleigh slued to one side of the road. Cursing inwardly, Emory knew the moment was lost, and he turned his attention to the mare in front of him, turning only when Rachel reached out her hand to brush the snow from his hair. He recoiled as if her touch were a flame.

"I thought only you might be cold," she said, hurt that he had pulled away from her.

"Some inner fire keeps me warm," was all Emory muttered, flicking the reins.

They went the rest of the way in silence. At Brenham Manor, Emory waited impatiently in the music room, while Rachel looked in on her mother. Louisa, thinner and bony cheeked, was wheezing and coughing, and she was feverish. Since Rebecca's death the life seemed to pass from her, but Rachel knew it was her father's continued silence that hurt the most.

"Have you heard nothing, Mother, in all these weeks?"

"Not a word, dear. Oh, how long must it go on? Haven't I been punished enough?"

"You have, indeed, Mother," replied Rachel solemnly.

And so have I, she thought during the silent trip back to the Hall. *So have I!*

That same evening, Rachel went to find her father-in-law. "I must speak with you, George. I have decided to leave Guersten Hall."

CHAPTER TWENTY-SIX

The old man wept openly. "I saw it coming," he said, tears streaming down his face, "and though I prayed it could be avoided, I guess it was inevitable."

Perhaps it was, thought Rachel, while George blew his nose and regained his composure, but just now, with all her reasons to remain now gone, it made little sense to delude herself further, to hope that anything meaningful could be salvaged from her marriage. That marriage had never been consummated, and she believed that Emory did not want her, and would no doubt be glad to see her gone.

"When?"

"As soon as I can make ready."

"I'm heartsick," moaned George, "for I love you dearly, Rachel, but I shan't stand in your way. Tisbury has sealed instructions concerning your welfare. You have only to call upon him. Need I say more?"

Rachel knew that her father-in-law would see her well cared for, but it mattered to her suddenly that he understand her decision to leave. Nearly in tears herself, she knelt by his chair.

"Tell me you understand George; that you know why I feel I must go. Tell me that it is not selfish finally, to be a little concerned about my own happiness."

She was silenced by a swift gesture of George's walking stick. "I do understand, and you have no cause for guilt, but your departure will grieve us all, even Emory, whether you believe it or not. Be sure you know what is at stake."

"The rest of my life is at stake, and I cannot bear the thought of spending it with a man whose emotions run hot and cold, and sometimes not at all; a man whose actions show he doesn't want me. Duncan wants me, even if Emory does not," she added, a bit petulantly.

"The doctor has said so?"

"Of course not! Duncan is too much of a gentleman to speak of love to another man's wife. He'll say nothing, as long as I'm legally bound to Emory."

"You are right there. Duncan is a complete gentleman, and he does care for you, any fool can see that. Have you told Emory, yet?" he asked her, though he already knew the answer, for it was clear Emory did not know, else his bellowing would have been heard in every corner of the house.

"No. Tomorrow will be soon enough. We're sure to quarrel yet again. I told you first because you would understand, he will not."

With red rimmed eyes, Stoddard supervised the serving of dinner that evening; having shrewdly put two and two together the moment Rachel requested that a trunk be brought down from the attic. Her face pinched, the cook glared at Emory as she passed in and out of the dining room, half tempted to rap him with a caddy of hot rolls. It simply never dawned on her that Emory knew nothing of Rachel's planned departure. After all, he was the cause of it, was he not?

"But where will you go?" asked Rachel's mother early the next day, having risen from her sickbed to drive straightaway to the Hall upon hearing the unsettling news.

"I have several choices open to me, Mother. There is the Guersten house at Eaton Square, Father's townhouse, and of course, I could always visit the Rowlands. I'm certain the future Lady Rowland could find a spot for an odd lady at her table."

"No doubt she could, but you can't very well flit about London with neither chaperone nor escort," uttered Louisa.

"It suited Edwina well enough, and little was said publicly about it!"

"Ah, yes, but remember, Edwina's husband is a powerful Lord . . ."

"and discreet gossip surfaced anyway," interjected George.

"Relax, both of you," said Rachel, pouring tea for them both. "I have no desire to take Lady Merrington's vacated place in society. After all, I am not going to London for diversion. I simply want to put some distance between Emory and myself. I need time to understand my own emotions and decide my own destiny. I have in mind a small rooming house operated by a friend of Miss Phillipps's."

"A rooming house!" Louisa did not bother to hide her dismay.

"It caters only to ladies, Mother, and it's quite proper and discreet, and it is adequately chaperoned," She passed a plate of tiny sandwiches to her mother. "I see this makes no sense to you," she added, dropping a lump of sugar into George's teacup.

"I confess it does not," said Louisa, puzzlement obvious in her blue eyes. "I always did what was expected of me, without questioning either my role or my duties. I will not offer unwanted advice, Rachel. I am here if you need me."

"As I am," said George, his voice sad, after Rachel had said a final good-bye to her mother. "While it pains me to see you go, the decision to do so is yours and you are free to make it. Just remember, whatever happens, if ever you are in need, or want, you have only to go to Tisbury."

Rachel bent to kiss the old man. "I thank you. I shall miss you most of all."

Gaffy and Granmam were sick with grief upon learning of Rachel's imminent departure, but Gaffy, at least, understood that she was only grasping at a well deserved chance for happiness. He wished for all others that marriage could bring the happiness and blessings that he and Granmam had shared these sixty odd years.

"Marriage is a graft to the tree of life," he told Rachel when she came to say a tearful good-bye. "Some take, some don't."

Though it was far from spontaneous, Rachel's decision to go had been made quickly, and once made; she sought to implement just as quickly. In her room, a large trunk filled rapidly and her bed became littered with lacy lingerie. "Just the winter things," she cautioned the two maids chosen to help her, as she selected which gowns and frocks would be packed and which would be sent later. The maids were blue, and finally Rachel could tolerate their sniffling no longer. With grated nerves she left them and went downstairs to the library.

She was there, marking Benjy's birth and Rebecca's death, her final entries, into the Guersten family book when Emory galloped in from the fields. Dismounting, he left Sultan under the porte cochere and stormed into the house, his heels pounding the marble floor all the way to library. There, he slammed the heavy door loudly. The noise made Rachel jump, and her quill pricked the page.

"Now look what you've done!" she said crossly, blotting up the spattered ink.

"Do you intend to nag right up until the time you leave?" he demanded angrily.

"So, then. You know."

"Yes, I know! And it seems I'm the last to know!"

Closing the thick journal, Rachel replaced it on its shelf, then returned to stand beside her gateleg desk. In a temper, Emory followed her there, the red scar broadcasting the extent of his fury.

"I suppose it was wrong of me not to tell you first, Emory, and I apologize for that. If you will keep a civil tongue perhaps we can dis-cuss it."

"Discuss it? Then it is true? You are leaving Guersten Hall?"

"No, I am not leaving the Hall. I am leaving you, and surely you know why. Our marriage was a mistake from the moment it was con-ceived by your father and mine, and I see no need to go into another long harangue about its merits now. From the start you wanted your freedom . . . well, now you will have it. There is really nothing more to be said."

"But there is, dammit," Emory exclaimed, "and I'm going to say it and for a change you're going to listen! I don't want my freedom!" he added, grasping her arms and pulling her close, though the desk was between them. In his excitement Emory was shouting at her, even from such close range. "I love you! I need you!"

"Aaah, Emory," whispered Rachel, extricating herself from his grasp. "If you but knew how I longed to hear you say those words! If you had only said them that day you struck me, I would have pledged my heart and asked only that you be gentle with it. I would have been a complete wife to you, then. As it is now, you state your case only to save your pride."

"Don't impugn my motives," Emory said, his voice rising again. "Just kiss me once, and then tell me you still want to leave!"

"I *am* leaving! My mind is made up."

"But I love you!"

"If only you had said so before . . ."

"Well, I've said it now! Unpack your things and let us be done with this foolishness!"

"No! It's too late."

"But why?"

"I don't believe you, that's why! And I'm tired of it all to boot; tired of the cavalier manner with which you toy with my emotions; tired of being ignored one moment and pursued the next. It won't do, Emory! I need something constant in my life, something stable and dependable."

"Or someone, eh? Like Ferguson?"

Rachel turned away from him, refusing to allow the doctor's name to be drawn into their argument. After all, Duncan had never kissed Rachel, never held her; had not even walked in the moonlight alone with her. Their relationship was pitifully platonic, and Duncan's conduct had been proper and gentlemanly at all times.

"He has played no part in any of this, Emory, and you know it. Further, need I remind you how well he has served us all?"

Admonished, Emory took up Rachel's hands, holding them tightly within his own. "Please!" he pleaded, in a gentler tone. "Won't you wait? Give it more time? Perhaps we can make it work yet."

"We've given it enough time already, Emory. It's been more than a year now, do you realize that? Our first anniversary passed two days ago."

Of course! The fifteenth of December! Emory's face fell as he remembered it now, too late. Perhaps forgetting was the catalyst that had prompted her leaving, yet under the circumstances, how could he be expected to remember one particular day, when all of last December was only a blur in his memory?

"You are angry because I forgot?"

"No," said Rachel in a calm voice, moving away from him. She turned to face the fireplace. "It simply doesn't matter anymore, Emory. Nothing does, except my leaving."

"And what about our marriage?"

"What about it? It had so little substance, and what there was is now gone. Let it die, Emory.

He came and stood beside her. "No!" he shouted, pounding his fist on the mantel. "I won't let you go!" His voice was fierce, yet trembling.

"Dear God, Emory! Must we ever quarrel? Can't you even say good-bye; wish me well, without lashing me with words? The choice to leave is mine! You have nothing to say about it!"

"That, my dear, has been precisely one of our problems. I've had nothing to say about anything, all along, or haven't you noticed? Like you, I was not consulted before our betrothal, only told about it afterward. I tried to live with it, and when I found I could not, I ran away. That was despicable, I admit, but I've apologized for it repeatedly. From the beginning, Father turned to you, as did Ermaline, but no one has ever considered my feelings, about anything!"

Leaning closer to Rachel, he continued. "Even so, after I saw you again, I hoped we could make another start. I made mistakes, yes, many, in fact, because somehow since you were no longer afraid of me, you disarmed me. Always it seemed, I undermined our relationship, losing whatever small ground I gained."

"You certainly did! That shouting and all that drinking!"

"I wasn't always as drunk as I appeared," muttered Emory. "Many times it was just a ruse!"

"A ruse?" Rachel was perplexed.

"Yes, a ruse!" he growled. "It was my intention to take you by force some night, letting you think it was the liquor."

"But why?" she asked, shocked by his confession.

"Why? To forestall this very moment! To prevent your departure! As long as our marriage remained unconsummated, I knew you might one day consider leaving, and I wanted to take that avenue of exit from you. If there was a child you would be forced to remain here. Even now, perhaps I might still do it!" he added, menacingly, standing close beside her.

"You would keep me here against my will?"

"I would do anything to keep you here! Dear God, Rachel, don't you understand? I'm half out of my head with the thought of your leaving. I love you! Granted, I was slow to accept it, but I do love you. I know now that I've always loved you. Won't you give me a chance to prove it?"

"You've had a dozen chances, and botched each and every one. Now, I simply don't believe you! I am leaving in the morning, as planned."

In anguish, Emory seized Rachel roughly, pulling her into his arms. His lips found hers. His kiss was passionate and demanding, his lips warm, his tongue an instrument of fire.

"Passion is not love," Rachel said coldly, avoiding his gaze as she pulled away from him.

"I know that now," he said, his green eyes ablaze with emotion. His forehead streaking, forcefully he gathered her into his arms a second time, holding her tight despite her resistance.

"Hear me out," he said, as she stood stiff and unbending before him. "I love you," he whispered again, looking down at her. "I've never said those words to any woman before this moment, Rachel; for I never knew a man could feel this way. I never believed there was any depth to love beyond passion, but I was wrong! There is, and because of it, I see and hear things of which I was never aware before. Don't leave me, not now, just when I'm learning to see the world through your eyes. Give me time, time to learn how to be a good husband, just as I've learned to be a good master."

Plaintive and passionate, Emory's outpourings touched Rachel's heart, weakening her resolve. She could only imagine how difficult it had been for him to bare his heart; still, she forced herself to remain unmoved by his words.

"I must go!" she whispered, still crushed in the circle of his arms. "Don't you see, Emory? I have things to learn also. Most importantly, I must learn to listen to my heart . . . discover where it leads. Rebecca taught me that."

Emory let his arms fall to his side, realizing at last that her decision was made. "I won't beg," he said, regaining his pride, but he was
crushed all the same, only now his anguish bordered on bitterness,
much of it hinging on the knowledge that he had held his tongue too
long. If only he'd spoken when his father had urged him to do so!

Valiantly, he struggled to control his emotions. Clenching his
fists, he momentarily considered striking her; perhaps he could yet
force her bodily to remain at Guersten Hall. Perhaps he should kiss her,
again and again, until her desire to leave was undermined by her own
passions, for Emory understood that the fire that smoldered within
Rachel's breast needed but a spark to ignite into a full-fledged flame.
And once lit . . . ?

But in the end, Emory took neither action, recognizing at last,
that their game was over. With Rachel's departure now only hours
away, he was forced to face reality. His love was not returned.

"I cannot change your mind?" was all that he said. Though it was
a question, it passed from his lips in the form of a statement, for he
already knew the answer.

"No," replied Rachel in confirmation.

"Will you return?"

She shrugged. Who could answer that? Theirs was such a stormy
relationship, had ever been, a kaleidoscope of tangled emotions, changing from moment to moment. Their eyes met and locked one last time,
but this time nothing passed between them.

"Will you not tell me good-bye," she asked again, "and wish me
well?"

Emory did not answer, but looked down at her for a long moment,
as if to memorize her face, and then turning on his heel, left the library.
Moments later she heard him ride away. It was the last she was to see
of him. The fact that he never did say good-bye was a blow that hurt
deeply.

Rachel sat alone in the elegant but empty dining room that last
evening, for George was far too heartsick to even feign an appetite.
After pushing her food about the plate, Rachel gave it up, also.

"Take it away, Stoddard," she said sadly, "and come sit with me. I
can't bear this aloneness another moment."

"Come down to my kitchen," said the older woman gently. "It's cheerier there, and I'll fix ye something hot to drink."

At one end of her scarred work table, Stoddard laid a spotless linen cloth and prepared tea for her beloved mistress one last time. From time to time, she, too, sniffed, and even wept openly when Steven's two daughters came into the kitchen to bid Rachel good-bye.

"I shall miss you both," Rachel told the sobbing sisters. "Do as Stoddard tells you and there will always be a place for you in this household, I am sure."

"Ye make my heart heavy," Stoddard said after the girls had gone. "Ye look so down in the mouth."

"I was thinking of the first night I came to Guersten Hall. Do you remember it?"

"Indeed I do! We had pork pies, and you took special pleasure at my pie crust. I remember also that you were sad and woeful that night, too."

"As bad as I felt then, Effie, tonight is even worse. My leaving is far more difficult than my coming. Why is that?"

"Rachel, dearie! The heart is involved now."

"Yes," sighed Rachel, rising to go upstairs, "it is. I came to love you all; all except the one that really mattered."

Early the next morning, Rachel climbed into a carriage and departed from Guersten Hall without a backward glance, made all the sadder by the knowledge that yet another Christmas would be spent alone, and lonely. Only Stoddard came to see her off, for her mother had returned to her sickbed, and George brooded morosely in his bedchamber.

Emory had disappeared. Well, he's no longer my concern, Rachel told herself as the carriage lurched down the road. If he chooses to return to his shiftless way, and drinks anew, then let him!

"I don't care!" she muttered aloud in the empty carriage. "None of it matters anymore!"

But if she had only chanced to look from her window as the carriage turned onto the Aylesbury road, she would have seen a familiar figure in black, now lonely, sitting tall and sober astride a dark stallion on a faraway ridge.

"Good-bye, little mouse!" called Emory into the mournful winter wind. "This time it is I who weeps."

Taking up his reins, he turned, and sadly went back to Guersten Hall, back to his aged father and his brother's child. *An old man and a baby!* That was his company! From now on his days, as well as his nights, would be lonely.

"Poetic justice, eh Sultan? As she suffered, so must I!

CHAPTER TWENTY-SEVEN

London was sooty, dirty, and after the snowy cleanness of the midlands, Rachel found it depressing, but Margaret Morton remembered her and welcomed her warmly without asking questions, for which Rachel was grateful. She was given a comfortable room in the rear of the house, overlooking a miniature courtyard, and the days began to blink by. Before the end of the month Rachel knew every brick in the courtyard wall, having counted them endless times. Lonely, much of her time through Christmas was spent reading, for there seemed little else to do. In need of female company, she renewed her friendship with Eleanora Scofield, enjoying the older woman's companionship as much as ever, and the two women took to dining together regularly several evenings a week at Eleanora's fashionable townhouse. Despite the gap in their ages, they were friends, good friends. It was a friendship Rachel needed badly, for her loneliness bore down on her like a crushing weight.

"If I don't shake myself from this mood soon," she told Eleanora one night, "I shall return to the Rachel of old. I seem always on the verge of tears these days."

"Many things have happened during the past year, my young friend," counseled Eleanora, "and some of them called for tears."

"True, but I fear once started the river will not stop. Come," she said, trying to be cheerful and changing the subject, "show me your designs for young Lady Creighton's wedding dress."

Eleanora was not given to meddling, and since Rachel did not burden her with the details of her departure from Guersten Hall, she did not interfere, but she knew without being told that Rachel's present state of unhappiness centered on her handsome husband.

"I had hoped they'd make a go of it," she told Mrs. Morton one day, "for I like that young man, even if he is a scoundrel."

Margaret Morton and Eleanora Scofield were also friends of long standing, and they joined forces now, taking it upon themselves to shake Rachel from her doldrums. As February faded into March their efforts were aided by some improvement in the weather, which gave a decided lift to Rachel's spirits. One afternoon, when Margaret wheeled a well-laden teacart into her immaculate front parlor, she found that she and Rachel were the only takers, for the fourth time that week.

"Time was there'd be a dozen or more for tea," she said, pouring. "Their chattering near drove me batty at times, but I do miss it."

"How do you explain the loss of your clientele?" asked Rachel. "A year ago you were full."

"I was always full, but with all these fancy new hotels in the city, it seems there is little need for safe havens for ladies these days."

Rachel bit into a second piece of Margaret's fluffy teacake. "Have you ever considered changing your image?"

"My image? How so, Rachel?"

"It's simply good business; you must keep pace with the times."

"Business! Bah! I've not much head for business, though I eked out a good living until now." She refilled their teacups and covered the pot with the cheerful cozy. "Still, tell me your idea anyway, my dear."

"You are on the very edge of the fastest growing shopping district in London; three new stores just since I arrived ten weeks ago, and all of them cater exclusively to women. A steady stream of ladies passes your door daily on their way to Eleanora's shoppe around the corner, yet between here and there, not a single establishment exists that offers necessaries or dining facilities to them, or even tea, for that matter," said Rachel, holding up her cup.

"I see it!" cried Margaret, with some excitement. "A tea room! A ladies dining room . . ."

"More perhaps," Rachel added. "What I have in mind would keep your ladies hotel in operation. Dress fittings are notoriously boring and frightfully tedious, as you well know. Perhaps some of your tea room patrons would relish a chance to rest; some place where they could put their feet up between fittings. Given your reputation for chaperoned and secure lodgings, ladies from the shires might even remain overnight. Their husbands would love you, for it would free them from coming into the city while their wives shopped for new wardrobes."

Margaret's face brightened visibly, cheered by the prospects of Rachel's suggestions. But after she surveyed the dining room with a critical eye she shook her head. "It's rather nondescript, don't you think? Somehow I don't see ladies of fashion flocking here."

"It needs only a facelift," tutted Rachel. "Remove this trestle table, add a few little ones instead, turn one of your front parlors into a tea room, and set aside the back one for a combination sitting room for the ladies' maids who will accompany your trade. Your location is an asset, Margaret. Capitalize on it. Frankly I do not think you'll find the renovations economically unsound."

"I do have some capital set aside," murmured Margaret, studying the room again. She began to visualize the changes to be made. "Perhaps I could borrow a leaf from Eleanora's book of success . . . choose a single color theme and make it my trademark."

"There! You are already thinking like a business woman. Just choose something distinctive, and keep it in good taste. Remember, their husbands must approve!"

"I'll try it!" announced Margaret, slapping the table decisively with her palm. "I've got nothing to lose, really, for I'll surely take a loss on the building if I'm forced to sell it as is. Will you help me?"

"I was hoping you'd ask," Rachel said with a wide grin. "I would relish the chance to be busy again."

Not three weeks later Rachel watched as her friend's little brownstone, repainted and redecorated, threw open its doors, receiving its first clientele that same day. More followed, all referred by Eleanora, who sagely saw what the ladies' conveniences would mean to her own still expanding business. Eleanora, who had recently added another twenty girls to her roster of seamstresses, had designed the simple brown dresses Margaret's serving girls now wore. In the dining room, now sporting new planked wainscoting, a terrazzo tiled floor had been laid. Its creamy color was picked up again in the table covers, and the girls' aprons and mobcaps. In the parlor, floral carpeting featured some of the same color, as did a pile of stationery that sat on the writing desk. Outside, a discreet little sign announced: *Tearoom . . . Dining Room,* and underneath: *Ladies Only.*

Daily the tea room was packed, and as word spread, more and more of Margaret's upstairs rooms were engaged by overnight guests, who took both supper and breakfast. The small and efficient operation was a pronounced success from its opening day.

With both of Rachel's friends now occupied by growing businesses, Rachel found that time, once again, became her enemy. When Ermaline and Henry Rowland returned to London, their six month honeymoon trip ended, Rachel turned to her sister-in-law for companionship. It was companionship that never materialized.

On an upper floor in that elaborate house in Knightsbridge, Ermaline and Henry had their own apartments, but the elder Mrs. Rowland's domain extended from the attic to the cellar just the same, and as a result, Ermaline had absolutely nothing to do. To stem her boredom, she jumped into the upper circles of London's society, and though she and Rachel visited regularly, Rachel found Ermaline much changed. She was now very much the frivolous new bride, her life calendared by one gay round of parties after another. Dozens of invitations arrived daily for the newlyweds, all received by Mrs. Rowland's own secretary. Each was carefully screened and Ermaline was advised which to accept and which to decline.

Nightly the happy couple pleaded with Rachel to join them in their round of balls and fetes, dinner parties, theater parties, after the concert parties. Quietly Rachel declined, for their happiness in each other's company made her feel lonelier than ever, and further, she recognized that repeated public appearances, unescorted, would bring forth a rash of invitations from just the sort of company she sought to avoid. Even when she dined at home with Ermaline and Henry upon occasion, Rachel usually found herself the odd lady, balancing the company at their dinner table.

While Ermaline was thrilled to see Rachel once again, was sorry to learn of her break with Emory, she was so completely involved in her own wholly new lifestyle that she was unable to offer much in the way of solace to Rachel. Now, without a care in the world about money, Ermaline had become a clothes-horse. She chattered incessantly about new gowns, parasols, slippers . . . this shoppe . . . that style. Her conversation became a jumble, with bits of information from home spattered between nothings. Half of what she babbled about was drivel, but Rachel was forced to listen intently, lest she miss some cherished bit of news from the Hall that concerned George, or the baby . . . or Emory.

"So you like this reticule, eh, Rachel?" asked Ermaline one day. "Hand beaded in Italy. Father's sister lived there. She's dead now. Father had a letter. I should have ordered a blue one, too, I think, to match my opera wrap."

"You heard from your father? He sent a letter?"

"Oh, yes, but I've misplaced it. Do you think this shade of rose complementary?"

"It is, Ermaline. But what did the letter say?"

"Nothing really. The cabbages are in the ground, Benjy is walking, and Emory is as grumpy as ever, that sort of thing. I'm going to have my apartments redecorated. What color would you suggest?"

"Already? You've only recently taken up residence, and Mrs. Rowland chose this shade of green especially for you. You will hurt her feelings by repainting so soon. What else did the letter say?"

"I suppose you are right, and this shade does flatter my hair. Father inherited Aunt Caroline's fortune. Edward has returned."

"Edward! Returned to the Hall? Then the enterprise at River Park failed!"

"Not at all! It turned out the soil wasn't good for much more than chicken scratching; so Emory said let them scratch! Edward turned River Park into a poultry farm! Largest egg farm in the shire, selling direct to Carperton's tommy shops and the mill towns. Later on an overseer will run it, but just now Peter wanted to stay in Lancashire. He found a girl, Miriam something or other. A cheesemonger's daughter.

Edward says she's a lovely lass. There! Now will you look at my dance program? I danced every dance last night. Oooh, those handsome officers! Those gorgeous uniforms!"

Rachel shook her head. Despite her concern over Ermaline's frivolity, she had to laugh at the young matron's contagious exuberance.

"You know, dear girl," Rachel said when it was time for her to leave, "you are beginning to sound a bit too much like Edwina Merrington!"

"I'm exactly like her!" confessed Ermaline, kissing her sister-in-law good-bye. "I love parties, and I love all the attention given to me, but don't fret, the only husband I shall ever bed is my own!"

"You must not let her become empty-headed," Rachel cautioned Henry when he escorted her to a waiting carriage. "One day Ermaline will take her place as lady of her own house. She must be prepared."

"I'm sure she will be; it's just that I love her so much I find it difficult not to indulge her. But the child will slow her down naturally, don't you think?"

"Child? What child? She spoke naught of it!"

"See? She's like a happy butterfly, flitting from flower to flower, and she feels so well I suspect she even forgets that she is expecting."

"Oh, Henry! Such glad tidings! My congratulations to you both."

Well, thought Rachel during the carriage ride back to Margaret's brownstone. *I've gleaned quite a bit of news this afternoon, but, oh! What I didn't have to endure to get it!* Though thrilled by Henry's news, Rachel was just a little concerned about Ermaline's new and frivolous personality. And yet, who could be more fluttery or flighty than the elder Mrs. Rowland herself, and she was an acclaimed success, sitting at the top of society's heap. As a matriarch she was a wizard, with an immaculate house and an orderly staff. *Just the same,* Rachel giggled, *right now I wouldn't trust Ermaline alone in my kitchen . . . if I had one!*

So Peter had found love? Rachel was happy for him, and happier still that Edward had returned to Guersten Hall. Without a mother, Benjy needed his father all the more. While George surely loved the little boy, Rachel knew that Emory would all but ignore the child. Squirming babies unsettled him, and now that Benjy was walking, he would be into everything. Rachel fought back tears at the remembrance of the little child. Oh, how she missed them all. Even Emory, she admitted with some reluctance.

At Mrs. Morton's, Rachel's existence continued its bored and lonely atmosphere until one evening a week or so later, she herself decided upon a turning point. She had been in London some time now, yet had avoided taking action on two important matters. The time had come to act; she simply couldn't muddle through many more empty days.

First, there was the unfinished business with her father. Rachel had made no recent effort to call upon him, no attempt to follow through on the deathbed pledge she'd given Rebecca. At least once, Rachel knew, she must try to bring about a reunion between her father and her sister's child. Benjamin must be convinced to at least recognize the little boy!

Secondly, there was a more important undertaking; the matter of her annulment. Rachel had put that off too, just why she didn't know. At first there had seemed to be no hurry. Now there seemed to be no reason not to go through with it. Tisbury had probably expected her weeks ago at his Fleet Street office; he must have wondered about her failure to appear. Surely, by now, he had drawn up the necessary papers. Her visit, her signature, was all that was needed to set the wheels into motion. Rachel made her decision. She would call on Tisbury; discuss the terms of the settlement, and be done with it.

"I will call on father first," Rachel told Eleanora over supper that evening, "and then see Tisbury next week. When I know where I stand, I will set a course for myself. I cannot remain at Margaret's forever," she added. "I have some money; I must find a place to live and something to do."

"You are determined to go through with this annulment then, eh, child?"

Rachel gave Eleanora a half smile and a matter-of-fact shrug. "I suppose so," she said. "The decision not to be Emory's wife was my own, after all, and I guess it's time I got myself . . . unmarried. "We'll both be free to start again."

Eleanora covered Rachel's hand with her own, in a friendly gesture. "Is that what you want? You are certain?"

Rachel shrugged again and looked hard at her friend. "What else is there? I cannot remain in this *wife-no-wife* limbo much longer. I must get on with my life."

"You could go back, Rachel, could you not?"

"Go back? But why? Emory doesn't want me! He never did!"

"He told you so?"

"No," admitted Rachel. "What he says, as a matter of fact, is just the opposite."

"Aaah! Then he does want you!"

"A man's wants are not grounds for marriage," said Rachel, shaking her curls. "I came by that bit of knowledge the hard way."

"As did I!" Eleanora stated, laughing, "and I agree, only it took three husbands to convince me! But somehow, I felt your Emory to be different."

"My Emory, indeed!"

Returning to Margaret's well lighted rooming house that same evening, an event occurred which turned Rachel's attentions to both her concerns in one fell swoop. One, the annulment, was pushed aside by the urgency of the other, for when Rachel entered through the front door, she found Margaret waiting in the foyer.

"You have a visitor," she whispered, taking Rachel's cloak. "A young woman, in service somewhere in the city. She has a message for you and was told to give it to no other."

"Really, Margaret! How mysterious! A message, you say?"

Margaret nodded. "I put the poor girl in the front parlor. She has been waiting for a long time."

Hurrying into the front parlor, Rachel closed the sliding doors behind her. Her visitor, curled up in a wing chair, was fast asleep, and Rachel studied the girl, deciding that she had never seen her before in her life. Young, plain, passably pretty, the girl was attired entirely in gray and wore sturdy side-buttoned shoes. From the quality of her garb, Rachel assessed she was in service to someone of means.

She shook the girl. "Wake up!"

The girl's eyes flew open and she hopped to her feet, embarrassed at being caught napping.

"Be at ease," said Rachel kindly. "The hour is late and I understand I kept you waiting."

"You are Mrs. Guersten?" asked the girl timidly.

"I am, and speak, lass. What is your message?"

"I have been sent to fetch you, ma'am," said the girl respectfully, making a little curtsey.

"Fetch me? At this hour? Fetch me where? Who sent you?"

"The doctor, ma'am. Dr. Ferguson."

"Duncan! But he doesn't know where I am!" Rachel had not seen Duncan since her last Sunday at Guersten Hall . . . ages ago! She had not discussed her departure with him at that time, and since then, had made special effort to keep distance between herself and him, for she did not wish his name to enter into the annulment proceedings in any way. Only afterward would she contact him.

"The doctor searched the city for you, ma'am," volunteered the girl. "Finally, Mr. Henry Rowland gave up this address."

Rachel knew that Henry would not have betrayed her confidence without good cause. "Why does the doctor not come himself?" she asked the gray clad girl.

"He cannot leave his patient, ma'am."

"His patient? What patient? Who?"

"Your father, ma'am. Mr. Benjamin Brenham."

"My fath . . . Speak, lass, will you? Spit it all out, at once!"

"Your father was took sick, ma'am. Even Dr. Ferguson thought he might die. He is some better, but the doctor cannot leave him to come for you himself. That is why he sent me when your address was learnt. Will you come, ma'am?"

"Yes, yes!" cried Rachel, flying off to retrieve her cloak again. "Does my mother know?" she asked the girl, who trailed behind.

"No, ma'am. There was no time, and Dr. Ferguson wants you to come first."

Hurrying now, Rachel buttoned her cloak about her shoulders. "How long has he been ill?"

"Near a week, ma'am."

"A week!" Oh my word, thought Rachel. A week! While I sat here doing nothing!

As Rachel prepared to go out again, Margaret stood by, wringing her hands nervously, eyeing the young female messenger with some suspicion.

"My dear, Rachel!! You simply can't go off in a stranger's carriage in the middle of the night like this! You've never seen this lass before. You might be putting yourself in danger!"

"Perhaps," admitted Rachel, now tying on her bonnet. "But I know only that my father is sick, and I must go at once!" she added, past animosities with him all but forgotten.

"Well, do find out where you are off to, at least! I shall worry less, then."

Rachel beckoned to the gray-clad girl who waited patiently by the door. "Where do you take me?" she asked. "Are you in my father's employ?"

"No, ma'am," answered the polite girl. "I work for Mrs. Bailey. We go to Trowbridge Road."

Mrs. Bailey! Oh, my God! Her father had been struck down while visiting his mistress! Rachel was shocked. No wonder Duncan had chosen not to send for her mother, but had searched her out instead!

Shooing the girl out to the front walk, Rachel spied a light carriage, with an old man up, waiting at the side gate.

"My father's," she said to Margaret. "I recognize it. Go to bed, and don't fret. The girl is legitimate anyway."

"And who on earth is Mrs. Bailey?"

"Like many men of wealth, Margaret, my father has a lady friend." Said Rachel, buttoning a glove.

"Aaaah, then that explains the mystery. Never fear, for I shall be discreet, but now you'd best be on your way. Who knows what you will find when you get to Trowbridge Road."

CHAPTER TWENTY-EIGHT

As the little carriage wheeled its way over cobblestoned streets, reeling down the narrow lanes, Rachel remembered a similar ride, long ago, on that day she'd first learned of Mrs. Bailey's existence. How shocked she'd been! Now, after a tumultuous year of marriage to a man like Emory Guersten, nothing much surprised her. She viewed man-woman relationships as something slightly bittersweet, but at her father's age? Such foolishness!

At the fringes of the dock area the carriage picked up speed, for London's streets were dangerous after dark. Alert, the old driver sat with his whip at the ready, and a heavy blackthorn stick lay close beside him. His precautions were unnecessary, though; the ride was uneventful, and at Trowbridge Road, Rachel left the carriage and climbed swiftly up the steep steps to the front door. Once it was opened by another gray-frocked maid, the quiet girl following behind disappeared. The front hall to which Rachel was admitted was quite gloomy, lit only by a single candle that spluttered smokily under a glass globe. Told to wait, Rachel suddenly found herself alone.

She scrutinized her surroundings. Only one piece of furniture, an oaken hall-tree with a small mirror attached to its front, stood in the front hall. A man's hat hung from one of the pegs, and Rachel picked it up to discover Benjamin's initials and Crofts' label inside. No doubt about it, her father was here.

Hearing a creak on the stairs behind her, Rachel spun about and faced the aged woman who descended them, guiding her way in the semi-darkness with one hand on the banister. A tall woman, neither thin nor heavy, Rachel guessed her to be well into her eighties, and like all the women in the household, she, too, was attired in the same dull gray, though her long sleeved dress was brightened by the placement of handmade and well-starched lace at cuff and collar.

Bold black eyes studied Rachel from behind a gentle face, a face framed by a mass of silvery gray hair laying neatly in rows of natural waves. It was evident that the old woman had once been quite attractive, and even now her lined skin was velvety and soft. Only her hands revealed the story of her lifetime of labor; they were gnarled and work-worn, rough and reddened.

"My father . . . Duncan . . . er, Dr. Ferguson? They are here?" began Rachel hesitantly.

"I will take you," the old woman said in a clear voice, and turning on her heel, started back up the stairs.

Rachel followed, up the stairs and then down a long hall, lined with a number of closed doors. Familiarly, the woman stepped past them all, moving very quietly, as though her tread would disturb whoever slept behind them, yet listening for any sound from within at the same time. Rachel heard nothing, saw no one, and presently they came to a halt before a heavy door at the back of the house. Without announcement, the woman turned the knob and stepped through, beckoning to Rachel to follow.

The room they entered was large, but so dark that at first Rachel could barely discern anything beyond that it was a bedchamber. Near the door one small lamp burned, and the place was stuffy, the air heavy. It was unmistakably a sick room, and before her, on a simple wooden bedstead, lay her father, his face as white as the linens that covered him.

Genuinely shocked, Rachel moved closer to his bedside. Her father's cheeks were hollow, dark rings encircled his closed eyes, and his chest rose and fell in a heavy slumber that Rachel felt certain had been drug induced.

As she stared in disbelief at him, the old woman moved to a shadowy corner of the room and nudged a sleeping form there. Duncan was on his feet in a flash, and spying Rachel, stepped into the dim light. She gasped, for at first glance the doctor looked almost as bad as his patient. Gaunt and weary, and in shirtsleeves, Duncan's hair was uncombed, his clothing rumpled and his gray eyes were tired and rimmed red. Lines of exhaustion marked his already thin face.

Rachel parted her lips to speak, for she had a thousand questions to put to him, but Duncan bid her be silent, and crossing to the bedside, felt for Benjamin's pulse. It was not strong, but it was no longer erratic and fading, and looking pleased, Duncan nodded to the old woman.

Rachel continued to study her father's face. When had she seen him last? That day on the bluff? *A year ago, almost!* How could twelve months so change a man? Benjamin's hair was now more white than gray, and he was thin to the point of boniness. *He looked old!*

Taking her arm, Duncan led Rachel away, into a smaller room which adjoined the sickroom. He closed the door behind them, leaving Benjamin in the care of the old woman.

"We can talk here, Rachel," he said, in a voice that harkened of his fatigue, "and don't worry, he is in good hands. That lady cares deeply for your father and will let no other nurse him. She has been at my side day and night for a week. You can trust her."

But Rachel's concern at that moment was not for the old woman; she had almost forgotten her, in fact, so great was her shock at her father's condition and appearance.

"Whatever happened to him, Duncan? Tell me! He looks terrible! Deathly!"

"Precisely the word, Rachel . . . precisely! It was his heart, and I can tell you now only that he will live." Duncan spoke gravely, his manner saying as much about the seriousness of Benjamin's condition as the words he uttered to describe it. "What goes on within that chest none can see, but I know without seeing that substantial damage has been done, that severe was his attack. What the future holds we will learn hour by hour, day by day, but I can assure you that your father is no longer the dynamic person you knew. No longer will there be a spring to his step, nor volume to his voice. He is now merely another man turned sixty, and a sick one, at that. Very sick, Rachel. Be prepared for a long recovery, and to break the news to your mother."

"Mother! I'd forgotten her!"

"In a few days you can send for her. She will want to be here when he wakens."

"He is not unconscious?"

Duncan shook his head. "He was, for some days, but now he merely sleeps. We must let his tired heart rest."

With worry shadowing her lovely face, Rachel dropped into a chair. "I don't understand any of this. Father always enjoyed excellent health. What brought about such a sudden change?"

"Many things contributed to it," advised the doctor. "He is a very stubborn man, as you know, and the rift that separated him from your mother caused him great distress, as did his arguments with you. To alleviate that stress he threw himself anew into his business ventures. Fatigue and overwork did the rest."

"But he thrived on hard work! His constitution was remarkable."

"Too much so, perhaps," stated Duncan. "It made him forget he was no longer a young man, and then, too," he added, gently, "I suspect that Rebecca's death played a prominent part in this."

"Then he read our letters after all? He knew of it!"

"No . . . in fact, I believe they still sit unread at his office. He learned of it from me, Rachel, inadvertently, only a month ago, for I naturally assumed he knew and made mention of it. The shock of it nearly felled him on the spot."

Holding back her tears, Rachel pressed a lace trimmed handkerchief to her eyes as a tapping was heard at the door. A third gray-clad girl entered, this one wearing a stiffly starched apron.

"Your supper is laid, Doctor, in Mrs. Bailey's sitting room."

"Come, Rachel," said Duncan, taking her arm again. "It's just down the hall, and your father will sleep awhile yet. Sit with me while I sup."

She objected, but the good doctor insisted, and after looking in on Benjamin once more, Duncan led the way down the long corridor to Mrs. Bailey's sitting room, situated near the top of the stairs. There another surprise awaited her, for Mrs. Bailey's sitting room turned out to be a tiny place with well used furniture and an everyday decor. It was hardly what Rachel had expected; perhaps mentally envisioning something on the grand scale of Edwina's private quarters, all purple and satiny. After all, Mrs. Bailey dallied with a man of considerable wealth, did she not?

Surrounded by chintz covered pillows, Rachel was soon settled on a comfortable settee with a cup of tea in her hand, listening as Duncan related the short and woeful tale of the onslaught of her father's sudden illness. Benjamin had been stricken here, in the Trowbridge Road house, on the stairs, and Mrs. Bailey had put him to bed.

"But how came they to seek your services, Duncan?" asked Rachel, puzzled, for the last she knew Duncan was still in the midlands, kept busy at his Peterborough clinic. Furthermore, until this very evening, she had not known that the doctor and her father were acquainted even.

"A little more than acquainted, Rachel," said Duncan wryly, setting down his cup. "For some time now your father and I have been working together on something that is of great importance to both of us. I was to meet him here that evening, but when I arrived the place was in turmoil. The maids were screaming, the children crying. Only Mrs. Bailey kept her head."

"Ah, yes, the children. I had forgotten them." A scowl darkened Rachel's lovely face. "You must excuse me, Duncan, it is just that you have been made privy to my father's . . . private life, while my mother and me seem to have been deliberately kept in the dark."

"Then neither of you know anything about the nature of this house . . . or of Mrs. Bailey?"

"I knew . . . of its existence, and hers. Mother does not. Perhaps it is better that way."

"I'm not certain I understand what you drive at, Rachel, but at any rate, it is not my place to discuss those matters which your father elected to keep secret. Just now I serve only as his physician. Later, when he improves," finished Duncan, with a motion of his arm, "he will explain all this himself."

"He will improve?"

"Oh, yes. Despite his present appearance I think he is out of immediate danger. He will see improvement, but never again robust good health. And now, dear Rachel," said Duncan, "my curiosity cannot be contained a moment more. What in God's name brought you to London, especially to that out of the way rooming house?"

"Mrs. Morton's? She is my friend, and I am here in the city . . . well, you might as well know the truth! I seek annulment from my marriage."

"Annulment?" repeated the astonished doctor. "You have left Guersten? But how? Annulment requires . . . certain grounds."

Rachel blushed, rather prettily. "I have grounds," she said demurely, after a pause, "grounds I choose not to discuss."

"I did not mean to pry, Rachel. Forgive me."

Yet even while the doctor made his simple apology, his face brightened considerably, and despite his fatigue his tired gray eyes began to sparkle. He smiled at Rachel.

"I suppose," he said, in a voice trembling with excitement, "that I should pretend some sadness. Will you forgive me if I do not?"

"You spent considerable time in that house, Duncan, and certainly you know my marriage to Emory had little chance at success. Besides, you are my friend, are you not?"

"I am! I mean . . . I was! Now, your news lets me dare hope that I may someday be more than that. If I speak prematurely, again, I beg forgiveness."

Duncan's voice took on a passionate quaver, as Rachel glanced up at him. The look he gave her stated clearly those words that, as a gentleman, he was not yet free to speak. His open adoration was plain to see, and under the circumstances, Rachel found it almost embarrassing.

"Whatever happens is in the future," was all she said, getting to her feet. "Just now the only future I am concerned with is Father's."

"Of course, of course!" replied the doctor, also rising. Still, he was heartened by Rachel's words. She had not ruled out the possibility that their futures might someday be joined. "It seems," he said, "that we are yet again brought together by illness. First there was George, and then Rebecca, and now, your father. But this time, despite the tragedy," he went on, "my heart takes flight. Your beauty leaves me as breathless as ever, and the sight of you has washed away my fatigue." Encouraged, he raised Rachel's hand, kissing her fingertips. "The time is not right, and I will say no more. For now."

Thus, allied as before, the two of them returned to Benjamin's bedside, and for the next few days Rachel remained there with Duncan, sharing the vigil. During this time, the old woman remained also. Nearly always present, she hovered over Benjamin's bed or was somewhere in the background. She seemed never to sleep, and Rachel learned only that her name was Hannah. Apparently, Hannah carried great weight in this house, for Rachel often saw her conversing with the other gray-clad figures, who always curtsied politely, and then promptly set about following whatever instructions the old woman dispensed.

Rachel's trunk was retrieved from Mrs. Morton's, and given a small room on the third floor, she became part of the peculiar household on Trowbridge Road. Rachel never went outside, and the household had no dinner regimen. Except for those she took with Duncan in the little sitting room at the top of the stairs, all of her meals were brought to her room on a tray.

Usually the house was silent, but occasionally Rachel heard the sound of children at play, or their shrill voices as they squabbled among themselves. Several times it was a baby she heard, crying thinly in the night. A sick baby, surmised Rachel from the sound, and was not surprised when Duncan disappeared now and again with old Hannah.

The children's presence in the house disturbed and troubled Rachel, and she was greatly surprised to discover there were so many of them. She had heard at least five different voices, possibly more, besides the crying infant's, but by the fourth day in the house she had yet to see a single one of them. Or, Mrs. Bailey!

Knowing her mother's heart would be broken just to learn of that woman's relationship with Benjamin, Rachel knew the presence of the children would shatter her more. Surely one of them was a boy! Had Benjamin found the son that Louisa had lost and never been able to replace? Was that Mrs. Bailey's hold over him? What else could it be? Certainly it wasn't social position or money. While the house was sturdy and sound, attractive and clean, and its address rimmed the edge of a once fashionable section of the city, still, it was quite obvious that Mrs. Bailey never entertained! There were no visitors to the house, and while the furniture was good, it was not unusual, and nothing in the entire place was fancy or ornate, gilded or jeweled. There were no oil paintings, no watercolors, no artwork of any kind, in fact, and the carpeting was all English, bright and sturdy Kidderminster's, with nary a single plush oriental in the lot.

The difference between this house and Benjamin's midland manor was startling, and Rachel wondered about it. Once, not long ago, her father had coveted Guersten Hall so much that he had sacrificed a daughter . . . nay, two of them, really, to lay claim to it. When that dream shattered, had he turned his back on the midlands and his family, choosing as a haven instead, this simple city house with its unseen mistress?

Still, if Duncan knew, or understood what it all meant, he spoke not a word of it, repeating only that Benjamin himself would explain it all when he was better.

That time came sooner than any of them expected, on a day that hinted boldly of spring's full-fledged arrival. Rays of late afternoon sun streamed through parted drapes at an open window, and Rachel, who was alone with her father, stood beside it, staring blankly at the busy street below.

Oh, how she hated the city! How she missed the midlands of Buckinghamshire! There, she knew, the symphony that was spring had already begun. The brooks, freed from winter's mantle of ice would gurgle and ripple with new life. Frogs would croak their ageless notes in the low meadow, and the larks and blackbirds would cry out in joy as they flitted above the just plowed earth, scrapping over the bounty turned up by the passing plow.

And the land! Bare brown earth . . . fragrant and ripe, soon to be clothed in new green and decked in flowery array. *Dear God,* thought Rachel, can it be that I am homesick for Guersten Hall, for my cabbages . . . for Emory even? *Yes!* She admitted to herself, I guess I am, and raising her hand, she wiped an errant tear from the corner of her eye.

"*Rachel!*"

At the sound of her father's hoarse whisper, Rachel spun around, to find him awake, his eyes open, one hand outstretched to her. He was weak, very weak, but he was fully awake and clearheaded.

"*Father! Praise God!*" sobbed Rachel, falling to her knees beside the low bed. She held her father's hand in hers and offered up a joyful prayer.

"Why do you weep by the window, child?"

"I was being silly, Father. I do believe I am homesick for the midlands. I miss those hills, and the wide fields, and all the little valleys tucked between."

"Homesick? Then I am not . . . where am I, Rachel? And where is your mother?"

"She is at Brenham Manor, but we are in London, at your Trowbridge Road house. You have been very ill. You are better, but you must rest."

"We must talk."

"Not now," cautioned Rachel. "I must send for Duncan and old Hannah. They will be most pleased to see you so alert."

"Hannah? You know about her then?"

"She and Duncan nursed, and I helped. We get along quite well, Hannah and I. I like her, but beyond that I really know little, Father, except that you are often here, with Mrs. Bailey and the children. I have not met them, and I judge you not, I simply state it as fact. But it is why I did not send for Mother; I thought it wiser to wait until you could be moved to your own townhouse."

"Judge . . . wait?" Benjamin gave Rachel a long and studied look, and then, sinking weakly back against his pillows, knitted his pale forehead into a sharp frown.

"Send for the others, Rachel. There is something you must learn."

"I am here!" called out Dr. Ferguson, just stepping over the threshold. "I hadn't expected you to rally so soon, and I hardly dared hope you would look so well when you did! And look, here comes Hannah with a bowl of her special broth. She'll have you sitting up in a day or two, I'll wager!"

Feeling for Benjamin's pulse, Duncan looked pleased that his patient was now roused from his long lethargy, but Hannah's joy was more pronounced. With a quick cry, she laid her tray on a table and went to Benjamin's side, bending to kiss his white cheek.

"You frighted me, lad. 'Tis glad I am to see you comin' round."

"Lad, indeed! Sixty I am, remember?"

"You'll always be my lad, and 'tis good to see you smile."

Benjamin clasped the old woman's hand in his and looked at her tenderly. Rachel watched them in wonderment from the far side of the bed, where she still knelt, taken by the thread of familiarity that ran between them. It was as if they had known each other a lifetime!

Duncan brought another pillow, propping Benjamin up on it, while Hannah pulled close a chair and began to spoon the hot broth into *her lad.* Between sips, Benjamin tried to talk, gesturing feebly with his hand.

"Rachel tells me that she hasn't been introduced to Mrs. Bailey yet? Can that be so?"

A strange smile flickered across Hannah's lips, and to hide it, she bent to her task, carefully transferring the broth from bowl to spoon, without spilling a single drop. At the foot of the bed, Duncan, too, was smiling.

"That is so," he said to Benjamin, "for the introduction should be yours to make. Besides, you swore me to secrecy, if you recall."

"So I did," replied Benjamin, "but I think it is time now for them to meet."

Frankly, at this very moment, Rachel didn't particularly care whether she met Mrs. Bailey or not! Not once, in all these days, to Rachel's knowledge, had that woman appeared in the sickroom or shown one ounce of concern for her generous benefactor.

"Please," she said now, "I am happy to see you better. It is enough for one day. I can meet Mrs. Bailey another time."

Benjamin's hand crept across the counterpane, covering Rachel's, which he squeezed as best he could. "You have already met her," he said, softly and tenderly, and then reaching across the bed with his other arm, joined hands with old Hannah, who laid down her spoon. "Rachel, this is Mrs. Bailey!"

The two women, one so old, the other so young, stared at each other across the bed, with Benjamin's sick figure sprawled between them.

"*You! You are Mrs. Bailey?*" muttered Rachel, in stunned surprise.

Rounding the bed to where Rachel knelt, Duncan lifted her to her feet, as Hannah rose from her chair and moved to Rachel's side.

"Actually," the old woman said, in that soft voice of hers, "there is no Mrs. Bailey. Bailey was my maiden name, and I use it now only in the operation of this house for your father."

"You run this house? But I don't understand," said Rachel, clearly baffled, looking first to her father and then back at Hannah. "If you are not Mrs. Bailey, then who are you?"

"You already know my first name. My last is . . . Brenham."

Brenham! Dizzied by the shock of it all, Rachel plopped herself rather unceremoniously on the edge of her father's bed, her brain awhirl. *Brenham!* Then old Hannah was her father's *mother!* And if that was so, then she was . . .

"You are my grandmother?" asked Rachel, in disbelief.

"Yes, child, I am your grandmother, and more than happy about it, too. You'll never know how badly I wanted to tell that very first night I saw you standing downstairs in the front hall! I knew I would like you, and no granddaughter could ever be dearer than you have become in just these few weeks.

"But, Father!" said Rachel, still not understanding fully, "why all the secrecy, and the children, what of them. I thought . . ."

Benjamin stilled her with a wave, and then placed a finger before his lips. "I know what you thought," he said, "but you were wrong. They are orphans, Rachel, all of them. Children from the slums and the docks. It is a long story, and Hannah and Duncan can piece it together for you later. Just now, kiss me and let me finish my soup. We will talk again tomorrow."

Kneeling again at her father's bedside, Rachel threw her arms about his neck.

"Oh, Father, how I have misjudged you!" she said, gazing at him through tear-filled eyes. "I'm ashamed, and I'm sorry. I love you."

"As I love you, girl. I, too, was wrong about a lot of things, and because of them, we spent most of last year misjudging each other. But go now, please, and send for your mother. I yearn to see her again. Tell her I need her. Add that I love her."

CHAPTER TWENTY-NINE

Drawn by a pair of high-stepping chestnuts, the shiny phaeton turned the path in St. James's Park for the second time in an hour. Duncan had engaged the open rig today, just as he had done these other warm spring afternoons, coaxing Rachel from her father's bedside now that he was improved.

Benjamin was not left alone, however, for some weeks ago Louisa had sped to his side, and after a reunion that was both happy and tearful, she had remained with him constantly ever since. She had taken to old Hannah just as readily as had Rachel, and when Benjamin's condition allowed, he was moved into a dark paneled room in his own townhouse. Louisa and Rachel had followed him there, and for now, at least, they were a family again.

Hannah remained at Trowbridge Road with her waifs, but Rachel went there frequently, and with her grandmother's help, was able to fit together the pieces of her father's secret life. Still trying to understand it all, Rachel discussed the subject with Duncan again and again.

"I met him one morning at the Bow Street Station," he had related to her on that same day she learned that Mrs. Bailey was her father's mother, and not his mistress, as Rachel had mistakenly believed for so long. "Your father had gone to Bow Street," continued Duncan, "to rescue some poor lad accused of pinching."

"A serious crime," Rachel had said. "What did the boy take?"

"Food . . . he was only hungry. After your father paid for his release he fed the lad, then put him to work in one of his loading sheds. Although we'd never met before, your father knew right off who I was, and we struck up a conversation. In passing, he stated that he had a pair of sick babies at Hannah's and asked if I would look at them. Naturally, I agreed, and later he fired off his proposal to me . . . that same evening! Of course, I accepted it on the spot."

"How quickly he took you into his confidence!" Rachel said, still reeling from the events that had been uncovered.

"My honest face and pleasant manner!" laughed Duncan, posturing, "or haven't you noticed?"

Rachel had, and admitted so. "Still," she commented, "I'm not sure I yet understand all this business about the children."

"It's really quite simple. For a long time now, your father wanted to found an orphanage, and felt he needed a medical man on the staff, as well as a capable administrator. He liked me, offered me both jobs, and was delighted when I accepted. Besides, now he only has to pay once!"

"But why this great concern for the children from the docks?"

"He came from those docks, Rachel, just as I came from the slums of Edinburgh. We're alike in many ways, your father and I, and like me, he never forgot his beginnings. Both of us were blessed with fortitude and both of us recognize that good fortune, as well as hard work, brought us success. Your mother's uncle gave your father early employment, but he knows that had he not married your mother, and her inherited fortune, he would likely be just another faithful clerk somewhere . . . like Potter."

"And you?" inquired Rachel, realizing how little she knew of the gentle doctor's past.

"My boyhood days were spent working in a charnel house. An old physician befriended me, saw something in my hands that I didn't know existed and guided my way through medical school. If not for him, I'd be an undertaker somewhere, working with the dead instead of the living. He died before I could repay him, but his concern, like your father's was for society's victims, the children, and I knew that if I aligned myself with Benjamin Brenham I could satisfy my own longings and repay my mentor as well."

"So you choose the children, too?"

"I do! It was long my own dream to found a hospital for them, and now, through your father's benevolence, I will have it, combined under one roof with his orphanage."

"Just how does old Hannah figure into all this?"

"While your father worked his way out of the docks, your grandmother remained where she was, in the very heart of that pesthole. It was the only life she had ever known, you see, and although she was respectable, she was uneducated. Your father brought her food and left her money to live on, and from time to time he brought something else . . . a child he had discovered abandoned in the streets, or a starving waif. Sometimes it was a sick baby, all found while making his rounds for Wittenham. Hannah cared for them, tended their needs, fed them and nursed them back to reasonably good health. One by one they were returned to the docks, displaced by others whose needs were greater When Hannah noticed that often the same child was filtered through their little reclamation center more than once, she and your father recognized the need to get them out the slums completely.

When your parents married, that way became clear. With Wittenham's money, he purchased the Trowbridge Road house and funneled the children through it. Hannah was able to keep them longer, until they were truly well, and she was able to take more of them. Eventually, your father found a way to send some of them south, to a farm somewhere in Bristol.

Many of them never repaid his kindnesses, but some did, and are even now in his employ, scattered throughout his warehouses, and each and every gray-clad girl in Hannah's house is a recipient of your father's largesse. If not for him, those girls would likely be dockside trollops, birthing children of their own into misery."

"I still don't understand why there was so much secrecy about it all," Rachel commented.

"Your father never wanted any recognition for his salvation of those poor tots. His concern for them was always genuine, a sort of there-might-go-I thing. In fact," Duncan had added, "in March your father deposited a small fortune in my name, to be used in the establishment of the complex we both seek. At his request his name appears nowhere in the undertaking, and if I were a man of another bent I could abscond with every penny."

"He trusts you," said Rachel simply.

"And be assured, I will never betray that trust. We share the same dream and I cherish his daughter."

"Even so," Rachel had said, pretending she hadn't heard Duncan's subtle declaration, "was it really necessary to keep Grandma Hannah's existence hidden from us all?"

"That was her own decision, Rachel, one she felt strongly about. Repeatedly, over the years, your father sought to get her to give up her role as Mrs. Bailey, wanting to take her to the clean midlands, but she would have none of it."

"But why?"

"That's simple. She felt needed at Trowbridge Road, and as she grew older, being needed grew in importance. Then, too, she felt that uneducated and unschooled in social graces, she could not help your father in any way in his quest for social recognition. In fact, your grandmother believed that she might even hinder him, but at Trowbridge Road she could help, and did. There, she was a vital part of her son's life, sharing something that was important to him. At Brenham Manor she would have been reduced to waiting, just as your mother has waited all these years.

Your father was ever aware of his background, Rachel. He never forgot it, and perhaps, in truth, he was a little ashamed of it, though he needn't have been. Few men from the docks have ever achieved so much, or been so generous along the way. Still, he longed to establish roots, acquire respectability . . ."

"But Father has always had those things!" interrupted Rachel.

"True enough, but what he really wanted was to be accepted, and in many ways he was, on his own merits, but he believed that he might be shunned socially if his humble beginnings became publicly known, so he hid them."

"But that's just so much foolishness!"

"He sees that now. I guess it was one peculiar facet of his pride, and too much pride is always foolish, is it not?"

That conversation had taken place weeks ago, and enjoying her excursion in the park, Rachel now leaned back against the upholstered cushions, made happy by the knowledge that never again would her parents be separated. Physically, Benjamin had been brought to a complete standstill, and it had given Louisa time to catch up. Her days of waiting were over, at last. Benjamin was never out of her sight for very long these days, something that was his choice, as well as hers. Yes, her mother was happy, and just thinking of it made Rachel smile.

Assuming that smile was intended for him, Duncan pressed closer on the seat, and then grimaced, looking over Rachel's shoulder.

"Drat!" he exclaimed. "I never seem to have you to myself for very long. There is your sister-in-law, with her cousins, on the path."

Indeed, it was Ermaline, strolling with Charlotte and Olivia. "Talk of delivering the innocents, eh?" she remarked when they came abreast of Rachel and Duncan. As a married woman, Ermaline now acted as chaperone for Adele's daughters. "Charlotte is older, and Olivia hungers for a man," she whispered, "yet Adele puts me to watching them."

"Ah! So she's set you to work matchmaking!"

"You might say that, since she believes her own presence keeps the fish from taking the bait, but she really doesn't trust me," she whispered. "She's parked in her rig over there," she added, motioning with her parasol, "by the main entrance to the park."

Rachel laughed at Ermaline's asides. "I see, and have the cousins had any bites."

"Not really, but they've had their share of nibbles. How the gentlemen do flock around, but I suspect they only want to learn the name of our dressmaker . . . for their mistresses!"

As usual, Ermaline was dressed to the nines, not that her cousins ran a poor second, for Eleanora had outdone herself. All of their costumes were dazzling.

Still smiling, Ermaline changed the subject. "Is this not the third time this week you've been out driving with our doctor friend here?" she asked, grinning openly at Duncan, who suddenly looked a bit uncomfortable.

"I believe it is," replied Rachel, "but how do you know that?"

"I know all manner of things," said Ermaline mysteriously.

"You sound like Lord Merrington, for heaven's sake!"

"My spy network is not nearly as good as his, but give it time, give it time!" responded Ermaline with a wink. She turned up the path again, for Charlotte and Olivia had wandered away just ahead of her. "I feel like a mother hen!" she expostulated. "I can't talk now, but do join us all for tea after your drive."

"We'd love to," called out Rachel. "Where?"

"Why, my apartments, of course, in Knightsbridge. See you there!"

"Do you think she disapproves of my seeing so much of you," asked Duncan, as the phaeton moved forward again.

"No, else she would say so. Ermaline is anything but subtle these days, and she did invite us to tea together. But I wonder how she learned so much about our outings?"

"Probably through Lord Merrington's grapevine. He knows everything!"

Rachel opened a ruffled parasol. "So it would seem. How *does* he do it?"

"Servants!" replied Duncan. "Don't forget, he has over a thousand in service, spread over four estates, a townhouse, a shooting lodge and even a yacht, I think. Every one of them has family, most likely in service somewhere, too . . . at places like Guersten Hall, Lady Rowland's and even the palace itself!"

"You mean they gossip?"

"They don't think of it as gossip, Rachel. They simply get quite involved with the families they work for. Sometimes they merely brag, others they are laid quite low when there is illness or unhappiness among us. They reflect our joy and our pain, but usually their loyalty cannot be doubted."

Later that afternoon, at Knightsbridge, tea time was much like their gay Sunday's of the past at Guersten Hall, and if Adele noticed that Duncan was openly adoring Rachel now, seemed on the verge of declaring himself, she wisely refrained from mentioning it. After all, she reasoned, Rachel was entitled to her own happiness, and Emory had made no effort to search her out or make any declarations of his own.

Rachel realized a lot of Duncan's attractiveness was his mind. He listened to her, discussed with her those things that interested her. She was drawn to him because of it, and because of it, she enjoyed his company even when he wasn't jovial, which happened frequently, for the gentle doctor was a very serious young man.

Thus, Duncan's pleasant outings with Rachel continued, spilling over to the theater and concerts. While Rachel enjoyed herself, sometimes it troubled her that their relationship was so one-sided, for now that she knew openly of Duncan's love, she wished sincerely that it might be returned.

Returning to her father's house from yet another drive one afternoon, she found her parents together in Benjamin's sickroom. While that in itself was not unusual, there was evidence that her mother had been weeping.

"My tears are all happy ones," sniffled Louisa, smiling at Benjamin, who appeared a little brim-eyed himself. "Your father has just told me once again that he loves me, and hearing it so often is all so wonderful. Then too, we were discussing Rebecca."

Remembering that Benjamin had previously scoffed at that intangible something that was love, Rachel was heartened by her mother's statement of happiness. He had steeled his heart closed as a young man and kept it steeled through all the years of his marriage. From the first, his will had overpowered Louisa's, and since she had never objected, Benjamin mistakenly assumed that she bent because she was no match for his stronger will. Only recently had he realized that she allowed it to be so because she adored him. It was about the same time that he also realized that he really loved her, had always loved her, and had always denied that love.

These revelations had taken place in the earlier days of his recovery, days when, too sick to move, he had only strength to think. Dwelling upon the past, he became unhappy at the way the facets of his private life were carved and shaped. Most of all, he recognized that he had never really put the loss of his son behind him, and to cover it, had set about filling his life with work, fronting himself with a brusqueness that kept others at arm's length. In doing so, he had deprived his wife of the knowledge that she was loved, and his daughters of the only grandparent they would ever know. He promised now to make amends to them all, as best he could.

"Some men drink, some gamble," he said with considerable humility. "My weakness was gnawing envy over Guersten Hall and its past. I let it color my entire life." Gently, he took Rachel's hand into his. "I've had plenty of time to think, and I know now that I was wrong to manipulate your life. In the past, I caused things to happen and they did; I prevented them from happening and they didn't. I merely extended that premise to my private life . . . your life, and Rebecca's. I know now it was wrong, and I'm sorry for the pain I've inflicted."

For a man of Benjamin's character, such an apology, a confession, actually, was indeed moving, and when he finished, neither Rachel nor her mother said anything, for Benjamin's suffering did not end there.

At his elbow was a stack of letters, including some that Rachel herself had written concerning the birth of Rebecca's child and her subsequent death, and Rachel knew it had taken courage on her father's part to read them now, for there was guilt . . . lots of it. He had closed his heart to his youngest daughter when she needed him the most. There was a hollow sadness in that part of Benjamin's heart that was hers alone, and it was a hollowness that he would take to the grave with him.

With tenderness, Rachel went to her father's side. "I understand about your guilt," she said softly, "but take care, Father. It is easy to make a pet of it, setting it on others who venture too close. Guilt is dangerous. It can be your downfall, in the end. If not physically, then spiritually."

"Well said, Rachel, and I shall remember it. But remember, too, your grief is behind you. Mine is just beginning."

"Neither grief nor guilt can help Rebecca now, Father, but you alone can, if you choose."

"Me? How so?"

At length, and in detail, Rachel related to her father the deathbed promise she had given Rebecca, repeating Rebecca's plaintive plea to see her father and her son joined in their rightful blood relationship. While she spoke, Benjamin listened stony faced, his expression revealing little.

"Did they think to soften my heart and open my purse by naming the child after me?"

"Rebecca's child is not named after you. He is the fifth Edward Guersten, and is called Benjy simply because he resembles you and Rebecca, and not his Guersten forbears."

"I see," said Benjamin quietly, sorry that he'd spoken so hastily and so sharply.

"*Do* you see, Father? They loved each other, and even if things came about a little backward, they were married by the vicar. Surely, if God can forgive them, you can. Won't you see the child?"

Closing his eyes, Benjamin rested his head on the back of his chair. "I can forgive Rebecca easily enough," he said sadly. "After all, she is gone and I loved her dearly. But young Guersten is another matter. I'm not quite ready for him."

"Don't ever blame Edward for what happened. Always remember, Rebecca chose him, and she died happy because of him. Poor Edward suffers now more than any of us."

The prolonged conversation and its upsetting nature had tired Benjamin, and Louisa signaled to Rachel to let the matter drop, and so she left the room without knowing whether her promise to Rebecca would be met or not. But at least it was all out in the open now. She had tried, and if need be, she would try again another time.

As Rachel dwelt further on that promise to Rebecca, her thoughts turned to her other piece of unsettled business. The matter of the annulment had been put off long enough. Going to the library, she penned a note, scheduling an appointment with Tisbury.

CHAPTER THIRTY

Lord Merrington's stout coach, newly painted a conservative gray, rocketed along the midland miles on its way to Guersten Hall. The Lord's ultimate destination was London, for he had business at Whitehall, but just now his more immediate concern was Emory Guersten, whom he looked upon as a friend. Unsettling rumors had reached Merrington's ear while he tarried at Northumberland, and the one that disturbed him most was the one that spoke of Rachel's departure from the Hall.

Merrington had wasted half his adult life barking up the wrong tree, as it were, when the true game was already snared and settled onto his hearth all the while. The crusty Lord was determined to see that his younger friend made not the same mistake, for he liked young Guersten and his beauteous wife. They were right for each other, both of them handsome and intelligent, physically strong and mentally quick. Together they could build an empire, lace it with healthy children to carry on, and if they were too stubborn, too blind to see it, why then the blunt old Lord would set 'em straight.

"Slow down!" he screamed through the little window to his coachman, as his gouty foot was buffeted against the opposite cushions again and again.

"Sorry, m'Lord! You said to hurry, and these roads are awful." Even as the coachman spoke, the wheels struck another bump, and Lord Merrington was bounced painfully against the far seat. "Shall I slow down, sir?" asked the coachman as Merrington moaned and swore again.

"No, no, dammit! I'm in a hurry! Just watch the ruts, boyo! My arse ain't springed, y' know!"

As the coach approached Guersten Hall, it was Emory himself, recognizing the emblazoned door, who galloped forward on Sultan to meet it. Riding up from the rear, he rode alongside and peered into the open window, bowing his head courteously to mark the Lord's rank. Merrington lowered the window glass all the way and poked out his head.

"Is it true? You let her go?" he demanded, without even greeting Emory.

While Emory was certainly pleased to see the Lord again, the smile of welcome that first spread across his face froze and then disappeared. "You rode all the way from Northumberland just to ask that? Has your spy system failed?"

"What?" cried the Lord over the racket of the wheels. "Get in!" he ordered curtly. "Can't hear ye!"

Expertly maneuvering Sultan close to the still moving carriage, Emory slipped from the saddle and entered the coach through the door that Merrington held open. Once inside, he settled his long frame onto the cushions opposite the Lord, taking special care not to jostle his friend's propped foot, made giant by layers and layers of swansdown.

Merrington wasted no time, but came right to the point of his visit. "Well . . . is it?"

"Is it true that Rachel left me?" asked Emory, laughing at the other's bluntness. "Yes, it's true . . . some months ago. And I repeat, has your spy system failed?"

"Hasn't! Knew she'd gone damned near as soon as you did. Just didn't want to believe it, that's all. Why didn't you stop her, for Chris' sake!"

"How?" responded Emory simply. "She left of her own accord, at a time of her own choosing. I bared my heart and pleaded with her for more time. I all but begged her to stay!"

"Perhaps you should have done that, too! She's no ordinary bit o' skirt and extraordinary measures were called for." But even as he said it, Merrington understood from the look on his friend's face that Rachel's departure had been a blow, one he'd not yet recovered from.

"What would you have me do, m'Lord? Tie her to the bed, keep her here by force? I love her . . . I told her that! She is my wedded wife . . . she knows that. Neither of those two things kept her at my side. While a lesser woman might have been convinced by my protestations of love, Rachel was not, and since I treated her so shabbily for so long, my arguments were without merit. She gave her all for my family and my estate, and under the circumstances, she had a right to go if she chose. There was nothing I could do."

"Has she instituted annulment proceedings yet? Have you heard from Tisbury? Has she been to see him?"

Emory shrugged off the Lord's questions. "I don't know, but I think not. It is the only thing that sustains me these days. We've had but two short notes, neither of which bore a return address. It appears Rachel went to London and disappeared."

"Disappeared, my foot! She's at her father's!"

"But I checked there . . . months ago!" said Emory, moving to sit straight and tall on the edge of the seat.

"Well, she's there now! Benjamin Brenham was struck down awhile back. Didn't you notice the mother had gone away?"

"Louisa? She sent a note saying she was joining Benjamin, but she didn't mention Rachel, and I thought nothing of it. I was happy for her; she and her husband had been separated long enough. I didn't realize that Benjamin was sick."

"Very sick, and he's being doctored by Ferguson."

At first, the inference of the Lord's remark escaped Emory. "Duncan? Well, Benjamin is in good hands," was all he said. But then, a swift second later, it hit him. "You mean Ferguson is there . . . every day? With Rachel?"

"He's there, all right! And I hear they're seen everywhere together . . . riding in Hyde Park, driving in St. James's, even dining together at your sister's table."

Instantly, Emory became depressed, but then that depression quickly gave way to anger. *So!* Rachel was in London, at her father's, and his illness had brought Duncan to her side. *How convenient!* While I wait with bated breath, hoping, nay, praying, that perhaps she might miss me . . . or the Hall! That somehow she might decide to return to us! Instead, she cavorts in the city on Duncan's arm, giving no thought to he who is still her husband.

"*Dammit!* I ought to go there and pound the good doctor senseless!" snarled Emory, making a fist. "I've longed to do it for some time."

"No doubt," muttered the Lord, "but then Rachel would be forced to defend him and you'd lose even more ground. Besides, Duncan's too gentlemanly for fisticuffs, and fisticuffs would only serve to point up the differences between you and him."

Glowering darkly, Emory sank against the padded seat. "You're right there. Rachel would consider fighting distasteful, as it is." With his elbows on his knees, Emory cupped his head in his hands, all the loneliness and torment of past months brought to the fore. Lord Merrington saw his friend's misery and was filled with passionate pity. He sighed, for there was nothing more pitiful than love not returned, and none more pitiful than the male, who'd already rendered himself wholly vulnerable by the mere admission that one woman, and one alone, had captured his heart.

Emory groaned inwardly, and so grievous was his plight that Merrington fathomed he heard it. Lifting his cane, he tapped the younger man on the shoulder.

"M'boy," he said, "fisticuffs are out, but still, you can't let her go without a fight. Go to London! Demand nothing, but court Rachel yourself. In the end, when she chooses between you and Ferguson, let it be the Emory she sees, and not the one she remembers. You've changed, lad. I spied it right away, and so will she. When she finds that you are steady and sober, and once she learns how well you are fulfilling your role here, well, maybe she'll reconsider . . . choose you over Duncan."

"Besides," added Emory, throwing out his chest in an attempt to be jestful, "am I not better looking than the lanky doctor?"

Lord Merrington's lips curled in a wry smile. "Glad to see you haven't lost your sense of humor, Emory, but don't be too smug about your good looks. Didn't Edwina choose me again over you? Love is all encompassing to a woman, never underestimate it! On that score, Rachel is no different than Edwina."

"Oh, but she is! Rachel doesn't love her husband, Edwina does. *There's* the difference."

Merrington smiled smugly at the reminder that Edwina loved him. How he basked in that love these days! What changes it had brought to his life! He considered himself indeed fortunate to have fallen in love with the same woman twice, and to have had that love returned both times.

"Well," he said to Emory, "if I was you, son, I'd be off to London. Go after her! Just remember, don't try to seduce her. You must court her! *There's* a difference to remember!"

"You're right, and I'll go at once!" announced Emory, slapping his hand against Merrington's leg for emphasis.

"*Thunderation!* Watch the foot! Edwina will never forgive you if you put me out of commission," roared the Lord as the coach rolled to a stop under the portico. Still apologizing, Emory tumbled out and helped the man lower his throbbing foot to the ground.

"And how is my friend Edwina?" asked Emory, as they moved inside. "Delivered safely of her babe, I pray."

Merrington beamed. "Aye! Months ago! My heir is a fine son, the only male in my family beside m'self. Edwina did herself proud!"

"Your joy is plain to see, m'Lord," said Emory earnestly, "and I share it." He hesitated, wanting to ask, but not knowing how. "The . . . er, child" he stammered.

"Is healthy, though a bit small. He looks to me like any other boy child, but Edwina assures he'll be quite handsome one day. For myself, I was content to see his eyes are bright, he hears well, and his wee cock's in the right place! Half my prayers have been answered," he said, "and time will tell about the other half." As he spoke, Merrington tapped the side of his head with a finger.

"Surely you don't suspect . . ."

"Nay, there's no evidence that he'll be dimwitted, but somehow I find my good fortune almost too much to believe. Suddenly, I find myself beholden to God."

Emory touched the older man's arm in a friendly gesture that was well received. "We stray sometimes, but some of us find our way back with the help of a good woman. And now, I leave you to my father," he added, as George rolled toward them. "I'm away to London after I change and pack."

"Come," said Lord Merrington to a confused and bewildered George, who watched as Emory rushed headlong up the stairs. Puzzled, he turned his chair and rolled after the limping Lord, just disappearing into the library. Upstairs, Emory was whistling loudly, and the sound of it filled the foyer below. George knew that only news of Rachel could have cheered him that much.

Emory *was* cheered. Sitting tall in the saddle he let Sultan find his own pace on the London road, and though the ride was tedious, hard on the ass, Emory did not stop at any of the inns and taverns along the way, sharp contrast to the old days when he would not have missed a single one. Sultan sensed Emory's urgency, and maintained a good and steady pace, his long stride covering the miles with relative ease. When they arrived at the Guerstens' house at Eaton Place about sundown, the stallion was not even breathing hard.

After stabling his mount, Emory then bathed and dressed, carefully, all in black, so excited by his errand in the city that he could barely contain himself. He would call on Rachel, as a gentleman calls on a lady, and if she would see him, then he would set about reconstructing that wonderful week they shared so long ago.

In the street he hired a hansom, and was soon rattling through London on his way to Benjamin's brownstone. On a corner near it he paid the cabbie, adding a generous tip that attested to his fine mood, and crossing the street, took up a position in a darkened doorway. There, he suddenly wavered, a bit unsure just how he should confront Rachel. Emory knew Merrington was right about one thing . . . there could be no blustery stances and shouted demands this time. If ever he was to recapture Rachel, lure her from the quiet doctor, it would have to be with gentle actions and soft words, and every gesture and word must be sincere. That above all, for Rachel would see through anything less, as she always had.

Yet, even as Emory watched the house, the front door opened and Rachel emerged on Duncan's arm, both of them in evening dress. Finding some amusement in something Duncan was saying, Rachel laughed up at him, while Emory seethed openly at the sight of them together. Shrinking further into the darkened doorway, he remained unseen there, struggling with an impulse to dash across the street and pummel the tall doctor. He continued to fume as a small cabriolet drew up to the curb and Rachel and Duncan headed for it, passing under a lighted lamp-post just across from him.

At that first full view of Rachel's lovely face, Emory's hands began to tremble and there came a roaring in his ears. As he watched, she moved to the carriage, while the night mist and street fog swirled in circles about her feet, reminding Emory of that night he'd glimpsed her galloping ghostlike across the Small Wood meadow. His head swam!

The driver of the carriage made a clucking sound and it moved forward, to be swallowed up by the night darkness. Jolted, Emory hailed another cab and followed after them, pressing a pair of coins into his driver's palm. When both carriages rolled to a stop again, one behind the other, it was at the steps of the galleried concert hall. There, a streak of blue that turned out to be the elder Mrs. Rowland's voluminous figure swooped down from the top step to greet Rachel, gathering her into the middle of a larger group that spilled over into the lobby of the hall. Emory spied his sister, Ermaline, there, standing between Charlotte and Olivia, and with them, chatting amicably, was the Lord High Mayor of the city, a pleasant fellow all decked out in his badge of office.

That place, at that time, was certainly not the spot to confront Rachel, and Emory stepped down from his hired cab to mingle with the crowd outside the hall, burning as though consumed by fever. That feverish state was a culmination of many emotions; desire and torment at seeing Rachel once again, coupled with the sweeping realization of just how much he really loved her, a realization loudly seconded by the thumping of his heart. Then too, he was overwhelmed by a mix of anger and anguish that was only heightened by Rachel's presence at Duncan's side. Furthermore, he was also swamped by loneliness, for while Rachel was welcomed and accepted by them all, he was now skulking about in the shadows outside, like a thief in the night. But since he was not dressed for the concert hall, Emory was forced to remain outside, and he paced there with long strides for well more than an hour, listening to the swell and ebb of the music as it filtered out to him. Emory knew not its composer, nor its title, but he recognized it as one of Rachel's favorites, one he'd heard her humming now and then, and he wished now that he had paid more attention to her likes and dislikes.

At intermission, when the doors to the hall were thrown open, Emory was startled to see Rachel and Duncan leaving already, moving side by side across the chandeliered lobby and down the steps to the curb, where Duncan whistled expertly for a hack. They passed so close by Emory this time that he could have touched Rachel's mantle, and he smelled that inimitable fragrance she always wore.

Once again Emory scurried after them, but this time he had to run half a block before finding a cab for himself, and he was surprised when the strange little cavalcade wound its way back to Benjamin's brownstone, near Waterloo Place. There, Duncan and Rachel went inside quickly, as Emory, again not sure of his next move, approached the house. Through a window he saw Rachel enter a dimly lighted room, the library, he guessed, with Duncan following behind her. The two of them stood close together, discussing something . . . something serious, thought Emory, judging from the serious expressions they both wore. They talked for a while, and then, stunned, Emory looked on as Duncan, in a swift movement, suddenly swept Rachel into his long arms. She offered no resistance, but lifted her face for his kiss, and placed one arm around his shoulder.

Watching them, Emory battled his rage, and in that instant, he knew real jealousy for the first time in his life. Not the simple rage of green envy, but the stomach wrenching shock of a blow to the heart! He recoiled, just as Rachel had recoiled at the sight of an earlier embrace, and Emory, understanding no more now than she did then, swore loudly.

In the house, Rachel looked up at Duncan with tears in her eyes. "I'm sorry," she said, disengaging herself from his arms.

"Why?" asked Duncan. "Because your lips are cold? Don't be! Your heart is warm, and I've known from the beginning that you don't love me."

"I want to, Duncan. Believe me, I've tried!"

"I know that, too, Rachel, and don't look so sad. Love cannot be compelled ... cannot be drawn from the heart as strength is drawn from the body or faith from the soul. Love is simpler. Passion is there or it isn't."

"I wanted it to be there, Duncan, I truly did. Once I am free, I would even marry you without it."

Duncan's lips moved slightly and he took Rachel's two hands between his and held them. "I believe that is the first foolish thing I have ever heard you say, my dear." Though there was pain in his heart, still, he smiled down at her. "You deserve more, and so do I. I may be quiet, but I have fire in my loins like other men, and someday I'll spend it on a woman who loves me with all her being. While I hoped that woman would be you, Rachel, as much as I love you, I'll settle for nothing less."

"And what becomes of us now?" asked Rachel in a low whisper. "Will this put an end to our friendship?"

Duncan was cheerful. "Of course not! I intend to call for you tomorrow as usual. I've rented a rig for our outing in the park." Bending his head, he kissed Rachel's fingertips, and his gray eyes became less piercing. "Be my friend, dear Rachel, forever and always. We live in an insane world, and I need all the sincerity and honesty I can glean from you. In place of passion let me have the best of your mind and heart. I pledge you the same. Now smile, and see me out."

He lifted Rachel's chin, kissed her soft cheek, and then left the room, appearing on the doorstep seconds later, let out by Rachel herself.

"I ought to kill you!" roared Emory when the doctor stepped into the circle of light shed by the street lamp.

"Guersten! I wondered if and when you'd ever show up! What brings you to London after all these months?"

"I heard rumors! It appears they're true!"

Duncan smiled. "Ah, Merrington's spies!" he said calmly. "Yes . . . they're all true! I've spent every moment I could with Rachel, trying to win her from you. In fact, tonight I even asked her to marry me!"

Emory's temple raged red, and even under the dim light of the lamp his scar could be seen burning brightly. "So that's what the kiss was all about! Damn you, Ferguson! Rachel's still my wife!"

Always collected and amenable, Duncan ignored Emory's menacing stance. "You and I are in a bind, Guersten," he said, "both of us in love with the same woman. Shall we discuss it like gentlemen?"

"I'd rather knock you down!" snarled Emory.

In a swift move, Duncan took Emory by the arm, and exhibiting surprising strength, propelled him across the street. "Walk with me awhile!" he commanded.

"I don't want to walk!"

"Dammit, Guersten, for once in your life shut up and do as you're told! I have something to say . . . for Rachel's sake, listen!"

Emory snatched his arm free of Duncan's vise-like grip, but for reasons unknown even to himself he held his tongue and fell into step beside the doctor, matching his stride to the doctor's longer one.

"It's strange you showed up tonight," Duncan said. "Neither Rachel nor I knew you were in the city, and yet I've felt your presence all evening, even though your name was never spoken."

"Not even when you asked my wife to marry you?"

"Not even then!" replied Duncan.

"Does she love you?"

"Let us just say that Rachel has great feeling for me."

"Then she agreed to marry you . . . after she visits Tisbury?"

"No."

"I'm confused," said Emory. "Just what did she say?"

"Nothing. But then she didn't have to, I knew the answer already, you see."

"I don't understand any of this! What the hell are you trying to say, Ferguson?"

"There is much in life that you don't have the capacity to understand, Emory, but there are many things I don't understand myself, so we are even. Why Rachel loves you is only one of them."

"She loves me? She said so?"

"No! I repeat . . . your name never came up. Rachel said nothing of loving you, simply because she doesn't know it herself yet."

"*Christ!* Now what nonsense do you speak?"

"I'm no fool, Guersten, and I've tasted cold lips before. I've been in communion with Rachel's mind for some time now, but someone else has already awakened the passion in her breast, stirred her woman's heart. I love her, and though I'm damned if I know why she chooses you, her happiness is all that matters to me. For now, I'll drop into the background."

With their long strides, the two men had come several blocks already. Emory suddenly stopped and turned, facing in the direction of Benjamin's brownstone. He couldn't even see the house from where he stood, but the simple knowledge that Rachel loved him was like a invisible beacon, lighting a path to where she was this very moment. He wanted to race down that path and sweep her into his arms, kiss her lips, listen to them saying what he wanted so badly to hear.

Duncan must have read his mind; with an outstretched arm he stayed Emory's impulse to run.

"I don't blame you," he said, "but will you heed some advice from one who also loves her? Rachel may be one of those rare women whose heart and mind never function in unison. At any given moment one of them alone is in command, and just now her heart needs more time. Give her that time, Emory. Let her discover that she loves you on her own. Your marriage will be all the stronger for it, and she'll come to you very soon, I think. Go back to Guersten Hall and wait."

Though Emory couldn't see Duncan's lean features in the dim light, still, he knew from the catch in the doctor's voice that his words, though remaining typically gentle, had been torn from his heart. Now, genuinely in love for the first time in his life, Emory understood what it was to come up empty-handed, to be left with an aching heart. Still, while he felt some sadness for the doctor, there was no pity, and he saw now what Rachel had always seen. Duncan was fine and compassionate; he would suffer Rachel's loss as a man, filling his lonely hours with constructive work, not drink and self-pity. Emory felt new respect for the man, and in the darkness, extended his hand.

"I thought you were my enemy. I would be pleased to call you friend."

But Duncan, in an untypical move, chose to ignore Emory's outstretched palm. "You're mistaken, Guersten. For her sake I will be friendly, but I'm not your friend. I love her dearly, and I want her badly. If she were not already your lawful wife I would fight tooth and nail for her, but I have always respected the sanctity of your marriage, even if you have not."

Turning on his heel, Duncan started off, then paused, and came back to where Emory still stood in the darkness. "You may think me a fool, and perhaps I am, but you see, Guersten, I love her, and her happiness means more to me than my own. While I shall never press, never overstep, never forget that I love her. I'll be just behind you . . . waiting. I've already captured her mind, and after you have crushed her love and grieved her heart, then I'll take her from you."

Duncan disappeared into the night for the second time. This time he did not return, and Emory knew then the depth of his love for Rachel, knew it to be just as deep as his own. Thoughtfully, Emory turned and walked slowly back to Benjamin's house, where Rachel lay in her bed on an upper floor, tossing fitfully, unaware of Emory's nearness. In the same darkened doorway he had occupied hours earlier, he took up a position and stood watching the house, while smoking a thin cheroot to its end. He was reminded of another night, another time that he watched from outside, only then he had turned away in despair. Tonight he would turn away again, but in buoyant happiness this time, and heeding Duncan's advice, he returned to Eaton Place and went to bed.

In the morning, Emory saddled Sultan and headed back to the midlands. Before he left the city he made two stops. One took him to the office of Sotheby's, the other to the green and white salon of Eleanora Scofield.

CHAPTER THIRTY-ONE

On the first day of June, Duncan left London to travel to the country-side to inspect several pieces of property for their suitableness as a site for the combined hospital-orphanage already chartered in his name by Benjamin. The good doctor wasn't gone a week before Rachel missed him terribly, for in his absence, she was once again reduced to reading and shopping in an attempt to relieve unending boredom. While she continued to spend a considerable amount of time with her father, who was recovering slowly, it was Louisa's company Benjamin really sought and enjoyed most these days.

By this time, Rachel and her father had come to terms with each other's distinctive personalities, and she discovered that in many ways she was more like him than she once imagined. Both of them were strong and determined, and both were somewhat stubborn. In addition, neither of them was blessed with insight to read what was in the heart. Because of this blind spot, Rachel, in her loneliness, became melancholy.

She tried to occupy herself with music, and one afternoon, at the pianoforte, her fingers idly brought forth a simple melody from the out-of-tune instrument as she tried to dispel her mood of somberness. Outside a light but steady rain fell, the aftermath of a torrential downpour that had fallen the night before, washing the city streets and rooftops of some of their accumulated dirt.

Not put off by the dampness, a visitor came to call, and Rachel was pleased when Ermaline burst into the music room without waiting to be announced.

"Thank heavens!" she exclaimed, greeting her sister-in-law with a smile of welcome. "I was just trying to cheer myself with a few lively airs. I'm low today. I miss Duncan, I guess. He's good for me . . . always finding something to do that keeps me from thinking of . . ." Rachel's voice trailed away, as she tried to put a name to just what it was that always seemed to occupy her thoughts these days.

"Emory?" asked Ermaline.

"Don't be silly!" said Rachel, with an air of dismissal. She arranged herself in a straight chair as Ermaline moved idly about the music room, plunking first the keys of the pianoforte and then the strings of the harp in the corner.

"It is you who are silly, Rachel," Ermaline said flatly. "It it Guersten Hall you miss . . . and Emory, not Duncan."

"That is a presumption, Ermaline, and a ridiculous one at that!"

"Is it? Then why do you play that same tune over and over? Often from what the maid tells me! Don't you recognize it? It is the very one you played that night at Guersten Hall when you saw Emory for the first time."

As Ermaline spoke, she advanced to where Rachel sat and stood over her, hands on her hips.

"Honestly, Rachel!" she said in an exasperated tone. "I could box your ears! You are so astute when it comes to the needs of others, yet continually you deny your own."

"You read far too much into a simple air, Ermaline," replied Rachel testily through tight lips, but she winced nonetheless, as if Ermaline had struck a nerve.

"Do I? Perhaps that little tune you play so often is the medium through which your heart speaks! Why don't you listen?"

"What nonsense you speak!" cried Rachel, a little vexed. "And here I thought you came by to cheer me!"

Thoroughly at ease in Rachel's presence, Ermaline dropped into a well padded chair and casually put her feet up on a low table.

"Frankly," she said to Rachel, "that was not the intent of my visit. I came by to invite you to dinner, but since the matter is out in the open, let us pursue it! Why don't you go back to my brother?"

Rachel leaped to her feet. "Really, Ermaline! You intrude!"

"Perhaps, but I love you both, and today I am going to be relentless! Why won't you give Emory another chance?"

"To do what? Humiliate me? Play upon my emotions? I can take no more of that!"

"Then don't! Try giving for a change. Throw off your yoke of reserve. Be a little wild, a little wanton! He'll adore you!"

"*Ermaline!* How indiscreetly you speak! It is you who must assume some reserve. You must be prepared to play out your role as Henry's wife."

"I am prepared! I play that role now," she said, wagging a finger. "Marriage is a dual role, but both must be kept in balance. In one, I am Henry's wife, and he knows that I am intelligent and will be efficient and capable in my future position, just as Emory knows by now that you have the same qualities and capabilities. In my other role, I am only a woman . . . Henry's wife. In that role I do not pretend to manage at all, for love cannot be managed. It must be allowed to happen."

Rachel threw up her hands. *How soon the novice learned! Already the new bride was dispensing advice!* Still, she winced again, for Ermaline's words had a familiar ring to them, reminding Rachel of something Lady Merrington once told her. Sooner or later, Edwina had said, you must be a woman!

"Ah, well," she said, wishing to brush away all thought of Edwina Merrington, "Emory and I could never work out our differences. It's hopeless! He's like that wild stallion of his, and I'm like a skitterish mare."

"But you're not!" exclaimed Ermaline. "If you were, you would have already been added to his stables and long forgotten, for Emory knows well how to handle skitterish mares! No, Rachel, it is your on-again, off-again personality that confuses him so, and you are far too serious. You must learn to be gay and light-hearted. Men adore our empty little heads."

"In that you may be right," Rachel sighed, "but it won't do for me. I dislike guile and deception. He's what he is, and I'm what I am, and in that one thing, at least, Emory and I are in agreement."

"Well, despite your differences, I still think your marriage could work, though it's apt to get a little lively at times." Ermaline laughed merrily, remembering some of the incidents that had shaken up the household at the Hall. "If you both try, perhaps you might get through one day without being throttled, and Emory, in his turn, might get through one night without being ousted from your bedroom!"

"Is that how we appear to others?" inquired Rachel, aghast.

"Forget what others say or think, love. They don't count! But isn't it possible that there is something between you which neither of you can nor will recognize?"

A shadow fell across Rachel's beautiful face as she remembered Emory's parting declaration of love. He had said then those words that she had longed to hear, had hurled them at her, in fact, but they had come too late.

"Perhaps one of us did," she said slowly to Ermaline, "and I refused to believe him."

Ermaline eyed the clock on the mantel. "Well, you have certainly entangled your heart in a dilemma, my sweet; one that I leave you to solve for yourself. I only came by to invite you to dinner tomorrow evening," she added, pulling on expensive kid gloves. "The Lord Mayor is dining with us again, and I need another woman. Will you come?"

Is that to be my role, mused Rachel, always the spare lady? Still, almost absent-mindedly she gave Ermaline her assent, and after a quick kiss, she departed in a whisk of silk and perfume.

Remaining in the music room, Rachel wandered about in an aimless fashion, returning again and again to the pianoforte, to stand staring down at the ivory keys as if they held some answer to her confused emotions. Perhaps Ermaline's presumptions did contain some substance, she thought. That little air did remind her of Emory. Is that why she played it, over and over? And was there perhaps some reason she had dragged her feet in the matter of the annulment? Had she used her father's illness as an excuse not to see Tisbury? And even now, though she had made the appointment, she had already cancelled it twice.

Rachel stood there, before the pianoforte, for a long, long time, when realization fell upon her like a bolt from the blue. "*Yes!*" she suddenly cried, striking the keys of the instrument discordantly with both hands. "*Yes! I miss him! I do think of him, constantly! And I don't want an annulment. I want to go . . . back! I want him!*"

Emory! Emory! *I love him!* sang Rachel's heart, and this time she listened. Her heart skipped a beat or two as she admitted it to herself, at long last, over and over. She said it aloud, as well. "*I love him! I love him!*"

Heart racing, Rachel's thoughts then ran wild, and Emory dominated them all. Emory . . . laughing, white teeth flashing. Emory . . . the red streak proclaiming his anger . . . his passion. Emory . . . his green, green eyes engulfing her. Emory . . . holding her, kissing her. She burned just remembering those kisses.

Burying her head on the keyboard, Rachel wondered why on earth she'd never known before this very moment that she truly loved him. Why had she denied her heart so long? Follow your heart, Rebecca had counseled, wherever it leads. Now, Rachel would do just that, hoping all the while that Emory would take her back, praying that in her absence his passion hadn't cooled . . . that he still wanted her.

He must! Now that she knew that she loved him, no other would ever do. She could love no other, give herself to no other. There was only Emory! She must go to him at once, she thought.

Upstairs in the quiet house just then, her mother sat at her father's bedside, valiantly taking notes as he waded through a sheaf of reports submitted by Potter. Rushing up the narrow stairs, skirts held high, Rachel raced to announce her joyous proclamation of love.

"I'm going home!" she cried, bursting in on them, "back to Guersten Hall where I belong."

Plainly startled by the news, her mother leaped to her feet, and Benjamin dropped his papers upon the counterpane. In amazement they watched Rachel, usually so reserved and decorous, bounding about the room, swinging excitedly on the bedpost.

"I love him! I'm going back!"

"Rachel! Calm yourself!" advised her mother. "Do sit down and start at the beginning. Whatever excites you so?"

But Rachel did not sit, could not, and what she said made little sense to either of her parents. *I love him,* was about all that they discerned from her frenzied words as she whirled round and round her father's bed until Louisa became concerned by such uncharacteristic behavior.

"What has come over you?" she said sternly. "Look at you, shouting, whirling. You look like . . ."

"Like Rebecca!" finished Benjamin quietly. "Exactly like Rebecca, Louisa, when she first recognized that she loved Edward! Come here, Rachel," he said, holding out his arms to his daughter. "So it's Emory, after all, eh?"

"Yes, Father! It's Emory, after all! How could I not have seen it? What took me so long?"

"Some of us are like that, dear," Benjamin said, reaching out for Louisa's hand. "You are sure?"

"Yes, and I must go to him at once."

"Then I give you my blessing, child. Go where your heart leads, and may you find happiness."

Rachel hugged her father tightly. "Oh, we mortals, we're such fools, are we not? To think I nearly made the same mistake that you did, so busy directing other people's lives that I ignored my heart."

Tenderly, Benjamin kissed his daughter's smooth cheek. Now, in the full bloom of love, she was more beautiful than ever. Her pink skin radiated with soft color and her eyes were heightened by a brilliance that was not there before.

"Return to your husband, and love him well. He is fortunate indeed. Your mother will help you pack, and I will have my best driver at the front door first thing in the morning."

"Before I go, Father . . . there is something else . . . ."

"Hush, Rachel, it need not be spoken of. Just now, it is still too painful, and there is my guilt to be dealt with. Give me time. When I am . . . better, I will consider Rebecca's child. I will see him."

"That's all she ever asked. It would make her happy."

In the front bedroom that was hers, Rachel began emptying drawers and wardrobes, packing yet again, only this time it was different. She was happy and excited! In no time, her bed was mounded with a high stack of gowns and bonnets, all scattered about in wild disarray.

"This is madness!" she said to her mother, who had come to help, and both of them laughed at the disorderly confusion Rachel had created. "I will take only what I need, and you can send the rest on later." When her mother didn't answer, Rachel turned around, expecting Louisa to be smiling. Instead, she stood by the window, folding and refolding a flowered gown.

"What is it, Mother? You've said so little. Are you not happy for me?"

Crossing the room, Louisa added the gown to the pile already on the bed and embraced her daughter tenderly. "Of course I am, and you have my blessings, too, my dear, but all the same, keep your head," she cautioned. "You may need it." She pushed Rachel onto the bed and sat down beside her. "You have been gone several long months, Rachel, and perhaps Emory will not return the love you carry to him."

"I know that, yet I don't care!" Rachel said. "Don't you see, Mother? Even if he lied when he said he loved me, it doesn't matter anymore, because I love him! I loved him before only I wouldn't admit it, even to myself. I chose to withhold my heart until he could prove that he was worthy of it. That was foolish! Love would have changed him naturally, and if not, then I would have learned to love him faults and all. I can only hope now that he still wants me."

"And if he doesn't?"

"Then I will live my life on the edge of his, and spend my days waiting to be noticed, for I know only this . . . I can love no other!"

"Then go to him," said her mother with some emotion. "The crumbs from love's table are better than nothing at all. I know . . . they sustained me for years. Go, and let there be happiness between the two of you; let love remain after the passion, let laughter return after the anger. I can wish you no more."

As promised, a fast coach and four were at the front door at sunup. Rachel sat close by the window the entire way, watching . . . watching, as the mileposts sped past. She had traveled this way so many times before, always in sadness or trepidation. Now, with expectant heart and lightened spirits, it all seemed so changed. Rachel could tell without being told the very moment they crossed into the midland shire of Buckingham, for the land was at once greener, the air purer. Under a blue sky the pungent fragrance of a variety of flowering trees and bushes filtered through the open window, and gentle breezes blew away the dust that rose up from the road.

At the inn at Aylesbury the horses were changed, while Rachel paced nervously back and forth beside the carriage. Horrick, her father's coachman, retired to the inn's kitchen for something to eat. He was gone only a short time, returning with half his dinner tucked under one arm, wrapped in clean cloth.

It was not my intent to make you feel guilty," Rachel said to the man. "You are entitled to your dinner."

"'Tis all right, Miss Rachel. Yer father told me you would be in a hurry. I'll finish it up," he said, pointing to his seat up in the box. "Now, in ye go and we're off again."

"I thank you, Horrick. I *am* in a hurry. I am going home!"

"So yer father did say, and the homeward miles . . . are they not the longest you'll ever travel?"

Eager though she was, Rachel developed a colossal case of the jitters as the powerful team ate up the miles. Her apprehension growing, her temples began to pound in a rhythm that matched the team's clattering hoofbeats. With sweaty palms and quavering heart, she contemplated the fact that she might be rushing headlong into heartbreak, for there was the chance that Emory had never meant those words he'd spoken in the library just before she left him. He might well have said them only to forestall her departure or until he had completed his conquest of her. Then too, had even that declaration of love been sincere, there was the possibility that in her absence Emory's ardor might have cooled. He simply might not want her now.

That thought devastated Rachel. Realistically, she knew she couldn't blame him if he had already turned away to find solace in some other who tended his wants, answered his needs. Emory was a man, a virile man, and Rachel had kept him at arm's length so very long. So much had happened that put distance between them, repeatedly, and the one thing that might have closed that distance had never come about.

As they neared the Hall, she fretted even more. Supposing that Emory cared not for her, wanted her not . . . what then? What if, even now, he was still anticipating his freedom from the marriage, was waiting patiently for some word from Tisbury that he already had it? He might be anticipating too, a return to that lifestyle he had so enjoyed until flagging finances and her presence at Guersten Hall had forced him to deny it . . . drinking, gambling, whoring. He might have already returned to it, perhaps was not even now present at the Hall. It was just possible that Rachel might find the estate abandoned yet again by its master, with old George and young Benjy left in the care of Stoddard and broken-hearted Edward, all of their fates and futures on the decline.

What will I do then? Pondered Rachel with faltering heart. Could she then leave again, abandoning them too . . . an invalided old man and her sister's child? Would she be reduced to waiting for Emory to appear, never knowing when he would come, or whether he would be sober when he did? Would she yearn for his kisses, hunger for caresses, and never know if he meant them or not? Would she? Could she?

"*Yes! Yes!*" she said to herself as the coach drew up under the porte cochere. I love them all . . . and I love him most of all, fully and completely! If that love now becomes bondage, chaining me inexorably to Guersten Hall forever, so be it. No matter what the future holds . . . *I am his!*

CHAPTER THIRTY-TWO

The wheels of the coach had barely stopped rolling before Rachel lifted the silver latch and leaped to the ground, leaving Horrick to see to the luggage. He tipped his hat in her direction by way of a polite good-bye as she hurried into the house, and then, since no one came to greet them, he deposited her trunk and two pieces of hand luggage just inside the heavy double doors. Having done so, he climbed back up to his seat, wheeled about, and drove the team and coach to the stables at Brenham Manor. In the five minutes he was in the drive of Guersten Hall, Horrick saw nary a soul, and none had spotted him or his coach, either.

Inside the mansion, Rachel stood at the foot of the grand stair-case, looking about. Everything sparkled, much as it had when she left, but there was a silence in the house that was unsettling. No one seemed to be about the place. Her heels clacked emptily on the polished marble as she scurried from room to room, searching for some member of the household . . . Angus, Stoddard . . . anybody. But there was no one, each room was as empty as the last, though Rachel noted in a quick perusal of each that nothing had been moved in her absence. Each piece of furniture, every object d'art sat just where it was on the day she left the Hall for London.

But then, entering the dining room, Rachel did discern some slight change. That room was empty, too, but the sideboard now held a footed tray upon which sat an assortment of brandy decanters. Spinning about, she hurried into the familiar library. It, too, was empty, and it, too, contained a variety of liquor bottles. Centered on the desk was a small round tray which held a single brandy bottle and a single glass. Behind the massive desk was a tall leather chair, which meant that Emory, or perhaps Edward, and not George, now used the desk regularly. Rachel guessed that the careful placement of the tray and its contents almost assured that it was Emory.

Touring the room, she found it otherwise unchanged, with nothing removed or re-positioned, until she crossed to the steps that led to the turreted platform. There, in the middle of the gateleg table that had served as her desk she spied another tray . . . another decanter, and another glass. Wine, this time.

The appearance of all those bottles and decanters alarmed Rachel. Was Emory drinking again? Was he using her gateleg desk for a wine table, as it appeared? Was it intended in any way to be a putdown of her? And if he was drinking, was he gambling also? Were their profits intact? Had he perhaps started on his Aunt Caroline's legacy, and the cash garnered from the sale of Abigail Prendergast's jewelry? And where were the servants? Had they been dismissed?

Troubled by these unanswered questions, Rachel headed back to the dining room, and passing through the serving pantry, came to a halt at the stairs that led down to Stoddard's kitchen. She called out, once . . . twice, but not a sound came up the stairwell. Nobody answered, nobody moved about below. She climbed the staircase to the second floor, only to find the upper rooms as deserted as the ones downstairs . . . George's room, the nursery . . . empty. Checking the salon, she chanced to look from the French windows across to the paddocks, and was very surprised to see Sultan there. The magnificent stallion stood alone near the fence; he was saddled, but appeared to be tethered in some way, something Rachel had never seen before. What did it all mean? Was Emory even now sleeping off a binge somewhere? In his room, perhaps?

She went directly there, and without bothering to knock, pushed open the door, certain that she would find him sprawled across the bed, snoring in sotted slumber. Instead, the room was vacant, quiet, with everything neatly in its place, from the unwrinkled bed to the picturesque seascapes that lined the walls. But Rachel's sharp eye did not miss the wine table standing in the center of the turret, on which stood another tray, another bottle, this one with a glass turned upside down over its neck.

Her concern grew to anger, anger that rose in her throat at the sight of that last bottle, and turning away, she sped off to her room, familiar with its cheery yellows and bright green. There, she removed her traveling clothes, determined to change into something comfortable, then to proceed onto the estate itself, learn what all this silence meant. Most of her day gowns were in the trunk sitting downstairs, and Rachel searched frantically for something light to wear. At first she found nothing, but then, turning, she spied her old leather breeches, laying on top of a small blanket chest. She pounced on them, and then set about finding a blouse of some sort, coming up with a brown tweed shirt. On a hook at the back of the wardrobe she was surprised to find her old cap, the same one she'd worn to confront Duggan's boys. Snatching it up, she left the room.

On impulse, Rachel returned to the salon again, this time stepping out onto the balcony. It was then that she spotted Stoddard in the yard below, weeding her little herb garden, close by the kitchen door.

"*Stoddard! Halloo!* Where is everybody?"

Straightening, Stoddard looked about, shielding her eyes with a hand.

"*Up here!*" cried Rachel. "Up on the balcony!"

Looking up, Stoddard spied Rachel, standing with her cap in her hand, and the older woman, recognizing those familiar breeches and high boots, gave a cry of happy surprise. Letting her hoe fall to the ground, she sped into the house.

Rachel ran to meet her, going so fast she nearly collided with the old cook when they both arrived in the serving pantry at the same time. They greeted each other with hugs and laughter.

"*Gor be!* I thought I be seein' things!"

"No, it's me . . . come back! But I'm puzzled. Where is everyone? George . . . Edward, Angus? Why is no one in the house? Where is Benjy? Where were you? Where are the maids?"

"Wait, wait, wait, Rachel! So many questions, and how you spew them out!" Effie laughed and caught her breath. "Everyone here," she said, waving her hand in a wide circle, "is out about the estate. George is out in his cart somewhere, happy to be watchin' the goin's-on. Edward is off in the woods, felling trees for the new sawmill, and all the house maids went to Coltenham to be fitted with new shoes. And I been pullin' weeds for nigh two hours!"

"And the baby?" inquired Rachel. "Where is little Benjy? His cradle is empty."

"Should think it is! Strappin' little buster outgrew that months back! Angus and Anna took him down to the park for a picnic, with their own two lads. They're all down under the willows by the stream."

"I see," said Rachel, her fears that something was wrong now allayed. "And where is . . . Emory?"

"Thought you'd never get around to asking," replied Stoddard, her pinched face softening under a broad smile. "Am I right in assuming he's the reason you came back?"

"Yes, Effie, he is! I discovered that I love him after all. Something Ermaline said made me see it quite unexpectedly, but I wonder just what I've come back to." A veil of doubt clouded Rachel's brown eyes, and she turned to the older woman with more questions.

"Is he . . . drinking again?" she asked guardedly. "Tell me, what does all this mean?" She pointed to all the decanters on the sideboard.

"I'll tell ye the truth," said Stoddard, speaking familiarly now, without bothering with the old formalities that marked their different stations. "Emory was drinking . . . heavily, for a while. The same day you left this house, in fact, he ordered all of the decanters put back. He was master, and I had no choice but to obey. He was heartbroken when you left, dear, and he drank himself silly trying to forget it until Edward came home. One night at dinner, Edward made him see that drinking was not the way to handle his grief. He told Emory that you had made *him* understand that he must bury his grief in work, and so must Emory.

"Winter had waned by then," continued Effie, "and it was nearing time to start the plowing again. Emory set aside his bottles, and the only wine he's taken since then is with his meals. He works day and night in the fields, has planted far more than you did last year, and is now badgerin' the old Warrenton sisters for their land so that he might plant even more. He is determined to double your success."

"And why is that?" asked Rachel. "Is there need for the extra capital, or is it just to best me?"

"Lord, no! Neither one! Emory just admits that you were right. An estate this size should not lie unproductive. It's that simple."

"How do you know this? He tells you?"

"Gor, no!" scoffed Stoddard, "but it is all they talk about, night after night at the table. T'would do your heart good to hear them," she added contentedly, "old George and his sons, banterin' back and forth with nary a cross word between 'em."

"I see," said Rachel softly. "Then all is well, after all?"

"It will be, now you're back, dearie."

"Then, why this? Why leave all these decanters placed so conspicuously?"

"Emory declared they were not to be moved. Apparently their presence helped him prove that he could get along without the drink, just as he got along . . ."

Stoddard paused, said no more, leaving her sentence unfinished, but Rachel did not have to hear those words to know what they were.

"Without me. Is that what you were going to say? Be honest, Effie, please. I must know what he . . . feels."

"He says nothing of what he feels. Nothing."

Rachel turned away, pensive, idly studying the dishes that lined the wall of the serving pantry. A colorful array, the numerous patterns and trademarks represented the best that England's potteries had to offer.

"He is well?" she asked at last, turning once again to face the cook.

"Aye, physically and mentally, but in here, I'm not so sure," Effie said, pointing a long finger at her own heart. "I hear him pacing in the night, and many's the morn I find his bed unused. Then, too, him and black are out constantly, whatever the weather."

Quite unexpectedly, watery tears flooded Stoddard's eyes. "Do you mean to stay, Rachel? If not . . . go now! Don't torture my lad!" she blurted. With that, she whirled, clattering down the wooden steps to her kitchen below, wiping her eyes as she went. It took Rachel some minutes to recover from the suddenness of the outburst, but then she ran down the steps after the cook. In the kitchen she found Effie sobbing by the larder wall, fallen to pieces by her own outburst.

"Stoddard!"

"I'm sorry, ma'am," said the weeping woman with humility. "I had no right to speak so. Please forgive me."

"It's all right," consoled Rachel, drawing the weeping woman close. "I understand that you spoke because you love him, too . . . have loved him for so many years. Because you do, I will tell you now, Effie, that by my return I am committed. For better or worse, I am home to stay . . . if he will have me."

That grand news set Stoddard to weeping anew; tears of joy this time, and Rachel was thankful when she collected herself again.

"Where will I find him?"

"Just beyond the dairy," cried Stoddard, her face brightening. "He's working on a new irrigation ditch there."

"But was that not his horse I saw tethered in the paddock."

"Aye. Sultan makes the cows skittish and it interferes with their milk. He was tied so he wouldn't follow after Emory, who went on foot. Now go to him," she said, herding Rachel out the door.

"Is Hunter available?" inquired Rachel.

"I believe Edward had him saddled just after lunch," stated the cook, her back turned, already making preparations for Rachel's homecoming dinner.

Not deterred by the fact that Hunter was already out, Rachel hurried off to the stables, assuming that some other mount would be available . . . Makira, perhaps. But Makira was gone, too. In fact, all the riders and hunters were gone from their stalls, and the stables were as empty as the house.

Vexed, Rachel leaned against the paddock gate. *Damn!* she thought, confounded by the lack of a mount. Why now, when her heart was aflutter with eagerness to see Emory again. Now, when she was so anxious to throw her arms about his neck and declare her love. Her conversation with Stoddard had made Rachel jubilant. Emory was well . . . everything was well, and he had missed her! Rachel was sure now that his earlier words of love were not false. He did love her! He did want her! And he would welcome her back!

It was then that Sultan snorted, loudly, almost as if he would be noticed. When Rachel turned in his direction, the stallion flicked his inky tail and whickered, the sound softer this time. He stood still, without flinching or prancing, as Rachel approached the fence.

"Aaah, Sultan! How grand you look! And what is this I hear . . . that you skitter the cows?"

I don't blame them, she thought, standing by the high fence. You are a fearful beast! Magnificent, yes, but fearful all the same.

She watched the black warily, and then, eyeing her in return, Sultan did a strange thing. Stepping forward, he came very close to where Rachel stood, until only the boards of the fence separated them. Then, with his great maned head, he nudged her, once . . . twice.

"What's this?" said Rachel in surprise, stroking his black nose. "After all this time you want to be friends? Is that because you know I love him, too, or are you only trying to entice me into loosing that tether? I know you don't like it." She touched the leather strap that held Sultan securely to the post, already bitten halfway through.

"You know where he is, don't you, Sultan? If I untied you, you'd be away in a minute. Would you take me to him? Are we friends enough for that? Can I trust you?"

Can I trust myself? she thought. *Am I truly rid of all my childhood fears, that I might ride such a beast as this? What if I am thrown? But no,* she said to herself positively. *I ride well enough, and Sultan will take me to Emory. I will chance it, for I must see him! My heart can wait no longer!*

Tucking her hair under her flatcap, Rachel climbed the board fence, and sitting on the top rail, leaned forward to pick up Sultan's tether, tugging at it hesitantly. Obediently, the great beast moved to her side. She had forgotten how huge he was, nearly as tall as the fence itself; all she need do is throw a leg over, and she would be able to drop right into the saddle. She did it quickly, before his intimidating size stripped away her courage.

Emory's saddle was uncomfortable, the seat much too wide, the stirrups too long. The stallion stood placidly while Rachel fitted her feet into them anyway.

"Now," she said, speaking to the back of Sultan's neck, "after I untie this strap, I'll lift the latch to the gate. Then, we'll be away in search of Emory."

With his ears laid back, Sultan stood perfectly still, appearing to be listening intently to Rachel's voice if not her words, but he remained still only until the very moment she loosed the leather strap. Then, without warning, he bolted.

The long legged stallion had no need for gates and latches! In a half dozen strides he was at full gallop, pounding across the paddock to the far fence, while Rachel held her breath and pressed her knees into his side to keep her seat. Crouched low in the saddle, she shortened the rein, anticipating that Sultan would jump the fence.

Jump he did, soaring effortlessly over the top, to land nicely on the other side, barely breaking stride, and then he was away in earnest, galloping down the dirt road at an even faster pace in search of his master while Rachel held on for dear life. The black's long mane came to life in the rushing wind, and it rose from his neck to wave in Rachel's face until she could barely see where she was going.

She remained low in the saddle, simply because that position was more comfortable. She relaxed now, exhilarated by the stallion's superb strength and great speed. His powerful muscles flexed and rippled under her thighs as together, they made their way across the back of the estate. The initial surge of fright she had experienced when Sultan bolted was now gone, though admittedly it was a toss-up whether she actually rode the black, or whether he merely carried her to Emory's side.

Thundering through the orchards at full tilt, she saw the workers there from the corner of her eye, dropping their tools and racing to the edge of the road to watch them pass, all of them certain that it must be a runaway horse. Vainly, one or two of them chased after the black, eating his dust for their trouble, for Sultan was out of sight in only a moment.

Just ahead, a rutted wagon track veered off to the left side of the road, and the stallion turned onto instinctively, choosing a route that led directly down the grassy strip running between the wheel ruts. Sultan, it appeared, knew the estate as well as Emory, who was not far from them at this moment, busy positioning boulders across a stream to form a small dam. When he heard the sound of galloping hoofbeats, he straightened from his labors.

"*Jesus Christ!*" he said aloud when he spied his own stallion bearing down on him. "Some damned dolt is tired of living!"

Watching the cloud of dust as it neared, Emory raised two fingers to his lips and whistled loudly. Sultan heard it, but he had already spotted his master, and his pace never slowed, not even when he reached the water's edge. Instead, he splashed right into the stream and started across to Emory's side, as Rachel, still bending low, hung on even more tightly, as midstream, she felt one foot slip from its stirrup, just as Emory shouted.

"*Whoaa! Halt!*"

On the spot, Sultan, ever obedient to his master's commands, halted, planting his feet on the stream's sandy bottom. When he did so, Rachel sailed out of the saddle, landing facedown in a foot and a half of water, one foot twisted in the stirrup. Unconcerned, Sultan bent and drank deeply from the cool stream.

Dunked thoroughly, Rachel raised herself up, rolling over onto her back as best she could, supporting herself uncomfortably on her elbows. In the process, her boot twisted even more, and only the fact that it was half off her foot saved her ankle from being snapped. With one hand, she reached up and removed her sodden cap. Rivers of water ran from it, and loosed from its confinement, her wet hair coiled limply around her shoulders, all semblance of coiffure or curl gone.

Emory stood on the bank, above her. With his jaw fallen open, and his arms slack at his side, he stared dumbly at the half drowned apparition that had dropped into the water before him, as futilely, Rachel tugged at the caught boot, attempting to free her foot, which remained solidly locked in the stirrup.

"Damn you, Emory Guersten! Now look what you've done!"

Rachel's furious words, hurled up at him, dispelled Emory's surprised look, and he advanced to the very edge of the bank. There, he planted his feet firmly on the grass, and placing his hands on his hips, stood looking down at Rachel, his green eyes sparkling mischievously.

"Well, well, well! It's you!"

"Of course it's me! And don't just stand there! Loose my foot!"

Not moving, Emory threw back his head and laughed his booming laugh, the sound of it full and filled with jollity. His obvious glee at her hapless predicament maddened Rachel all the more, and she flung her sodden cap at him. It sailed limply over the water, to fall short of its mark, landing harmlessly at his feet with a wet *plop*. Amused, Emory's laughter boomed again.

"Get me out of here!"

"Here, here, Rachel! You haven't even said hello, yet you're already spouting orders!"

"Well, what do you expect? If you hadn't whistled or shouted at Sultan I wouldn't be sitting here in the middle of your damned pond!"

"I only meant to rescue you! Sultan can be dangerous. You might have been killed!"

"I do ride, you know, and rather well! Now stop jawing and get me out of here!"

"Oh, but you still haven't said hello!"

Rachel glared up at him, her furor mounting. She was wet, she was cold, and besides, beneath her, a good sized stone was cutting into her backside.

"All right, all right! *Helloandallthatrot!* Now come loose my boot!"

But Emory was enjoying the moment, and used it to advantage, playing his game. "Just one moment, my dear. This is a perfect time for you and I to have a talk is it not? You can't run away, and you'll have to listen to what I have to say, eh?"

"Damn you!" she shouted up at him.

"Tut, tut, my dear," he said. "We can't talk if you continue to shout. And take care you don't make Sultan nervous. If he moves you might be dunked again." Rubbing his chin with one hand, Emory pretended a pensive gesture. "Hmm. Perhaps I should whistle again, let him drag you here to my feet."

"Damn you, damn you, damn you!" screamed Rachel, even louder this time.

But Sultan did not move, never flinched, although his ears raised and lowered as Rachel and Emory shouted at one another across the water. Her arms were growing tired, and whenever she relaxed even a little, the stream's sparkling water gurgled and bubbled uncomfortably close to her chin.

Emory now knelt on the bank, and despite her fury and her discomfort, Rachel couldn't help noticing how very handsome he was. She raised her face, studying him with her brown eyes. Typically, his shirt was unbuttoned nearly to the waist, the sleeves rolled above his elbows, and he was wearing taut riding breeches and brown boots. Tall and powerful, his muscular frame was hewn to perfection by exercise and hard work, and he was well browned from hours in the open sun. Emory had always disdained hats, and now his face, with its high forehead, was especially well tanned, all except for the jagged three inch scar over his left eye. That taut tissue remained unshaded, and now appeared white in contrast to the bronzed flesh that surrounded it. Black wavy hair formed a thick cap around his head, and under it, those green, green eyes glinted back at her.

From his vantage point on the bank Emory, in his turn, studied Rachel. The open necked shirt she wore had fallen away from her throat and the crystal clear water lapped enticingly at her breasts. Her long hair lay in wet coils across her shoulders, and he knew the well soaked leather breeches were probably cold and clammy by now. Her face, with its creamy complexion and velvety skin was just as he remembered it, for every graceful curve had been etched into his memory on a misty moonlight night long ago. But no, he decided, gazing at her sprawled form, his heart and mind had not served him well, after all. Here, now, disheveled and soaking wet, with curls askew and fury in her eyes, his Rachel was more beautiful than ever before, if that was possible.

Sultan snorted, breaking the silence.

"So!" Emory said, standing up. "You have returned!"

"Yes," she replied. "I have returned."

Dropping from the bank, Emory waded into the stream to stand over her, looking down.

"You've been gone a long time. What brought you back?"

"Really, Emory! Don't play the fool. You know perfectly well what brought me back."

"I do," he said evenly, "but I want to hear you say it."

Rachel pressed her lips together and squirmed, as the hard stone bit again into her bottom.

"Say it!" he bellowed, bending even closer.

"All right!" shouted Rachel in return. "I am your wife! I came back because I need you."

"And?" he thundered.

"And because I want you!" Shouting at the top of her lungs now, Rachel damned him mentally as the cold water lapped again at her chin.

"Aaaaah, and what if I refuse to take you back, eh? Perhaps I no longer want you! Have you considered that?"

"But you *must* take me back, Emory!" cried Rachel in a panic as he teased her with those dreaded words. "I know now I cannot live without you! I will be your proper wife, your mistress, even . . . anything, only tell me that you want me too!"

"Aaaaah! Much better, my dear, much better! Perhaps I might take you back after all. But first, there are some conditions to be met, and you must agree to them."

Before him, Rachel squirmed uneasily, and not just because of her uncomfortable position or that blasted stone. Emory would have his moment! His game! She was trapped, and defeated, nodded her ahead in agreement.

"I am your husband!" he thundered once again. "And I will be obeyed! *I* will wear the trousers in this household! Those damned leather pants must go!" he added, slapping her leg familiarly.

"But I need them!" said Rachel curtly, shifting her weight again in a vain attempt to be comfortable. "I cannot ride without them. Surely, you can't expect me to go back to a lady's saddle after all this time."

"The pants go!" repeated Emory. "Get yourself one of those new split riding skirts."

"All right, all right!" said Rachel in exasperation. "Just get my foot out of this blasted stirrup!"

Smug and satisfied that he had made Rachel openly admit her need and acknowledge him as her master, Emory turned to set about freeing her boot from Sultan's stirrup. He bent forward, his back to her, reaching across her extended leg to fumble with her boot. When she felt her foot beginning to slide from the boot at last, she raised her free leg and, placing her foot against Emory's inviting backside, gave him a push. From her position in the middle of the stream, it was a feeble push, one without strength behind it, and Emory never would have fallen had Sultan not moved just then.

But Sultan did move, just as Emory leaned forward to brace himself against the stallion's flanks with an outstretched arm. When his support vanished, Emory pitched headlong into nothingness, to land with a sizeable splash, just as Rachel had done moments before, facedown in the rippling water.

He came up spluttering with indignant rage, brought about by the fact that Rachel had gotten the best of him. With her foot now free, she sat up, laughing merrily at his discomfort, chortling even more when Sultan raised his black-maned head and snorted loudly.

"Now what the hell did you do that for?" Emory bellowed.

"You may consider it a warning! Don't resume your childish game of intimidation, for each time you do, I shall even the score!"

Suddenly both of them were laughing, and just as suddenly, the laughter stopped. Rachel's brown eyes searched his green ones. She saw mirrored there all the love that Emory's heart could no longer contain, no longer hide. Their eyes locked, and that magic something that is love, known, seen, and heard only by lovers, descended upon them, covering them as solidly as if it were a blanket.

"I knew you'd be back," said Emory in a choked voice. "Duncan told me . . . some weeks ago."

"Ah! And something he said led you to believe I would drop in . . . like this?"

"He merely said you would return, sooner or later, when your heart spoke."

Emory clambered to his feet, splashing water all over Rachel, and coming to stand over her, he gave her a long look, one heavy and charged with emotion as lightning charged the night sky, and then he extended both his hands to her. Rachel reached out for them, and he pulled her gently to her feet.

They stood close together in the stream, while rivers of water poured from their clothing and Rachel's boots overflowed. Gathering her into his arms, Emory bent to kiss her. Their wet lips met and were warmed by love, for that gentle kiss became a declaration of their love for each other. It was a pledge, a seal of love, like no other kiss they had ever shared before. Its surface was gentle, filled with tenderness, and spoke of love that flooded their hearts, while its depth hinted boldly of the wild and abandoned passion that they would share in bodily union later.

"I love you, Emory. I love you," said Rachel breathlessly, as her arms went about her husband's wide shoulders. They were simple words, timeworn words, and they had been said so many times before, but not by her, and not to him. They were old words, words that passed from Rachel's lips, but they came from her heart, and that made them new . . . her gift to him. And being new, they brought such joy to him who heard them, and brought equal joy to her who spoke them, for in speaking them, Rachel became a woman.

CHAPTER THIRTY-THREE

Arm in arm, they finally waded from the stream, both of them dripping wet. Once on the bank, Emory swept Rachel into his arms again, kissing her willing lips repeatedly.

"Aaah!" he said. "We've been such fools, Rachel! We've wasted so much time!"

"I know," she replied, lifting her face for another kiss, "but we've saved our marriage, and the best is yet to come."

"That it is!" agreed Emory, emitting a lascivious chuckle that made Sultan lift his head. A strange look darkened Emory's flashing eyes; they became sober and serious. "Oh, how I love you, Rachel," he said to her passionately. "I think now that I've always loved you. Why I denied it . . . fought it, I cannot say, but this I do know, my love. I may err now and again, and I may try your patience upon occasion, but I will always love you. Never lose sight of it. Beyond that, I will try my damndest to make you happy."

"That you love me makes me happy," sighed Rachel. "And that you still want me makes me ecstatic. I will love you in return, completely, and try not to judge . . ."

"You were right to judge, Rachel. I know that now, too. I was always halfway between here and nowhere, and I had to learn that. I had trapped myself somewhere in the middle, but now I'm rescued by your love." Suddenly, he pulled her roughly against his length. "Don't ever leave me again!" he said in her ear, almost vehemently.

"I won't, I promise," she whispered, gazing up at him happily. In her eyes, Emory could see what Edward had seen in Rebecca's . . . what all who love can see when love is returned.

"Come," Emory said huskily, "before I take you behind yon bush! Let us find the others. They deserve to share my happiness."

With ease, Emory lifted her onto his saddle, hoisting himself up behind her. She snuggled against him, content to be enveloped in his love as Sultan galloped away across the fields.

They encountered the two old men first, George and Gaffy, their little carts parked side by side in the sun, where it was bright and warm. Daily, from their padded seats, they surveyed the estate in their roles as silent overseers. Now, hearing Sultan's approaching hoofbeats, they turned in those seats, almost in unison. At first, given the distance, neither of them sighted Rachel, cradled close in Emory's arms, but when she spotted them, she shouted and waved her arms wildly. George, whose old eyes were a mite sharper than Gaffy's, saw the streaming brown hair and the smile that wreathed Emory's face. Only one person could have returned that smile to his son's lips, and George knew at once who it was.

"She's back!" he cried out, waving his walking stick excitedly in the air with his good arm. "She's back! Our girl is home again!"

Struggling to hold back happy tears, Rachel slid from Emory's arms, running across the grass to hug and kiss them both.

"Praise God!" said George, bobbing his white head up and down merrily. "You've saved my lad from a life of loneliness."

"No," said Rachel, teary eyed. "Love saved us both from that awful fate."

"The graft took, after all," she whispered into Gaffy's ear a moment later.

"Aye! Hoped it would! Some take longer than others, girl, but they're all the stronger for it."

Emory, who had not left his saddle, became impatient to show Rachel all that he had accomplished on his own and, reaching down, lifted her before him again, encircling her waist possessively with both arms. His happiness, as she nestled against him, was plain for all to see, and it added to the old men's joy.

Curious, Gaffy pointed a finger to the water still dripping from their clothes. "Thet must've been some reunion! Wish't I'd been there!" he said with a sagacious grin, slapping his thigh.

Rachel put both arms around Emory's waist and held on tightly. "Just say, we came to an understanding . . . in the middle of the stream!" She laughed. "He has promised to abandon his games, and I think I promised to be an obedient wife."

"And I shall dunk her again and again whenever it becomes necessary!" chimed Emory in mock fierceness as he turned Sultan. "And now we're off . . . I'm going to give Rachel a grand tour."

"I want to see how well he took care of my cabbages!"

But there was no question of Emory's competence these days, for there were visible signs of it everywhere at the Hall. A number of additions and improvements he had made attested to his attentiveness, and now there was a new road cut through the woods, one that intersected with the Peterborough road, which saved time on the many daily runs made to Duggan's tommy shop.

After viewing the sawmill and tearfully greeting a sober and thinner Edward, Emory pointed out a new building, erected just where the old makeshift loading shed had once stood within the tight circle of beeches that ringed Guersten Hall's best fields. The long wooden building was a combination of packing house and loading shed, and one corner was piled high with new crates of white wood. The end of each was marked with a colorful label that read *Guersten Brothers*, with all the letters circled neatly inside a ring of beeches.

"I'm glad that you included Edward," Rachel told Emory, viewing the labels with pride. "It must have pleased your father."

"It did," he said, "and all the egg crates at River Park carry that same marking. Edward has always loved this place, and had I set a better example, we two might had accomplished this years ago, and besides, he has worked as hard as any toward its success, while I am only a late comer on that score. Somehow, *Guersten Brothers* just seemed fitting."

Everyone on the estate was made happy by Rachel's return, and under the willows in the park she was greeted with smiles by Angus and Anna, kisses by Stevens's two young daughters, and strained reserve by little Benjy and MacKinder's two sons, none of them at all sure who she was. But Benjy's restraint broke, shrewd little lad that he was, when he decided that Rachel's presence made Uncle Emory smile a lot, and at last he relented and allowed Rachel to lift him. Moments later, in fact, he clutched at her with sturdy little arms as the three of them piled on Sultan's back and rode away up to the manor house.

Dinner that evening was a happy and high-spirited affair, replete with Stoddard's best. There was salmon and game fowl served with a bread sauce, and tender beef cooked to perfection. With it were tender new vegetables from their own fields, and delicious strawberry tarts to finish the fare.

No sooner had they left the dining room than Emory led Rachel into the paneled library, kicking the door shut with one foot. When it closed behind them, they were in each other's arms, Rachel's lips melting passionately under his.

"What do you think should happen now?" Emory asked in a jesting tone as he pressed Rachel closer.

"I assume," she said, offering her lips for another kiss, "that tonight we will seal our marriage with love, but if you need to ask, dear husband, then perhaps we have a problem."

"There is indeed a problem," Emory said, his voice suddenly quite sober. "And it has to do with the way I feel," he added, ushering Rachel onto the long sofa before the fireplace.

He crowded close beside her. "I want to marry you!"

Rachel laughed delightedly, still supposing he jested. "What game is this you tease me with?" she asked. "We *are* married, and well you know it!"

"You may be, but Hugh took my place that day, and there is the rub. I want to stand beside you myself, speak my own vows of matrimony."

Rachel searched Emory's serious face, and what she saw there told her that he was not jesting. Proclaiming Rachel to be his bride, his wife, before God and all mankind was suddenly terribly important to him, and it showed. With tenderness, she laid her fingertips against his warm lips.

"The unpleasantries that once stood in the path of our love are all but forgotten now, dear love. In years to come, perhaps we will even laugh about them. All that matters now is that I love you and that you love me. I am already your wife, Emory, but if it's important to you to speak your own vows, then by all means send for the vicar. I am honored that you care."

"I do care, and it is important to me. Everything is in its proper perspective at last. I cannot love you more, Rachel, but let us go back and begin again."

Emory's strange proposal of sorts was sealed with another long and passionate kiss, after which Rachel snuggled into his arms, deliriously happy.

"So until the vicar comes, I am yet to sleep alone, eh, my sweet?" she asked, not bothering to hide her disappointment.

"I weighed that mightily, love, for all those days and nights you were gone did little to quell the passion that even now consumes me. How I ache for you! But," he said, grinning, "it will be for this one night only, I saw to that. I sent word away while you dressed for dinner. The vicar comes tomorrow . . . early."

"Tomorrow? Oh, but what will I wear? The best of my frocks are still in London!"

"Come with me!" said Emory excitedly. "I have something to show you!"

Jumping to his feet, he led Rachel from the library and up the marble stairs, taking them two at a time as she raced to keep up.

"Wait, wait!" she cried at the top, falling breathless into his arms. "What is it you would show me?"

Without a word, Emory took Rachel to the door of the square bedchamber beside the salon. Rachel's laughter disappeared, replaced by a frown, as Emory reached for the doorknob.

"Were you here earlier," he asked, "when you were searching for us all?"

"No," replied Rachel. "It was the one room I avoided. I'd hoped to avoid it even now."

"You cannot, Rachel. You are mistress here. This room is yours to occupy, by right of station."

"I know that," she whispered, clutching at his coat front, "and in time I suppose I will. But it is such a dark room, and it is where we lost Rebecca."

"It is also where we gained Benjy, remember? In a way, this room is the lifeblood of the estate, for its future lies with its women."

Rachel's face became a little crestfallen. "What you say is true, and yet . . . I'd hoped not to have to spend our first night . . . here."

"I considered all that, and remembering that in almost every room in this house we've had our little sallies, I thought it better for us both to have our first union take place somewhere else, someplace that will hold only those memories we bring to it."

"Oh, Emory! That sounds perfect! What do you have in mind? And where?"

"We'll travel up to Greycliffe, Adele's seaside home. The season hasn't started, and we'll be all alone there, except for the housekeeper. We can stay a few days and then return, and when we do, you will truly be my wife, mistress of this great Hall."

The frown and the dark mood were gone, and Rachel's eyes reflected her ecstatic bliss. "Perhaps then I'll consider this room," she said, "after I've brightened it some! Now show me your surprise!"

The furniture in the darkened bedroom was shrouded in wraps. Emory steered Rachel to a far corner near one of the windows. There, he drew open the drapes, positioning Rachel before a triple-folding screen. Behind it stood a mannequin, fully enveloped in white sheeting, and standing close to her, Emory put his arms around Rachel's waist.

"When I learned from Duncan that you would return to me, I went to see Mrs. Scofield at her London shoppe . . ."

"Eleanora? But we are friends! She said nothing to me of your visit."

"Simply because I asked her not to." Carefully, Emory unwound the wide swath of sheeting, then he stepped back, dropping the cloth on the floor behind them, as Rachel gasped in stunned surprise. "At my request and suggestions, Eleanora executed this creation just for you. It is my gift to you, Rachel."

On the mannequin was a wedding dress, a gown so extraordinarily beautiful that it literally took Rachel's breath away. Made of pristine silk-faced satin, it covered the mannequin from top to toe in whiteness. The high scalloped collar and set-in yoke were fashioned of Italian lace, its pattern of leafy fans heavily beaded with tiny pearls. The bodice and the front of the wide skirt were appliquéd and beaded similarly, and a delicate edging of pearled lace whispered its way around the circular hem.

Peaked and belled, the oversleeves ended at the elbow, edged with the same trim that adorned the hem, and extended over long close-fitting sleeves of more beaded lace to end at the wrist. As a finishing touch, twenty-seven tiny satin buttons paraded downward from the waistline to meet one of the beaded fans adorning the skirt.

Rachel was left speechless by the sight of the dress, her surprise greatly enhanced by the fact that Emory had ordered it especially for her, had suggested its design, and had lived on the hope that she would one day return to the Hall to wear it. Turning, she flung herself wildly into his arms and was received there joyously.

"Oh, Emory! I don't know what to say," she said, almost in tears, quite moved that claiming her as his bride meant so much to him.

He kissed her lips lightly. "It is a symbol of my love," he said throatily into her hair. "Wear it tomorrow . . . for me."

That night Rachel occupied her yellow-and-green bedroom, next to Emory's turreted one, for the last time. Half the night he pounded on the wall that separated them, and they laughed about it, remembering all the other times he had done the same thing. Twice, they met in the hallway between their doors to exchange passionate kisses, and in the morning, Rachel was out of bed early, eager for the day to begin.

After bathing, she dressed her hair in a high upsweep, to allow the scalloped lace at her throat to set off her slender neck. She felt quite beautiful after slipping into the cool satin of Emory's gift. Carefully fastening the family heirlooms in place, she screwed the pearl eardrops into her ears and clasped the heavy pearl pendant about her neck. The luminous gem lay positioned perfectly, sitting at exactly that spot where the lace yoke ended and the swell of her breasts began.

She was ready and, with pounding heart, headed for the stairs, blushing under the emotional stares of Stoddard and a gathering of maids. At the bottom of the marble stairs Emory waited for her, handsome all in black, with the ruffles of a lacy jabot spilling over a white brocaded waistcoat.

As for him, his pulse raced as he watched her descend the long stairs and come to stand beside him. As always, he was awed by her beauty, and someday, he was thinking, he would have Landseer paint her portrait in that dress. Reaching out, she touched his cheek with cool fingers, and he clutched at them, holding them tightly in his.

"I thought the music room appropriate," he said at last, finding his voice. "The vicar waits for us there, but first, come into the library with me. I have one more gift for you."

There, Emory removed a large white box from the desk, handing it to Rachel without ceremony. Inside, on a bed of white satin, was a platinum-and-diamond coronet, one Rachel recognized immediately, though she'd never seen it before then, for it matched exactly, in beauty and craftsmanship, the pendant that lay about her throat.

"The Guersten coronet!" she exclaimed. "Wherever did you find it? Your father was positive it had been melted down long ago and the stones sold!"

"I feared as much myself," admitted Emory, "but a friend at Sotheby's spread the word that I wanted it back intact. It turned up at Christie's only recently. Father agreed that we should recover it, though what we were forced to pay for its return was damned near ransom! But I would have paid twice that price, for I wanted you to wear it with that dress."

Emory took the glittering coronet from Rachel's hands and, stepping before her, placed it carefully upon her head. He spoke not a word, for none were needed, and their lips met in a seal of love.

"Now," he said, "let us go. We've let the vicar cool his heels long enough."

"Wait, Emory! I have a gift for you, though nothing so grand," Rachel said. Smiling, she signaled him to follow and went to the glass-fronted bookcases, where she removed the Guersten family book. From it she withdrew a folded sheet, handing it over to him. Emory groaned audibly, but smiled broadly, recognizing the paper even before he unfolded that letter of proxy he had scribbled to his father, just hours before running away from Rachel.

"I thought perhaps you might like to have it back."

"I certainly do! I've searched for it several times, wanting to destroy it."

"It was here, all the time," said Rachel, touching the family ledger, her eyes twinkling. "You mean to say you don't want to save it . . . to show your heirs?"

"Hell, no! I'm not about to admit my foolishness to my grandchildren one day!"

Promptly, Emory put a match to the document, casting it into the fireplace. In silence, they watched it burn.

"Nothing you could have given me today could mean more," he said. "With that dratted paper now turned to ashes, my foolish past is truly behind me. Today I feel like a bridegroom, and tonight I'll truly be a husband."

Emory was transformed, and not just by the words he uttered, and Rachel saw him in a whole new light. Never before had she seen him quite so serious, and she knew then just how important this day was to him. Rachel had been married on a snowy winter day well more than a year ago, but today, June the fifteenth, would forever after be Emory's wedding day, and taking up a feathered quill, Rachel opened the heavy tome once more and recorded the date, and its significance, on a blank page. Pleased, Emory blotted the page, and together they went to the music room.

The ceremony was brief and private. Only George and Edward, of all the household, were allowed to enter the little room, and only one small basket of garden blooms marked the affair with any color. Rachel had chosen Stoddard, who loved them both, to stand as her witness, as Edward would for Emory, and just now, Emory was almost as somber and serious as the musty old vicar himself.

But his solemn mood was short-lived, to be replaced by his natural jollity when the dark robed cleric creaked up to Rachel. The man was instantly confused, registering a frown that furrowed his brow as he peered over wire spectacles at her.

"Did I not wed thee already to a tall young man who wears a dark mustache?"

"That was my sister, Rebecca, good vicar," replied Rachel courteously, while smothering a smile.

"And my brother, Edward," chimed Emory.

"About a year ago," clarified Rachel.

"That was the lass we lost," remarked George softly to the vicar, from his position behind them.

"Aaaah," said the vicar. "I remember now." Still, he continued to study Rachel further, rather pointedly, and finally, lifting a bony finger, stabbed the air with it.

"Before that then," he said to her, "did I not join thee in wedlock on a winter day with an older man . . . a rather rotund gentleman?"

"That was indeed me," said Rachel, "but the gentleman in question was Sir Hugh Chandler . . .."

"Who is my uncle," interrupted Emory.

"Sir Hugh graciously stood as proxy for my son that day," George explained for the vicar's sake.

"Aaaah," muttered the vicar again in his croaky voice, as though he understood, which he did not. With his finger, he seesawed back and forth, pointing first at Rachel, then to Emory. "Then I have wed thee . . . and thee . . . already?"

"Yes, sir," answered Rachel, smiling openly now.

"No sir!" said Emory with emphasis, at exactly the same moment. "I have never exchanged vows with any woman. I wish to do so now."

The stooped clergyman turned away from Emory, and stepping closer to Rachel, spoke directly to her.

"Is this man your husband or is he not?" he inquired over the rim of his glasses, pointing in Emory's direction.

"He is," said Rachel in a clear voice.

The vicar then cocked his head and looked up at Emory, who towered over him.

"Then the two of you are already married, are you not?"

"She is," said Emory, "but I feel not to be. It is why you were summoned."

The confused elder called to his assistant for a chair, sitting down heavily when it was brought.

"Dear me," he said to himself. "I married them, but they are not wed. How can that be?"

To resolve the man's confusion, George rolled himself to the beleaguered vicar's side, and using his fingers, explained as best he could how two sisters, and two brothers, forming only two couples, needed three wedding ceremonies to achieve a proper state of matrimony. The old cleric's head bobbed up and down as he watched George's fingers recite the litany of numbers, and finally, with a what-does-it-matter shrug, he creaked from his chair and joined Rachel and Emory again in holy wedlock.

Afterward, while Rachel and Emory struggled to withhold their laughter, the man departed, rather hastily, convinced at last that he was growing old. He was seen slumped into a corner of his carriage, while his assistant sat straight and tall beside him, as befits a man soon to be appointed vicar.

After a happy wedding breakfast in the dining room, Rachel and Emory changed and prepared to set off for Norwich, with Sultan and Hunter tethered behind their carriage. Before pulling away from the porte cochere though, Rachel went to kneel at her father-in-law's side. The white haired old man sat in his wheelchair in the long gallery waiting to say good-bye to her. His round face beamed pinkly.

"My happiness knows no bounds," he whispered to Rachel, brushing her cheek with his lips. "I knew it would all work out one day, and I'm glad you both found love. Just the same," he added, "I'm beholden to you for saving Emory. Until you came into his life he was like a branch, fallen from our family tree. Thanks to you, and your love for each other, new life has been sparked into the decaying branch, and miraculously, it is healthy once more. It bodes well for the future, my dear, a future that you and Emory will shape together. Now be off . . . love has its own rewards, and you will find them at Greycliffe, I'm sure."

With a wave, the lovers set off from Guersten Hall, making their way toward Greycliffe excitedly, both of them caught up by their mutual love and the anticipation of uninterrupted time there.

"Will we really be all alone?" inquired Rachel, lovely in a mauve colored traveling outfit and a ribbon trimmed bonnet.

"All alone, except for the housekeeper and her son," said Emory happily, smothering her face with kisses again and again.

The morning swept away, and the journey neared its end with neither of them taking any real notice of the lovely countryside, so absorbed in each other were they. Just past Norwich, they traveled through a sleepy hamlet situated by a little harbor carved by nature's hand along the shore. Perched alone on a cliffed promontory above it sat Greycliffe, squat and square, its gardens sloping clear to the cliff's lip on one side, and to the very edge of the Norfolk woods on the other. In front, a wide swath of green ran around the house, well dotted with wind-swept plantings and flowering shrubs. Flocks of noisy gulls dipped and careened over the water, chattering incessantly all the while, and overhead, more white breasted birds soared, then glided downward on the wind.

In the yard, Emory took their luggage into the house himself, and he charmed the old housekeeper off her feet, as he always had, smacking her cheek and swinging her into the air. Her son turned out to be a slow-witted man of fifty, at least, a solemn creature so awed by Rachel that he never spoke a word to her the entire time she remained at Greycliffe, and old Berta herself had been alone in the house by the sea so long that most of the time she retreated into a world of her own. She maintained a decent house, though, and their meals would be hot, tasty, and on time, however informal they were.

"Shall I open two bedrooms?" asked Berta coyly, when Emory introduced Rachel as his wife, "or just one?" Since their arrival was virtually unheralded, every room in the house was closed and shuttered.

"One will do, you scamp!" said Emory to the housekeeper, laughing. "And make it my old one . . . on the third floor." Fishing into a wicker basket, he retrieved a bottle of champagne and handed it to Berta. "Chill this good," he advised, "and prepare a simple supper for us. Remember, though, it is our nuptial supper . . . give it care. While you're accomplishing all that, I'm going to take Rachel down and show her my beach."

They went on foot after Emory had stabled the horses, winding their way hand in hand down the steep path that led from the cliff to the beach below. Enraptured with each other, they spent the better part of the afternoon there, tramping the sands, wading in the roiling surf and exploring the many hidden coves that Emory knew so well. Oblivious to windblown hair and wet skirts, Rachel reveled in Emory's attentions and his caresses, and he was equally happy, glorying in the passionate kisses they shared, and more in the way Rachel now welcomed his embraces.

Later, while watching the sun sink into the sea, they supped on a verandah high above the crashing surf. Berta brought them platters of steamed mussels and spit-grilled lamb with salmon, which they washed down with the bubbly champagne, cooled in the well. Emory appeared to be pleasantly mulled after a while, but Rachel relaxed, having decided he was more intoxicated by his happiness than the wine. The meal was unhurried, but no sooner was it over than they retired for the night to his room on the third floor.

It was an immense place which ran the length of the back of the house, with a wall of tall windows curving high above the sea. Sparsely but comfortably furnished, its walls were lined with seascapes, and the polished floor of wide planking was bare except for a throw carpet beside the big bed.

Berta had prepared a bath, and Rachel went there to prepare herself for her husband, but Emory was out of his clothes almost as soon as they closed the door behind them. When Rachel emerged from the tiny dressing room in a diaphanous nightgown, she found him strutting about the room, wholly unabashed by his nakedness.

"Will you always be parading about like that?" she asked, with laughing eyes. She was no longer shocked by the sight of his masculine body, but just the same, it was going to take some time for her to become used to his nudity, and his naturalness concerning it.

"Whenever I can," he said frankly. "It gives me a feeling of complete freedom, and I get it nowhere as much as I do in this very room." He motioned to the many curved windows, and the panoramic view of the sea, where the moonlight blazoned a swath across the water. "As a boy I spent hours and hours up here, all by myself, pretending I was at the wheel of my own sailing ship. Look!" he cried with excitement, peering through a long glass. "There's a ship out there now, passing by the point! Do you see it?" he asked Rachel, as she squinted through the unfamiliar glass. "A brigantine, I'd guess, from her sails!"

"You really do love the sea, don't you?"

"I love you, and only you!" said Emory fiercely, pulling her into his arms. "I'm now captain of a great midland estate, and I know I must put all thoughts of the sea from my head forever. Still, it beckons me . . . tempts me, like a woman, and whenever I see a sail, or the sea as it is tonight, so calm and shining, I know that this feeling will never leave me, no matter how old I grow."

"The sea is not always calm and shining, Emory," said Rachel, as they stood with their arms about one another, looking out at the dark water. "It can be cruel and merciless, sometimes."

"True!" he replied, "but when it is black and roiling, it excites me even more!" He turned her in his arms, and kissed her, loving the way her lips parted freely to meet his. "Almost as much as you do!" he whispered hoarsely, as his body stirred, responding to her nearness. "Now come," he added in a passionate voice, "our nuptial bed awaits, and I am eager for you. I have waited a long time for you, Rachel, my love!"

"I know that, but I, too, am now eager," she said softly against his skin, "and never again will I be like a ship without a master. You are my captain, my husband . . . and I will love you always."

His body aching for fulfillment, Emory went to the bed and sat upon the edge of it, leaning forward to blow out the single lamp that burned beside it. Instantly, the room was flooded with moonlight, which patterned a square upon the floor precisely where Rachel still stood beside the long glass. Through the sheer gown Emory saw the shadowy outline of her lush body, and his blood stirred even more, knowing he would soon claim it in love.

Without modesty, Rachel turned to face him, loosening the ribbons of her nightdress. The delicate gown fluttered to the floor, forgotten, and naked, Rachel approached the bed, where Emory waited for her, his burning body poised and ready.

"Emory! Emory!" she whispered, slipping into his arms, as their lips met in a searing kiss that burned them both with its fire. Gently, his fingers brushed lightly across the swell of her breasts, and arms and legs became entangled as they fell back upon the bed, totally engulfed by their mutual desire. As Emory knew she would, Rachel responded to the whispered touch of his flesh upon hers, and her light fingers breathed new life into the nerves of his body.

He took her then, whispering her name again and again, as she called out to him, and he would take her again that first night of love, as, in time worn fashion, physical love between a man and woman circled full around. In loving tenderness, each gave and each received, until the mutual desire burst into a passionate flame. Together they were one, soaring like gulls on the wind above the silver splashed sea outside, until release brought them fulfillment.

Their lovemaking was unhurried, and afterward, still cradled in Emory's arms, Rachel fell asleep. Peculiarly, he was unable to sleep and, in a pensive mood, lay quietly, watching her still-naked breast rise and fall in even slumber. In many ways the physical act was no different than others Emory had experienced. His body had responded as it always had, it flushed and filled, then emptied, as before, with others. And yet, this time something *was* different! Something of himself had poured into Rachel with this release, and it had been drawn from his heart, as well as his body. Never before, even in his wildest couplings with Edwina, had Emory ever felt so fulfilled, so satisfied afterward.

He knew now that love made all the difference, and would remain the difference, as together he and Rachel set out on a new beginning. Their future was secure, of that he was certain. Her body, her passions, were adequate to answer the needs of his, and in her heart was a love that matched his. Her level head would bring him up short whenever he went off half-cocked on some wild tangent, and if her sharp tongue required silencing now and again, then he would do it with kisses.

Yes, their future was secure and bright, all because of love. She had been wise, very wise, he admitted to himself now, to resist all of his earlier advances, for if she had succumbed then, he would have taken her physically, but their hearts and minds would never have touched in union, and in time, he would have gone his way, leaving her at the Hall with nothing but his name . . . and perhaps a child.

A child! Suddenly the idea thrilled him. *His child!* More than likely it would happen, and probably soon, for their unions would be frequent and passionate. But all that was ahead of them, part of their future. For now, Emory was happy, made content with the simple knowledge that Rachel was his wife, that he loved her completely. *He loved her!* He must tell her! Often!

Rolling onto his stomach, he coiled one of her long curls around his fingers, then tugged at it gently.

"Rachel! Wake up! I must tell you again how much I love you! Do you hear me? I love you! I love you!"

She stirred, then smiled. "I surely hope so!" she murmured sleepily. "After that exhibition!"

Opening her arms, Emory rushed into them and their lips met. They clung together, not in passion this time, but in a mutual closeness that needed no words to express what it was that they both felt.

"And I love you," Rachel whispered, kissing her husband's shoulder. "Now sleep. In the morning, I'll show you again how much."

All too soon, pleasant days and passion-filled nights slipped away, and on their last day at Greycliffe, Emory saddled Sultan and Hunter for one last ride on the beach. With Rachel leading the way, they pounded the stallions through the surf, surrounded by foam and spray, and later, they swam in a sun-warmed pool, relishing the feel of the sun on their naked bodies. Abandoning herself completely to love was still a new experience for Rachel, and in its newness she discovered she was more attuned to the needs of Emory's body than once she dreamed possible, and he, loving her with all his being, was amazed to find that often, their thoughts ran parallel, too.

Thus, united in every way, close in heart and mind, as well as body, they left Greycliffe reluctantly. At the same time, both them were anxious to return to Guersten Hall, eager to get on with the business of sharing their lives together.

CHAPTER THIRTY-FOUR

Summer, in all its glory, came to the midlands again, winding its way through June and July, when haying time came again. This time, Emory labored side by side with the rest of the Hall's men to store away all that could be of the winter forage. Rachel became sunburned from hours spent toiling under the brassy sun, made happy half a dozen times a day when Emory rode to her side for a kiss or waved to her from a distance as he went about his own chores.

The hot days and sultry nights of August seemed only to fire their desires more, and Emory spent almost every night with Rachel in the big square bedroom beside the salon, now lightened with a soft green rug and creamy curtains. On occasion, it was Rachel who woke from slumber, wanting his touch and his kiss, unashamed of her need, frank in her expression of it.

Out on the estate, under Emory's guidance, Rachel's plan, as he still called it, was now even more successful in its second summer. The enterprise thrived, growing and flourishing almost as much as did little Benjy.

Rachel loved the little fellow with all her heart, and he returned that love. It was natural that Rachel would become a surrogate mother to the child, filling the void in Rebecca's place. In the house, Benjy appeared almost mysteriously whenever Rachel did, much to the consternation of Anna, who was charged with his care and who feared the stairs, although Benjy was able to manipulate them with ease on his hands and knees.

He was an exceptional little boy; good humored, alert and curious, fascinated by all that moved and all that did not. Reaching out to the world about him, he focused on every subtle change in texture, reflecting pensively on the varied differences to be discovered. Rachel found him to be eager, but not aggressive; placid, but not passive. He was never violent or cranky, and almost never ailed. Bright and gentle, dear little Benjy brought a distinct measure of simple joy to all their lives.

To old George, though, the child became all things . . . a companion, someone to laugh at, or with. Then too, the toddler renewed the old man's sense of worth, for lately, able to do so very little for himself, George had begun to feel burdensome. But the little boy was also helpless, required care, and yet he gave so much to the household each day. Borrowing a page from Benjy's book, George took heart and felt redeemed.

In October, Rachel's parents returned to Brenham Manor for a visit. They arrived without advance notice, bringing old Hannah with them, and Louisa let Benjamin rest for a day or two before sending word to the Hall of their presence there.

On a day that was bright and sunny, Emory saddled the stallions, and he and Rachel galloped through the Small Wood and up to the pretty house where she was born. The ride was exhilarating, the crisp morning air announcing plainly that a change in the seasons was underway.

Louisa was alone in the morning room when they arrived. Renewed, spirited, she opened her arms and greeted them warmly.

"I don't need to ask if you are happy," she said to both of them. "You are, and it shows."

"We *are* happy, Mother," confirmed Rachel, "and our happiness grows every day."

"As does our love," added Emory, circling Rachel's slender waist with a long arm.

He flashed a brilliant smile. "Give us no thoughts but good ones."

"And you, Mother? You look well, happy. Do things continue to go well for you and Father?"

"Yes, yes," replied Louisa, actually turning pink. "We've learned a great deal about each other these past few months, things that we were too busy or too timid to discover before. Our relationship is good," she added simply, "and your father is better. He occupies himself an hour or two a day with papers submitted by Potter, but he is careful not to overdo. He has adjusted quite well, considering that his retirement was forced upon him."

"Where is he now? We would like to see him."

"Believe it or not, he felt an urge to go up to his bluff, one he couldn't smother. He promised to be careful, and said he wouldn't stay too long. Will you wait? Your grandmother is here now with us, and will be a permanent fixture in our lives whether we are here or in London. She has agreed it is time for her to fill her days with enjoyment instead of work."

"Oh, I must see her again. Where is she just now?"

"She and Lydia are settled into the library for a long and detailed conversation. Lydia has agreed to take Hannah's place at Trowbridge Road, and later, when the hospital and orphanage become reality, she will work with Duncan in its administration. Lydia was over the moon about being asked to take Hannah's place, and welcomes another chance to be busy in the care and nurturing of children. She much prefers this opportunity than to spend her days doing nothing of importance. I guess it is all about being needed, dear."

"How wonderful for you all, to have things working out so well. Duncan, too, must be pleased. He is expected at the Hall sometime soon, to follow up on George's care, and I will have you and Father, and grandmother and Lydia for dinner one Sunday. It will be like Sunday's past. I will return to visit with Hannah another day, but for now, let us ride out and meet Father!" She turned to Emory. "I'll race you!"

As they went outside, Rachel was already well ahead of Emory, and he let her go, let her lead the way. Not because Sultan couldn't outdistance Hunter had he let him, but more because Emory was yet uncertain whether his presence on the bluff would be welcomed. A long time back, Benjamin Brenham had his fill of Guerstens, and had said so, openly. Feeling cheated, he had been bitter, that Emory knew, having been forewarned by his friend the Lord, who'd gleaned that information from his grapevine. While illness had made Benjamin reflective, enabling him to make his peace with Rachel, was he ready to extend that peace to a Guersten?

Proceeding carefully, Emory cleared the last of the tall evergreens and mounted the bluff. Beside a huge gray boulder, Rachel stood in the circle of her father's arms, both of them smiling.

"What do you think of, Father, as you look out there?" she asked, wondering if perhaps he yet harbored some faint vision of obtaining the Hall as his own.

"Nothing, daughter, nothing. I see things clearly now. It's just a house. More beautiful than most, but still just brick and timber, glass and chimneys, nothing more. I've come to realize that roots and heritage are not acquired like property, but are built, nurtured through long years of toil and pride in what is your own. It was a valuable lesson," he added. "Perhaps I never had the makings of a true country gentleman, after all. I find I don't have the thinking for it. I should have stayed in the city, where I belonged. I'm a businessman, and a damned good one at that! From now on I'll stick to what I know best. Now, I must go down, for I promised your mother I'd not tarry." He turned, taking up Patch's rein. He patted her neck affectionately, then, unexpectedly, thrust one hand toward Emory, who had dismounted and approached slowly.

"Hello, son," he said. "Welcome and take care of my girl."

"Thank you," replied Emory, taking his father-in-law's outstretched hand. "I love her very much, and you can be sure that I'll work very hard to make her happy." He looked at Rachel, and then smiled. "I've learned some lessons of my own. Before Rachel came into my life, I always thought heritage like ours to be fairly worthless, because I couldn't see it . . . touch it. But she made me understand that it can be seen, can be touched. It's there," he said, his arm sweeping in a wide arc that took in the forest and the fields, the cream colored mansion and the barns behind it. "Heritage *is* tangible, and it represents the future, as well as the past. Rachel taught me that."

Benjamin nodded, pleased with the solidity of Emory's thinking, and shaking hands once more, the two men parted amicably. After Rachel kissed her father, he mounted and rode off down the path, to make his way back to the pink brick manor house where Louisa waited on the verandah.

Together, Rachel and Emory watched him until he disappeared, and then they turned to view the landscape spread below them. In the distance, ripening fields were ready for harvesting, and white sheep dotted the far pastures. Closer by, a straggly parade of milk cows wended their way to the low meadow beyond the dairy, and a row of springed wagons was just pulling away from under the loading sheds, headed for markets in Coltenham, Aylesbury and Peterborough.

"I've made a few discoveries of my own," admitted Rachel, encircling her husband's waist with both arms, "beside the one that I love you! There is much in my life that can be changed, and I must strive to make those changes, but there is also much that cannot be altered, perhaps should not be, and I must learn to recognize those things; learn to live with them."

"Somewhere in the middle of all that," said Emory, his mouth coming down hard on hers, "is our love. It will change and grow, as we change and grow, and yet . . . just now I don't want anything to change. My heart still pounds at the sight of you, my body quickens at your touch. It is enough," he added, "and I hope it will always remain so."

"It will, I know," whispered Rachel, offering her lips again. Emory reached out his hand, removing the ribbon that confined her auburn curls. Freed, the silken tresses tumbled loose, and he fingered their softness. As their lips met again, his other hand moved to cup the fullness of her breast, and holding it there, she slipped to her knees on the mossy ground, drawing him to her side.

"Come," she whispered, her voice quivering with rising desire. "Love me, here . . . in the open, on this little bluff that looks down on all that is our past, and all that is our future."

They shed their clothes quickly, and Rachel lay down next to the shaded boulder, where the moss was soft and cool against her back. Her skin flushed pink in her eagerness to be taken, and Emory knelt over her, his own body poised, pointed, ready. When he mounted her, it was like no other time before, even though their frequent couplings had been fulfilling to them both. This time, their lovemaking was wild, abandoned, frantic and frenzied, and something in each of the rose higher and higher, meeting in a crescendo that quickened Rachel's heart. When it occurred to her that she might become pregnant, right here on the bluff, the thought of it fired her loins again, and she circled his shoulders with her arms, crying out his name. Emory remained locked in her embrace until he, too, matched her passion and met it anew, his emotions pouring forth hotly in a straight line connecting heart and loins.

The act was gentler the second time, accomplished in a slow and mounting rhythm that enveloped them in their love for each other. Afterward, spent, they lay awhile, locked together.

"This is how it should be, always," murmured Emory, tracing a rivulet of perspiration that trailed its way across the rosy flesh of one breast. "We must come here often."

"No," said Rachel, touching his lips. "These moments are rare, and should remain so. They are the ones I will remember when I am old . . . when my blood no longer runs hot. But perhaps," she added, laughing up at him, "given your temper and my tongue, we will come here often at that, for each time we have a falling out I will come here. Follow me, then, and we will renew our love here, overlooking all that is now our future."

Only a few mornings later, after breakfast, Angus placed George in the seat of his little brake cart. One of the housemaids climbed beside him, and Rachel placed little Benjy in the girl's lap, then handed the child a half loaf of bread, wrapped in a cloth napkin.

"For the swans, Benjy. Break it into pieces before you throw it to them."

The cart moved down the drive, heading for the oval pool that separated Guersten Hall from Brenham Manor. Feeding the swans had become daily ritual for the old man and his grandson, weather permitting, and they were precious moments the old man treasured. Jealously, he even resented the presence of the maid, but he recognized that she was necessary to their outings, for he could neither hold nor lift the active child, now already six months past his first birthday.

At the familiar footbridge by the pool, Baybelle halted without needing to be told, and the maid clambered down to set the child on his feet. Obediently, Benjy took her hand, and together they proceeded to the water's edge, where a sizeable flock of swans waited to be fed.

While Benjy set about tearing the bread into pieces, tossing it upon the water, George noticed a tall figure watching them from a vantage point near the summerhouse on the other side of the pool. Slowly, Benjamin Brenham moved to the footbridge, and the two men studied each other in silence across the water. They had not come face to face with one another since that wintry December day when Rachel became Emory's wife.

George broke the silence. "Brenham!" he called out. "You're looking well! You are better?"

At first, Benjamin did not answer, merely eyed George from the distance, but then, he moved across the little footbridge, coming to a halt only a foot or two from George's cart.

"I am improved," he said at last, though his manner remained stiff. "Able to leave my bed, at least, though my activities must always remain curtailed."

"As are mine," said George, tapping his walking stick against his useless legs. "It seems that if we do not slow our pace, nature does it for us, eh?"

An awkward and uncomfortable silence fell between the two men, until George spoke once again.

"It's been a long time, Benjamin, and a lot has happened since we struck our deal, much that neither of us counted on."

"True, true," replied Benjamin, exhaling heavily, "and I'm as much to blame as any for what happened, since I let myself be duped. Knowing I had no sons, did you think to gain control of my fortune through my daughters? You must have known Rebecca was already pregnant when you baited me with your offer for Rachel's hand. To my shame, I bought it!"

Benjamin looked away, and George eyed him warily, tapping idly with his walking stick. "I'd hoped you wouldn't be bitter," he said, somberly, "but I must tell you that you are wrong in that, Brenham. Dead wrong! I knew naught about that babe until Rachel told me, and that was several months after she and Emory were wed. And as far as Rachel is concerned, I'm not sorry that I was instrumental in bringing her to Guersten Hall. If that sounds selfish, well, perhaps it is, but she is the best thing that has happened around here in two hundred years. Thanks to her, both my sons are men now, and my daughter is married into a fine old family. Furthermore," he went on, "the estate is flourishing for the first time since my father died. I can understand why you felt duped, and I'll admit that I considered Emory, as I knew him then, and Rachel, as I remembered her, to be expendable, but that December day when I saw her again in your library, I knew my fortunes were on the rise again. Somehow I knew that they would fall in love in time . . . the rogue and the mouse, and all of us would be the better for it. Theirs has been a stormy love affair, and only a fool would believe their marriage won't have its share of dark clouds, but their love will see them through. It will endure and grow even stronger, and with it your fortunes and mine."

The extended conversation left George somewhat winded, and he paused to catch his breath, while placing his hands, one atop the other, on the knob of his walking stick. "I'm getting on now, Benjamin," he said at last, "just waiting for Time's broom to sweep me away. Rachel was just the shot in the arm this tired old family needed, and thanks to her I can fall into my dotage without a worry about the Guerstens yet to come. It's a good feeling, but if you were to set aside your bitterness and join us in our happiness, I'd feel even better!"

The set of Benjamin's firm, square jaw softened, and his stiffness vanished. "I'm not bitter," he said to George, offering his hand as proof. "It's just that old habits die hard, and I've not yet learned to temper my tongue."

"Glad to hear that's all it is," replied George, gripping the other's hand with all the strength he could muster. "Edward will be, too, I know. He worries that you hold him . . ."

"Aaaah, Edward! Rachel tells me he still grieves, after all this time. Ask him to come round, would you? Perhaps we can help each other . . . with our grief."

"I'll do that and soon. Rachel tells me she is planning a reunion dinner for our two families in the immediate future. Perhaps we can all share our good fortune, and observe our children's happiness over dinner and brandy."

"But now," said George, pointing to where little Benjy was throwing crusts of yesterday's bread to the gliding swans, "don't you think it's time you met your grandson?"

Turning ever so slowly, Benjamin looked toward the child, studying him for a long moment, and then, with a wave of his hand to George, he moved toward Benjy, whose interest was now captured by a fat bullfrog sitting on a lily pad. At Benjamin's approach, and a signal from George, the maid blended into the background, leaving the tall man and the child alone.

By what instinct does a child know his grandfather? Who can say, yet while Benjamin did not resemble in the least the round and white haired George, who rode about on wheels, little Benjy knew at once that the older man who approached him now was also someone special.

"See! See!" he chortled, tugging at Benjamin's trouser leg, as he pointed a finger at the frog. A moment later, he raised his chubby arms to Benjamin, and waited to be lifted.

Benjamin choked at the sight of him, for as he had grown; Benjy had changed, and was now so much like Rebecca that it defied description. There was her mouth, with its radiant smile, and there was that same elfin face, surrounded by a mass of dark curls that tumbled every which way. Only in the eyes did Benjy not resemble his mother; instead of being blue, they were gray and smoky, like Benjamin's own.

A tingling sensation began somewhere at the back of Benjamin's nose, and a tear formed in his eye. He swallowed hard, and then, stooping, picked up the child.

"Come," he said to his grandson, as the baby's trusting arms went about his neck, "let us visit your mama."

"Mama, Mama," repeated the little boy gamely, as Benjamin crossed the footbridge, walking toward the slope that overlooked the summerhouse, where Rebecca's gravesite was warmed by the October sun.

Rachel and Stoddard spent some hours in the planning of the special dinner for the families, planned for the first Sunday in November. It was a grand spread, and a full table, and included everyone at Brenham Manor; her parents, her grandmother, Lydia, and even Agatha, who loved them all. Duncan arrived early that Sunday, that he might examine and talk with George about his health, and when Adele and Hugh turned up with the cousins, all of them richly garbed in new winter Scofield creations, Rachel and Emory strolled in the empty ballroom, arms entwined, pleased with the happy chattering coming from the drawing room. "Our families are truly joined now, Emory, and will remain so. I never thought it would come about so easily, but I am glad for Rebecca's sake that Father and Benjy get along so well. And imagine, he now has a grandmother and a great-grandmother! How he dotes on the attention!"

Emory turned, as another round of laughter filtered from the drawing room. "From the sound, I'd guess Benjy is mastering the art of being entertaining. He finally learned how to somersault, and must be rolling all over the carpeting showing off his expertise. Come, let us join them all. We are missing the show!"

Some months later, when the first blush of spring spread across the fields of Guersten Hall, and long after Benjamin and Louisa had returned to London, with Hannah and Lydia, a thick sealed packet of papers arrived at Guersten Hall, delivered by a special courier from Durklin's office. Among them was the deed to Brenham Manor and all its acreage, accompanied by a letter Benjamin had written to Edward. In essence, the estate was now little Benjy's, with Edward appointed as its administrator until the child reached his majority.

"But it is my fervent hope," wrote Benjamin, "that someday in the future, the lands of Brenham Manor will be rejoined to those of Guersten Hall, from which they were carved more than thirty years ago." Further, Benjamin had added, he hoped that Edward would be allowed to assume fully the role of overseer for Rachel's agricultural enterprise. "Though begun on a small scale," the letter said, "if properly nurtured, Guersten Brothers will one day be an entity to be reckoned with."

Edward was perplexed. "But how can that be?" he asked, as they sat around the dining room table having breakfast. "I am not the master of the Hall . . . Emory is!" He turned to face Rachel, holding her father's letter in his hand. "None of this makes any sense!"

"It does if you read this!" remarked Emory chokingly, holding out a letter of his own, one delivered by the same courier. In it, Benjamin invited Emory to visit him at his London brownstone, explaining that he intended to offer Emory, after proper indoctrination, the reins to his complex business holdings.

"Recognizing that without younger blood, my empire will be whittled away by competition until nothing remains," said Emory's letter, "I offer its administration to you now, and to your son and heir, in the future."

"That part puzzles me," said Emory. "I don't have a son! In fact, I don't have any heirs yet."

Something made him turn just then, to look at Rachel, who sat at the far end of the table with an *I-know-something-you-don't-know* smile playing about her mouth.

"Or do I?" he inquired hesitantly.

Smiling at him from across the table, Rachel's face wreathed into a wide grin. "Well, I . . ."

She got no further. Emory let out a whoop and raced around to her side and, scooping her into his arms, kissed her madly, over and over. Benjy, thinking it was a game of some sort, and not wanting to be excluded, tugged frantically at Rachel's skirts until she picked him up, and the three of them then danced about the room joyfully. Benjy laughed merrily when Uncle Emory planted kisses on his nose and ears as well as Rachel's.

"Da! Da!" cried the little fellow to his father, but Edward didn't answer, for he was engrossed in the rest of his brother's letter. In it, Benjamin stated that he and Louisa had chosen to live out the remainder of their years in the London brownstone they had occupied when they were first married. Old Hannah, Rachel's grandmother, would live there with them, too. In failing health, Benjamin wanted to be near his Thameside offices. He wrote that Durklin, his solicitor, and Potter, his clerk, would impart to Emory whatever technical information he needed to know about the business, but Benjamin himself would provide the unique and necessary expertise that had made it flourish throughout the years.

"Rachel has written of your lure of the sea," he had added in a footnote to Emory, "and your fascination with it, and it is my hope and expectation that before this time next year we will be able to solidify some plans I have drawn for overseas expansion. I have in mind Charleston, South Carolina, the feasibility of which has already been established by my agents in the United States, who even now await your visit."

"Well, well, well, Father!" said Edward, expelling his breath in a long whistle. "Emory's going to sea! What do you think of that?"

George daubed at his eyes and looked across the room to see his happy daughter-in-law crushed within Emory's embrace. The old man remained silent, for it was only with the greatest difficulty that he was able to keep his emotions in check.

Retrieving his son from Rachel's arms, Edward placed the child in his grandfather's lap and pushed the chair from the dining room.

"It's off to the ballroom terrace for the three of us! It's a lovely new day, and these two need a moment together."

Alone at last, Emory drew Rachel close, holding her tightly against his wide chest. "Ah, Rachel!" he whispered into her hair. "Why does news of a coming child make a man feel so complete?"

"Then it makes you happy?"

"Happy! I am beside myself!"

Rachel went to the sideboard and, removing the stopper of a crystal decanter there, poured a measure of brandy into a small glass.

"Some things in life call for a drink, a toast, and this is one of those times," she said.

Taking up the glass, Emory raised it to his wife in a silent salute, and then tossed it away neatly, returning the glass to the sideboard. Then he swept Rachel into his arms.

"Aaaah, mouse! To think I once needed that! How I love you! How I adore you! And my happiness is only beginning! *Our* happiness!"

He reached for Rachel's hand, and together they went outside, across the terrace and past the others, turning toward the stone summerhouse. There they stood silently, arm in arm, viewing the grandeur that was Guersten Hall. Rachel's determination had reclaimed it, and Emory's would now forever preserve it. Anchored by love, the future was secure, not only for them, but for the child she carried within her, and for generations of Guerstens yet to come.

THE END

ABOUT THE AUTHOR

Ethel says nothing much to write here about! After high school, she enlisted in the Women's Army Corps and attended clerical and short-hand schooling followed by assignment to a Counter Intelligence Corps base in Maryland. As the only WAC on that base cleared for top secret, she was instrumental in working at the Pentagon selecting officers for assignment to agent classes. Leaving the WAC in 1953 as staff sergeant, she was hired by an engineering company that designed and manufactured electrical power distribution switchboards, dimmer boards, and panel boards.

Ethel met her husband, Fred, at that company, and they were married in 1957, moving to Quincy, Massachusetts, where they raised their five children and operated a mom-and-pop variety store for thirty-two years. She returned to work full-time in financial services when their children approached college age. They retired to Vero Beach, Florida, returning later to Massachusetts in 2003. Presently, she is just a wife, mother, grandmother, and hopefully, a successful writer, living happily in West Bridgewater, Massachusetts, with her husband. Life is good, all about faith and family.

CPSIA information can be obtained
at www.ICGtesting.com
Printed in the USA
FFOW01n2141171215
19499FF